IR

D0016135

Westminster Public Library
3705 W. 112th Avenue
Westminster, CO 80031

DISCARD

APR   2002

THE
PUSHCART
BOOK OF SHORT STORIES

The Pushcart
Book of
Short Stories

The best short stories
from a quarter-century
of The Pushcart Prize

Bill Henderson,
Editor

PUSHCART PRESS
Wainscott, New York

© 2002 Pushcart Press
all rights reserved
ISBN 1-888889-23-3
    1-88889-28-4 (paperback)
LC: 2001 126961

Stories are reprinted with permission
of authors, or their agents or publishers.
Rights revert on publication.

For information address
Pushcart Press
PO Box 380
Wainscott, New York 11975

distributed by W.W. Norton & Co.

INTRODUCTION

It all started like this in 1976:

"Think you know what's happening in literature today? Approximately 2,000 alternative publishers now exist in the United States and their number is mushrooming . . . during the same period many large commercial houses have been absorbed by conglomerates more interested in parking lots, television, motion pictures and it was gravely rumored for a forthcoming takeover (and gravely denied) in breakfast cereal . . ."

With these introductory words, the first edition of the *Pushcart Prize* was published from a studio apartment in Yonkers, New York a quarter century ago. The projected series had a miniscule budget, no grants, and only one publisher/package wrapper—this writer. But it enjoyed an impressive array of Founding Editors, among them Anais Nin, Buckminster Fuller, Ishmael Reed, Len Fulton, Joyce Carol Oates, Reynolds Price, Ted Wilentz, Ralph Ellison and Paul Bowles. And behind them stood a solid tradition of small press heroes: Edgar Allan Poe, Walt Whitman, Stephen Crane, Upton Sinclair, Carl Sandburg, Erza Pound, James Joyce, D.H. Lawrence and the entire Russian *samizdat* movement.

It was the hope of our Founding Editors and myself that we could remind readers of this tradition and encourage writers to ignore the commercial publishing forces that tend to favor only authors with dollar signs around their necks. It couldn't get much worse than it was for writers in 1976, we figured.

We were right and we were also wrong.

The commercial world did get worse. Currently five international conglomerates control most of our general publishing: Viacom, News

Corporation, Germany's Holtzbrinck and Bertelsmann and England's Longmans Pearson, and two huge chains rule most of the bookstore trade: Barnes & Noble and Borders.

But it got better too. As the conglomerates passed up all but the bankable, small press publishers thrived. The worse it got in New York and LA, the better it got in the heartland. The last quarter of the 20th Century saw an amazing literary renaissance, thanks to hundreds of unsung editors and writers scattered across the nation.

The history of *The Pushcart Prize* series is a measure of their devotion. In our very first edition we discovered a story by an unknown named Raymond Carver from a now defunct little mag called *Spectrum*. In the next editions more newcomers surfaced: Tim O'Brien and John Irving. Soon thereafter nominations for people named Lynne Sharon Schwartz, Andre Dubus, Jayne Anne Phillips, Charles Baxter, Bobbie Ann Mason, Susan Minot, Mona Simpson, Richard Ford, and D. R. MacDonald were reprinted from a variety of presses.

As the publishing world began to take notice of the sources of these astonishing authors, the presses who nurtured them were also acclaimed, as was the annual *Pushcart Prize*. "A distinguished annual literary event" said Anne Tyler in a *New York Times* review. "When it comes to contemporary American literature, the small press is where the action is . . . Of all the anthologies, Pushcart's is the most rewarding to read straight through," noted the *Chicago Tribune*. "A treasure trove" said the *Los Angeles Times* in reviewing our *Prize*.

As the commercial world became more and more dependent on celebrity, sex, self-help and the merely trendy, small presses became a reliable outlet for what was beyond the usual and the bankable. Wonder resurfaced.

This book is but a sampler of such wonder. Over 500 fictions appeared in the first quarter century of *The Pushcart Prize*. Here we are able to reprint only 43. If space permitted I would have included almost all 500 plus. Most major libraries shelve the *Pushcart Prize* series. You may wish to browse our editions and make your own selection of the best of the best.

I am tempted to talk about every story that follows. They have stayed with me, in memory, in appreciation, for years, indeed decades. To paraphrase any of these tales would perhaps diminish their impact on the reader, who should come to them fresh, without editorial prejudice.

Other collections have appeared recently—the best stories of the century some proclaimed themselves to be. But Pushcart makes no such claim. These are fictions of our time, from our heartland, presented without commercial interruption. They exist on these pages because of the dedication of editors who were not interested in the latest "hype and rep and hullabaloo . . . the New Thing, or the Big Thing, or even the Old Thing," as Russell Banks expressed it in his Introduction to *Pushcart Prize XV*.

Our thanks then to the editors of the following presses with stories included here: *Crazyhorse*, David Godine, *Ontario Review, Massachusetts Review, Ascent, Grand Street, Sewanee Review, Antaeus, Iowa Review, Story, Glimmer Train, TriQuarterly, Milkweed Editions, News From the Republic of Letters, Doubletake, Partisan Review, Conjunctions, Michigan Quarterly Review, Ploughshares, ZYZZYVA, Threepenny Review, Paris Review, Laurel Review, Missouri Review, Shenandoah, Fiction International, Agni, Georgia Review.*

Thanks also to the people who originally nominated these stories for the *Pushcart Prize*: Seymour Lawrence, Joyce Carol Oates, Ted Wilentz, DeWitt Henry, Robin Hemley, Susan Moon, Robert Phillips, Tomás Filer, Sandy Huss, Lloyd Schwartz, Henry Carlile, Dennis Vannatta, David Wojahn, Richard Burgin, Pat Strachan, David Jauss, Carolyn Kizer, James Linville, Sam Halpert, Sara Vogan, Brigit Kelly, Kate Walbert, Robert Schirmer, Josip Novakovich, Ellen Wilbur, Mark Halliday, Raymond Carver, Marry Morris, T. C. Boyle, Edmund Keeley, John Daniel, Helen Handley, Sigrid Nunez, Daniel Menaker, Elizabeth Inness-Brown, George Plimpton, Patricia Zelver, Harry Smith, Lynne Spaulding, Joe Ashby Porter, Nona Balakian, Gordon Lish, and Robert Boyers.

"Definitive" is a word over-used in publishing. But try it on as it applies to *The Pushcart Book of Short Stories*. I doubt if any more complete or astonishing collection of contemporary fiction will come along very soon. These authors tell us who we are—the secret life our culture.

Bill Henderson

THE STORIES

THE
PUSHCART
BOOK OF SHORT STORIES

CORDIALS

by DAVID KRANES

from TRIQUARTERLY

IT WASN'T UNTIL THE WAITRESS brought her Benedictine and she felt her first contraction that Lynn even thought of herself as being pregnant. She was anatomically thin and had managed to conceal the fact for well over seven months, with a regimen of boiled turnips and cold consommé—and the reminder was badly timed to say the least. She had wanted to sleep with David Marker from the moment she and Jack had spent a Saturday with the Markers sailfishing three months ago out at Wildwood, but there'd been interferences at just about every point. She had called him; he had called her; they had tried one afternoon at her apartment only to find her son Adam home from Hotchkiss as a surprise. Fall in New York is a difficult time to have an affair: everything starting up, schedules over-crowded again; and so this evening was to have been an island for both of them.

"Something the matter?" David asked her.

She smiled. "No."

"You winced."

"Just anxious, I guess."

"As am I."

She rubbed the knuckles of his hand, climbing each ridge, kneading the loose skin in the depressions with her forefinger and thumb.

"Do you want to leave now?" he asked.

"Let's finish our drinks," she said, her eyes partly on her watch, wondering when the next contraction would come. It came seven minutes later. She drained her glass: "All through," she said.

David smiled, breathed in his Drambuie and drained it. "Let's go," he said.

He helped her on with her coat. "Where are we . . . ?"

"A friend lent me his studio."

"Where?"

"Rowayton."

"That's an hour."

"Fifty minutes. And it's a nice Indian summer. We'll drive with the windows down. Sea smell's an aphrodisiac."

"I don't need an aphrodisiac." Her voice was surprisingly soft and quiet.

David nodded to the maitre de, and pushed the door open; she went out. "It's a great place—this place—this studio."

Lynn breathed the late September West 52nd Street smells, and felt another contraction coming on.

When they cloverleafed onto the Merritt Parkway, the tugs were coming regularly, just under five minutes. Both the front windows were down. David had the heater on, her coat off. She had her face against his neck, her jaw pressed there. She'd worn no bra—she didn't really need to—and he was moving the tips of his right middle fingers over the nipple, under her burgundy knit.

"You're perspiring," he said, trying to make it sound playful.

"Yes." She bit at him. "It's the heater. The blower's going right up my dress." She knew, in fact, it was probably lactating.

"Rowayton?" There was a hum in her voice.

16

"There are fourteen-foot ceilings," David traced her neck. "And a fireplace."

"Had you planned on using the fireplace?"

"For a fire, sure; not for us."

"I don't know if I can wait." Lynn felt her body tightening again, watched the speedometer climb from 70 to 85.

"You'll love it," David said to her; "it's on the shore. You can hear the ocean. Waves. It's a great rhythm. Great keeping time to. Natural. Nothing rushed." He let his hand slide slowly down to her leg. She picked it up, kissed it. She looked at her watch: three minutes and twenty seconds; she picked up and kissed his hand when she felt the next contraction again; three minutes and fifteen.

"How long until we get there?" she asked him.

"Twenty—twenty-five minutes." He played with her nipple again. She held her breath. "You're really remarkable," he told her. "I've been clawing half New York's concrete for three months."

"Me too," she said. "I've been having the most amazing fantasies."

"I'm not very good at waiting," David told her, then smiled.

"Nor am I." She thought about it; it was true. "I wait for very few things."

"Waiting fantasies are strange." He began to slide his hand down to her abdomen. "They make you feel almost adolescent." She picked his hand up again, kissed it, checked her watch. "Your heart's jumping."

"There's a motel in Mamaroneck," she said.

"One quarter hour, *max*," he told her. The pains were coming every two minutes plus.

When they pulled in beside the studio and cut their lights, Lynn's spasms were only a minute, or slightly more, apart. Like a school-boy, David started to undress her in the car; she put two hands against his chest: "Let's go inside."

He smiled; "O.K.," then kissed her eyes, let himself out, and walked around to her door. She could smell the sea, as he'd predicted, and it smelled as though her own body had become huge, grown unlit and infinite and moved outside to become anatomy in the night around her. She became her own child briefly— undelivered though dependent and scared. She thought of when she was fourteen, parking out near Coney Island with a boy named Arnold, the "Tennessee Waltz" on the car radio, how her whole

17

mouth had trembled, how her thigh muscles had gone slack. She heard the door button click, felt the sea wind against her hair, smelled the blown redolence of herself.

Lynn didn't like being aggressive. She had always hated that role, it ruined everything; but she pulled David inside and when he wanted to get a fire going, she said *no*.

"Why?"

"Please."

"Lynn, that's the whole . . ."

"Afterward!"

"I may want to sleep."

"Please!"

"O.K."

She pulled him to the bed.

She had continually fantasized David's undressing her, three months lived it in her mind: its being gentle, slow; kisses, where he placed them, breast, belly, hip; when they came. And so against her better judgment she let him, let it work out, let the mind come true. True: she stood there, in the dark, arching, moving, turning slightly for him on the balls of her heels. And David carried it off: it was worth the concealment, worth the pain. The hands played, the kisses came on time, in form. She felt the zipper on her dress move down, slipped her arms out, felt the dress fall around her hips. She felt her water break. "David," she said, and pulled him in.

She dug at him, made his shoulder bleed, bit his face. It helped to get the pain out. He was trembling, "Jesus! Jesus-God! Jesus, Lynn," he said. "God, come on! Off our feet! Off our feet! Talk about adolescents! God!"

"Then get undressed," she told him.

"You!"

"David . . ."

"Do it. You—"

His jacket was already off. His neck was moving on its base; his breath, heavy, wet. "Christ, you're incredible! You're incredible!" he said.

She couldn't help it. They were somewhere between twenty and thirty seconds apart now, and the pain and pressure was too much. She grabbed the collar of his shirt and tore, ripped it down, spread it, snapping all the buttons in a line. They landed, light as crickets, on the rug. "Fantastic!" David was moaning. "Oh, fantastic! Wow!"

18

She yanked his belt. "Oh, God!" She felt it uncinch. She broke the button above the fly and heard the zipper whine. The pants fell past his knees.

"O.K." she managed, her voice strained and tight, "You do the rest."

"No. Please." He was rocking. "You. The shoes!"

"David . . . "

"O.K. I'm sorry," He stepped out of things. "I'm sorry." He let other things drop. She saw his shape sit on the bed's edge, pull his shoes off. She didn't know how she was going to make it as she removed her panties and came close.

He pulled the bedspread down. She found a wastebasket and slid it beside the bed. She moved against him, kept his hands on her back, pressing her whole anatomy hard, violently down, against, trying to create hard enough pressure to displace some of the pain. She screamed. She dug in. She fought against him with her fists and knees. He kept bellowing sounds to match hers, saying things like: *God*—he thought his fantasies were pretty advanced, but— *Jesus*—he realized now that they were—*Christ*—naive. But as they tore and fought against each other, Lynn felt herself giving way and knew that what she'd hoped for was impossible. She could not last. She could not hold out.

She slid down his body slowly, marking it with her teeth, clearing herself as where she could. When the baby came, it came easily and she was able crudely to slice the cord, get everything in the wastebasket and cover it with the bedspread without really losing much of the rhythm of the foreplay. She submitted to David pulling at her, at her shoulders, slid back up along him, joining, both of them, three minutes later, coming almost together under the bloodsoak of sheets.

David lay with his head off the far edge of the bed, making sounds. Lynn played one hand over his ribs, blew breath gently against his sweat. She could smell herself—herself, the ocean and her own birth, but could not keep them apart. She thought she heard a steamer, way out in Long Island Sound. Shortly afterward, when David showered, she took the basket out to the small pier of the studio front and emptied it into the sea. Standing there briefly, she tasted herself again, her own fetality, felt the darkness—warm, salty, moist, in membranes layered out and out around her. The moon, real and untelevised above, seemed a strange opening in

19

space, a place she might ultimately move to, go. She ached, but could not feel her body. It was an abstract ache, one in air.

Inside, they came together one more time: much quicker, less violent, more studied, more synchronized. David did not shower. Instead, he dressed himself hurriedly and lit a long cigar.

"Did I hurt you?" he asked. "I'm always afraid . . . "

"No," Lynn reassured him from the bathroom. She stopped herself with toilet paper, pulled on her panties, and dropped her dress over her head. "No." Somehow it was true.

"Hey—you start?"

"What?"

"Your period start?"

" . . . Yes."

In the car, on the way back to Manhattan, they talked enthusiastically about St. Croix.

Her husband, Jack, was sitting on the long couch going through briefs in his blue bathrobe when she came in. There was a small snifter of crème de cacao on the coffee table to his right. They said hello. She kissed him on his forehead and hung up her coat.

"Where you been?"

"Theater."

"What'd you see?"

"*Long Day's Journey.*"

"How was it?"

"Fantastic.' ' She straightened her hair.

"Great play." Jack wrote a sentence in the margin of his brief.

"There's some triple sec there, if you want."

"Thanks."

"Picked it up on the way home."

She poured a cordial glass half full. The smell of orange reminded her somehow of Christmas, kumquats from Florida fruit packages she had bitten into in lost distant Decembers as a child. She crossed the room. She stood in front of their window wall, looking out. The lights beyond, below, all the bunched thousands of them, looked like perforations. She stared at the reflected milk stains on her dress, her reflection seeming to spread out across the perforations to surround her until, searching the distance, she was gone.

"Did you find it?"

"Hmmm?"

"Find the triple sec."

"Yes. Fine. Thanks."

"See the letter from Ad?"

"No. What's he say?"

"They beat Taft 21 to 20. He pulled a ligament in his knee. He's been having whirlpools. Nothing serious. They took X rays at the Sharon Hospital. He's seeing Cynthia Kaufmann this weekend. Listen—do you want to?"

"Hmmm?"

"You at all horny?"

She pressed the cordial glass against her lips. The fruity taste rose up, viscous, wet; it made orange seeds of her eyes. "Maybe later," she said.

"Can't hear you."

She took the glass away, wet her lips. "Maybe later."

"Sure, O.K."

Her eyes watered. She experienced the only moment akin to incest she had ever felt. She thought of her son, Adam, in the whirlpool. Her knee hurt.

1976

THE PENSION
GRILLPARZER

by JOHN IRVING

from ANTAEUS

$\mathbf{M}$Y FATHER WORKED for the Austrian Tourist Bureau. It was my mother's idea that our family travel with him when he went on the road as a Tourist Bureau spy. My mother and brother and I would accompany him on his secretive missions to uncover the discourtesy, the dust, the badly cooked food, the short cuts taken by Austria's restaurants and hotels and pensions. We were instructed to create difficulties whenever we could, to never order exactly what was on the menu, to imitate a foreigner's odd requests—the hours we would like to have our baths, the need for aspirin and directions to the zoo. We were instructed to be civilized but troublesome; and when the visit was over, we reported to my father in the car.

My mother would say, "The hairdresser is always closed in the morning. But they make suitable recommendations outside. I guess it's all right, provided they don't claim to have a hairdresser actually *in* the hotel."

"Well, they *do* claim it," my father would say. He'd note this on a giant pad.

I was always the driver. I said, "The car is parked off the street, but someone put fourteen kilometers on the gauge between the time we handed it over to the doorman and picked it up at the hotel garage."

"That is a matter to report directly to the management," my father said, jotting it down.

"The toilet leaked," I said.

"I couldn't open the door to the W.C.," said my brother, Robo.

"Robo," mother said, "you always have trouble with doors."

"Was that supposed to be Class C?" I asked.

"I'm afraid not," father said. "It is still listed as Class B." We drove for a short while in silence. Our most serious judgment concerned changing a hotel's or a pension's class standing: we did not suggest it frivolously.

"I think this calls for a letter to the management," mother suggested. "Not too nice a letter, but not a really rough one. Just state the facts."

"Yes, I rather liked him," father said. He always made a point of getting to meet the managers.

"Don't forget the business of driving the car," I said. "That's really unforgivable."

"And the eggs were bad," said Robo; he was not yet ten and his judgments were not seriously considered.

We became a far harsher team of evaluators when my grandfather died and we inherited grandmother—my mother's mother, who thereafter accompanied us on our travels. A regal dame, Johanna was accustomed to Class A travel, and my father's duties more frequently called for investigations of Class B and Class C lodgings. They were the places, the B and C hotels (and the pensions), that most interested the tourists. At restaurants we did a little better. People who couldn't afford the classy places to sleep were still interested in the best places to eat.

"I shall not have dubious food tested on me," Johanna told us. "This strange employment may give you all glee about having free vacations, but I can see there is a terrible price paid: the anxiety of not knowing what sort of quarters you'll have for the night. The Americans may find it charming that we still have rooms without baths and toilets, but I am an old woman and I'm not charmed by walking down a public corridor in search of cleanliness and my relievement. The anxiety is only half of it. Actual diseases are possible—and not only from food. If the bed is questionable, I promise I shan't put my head down. And the children are young and impressionable; you should think of the clientele in some of these lodgings and seriously ask yourselves about the influences." My mother and father nodded; they said nothing. "Slow down!" grandmother said to me. "You're just a young boy who likes to show off." I slowed down. "Vienna," grandmother sighed. "In Vienna I always stayed at the Ambassador."

"Johanna, the Ambassador is not under investigation," father said.

"I should think not," Johanna said. "I suppose we're not even headed toward a Class A place?"

"Well, it's a B trip," my father admitted. "For the most part."

"I trust," grandmother said, "that you mean there is one A place en route?"

"No," father admitted. "There is one C place."

"It's okay," Robo said. "There are fights in Class C."

"I should imagine so," Johanna said.

"It's a Class C pension, very small," father said, as if the size of the place forgave it.

"And they're applying for a B," said mother.

"But there have been some complaints," I added.

"I'm sure there have," Johanna said.

"And animals," I added. My mother gave me a look.

"Animals?" said Johanna.

"Animals," I admitted.

"A *suspicion* of animals," my mother corrected me.

"Yes, be fair," father said.

"Oh wonderful," grandmother said. "A suspicion of animals. Their hair on the rugs? Their terrible waste in the corners! Did you know that my asthma reacts, severely, to any room in which there has recently been a cat?"

"The complaint was not about cats," I said. My mother elbowed me sharply.

"Dogs?" Johanna said. "Rabid dogs! Biting you on the way to the bathroom . . ."

"No," I said. "Not dogs."

"Bears!" Robo cried.

But my mother said, "We don't know for sure about any bear, Robo."

"This isn't serious?" Johanna said.

"Of course it's not serious," father said. "How could there be bears in a pension?"

"There was a letter saying so," I said. "Of course, the Tourist Bureau assumed it was a crank complaint. But then there was another sighting—and a second letter claiming there had been a bear."

My father used the rear-view mirror to scowl at me, but I thought that if we were all supposed to be in on the investigation, it would be wise to have grandmother on her toes.

"It's probably not a real bear," Robo said, with obvious disappointment.

"A man in a bear suit!" Johanna cried. "What unheard-of perversion is *that*? A *beast* of a man sneaking about in disguise! Up to what? It's a man in a bear suit, I know it is," she said. "I want to go to that one first. If there's going to be a Class C experience on this trip, let's get it over with as soon as possible."

"But we haven't got reservations for tonight," mother said.

"Yes, we might as well give them a chance to be at their best," father said. Although he never revealed to his victims that he worked for the Tourist Bureau, father believed that reservations were simply a decent way of allowing the personnel to be as prepared as they could be.

"I'm sure we don't need to make a reservation in a place frequented by men who disguise themselves as animals," Johanna said. "I'm sure there is always a vacancy there. I'm sure the guests are regularly dying in their beds—of fright, or else of whatever unspeakable injury the madman in the foul bear suit does to them."

"It's probably a real bear," Robo said, hopefully—for in the turn the conversation was taking, he certainly saw that a real bear would be preferable to grandmother's imagined ghoul. Robo had no fear, I think, of a real bear.

I drove us as inconspicuously as possible to the dark, dwarfed corner of Planken and Seilergasse. We were looking for the Class C pension that wanted to be a B.

"No place to park," I said to father, who was already making note of it in his pad.

"The Pension Grillparzer," my mother read aloud to us, pointing out the tiny sign.

"What dreadful pretension," grandmother said.

I double parked and we sat in the car and peered up at the Pension Grillparzer; it rose only four slender stories between a pastry shop and a Tabak Trafik.

"See?" father said. "No bears!"

"No *men*, I hope," said grandmother.

"They come at night," Robo said, looking cautiously up and down the street.

We went inside to met the manager, a Herr Theobald who instantly put Johanna on her guard. "Three generations traveling together!" he cried. "Like the old days," he added, especially to grandmother, "before all these divorces and the young people wanting to live in apartments by themselves. This is a *family* pension! I just wish you had made a reservation so I could put you more closely together."

"We're not accustomed to sleeping in the same room," grandmother told him.

"Of course not!" Theobald cried. "I just meant I wished that your *rooms* could be closer together." This worried grandmother, clearly.

"How far apart must we be put?" she asked.

"Well, I've only two rooms left," he said. "And only one of them is large enough for the two boys and their parents. We have some portable cots we can move in, you see."

"We're not usually together," father said.

"And my room is how far from theirs?" Johanna asked coolly.

"You're right across from the W.C.!" Theobald told her, as if this were a plus.

But as we were shown to our rooms, grandmother staying with father—contemptuously to the rear of our procession—I heard her mutter: "This is not how I conceived of my retirement. Across the hall from a W.C., listening to all the visitors."

"Not one of these rooms is the same," Theobald told us. "The furniture is all from my family." We could believe it. The one large room Robo and I were to share with my parents was a hall-sized museum of knick-knacks, every dresser with a different style of knob. On the other hand, the sink had brass faucets and the head-board of the bed was carved. I could see my father balancing things up for future notation in the giant pad.

"You may do that later," Johanna informed him. "Where do *I* stay?"

As a family, we dutifully followed Theobald and my grandmother down the long, twining hall—my father counting the paces to the W.C. The hall rug was thin, the color of a shadow. Along the walls were old photographs of speed-skating teams—on their feet the strange blades curled at the tips like court jesters' shoes or the runnners of ancient sleds.

Robo, running far ahead, announced his discovery of the W.C.

Grandmother's room was full of china, polished wood and the hint of mold. The drapes were damp. The bed had an unsettling ridge at its center, almost as if a very slender body lay stretched beneath the spread.

Grandmother said nothing, and when Theobald reeled out of the room like a wounded man who's been told he'll live, grandmother asked my father, "On what basis can the Pension Grillparzer hope to get a B?"

"Quite decidedly C," I said.

"I would say, myself, that it was E or F," grandmother told us.

My mother ran her hand along the window sill. "Very clean, though," she said.

"I imagine," said grandmother, pulling back the heavy bedspread, "that these things absorb quite a lot."

* * *

In the dim tea room a man without a tie sang a Hungarian song. "It does not mean he's Hungarian," father reassured Johanna, but she was skeptical.

"I'd say the odds are not in his favor," she suggested; she would not have tea or coffee. Robo ate a little cake, which he claimed to like. My mother and I smoked a cigarette; she was trying to quit and I was trying to start, with moderation; therefore, we shared a cigarette between us—in fact, we'd promised never to smoke a whole one alone.

"He's a great guest," Herr Theobald whispered to my father; he indicated the singer. "He knows songs from all over."

"From Hungary, at least," grandmother said, but she smiled.

27

A small man, clean-shaven but with that permanent gun-blue shadow of a beard on his lean face, spoke to my grandmother. He wore a clean shirt (but yellow from age and laundering), suit pants and an unmatching jacket.

"Pardon me?" said grandmother.

"I said that I tell dreams," the man informed her.

"You *tell* dreams," grandmother said. "Meaning, you have them?"

"Have them and tell them," he said mysteriously. The singer stopped singing.

"Any dream you want to know," said the singer, "he can tell it."

"I'm quite sure I don't want to know any," grandmother said. She viewed with displeasure the ascot of dark hair bursting out at the open throat of the singer's shirt. She would not regard the man who "told" dreams, at all.

"I can see you are a lady," the dream man told grandmother. "You don't respond to just every dream that comes along."

"Certainly not," said grandmother; she shot my father one of her how-could-you-have-let-this-happen-to-me? looks.

"But I know one," said the dream man; he shut his eyes. The singer slipped a chair forward and we suddenly realized he was sitting very close to us. Robo, though he was much too old for it, sat in father's lap. "In a great castle," the dream man began, "a woman lay beside her husband; she was wide awake, suddenly, in the middle of the night. She woke up without the slightest idea of what had awakened her, and she felt as alert as if she'd been up for hours. It was also clear to her, without a look, a word or a touch, that her husband was wide awake too—and just as suddenly."

"I hope this is suitable for the child to hear, ha ha," Herr Theobald said, but no one even looked at him. My grandmother folded her hands in her lap and stared at them—her knees together, her heels tucked under her straight-backed chair. My mother held my father's hand.

I sat next to the dream man, whose jacket smelled like the hay that animals sleep on. He said: "The woman and her husband lay awake listening for sounds in the castle, which they were renting and did not know intimately. They listened for sounds in the courtyard, which they never bothered to lock. The village people always took walks by the castle; the village children were allowed to swing on the great courtyard door. What had awakened them?"

"Bears?" said Robo, but father touched his fingertips to Robo's mouth.

"They heard horses," said the dream man. Old Johanna, her eyes shut, her head inclined toward her lap, seemed to shudder in her stiff chair. "They heard the breathing and stamping of horses who were trying to keep still. The husband reached out and touched his wife. 'Horses?' he said. The woman got out of bed and went to the courtyard window. She would swear to this day that the courtyard was full of soldiers on horseback—but *what* soldiers they were! They wore *armor!* The visors on their helmets were closed and their murmuring voices were as tinny and difficult to hear as voices on a fading radio station. Their armor clanked as their horses shifted restlessly under them.

"There was an old dry bowl of a former fountain, there in the castle's courtyard, but the woman saw that the fountain was flowing; the water slapped over the worn curb and the horses were drinking it. The knights were wary, they would not dismount; they looked up at the castle's dark windows, as if they knew they were uninvited at this watering trough—this rest station on their way, somewhere.

"In the moonlight the woman saw their big shields glint. She crept back to bed and lay rigidly against her husband. 'What is it?' he asked her.

"'Horses,' she told him.

"'I thought so,' he said. 'They'll eat the flowers.'

"'Who built this castle?' she asked him. It was a very old castle, they both knew that.

"'Charlemagne,' he told her; he was going back to sleep.

"But the woman lay awake, listening to the water which now seemed to be running all through the castle, gurgling in every drain, as if the old fountain were drawing water from every available source. And there were the distorted voices of the whispering knights—Charlemagne's soldiers speaking their dead language! And the horses kept drinking.

"The woman lay awake a long time, waiting for the soldiers to leave; she had no fear of attack from them; she was sure they were on a journey and had only stopped to rest at a place they once knew. But for as long as the water ran she felt that she mustn't disturb the castle. When she fell asleep, she thought Charlemagne's men were still there.

"In the morning her husband asked her, 'Did you hear water running, too?' Yes, she had. But the fountain was dry, of course, and out the window they could see that the flowers weren't eaten—and everyone knows horses eat flowers.

"But the woman knew that the good knights would never have let their horses trample the flower beds. She threw open the window and the strong smell of horses was rich in the courtyard—their sweat, their sweet hair, their dung.

"'But look,' said her husband; he went into the courtyard with her. 'There are no hoofprints, there are no droppings. We must have dreamed we heard them.' She did not tell him that she had *seen* them, too, or that there were soldiers; or that, in her opinion, it was unlikely that two people would dream the same dream. She did not remind him that he was a heavy smoker who never smelled the soup simmering; the aroma of horses in the fresh air would, understandably, be too subtle for him.

"She saw the soldiers, or dreamed them, twice more while they stayed there, but her husband never again woke up with her. It was always sudden. Once she woke with the taste of metal on her tongue, as if she'd touched some old, sour iron to her mouth—a sword, a chest plate, chain mail, a thigh guard. They were out there again, in colder weather. From the water in the fountain a dense fog surrounded them; the horses were snowy with frost. And there were not so many of them the next time—as if the winter or their skirmishes were reducing their numbers. The last time the horses looked gaunt to her, and the men looked more like unoccupied suits of armor balanced delicately in the saddles. The horses wore long masks of ice on their muzzles, their breathing (or the men's breathing) was congested.

"Her husband," said the dream man, "would die of a respiratory infection, but the woman did not know it when she dreamed this dream."

My grandmother looked up from her lap and slapped the dream man's beard-grey face. Robo stiffened in my father's lap; my mother caught her mother's hand. The singer shoved back his chair and jumped to his feet, frightened, or ready to fight someone, but the dream man simply bowed to grandmother and left the gloomy tea room. It was as if he'd made a contract with Johanna which was final but gave neither of them any joy. My father wrote something in the giant pad.

30

"Well, wasn't *that* some story?" said Herr Theobald. "Ha ha." He rumpled Robo's hair—something Robo always hated.

"Herr Theobald," my mother said, still holding Johanna's hand, "my father died of a respiratory infection."

"Oh dear," said Herr Theobald. "I'm sorry, *meine Frau*," he told grandmother, but old Johanna would not speak to him.

We took grandmother out to eat in a Class A restaurant, but she hardly touched her food. "That person was a gypsy," she told us, "a satanic being."

"Please, mother," my mother said. "He couldn't have known about father."

"He knew more than you know," grandmother snapped.

"The schnitzel is excellent," father said, writing in the pad. "The Gumpoldskirchner is just right with it. But the Bohnensalat is too wet."

"The Kalbsnieren are fine," I said.

"The eggs are okay," said Robo.

Grandmother said nothing until we returned to the Pension Grillparzer, where we noticed that the door to the W.C. was hung a foot or more off the floor, so that it resembled the bottom half of an American toilet stall door, or a saloon door in the Western movies. "I'm certainly glad I used the W.C. at the restaurant," grandmother said. "How revolting! I shall try to pass the night without exposing myself where every passer-by can peer at my ankles."

In our family room father said, "Didn't Johanna live in a castle before you were born? I thought she and Grandpa rented some castle."

"Yes!" mother said. "They rented Schloss Katzelsdorf. I still have the photographs."

"Well, that's why the Hungarian's dream upset her," father said.

"Someone is riding a bike in the hall," Robo said. "I saw a wheel go by, under our door."

"Robo, go to sleep," mother said.

"It went 'squeak-squeak,'" Robo said.

"Good night, boys," said father.

"If you can talk, we can talk," I said.

"Then talk to each other," father said. "I'm talking to your mother."

"I want to go to sleep," mother said. "I wish no one would talk."

31

We tried. Perhaps we slept. Then Robo whispered to me that he had to use the W.C.

"You know where it is," I said.

Robo went out the door, leaving it slightly open; I heard him walk down the corridor, brushing his hand along the wall. He was back very quickly.

"There's someone *in* the W.C.," he said.

"Well, wait for them to finish," I said.

"The light wasn't on," Robo said, "but I could still see under the door. Someone is in there, in the dark."

"I prefer the dark myself," I said.

But Robo insisted on telling me exactly what he'd seen. He said that under the door was a pair of *hands*.

"Hands?" I said.

"Yes, where the feet should have been," Robo said; he claimed that there was a hand on either side of the toilet—instead of a foot.

"Get out of here, Robo!" I said.

"Please come see," he begged. I went down the hall with him but there was no one in the W.C. "They've gone," he said.

"Walked off on their hands, no doubt," I said. "Go pee, I'll wait for you."

He went into the W.C. and peed sadly in the dark. When we were almost back to our room together, a small dark man with the same kind of skin and clothes as the dream man who had angered grandmother passed us in the hall. He winked at us, and smiled. I had to notice that he was walking on his hands.

"You see?" Robo whispered to me. We went into our room and shut the door.

"What is it?" mother said.

"A man walking on his hands," I said.

"A man *peeing* on his hands," Robo said.

"Class C," father murmured in his sleep; he often dreamed that he was making notes in the giant pad.

"We'll talk about it in the morning," mother said.

"He was probably just an acrobat who was showing off for you, because you're a kid," I told Robo.

"How did he know I was a kid when he was in the W.C.?" Robo asked me.

"Go to sleep," mother whispered.

We heard grandmother scream down the hall.

32

Mother put on her pretty green dressing gown; father put on his bathrobe and his glasses; I pulled on a pair of pants, over my pajamas. Robo was in the hall first. We saw the light coming from under the W.C. door; grandmother was screaming rhythmically in there.

"Here we are!" I called to her.

"Mother, what is it?" mother asked.

We gathered in the broad slot of light. We could see grandmother's mauve slippers and her porcelain-white ankles under the door. She stopped screaming. "I heard whispers when I was in my bed," she said.

"It was Robo and me," I told her.

"Then, when everyone seemed to have gone, I came into the W.C.," Johanna said. "I left the light off. I was very quiet," she told us. "Then I saw and heard the wheel."

"The *wheel*?" father asked.

"A wheel went by the door a few times," grandmother said. "It rolled by and came back and rolled by again."

Father made his fingers roll like wheels alongside his head; he made a face at mother. "Somebody needs a new set of wheels," he whispered, but mother looked crossly at him.

"I turned on the light," grandmother said, "and the wheel went away."

"I told you there was a bike in the hall," said Robo.

"Shut up, Robo," father said.

"No, it was not a bicycle," grandmother said. "There was only one wheel."

Father was making his hands go crazy beside his head. "She's got a wheel or two missing," he hissed at my mother, but she cuffed him and knocked his glasses askew.

"Then someone came and looked under the door," grandmother said, "and that is when I screamed."

"Someone?" said father.

"I saw his hands, a man's hands—there was hair on his knuckles," grandmother said. "His hands were on the rug right outside the door. He must have been looking up at me."

"No, grandmother," I said. "I think he was just standing out here on his hands."

"Don't be fresh," my mother whispered.

"But we saw a man walking on his hands," Robo said.

33

"You did *not*," father said.

"We did," I said. "And Robo saw him earlier, in the W.C. He was standing on his hands in the W.C."

"We're going to wake up everyone," mother cautioned us.

The toilet flushed and grandmother shuffled out the door with only a little of her former dignity intact. She was wearing a gown over a gown over a gown; her neck was very long and her face was creamed white. She looked like a troubled goose. "He was evil and vile," she said to us. "He knew terrible magic."

"The man who looked at you?" mother said.

"That man who told my dream," grandmother said. Now a tear made its way through her furrows of face cream. "That was *my* dream," she said, "and he told everyone. It is unspeakable that he even *knew* it," she hissed at us. "*My* dream—Charlemagne's horses and soldiers—*I* am the only one who should know it. I had the dream before you were born," she told mother. "And the vile evil magic man told my dream as if it were *news*.

"I never even told your father all there was to that dream. I was never sure that it *was* a dream. And now there are men on their hands, and their knuckles are hairy, and there are magic wheels. I want the boys to sleep with me."

So that was how Robo and I came to share the large family room, far away from the W.C., with grandmother, who lay on my mother's and father's pillows with her creamed face shining like the face of a wet ghost. Robo lay awake watching her. I do not think Johanna slept very well; I imagined she was dreaming her dream of horses, again—reliving the last winter of Charlemagne's cold soldiers with their strange metal clothes covered with frost and their armor frozen shut.

When it was obvious that I had to go to the W.C., Robo's round bright eyes followed me to the door.

There was someone in the W.C. There was no light shining from under the door, but there was a unicycle parked against the wall outside. Its rider sat in the dark W.C.; the toilet was flushing over and over again—like a child, the person was not giving the tank time to refill—and there was quite a terrible stench. I remembered my father saying, as he ushered my mother into Johanna's abandoned room: "If a man tried to pee while standing on his hands, it seems it would go all over his chin."

I went closer to the gap under the W.C. door, but the occupant

34

was not standing on his or her hands. I saw what were clearly feet, in almost the expected position—but *what* feet they were! The feet were shoed with fur—more hair, surely, than the hair on the knuckles grandmother had seen. The feet did not touch the floor; their soles tilted up toward me—dark bruise-colored pads. They were huge feet attached to short, furry shins. They were a bear's feet, only there were no claws. A bear's claws are not retractable, like a cat's; if a bear had claws, you would see them. Here was an imposter in a bearsuit, or a de-clawed bear. A domestic bear? At least—by its presence in the W.C.—a housebroken bear. For by its smell I could tell it was no man in a bearsuit: it was all bear. It was real bear.

I backed into the door of grandmother's room, behind which my father lurked, waiting for further disturbances. He snapped open the door and I fell inside, frightening us both. Mother sat up in bed and pulled the feather quilt over her head. "Got him!" father cried, dropping down on me. The floor trembled; the bear's unicycle slipped against the wall and fell into the door of the W.C., out of which the bear suddenly shambled, stumbling over its unicycle and lunging for its balance. Worriedly, it stared across the hall, through the open door, at father sitting on my chest. It picked up the unicycle in its front paws. "*Grauf?*" said the bear. Father slammed the door.

Down the hall we heard a woman call: "Where are you, Duna?"

"*Harf!*" the bear said.

Father and I heard the woman come closer. She said, "Oh, Duna, practicing again? Always practicing. But it's better in the daytime." The bear said nothing. Father opened the door.

"Don't let anyone else in," mother said, still under the featherbed.

In the hall a pretty, aging woman stood beside the bear who now balanced in place on its unicycle, one huge paw on the woman's shoulder. She wore a vivid red turban and a long wrap-around dress that resembled a curtain. Perched on her high bosom was a necklace strung with bear claws; her earrings touched the shoulder of her curtain-dress and her other, bare shoulder where my father and I stared at her fetching mole. "Good evening," she said to father. "I'm sorry if we've disturbed you. Duna is forbidden to practice at night, but he loves his work."

The bear muttered, pedaling away from the woman. The bear had very good balance but he was careless; he brushed against the walls of the hall and touched the photographs of the speed-skating teams with his paws. The woman, bowing away from father, went after the bear, calling "Duna, Duna, Duna. . ." and straightening the photographs as she followed him down the hall.

"*Duna* is the Hungarian word for the Danube," father told me. "That bear is named after our beloved *Donau*."

"*What* bear?" said mother. "I heard a *woman*. Did you drag a bear into our room? Is there another woman here?"

But I left father to explain it all to her. I knew that in the morning Herr Theobald would have much to explain, and I would hear everything reviewed at that time. I went across the hall to the W.C. My task there was hurried by the bear's lingering odor and by suspicion of bear hair on everything; it was only my suspicion, though, for the bear had left everything quite tidy—or at least neat for a bear.

"I saw the bear," I whispered to Robo, back in our room, but Robo had crept into grandmother's bed and had fallen asleep beside her. Old Johanna was awake, however—or she only *appeared* to be: her eyes were open and she turned somewhat in my direction when I whispered to Robo.

"I saw fewer and fewer soldiers," she said. "That last time they came there were only nine of them. Everyone looked so hungry; they must have eaten the extra horses. It was so cold. Of course I wanted to help them, but we weren't alive at the same time; how could I help them if I wasn't even born? Of course I knew they would die, but it took such a long time!

"The last time they came, the fountain was frozen. They used their swords and hatchets and long pikes to break the ice into chunks. They built a fire and melted the ice in a pot. They took bones from their saddlebags—bones of all kinds—and threw them in the soup. It must have been a very thin broth because the bones had long ago been gnawed clean. I don't know what bones they were. Rabbits, I suppose and maybe a deer or a wild boar. Maybe the extra horses. I do not choose to think that they were the bones of the missing soldiers."

"Go to sleep, grandmother," I said.

"Don't worry about the bear," she said.

* * *

In the breakfast room of the Pension Grillparzer—the same room as the tea room, in brighter light—we confronted Herr Theobald

36

with the menagerie of his other guests who had disrupted our evening. I knew that (as never before) my father was planning to reveal himself as a Tourist Bureau spy.

"Men walking about on their hands," father said.

"Men looking under the door of the W.C.," said grandmother. "*That* man," I said, and pointed to the small, sulking fellow at the corner table, seated for breakfast with his cohorts—the dream man and the Hungarian singer.

"He does it for his living," Herr Theobald told us, and as if to demonstrate that this was so, the man who stood on his hands began to stand on his hands.

"Make him stop that," father said. "We know he can do it."

"But did you know that he can't do it any other way?" the dream man asked suddenly, though he was not hostile. "Did you know his legs are useless? He has no shin bones. It is *wonderful* that he can walk on his hands! Otherwise, he wouldn't walk at all." The man, although it was clearly hard to do while standing on his hands, nodded his head.

"Please sit down," mother said.

"It is perfectly all right to be crippled," grandmother said, boldly. "But *you* are evil," she told the dream man. "You know things you have no right to know. He knew my *dream*," she told Herr Theobald, as if she were reporting a theft from her room.

"He is a *little* evil, I know," Theobald admitted. "But not usually! And he behaves better and better. He can't help what he knows."

"I was just trying to straighten you out," the dream man told grandmother. "I thought it would do you good. Your husband has been dead quite a while, after all, and it's about time you stopped making so much of that dream. You're not the only person who's had such a dream."

"Stop it!" grandmother shouted.

"Well, you ought to know," said the dream man.

"No, be quiet please," Herr Theobald told him.

"I am from the Tourist Bureau," father announced, probably because he couldn't think of anything else to say.

"Oh my God," Herr Theobald said.

"It's not Theobald's fault," said the singer. "It's our fault. He's nice to put up with us, though it costs him his reputation."

"They married my sister," Theobald told us. "They are *family*, you see. What can I do?"

"'They' married your sister?" mother said.

"Well, she married me first," said the dream man.

"And then she heard me sing!" laughed the singer.

"She's never been married to the other one," Theobald said, and everyone looked apologetically toward the man could only walk on his hands.

"But one day she will!" he cried. The dream man playfully hit him with a bun. The singer hooted with his mouth full, spraying crumbs.

"I don't think you could catch her!" the dream man hollered, and all three of them burst out laughing.

"Please!" cried Herr Theobald. "What will these people think?" The three misbehavers were sheepish and quiet. Theobald said, "They were once a circus act, but politics got them in trouble."

"We were the best in Hungary," said the singer. "You ever hear of the Circus Szolnok?"

"No, I'm afraid not," father said, seriously.

"We played in Miskolc, in Szeged, in Drebrecen," said the dream man.

"*Twice* in Szeged," the singer said.

"We would have made it to Budapest if it hadn't have been for the Russians," said the man who walked on his hands.

"Yes, it was the Russians who removed his shin bones," said the dream man.

"Tell the truth," the singer said. "He was *born* without shin bones. But it's true that we couldn't get along with the Russians."

"They tried to jail the bear," said the dream man.

"This is partly true," Theobald admitted.

"And we rescued his sister from them," said the man who walked on his hands.

"So of course I must put them up," said Herr Theobald, "and they work as hard as they can. But who is interested in their act in this country? It's a Hungarian thing. There is no *tradition* of bears on unicycles here," Theobald told us. "It means nothing to us Viennese."

"Tell the truth," said the dream man. "It is because I have told the wrong dreams. We worked a nightclub on the Kaerntnerstrasse, but then we were banned."

"You should never have told *that* dream," the singer said gravely.

"Well, it was your wife's responsibility too!" the dream man said.

"She was *your* wife, then," the singer said.

"And she will be mine!" sang the man who walked on his hands.

"Please stop it!" screamed Theobald.

"We get to do the balls for children's diseases," the singer said. "And some of the state hospitals—especially at Christmas. Or for some bigwig's birthday."

"If you would only do more with the bear," Herr Theobald advised them.

"Speak to your sister about that," said the dream man. "It's *her* bear, she's trained him, she's let him get lazy and sloppy and full of bad habits."

"He is the only one of you who never makes fun of me," said the man who could only walk on his hands.

"I would like to leave," grandmother said. "This is, for me, an awful experience."

"Please, dear lady," Herr Theobald said, "we only wanted to show you that we meant no offense. These are hard times. I need a B rating to attract more tourists, and I can't—in my heart—throw out the Circus Szolnok."

" 'In his heart,' my ass!" said the dream man. "He's afraid of his sister; he wouldn't dream of throwing us out."

"If he dreamed it, you would know it!" cried the man on his hands.

"I am afraid of the bear," Herr Theobald said. "It does everything she tells it to do."

"Say 'he,' not 'it,' " said the man on his hands. "He is a fine bear, and he never hurt anybody. He has no claws, as you know, and very few teeth either."

"The poor thing has a terribly hard time eating," Herr Theobald admitted. "He is quite old."

Over my father's shoulder, I saw him write in the giant pad: "An old bear and an unemployed circus act. This family is centered on the sister."

At that moment, out on the sidewalk, we could see her tending to the bear. It was early morning and the street was not especially busy. By law, of course, she had the bear on a leash, but it was a token control. In her startling red turban the woman walked up and down the sidewalk, following the lazy movements of the bear on his unicycle. The animal pedaled easily from parking meter to parking meter, sometimes leaning a paw on the meter as he turned. When he used the meter that way, the woman would scold him and bat at his paw. But the bear got away with what he could. He was very talented on the unicycle, you could tell; but you could also tell that the unicycle was a dead end for him. You could see that the bear felt he could go no further with unicycling.

"She should bring him off the street now," Herr Theobald fretted. "The people in the pastry shop next door complain to me," he told us. "They say the bear drives their customers away."

"But he makes them *come!*" said the man on his hands.

"It makes some people come, and it turns some away," the dream man said. He was suddenly somber, as if this profundity had depressed him.

But we had been so taken up with the antics of the Circus Szolnok that we had neglected old Johanna. When my mother saw that grandmother was quietly crying, she told me to bring the car around.

"It's been too much for her," my father whispered to Theobald. The Circus Szolnok looked ashamed of themselves.

At the door to the elevator grandmother said to Herr Theobald, "You have all gone too far, simply too far." Theobald seemed to accept this judgment; he said nothing. But the dream man was standing unpleasantly close to him, as if he were about to whisper an alarming dream in his ear, and even the usually cheerful singer looked potentially violent. The man who walked on his hands had not come to the elevator to see us off.

Outside on the sidewalk the bear pedaled up to me and handed me the keys; the car was parked at the curb. "Not everyone likes to be given the keys in that fashion," Herr Theobald told his sister.

"Oh, I thought he'd rather like it," she said, rumpling my hair. She was as appealing as a barmaid, which is to say that she was more appealing at night; in the daylight I could see that she was older than her brother, and older than her husbands too—and in time, I imagined, she would cease being lover and sister to them, respectively, and become a mother to them all. She was already a mother to the bear.

"Come over here," she said to him. He pedaled listlessly in place on his unicycle, hanging to a parking meter for support. He licked the little glass face of the meter. She tugged his leash. He stared at her. She tugged again. Insolently, the bear began to pedal—first one way, then the next. It was as if he took interest, seeing that he had an audience. He began to show off.

"Don't try anything," the sister said to him, but the bear pedaled

40

faster and faster, going forward, going backward, angling sharply
and veering among the parking meters; the sister had to let go of the
leash. "Duna, stop it!" she cried, but the bear was out of control. He
let the wheel roll too close to the curb and the unicycle pitched him
hard into the fender of a parked car. He sat on the sidewalk with the
unicycle beside him; you could tell that he hadn't injured himself,
but he looked very embarrassed and nobody laughed. The bear
looked like an old man who had taken a clumsy dump in the midst of
a sporting event meant for much younger people, and he sat wishing
for his dignity back while, in fact, he felt foolish and old and ashamed
of his awkwardness, his matted hair, and what terrible vanity had
ever made him attempt such a display. "Oh Duna," the sister said,
scoldingly, but she went over and crouched beside him at the curb.
"Duna, Duna," she reproved him, gently. He shook his big head; he
would not look at her. There was some saliva strung on the fur near
his mouth and she wiped this away with her hand; he pushed her
hand away with his paw.

"Come back again!" cried Herr Theobald, miserably, as we got
into the car.

"That bear is just like everyone else," Robo said.

Mother sat in the car with her eyes closed and her fingers massag-
ing her temples; this way she seemed to hear nothing we said. She
claimed it was her defense against traveling with such a contentious
family.

I steered us off through the tiny streets; I took Spiegelgasse to
Lobkowitzplatz. Spiegelgasse is so narrow that you can see the reflection of your own car in the windows of the shops you pass, and I felt
our movement through Vienna was superimposed—like a trick with
a movie camera, as if we made a fairy tale journey through a toy city.

I did not want to report on the usual business concerning the care
of the car, but I saw that father was trying to maintain order and
calm; he had the giant pad spread in his lap as if we'd just completed
a routine investigation. "What does the gauge tell us?" he asked.

"Someone put thirty-five kilometers on it," I said.

"That bear has been in here," grandmother said. "There are hairs
from the beast in the back seat, and I can smell him."

"I don't smell anything," father said.

"And the perfume of that slattern in the turban," grandmother
said. "It is hovering near the ceiling of the car." Father sniffed.
Mother continued to massage her temples.

41

On the floor by the brake and clutch pedals I saw several of the mintgreen toothpicks that the Hungarian singer was in the habit of wearing like a scar at the corner of his mouth. I didn't mention them. It was enough to imagine them all, out of the town in our car. The singing driver, the man on his hands beside him—waving out the window with his feet. And in back, separating the dream man from his former wife, the old bear slouched like a benign drunk, his great head brushing the upholstered roof, his mauling paws relaxed in his large lap.

"Those poor people," mother said, her eyes still closed.

"Liars and criminals," grandmother said. "Mystics and refugees and broken-down animals."

"They were trying hard," father said, "but they weren't coming up with the prizes."

"Better off in a zoo," said grandmother.

"I had a good time," Robo said.

"It's hard to break out of Class C," I said.

"They have fallen past Z," said old Johanna. "They have disappeared from the human alphabet."

"I think this calls for a letter," mother said.

But father raised his hand as if his other hand were touching a Bible, and we were quiet. He was writing in the giant pad and wished to be undisturbed. His face was stern. I knew that grandmother felt confident of his verdict. Mother knew it was useless to argue. Robo was already bored, and it was not until later that I read the final entry of the Pension Grillparzer.

Application for a B rating: approved. Father's reason: a lively family with lots of personality. And under the heading "Suspicion of Animals" father wrote (ambiguously): Just like everyone else.

When grandmother was asleep in the car, mother said, "I don't suppose that in this case a change in the rating will matter very much, one way or another."

"No," father said, "not much at all." He was right about that, though it would be years until I saw the Pension Grillparzer again.

* * *

When grandmother died, rather suddenly in her sleep, mother announced that she was tired of traveling. The real reason, however, was that she began to find herself plagued by grandmother's dream. "The horses are so thin," she told me once. "I mean, I always knew they would be thin, but not *this* thin. And the soldiers—I knew they were miserable," she said, "but not *that* miserable."

Father resigned from the Tourist Bureau and found a job with a local detective agency specializing in hotels and department stores. It was a satisfactory job for him, though he refused to work during the Christmas season—when, he said, some people ought to be allowed to steal a little.

My parents seemed to me to relax as they got older, and I really felt they were fairly happy near the end. I know that the strength of grandmother's dream was dimmed by the real world, and specifically by what happened to Robo. He went to a private school and was well liked there, but he was killed by a homemade bomb in his first year at the university. He was not even "political." In his last letter to my parents he wrote: "The self-seriousness of the radical factions among the students is much overrated. And the food is execrable." Then Robo went to his history class, and his classroom was blown apart.

It was after my parents died that I gave up smoking and took up traveling again. I took my second wife back to the Pension Grillparzer; with my first wife, I never got as far as Vienna.

The Grillparzer had not kept its B rating very long, and it had fallen from the ratings altogether by the time I returned to it. Herr Theobald's sister was in charge of the place. Gone was her tart appeal and in its place was the sexless cynicism of some maiden aunts. She was shapeless and her hair was dyed a sort of bronze, so that her head resembled one of those copper scouring pads that you use on a pot. She did not remember me and was suspicious of my questions. Because I appeared to know so much about her past associates, she probably thought I was with the police.

The Hungarian singer had gone away—another woman thrilled by his voice. The dream man had been *taken* away—to an institution. His own dreams had turned to nightmares and he'd awakened the pension each night with his horrifying howls. His removal from the seedy premises, said Herr Theobald's sister, was almost simultaneous with the loss of the Grillparzer's B rating.

Herr Theobald was dead. He had dropped down clutching his heart in the hall, where he ventured one night to investigate what he thought was a prowler. It was only Duna, the malcontent bear, who was dressed in the dream man's pin-striped suit. Why Theobald's sister had dressed the bear in this manner was not explained to me,

43

but the shock of the sullen animal unicycling in the lunatic's left-behind clothes had been enough to scare Herr Theobald to death.

The man who could only walk on his hands had also fallen into the gravest trouble. His wristwatch band snagged on a tine of an escalator and he was suddenly unable to hop off; his necktie, which he rarely wore because it dragged on the ground when he walked on his hands, was drawn under the step-off grate at the end of the escalator, where he was strangled. Behind him a line of people formed, marching in place by taking one step back and allowing the escalator to carry them forward, then taking another step back. It was quite a while before anyone got up the nerve to step over him. The world has many unintentionally cruel mechanisms that are not designed for people who walk on their hands.

After that, Theobald's sister told me, the Pension Grillparzer went from Class C to much worse. As the burden of management fell more heavily on her, she had less time for Duna and her bear grew senile and indecent in his habits. Once he bullied a mailman down the marble staircase at such a ferocious pace that the man fell and broke his hip; the attack was reported and an old city ordinance forbidding unrestrained animals in places open to the public was enforced. Duna was outlawed at the Pension Grillparzer.

For a while, Theobald's sister kept the bear in the cage in the courtyard of the building, but he was taunted by dogs and children, and food (and worse) was dropped into his cage from the apartments that faced the courtyard. He grew devious—only pretending to sleep—and he ate someone's cat. Then he was poisoned twice and became afraid to eat in this perilous enviroment. There was no alternative but to donate him to the Schoenbrunn Zoo, but there was even some doubt as to his acceptability. He was toothless and ill, perhaps contagious, and his long history of having been treated as a human being did not prepare him for the gentler routines of zoo life. His outdoor sleeping quarters in the courtyard of the Grillparzer had inflamed his rheumatism, and even his one talent—unicycling—was irretrievable. When he first tried it in the zoo, he fell. Someone laughed. Once anyone laughed at something Duna did, Theobald's sister explained, Duna would never do that thing again. He became, at last, a kind of charity case of Schoenbrunn, where he died a short two months after he'd taken up his new lodgings. In the opinion of Theobald's sister, Duna died of mortification—the result of a rash that had spread over his chest, which then had to be shaved.

In the cold courtyard of the building I looked in the bear's empty cage. The birds hadn't left a fruit seed, but in a corner of his cage was a looming mound of the bear's ossified droppings—as void of life, and even odor, as the corpses captured by the holocaust of Pompeii. I couldn't help thinking of Robo; of the bear, there were more remains.

In the car I was further depressed to notice that not one kilometer had been added to the gauge, not one kilometer had been driven in secret. There was no one around to take liberties anymore.

"When we're a safe distance away from your precious Pension Grillparzer," my second wife said to me, "I'd like you to tell me why you brought me to such a shabby place."

"It's a long story," I told her.

I was thinking I had noticed a curious lack of either enthusiasm or bitterness in the account of the world by Theobald's sister. There was in her story the flatness one associates with a storyteller who is accepting of unhappy endings, as if her life and her companions had never been exotic to *her*—as if they had always been staging a ludicrous and doomed effort at reclassification.

1977

45

GOING AFTER CACCIATO

by Tim O'Brien

from PLOUGHSHARES

I**T WAS A BAD TIME.** Billy Boy Watkins was dead, and so was
Frenchie Tucker. Billy Boy had died of fright, scared to death on the
field of battle, and Frenchie Tucker had been shot through the neck.
Lieutenants Sidney Martin and Walter Gleason had died in tunnels.
Pederson was dead and Bernie Lynn was dead. Buff was dead. They
were all among the dead. The war was always the same, and the rain
was part of the war. The rain fed fungus that grew in the men's socks
and boots, and their socks rotted, and their feet turned white and
soft so that the skin could be scraped off with a fingernail, and Stink
Harris woke up screaming one night with a leech on his tongue.
When it was not raining, a low mist moved like sleep across the

46

paddies, blending the elements into a single gray element, and the war was cold and pasty and rotten. Lieutenant Corson, who came to replace Lieutenant Martin, contracted the dysentery. The tripflares were useless. The ammunition corroded and the foxholes filled with mud and water during the nights, and in the mornings there was always the next village and the war was always the same. In early September Vaught caught an infection. He'd been showing Oscar Johnson the sharp edge on his bayonet, drawing it swiftly along his forearm and peeling off a layer of mushy skin. "Like a Gillette blueblade," Vaught had grinned. It did not bleed, but in a few days the bacteria soaked in and the arm turned yellow, and Vaught was carried aboard a Huey that dipped perpendicular, blades clutching at granite air, rising in its own wet wind and taking Vaught away. He never returned to the war. Later they had a letter from him that described Japan as smoky and full of bedbugs, but in the enclosed snapshot Vaught looked happy enough, posing with two sightly nurses, a long-stemmed bottle of wine rising from between his thighs. It was a shock to learn that he'd lost the arm. Soon afterward Ben Nystrom shot himself in the foot, but he did not die, and he wrote no letters. These were all things to talk about. The rain, too. Oscar said it made him think of Detroit in the month of May. "Not the rain," he liked to say. "Just the dark and gloom. It's Number One weather for rape and looting. The fact is, I do ninety-eight percent of my total rape and looting in weather just like this." Then somebody would say that Oscar had a pretty decent imagination for a nigger.

That was one of the jokes. There was a joke about Oscar. There were many jokes about Billy Boy Watkins, the way he'd collapsed in fright on the field of glorious battle. Another joke was about the lieutenant's dysentery, and another was about Paul Berlin's purple biles. Some of the jokes were about Cacciato, who was as dumb, Stink said, as a bullet, or, Harold Murphy said, as an oyster fart.

In October, at the end of the month, in the rain, Cacciato left the war.

"He's gone away," said Doc Peret. "Split for parts unknown."

The lieutenant didn't seem to hear. He was too old to be a lieutenant, anyway. The veins in his nose and cheeks were shattered by booze. Once he had been a captain on the way to being a major, but whiskey and the fourteen dull years between Korea and Vietnam had ended all that, and now he was just an old lieutenant with the

47

dysentery. He lay on his back in the pagoda, naked except for green socks and green undershorts.

"Cacciato," Doc Peret repeated. "He's gone away. Split, departed."

The lieutenant did not sit up. He held his belly with both hands as if to contain the disease.

"He's gone to Paris," Doc said. "That's what he tells Paul Berlin, anyhow, and Paul Berlin tells me, so I'm telling you. He's gone, packed up and gone."

"Paree," the lieutenant said softly. "In France, Paree? *Gay Paree?*"

"Yes, sir. That's what he says. That's what he told Paul Berlin, and that's what I'm telling you. You ought to cover up, sir."

The lieutenant sighed. He pushed himself up, breathing loud, then sat stiffly before a can of Sterno. He lit the Sterno and cupped his hands around the flame and bent down drawing in the heat. Outside, the rain was steady. "Paree," he said wearily. "You're saying Cacciato's left for gay Paree, is that right?"

"That's what he said, sir. I'm just relaying what he told to Paul Berlin. Hey, really, you better cover yourself up."

"Who's Paul Berlin?"

"Right here, sir. This is Paul Berlin."

The lieutenant looked up. His eyes were bright blue, oddly out of place in the sallow face. "You Paul Berlin?"

"Yes, sir," said Paul Berlin. He pretended to smile.

"Geez, I thought you were Vaught."

"Vaught's the one who cut himself, sir."

"I thought that was you. How do you like that?"

"Fine, sir."

The lieutenant sighed and shook his head sadly. He held a boot to dry over the burning Sterno. Behind him in the shadows sat the crosslegged, roundfaced Buddha, smiling benignly from its elevated perch. The pagoda was cold. Dank and soggy from a month of rain, the place smelled of clays and silicates and old incense. It was a single square room, built like a pillbox with a flat ceiling that forced the soldiers to stoop and kneel. Once it might have been an elegant house of worship, neatly tiled and painted and clean, candles burning in holders at the Buddha's feet, but now it was bombed-out junk. Sandbags blocked the windows. Bits of broken pottery lay under chipped pedestals. The Buddha's right arm was missing and his fat

48

groin was gouged with shrapnel. Still, the smile was intact. Head cocked, he seemed interested in the lieutenant's long sigh. "So. Cacciato's gone away, is that it?"

"There it is," Doc Peret said. "You've got it now."

Paul Berlin smiled and nodded.

"To gay Pareee," the lieutenant said. "Old Cacciato's going to Paree in France." He giggled, then shook his head gravely. "Still raining?"

"A bitch, sir."

"You ever seen rain like this? I mean, ever?"

"No, sir," Paul Berlin said.

"You Cacciato's buddy, I suppose?"

"No, sir," Paul Berlin said. "Sometimes he'd tag along, but not really."

"Who's his buddy?"

"Vaught, sir. I guess Vaught was, sometime."

"Well," the lieutenant said, dropping his nose inside the boot to smell the sweaty leather, "well, I guess we should just get Mister Vaught in here."

"Vaught's gone, sir. He's the one who cut himself—gangrene, remember?"

"Mother of Mercy."

Doc Peret draped a poncho over the lieutenant's shoulders. The rain was steady and thunderless and undramatic. Though it was mid-morning, the feeling was of endless dusk.

"Paree," the lieutenant murmured. "Cacciato's going to gay Paree—pretty girls and bare ass and Frogs everywhere. What's wrong with him?"

"Just dumb, sir. He's just awful dumb, that's all."

"And he's walking? He says he's walking to gay Paree?"

"That's what he says, sir, but you know how Cacciato can be."

"Does he know how far it is?"

"Six thousand eight hundred statute miles, sir. That's what he told me—six thousand eight hundred miles on the nose. He had it down pretty well. He had a compass and fresh water and maps and stuff."

"Maps," the lieutenant said. "Maps, flaps, schnaps. I guess those maps will help him cross the oceans, right? I guess he can just rig up a canoe out of those maps, no problem."

"Well, no," said Paul Berlin. He looked at Doc Peret, who shrugged. "No, sir. He showed me on the maps. See, he says he's going

49

through Laos, then into Thailand and Burma, and then India, and then some other country, I forget, and then into Iran and Iraq, and then Turkey, and then Greece, and the rest is easy. That's exactly what he said. The rest is easy, he said. He had it all doped out."

"In other words," the lieutenant said, lying back, "in other words, fuckin AWOL."

"There it is," said Doc Peret. "There it is."

The lieutenant rubbed his eyes. His face was sallow and he needed a shave. For a time he lay very still, listening to the rain, hands on his belly, then he giggled and shook his head and laughed. "What for? Tell me—what the fuck for?"

"Easy," Doc said. "Really, you got to stay covered up, sir, I told you that."

"What for? I mean, what for?"

"Shhhhhhh, he's just dumb, that's all."

The lieutenant's face was yellow. He laughed, rolling onto his side and dropping the boot. "I mean, why? What sort of shit is this—walking to fucking gay Paree? What kind of bloody war is this, tell me, what's wrong with you people? Tell me—what's *wrong* with you?"

"Shhhhhh," Doc purred, covering him up and putting a hand on his forehead. "Easy does it."

"Angel of Mercy, Mother of Virgins, what's *wrong* with you guys? Walking to gay Paree, what's *wrong*?"

"Nothing, sir. It's just Cacciato. You know how Cacciato can be when he puts his head to it. Relax now and it'll be all fine. Fine. It's just that rockhead, Cacciato."

The lieutenant giggled. Without rising, he pulled on his pants and boots and a shirt, then rocked miserably before the blue Sterno flame. The pagoda smelled like the earth, and the rain was unending. "Shoot," the lieutenant sighed. He kept shaking his head, grinning, then looked at Paul Berlin. "What squad you in?"

"Third, sir."

"That's Cacciato's squad?"

"Yes, sir."

"Who else?"

"Me and Doc and Eddie Lazzutti and Stink and Oscar Johnson and Harold Murphy. That's all, except for Cacciato."

"What about Pederson and Buff?"

"They're the dead ones, sir."

"Shoot." The lieutenant rocked before the flame. He did not look well. "Okay," he sighed, getting up. "Third Squad goes after Cacciato."

Leading to the mountains were four clicks of level paddy. The mountains jerked straight out of the rice, and beyond those mountains and other mountains was Paris.

The tops of the mountains could not be seen for the mist and clouds. The rain was glue that stuck the sky to the land.

The squad spent the night camped at the base of the first mountain, then in the morning they began the ascent. At mid-day Paul Berlin spotted Cacciato. He was half a mile up, bent low and moving patiently, steadily. He was not wearing a helmet—surprising, because Cacciato always took great care to cover the pink bald spot at the crown of his skull. Paul Berlin spotted him, but it was Stink Harris who spoke up.

Lieutenant Corson took out the binoculars.

"Him, sir?"

The lieutenant watched while Cacciato climbed towards the clouds.

"That him?"

"It's him. Bald as an eagle's ass."

Stink giggled. "Bald as Friar Tuck—it's Cacciato, all right. Dumb as a dink."

They watched until Cacciato was swallowed in the rain and clouds.

"Dumb-dumb," Stink giggled.

They walked fast, staying in a loose column. First the lieutenant, then Oscar Johnson, then Stink, then Eddie Lazzutti, then Harold Murphy, then Doc, then, at the rear, Paul Berlin. Who walked slowly, head down. He had nothing against Cacciato. The whole episode was silly, of course, a dumb and immature thing typical of Cacciato, but even so he had nothing special against him. It was just too bad. A waste of time in the midst of infinitely wider waste.

Climbing, he tried to picture Cacciato's face. The image came out fuzzed and amorphous and bland—entirely compatible with the boy's personality. Doc Peret, an acute observer of such things, hypothesized that Cacciato had missed Mongolian idiocy by the breadth of a single, wispy genetic hair. "Could have gone either way," Doc had said confidentially. "You see the slanting eyes? The

51

pasty flesh, just like jelly, right? The odd-shaped head? I mean, hey, let's face it—the guy's fuckin ugly. It's only a theory, mind you, but I'd wager big money that old Cacciato has more than a smidgen of the Mongol in him."

There may have been truth to it. Cacciato looked curiously unfinished, as though nature had struggled long and heroically but finally jettisoned him as a hopeless cause, not worth the diminishing returns. Open-faced, round, naive, plump, tender-complected and boyish, Cacciato lacked the fine detail, the refinements and final touches that maturity ordinarily marks on a boy of seventeen years. All this, the men concluded, added up to a case of simple gross stupidity. He wasn't positively disliked—except perhaps by Stink Harris, who took instant displeasure with anything vaguely his inferior—but at the same time Cacciato was no one's friend. Vaught, maybe. But Vaught was dumb, too, and he was gone from the war. At best, Cacciato was tolerated. The way men will sometimes tolerate a pesky dog.

It was just too bad. Walking to Paris, it was one of those ridiculous things Cacciato would do. Like winning the Bronze Star for shooting a dink in the face. Dumb. The way he was forever whistling. Too blunt-headed to know better, blind to the bodily and spiritual danger of human combat. In some ways this made him a good soldier. He walked point like a boy at his first county fair. He didn't mind the tunnel work. And his smile, more decoration than an expression of emotion, stayed with him in the most lethal of moments—when Billy Boy turned his last card, when Pederson floated face-up in a summer day's paddy, when Buff's helmet overflowed with an excess of red and gray fluids.

It was sad, a real pity.

Climbing the mountain, Paul Berlin felt an odd affection for the kid. Not friendship, exactly, but—real pity.

Not friendship. Not exactly. Pity, pity plus wonder. It was all silly, walking away in the rain, but it was something to think about.

They did not reach the summit of the mountain until midafternoon. The climb was hard, the rain sweeping down, the mountain oozing from beneath their feet. Below, the clouds were expansive, hiding the paddies and the war. Above, in more clouds, were more mountains.

Oscar Johnson found where Cacciato had spent the first night, a rock formation with an outcropping ledge as a roof, a can of burnt-out

Sterno, a chocolate wrapper, and a partly burned map. On the map, traced in red ink, was a dotted line that ran though the paddyland and up the first small mountain of the Annamese Cordillera. The dotted line ended there, apparently to be continued on another map.

"He's serious," the lieutenant said softly. "The blockhead's serious." He held the map as if it had a bad smell.

Stink and Oscar and Eddie Lazzutti nodded.

They rested in Cacciato's snug rock nest. Tucked away, looking out on the slate rain toward the next mountain, the men were quiet. Paul Berlin laid out a game of solitaire. Harold Murphy rolled a joint, inhaled, then passed it along, and they smoked and watched the rain and clouds and wilderness. It was peaceful. The rain was nice.

No one spoke until the ritual was complete.

Then, in a hush, all the lieutenant could say was, "Mercy."

"Shit," was what Stink Harris said.

The rain was unending.

"We could just go back," Doc Peret finally said. "You know, sir? Just head on back and forget him."

Stink Harris giggled.

"Seriously," Doc kept on, "we could just let the poor kid go. Make him MIA, strayed in battle, the lost lamb. Sooner or later he'll wake up, you know, and he'll see how insane it is and he'll come back."

The lieutenant stared into the rain. His face was yellow except for the network of broken veins.

"So what say you, sir? Let him go?"

"Dumber than a rock," Stink giggled.

"And smarter than Stink Harris."

"You know *what*, Doc."

"Pickle it."

"Who's saying to pickle it?"

"Just pickle it," said Doc Peret. "That's what."

Stink giggled but he shut up.

"What do you say, sir? Turn back?"

The lieutenant was quiet. At last he shivered and went into the rain with a wad of toilet paper. Paul Berlin sat alone, playing solitaire in the style of Las Vegas. Pretending, of course. Pretending to pay thirty thousand dollars for the deck, pretending ways to spend his earnings.

53

When the lieutenant returned he told the men to saddle up.

"We turning back?" Doc asked.

The lieutenant shook his head. He looked sick.

"I knew it!" Stink crowed. "Damn straight, I knew it! Can't hump away from a war, isn't that right, sir? The dummy has got to learn you can't just hump your way out of a war." Stink grinned and flicked his eyebrows at Doc Peret. "I knew it. By golly, I knew it!"

Cacciato had reached the top of the second mountain. Standing bareheaded, hands loosely at his sides, he was looking down on them through a blur of rain. Lieutenant Corson had the binoculars on him.

"Maybe he don't see us," Oscar said. "Maybe he's lost."

"Oh, he sees us. He sees us fine. Sees us real fine. And he's not lost. Believe me, he's not."

"Throw out smoke, sir?"

"Why not?" the lieutenant said. "Sure, why not throw out pretty smoke, why not?" He watched Cacciato through the glasses while Oscar threw out the smoke. It fizzled for a time and then puffed up in a heavy cloud of lavender. "Oh, he sees us," the lieutenant whispered. "He sees us fine."

"The bastard's *waving*!"

"I can see that, thank you. Mother of Saints."

As if stricken, the lieutenant suddenly sat down in a puddle, put his head in his hands and began to rock as the lavender smoke drifted up the face of the mountain. Cacciato was waving both arms. Not quite waving. The arms were flapping. Paul Berlin watched through the glasses. Cacciato's head was huge floating like a balloon in the high fog, and he did not look at all frightened. He looked young and stupid. His face was shiny. He was smiling, and he looked happy.

"I'm sick," the lieutenant said. He kept rocking. "I tell you, I'm a sick, sick man."

"Should I shout up to him?"

"Sick," the lieutenant moaned. "Sick, sick. It wasn't this way on Pusan, I'll tell you that. Sure, call up to him—I'm sick."

Oscar Johnson cupped his hands and hollered, and Paul Berlin watched through the glasses. For a moment Cacciato stopped waving. He spread his arms wide, as if to show them empty, slowly spreading them out like wings, palms up. Then his mouth opened wide, and in the mountains there was thunder.

"What'd he say?" The lieutenant rocked on his haunches. He was clutching himself and shivering. "Tell me what he said."

"Can't hear, sir. Oscar—?"

There was more thunder, long lasting thunder that came in waves from deep in the mountains. It rolled down and moved the trees and grasses.

"Shut the shit up!" The lieutenant was rocking and shouting at the rain and wind and thunder. "What'd the dumb fucker say?"

Paul Berlin watched through the glasses, and Cacciato's mouth opened and closed and opened, but there was only more thunder. Then his arms began flapping again. Flying, Paul Berlin suddenly realized. The poor kid was perched up there, arms flapping, trying to fly. Fly! Incredibly, the flapping motion was smooth and practiced and graceful.

"A chicken!" Stink squealed. "Look it! A squawking chicken!"

"Mother of Children."

"Look it!"

"A miserable chicken, you see that? A chicken!"

The thunder came again, breaking like Elephant Feet across the mountains, and the lieutenant rocked and held himself.

"For Christ sake," he moaned," "What'd he say? Tell me."

Paul Berlin could not hear. But he saw Cacciato's lips move, and the happy smile.

"Tell me."

So Paul Berlin, watching Cacciato fly, repeated it. "He said goodbye."

In the night the rain hardened into fog, and the fog was cold. They camped in the fog, near the top of the mountain, and the thunder stayed through the night. The lieutenant vomited. Then he radioed that he was in pursuit of the enemy.

"Gunships, Papa Two-Niner?" came the answer from far away.

"Negative," said the old lieutenant.

"Arty? Tell you what. You got a real sweet voice, Papa Two-Niner. No shit, a lovely voice." The radio-voice paused. "So, here's what I'll do, I'll give you a bargain on the arty—two for the price of one, no strings and a warranty to boot. How's that? See, we got this terrific batch of new 155 in, first class ordinance, I promise you, and what we do, what we do is this. What we do is we go heavy on volume here, you know? Keeps the prices low."

"Negative," the lieutenant said.

"Well, geez. Hard to please, right? Maybe some nice illum, then? Willie Peter, real boomers with some genuine sparkles mixed in. We're having this close-out sale, one time only."

"Negative. Negative, negative, negative."

"You'll be missing out on some fine shit."

"Negative, you monster."

"Okay," the radio-voice said, disappointed-sounding "but you'll wish . . . No offense, Papa Two-Niner. Have some happy hunting."

"Mercy," said the lieutenant into the blaze of static.

The night fog was worse than the rain, colder and more saddening. They lay under a sagging lean-to that seemed to catch and hold the fog like a net. Oscar and Harold Murphy and Stink and Eddie Lazzutti slept anyway, curled around one another like lovers. They could sleep and sleep.

"I hope he's moving," Paul Berlin whispered to Doc Peret. "I just hope he keeps moving. He does that, we'll never get him."

"Then they'll chase him with choppers. Or planes or something."

"Not if he gets himself lost," Paul Berlin said. "Not if he hides."

"What time is it?"

"Don't know."

"What time you got, sir?"

"Very lousy late," said the lieutenant from the bushes.

"Come on."

"Four o'clock. O-four-hundred, which is to say a.m. Got it?"

"Thanks."

"Charmed." His ass, hanging six inches from the earth, made a soft warm glow in the dark.

"You okay, sir?"

"I'm wonderful. Can't you see how wonderful I am?"

"I just hope Cacciato keeps moving," Paul Berlin whispered. "That's all I hope—I hope he uses his head and keeps moving."

"It won't get him anywhere."

"Get him to Paris maybe."

"Maybe," Doc sighed, turning onto his side, "and where is he then?"

"In Paris."

"No way. I like adventure, too, but, see, you can't walk to Paris from here. You just can't."

"He's smarter than you think," Paul Berlin said, not quite believing it. "He's not all that dumb."

"I know," the lieutenant said. He came from the bushes. "I know all about that."

"Impossible. None of the roads go to Paris."

"Can we light a Sterno, sir?"

"No," the lieutenant said, crawling under the lean-to and lying flat on his back. His breath came hard. "No, you can't light a fucking Sterno, and no, you can't go out to play without your mufflers and galoshes, and no, kiddies and combatants, no, you can't have chocolate sauce on your broccoli. No."

"All right."

"No!"

"You saying no, sir?"

"No," the lieutenant sighed with doom. "It's still a war, isn't it?"

"I guess."

"There you have it. It's still a war."

The rain resumed. It started with thunder, then lightning lighted the valley deep below in green and mystery, then more thunder, then it was just the rain. They lay quietly and listened. Paul Berlin, who considered himself abnormally sane, uncluttered by high ideas or lofty ambitions or philosophy, was suddenly struck between the eyes by a vision of murder. Butchery, no less. Cacciato's right temple caving inward, a moment of black silence, then the enormous explosion of outward-going brains. It was no metaphor; he didn't think in metaphors. No, it was a simple scary vision. He tried to reconstruct the thoughts that had led to it, but there was nothing to be found—the rain, the discomfort of mushy flesh. Nothing to justify such a bloody image, no origins. Just Cacciato's round head suddenly exploding like a pricked bag of helium: boom.

Where, he thought, was all this taking him, and where would it end? Murder was the logical circuit-stopper, of course; it was Cacciato's rightful, maybe inevitable due. Nobody can get away with stupidity forever, and in war the final price for it is always paid in purely biological currency, hunks of toe or pieces of femur or bits of exploded brain. And it *was* still a war, wasn't it?

Pitying Cacciato with wee-hour tenderness, and pitying himself for the affliction that produced such visions, Paul Berlin hoped for a miracle. He was tired of murder. Not scared by it—not at that particular moment—and not awed by it, just fatigued.

57

"He did some awfully brave things," he whispered. Then realized that Doc was listening. "He did. The time he dragged that dink out of his bunker, remember that."

"Yeah."

"The time he shot the kid in the kisser."

"I remember."

"At least you can't call him a coward, can you? You can't say he ran away because he was scared."

"You can say a lot of other shit, though."

"True. But you can't say he wasn't brave. You can't say that."

"Fair enough," Doc said. He sounded sleepy.

"I wonder if he talks French."

"You kidding, partner?"

"Just wondering. You think it's hard to learn French, Doc?"

"Cacciato?"

"Yeah, I guess not. It's a neat thing to think about, though, old Cacciato walking to Paris."

"Go to sleep,," Doc Peret advised. "Remember, pal, you got your own health to think of."

They were in the high country.

It was country far from the war, high and peaceful country with trees and thick grass, no people and no dogs and no lowland drudgery. Real wilderness, through which a single trail, liquid and shiny, kept taking them up.

The men walked with their heads down. Stink at point, then Eddie Lazzutti and Oscar, next Harold Murphy with the machine gun, then Doc, then the lieutenant, and last Paul Berlin.

They were tired and did not talk. Their thoughts were in their legs and feet, and their legs and feet were heavy with blood, for they'd been on the march many hours and the day was soggy with the endless rain. There was nothing symbolic, or melancholy, about the rain. It was simple rain, everywhere.

They camped that night beside the trail, then in the morning continued the climb. Though there were no signs of Cacciato, the mountain had only one trail and they were on it, the only way west.

Paul Berlin marched mechanically. At his sides, balancing him evenly and keeping him upright, two canteens of Kool-Aid lifted and fell with his hips, and the hips rolled in their ball-and-socket joints.

He respired and sweated. His heart hard, his back strong, up the high country.

They did not see Cacciato, and for a time Paul Berlin thought they might have lost him forever. It made him feel better, and he climbed the trail and enjoyed the scenery and the sensations of being high and far from the real war, and then Oscar found the second map.

The red dotted line crossed the border into Laos.

Farther ahead they found Cacciato's helmet and armored vest, then his dogtags, then his entrenching tool and knife.

"Dummy just keeps to the trail," the lieutenant moaned. "Tell me why?" Why doesn't he leave the trail?"

"It's the only way to Paris," Paul Berlin said.

"A rockhead," said Stink Harris. "That's why."

Liquid and shiny, a mix of rain and red clay, the trail took them higher.

Cacciato eluded them but he left behind the wastes of his march—empty tins, bits of bread, a belt of golden ammo dangling from a dwarf pine, a leaking canteen, candy wrappers and worn rope. Clues that kept them going. Tantalizing them on, one step then the next—a glimpse of his bald head, the hot ash of a breakfast fire, a handkerchief dropped coyly along the path.

So they kept after him, following the trails that linked one to the next westward in a simple linear direction without deception. It was deep, jagged, complex country, dark with the elements of the season, and ahead was the frontier.

"He makes it that far," Doc Peret said, pointing to the next line of mountains, "and we can't touch him."

"How now?"

"The border," Doc said. The trail had leveled out and the march was easier. "He makes it to the border and it's bye-bye Cacciato."

"How far?"

"Two clicks maybe. Not far."

"Then he's made it," whispered Paul Berlin.

"Maybe so."

"By God!"

"Maybe so," Doc said.

"Boy, lunch at Tour d'Argent! A night at the old opera!"

"Maybe so."

The trail narrowed, then climbed, and a half-hour later they saw him.

He stood at the top of a small grassy hill, two hundred meters ahead. Loose and at ease, smiling, Cacciato already looked like a civilian. His hands were in his pockets and he was not trying to hide himself. He might have been waiting for a bus, patient and serene and not at all frightened.

"Got him!" Stink yelped. "I knew it! Now we got him!"

The lieutenant came forward with the glasses.

"I knew it," Stink crowed, pressing forward. "The blockhead's finally giving it up—giving up the old ghost, I knew it!"

"What do we do, sir?"

The lieutenant shrugged and stared through the glasses.

"Fire a shot?" Stink held his rifle up and before the lieutenant could speak he squeezed off two quick rounds, one a tracer that turned like a corkscrew through the mist. Cacciato smiled and waved.

"Look at him," Oscar Johnson said. "I do think we got ourselves a predicament. Truly a predicament."

"There it is," Eddie said, and they both laughed, and Cacciato kept smiling and waving.

"A true predicament."

Stink Harris took the point, walking fast and chattering, and Cacciato stopped waving and watched him come, arms folded and his big head cocked as if listening for something. He looked amused.

There was no avoiding it.

Stink saw the wire as he tripped it, but there was no avoiding it.

The first sound was that of a zipper suddenly yanked up; next, a popping noise, the spoon releasing and primer detonating; then the sound of the grenade dropping; then the fizzling sound. The sounds came separately but quickly.

Stink knew it as it happened. With the next step, in one fuzzed motion, he flung himself down and away, rolling, covering his skull, mouth open, yelping a funny, trivial little yelp.

They all knew it.

Eddie and Oscar and Doc Peret dropped flat, and Harold Murphy bent double and did an oddly graceful jackknife for a man of his size, and the lieutenant coughed and collapsed, and Paul Berlin, seeing purple, closed his eyes and fists and mouth, brought his knees to his belly, coiling, and let himself fall.

Count, he thought, but the numbers came in a tangle without sequence.

His belly hurt. That was where it started. First the belly, a release of fluids in the bowels next, a shitting feeling, a draining of all the pretensions and silly hopes for himself, and he was back where he started, writhing. The lieutenant was beside him. The air was windless—just the misty rain. His teeth hurt. Count, he thought, but his teeth hurt and no numbers came. I don't want to die, he thought lucidly, with hurting teeth.

There was no explosion. His teeth kept hurting and his belly was floating in funny ways.

He was ready, steeled. His lungs hurt now. He was ready, but there was no explosion. Then came a fragile pop. Smoke, he thought without thinking, smoke.

"Smoke," the lieutenant moaned, then repeated it, "fucking smoke."

Paul Berlin smelled it. He imagined its velvet color, purple, but he could not open his eyes. He tried, but he could not open his eyes or unclench his fists or uncoil his legs, and the heavy fluids in his stomach were holding him down, and he could not wiggle or run to escape. There was no explosion.

"Smoke," Doc said softly. "Just smoke."

It was red smoke, and the message seemed clear. It was all over them. Brilliant red, thick, acid-tasting. It spread out over the earth like paint, then began to climb against gravity in a lazy red spiral.

"Smoke," Dock said. "Smoke."

Stink Harris was crying. He was on his hands and knees, chin against his throat, bawling and bawling. Oscar and Eddie had not moved.

"He had us," the lieutenant whispered. His voice was hollowed out, senile sounding, almost a reminiscence. "He could've had all of us."

"Just smoke," Doc said. "Lousy smoke is all."

"The dumb fucker could've had us."

Paul Berlin could not move. He felt entirely conscious, a little embarrassed but not yet humiliated, and he heard their voices, heard Stink weeping and saw him beside the trail on his hands and knees, and he saw the red smoke everywhere, but he could not move.

* * *

61

"He won't come," said Oscar Johnson, returning under a white flag. "Believe me, I tried, but the dude just won't play her cool."

It was dusk and the seven soldiers sat in pow-wow.

"I told him it was crazy as shit and he'd probably end up dead, and I told him how his old man would shit when he heard about it. Told him maybe things wouldn't go so hard if he just gave up and come back right now. I went through the whole spiel, top to bottom. The dude just don't listen."

The lieutenant was lying prone, Doc's thermometer in his mouth, sick-looking. It wasn't his war. The skin on his arms and neck was loose around deteriorating muscle.

"I told him—I told him all that good shit. Told him it's ridiculous, dig? I told him it won't work, no matter what, and I told him we're fed up. Fed up."

"You tell him we're out of rations?"

"Shit, yes, I told him that. And I told him he's gonna starve his own ass if he keeps going, and I told him we'd have to call in gunships if it came to it."

"You tell him he can't walk to France?"

Oscar grinned. He was black enough to be indistinct in the dust. "Maybe I forgot to tell him that."

"You should've told him."

The lieutenant slid a hand behind his neck and pushed against it as if to relieve some spinal pressure. "What else?" he asked. "What else did he say?"

"Nothing, sir. He said he's doing okay. Said he was sorry to scare us with the smoke."

"The bastard." Stink kept rubbing his hands against the black stock of his rifle.

"What else?"

"Nothing. You know how he is, sir. Just a lot of smiles and stupid stuff. He asked how everybody was, so I said we're fine, except for the scare with the smoke boobytrap, and then he said he was sorry about that, so I told him it was okay. What can you say to a dude like that?"

The lieutenant nodded, pushing against his neck. He was quiet awhile. He seemed to be making up his mind. "All right," he finally sighed. "What'd he have with him?"

"Sir?"

"Musketry," the lieutenant said. "What kind of weapons?"

"His rifle. That's all, his rifle and some bullets. I didn't get much of a look."

"Claymores?"

Oscar shook his head. "I didn't see none. Maybe so."

"Grenades?"

"I don't know. Maybe a couple."

"Beautiful recon job, Oscar. Real pretty."

"Sorry, sir. He had his stuff tight, though."

"I'm sick."

"Yes, sir."

"Dysentery's going through me like coffee. What you got for me, Doc?"

Doc Peret shook his head. "Nothing, sir. Rest."

"That's it," the lieutenant said. "What I need is rest."

"Why not let him go, sir?"

"Rest," the lieutenant said, "is what I need."

Paul Berlin did not sleep. Instead he watched Cacciato's small hill and tried to imagine a proper ending.

There were only a few possiblities remaining, and after what had happened it was hard to see a happy end to it. Not impossible, of course. It could still be done. With skill and boldness, Cacciato might slip away and cross the frontier mountains and be gone. He tried to picture it. Many new places. Villages at night with barking dogs, people whose eyes and skins would change in slow evolution and counterevolution as Cacciato moved westward with whole continents before him and the war far behind him and all the trails connecting and leading toward Paris. It could be done. He imagined the many dangers of Cacciato's march, treachery and deceit at every turn, but he also imagined the many good times ahead, the stinging feel of aloneness, and new leanness and knowledge of strange places. The rains would end and the trails would go dry and be baked to dust, and there would be changing foliage and great expanses of silence and songs and pretty girls in straw huts and, finally, Paris.

It could be done. The odds were like poison, but it could be done.

Later, as if a mask had been peeled off, the rain ended and the sky cleared and Paul Berlin woke to see the stars.

They were in their familiar places. It wasn't so cold. He lay on his back and counted the stars and named those that he knew, named the constellations and the valleys of the moon. It was just too bad.

Crazy, but still sad. He should've kept going—left the trails and waded through streams to rinse away the scent, buried his feces, swung from the trees branch to branch; he should've slept through the days and ran through the nights. It might have been done.

Toward dawn he saw Cacciato's breakfast fire. He heard Stink playing with the safety catch on his M-16, a clicking noise like a slow morning cricket. The sky lit itself in patches.

"Let's do it," the lieutenant whispered.

Eddie Lazzutti and Oscar and Harold Murphy crept away toward the south. Doc and the lieutenant waited a time then began to circle west to block a retreat. Stink Harris and Paul Berlin were to continue up the trail.

Waiting, trying to imagine a rightful and still happy ending, Paul Berlin found himself pretending, in a vague sort of way, that before long the war would reach a climax beyond which everything else would become completely commonplace. At that point he would stop being afraid. All the bad things, the painful and grotesque things, would be in the past, and the things ahead, if not lovely, would at least be tolerable. He pretended he had crossed that threshold.

When the sky was half-light, Doc and the lieutenant fired a red flare that streaked high over Cacciato's grassy hill, hung there, then exploded in a fanning starburst like the start of a celebration. Cacciato Day, it might have been called. October something, in the year 1968, the year of the Pig.

In the trees at the southern slope of the hill Oscar and Eddie and Harold Murphy each fired red flares to signal their advance.

Stink went into the weeds and hurried back, zipping up his trousers. He was very excited and happy. Deftly, he released the bolt on his weapon and it slammed hard into place.

"Fire the flare," he said, "and let's go."

Paul Berlin took a long time opening his pack.

But he found the flare, unscrewed its lid, laid the firing pin against the primer, then jammed it in.

The flare jumped away from him. It went high and fast, rocketing upward and taking a smooth arc that followed the course of the trail, leaving behind a dirty wake of smoke.

At its apex, with barely a sound, the flare exploded in a green dazzle over Cacciato's hill. It was a fine, brilliant shade of green.

"Go," whispered Paul Berlin. It did not seem enough. "Go," he said, and then he shouted, "Go."   *1977*

ROUGH STRIFE

by LYNNE SHARON SCHWARTZ

from ONTARIO REVIEW

> Now let us sport us while we may;
> And now, like am'rous birds of prey
> . . . tear our pleasure with rough strife
> Through the iron gates of life.
> —*Andrew Marvell*

CAROLINE AND IVAN finally had a child. Conception stunned them; they didn't think, by now, that it could happen. For years they had tried and failed, till it seemed that a special barren destiny was preordained. Meanwhile, in the wide spaces of childlessness, they had created activity: their work flourished. Ivan, happy and moderately powerful in a large foundation, helped decide how to distribute money for artistic and social projects. Caroline taught mathematics at a small suburban university. Being a mathematician, she found, conferred a painful private wisdom on her efforts to conceive. In her brain, as Ivan exploded within her, she would involuntarily calculate probabilities; millions of blind sperm and one reluctant egg clustered before her eyes in swiftly transmuting geometric patterns. She lost her grasp of pleasure, forgot what it could feel like without a goal. She had no idea what Ivan might be thinking about, scattered seed money, maybe. Their passion became courteous and automatic until, by attrition, for months they didn't make love—it was too awkward.

One September Sunday morning she was in the shower, watching, through a crack in the curtain, Ivan naked at the washstand. He was shaving, his jaw tilted at an innocently self-satisfied angle. He wasn't aware of being watched, so that a secret quality, an essence of Ivan, exuded in great waves. Caroline could almost see it, a cloudy aura. He stroked his jaw vainly with intense concentration, a self-absorption so contagious that she needed, suddenly, to possess it with him. She stepped out of the shower.

"Ivan."

He turned abruptly, surprised, perhaps even annoyed at the interruption.

"Let's not have a baby any more. Let's just . . . come on." When she placed her wet hand on his back he lifted her easily off her feet with his right arm, the razor still poised in his other, outstretched hand.

"Come on," she insisted. She opened the door and a draft blew into the small steamy room. She pulled him by the hand toward the bedroom.

Ivan grinned. "You're soaking wet."

"Wet, dry, what's the difference?" It was hard to speak. She began to run, to tease him; he caught her and tossed her onto their disheveled bed and dug his teeth so deep into her shoulder that she thought she would bleed.

Then with disinterest, taken up only in this fresh rushing need for him, weeks later Caroline conceived. Afterwards she liked to say that she had known the moment it happened. It felt different, she told him, like a pin pricking a balloon, but without the shattering noise, without the quick collapse. "Oh, come on," said Ivan. "That's impossible."

But she was a mathematician, after all, and dealt with infinitesimal precise abstractions, and she did know how it had happened. The baby was conceived in strife, one early October night, Indian summer. All day the sun glowed hot and low in the sky, settling an amber torpor on people and things, and the night was the same, only now a

66

dark hot heaviness sunk slowly down. The scent of the still-blooming honeysuckle rose to their bedroom window. Just as she was bending over to kiss him, heavy and quivering with heat like the night, he teased her about something, about a mole on her leg, and in reply she punched him lightly on the shoulder. He grabbed her wrists, and when she began kicking, pinned her feet down with his own. In an instant Ivan lay stretched out on her back like a blanket, smothering her, while she struggled beneath, writhing to escape. It was a silent, sweaty struggle, interrupted with outbursts of wild laughter, shrieks and gasping breaths. She tried biting but, laughing loudly, he evaded her, and she tried scratching the fists that held her down, but she couldn't reach. All her desire was transformed into physical effort, but he was too strong for her. He wanted her to say she gave up, but she refused, and since he wouldn't loosen his grip they lay locked and panting in their static embrace for some time.

"You win," she said at last, but as he rolled off she sneakily jabbed him in the ribs with her elbow.

"Aha!" Ivan shouted, and was ready to begin again, but she quickly distracted him. Once the wrestling was at an end, though, Caroline found her passion dissipated, and her pleasure tinged with resentment. After they made love forcefully, when they were covered with sweat, dripping on each other, she said, "Still, you don't play fair."

"I don't play fair! Look who's talking. Do you want me to give you a handicap?"

"No."

"So?"

"It's not fair, that's all."

Ivan laughed gloatingly and curled up in her arms. She smiled in the dark.

That was the night the baby was conceived, not in high passion but rough strife.

She lay on the table in the doctor's office weeks later. The doctor, whom she had known for a long time, habitually kept up a running conversation while he probed. Today, fretting over his weight problem, he outlined his plans for a new diet. Tensely she watched him, framed and centered by her raised knees, which were still bronzed from summer sun. His other hand was pressing on her stomach. Caroline was nauseated with fear and trembling, afraid of the verdict. It was taking so long, perhaps it was a tumor.

67

"I'm cutting out all starches," he said. "I've really let myself go lately."

"Good idea." Then she gasped in pain. A final, sickening thrust, and he was out. Relief, and a sore gap where he had been. In a moment, she knew, she would be retching violently.

"Well?"

"Well, Caroline, you hit the jackpot this time."

She felt a smile, a stupid, puppet smile, spread over her face. In the tiny bathroom where she threw up, she saw in the mirror the silly smile looming over her ashen face like a dancer's glowing grimace of labored joy. She smiled through the rest of the visit, through his advice about milk, weight, travel and rest, smiled at herself in the window of the bus, and at her moving image in the fenders of parked cars as she walked home.

Ivan, incredulous over the telephone, came home beaming stupidly just like Caroline, and brought a bottle of champagne. After dinner they drank it and made love.

"Do you think it's all right to do this?" he asked.

"Oh, Ivan, honestly. It's microscopic."

He was in one of his whimsical moods and made terrible jokes that she laughed at with easy indulgence. He said he was going to pay the baby a visit and asked if she had any messages she wanted delivered. He unlocked from her embrace, moved down her body and said he was going to have a look for himself. Clowning, he put his ear between her legs to listen. Whatever amusement she felt soon ebbed away into irritation. She had never thought Ivan would be a doting parent—he was so preoccupied with himself. Finally he stopped his antics as she clasped her arms around him and whispered, "Ivan, you are really too much." He became unusually gentle. Tamed, and she didn't like it, hoped he wouldn't continue that way for months. Pleasure lapped over her with a mild, lackadaisical bitterness, and then when she could be articulate once more she explained patiently, "Ivan, you know, it really is all right. I mean, it's a natural process."

"Well I didn't want to hurt you."

"I'm not sick."

Then, as though her body were admonishing that cool confidence, she did get sick. There were mornings when she awoke with such paralyzing nausea that she had to ask Ivan to bring her a hard roll from the kitchen before she could stir from bed. To move from her awakening position seemed a tremendous risk, as if she might spill out. She rarely threw up—the nausea resembled violent hunger. Something wanted to be filled, not expelled, a perilous vacuum occupying her insides. The crucial act was getting the first few mouthfuls down. Then the solidity and denseness of the hard unbuttered roll stabilized her, like a heavy weight thrown down to anchor a tottering ship. Her head ached. On the mornings when she had no classes she would wander around the house till almost noon clutching the partly-eaten roll in her hand like a talisman. Finishing one roll, she quickly went to the breadbox for another; she bought them regularly at the bakery a half-dozen at a time. With enough roll inside her she could sometimes manage a half-cup of tea, but liquids were risky. They sloshed around inside and made her envision the baby sloshing around too, in its cloudy fluid. By early afternoon she would feel fine. The baby, she imagined, claimed her for the night and was reluctant to give up its hold in the morning: they vied till she conquered. She was willing to yield her sleeping hours to the baby, her dreams even, if necessary, but she wanted the daylight for herself.

The mornings that she taught were agony. Ivan would wake her up early, bring her a roll, and gently prod her out of bed.

"I simply cannot do it," she would say, placing her legs cautiously over the side of the bed.

"Sure you can. Now get up."

"I'll die if I get up."

"You have no choice. You have a job." He was freshly showered and dressed, and his neatness irritated her. He had nothing more to do—the discomfort was all hers. She rose to her feet and swayed.

Ivan looked alarmed. "Do you want me to call and tell them you can't make it?"

"No, no." That frightened her. She needed to hold on to the job, to defend herself against the growing baby. Once she walked into the classroom she would be fine. A Mondrian print hung on the back wall—she could look at that, and it would steady her. With waves of nausea roiling in her chest, she stumbled into the bathroom.

She liked him to wait until she was out of the shower before he left for work, because she anticipated fainting under the impact of the water. Often at the end she forced herself to stand under an ice cold flow, leaning her head way back and letting her short fair hair drip down behind her. Though it was torture, when she emerged she felt more alive.

After the shower had been off a while Ivan would come and open the bathroom door. "Are you O.K. now, Caroline? I've got to go." It made her feel like a child. She would be wrapped in a towel with her hair dripping on the mat, brushing her teeth or rubbing cream into her face. "Yes, thanks for waiting, I guess this'll end soon. They say it's only the first few months."

He kissed her lips, her bare damp shoulder, gave a parting squeeze to her toweled behind, and was gone. She watched him walk down the hall. Ivan was very large. She had always been drawn and aroused by his largeness, by the huge bones and the taut legs that felt as though he had steel rods inside. But now she watched with some trepidation, hoping Ivan wouldn't have a large, inflexible baby.

Very slowly she would put on clothes. Selecting each article seemed a much more demanding task than ever before. Seeing how slow she had become, she allowed herself over an hour, keeping her hard roll nearby as she dressed and prepared her face. All the while, through the stages of dressing, she evaluated her body closely in the full-length mirror, first naked, then in bra and underpants, then with shoes added, and finally with a dress. She was looking for signs, but the baby was invisible. Nothing had changed yet. She was still as she had always been, not quite slim yet somehow appearing small, almost delicate. She used to pride herself on strength. When they moved in she had worked as hard as Ivan, lugging furniture and lifting heavy cartons. He was impressed. Now, of course, she could no longer do that—it took all her strength to move her own weight.

With the profound sensuous narcissism of women past first youth, she admired her still-narrow waist and full breasts. She was especially fond of her shoulders and prominent collarbone, which had a fragile, inviting look. That would all be gone soon, of course, gone soft. Curious about how she would alter, she scanned her face for the pregnant look she knew well from the faces of friends. It was far less a tangible change than a look of transparent vulnerability that took over the face: nearly a pleading look, a beg for help like a message from a powerless invaded country to the rest of the world. Caroline did not see it on her face yet.

From the tenth to the fourteenth week of her pregnancy she slept, with brief intervals of lucidity when she taught her classes. It was a strange dreamy time. The passionate nausea faded, but the lure of the bed was irresistible. In the middle of the day, even, she could pass by the bedroom, glimpse the waiting bed and be overcome by the soft heavy desire to lie down. She fell into a stupor immediately and did not dream. She forgot what it was like to awaken with energy and move through an entire day without lying down once. She forgot the feeling of eyes opened wide without effort. She would have liked to hide this strange, shameful perversity from Ivan, but that was impossible. Ivan kept wanting to go to the movies. Clearly, he was bored with her. Maybe, she imagined, staring up at the bedroom ceiling through slitted eyes, he would become so bored he would abandon her and the baby and she would not be able to support the house alone and she and the baby would end up on the streets in rags, begging. She smiled. That was highly unlikely. Ivan would not be the same Ivan without her.

"You go on, Ivan. I just can't."

Once he said, "I thought I might ask Ruth Forbes to go with me to see the Charlie Chaplin in town. I know she likes him. Would that bother you?"

She was half-asleep, slowly eating a large apple in bed and watching *Medical Center* on television, but she roused herself to answer. "No, of course not." Ruth Forbes was a divorced woman who lived down the block, a casual friend and not Ivan's type at all, too large, loud and depressed. Caroline didn't care if he wanted her company. She didn't care if he held her hand on his knee in the movies as he liked to do, or even if, improbably, he made love to her afterwards in her sloppy house crawling with children. She didn't care about anything except staying nestled in bed.

She made love with him sometimes, in a slow way. She felt no specific desire but didn't want to deny him, she loved him so. Or had, she thought vaguely, when she was alive and strong. Besides, she knew she could sleep right after. Usually there would be a moment when she came alive despite herself, when the reality of his body would strike her all at once with a wistful throb of lust, but mostly she was too tired to see it through, to leap towards it, so she let it subside, merely nodding at it gratefully as a sign of dormant life. She felt sorry for Ivan, but helpless.

Once to her great shame, she fell asleep while he was inside her. He woke her with a pat on her cheek, actually, she realized from the faint sting, a gesture more like a slap than a pat. "Caroline, for Christ's sake, you're sleeping."

"No, no, I'm sorry. I wasn't really sleeping. Oh, Ivan, it's nothing. This will end." She wondered, though.

Moments later she felt his hands on her thighs. His lips were brooding on her stomach, edging, with expertise, lower and lower down. He was murmuring something she couldn't catch. She felt an ache, an irritation. Of course he meant well, Ivan always did. Wryly, she appreciated his intentions. But she couldn't bear that excitement now.

"Please," she said. "Please don't do that."

He was terribly hurt. He said nothing, but leaped away violently and pulled all the blankets around him. She was contrite, shed a few private tears and fell instantly into a dreamless dark.

He wanted to go to a New Year's Eve party some close friends were giving, and naturally he wanted her to come with him. Caroline vowed to herself she would do this for him because she had been giving so little for so long. She planned to get dressed and look very beautiful, as she could still look when she took plenty of time and tried hard enough; she would not drink very much—it was sleep-inducing—and she would not be the one to suggest going home. After sleeping through the day in preparation, she washed her hair, using something she found in the drugstore to heighten the blonde flecks. Then she put on a long green velvet dress with gold embroidery, and inserted the gold hoop earrings Ivan bought her some years ago for her twenty-fifth birthday. Before they set out she drank a cup of black coffee. She would have taken No-Doze but she was afraid of drugs, afraid of giving birth to an armless or legless baby who would be a burden and a heartache to them for the rest of their days.

At the party of mostly university people, she chatted with everyone equally, those she knew well and those she had never met. Sociably, she held a filled glass in her hand, taking tiny sips. She and Ivan were not together very much—it was crowded, smoky and loud; people kept moving and encounters were brief—but she knew he was aware of her, could feel his awareness through the milling bodies. He was aware and he was pleased. He deserved more than the somnambulist she had become, and she was pleased to please him. But after a while her legs would not support her for another instant. The skin tingled: soft warning bells rang from every pore.

She allowed herself a moment to sit down alone in a small alcove off the living room, where she smoked a cigarette and stared down at her lap, holding her eyes open very wide. Examining the gold and rose-colored embroidery on her dress, Caroline traced the coiled pattern, mathematical and hypnotic, with her index finger. Just as she was happily merging into its intricacies, a man, a stranger, came in, breaking her trance. He was a very young man, twenty-three, maybe, of no apparent interest.

"Hi. I hear you're expecting a baby," he began, and sat down with a distinct air of settling in.

"Yes. That's quite an opening line. How did you know?"

"I know because Linda told me. You know Linda, don't you? I'm her brother."

He began asking about her symptoms. Sleepiness? Apathy? He knew, he had worked in a clinic. Unresponsive, she retorted by inquiring about his taste in music. He sat on a leather hassock opposite Caroline on the couch, and with every inquisitive sentence drew his seat closer till their knees were almost touching. She shifted her weight to avoid him, tucked her feet under her and lit another cigarette, feeling she could lie down and fall into a stupor quite easily. Still, words were coming out of her mouth, she heard them; she hoped they were not encouraging words but she seemed to have very little control over what they were.

"I—" he said. "You see—" He reached out and put his hand over hers. "Pregnant women, like, they really turn me on. I mean, there's a special aura. You're sensational."

She pulled her hand away. "God almighty."

"What's the matter? Honestly, I didn't mean to offend you."

"I really must go." She stood up and stepped around him.

"Could I see you some time?"

"You're seeing me now. Enjoy it."

He ran his eyes over her from head to toe, appraising. "It doesn't show yet."

Gazing down at her body, Caroline stretched the loose velvet dress taut over her stomach. "No, you're right, it doesn't." Then, over her shoulder, as she left their little corner, she tossed, "Fuck you, you pig."

With a surge of energy she downed a quick Scotch, found Ivan and tugged at his arm. "Let's dance."

Ivan's blue eyes lightened with shock. At home she could barely walk.

"Yes, let's." He took her in his arms and she buried her face against his shoulder. But she held her tears back, she would not let him know.

Later she told him about it. It was three-thirty in the morning, they had just made love drunkenly, and Ivan was in high spirits. She knew why—he felt he had her back again. She had held him close and uttered her old sounds, familiar moans and cries like a poignant, nearly-forgotten tune, and Ivan was miraculously restored, his impact once again sensible to eye and ear. He was making her laugh hysterically now, imitating the eccentric professor of art history at the party, an owlish émigré from Bavaria who expounded on the dilemmas of today's youth, all the while pronouncing "youth" as if it rhymed with "mouth." Ivan had also discovered that he pronounced "unique" as if it were "eunuch." Then, sitting up in bed cross-legged, they competed in making up pretentious scholarly sentences that included both "unique" and "youth" mispronounced.

"Speaking of 'yowth,'" Caroline said, "I met a weird one tonight, Linda's brother. A very eunuch yowth, I must say." And giggling, she recounted their conversation. Suddenly at the end she unexpectedly found herself in tears. Shuddering, she flopped over and sobbed into her pillow.

"Caroline," he said tenderly, "please. For heaven's sake, it was just some nut. It was nothing. Don't get all upset over it." He stroked her bare back.

"I can't help it." she wailed. "It made me feel so disgusting."

"You're much too sensitive. Come on." He ran his hand slowly through her hair, over and over.

She pulled the blanket around her. "Enough. I'm going to sleep."

A few days later, when classes were beginning again for the new semester, she woke early and went immediately to the shower, going through the ritual motions briskly and automatically. She was finished and brushing her teeth when she realized what had happened. There she was on her feet, sturdy, before eight in the morning, planning how she would introduce the topic of the differential calculus to her new students. She stared at her face in the mirror with unaccustomed recognition, her mouth dripping white foam, her dark eyes startled. She was alive. She didn't know how the miracle had happened, nor did she care to explore it. Back in the bedroom she dressed quickly, zipping up a pair of slim rust-colored woolen slacks with satisfaction. It didn't show yet, but soon.

"Ivan, time to get up."

He grunted and opened his eyes. When at last they focused on Caroline leaning over him they burned blue and wide with astonishment. He rubbed a fist across his forehead. "Are you dressed already?"

"Yes. I'm cured."

"What do you mean?"

"I'm not tired any more. I'm slept out. I've come back to life."

"Oh." He moaned and rolled over in one piece like a seal.

"Aren't you getting up?"

"In a little while. I'm so tired. I must sleep for a while." The words were thick and slurred.

"Well!" She was strangely annoyed. Ivan always got up with vigor. "Are you sick?"

"Uh-uh."

After a quick cup of coffee she called out, "Ivan, I'm leaving now. Don't forget to get up." The January air was crisp and exhilarating, and she walked the half-mile to the university at a nimble clip, going over her introductory remarks in her head.

Ivan was tired for a week. Caroline wanted to go out to dinner every evening—she had her appetite back. She had broken through dense earth to fresh air. It was a new year and soon they would have a new baby. But all Ivan wanted to do was stay home and lie on the bed and watch television. It was repellent. Sloth, she pointed out to him more than once, was one of the seven deadly sins. The fifth night she said in exasperation, "What the hell is the matter with you? If you're sick go to a doctor."

"I'm not sick. I'm tired. Can't I be tired too? Leave me alone. I left you alone, didn't I?"

"That was different."

"How?"

"I'm pregnant and you're not, in case you've forgotten."

"How could I forget?"

She said nothing, only cast him an evil look.

One evening soon after Ivan's symptoms disappeared, they sat together on the living-room sofa sharing sections of the newspaper.

Ivan had his feet up on the coffee table and Caroline sat diagonally, resting her legs on his. She paused in her reading and touched her stomach.

"Ivan."

"What?"

"It's no use. I'm going to have to buy some maternity clothes."

He put down the paper and stared. "Really?" He seemed distressed.

"Yes."

"Well, don't buy any of those ugly things they wear. Can't you get some of those, you know, sort of Indian things?"

"Yes. That's a good idea. I will."

He picked up the paper again.

"It moves."

"What?"

"I said it moves. The baby."

"It moves?"

She laughed. "Remember Galileo? *Eppure, si muove*." They had spent years together in Italy in their first youth, in mad love, and visited the birthplace of Galileo. He was a hero to both of them, because his mind remained free and strong though his body succumbed to tyranny.

Ivan laughed too. "*Eppure, si muove*. Let me see." He bent his head down to feel it, then looked up at her, his face full of longing, marvel and envy. In a moment he was scrambling at her clothes in a young eager rush. He wanted to be there, he said. Caroline, taken by surprise, was suspended between laughter and tears. He had her on the floor in silence, and for each it was swift and consuming.

Ivan lay spent in her arms. Caroline, still gasping and clutching him, said, "I could never love it as much as I love you." She wondered, then, hearing her words fall in the still air, whether this would always be true.

Shortly after she began wearing the Indian shirts and dresses, she noticed that Ivan was acting oddly. He stayed late at the office more than ever before, and often brought work home with him. He appeared to have lost interest in the baby, rarely asking how she felt, and when she moaned in bed sometimes, "Oh, I can't get to sleep, it keeps moving around," he responded with a grunt or not at all. He asked her, one warm Sunday in March, if she wanted to go bicycle riding.

76

"Ivan, I can't go bicycle riding. I mean, look at me."

"Oh, right. Of course."

He seemed to avoid looking at her, and she did look terrible, she had to admit. Even she looked at herself in the mirror as infrequently as possible. She dreaded what she had heard about hair falling out and teeth rotting, but she drank her milk diligently and so far neither of those things had happened. But besides the grotesque belly, her ankles swelled up so that the shape of her own legs was alien. She took diuretics and woke every hour at night to go to the bathroom. Sometimes it was impossible to get back to sleep so she sat up in bed reading. Ivan said, "Can't you turn the light out? You know I can't sleep with the light on."

"But what should I do? I can't sleep at all."

"Read in the living room."

"It's so cold in there at night."

He would turn away irritably. Once he took the blanket and went to sleep in the living room himself.

They liked to go for drives in the country on warm weekends. It seemed to Caroline that he chose the bumpiest, most untended roads and drove them as rashly as possible. Then when they stopped to picnic and he lay back to bask in the sharp April sunlight, she would always need to go and look for a bathroom, or even a clump of trees. At first this amused him, but soon his amusement became sardonic. He pulled in wearily at gas stations where he didn't need gas and waited in the car with folded arms and a sullen expression that made her apologetic about her ludicrous needs. They were growing apart. She could feel the distance between them like a patch of fog, dimming and distorting the relations of objects in space. The baby that lay between them in the dark was pushing them apart.

Sometimes as she lay awake in bed at night, not wanting to read in the cold living room but reluctant to turn on the light (and it was only a small light, she thought bitterly, a small bedside light), Caroline brooded over the horrible deformities the baby might be born with. She was thirty-one years old, not the best age to bear a first child. It could have cerebral palsy, cleft palate, two heads, club foot. She wondered if she could love a baby with a gross defect. She wondered if Ivan would want to put it in an institution, and if there were any decent institutions in their area, and if they would be spending every Sunday afternoon for the rest of their lives visiting the baby and driving home heartbroken in silence. She lived through these visits to the institution in vivid detail till she knew the doctors' and nurses' faces well. And there would come a point when Ivan would refuse to go any more—she knew what he was like, selfish with his time and impatient with futility—and she would have to go alone. She wondered if Ivan ever thought about these things, but with that cold mood of his she was afraid to ask.

One night she was desolate. She couldn't bear the loneliness and the heaviness any more, so she woke him.

"Ivan, please. Talk to me. I'm so lonely."

He sat up abruptly. "What?" He was still asleep. With the dark straight hair hanging down over his lean face he looked boyish and vulnerable. Without knowing why, she felt sorry for him.

"I'm sorry. I know you were sleeping but I—" Here she began to weep. "I just lie here forever in the dark and think awful things and you're so far away, and I just—"

"Oh, Caroline. Oh, God." Now he was wide awake, and took her in his arms.

"You're so far away," she wept. "I don't know what's the matter with you."

"I'm sorry. I know it's hard for you. You're so—everything's so different, that's all."

"But it's still me."

"I know. I know it's stupid of me. I can't—"

She knew what it was. It would never be the same. They sat up all night holding each other, and they talked. Ivan talked more than he had in weeks. He said of course the baby would be perfectly all right, and it would be born at just the right time, too, late June, so she could finish up the term, and they would start their natural childbirth group in two weeks so he could be with her and help her, though of course she would do it easily because she was so competent at everything, and then they would have the summer for the early difficult months, and she would be feeling fine and be ready to go back to work in the fall, and they would find a good person, someone like a grandmother, to come in, and he would try to stagger his schedule so she would not feel overburdened and trapped, and in short everything would be just fine, and they would make love again like they used to and be close again. He said exactly what she needed to hear, while she huddled against him, wrenched with pain to realize that he had known all along the right words to say but hadn't thought to say them till she woke him in desperation. Still, in the dawn she slept contented. She loved him. Every now and then she perceived this like a fact of life, an ancient tropism.

Two weeks later they had one of their horrible quarrels. It happened at a gallery, at the opening of a show by a group of young local artists Ivan had discovered. He had encouraged them to apply to his foundation for money and smoothed the way to their success. Now at their triumphant hour he was to be publicly thanked at a formal dinner. There were too many paintings to look at, too many people to greet, and too many glasses of champagne thrust at Caroline, who was near the end of her eighth month now. She walked around for an hour, then whispered to Ivan, "Listen, I'm sorry but I've got to go. Give me the car keys, will you? I don't feel well."

"What's the matter?"

"I can't stop having to go to the bathroom and my feet are killing me and my head aches, and the kid is rolling around like a basketball. You stay and enjoy it. You can get a ride with someone. I'll see you later"

"I'll drive you home," he said grimly. "We'll leave."

An awful knot gripped her stomach. The knot was the image of his perverse resistance, the immense trouble coming, all the trouble congealed and solidified and tied up in one moment. Meanwhile they smiled at the passers-by as they whispered ferociously to each other.

"Ivan, I do not want you to take me home. This is your event. Stay. I am leaving. We are separate people."

"If you're as sick as you say you can't drive home alone. You're my wife and I'll take you home."

"Suit yourself," she said sweetly, because the director of the gallery was approaching. "We all know you're much bigger and stronger than I am." And she smiled maliciously.

Ivan waved vaguely at the director, turned and ushered her to the door. Outside he exploded.

"Shit, Caroline! We can't do a fucking thing anymore, can we?"

"You can do anything you like. Just give me the keys. I left mine home."

"I will not give you the keys. Get in the car. You're supposed to be sick."

"You big resentful selfish idiot. Jealous of an embryo." She was screaming now. He started the car with a rush that jolted her forward against the dashboard. "I'd be better off driving myself. You'll kill me this way."

"Shut up," he shouted. "I don't want to hear any more."

"I don't care what you want to hear or not hear."

"Shut the hell up or I swear I'll go into a tree. I don't give a shit anymore."

It was starting to rain, a soft silent rain that glittered in the drab dusk outside. At exactly the same moment they rolled up their windows. They were sealed in together. Caroline thought, like restless beasts in a cage. The air in the car was dank and stuffy.

When they got home he slammed the door so hard the house shook. Caroline had calmed herself. She sank down in a chair, kicked off her shoes and rubbed her ankles. "Ivan, why don't you go back? It's not too late. These dinners are always late anyway. I'll be O.K."

"I don't want to go anymore," he yelled. "The whole thing is spoiled. Our whole lives are spoiled from now on. We were better off before. I thought you had gotten over wanting it. I thought it was a dead issue." He stared at her bulging stomach with such loathing that she was shocked into horrid, lucid perception.

"You disgust me," she said quietly. "Frankly, you always have and probably always will." She didn't know why she said that. It was quite untrue. It was only true that he disgusted her at this moment, yet the rest had rolled out like string from a hidden ball of twine.

"So why did we ever start this in the first place?" he screamed.

She didn't know whether he meant the marriage or the baby, and for an instant she was afraid he might hit her, there was such compressed force in his huge shoulders.

"Get the hell out of here. I don't want to have to look at you."

"I will. I'll go back. I'll take your advice. Call your fucking obstetrician if you need anything. I'm sure he's always glad of an extra feel."

"You ignorant pig. Go on. And don't hurry back. Find yourself a skinny little art student and give her a big treat."

"I just might." He slammed the door and the house shook again.

He would be back. This was not the first time. Only now she felt no secret excitement, no tremor, no passion that could reshape into lust; she was too heavy and burdened. It would not be easy to make it up—she was in no condition. It would lie between them silently like a dead weight till weeks after the baby was born, till Ivan felt he

80

could reclaim his rightful territory. She knew him too well. Caroline took two aspirins. When she woke at three he was in bed beside her, gripping the blanket in his sleep and breathing heavily. For days afterward they spoke with strained, subdued courtesy.

They worked diligently in the natural childbirth classes once a week, while at home they giggled over how silly the exercises were, yet Ivan insisted she pant her five minutes each day as instructed. As relaxation training, Ivan was supposed to lift each of her legs and arms three times and drop them, while she remained perfectly limp and passive. From the very start Caroline was excellent at this routine, which they did in bed before going to sleep. A substitute, she thought, yawning. She could make her body so limp and passive her arms and legs bounced on the mattress when they fell. One night for diversion she tried doing it to Ivan, but he couldn't master the technique of passivity.

"Don't do anything, Ivan. I lift the leg and I drop the leg. You do nothing. Do you see? Nothing at all," she smiled.

But that was not possible for him. He tried to be limp but kept working along with her; she could see his muscles, precisely those leg muscles she found so desirable, exerting to lift and drop, lift and drop.

"You can't give yourself up. Don't you feel what you're doing? You have to let me do it to you. Let me try just your hand, from the wrist. That might be easier."

"No, forget it. Give me back my hand." He smiled and stroked her stomach gently. "What's the difference? I don't have to do it well. You do it very well."

She did it very well indeed when the time came. It was a short labor, less than an hour, very unusual for a first baby, the nurses kept muttering. She breathed intently, beginning with the long slow breaths she had been taught, feeling quite remote from the bustle around her. Then, in a flurry, they raced down the hall on a wheeled table with a train of white-coated people trotting after, and she thought, panting, No matter what I suffer, soon I will be thin again, I will be more beautiful than ever.

The room was crowded with people, far more people than she would have thought necessary, but the only faces she singled out were Ivan's and the doctor's. The doctor, with a new russet beard and his face a good deal thinner now, was once again framed by her knees, paler than before. Wildly enthusiastic about the proceedings, he yelled, "Terrific, Caroline, terrific," as though they were in a noisy public place. "O.K., start pushing."

They placed her hands on chrome rails along the table. On the left, groping, she found Ivan's hand and held it instead of the rail. She pushed. In surprise she became aware of a great cleavage, like a mountain of granite splitting apart, only it was in her, she realized, and if it kept on going it would go right up to her neck. She gripped Ivan's warm hand, and just as she opened her mouth to roar someone clapped an oxygen mask on her face so the roar reverberated inward on her own ears. She wasn't supposed to roar, the natural childbirth teacher hadn't mentioned anything about that, she was supposed to breathe and push. But as long as no one seemed to take any notice she might as well keep on roaring, it felt so satisfying and necessary. The teacher would never know. She trusted that if she split all the way up to her neck they would sew her up somehow—she was too far gone to worry about that now. Maybe that was why there were so many of them, yes, of course, to put her back together, and maybe they had simply forgotten to tell her about being bisected; or maybe it was a closely guarded secret, like an initiation rite. She gripped Ivan's hand tighter. She was not having too bad a time, she would surely survive, she told herself, captivated by the hellish bestial sounds going from her mouth to her ear; it certainly was what her students would call a peak experience, and how gratifying to hear the doctor exclaim, "Oh, this is one terrific girl! One more, Caroline, give me one more push and send it out. Sock it to me."

She always tried to be obliging, if possible. Now she raised herself on her elbows and, staring straight at him—he too, after all, had been most obliging these long months—gave him with tremendous force the final push he asked for. She had Ivan's hand tightly around the rail, could feel his knuckles bursting, and then all of a sudden the room and the faces were obliterated. A dark thick curtain swiftly wrapped around her and she was left all alone gasping, sucked violently into a windy black hold of pain so explosive she knew it must be death, she was dying fast, like a bomb detonating. It was all right, it was almost over, only she would have liked to see his blue eyes one last time.

From somewhere in the void Ivan's voice shouted in exultation, "It's coming out," and the roaring stopped and at last there was peace and quiet in her ears. The curtain fell away, the world returned. But her eyes kept on burning, as if they had seen something not meant for living eyes to see and return from alive.

"Give it to me," Caroline said, and held it. She saw that every part was in the proper place, then shut her eyes.

They wheeled her to a room and eased her onto the bed. It was past ten in the morning. She could dimly remember they had been up all night watching a James Cagney movie about prize-fighting while they timed her irregular mild contractions. James Cagney went blind from blows given by poisoned gloves in a rigged match, and she wept for him as she held her hands on her stomach and breathed. Neither she nor Ivan had slept or eaten for hours.

"Ivan, there is something I am really dying to have right now."

"Your wish is my command."

She asked for a roast beef on rye with ketchup, and iced tea. "Would you mind? It'll be hours before they serve lunch."

He brought it and stood at the window while she ate ravenously.

"Didn't you get anything for yourself?"

"No, I'm too exhausted to eat." He did, in fact, look terrible. He was sallow; his eyes, usually so radiant, were nearly drained of color, and small downward-curving lines around his mouth recalled his laborious vigil.

"You had a rough night, Ivan. You ought to get some sleep. What's it like outside?"

"What?" Ivan's movements seemed to her extremely purposeless. He was pacing the room with his hands deep in his pockets, going slowly from the foot of the bed to the window and back. Her eyes followed him from the pillow. Every now and then he would stop to peer at Caroline in an unfamiliar way, as if she were a puzzling stranger.

"Ivan, are you O.K.? I meant the weather. What's it doing outside?" It struck her, as she asked, that it was weeks since she had cared to know anything about the outside. That there was an outside, now that she was emptied out, came rushing at her with the most urgent importance, wafting her on a tide of grateful joy.

"Oh," he said vaguely, and came to sit on the edge of her bed. "Well, it's doing something very peculiar outside, as a matter of fact. It's raining but the sun is shining."

She laughed at him. "But haven't you ever seen it do that before?"

"I don't know. I guess so." He opened his mouth and closed it several times. She ate, waiting patiently. Finally he spoke. "You know, Caroline, you really have quite a grip. When you were holding my hand in there, you squeezed it so tight I thought you would break it."

"Oh, come on, that can't be."

"I'm not joking." He massaged his hand absently. Ivan never complained of pain; if anything he understated. But now he held out his right hand and showed her the raw red knuckles and palm, with raised flaming welts forming.

She took his hand. "You're serious. Did I do that? Well, how do you like that?"

"I really thought you'd break my hand. It was killing me." He kept repeating it, not resentfully but dully, as though there were something secreted in the words that he couldn't fathom.

"But why didn't you take it away if it hurt that badly?" She put down her half-eaten sandwich as she saw the pale amazement ripple over his face.

"Oh, no, I couldn't do that. I mean—if that was what you needed just then—" He looked away, embarrassed. "Listen," he shrugged, not facing her, "we're in a hospital, after all. What better place? They'd fix it for me."

Overwhelmed, Caroline lay back on the pillows. "Oh, Ivan. You would do that?"

"What are you crying for?" he asked gently. "You didn't break it, did you? Almost doesn't count. So what are you crying about. You just had a baby. Don't cry."

And she smiled and thought her heart would burst.

1978

THE FAT GIRL

by ANDRE DUBUS

from ADULTERY AND OTHER CHOICES (The Godine Press)

HER NAME WAS LOUISE. Once when she was sixteen a boy kissed her at a barbecue; he was drunk and he jammed his tongue into her mouth and ran his hands up and down her hips. Her father kissed her often. He was thin and kind and she could see in his eyes when he looked at her the lights of love and pity.

It started when Louise was nine. You must start watching what you eat, her mother would say. I can see you have my metabolism. Louise also had her mother's pale blonde hair. Her mother was slim and pretty, carried herself erectly, and ate very little. The two of them would eat bare lunches, while her old brother ate sandwiches and potato chips, and then her mother would sit smoking while

Louise eyed the bread box, the pantry, the refrigerator. Wasn't that good, her mother would say. In five years you'll be in high school and if you're fat the boys won't like you; they won't ask you out. Boys were as far away as five years, and she would go to her room and wait for nearly an hour until she knew her mother was no longer thinking of her, then she would creep into the kitchen and, listening to her mother talking on the phone, or her footsteps upstairs, she would open the bread box, the pantry, the jar of peanut butter. She would put the sandwich under her shirt and go outside or to the bathroom to eat it.

Her father was a lawyer and made a lot of money and came home looking pale and happy. Martinis put color back in his face, and at dinner he talked to his wife and two children. Oh give her a potato, he would say to Louise's mother. She's a growing girl. Her mother's voice then became tense: If she has a potato she shouldn't have dessert. She should have both, her father would say, and he would reach over and touch Louise's check or hand or arm.

In high school she had two girl friends and at night and on week-ends they rode in a car or went to movies. In movies she was fascinated by fat actresses. She wondered why they were fat. She knew why she was fat: she was fat because she was Louise. Because God had made her that way. Because she wasn't like her friends Barbara and Marjorie, who drank milk shakes after school and were all bones and tight skin. But what about those actresses, with their talents, with their broad and profound faces? Did they eat as heedlessly as Bishop Humphries and his wife who sometimes came to dinner and, as Louise's mother said, gorged between amenities? Or did they try to lose weight, did they go about hungry and angry and thinking of food? She thought of them eating lean meats and salads with friends, and then going home and building strange large sandwiches with Italian bread. But mostly she believed they did not go through these failures; they were fat because they chose to be. And she was certain of something else too: she could see it in their faces: they did not eat secretly. Which she did: her creeping to the kitchen when she was nine became, in high school, a ritual of deceit and pleasure. She was a furtive eater of sweets. Even her two friends did not know her secret.

Barbara was thin, gangling, and flat-chested; she was attractive enough and all she needed was someone to take a second look at her face, but the school was large and there were pretty girls in every classroom and walking all the corridors, so no one ever needed to take a second look at Barbara. Marjorie was thin too, an intense, heavy-smoking girl with brittle laughter. She was very intelligent, and with boys she was shy because she knew she made them uncomfortable, and because she was smarter than they were and so could not understand or could not believe the levels they lived on. She was to have a nervous breakdown before earning her PhD. in philosophy at the University of California, where she met and married a physicist and discovered within herself an untrammelled passion: she made love with her husband on the couch, the carpet, in the bathtub, and on the washing machine. By that time much had happened to her and she never thought of Louise. Barbara would finally stop growing and begin moving with grace and confidence. In college she would have two lovers and then several more during the six years she spent in Boston before marrying a middleaged editor who had two sons in their early teens, who drank too much, who was tenderly, boyishly grateful for her love, and whose wife had been killed while rock-climbing in New Hampshire with her lover. She would not think of Louise either, except in an earlier time, when lovers were still new to her and she was ecstatically surprised each time one of them loved her and, sometimes at night, lying in a man's arms, she would tell how in high school no one dated her, she had been thin and plain (she would still believe that: that she had been plain; it had never been true) and so had been forced into the week-end and night-time company of a neurotic smart girl and a shy fat girl. She would say this with self-pity exaggerated by scotch and her need to be more deeply loved by the man who held her.

She never eats, Barbara and Marjorie said of Louise. They ate lunch with her at school, watched her refusing potatoes, ravioli, fried fish. Sometimes she got through the cafeteria line with only a salad. That is how they would remember her: a girl whose hapless body was destined to be fat. No one saw the sandwiches she made and took to her room when she came home from school. No one saw the store of Milky Ways, Butterfingers, Almond Joys, and Hersheys far back on her closet shelf, behind the stuffed animals of her childhood. She was not a hypocrite. When she was out of the house she truly believed she was dieting; she forgot about the candy, as a man speaking into his office dictaphone may forget the lewd photographs hidden in an old shoe in his closet. At other times, away from the home, she thought of the waiting candy with near lust. One

87

night driving home from a movie, Marjorie said: 'You're lucky you don't smoke; it's *incredible* what I go through to hide it from my parents.' Louise turned to her a smile which was elusive and mysterious; she yearned to be home in bed, eating chocolate in the dark. She did not need to smoke; she already had a vice that was insular and destructive.

She brought it with her to college. She thought she would leave it behind. A move from one place to another, a new room without the haunted closet shelf, would do for her what she could not do for herself. She packed her large dresses and went. For two weeks she was busy with registration, with shyness, with classes; then she began to feel at home. Her room was no longer like a motel. Its walls had stopped watching her, she felt they were her friends, and she gave them her secret. Away from her mother, she did not have to be as elaborate; she kept the candy in her drawer now.

The school was in Massachusetts, a girls' school. When she chose it, when she and her father and mother talked about it in the evenings, everyone so carefully avoided the word boys that sometimes the conversations seemed to be about nothing but boys. There are no boys there, the neuter words said; you will not have to contend with that. In her father's eyes were pity and encouragement; in her mother's was disappointment, and her voice was crisp. They spoke of courses, of small classes where Louise would get more attention. She imagined herself in those small classes; she saw herself as a teacher would see her, as the other girls would; she would get no attention.

The girls at the school were from wealthy families, but most of them wore the uniform of another class: blue jeans and work shirts, and many wore overalls. Louise bought some overalls, washed them until the dark blue faded, and wore them to classes. In the cafeteria she ate as she had in high school, not to lose weight nor even to sustain her lie, but because eating lightly in public had become as habitual as good manners. Everyone had to take gym, and in the locker room with the other girls, and wearing shorts on the volleyball and badminton courts, she hated her body. She liked her body most when she was unaware of it: in bed at night, as sleep gently took her out of her day, out of herself. And she liked parts of her body. She liked her brown eyes and sometimes looked at them in the mirror: they were not shallow eyes, she thought; they were indeed windows of a tender soul, a good heart. She liked her lips and nose, and her chin, finely shaped between her wide and sagging cheeks. Most of all she liked her long pale blonde hair, she liked washing and drying it and lying naked on her bed, smelling of shampoo, and feeling the soft hair at her neck and shoulders and back.

Her friend at college was Carrie, who was thin and wore thick glasses and often at night she cried in Louise's room. She did not know why she was crying. She was crying, she said, because she was unhappy. She could say no more. Louise said she was unhappy too, and Carrie moved in with her. One night Carrie talked for hours, sadly and bitterly, about her parents and what they did to each other. When she finished she hugged Louise and they went to bed. Then in the dark Carrie spoke across the room: 'Louise? I just wanted to tell you. One night last week I woke up and smelled chocolate. You were eating chocolate, in your bed. I wish you'd eat it in front of me, Louise, whenever you feel like it.'

Stiffened in her bed, Louise could think of nothing to say. In the silence she was afraid Carrie would think she was asleep and would tell her again in the morning or tomorrow night. Finally she said Okay. Then after a moment she told Carrie if she ever wanted any she could feel free to help herself; the candy was in the top drawer. Then she said thank you.

They were roommates for four years and in the summers they exchanged letters. Each fall they greeted with embraces, laughter, tears, and moved into their old room, which had been stripped and cleansed of them for the summer. Neither girl enjoyed summer. Carrie did not like being at home because her parents did not love each other. Louise lived in a small city in Louisiana. She did not like summer because she had lost touch with Barbara and Marjorie; they saw each other, but it was not the same. She liked being with her father but with no one else. The flicker of disappointment in her mother's eyes at the airport was a vanguard of the army of relatives and acquaintances who awaited her: they would see her on the streets, in stores, at the country club, in her home, and in theirs; in the first moments of greeting, their eyes would tell her she was still fat Louise, who had been fat as long as they could remember, who had gone to college and returned as fat as ever. Then their eyes dismissed her, and she longed for school and Carrie, and she wrote letters to her friend. But that saddened her too. It wasn't simply that Carrie was her only friend, and when they finished college they might never see each other again. It was that her existence in the world was so divided; it had begun when she was a child creeping to the kitchen; now that division was much sharper, and her friendship with Carrie seemed disproportionate and perilous. The world she was destined to live in had nothing to do with the intimate nights in their room at school.

In the summer before their senior year, Carrie fell in love. She wrote to Louise about him, but she did not write much, and this hurt Louise more than if Carrie had shown the joy her writing tried to conceal. That fall they returned to their room; they were still close and warm, Carrie still needed Louise's ears and heart at night as she spoke of her parents and her recurring malaise whose source the two friends never discovered. But on most week-ends Carrie left, and caught a bus to Boston where her boy friend studied music. During the week she often spoke hesitantly of sex; she was not sure if she liked it. But Louise, eating candy and listening, did not know whether Carrie was telling the truth or whether, as in her letters of the past summer, Carrie was keeping from her those delights she may never experience.

Then one Sunday night when Carrie had just returned from Boston and was unpacking her overnight bag, she looked at Louise and said: 'I was thinking about you. On the bus coming home tonight.' Looking at Carrie's concerned, determined face, Louise prepared herself for humiliation. 'I was thinking about when we graduate. What you're going to do. What's to become of you. I want you to be loved the way I love you. Louise, if I help you, *really* help you, will you go on a diet?'

Louise entered a period of her life she would remember always, the way some people remember having endured poverty. Her diet did not begin the next day. Carrie told her to eat on Monday as though it were the last day of her life. So for the first time since grammar school Louise went into a school cafeteria and ate everything she wanted. At breakfast and lunch and dinner she glanced around the table to see if the other girls noticed the food on her tray. They did not. She felt there was a lesson in this, but it lay beyond her grasp. That night in their room she ate the four remaining candy bars. During the day Carrie rented a small refrigerator, bought an electric skillet, an electric broiler, and bathroom scales.

On Tuesday morning Louise stood on the scales, and Carrie wrote in her notebook: *October 14: 184 lbs.* Then she made Louise a cup of black coffee and scrambled one egg and sat with her while she ate. When Carrie went to the dining room for breakfast, Louise walked about the campus for thirty minutes. That was part of the plan. The campus was pretty, on its lawns grew at least one of every tree native to New England, and in the warm morning sun Louise felt a new hope. At noon they met in their room, and Carrie broiled her a piece of hamburger and served it with lettuce. Then while Carrie ate in the dining room Louise walked again. She was weak with hunger and she felt queasy. During her afternoon classes she was nervous and tense, and she chewed her pencil and tapped her heels on the floor and tightened her calves. When she returned to her room late that afternoon, she was so glad to see Carrie that she embraced her; she had felt she could not bear another minute of hunger, but now with Carrie she knew she could make it at least through tonight. Then she would sleep and face tomorrow when it came. Carrie broiled her a steak and served it with lettuce. Louise studied while Carrie ate dinner, then they went for a walk.

That was her ritual and her diet for the rest of the year, Carrie alternating fish and chicken breasts with the steaks for dinner, and every day was nearly as bad as the first. In the evenings she was irritable. In all her life she had never been afflicted by ill temper and she looked upon it now as a demon which, along with hunger, was taking possession of her soul. Often she spoke sharply to Carrie. One night during their after-dinner walk Carrie talked sadly of night, of how darkness made her more aware of herself, and at night she did not know why she was in college, why she studied, why she was walking the earth with other people. They were standing on a wooden foot bridge, looking down at a dark pond. Carrie kept talking; perhaps soon she would cry. Suddenly Louise said; 'I'm sick of lettuce. I never want to see a piece of lettuce for the rest of my life. I hate it. We shouldn't even buy it, it's immoral.'

Carrie was quiet. Louise glanced at her, and the pain and irritation in Carrie's face soothed her. Then she was ashamed. Before she could say she was sorry, Carrie turned to her and said gently: 'I know. I know how terrible it is.'

Carrie did all the shopping, telling Louise she knew how hard it was to go into a supermarket when you were hungry. And Louise was always hungry. She drank diet soft drinks and started smoking Carrie's cigarettes, learned to enjoy inhaling, thought of cancer and emphysema but they were as far away as those boys her mother had talked about when she was nine. By Thanksgiving she was smoking over a pack a day and her weight in Carrie's notebook was one hundred and sixty-two pounds. Carrie was afraid if Louise went home at Thanksgiving she would lapse from the diet, so Louise spent the vacation with Carrie, in Philadelphia. Carrie wrote her family about the diet, and told Louise that she had. On the plane to Philadelphia, Louise said: 'I feel like a bedwetter. When I was a little girl I had a friend who used to come spend the night and Mother would put a rubber sheet on the bed and we all pretended there wasn't a rubber sheet and that she hadn't wet the bed. Even me, and I slept with her.' At Thanksgiving dinner she lowered her eyes as Carrie's father put two slices of white meat on her plate and passed it to her over the bowls of steaming food.

When she went home at Christmas she weighed a hundred and fifty-five pounds; at the airport her mother marvelled. Her father laughed and hugged her and said: 'But now there's less of you to love.' He was troubled by her smoking but only mentioned it once; he told her she was beautiful and, as always, his eyes bathed her with love. During the long vacation her mother cooked for her as Carrie had, and Louise returned to school weighing a hundred and forty-six pounds.

Flying north on the plane she warmly recalled the surprised and congratulatory eyes of her relatives and acquaintances. She had not seen Barbara or Marjorie. She thought of returning home in May, weighing the hundred and fifteen pounds which Carrie had in October set as their goal. Looking toward the stoic days ahead, she felt strong. She thought of those hungry days of fall and early winter (and now: she was hungry now: with almost a frown, almost a brusque shake of the head, she refused peanuts from the stewardess): those first weeks of the diet when she was the pawn of an irascibility which still, conditioned to her ritual as she was, could at any moment take command of her. She thought of the nights of trying to sleep while her stomach growled. She thought of her addiction to cigarettes. She thought of the people at school: not one teacher, not one girl, had spoken to her about her loss of weight, not even about her absence from meals. And without warning her spirit collapsed. She did not feel strong, she did not feel she was committed to and within reach of achieving a valuable goal. She felt that somehow she had lost more than pounds of fat; that some time

92

during her dieting she had lost herself too. She tried to remember what it had felt like to be Louise before she had started living on meat and fish, as an unhappy adult may look sadly in the memory of childhood for lost virtues and hopes. She looked down at the earth far below, and it seemed to her that her soul, like her body aboard the plane, was in some rootless flight. She neither knew its destination nor where it had departed from; it was on some passage she could not even define.

During the next few weeks she lost weight more slowly and once for eight days Carrie's daily recording stayed at a hundred and thirty-six. Louise woke in the morning thinking of one hundred and thirty-six and then she stood on the scales and they echoed her. She became obsessed with that number, and there wasn't a day when she didn't say it aloud, and through the days and nights the number stayed in her mind, and if a teacher had spoken those digits in a classroom she would have opened her mouth to speak. What if that's me, she said to Carrie. I mean what if a hundred and thirty-six is my real weight and I just can't lose anymore. Walking hand-in-hand with her despair was a longing for this to be true, and that longing angered her and wearied her, and every day she was gloomy. On the ninth day she weighed a hundred and thirty-five and a half pounds. She was not relieved; she thought bitterly of the months ahead, the shedding of the last twenty and a half pounds.

On Easter Sunday, which she spent at Carrie's, she weighed one hundred and twenty pounds, and she ate one slice of glazed pineapple with her ham and lettuce. She did not enjoy it: she felt she was being friendly with a recalcitrant enemy who had once tried to destroy her. Carrie's parents were laudative. She liked them and she wished they would touch sometimes, and look at each other when they spoke. She guessed they would divorce when Carrie left home, and she vowed that her own marriage would be one of affection and tenderness. She could think about that now: marriage. At school she had read in a Boston paper that this summer the cicadas would come out of their seventeen year hibernation on Cape Cod, for a month they would mate and then die, leaving their young to burrow into the ground where they would stay for seventeen years. That's me, she had said to Carrie. Only my hibernation lasted twenty-one years.

Often her mother asked in letters and on the phone about the diet, but Louise answered vaguely. When she flew home in late May she weighed a hundred and thirteen pounds, and at the airport her mother cried and hugged her and said again and again: You're so *beaut*iful. Her father blushed and bought her a martini. For days her relatives and acquaintances congratulated her, and the applause in their eyes lasted the entire summer, and she loved their eyes, and swam in the country club pool, the first time she had done this since she was a child.

She lived at home and ate the way her mother did and every morning she weighed. Her mother liked to take her shopping and buy her dresses and they put her old ones in the Goodwill box at the shopping center; Louise thought of them existing on the body of a poor woman whose cheap meals kept her fat. Louise's mother had a photographer come to the house, and Louise posed on the couch and standing beneath a live oak and sitting in a wicker lawn chair next to an azalea bush. The new clothes and the photographer made her feel she was going to another country or becoming a citizen of a new one. In the fall she took a job of no consequence, to give her something to do.

Also in the fall a young lawyer joined her father's firm, he came one night to dinner, and they started seeing each other. He was the first man outside her family to kiss her since the barbecue when she was sixteen. Louise celebrated Thanksgiving not with rice dressing and candied sweet potatoes and mince meat and pumpkin pies, but by giving Richard her virginity which she realized, at the very last moment of its existence, she had embarked on giving him over thirteen months ago, on that Tuesday in October when Carrie had made her a cup of black coffee and scrambled one egg. She wrote this to Carrie, who replied happily by return mail. She also, through glance and smile and innuendo, tried to tell her mother too. But finally she controlled that impulse, because Richard felt guilty about making love with the daughter of his partner and friend. In the spring they married. The wedding was a large one, in the Episcopal church, and Carrie flew from Boston to be maid of honor. Her parents had recently separated and she was living with the musician and was still victim of her unpredictable malaise. It overcame her on the night before the wedding, so Louise was up with her until past three and woke next morning from a sleep so heavy that she did not want to leave it.

Richard was a lean, tall, energetic man with the metabolism of a pencil sharpener. Louise fed him everything he wanted. He liked Italian food and she got recipes from her mother and watched him eating spaghetti with the sauce she had only tasted, and ravioli and lasagna, while she ate antipasto with her chianti. He made a lot of money and borrowed more and they bought a house whose lawn sloped down to the shore of a lake; they had a wharf and a boathouse, and Richard bought a boat and they took friends waterskiing. Richard bought her a car and they spent his vacations in Mexico, Canada, the Bahamas, and in the fifth year of their marriage they went to Europe and, according to their plan, she conceived a child in Paris. On the plane back, as she looked out the window and beyond the sparkling sea and saw her country, she felt that it was waiting for her, as her home by the lake was, and her parents, and her good friends who rode in the boat and waterskied; she thought of the accumulated warmth and pelf of her marriage, and how by slimming her body she had bought into the pleasures of the nation. She felt cunning, and she smiled to herself, and took Richard's hand.

But these moments of triumph were sparse. On most days she went about her routine of leisure with a sense of certainty about herself that came merely from not thinking. But there were times, with her friends, or with Richard, or alone in the house, when she was suddenly assaulted by the feeling that she had taken the wrong train and arrived at a place where no one knew her, and where she ought not to be. Often, in bed with Richard, she talked of being fat: 'I was the one who started the friendship with Carrie, I chose her, I started the conversations. When I understood that she was my friend I understood something else: I had chosen her for the same reason I'd chosen Barbara and Marjorie. They were all thin. I was always thinking about what people saw when they looked at me and I didn't want them to see two fat girls. When I was alone I didn't mind being fat but then I'd have to leave the house again and then I didn't want to look like me. But at home I didn't mind except when I was getting dressed to go out of the house and when Mother looked at me. But I stopped looking at her when she looked at me. And in college I felt good with Carrie; there weren't any boys and I didn't have any other friends and so when I wasn't with Carrie I thought about her and I tried to ignore the other people around me, I tried to make them not exist. A lot of the time I could do that. It was strange, and I felt like a spy.'

If Richard was bored by her repetition he pretended not to be.

95

But she knew the story meant very little to him. She could have been telling him of a childhood illness, or wearing braces, or a broken heart at sixteen. He could not see her as she was when she was fat. She felt as though she were trying to tell a foreign lover about her life in the United States, and if only she could command the language he would know and love all of her and she would feel complete. Some of the acquaintances of her childhood were her friends now, and even they did not seem to remember her when she was fat.

Now her body was growing again, and when she put on a maternity dress for the first time she shivered with fear. Richard did not smoke and he asked her, in a voice just short of demand, to stop during her pregnancy. She did. She ate carrots and celery instead of smoking, and at cocktail parties she tried to eat nothing, but after her first drink she ate nuts and cheese and crackers and dips. Always at these parties Richard had talked with his friends and she had rarely spoken to him until they drove home. But now when he noticed her at the hors d'oeuvres table he crossed the room and, smiling, led her back to his group. His smile and his hand on her arm told her he was doing his clumsy, husbandly best to help her through a time of female mystery.

She was gaining weight but she told herself it was only the baby, and would leave with its birth. But at other times she knew quite clearly that she was losing the discipline she had fought so hard to gain during her last year with Carrie. She was hungry now as she had been in college, and she ate between meals and after dinner and tried to eat only carrots and celery, but she grew to hate them, and her desire for sweets was as vicious as it had been long ago. At home she ate bread and jam and when she shopped for groceries she bought a candy bar and ate it driving home and put the wrapper in her purse and then in the garbage can under the sink. Her cheeks had filled out, there was loose flesh under her chin, her arms and legs were plump, and her mother was concerned. So was Richard. One night when she brought pie and milk to the living room where they were watching television, he said: 'You already had a piece. At dinner.'

She did not look at him.

'You're gaining weight. It's not all water, either. It's fat. It'll be summertime. You'll want to get into your bathing suit.'

The pie was cherry. She looked at it as her fork cut through it; she

96

speared the piece and rubbed it in the red juice on the plate before lifting it to her mouth.

'You never used to eat pie,' he said. 'I just think you ought to watch it a bit. It's going to be tough on you this summer.'

In her seventh month, with a delight reminiscent of climbing the stairs to Richard's apartment before they were married, she returned to her world of secret gratification. She began hiding candy in her underwear drawer. She ate it during the day and at night while Richard slept, and at breakfast she was distracted, waiting for him to leave.

She gave birth to a son, brought him home, and nursed both him and her appetites. During this time of celibacy she enjoyed her body through her son's mouth; while he suckled she stroked his small head and back. She was hiding candy but she did not conceal her other indulgences: she was smoking again but still she ate between meals, and at dinner she ate what Richard did, and coldly he watched her, he grew petulant, and when the date marking the end of their celibacy came they let it pass. Often in the afternoons her mother visited and scolded her and Louise sat looking at the baby and said nothing until finally, to end it, she promised to diet. When her mother and father came for dinners, her father kissed her and held the baby and her mother said nothing about Louise's body, and her voice was tense. Returning from work in the evenings Richard looked at a soiled plate and glass on the table beside her chair as if detecting traces of infidelity, and at every dinner they fought.

'Look at you,' he said. 'Lasagna, for God's sake. When are you going to start? It's not simply that you haven't lost any weight. You're gaining. I can see it. I can feel it when you get in bed. Pretty soon you'll weigh more than I do and I'll be sleeping on a trampoline.'

'You never touch me anymore.'

'I don't want to touch you. Why should I? Have you *looked* at yourself?'

'You're cruel,' she said. 'I never knew how cruel you were.'

She ate, watching him. He did not look at her. Glaring at his plate, he worked with fork and knife like a hurried man at a lunch counter.

'I bet you didn't either,' she said.

That night when he was asleep she took a Milky Way to the bathroom. For a while she stood eating in the dark, then she turned on the light. Chewing, she looked at herself in the mirror; she looked at her eyes and hair. Then she stood on the scales and looking at the numbers between her feet, one hundred and sixty-two, she remembered when she had weighed a hundred and thirty-six pounds for eight days. Her memory of those eight days was fond and amusing, as though she were recalling an Easter egg hunt when she was six. She stepped off the scales and pushed them under the lavatory and did not stand on them again.

It was summer and she bought loose dresses and when Richard took friends out on the boat she did not wear a bathing suit or shorts; her friends gave her mischievous glances, and Richard did not look at her. She stopped riding on the boat. She told them she wanted to stay with the baby, and she sat inside holding him until she heard the boat leave the wharf. Then she took him to the front lawn and walked with him in the shade of the trees and talked to him about the blue jays and mockingbirds and cardinals she saw on their branches. Sometimes she stopped and watched the boat out on the lake and the friend skiing behind it.

Every day Richard quarrelled, and because his rage went no further than her weight and shape, she felt excluded from it, and she remained calm within layers of flesh and spirit, and watched his frustration, his impotence. He truly believed they were arguing about her weight. She knew better: she knew that beneath the argument lay the question of who Richard was. She thought of him smiling at the wheel of his boat, and long ago courting his slender girl, the daughter of his partner and friend. She thought of Carrie telling her of smelling chocolate in the dark and, after that, watching her eat it night after night. She smiled at Richard, teasing his anger.

He is angry now. He stands in the center of the living room, raging at her, and he wakes the baby. Beneath Richard's voice she hears the soft crying, feels it in her heart, and quietly she rises from her chair and goes upstairs to the child's room and takes him from the crib. She brings him to the living room and sits holding him in her lap, pressing him gently against the folds of fat at her waist. Now Richard is pleading with her. Louise thinks tenderly of Carrie broiling meat and fish in their room, and walking with her in the evenings. She wonders if Carrie still has the malaise. Perhaps she will come for a visit. In Louise's arms now the boy sleeps.

'I'll help you,' Richard says. 'I'll eat the same things you eat.'

But his face does not approach the compassion and determination and love she had seen in Carrie's during what she now recognizes as the worst year of her life. She can remember nothing about that year except hunger, and the meals in her room. She is hungry now. When she puts the boy to bed she will get a candy bar from her room. She will eat it here, in front of Richard. This room will be hers soon. She considers the possibilities: all these rooms and the lawn where she can do whatever she wishes. She knows he will leave soon. It has been in his eyes all summer. She stands, using one hand to pull herself out of the chair. She carries the boy to his crib, feels him against her large breasts, feels that his sleeping body touches her soul. With a surge of vindication and relief she holds him. Then she kisses his forehead and places him in the crib. She goes to the bedroom and in the dark takes a bar of candy from her drawer. Slowly she descends the stairs. She knows Richard is waiting but she feels his departure so happily that, when she enters the living room, unwrapping the candy, she is surprised to see him standing there.

1978

HOME

by JAYNE ANNE PHILLIPS

from THE IOWA REVIEW

I'M AFRAID Walter Cronkite has had it, says Mom. Roger Mudd always does the news now. How would you like to have a name like that? Walter used to do the conventions and a football game now and then. I mean he would sort of appear, on the sidelines. Didn't he? But you never see him anymore. Lord. Something is going on.

Mom, I say. Maybe he's just resting. He must have made a lot of money by now. Maybe he's tired of talking about elections and mine disasters and the collapse of the franc. Maybe he's in love with a young girl.

He's not the type, says my mother. You can tell *that* much. No, she says, I'm afraid it's cancer.

My mother has her suspicions. She ponders. I have been home with her for two months. I ran out of money and I wasn't in love, so I have come home to my mother. She is an educational administrator. All winter long after work she watches television and knits afghans.

Come home, she said. Save money.

I can't possibly do it, I said. Jesus, I'm twenty-three years old.

Don't be silly, she said. And don't use profanity.

She arranged a job for me in the school system. All day I tutor children in remedial reading. Sometimes I am so discouraged that I lie on the couch all evening and watch television with her. The shows are all alike. Their laugh tracks are conspicuously similar; I think I recognize a repetition of certain professional laughters. This laughter marks off the half hours.

Finally I make a rule: I won't watch television at night. I will watch only the news, which ends at 7:30. Then I will go to my room and do God knows what. But I feel sad that she sits there alone, knitting by the lamp. She seldom looks up.

Why don't you ever read anything? I ask.

I do, she says. I read books in my field. I read all day at work, writing those damn proposals. When I come home I want to relax.

Then let's go to the movies.

I don't want to go to the movies. Why should I pay money to be upset or frightened?

But feeling something can teach you. Don't you want to learn anything?

I'm learning all the time, she says.

She keeps knitting. She folds yarn the color of cream, the color of snow. She works it with her long blue needles, piercing, returning, winding. Yarn cascades from her hands in long panels. A pattern appears and disappears. She stops and counts; so many stitches across, so many down. Yes, she is on the right track.

Occasionally I offer to buy my mother a subscription to something mildly informative: *Ms, Rolling Stone, Scientific American*.

I don't want to read that stuff, she says. Just save your money. Did you hear Cronkite last night? Everyone's going to need all they can get.

Often I need to look at my mother's old photographs. I see her sitting in knee-high grass with a white gardenia in her hair. I see her dressed up as the groom in a mock wedding at a sorority party, her

101

black hair pulled back tight. I see her formally posed in her cadet nurse's uniform. The photographer has painted her lashes too lushly, too long; but her deep red mouth is correct.

The war ended too soon. She didn't finish her training. She came home to nurse only her mother and to meet my father at a dance. She married him in two weeks. It took twenty years to divorce him.

When we traveled to a neighboring town to buy my high school clothes, my mother and I would pass a certain road that turned off the highway and wound to a place I never saw.

There it is, my mother would say. The road to Wonder Bar. That's where I met my Waterloo. I walked in and he said, 'There she is. I'm going to marry that girl.' Ha. He sure saw me coming.

Well, I asked, why did you marry him?

He was older, she said. He had a job and a car. And mother was so sick.

My mother doesn't forget her mother.

Never one bedsore, she says. I turned her every fifteen minutes. I kept her skin soft and kept her clean, even to the end.

I imagine my mother at twenty-three; her black hair, her dark eyes, her olive skin and that red lipstick. She is growing lines of tension in her mouth. Her teeth press into her lower lip as she lifts the woman in the bed. The woman weighs no more than a child. She has a smell. My mother fights it continually; bathing her, changing her sheets, carrying her to the bathroom so the smell can be contained and flushed away. My mother will try to protect them both. At night she sleeps in the room on a cot. She struggles awake feeling something press down on her and suck her breath: the smell. When my grandmother can no longer move, my mother fights it alone.

I did all I could, she sighs. And I was glad to do it. I'm glad I don't have to feel guilty.

No one has to feel guilty, I tell her.

And why not? says my mother. There's nothing wrong with guilt. If you are guilty, you should feel guilty.

My mother has often told me that I will be sorry when she is gone.

I think. And read alone at night in my room. I read those books I never read, the old classics, and detective stories. I can get them in the library here. There is only one bookstore; it sells mostly newspapers and *True Confessions* oracles. At Kroger's by the checkout

102

counter I buy a few paperbacks, best sellers, but they are usually bad.

The television drones on downstairs.

I wonder about Walter Cronkite.

When was the last time I saw him? It's true his face was pouchy, his hair thinning. Perhaps he is only cutting it shorter. But he had that look about the eyes. . . .

He was there when they stepped on the moon. He forgot he was on the air and he shouted, 'There . . . there . . . now . . . . We have contact!' Contact. For those who tuned in late, for the periodic watchers, he repeated: 'One small step. . . .'

I was in high school and he was there with the body count. But he said it in such a way that you knew he wanted the war to end. He looked directly at you and said the numbers quietly. Shame, yes, but sorrowful patience, as if all things had passed before his eyes. And he understood that here at home, as well as in starving India, we would pass our next lives as meager cows.

My mother gets *Reader's Digest*. I come home from work, have a cup of coffee, and read it. I keep it beside my bed. I read it when I am too tired to read anything else. I read about Joe's kidney and Humor in Uniform. Always, there are human interest stories in which someone survives an ordeal of primal terror. Tonight it is Grizzly! Two teenagers camping in the mountains are attacked by a bear. Sharon is dragged over a mile, unconscious. She is a good student loved by her parents, an honest girl loved by her boyfriend. Perhaps she is not a virgin; but in her heart, she is virginal. And she lies now in the furred arms of a beast. The grizzly drags her quietly, quietly. He will care for her all the days of his life. . . . Sharon, his rose.

But alas. Already, rescuers have organized. Mercifully her boyfriend is not among them. He is sleeping en route to the nearest hospital; his broken legs have excused him. In a few days, Sharon will bring him his food on a tray. She is spared. She is not demure. He gazes on her face, untouched but for a long thin scar near her mouth. He thinks of the monster and wonders at its delicate mark. Sharon says she remembers nothing of the bear. She only knows the tent was ripped open, that its heavy canvas fell across her face.

I turn out my light when I know my mother is sleeping. By then my eyes hurt and the streets of the town are deserted.

My father comes to me in a dream. He kneels beside me, touches my mouth. He turns my face gently toward him.

Let me see, he says. Let me see it.

He is looking for a scar, a sign. He wears only a towel around his waist. He presses himself against my thigh, pretending solicitude. But I know what he is doing; I turn my head in repulsion and stiffen. He smells of a sour musk and his forearms are black with hair. I think, it's been years since he's had an erection. . . .

Finally he stands. Cover yourself, I tell him.

I can't, he says. I'm hard.

On Saturdays I go to the Veterans of Foreign Wars rummage sales. They are held in the drafty basement of a church, rows of collapsible tables piled with objects. Sometimes I think I recognize the possessions of old friends: a class ring, yearbooks, football sweaters with our high school insignia. Would this one have fit Jason?

He used to spread it on the seat of the car on winter nights when we parked by country churches and graveyards. There seemed to be no ground, just water, a rolling, turning, building to a dull pain between my legs.

What's wrong? What is it?

Jason, I can't. . . . This pain. . . .

It's only because you're afraid. If you'd let me go ahead. . . .

I'm not afraid of you, I'd do anything for you. But Jason, why does it hurt like this?

We would try. But I couldn't. We made love with our hands. Our bodies were white. Out the window of the car, snow rose up in mounds across the fields. Afterward, he looked at me peacefully, sadly.

I held him and whispered, soon, soon. . . . we'll go away to school.

His sweater. He wore it that night we drove back from the football awards banquet. Jason made All State but he hated football.

I hate it, he said. So what? he said. That I'm out there puking in the heat? Screaming 'kill' at a sandbag?

I held his award in my lap, a gold man frozen in mid-leap. Don't play in college, I said. Refuse the money.

He was driving very slowly.

I can't see, he said. I can't see the edges of the road. . . . Tell me if I start to fall off.

Jason, what do you mean?

He insisted I roll down the window and watch the edge. The banks of the road were gradual, sloping off in brush and trees on either side. White lines at the edge glowed in dips and turns.

We're going to crash, he said.

No, Jason. You've driven this road before. We won't crash.

We're crashing, I know it, he said. Tell me, tell me I'm OK. . . .

Here on the rummage sale table, there are three football sweaters. I see they are all too small to have belonged to Jason. So I buy an old soundtrack, "The Sound of Music." Air, Austrian mountains. And an old robe to wear in the mornings. It upsets my mother to see me naked; she looks at me so curiously, as though she didn't recognize my body.

I pay for my purchases at the cash register. Behind the desk I glimpse stacks of *Reader's Digests*. The Ladies' Auxiliary turns them inside out, stiffens and shellacs them. They make wastebaskets out of them.

I give my mother the record. She is pleased. She hugs me.

Oh, she says, I used to love the musicals. They made me happy. Then she stops and looks at me.

Didn't you do this? she says. Didn't you do this in high school?

Do what?

Your class, she says. You did "The Sound of Music."

Yes, I guess we did.

What a joke. I was the beautiful countess meant to marry Captain Von Trapp before innocent Maria stole his heart. Jason was a threatening Nazi colonel with a bit part. He should have sung the lead but sports practices interfered with rehearsals. Tall, blond, aged in make-up under the lights, he encouraged sympathy for the bad guys and overshadowed the star. He appeared just often enough to make the play ridiculous.

My mother sits in the blue chair my father used for years.

Come quick, she says. Look. . . .

She points to the television. Flickerings of Senate chambers, men in conservative suits. A commentator drones on about tax rebates.

There, says my mother. Hubert Humphrey. Look at him .

It's true. Humphrey is different, changed from his former toady self to a desiccated old man, not unlike the discarded shell of a locust. Now he rasps into the microphone about the people of these great states.

Old Hubert's had it, says my mother. He's a death mask.

That's what he gets for sucking blood for thirty years.

No, she says. No, he's got it too. Look at him! Cancer. Oh.

For God's sake, will you think of something else for once?

I don't know what you mean, she says. She goes on knitting.

All Hubert needs, I tell her, is a good roll in the hay.

You think that's what everyone needs.

Everyone does need it.

They do not. People aren't dogs. I seem to manage perfectly well without it, don't I?

No, I wouldn't say that you do.

Well, I do. I know your mumbo-jumbo about sexuality. Sex is for those who are married, and I wouldn't marry again if it was the Lord himself.

Now she is silent. I know what's coming.

Your attitude will make you miserable, she says. One man after another. I just want you to be happy.

I do my best.

That's right, she says, be sarcastic.

I refuse to answer. I think about my growing bank account. Graduate school, maybe in California. Hawaii. Somewhere beautiful and warm. I will wear few clothes and my skin will feel the air.

What about Jason, says my mother. I was thinking of him the other day.

Our telepathy always frightens me. Telepathy and beyond. Before her hysterectomy, our periods often came on the same day.

If he hadn't had that nervous breakdown, she says softly, do you suppose. . . .

No, I don't suppose.

I wasn't surprised that it happened. When his brother was killed, that was hard. But Jason was so self-centered. He thought everyone was out to get him. You were lucky to be rid of him. Still, poor thing. . . .

Silence. Then she refers in low tones to the few months Jason and I lived together before he was hospitalized.

You shouldn't have done what you did when you went off to college. He lost respect for you.

106

It wasn't respect for me he lost—He lost his fucking mind, if you remember—

I realize I'm shouting. And shaking. What is happening to me?

My mother stares.

We'll not discuss it, she says.

She gets up. I hear her in the bathroom. Water running into the tub. Hydrotherapy. I close my eyes and listen. Soon, this weekend. I'll get a ride to the university a few hours away and look up an old lover. I'm lucky. They always want to sleep with me. For old time's sake.

I turn down the sound of the television and watch its silent pictures. Jason's brother was a musician; he taught Jason to play the pedal steel. A sergeant in uniform delivered the message two weeks before the state playoff games. Jason appeared at my mother's kitchen door with the telegram. He looked at me, opened his mouth, backed off wordless in the dark. I pretend I hear his pedal steel; its sweet country whine might make me cry. And I recognize this silent movie. . . . I've seen it four times. Gregory Peck and his submarine crew escape fallout in Australia, but not for long. The cloud is coming. And so they run rampant in auto races and love affairs. But in the end, they close the hatch and put out to sea. They want to go home to die.

Sweetheart? My mother calls from the bathroom. Could you bring me a towel?

Her voice is quavering slightly. She is sorry. But I never know which part of it she is sorry about. I get a towel from the linen closet and open the door of the steamy bathroom. My mother stands in the tub, dripping, shivering a little. She is so small and thin; she is smaller than I. She has two long scars on her belly, operations of the womb, and one breast is misshapen, sunken, indented near the nipple.

I put the towel around her shoulders and my eyes smart. She looks at her breast.

Not too pretty is it, she says. He took out too much when he removed that lump.

Mom, it doesn't look so bad.

I dry her back, her beautiful back which is firm and unblemished. Beautiful, her skin. Again, I feel the pain in my eyes.

But you should have sued the bastard, I tell her. He didn't give a shit about your body.

107

We have an awkward moment with the towel when I realize I can't touch her any longer. The towel slips down and she catches it as one ends dips into the water.

Sweetheart, she says. I know your beliefs are different from mine. But have patience with me. You'll just be here a few more months. And I'll always stand behind you. We'll get along.

She has clutched the towel to her chest. She is so fragile, standing there, naked, with her small shoulders. Suddenly I am horribly frightened.

Sure, I say, I know we will.

I let myself out of the room.

Sunday my mother goes to church alone. Daniel calls me from D.C. He's been living with a lover in Oregon. Now he is back east; she will join him in a few weeks. He is happy, he says. I tell him I'm glad he's found someone who appreciates him.

Come on now, he says. You weren't that bad.

I love Daniel, his white and feminine hands, his thick chestnut hair, his intelligence. And he loves me, though I don't know why. The last few weeks we were together I lay beside him like a piece of wood. I couldn't bear his touch; the moisture his penis left on my hips as he rolled against me. I was cold, cold. I huddled in blankets away from him.

I'm sorry, I said. Daniel, I'm sorry please . . . what's wrong with me? Tell me you love me anyway. . . .

Yes, he said. Of course I do. I always will. I do.

Daniel says he has no car, but he will come by bus. Is there a place for him to stay?

Oh yes, I say. There's a guest room. Bring some Trojans. I'm a hermit with no use for birth control. Daniel, you don't know what it's like here.

I don't care what it's like. I want to see you.

Yes, I say. Daniel, hurry.

When he arrives the next weekend, we sit around the table with my mother and discuss medicine. Daniel was a medic in Vietnam. He smiles at my mother. She is charmed though she has reservations; I see them in her face. But she enjoys having someone else in the house, a presence: a male. Daniel's laughter is low and modulated. He talks softly, smoothly: a dignified radio announcer, an accomplished anchor man.

But when I lived with him, he threw dishes against the wall. And jerked in his sleep, mumbling. And ran out of the house with his hands across his eyes.

After we first made love, he smiled and pulled gently away from me. He put on his shirt and went to the bathroom. I followed and stepped into the shower with him. He faced me, composed, friendly, and frozen. He stood as though guarding something behind him.

Daniel, turn around. I'll soap you back.

I already did.

Then move, I'll stand in the water with you.

He stepped carefully around me.

Daniel, what's wrong? Why won't you turn around?

Why should I?

I'd never seen him with his shirt off. He'd never gone swimming with us, only wading, alone, disappearing down Point Reyes Beach. He wore longsleeved shirts all summer in the California heat.

Daniel, I said, you've been my best friend for months. We could have talked about it.

He stepped backwards, awkwardly, out of the tub and put his shirt on.

I was loading them on copters, he told me. The last one was dead anyway; he was already dead. But I went after him, dragged him in the wind of the blades. Shrapnel and napalm caught my arms, my back. Until I fell, I thought it was the other man's blood in my hands.

They removed most of the shrapnel, did skin grafts for the burns. In three years since, Daniel made love five times; always in the dark. In San Francisco he must take off his shirt for a doctor; tumors have grown in his scars. They bleed through his shirt, round rust-colored spots.

Face-to-face in bed, I tell him I can feel the scars with my fingers. They are small knots on his skin. Not large, not ugly. But he can't let me, he can't let anyone, look: he says he feels wild, like raging, and then he vomits. But maybe, after they removed the tumors. . . . Each time they operate, they reduce the scars.

We spend hours at the Veterans's Hospital waiting for appointments. Finally they schedule the operation. I watch the black-ringed wall clock, the amputees gliding by in chairs that tick on the linoleum floor. Daniel's doctors run out of local anesthetic during the procedure and curse about lack of supplies; they bandage him with

109

gauze and layers of Band-Aids. But it is all right. I buy some real bandages. Every night I cleanse his back with a sponge and change them.

In my mother's house, Daniel seems different. He has shaved his beard and his face is too young for him. I can grip his hands.

I show him the house, the antiques, the photographs on the walls. I tell him none of the objects move; they are all cemented in place. Now the bedrooms, my room.

This is it, I say. This is where I kept my Villager sweaters when I was seventeen, and my dried corsages. My cups from the Tastee Freez labeled with dates and boys' names.

The room is large, blue. Baseboards and wood trim are painted a spotless white. Ruffled curtains, ruffled bedspread. The bed itself is so high one must climb into it. Daniel looks at the walls, their perfect blue and white.

It's a piece of candy, he says.

Yes, I say, hugging him, wanting him.

What about your mother?

She's gone to meet friends for dinner. I don't think she believes what she says, she's only being my mother. It's all right.

We take off our clothes and press close together. But something is wrong. We keep trying. Daniel stays soft in my hands. His mouth is nervous; he seems to gasp at my lips.

He says his lover's name. He says they aren't seeing other people.

But I'm not other people. And I want you to be happy with her.

I know. She knew . . . I'd want to see you.

Then what?

This room, he says. This house. I can't breathe in here.

I tell him we have tomorrow. He'll relax. And it is so good just to see him, a person from my life.

So we only hold each other, rocking.

Later, Daniel asks about my father.

I don't see him, I say. He told me to choose.

Choose what?

Between them.

My father. When he lived in this house, he stayed in the dark with his cigarette. He sat in his blue chair with the lights and television off, smoking. He made little money; he said he was self-employed. He was sick. He grew dizzy when he looked up suddenly. He slept in the basement. All night he sat reading in the bathroom. I'd hear him walking up and down the dark steps at night. I lay in the dark and listened. I believed he would strangle my mother, then walk upstairs and strangle me. I believed we were guilty; we had done something terrible to him.

Daniel wants me to talk.

How could she live with him, I ask. She came home from work and got supper. He ate it, got up and left to sit in his chair. He watched the news. We were always sitting there, looking at his dirty plates. And I wouldn't help her. She should wash them, not me. She should make the money we lived on. I didn't want her house and his ghost with its cigarette burning in the dark like a sore. I didn't want to be guilty. So she did it. She did it all herself. She sent me to college; she paid for my safe escape.

Daniel and I go to the Rainbow, a bar and grill on Main Street. We hold hands, play country songs on the juke box, drink a lot of salted beer. We talk to the barmaid and kiss in the overstuffed booth. Twinkle lights blink on and off above us. I wore my burgundy stretch pants in here when I was twelve. A senior pinched me, then moved his hand slowly across my thigh, mystified, as though erasing the pain.

What about tonight? Daniel asks. Would your mother go out with us? A movie, a bar? He sees me in her, he likes her. He wants to know her.

Then we will have to watch television.

We pop popcorn and watch the late movies. My mother stays up with us, mixing whiskey sours and laughing. She gets a high color in her cheeks and the light in her eyes glimmers up; she is slipping, slipping back and she is beautiful, oh, in her ankle socks, her red mouth and her armour of young girl's common sense. She has a beautiful laughter. She and Daniel end by mock armwrestling; he pretends defeat and goes upstairs to bed.

My mother hears his door close. He's nice, she says. You've known some nice people, haven't you?

I want to make her back down.

Yes, he's nice, I say. And don't you think he respects me? Don't you think he truly cares for me, even though we've slept together?

He seems to, I don't know. But if you give them that, it costs them nothing to be friends with you.

111

Why should it cost? The only cost is what you give, and you can tell if someone is giving it back.

How? How can you tell? By going to bed with every man you take a fancy to?

I wish I took a fancy oftener, I tell her. I wish I wanted more, I can be good to a man, but I'm afraid . . . I can't be physical, not really. . . .

You shouldn't.

I should. I want to, for myself as well. I don't think . . . I've ever had an orgasm.

What? she says. Never? Haven't you felt a sort of building up, and then a dropping off . . . a conclusion? Like something's over?

No, I don't think so.

You probably have, she assures me. It's not necessarily an explosion. You were just thinking too hard, you think too much.

But she pauses.

Maybe I don't remember right, she says. It's been years, fifteen years, and in the last years of the marriage I would have died if your father had touched me. But before, I know I felt something. That's partly why I haven't . . . since . . . what if I started wanting it again? Then it would be hell.

But you have to try to get what you want. . . .

No, she says. Not if what you want would ruin everything. And now, anyway. Who would want me.

I stand at Daniel's door. The fear is back; it has followed me upstairs from the dead dark bottom of the house. My hands are shaking. I'm whispering . . . Daniel, don't leave me here.

I go to my room to wait. I must wait all night, or something will come in my sleep. I feel its hands on me now, dragging, pulling. I watch the lit face of the clock: three, four, five. At seven I go to Daniel. He sleeps with his pillow in his arms. The high bed creaks as I get in. Please now, yes . . . he is hard. He always woke with erections . . . inside me he feels good, real, and I tell him no, stop, wait . . . I hold the rubber, stretch its rim away from skin so it smooths on without hurting and fills with him . . . now again, here, yes but quiet, be quiet . . . oh Daniel . . . the bed is making noise . . . yes, no, but be careful, she . . . We move and turn and I forget about the sounds. We push against each other hard, he is almost there and I am almost with him and just when it is over I think I hear my mother in the room directly under us. . . . But I am half dreaming. I move to get out of bed and Daniel holds me. No, he says. Stay. . . .

We sleep and wake to hear the front door slam.

Daniel looks at me.

There's nothing to be done, I say. She's gone to church.

He looks at the clock. I'm going to miss that bus, he says. We put our clothes on fast and Daniel moves to dispose of the rubber . . . how? The toilet, no, the wastebasket. . . . He drops it in, bends over, retrieves it. Finally he wraps it in a Kleenex and puts it in his pocket. Jesus, he swears. He looks at me and grins. When I start laughing, my eyes are wet.

I take Daniel to the bus station and watch him out of sight. I come back and strip the bed, bundle the sheets in my arms. This pressure in my chest . . . I have to clutch the sheets tight, tighter. . . .

A door clicks shut. I go downstairs to my mother. She refuses to speak or let me near her. She stands by the sink and holds her small square purse with both hands. The fear comes. I hug myself, press my hands against my arms to stop shaking. My mother runs hot water, soap, takes dishes from the drainer. She immerses them, pushes them down, rubbing with a rag in a circular motion.

Those dishes are clean, I tell her. I washed them last night.

She keeps washing, rubbing. Hot water clouds her glasses, the window in front of us, our faces. We all disappear in steam. I watch the dishes bob and sink. My mother begins to sob. I move close to her and hold her. She smells as she used to smell when I was a child and slept with her.

I heard you, I heard it, she says. Here, in my own house. Please . . . how much can you expect me to take? I don't know what to do about anything. . . .

She looks into the water, keeps looking. And we stand here just like this.

1979

113

LEVITATION

by CYNTHIA OZICK

from PARTISAN REVIEW

A PAIR OF NOVELISTS, husband and wife, gave a party. The husband was also an editor; he made his living at it. But really he was a novelist. His manner was powerless; he did not seem like an editor at all. He had a nice plain pale face, likable. His name was Feingold.

For love, and also because he had always known he did not want a Jewish wife, he married a minister's daughter. Lucy too had hoped to marry out of her tradition. (These words were hers. "Out of my tradition," she said. The idea fevered him.) At the age of twelve she felt herself to belong to the people of the Bible. ("A

Hebrew," she said. His heart lurched, joy rocked him.) One night from the pulpit her father read a Psalm; all at once she saw how the Psalmist meant *her*; then and there she became an Ancient Hebrew.

She had huge, intent, sliding eyes, disconcertingly luminous, and copper hair, and a grave and timid way of saying honest things.

They were shy people, and rarely gave parties.

Each had published one novel. Hers was about domestic life; he wrote about Jews.

All the roil about the State of the Novel had passed them by. In the evening after the children had been put to bed, while the portable dishwasher rattled out its smell of burning motor oil, they sat down, she at her desk, he at his, and began to write. They wrote not without puzzlements and travail; nevertheless as naturally as birds. They were devoted to accuracy, psychological realism, and earnest truthfulness; also to virtue, and even to wit. Neither one was troubled by what had happened to the novel: all those declarations about the end of Character and Story. They were serene. Sometimes, closing up their notebooks for the night, it seemed to them that they were literary friends and lovers, like George Eliot and George Henry Lewes.

In bed they would revel in quantity and murmur distrustingly of theory. "Seven pages so far this week." "Nine-and-a-half, but I had to throw out four. A wrong tack." "Because you're doing first person. First person strangles. You can't get out of their skin." And so on. The one principle they agreed on was the importance of never writing about writers. Your protagonist always has to be someone *real,* with real work-in-the-world—a bureaucrat, a banker, an architect (ah, they envied Conrad his shipmasters!)—otherwise you fall into solipsism, narcissism, tedium, lack of appeal-to-the-common-reader; who knew what other perils.

This difficulty—seizing on a concrete subject—was mainly Lucy's. Feingold's novel—the one he was writing now—was about Menachem ben Zerach, survivor of a massacre of Jews in the town of Estella in Spain in 1328. From morning to midnight he hid under a pile of corpses, until a "compassionate knight" (this was the language of the history Feingold relied on) plucked him out and took him home to tend his wounds. Menachem was then twenty; his father and mother and four younger brothers had been cut down in the terror. Six thousand Jews died in a single day in

115

March. Feingold wrote well about how the mild winds carried the salty fragrance of fresh blood, together with the ashes of Jewish houses, into the faces of the marauders. It was nevertheless a triumphant story: at the end Menachem ben Zerach becomes a renowned scholar.

"If you're going to tell about how after he gets to be a scholar he just sits there and *writes*," Lucy protested, "then you're doing the Forbidden Thing." But Feingold said he meant to concentrate on the massacre, and especially on the life of the "compassionate knight." What had brought him to this compassion? What sort of education? What did he read? Feingold would invent a journal for the compassionate knight, and quote from it. Into this journal the compassionate knight would direct all his gifts, passions, and private opinions.

"Solipsism," Lucy said. "Your compassionate knight is only another writer. Narcissism. Tedium."

They talked often about the Forbidden Thing. After a while they began to call it the Forbidden City, because not only were they (but Lucy especially) tempted to write—solipsistically, narcissistically, tediously, and without common appeal—about writers, but, more narrowly yet, about writers in New York.

"The compassionate knight," Lucy said, "lived on the Upper West Side of Estella. He lived on the Riverside Drive, the West End Avenue, of Estella. He lived in Estella on Central Park West."

The Feingolds lived on Central Park West.

In her novel—the published one, not the one she was writing now—Lucy had described, in the first person, where they lived:

By now I have seen quite a few of those West Side apartments. They have mysterious layouts. Rooms with doors that go nowhere—turn the knob, open: a wall. Someone is snoring behind it, in another apartment. They have made two and three or even four and five flats out of these palaces. The toilet bowls have antique cracks that shimmer with moisture like old green rivers. Fluted columns and fireplaces. Artur Rubinstein once paid rent here. On a gilt piano he raced a sonata by Beethoven. The sounds went spinning like mercury. Breathings all lettered now. Editors. Critics. Books, old, old books, heavy as centuries. Shelves built into the cold fireplace; Freud on the grate, Marx on the hearth, Melville, Hawthorne, Emerson. Oh God, the weight, the weight.

Lucy felt herself to be a stylist; Feingold did not. He believed in putting one sentence after another. In his publishing house he had no influence. He was nervous about his decisions. He rejected most manuscripts because he was afraid of mistakes; every mistake lost money. It was a small house panting after profits; Feingold told Lucy that the only books his firm respected belonged to the accountants. Now and then he tried to smuggle in a novel after his own taste, and then he would be brutal to the writer. He knocked the paragraphs about until they were as sparse as his own. "God knows what you would do to mine," Lucy said; "bald man, bald prose." The horizon of Feingold's head shone. She never showed him her work. But they understood they were lucky in each other. They pitied every writer who was not married to a writer. Lucy said: "At least we have the same premises."

Volumes of Jewish history ran up and down their walls; they belonged to Feingold. Lucy read only one book—it was *Emma*— over and over again. Feingold did not have a "philosophical" mind. What he liked was event. Lucy liked to speculate and ruminate. She was slightly more intelligent than Feingold. To strangers he seemed very mild. Lucy, when silent, was a tall copper statue.

They were both devoted to omniscience, but they were not acute enough to see what they meant by it. They thought of themselves as children with a puppet theater: they could make anything at all happen, speak all the lines, with gloved hands bring all the characters to shudders or leaps. They fancied themselves in love with what they called "imagination." It was not true. What they were addicted to was counterfeit pity, and this was because they were absorbed by power, and were powerless.

They lived on pity, and therefore on gossip: who had been childless for ten years, who had lost three successive jobs, who was in danger of being fired, which agent's prestige had fallen, who could not get his second novel published, who was *persona non grata* at this or that magazine, who was drinking seriously, who was a likely suicide, who was dreaming of divorce, who was secretly or flamboyantly sleeping with whom, who was being snubbed, who counted or did not count; and toward everyone in the least way victimized they appeared to feel the most immoderate tenderness. They were, besides, extremely "psychological": kind listeners, helpful, lifting hot palms they would gladly put to anyone's anguished temples. They were attracted to bitter lives.

About their own lives they had a joke: they were "secondary-

117

level" people. Feingold had a secondary-level job with a secondary-level house. Lucy's own publisher was secondary-level; even the address was Second Avenue. The reviews of their books had been written by secondary-level reviewers. All their friends were secondary-level: not the presidents or partners of the respected firms, but copy editors and production assistants; not the glittering eagles of the intellectual organs, but the wearisome hacks of small Jewish journals; not the fiercely cold-hearted literary critics, but those wan and chattering daily reviewers of film. If they knew a playwright, he was off-off-Broadway in ambition and had not yet been produced. If they knew a painter, he lived in a loft and had exhibited only once, against a wire fence in the outdoor show at Washington Square in the spring. And this struck them as mean and unfair; they liked their friends, but other people—why not they?—were drawn into the deeper caverns of New York, among the lions.

New York! They risked their necks if they ventured out to Broadway for a loaf of bread after dark; muggers hid behind the seesaws in the playgrounds, junkies with knives hung upside down in the jungle gym. Every apartment a lit fortress; you admired the lamps and the locks, the triple locks on the caged-in windows, the double locks and the police rods on the doors, the lamps with timers set to make burglars think you were always at home. Footsteps in the corridor, the elevator's midnight grind; caution's muffled gasps. Their parents lived in Cleveland and St. Paul, and hardly ever dared to visit. All of this: grit and unsuitability (they might have owned a snowy lawn somewhere else); and no one said their names, no one had any curiosity about them, no one ever asked whether they were working on anything new. After half a year their books were remaindered for eighty-nine cents each. Anonymous mediocrities. They could not call themselves forgotten because they had never been noticed.

Lucy had a diagnosis: they were, both of them, sunk in a ghetto. Feingold persisted in his morbid investigations into Inquisitional autos-de-fé in this and that Iberian marketplace. She herself had supposed the inner life of a housebound woman—she cited *Emma*—to contain as much comedy as the cosmos. Jews and women! They were both beside the point. It was necessary to put aside pity; to look to the center; to abandon selflessness; to study power.

They drew up a list of luminaries. They invited Irving Howe,

Susan Sontag, Alfred Kazin, and Leslie Fiedler. They invited
Norman Podhoretz and Elizabeth Hardwick. They invited Philip
Roth and Joyce Carol Oates and Norman Mailer and William
Styron and Donald Barthelme and Jerzy Kosinski and Truman
Capote. None of these came; all of them had unlisted numbers, or
else machines that answered the telephone, or else were in Prague
or Paris or out of town. Nevertheless the apartment filled up. It
was a Saturday night in a chill November. Taxis whirled on patches
of sleet. On the inside of the apartment door a mound of rainboots
grew taller and taller. Two closets were packed tight with rain coats
and fur coats; a heap of coats smelling of skunk and lamb fell
tangled off a bed.

The party washed and turned like a sluggish tub; it lapped at all
the walls of all the rooms. Lucy wore a long skirt, violet-colored,
Feingold a lemon shirt and no tie. He looked paler than ever. The
apartment had a wide center hall, itself the breadth of a room; the
dining room opened off it to the left, the living room to the right.
The three party-rooms shone like a triptych: it was as if you could
fold them up and enclose everyone into darkness. The guests were
free-standing figures in the niches of a cathedral; or else dressed-up
cardboard dolls, with their drinks, and their costumes all meticul-
ously hung with sashes and draped collars and little capes, the
women's hair variously bound, the men's sprouting and spilling:
fashion stalked, Feingold moped. He took in how it all flashed,
manhattans and martinis, earrings and shoe-tips—he marveled,
but knew it was a falsehood, even a figment. The great world was
somewhere else. The conversation could fool you; how these
people talked! From the conversation itself—grains of it, carried
off, swallowed by new eddyings, swirl devouring swirl, every
moment a permutation in the tableau of those free-standing figures
or dolls, all of them afloat in a tub—from this or that hint or syllable
you could imagine the whole universe in the process of ultimate
comprehension. Human nature, the stars, history—the voices
drummed and strummed. Lucy swam by blank-eyed, pushing a
platter of mottled cheeses. Feingold seized her: "It's a waste!" She
gazed back. He said, "No one's here!" Mournfully she rocked a
stump of cheese; then he lost her.

He went into the living room: it was mainly empty, a few lumps
on the sofa. The lumps wore business suits. The dining room was
better. Something in formation: something around the big table:

coffee cups shimmering to the brim, cake cut onto plates (the mock-Victorian rosebud plates from Boots' drug store in London: the year before their first boy was born Lucy and Feingold saw the Brontës' moors; Coleridge's house in Highgate; Lamb House, Rye, where Edith Wharton had tea with Henry James; Bloomsbury; the Cambridge stairs Forster had lived at the top of)—it seemed about to become a regular visit, with points of view, opinions; a discussion. The voices began to stumble; Feingold liked that, it was nearly human. But then, serving round the forks and paper napkins, he noticed the awful vivacity of their falsetto phrases: actors, theater chatter, who was directing whom, what was opening where; he hated actors. Shrill puppets. Brainless. A double row of faces around the table; gurgles of fools.

The center hall—swept clean. No one there but Lucy, lingering.

"Theater in the dining room," he said. "Junk."

"Film. I heard film."

"Film too," he conceded. "Junk. It's mobbed in there."

"Because they've got the cake. They've got all the food. The living room's got nothing."

"My God," he said, like a man choking, "do you realize *no one came?*"

The living room had—had once had—potato chips. The chips were gone, the carrot sticks eaten, of the celery sticks nothing left but threads. One olive in a dish; Feingold chopped it in two with vicious teeth. The business suits had disappeared. "It's awfully early," Lucy said; "a lot of people had to leave." "It's a cocktail party, that's what happens," Feingold said. "It isn't *exactly* a cocktail party," Lucy said. They sat down on the carpet in front of the fireless grate. "Is that a real fireplace?" someone inquired. "We never light it," Lucy said. "Do you light those candlesticks ever?" "They belonged to Jimmy's grandmother," Lucy said, "we never light them."

She crossed no-man's-land to the dining room. They were serious in there now. The subject was Chaplin's gestures.

In the living room Feingold despaired; no one asked him, he began to tell about the compassionate knight. A problem of ego, he said: compassion being super-consciousness of one's own pride. Not that he believed this; he only thought it provocative to say something original, even if a little muddled. But no one responded. Feingold looked up. "Can't you light that fire?" said a

120

man. "All right," Feingold said. He rolled a paper log made of last Sunday's *Times* and laid a match on it. A flame as clear as a streetlight whitened the faces of the sofa-sitters. He recognized a friend of his from the Seminary—he had what Lucy called "theological" friends—and then and there, really very suddenly, Feingold wanted to talk about God. Or, if not God, then certain historical atrocities, abominations: to wit, the crime of the French nobleman Draconet, a proud Crusader, who in the spring of the year 1247 arrested all the Jews of the province of Vienne, castrated the men, and tore off the breasts of the women; some he did not mutilate, and only cut in two. It interested Feingold that Magna Carta and the Jewish badge of shame were issued in the same year, and that less than a century afterward all the Jews were driven out of England, even families who had been settled there seven or eight generations. He had a soft spot for Pope Clement IV, who absolved the Jews from responsibility for the Black Death. "The plague takes the Jews themselves," the Pope said. Feingold knew innumerable stories about forced conversions, he felt at home with these thoughts, comfortable, the chairs seemed dense with family. He wondered whether it would be appropriate—at a cocktail party, after all!—to inquire after the status of the Seminary friend's agnosticism: was it merely that God had stepped out of history, left the room for a moment, so to speak, without a pass, or was there no Creator to begin with, nothing had been created, the world was a chimera, a solipsist's delusion?

Lucy was uneasy with the friend from the Seminary; he was the one who had administered her conversion, and every encounter was like a new stage in a perpetual examination. She was glad there was no Jewish catechism. Was she a backslider? Anyhow she felt tested. Sometimes she spoke of Jesus to the children. She looked around—her great eyes wheeled—and saw that everyone in the living room was a Jew.

There were Jews in the dining room too, but the unruffled, devil-may-care kind: the humorists, the painters, film reviewers who went off to studio showings of "Screw on Screen" on the eve of the Day of Atonement. Mostly there were Gentiles in the dining room. Nearly the whole cake was gone. She took the last piece, cubed it on a paper plate, and carried it back to the living room. She blamed Feingold, he was having one of his spasms of fanaticism. Everyone normal, everyone with sense—the humanists and

121

humorists, for instance—would want to keep away. What was he now, after all, but one of those boring autodidacts who spew out everything they read? He was doing it for spite, because no one had come. There he was, telling about the blood-libel. Little Hugh of Lincoln. How in London, in 1279, Jews were torn to pieces by horses, on a charge of having crucified a Christian child. How in 1285, in Munich, a mob burned down a synagogue on the same pretext. At Eastertime in Mainz two years earlier. Three centuries of beatified child martyrs, some of them figments, all called "Little Saints." The Holy Niño of LaGuardia. Feingold was crazed by these tales, he drank them like a vampire. Lucy stuck a square of chocolate cake in his mouth to shut him up. Feingold was waiting for a voice. The friend from the Seminary, pragmatic, licked off his bit of cake hungrily. It was a cake sent from home, packed by his wife in a plastic bag, to make sure there was something to eat. It was a guaranteed nolard cake. They were all ravenous. The fire crumpled out in big paper cinders.

The friend from the Seminary had brought a friend. Lucy examined him: she knew how to give catechisms of her own, she was not a novelist for nothing. She catechized and catalogued: a refugee. Fingers like long wax candles, snuffed at the nails. Black sockets: was he blind? It was hard to tell where the eyes were under that ledge of skull. Skull for a head, but such a cushioned mouth, such lips, such orderly expressive teeth. Such a bone in such a dry wrist. A nose like a saint's. The face of Jesus. He whispered. Everyone leaned over to hear. He was Feingold's voice: the voice Feingold was waiting for.

"Come to modern times," the voice urged. "Come to yesterday." Lucy was right: she could tell a refugee in an instant, even before she heard any accent. They all reminded her of her father. She put away this insight (the resemblance of Presbyterian ministers to Hitler refugees) to talk over with Feingold later: it was nicely analytical, it had enough mystery to satisfy. "Yesterday," the refugee said, "the eyes of God were shut." And Lucy saw him shut his hidden eyes in their tunnels. "Shut," he said, "like iron doors"—a voice of such nobility that Lucy thought immediately of that eerie passage in Genesis where the voice of the Lord God walks in the Garden in the cool of the day and calls to Adam, "Where are you?"

They all listened with a terrible intensity. Again Lucy looked

122

around. It pained her how intense Jews could be, though she too was intense. But she was intense because her brain was roiling with ardor, she wooed mind-pictures, she was a novelist. *They* were intense all the time; she supposed the grocers among them were as intense as any novelist; was it because they had been Chosen, was it because they pitied themselves every breathing moment?

Pity and shock stood in all their faces.

The refugee was telling a story. "I witnessed it," he said. "I am the witness." Horror; sadism; corpses. As if—Lucy took the image from the elusive wind that was his voice in its whisper—as if hundreds and hundreds of Crucifixions were all happening at once. She visualized a hillside with multitudes of crosses, and bodies dropping down from big bloody nails. Every Jew was Jesus. That was the only way Lucy could get hold of it: otherwise it was only a movie. She had seen all the movies, the truth was she could feel nothing. That same bulldozer shoveling those same sticks of skeletons, that same little boy in a cap with twisted mouth and his hands in the air—if there had been a camera at the Crucifixion Christianity would collapse, no one would ever feel anything about it. Cruelty came out of the imagination, and had to be witnessed by the imagination.

All the same, she listened. What he told was exactly like the movies. A gray scene, a scubby hill, a ravine. Germans in helmets, with shining tar-black belts, wearing gloves. A ragged bundle of Jews at the lip of the ravine—an old grandmother, a child or two, a couple in their forties. All the faces stained with grayness, the stubble of the ground stained gray, the clothes on them limp as shrouds but immobile, as if they were already under the dirt, shut off from breezes, as if they were already stone. The refugee's whisper carved them like sculptures—there they stood, a shadowy stone asterisk of Jews, you could see their nostrils, open as skulls, the stony round ears of the children, the grandmother's awful twig of a neck, the father and mother grasping the children but strangers to each other, not a touch between them, the grandmother cast out, claiming no one and not claimed, all prayerless stone gums. There they stood. For a long while the refugee's voice pinched them and held them, so that you had to look. His voice made Lucy look and look. He pierced the figures through with his whisper. Then he let the shots come. The figures never teetered never shook: the stoniness broke all at once and they fell cleanly,

123

like sacks, into the ravine. Immediately they were in a heap, with random limbs all tangled together. The refugee's voice like a camera brought a German boot to the edge of the ravine. The boot kicked sand. It kicked and kicked, the sand poured over the family of sacks.

Then Lucy saw the fingers of the listeners—all their fingers were stretched out.

The room began to lift. It ascended. It rose like an ark on waters. Lucy said inside her mind, "This chamber of Jews." It seemed to her that the room was levitating on the little grains of the refugee's whisper. She felt herself alone at the bottom, below the floorboards, while the room floated upward, carrying Jews. Why did it not take her too? Only Jesus could take her. They were being kidnapped, these Jews, by a messenger from the land of the dead. The man had a power. Already he was in the shadow of another tale: she promised herself she would not listen, only Jesus could make her listen. The room was ascending. Above her head it grew smaller and smaller, more and more remote, it fled deeper and deeper into upwardness.

She craned after it. Wouldn't it bump into the apartment upstairs? It was like watching the underside of an elevator, all dirty and hairy, with dust-roots wagging. The black floor moved higher and higher. It was getting free of her, into loftiness, lifting Jews.

The glory of their martyrdom.

Under the rising eave Lucy had an illumination: she saw herself with the children in a little city park. A Sunday afternoon early in May. Feingold has stayed home to nap, and Lucy and the children find seats on a bench and wait for the unusual music to begin. The room is still levitating, but inside Lucy's illumination the boys are chasing birds. They run away from Lucy, they return, they leave. They surround a pigeon. They do not touch the pigeon; Lucy has forbidden it. She has read that city pigeons carry meningitis. A little boy in Red Bank, New Jersey, contracted sleeping sickness from touching a pigeon; after six years, he is still asleep. In his sleep he has grown from a child to an adolescent; puberty has come on him in his sleep, his testicles have dropped down, a benign blond beard glints mildly on his cheeks. His parents weep and weep. He is still asleep. No instruments or players are visible. A woman steps out onto a platform. She is an anthropologist from the Smithsonian Institute in Washington, D.C. She explains that there

124

will be no "entertainment" in the usual sense; there will be no "entertainers." The players will not be artists; they will be "real peasants." They have been brought over from Messina, from Calabria. They are shepherds, goatherds. They will sing and dance and play just as they do when they come down from the hills to while away the evenings in the taverns. They will play the instruments that scare away the wolves from the flock. They will sing the songs that celebrate the Madonna of Love. A dozen men file onto the platform. They have heavy faces that do not smile. They have heavy dark skins, cratered and leathery. They have ears and noses that look like dried twisted clay. They have gold teeth. They have no teeth. Some are young; most are in their middle years. One is very old; he wears bells on his fingers. One has an instrument like a butter churn: he shoves a stick in and out of a hole in a wooden tub held under his arm, and a rattling screech spurts out of it. One blows on two slender pipes simultaneously. One has a long strap, which he rubs. One has a frame of bicycle bells; a descendant of the bells the priests used to beat in the temple of Minerva.

The anthropologist is still explaining everything. She explains the "male" instrument: three wooden knockers; the innermost one lunges up and down between the other two. The songs, she explains, are mainly erotic. The dances are suggestive.

The unusual music commences. The park has filled with Italians—greenhorns from Sicily, settled New Yorkers from Naples. An ancient people. They clap. The old man with the bells on his fingers points his dusty shoe-toes and slowly follows a circle of his own. His eyes are in trance, he squats, he ascends. The anthropologist explains that up-and-down dancing can also be found in parts of Africa. The singers wail like Arabs; the anthropologist notes that the Arab conquest covered the southernmost portion of the Italian boot for two hundred years. The whole chorus of peasants sings in a dialect of archaic Greek; the language has survived in the old songs, the anthropologist explains. The crowd is laughing and stamping. They click their fingers and sway. Lucy's boys are bored. They watch the man with the finger-bells; they watch the wooden male pump up and down. Everyone is clapping, stamping, clicking, swaying, thumping. The wailing goes on and on, faster and faster. The singers are dancers, the dancers are singers, they turn and turn, they are smiling the drugged smiles of dervishes. At home they grow flowers. They follow the sheep into the deep grass. They drink wine in the taverns at night. Calabria and Sicily in New York, sans wives, in sweat-blotched shirts and wrinkled dusty pants, gasping before strangers who have never smelled the sweetness of their village grasses!

Now the anthropologist from the Smithsonian has vanished out of Lucy's illumination. A pair of dancers seize each other. Leg winds over leg, belly into belly, each man hopping on a single free leg. Intertwined, they squat and rise, squat and rise. Old Hellenic syllables fly from them. They send out high elastic cries. They celebrate the Madonna, giver of fertility and fecundity. Lucy is glorified. She is exalted. She comprehends. Not that the musicians are peasants, not that their faces and feet and necks and wrists are blown grass and red earth. An enlightenment comes on her: she sees what is eternal: before the Madonna there was Venus; before Venus, Aphrodite; before Aphrodite, Astarte. Her womb is garden, lamb, and babe. She is the river and the waterfall. She causes grave men of business—goatherds are men of business—to cavort and to flash their gold teeth. She induces them to blow, beat, rub, shake and scrape objects so that music will drop out of them.

Inside Lucy's illumination the dancers are seething. They are writhing. For the sake of the goddess, for the sake of the womb of the goddess, they are turning into serpents. When they grow still they are earth. They are from always to always. Nature is their pulse. Lucy sees: she understands: the gods are God. How terrible to have given up Jesus, a man like these made of earth like these, with a pulse like these, God entering nature to become god! Jesus, no more miraculous than an ordinary goatherd; is a goatherd miracle? Is a leaf? A nut, a pit, a core, a seed, a stone? Everything is miracle! Lucy sees how she has abandoned nature, how she has lost true religion on account of the God of the Jews. The boys are on their bellies on the ground, digging it up with sticks. They dig and dig: little holes with mounds beside them. They fill them with peach pits, cherry pits, cantaloupe rinds. The Sicilians and Neapolitans pick up their baskets and purses and shopping bags and leave. The benches smell of eaten fruit, running juices, insect-mobbed. The stage is clean.

The living room has escaped altogether. It is very high and extremely small, no wider than the moon on Lucy's thumbnail. It is still sailing upward, and the voices of those on board are so faint that

Lucy almost loses them. But she knows which word it is they mainly use. How long can they go on about it? How long? A morbid cud-chewing. Death and death and death. The word is less a human word than an animal's cry; a crow's. Caw caw. It belongs to storms, floods, avalanches. Acts of God. "Holocaust," someone caws dimly from above; she knows it must be Feingold. He always says this word over and over and over. History is bad for him: how little it makes him seem! Lucy decides it is possible to become jaded by atrocity. She is bored by the shootings and the gas and the camps, she is not ashamed to admit this. They are as tiresome as prayer. Repetition diminishes conviction; she is thinking of her father leading the same hymns week after week. If you said the same prayer over and over again, wouldn't your brain turn out to be no better than a prayer wheel?

In the dining room all the springs were running down. It was stale in there, a failed party. They were drinking beer or Coke or whiskey-and-water and playing with the cake crumbs on the table-cloth. There was still some cheese left on a plate, and half a bowl of salted peanuts. "The impact of Romantic Individualism," one of the humanists objected. "At the Frick?" "I never saw that." "They certainly are deliberate, you have to say that for them." Lucy, leaning abandoned against the door, tried to tune in. The relief of hearing atheists. A jacket designer who worked in Feingold's art department came in carrying a coat. Feingold had invited her because she was newly divorced; she was afraid to live alone. She was afraid of being ambushed in her basement while doing laundry. "Where's Jimmy?" the jacket designer asked. "In the other room." "Say goodbye for me, will you?" "Goodbye," Lucy said. The humanists—Lucy saw how they were all compassionate knights—stood up. A puddle from an overturned saucer was leaking onto the floor. "Oh, I'll get that," Lucy told the knights, "don't think another thought about it."

Overhead Feingold and the refugee are riding the living room. Their words are specks. All the Jews are in the air.

1980

PRETEND DINNERS

by W. P. KINSELLA

from CRAZY HORSE

For Barbara Kostynyk

It was Oscar Stick she married. The thing that surprise me most about Oscar and Bonnie getting together is that Oscar be a man who don't really like women, and Bonnie seem to me a woman who need more love than anybody I ever knowed.

She was Bonnie Brightfeathers to start with and a girl who always been into this here Women's Lib stuff. She been three years older than me for as long as I can remember. That age make quite a difference at times. When she was eighteen she don't even talk to a kid like me, but now that she's 23 and I'm 20, it don't seem to make any difference at all.

Bonnie Brightfeathers graduate the grade twelve class at the Residential School with really good report cards. She hold her head up, walk with long steps like she going someplace, and she don't chase around with guys or drink a lot. Her and Bedelia Coyote is friends and they always say they don't need men for nothing.

"A woman without a man be like a fish without a bicycle," Bedelia say all the time. She read that in one of these MS Magazines that she subscribe to, and she like to say it to my girlfriend Sadie One-wound when she see us walk along the road have our arms around each other.

After high school Bonnie get a job with one of these night patrol and security companies in Wetaskiwin. Northwest Security and Investigations is the right name. She wear a light brown uniform and carry on her hip in a holster what everybody say is a real gun. She move away from her parents who got more kids than anything else except maybe beer bottles what been throwed through the broke front window of their cabin and lay in the yard like cow chips. She move from the reserve to Wetaskiwin after her first pay cheque. Pretty soon she got her own little yellow car and an apartment in a new building at the end of 51st avenue.

All this before she was even nineteen. It was almost a year later that I got to know her good. A Government looking letter come to the reserve for her and her father ask me to take it up to Wetaskiwin the next time I go. That same night I went in Blind Louis Coyote's pickup truck and Bonnie invite me up to her apartment after I buzzed the talk-back machine in the lobby.

It be an apartment where the living room/bed room be all one. The kitchen is about as big as most closets but she got the whole place fixed up cheerful: soft cushions all over the place, lamps with colored bulbs, and pretty dishes. She got too a record player and a glass coffee table with chrome legs. The kitchen table be so new that it still smell like the inside of a new car. There are plants too, hang on a wool rope from the ceiling and brush my shoulder when I cross the room to sit on her sofa. Whole apartment ain't big enough to swing a cat in, but it is a soft, warm place to be, like the inside of a sleeping bag.

Bonnie is a real pretty person remind me some of my sister Illianna. She got long hair tied in kind of a pony-tail on each side of her head and dark eyes just a little too big for her face. Her skin is a browny-yellow color like furniture I seen in an antique store window. She is a lot taller than most Indian girls and real slim. She wear cut off jeans and a scarlet blouse the night I come to see her.

She give me a beer in a tall glass. I don't even get to see the bottle except when she take it out of the fridge. She put out for us some peanuts in a sky-blue colored dish the shape of a heart while she talk to me about how happy she is.

This is about the time that I write down my first stories for Mr. Nichols. Being able to do something that I want to do sit way off in the future like a bird so high in the sky that it be just a speck, but I can understand how proud Bonnie feel to see her life turning out good.

"Someday, Silas, I'm going to have me a whole big house. I babysit one time for people in Wetaskiwin who got a living room bigger than this whole apartment." She pour herself a beer and come sit down beside me.

"You know what they teached us at the Home Economics class in high school? About something called gracious living. Old Miss Lupus, she show us how to set a table for a dinner party of eight. She show us what forks to put where and learned us what kind of wine to serve with what dish."

Bonnie got at the end of her room the top half of a cupboard with doors that are like mirrored sunglasses, all moonlight colored and you can sort of see yourself in them. When she tell me the cupboard is called a hutch I make jokes about how many rabbits she could keep in there.

"I remember Bedelia Coyote saying, 'Hell, we have a dinner party for fifteen every night, but we only got eleven plates so the late ones get to wait for a second setting, if the food don't run out first.' "

After a while Bonnie show me the inside of the cupboard. She got two dinner plates be real white and heavy, two sets of silver knives, spoon, and fat and thin forks, two wine glasses with stems must be six inches long, and four or five bottles of wine and liquor. The bottles be all different colors and shapes.

"Most everybody make fun of that stuff Miss Lupus teach us, but I remember it all good and I'm gonna use it someday. One time Sharon Fence-post asked, 'What kind of wine do you serve with Kraft Dinner?' and Miss Lupus try to give her a straight answer, but everybody laugh so hard we can't hear what she say."

Bonnie take down the bottles from the cabinet to show me. "I buy them because they look pretty. See, I never even crack the seals," and she take out a tall bottle of what could be lemon pop except the label say, *Galliano*. She got too a bottle of dark green with a neck over a foot long and it have a funny name that I have to write down on the back of a match book, *Valpolicella*.

"We put on pretend dinners up there at the school. They got real fancy wine glasses, look like a frosted window, and real wine bottles except they got in them only water and food coloring. We joke about how Miss Lupus and Mr. Gortner, the principal, drink up all the real wine before they fill up the bottles for us to pretend with. Vicki Crowchild took a slug out of one of them bottles, then spit it clean across the room and say, 'This wine tastes like shit.' Miss Lupus suspended her for two weeks for that.

"See this one," Bonnie say, and show me a bottle that be both a bottle and a basket, all made of glass and filled with white wine. "Rich people do that," she say, "put out wine bottles in little wood baskets. They sit it up on the table just like a baby lay in a crib."

There is a stone crock of blue and white got funny birds fly around on it, and one that be stocky and square like a bottle of Brute Shaving Lotion, and be full of a bright green drink called *Sciarda*. I'd sure like to taste me that one sometime.

It is like we been friends, Bonnie and me, for a long time, or better than friends, maybe a brother and sister. Bonnie got in her lamp soft colored light bulbs that make the room kind of golden. She put Merle Haggard on the record player and we talk for a long time. Later on, my friends Frank and Rufus give me a bad time 'cause I stay there maybe three hours and leave them wait in the truck. They tease me about what we maybe done up there, but I know we are just friends and what anybody else think don't matter.

"Sit up to the table here, Silas, and I make for you a pretend dinner," Bonnie say. She put that heavy plate, white as new snow, in front of me, and she arrange the knife and other tools in the special way she been taught.

"Put your beer way off to the side there. Beer got no place at pretend dinners," and she set out the tall wine glasses and take the glass bottle and basket and make believe she fill up our glasses. "Know what we having for dinner?"

"Roast moose," I say.

Bonnie laugh pretty at that, but tell me we having chicken or maybe fish 'cause when you having white wine you got to serve only certain things like that with it.

"I remember that, the next time we have a bottle in the bushes outside Blue Quills Hall on Saturday night," I tell her.

Bonnie make me a whole pretend dinner, right from things she say is appetizers to the roast chicken stuffed with rice. "What do you want for dessert?" she ask me. When I say chocolate pudding, she say I should have a fancy one like strawberry shortcake or peaches with brandy. "Might as well have the best when you making believe."

I stick with chocolate pudding. I like the kind that come in a can what is painted white inside.

"Some of this here stuff is meant to be drunk after dinner," Bonnie say, waving the tall yellow bottle that got the picture of an old fashioned soldier on the label. "I ain't got the right glasses for this yet. Supposed to use tiny ones no bigger than the cap off a whiskey bottle. This time you got to pretend both the bottle and glass. Miss Lupus tell us that people take their after dinner drinks to the living room, have their cigarette there and relax their stomach after a big meal."

I light up Bonnie's cigarette for her and we pretend to relax our stomachs.

"I'm gonna really do all this oneday, Silas. I'm gonna get me a man who likes to share real things with me, but one who can make believe too."

"Thought you and Bedelia don't like men?"

"Bedelia's different from me. She really believe what she say, and she's strong enough to follow it through. I believe women should have a choice of what they do, but that other stuff, about hating men, and liking to live all alone, for me at least that just be a front that is all pretend like these here dinners."

She say something awful nice to me then. We talking in Cree and it be a hard language to say beautiful things in. What Bonnie say to me come up because we carried on talking about love. I say I figure most everybody find someone to love at least once or twice.

"How many people you know who is happy in their marriage?" Bonnie say.

"Maybe only one or two," I tell her.

"I don't want no marriage like I seen around here. For me it got to be more. I want somebody to twine my nights and days around, the way roses grow up a wire fence."

When I tell her how pretty I figure that is her face break open in a great smile and the dimples on each side of her mouth wink at me. I wish her luck and tell her how much I enjoy that pretend dinner of hers. Bonnie got a good heart. I hope she find the kind of man she looking for.

That's why it be such a surprise when she marry Oscar Stick.

Oscar is about 25. He is short and stocky with bowed legs. He walk rough, drink hard, and fist-fight anybody who happen to meet his eye. He like to stand on the step of the Hobbema General Store with his thumbs in his belt loops. Oscar can roll a cigarette with only one hand and he always wear a black felt hat that make him look most a foot taller than he really is. He rodeo all summer and do not much in the winter.

Oscar be one of these mean, rough dudes who like to see how many women he can get and then he brag to everybody and tell all about what he done with each one.

"A woman is just a fuck. The quicker you let her know that the better off everybody is." Oscar say that to us guys one night at the pool hall. He is giving me and my friend Frank Fence-post a bad time 'cause we try to be mostly nice to our girlfriends.

"Always let a woman know all you want to do is screw her and get to hell away from her. It turns them on to think you're like that. And everyone thinks they is the one gonna change your mind. You should see how hard they try, and the only way a woman know to change you is to fuck you better. . ." and he laugh, wink at us guys, and light up a cigarette by crack a blue-headed match with his thumbnail.

Guess Bonnie must of thought she could change him.

"Bedelia's never once said 'I told you so' to me. She been a good friend." It is last week already and it is Bonnie Stick talking to me.

Not long after that time three years ago when her and Oscar married, her folks got one of them new houses that the Indian Affairs Department build up on the ridge. After things start going bad for Oscar and Bonnie they move into Brightfeathers' old cabin on the reserve.

"It was Bedelia who got the Welfare for me when Oscar went off to rodeo last summer and never sent home no money."

I met Bonnie just about dusk walking back to her cabin from

Hobbema. She carrying a package of tea bags, couple of Kraft Dinner, and a red package of DuMaurier cigarettes. She invite me to her place for tea.

We've seen each other to say hello to once in a while but we never have another good visit like we did in Wetaskiwin. I am just a little bit shy to talk to her 'cause I know about her dreams and I only have to look at her to tell that things turned out pretty bad so far.

She still wear the tan colored pants from her uniform but by now they is faded, got spots all over them, and one back pocket been ripped off. Bonnie got a tooth gone on her right side top and it make her smile kind of crooked. She got three babies and look like maybe she all set for a fourth by the way her belly bulge. I remember Oscar standing on the steps of the store saying, "A woman's like a rifle: should be kept loaded up and in a corner."

She boil up the tea in a tin pan on the stove. We load it up with canned milk and sugar. Bonnie look over at the babies spread out like dolls been tossed on the bed. The biggest one lay on her stomach with her bum way up in the air. "We got caught the first time we ever done it, Oscar and me," and she make a little laugh as she light up a cigarette. "This here coal-oil lamp ain't as fancy as what I had in the apartment, eh?"

We talk for a while about that apartment.

"I really thought it would be alright with Oscar. I could of stayed working if it weren't for the babies. They took back the car and all my furniture 'cause I couldn't pay for it. At first Oscar loved me so good, again and again, so's I didn't mind living in here like this," and she wave her hand around the dark cabin with the black woodstove and a few pieces of broke furniture. "Then he stopped. He go off to the rodeo for all summer, and when he is around he only hold me when he's drunk and then only long enough to make himself happy.

"I shouldn't be talking to you like this, Silas. Seems like every time I see you I tell you my secrets."

I remind her about those pretty words she said to me about twining around someone. She make a sad laugh. "You can only pretend about things like that. . .they don't really happen," and she make that sad laugh again. "Sometimes I turn away from him first just to show I don't give a care for him either. And sometimes I

134

feel like I'm as empty inside as a meadow all blue with moonlight, and that I'm gonna die if I don't get held. . ."

Bonnie come up to me and put her arms around me then. She fit herself up close and put her head on my chest. She hang on to me so tight, like she was going to fall a long way if she was to let go. I feel my body get interested in her and I guess she can too 'cause we be so close together. I wonder if she is going to raise her face up to me and maybe fit her mouth inside mine the ways girls like to do.

But she don't raise her face up. "It ain't like you think," she say into my chest. "I know you got a woman and I got my old man, wherever he is. It's just that sometimes. . ." and her voice trail off.

I kind of rub my lips against the top of her head. Her arms been holding me so long that they started to tremble. "I charge up my batteries with you, Silas. Then I can go along for another while and pretend that everything is going to be okay. Hey, remember the time that I made up the pretend dinner for you? I still got the stuff," she say, and take her arms from around me. From under the bed she bring out a cardboard box say Hoover Vacuum Cleaner on the side, and take out that tall wine bottle, and the heavy white plates, only one been broke and glued back together so it got a scar clean across it.

She clear off a space on the table and set out the plates and wine glasses. One glass got a part broken out of it, a V shape, like the beak of a bird. The wine bottles is dusty and been empty for a long time.

"Oscar drink them up when he first moved in with me, go to sloop with his head on the fancy table of mine," Bonnie say as she tip up the tall bottle. She laugh a little and the dimples show on each side of her mouth.

"I'll take the broke glass," she say, "though I guess it not make much difference if we don't have no wine. If you're hungry, Silas, I make some more tea and there's buscuits and syrup on the counter."

"No thanks," I say. "We don't want to spoil these here pretend dinners by having no food."

1980

135

LOST TIME ACCIDENT

by GAYLE BANEY WHITTIER

from THE MASSACHUSETTS REVIEW

DON'T GET THAT STUFF near your mouth!"

"Why not? What'd happen?"

"It could kill you." But he deals this out easily, a man who moves daily among fatalities. My mother, fixing dinner, frowns: "I simply fail to see why you bring that poison home!"

He winks at me. "Why, that's not poison you're lookin' at, Lizzie, that's money."

"Oh, *sure.*"

"Besides, Annie'll be the only kid in her class who's got *samples* for her project," he justifies. "Even Old Brown's daughter won't have nothin' like this!" A smile bonds him, the father, me the girlchild: Old Brown may be his boss's boss, but in school I get higher marks than Nancy Brown in every subject. In school, we get even. "Brown wouldn't even know where to *look for* samples," my father adds complacently.

"I still don't like it."

What she doesn't like lies in front of me: little vials of soft-looking abrasive dust, in various grinds like coffee or like spice; the lethal bead of mercury which, if smashed, reforms itself at once into a chain of smaller spheres; sharp green and black and rose-colored, manmade crystals, products of Diamonid, where my father works. A public relations booklet, "How Diamonid is Made," lies on the kitchen table too. But I already know that story.

"They heat up all them chemicals in furnaces—you know, you seen 'em—till it gets harder than diamonds. They even use this stuff to *cut* diamonds. What d'ya think of *that*?"

Reverently, my finger tries the needle tip of one of the crystals. It feels true: HARDER THAN DIAMONDS. That is the electric promise on a big sign between the factory's twin chimneys. Below it, a smaller legend swings in the cloudy wind along the riverfront:"—Days Since the Last LTA." LTA stands for "Lost Time Accident," my father says. As the crystal dimples my fingertip, imminent danger draws me nearer to my father and my father's world. I imagine how close to the surface our blood is.

He works in dangers, where a man should work, and wears the steel-toed "safety shoes" to prove it. So do my uncles and my male cousins, those who are old enough to quit school and get a job. "Wouldn't catch me in no office!" they all boast. Looking down now at the luminous bead of mercury, a bead pregnant with my own suddenly possible death, I feel the strict enchantment of my father's otherness; and I divine the high and final line where violence marries beauty. Risk is my father's legacy to me: my mother's will be different.

"Don't breathe!" she always cries out, in those nights when we drive homeward from a family party or a movie, following the ancient crescent of the Niagara River which will outlast us all. "Don't breathe it! Hold your breath!"—distrustful of the silicon and pungent air around the factories, blind to the terrible loveliness of their smoking, glowing slagheaps in our ordinary night. When the stench begins, my mother and father both take big, ostentatious breaths; he plants his foot down hard on the gas pedal;

137

the car jumps forward as if at the sound of a starting gun. A mile later, just beyond the row of factories, they surface, gasping. But although I always join them at the start, always draw my deep underwater-swimmer's breath too, I can't resist knowing what danger tastes like. Surreptitiously, I breathe them in: rancid, acid, strange odors that beg analysis even when they most disgust me. My throat is full of them, their sharpness and their exotic new complexities. Tasting them, I taste as well my coming sensuality, which will set experiment ahead of judgment, pleasure above safety, every time. That is why I disobey them both so secretly, seeming to gasp too, for the air which we pretend is safe again.

They would be worth a life or two, those alchemical fires glimpsed over my shoulder as we drive away. I try to read by colors what is smelted there: yellow for sulphur, framed in blue; the neon green, leafbright, to speak for copper; and a mysterious quiet mound, banked and smouldering pink as roses. Full of wonder, I feel myself moving towards a prayer in praise of my own human-kind, rash dreamers and builders of all that I behold. The words of awe rise upward on my young but going breath. In my mouth they turn back into air just as I start to speak them. Music, sometimes, even now, revives those visions and the troubling, stubborn vener-ation that I feel yet before the face of power.

Power is my native city's rightful name. The Power City. It rides on the neck of the rough white river, deadly too, like a leash on the leviathan. My father's maleness goes with it in its power, runs outward from the city's metal core into the country's infinite iron body. The river clasps Grand Island in a dread embrace, then parts like the branches of the human heart. But it feels nothing. America—this was my earliest lesson after God—is built on what he does.

But what exactly *does* he do? Like all my other childhood mysteries, this one will never yield its final name. "My husband works for the Diamonid," my mother merely says. Her brothers and his do, too—or for Hooker or Dupont or Olin. "He works at Olin." That's my Uncle Joe.

"What does he do?" I ask.

Her answer trades me word for unknown word. "He works in Shipping and Receiving. On the night shift now." Or, "Why, he makes *big money*. He's getting star rate now."

But what does he do? The proud-eyed men in my family come

back to mind: their serious, important look, the rare and hefty laughter salvaged when they "let themselves go": Thinking of their splendor, physical and brief, their dignity mined somehow from a day of taking orders—thinking of my childhood love which has outlasted them, I see that I am blessed not to know. They sold the only thing the poor have to sell, their breath and blood. And I confess the child I was. I would have loved my Uncle Casey, that night singer, less if I had known he spent the workday heaving sacks of concrete from a platform to a shed. And what if I had numbered, even once, my own father's compromises, counted out the daily spirit-killing facts behind his "steady job?" His pride is my pride too. If I had known, I could not have volunteered, when the teacher went around the room asking what all the fathers did, I could not have answered with such easy, innocent pride, "*My father works for Diamonid.*"

"That filthy place!"

Whenever the industrial stench, the greasy dust, invades our house, my mother curses and mourns her missed life elsewhere, with another sort of man, in another sort of place. "I could have married Leonard Price. My mother *begged* me to. And he's a lawyer now, he lives on the Escarpment. Oh, I was beautiful, just beautiful. . . ."

"Goddamighty," my father reminds her wearily, "that dust is what we live off, Lizzie. You can thank your lucky stars for it, if you got any sense." He has "seniority" now, then a promotion and another one. No longer paid from week to slender week, he gets his paycheck once a month, like the management. "Unless there's a big layoff," my father promises, he will always bring home his paycheck and his bonus at Christmas, every month, every year, for as long as I need him. Forever.

"Oh, they just give you a fancy title and less money," my mother sneers. "Why, my baby brother on the assembly line's earning more than you."

"Yeah, and doin' what?" he counters.

"Don't you insult my brother! Good honest work and nobody can say it ain't!" I listen to her slip back into the dialect she hoped to leave behind her.

"I'm sorry, Liz. By God, I'm sorry."

"I should hope so!" she tells him. "That filthy place. Why. . . ."

139

"Ahh, stop bitin' the hand that feeds you." He strides out of the room.

"Mr. High-and-Mighty," she mutters behind his back. Then she notices me. "Why, that man owes everything he is to me! When we got married, he couldn't even read. I used to teach him. Don't you ever tell him that I told you."

"I won't," I swear, I who will remember this forever.

Our day turns as evenly to the whistles of Diamonid as a monk's day to bells. It opens in my sleep. Sometimes I rouse myself dimly when my father leaves. The noise of his Studebaker unsettles my deep child's sleep long enough for me to feel and mourn his absence in the house. Later I wake up to find him gone. And until he comes home again, nothing sits in its right minute or right place.

"When's supper? What're we having?"

"Don't call it 'supper.' It's dinner; we aren't farmers."

No. Coal miners, my father's people were, used to laboring in blackness and in early deaths. Hers marched a safe and charted course as civil servants. The stamp of these ancestral trades imprints them both, but she has married him, drawn to that breakfree energy that sent him to Diamonid, that promoted him through the war, that brought him, finally, a crew of men.

Our family begins, then, only at four-fifteen in the afternoon, on the shrill distant note of the quitting whistle. My mother, newly fragrant with Friendship Garden, her pincurled hair unfurled around her solemn face, pretends to leisure, ties a ruffled apron over her clean dress. Then his car rushes into the driveway, the door's lock gives way with a click of metal like a broken bone. His footsteps. They are unique; the man himself is in them—a man no longer young, a man too old, really to have a child as small as I, an accidental blessing.

"*Was* I an accident?" I dare to ask my mother once.

"Who told you that?"

"Nobody. *Was* I?"

"You were a big *surprise*," she finally allows.

"Surprise!" my father shouts, bursting through the door. Behind it, almost flattened, we stand silently, SHHH, pantomimes my mother, raising a newly manicured finger to her lips. Something like an old, remembered joy brightens her features momentarily.

"Hey, anybody home?" he asks, pretending to look for us. "Hey, where is everybody? Ain't nobody here?" Mock worries. Then "BOO!" he's found us. And in his hand, a chocolate bar, a suitor's rose: for me, a sunset sheath of scrap papers, or carbons the color of midnight. Out of the giving and his old return, even my obdurate loneliness melts. "Daddy!" I shout, and we are home.

"Well, will you just look at my two beautiful ladies!" he lies. "Don't you look good enough to eat!"

"Oh, blarney," my mother says, but smiles a younger smile. I feel his lie, a long one by the time that I am born and stand beside her, sharing unevenly in all of his old compliments.

"Somethin' smells good! You got somethin' in the oven, Lizzie?" And he winks a broad vaudevillian wink.

"Herb!"

"Well, have ya?"

"Don't you hold your breath," she tells him, eyes snapping.

I understand them just enough to know that their teasing predates me, that they are remembering each other as they were alone. I am lonely again myself. What does he mean? What could be in the oven except one of my mother's thrifty casseroles, almost unsalted and tending towards one even color? Suspicious of daily pleasure, she cooks "plain." But we must be grateful for it because of all the children who are starving in Europe. Not even Grace can sweeten what she serves.

Now, "Don't get any of that filth on my clean floor!" she warns, as he pretends to lunge at her. "And don't get *near* that carpet! Why, it'd cut it all to pieces. Go wash up," she commands, turning into his mother too. And their flirtation is over for the day.

The Company follows him home. *Don't breathe it.* But the silent, ubiquitous black Diamonid dust collects invisibly in the folds of his clothing, sifts out unseen into a fine glittering shadow which outlines the place where he has stood. All at once you look down and see it there, pooled around his safety shoes with their steelcapped toes ("Company rule, cuts down on accidents") covering his own crooked, comical ones. Diamonid dust destroys whatever it touches; but every night my father comes back to us preserved, saved by his safety shoes and by his ready Irish wits. He comes home "on the dot," my mother boasts to her less-fortunately married friends, the wives of "ladies' men" or drunkards—which is

141

the worst thing a man can be, because if he drinks he will not be a "good provider."

"I'd trust him anywhere," my mother sings. But she too clocks his fifteen minutes between the company gates and our back door. Suddenly, in the midst of one of their quarrels, I will hear her cry, "You work in a filthy place! Your secretary. . ." before his hand bruises her into silence. And I understand that there is moral filth, too, just outside her jurisdiction, in the subtle colors of the air where our livelihood inhales and exhales.

"Back in a jiffy," he tells us now, disappearing into the cellar. Bent over the washtub, he violently scrubs away the company dirt, puts on fresh clothes for the second half of his daily life.

Above him, just as energetically, my mother sweeps up the dark dust. It winks and glistens in her dustpan among our duller household kind. "I want to be sure I get it all," my mother says, as if acknowledging that it is aristocratic, powerful as if it had fallen from a magician's pack stamped with an open trademark diamond around the letter D.

"Diamonid," I try the latinate word, echoing an inventor who named, but did not make, that terrible powder with his own two hands, his nostrils, or his broken lungs. "Diamonid." I am softly in love with its strangeness. When I touch the dust my finger leaves its print, and the dust sets its shiny smudge against my skin.

He washes it away with a soap hard and yellow as a brick of amber. Coming back upstairs, he smells of the soap, acid and golden-brown and potent as the man himself. "Clean as a whistle," he supposes.

But in my father's lungs, invisibly, the black pollen settles, cutting and hardening into what will be his distant death. Some other day, coming back ashen from the doctor's office, "Oh, my God," he'll cry to us, "I got emphysema. Advanced, he says. Do you know what that is? That's just a new name for Black Lung, that's all. That's all." And he will recount, over and over, his grandfather's tortured death, the miner's death he thought he had outrun, until my mother ends it: "For the love of God, shut up! You think that you're the only one. . .?"

Now, that day unguessed, my mother serves dinner to us, I set the table, he lifts up his voice to tell us about Work. He spins stories out of it, takes male sustenance there, and somehow, miraculously, dreams a tall and fugitive pride in what he does. After the second story, or the third, I imagine that I stand in the stone and concrete of his masculine world. Sometimes, crushed, he seconds my mother's bitter knowledge: "Christ, what a hole that place is!" But, "You'll never have to work in a place like that, Annie," he promises us both. "You're real smart. Your teacher said. *You* won't end up in there."

It puzzles me. No other woman in my family works anywhere at all, except the wife of my uncle-the-gambler. *Men* work. Women marry them. Why would I ever have to work? Listening to my father, I suddenly guess that I am not pretty. I feel a confused shame, but he goes on: "You're college material. Get yourself a real good job," he is advising me. "Something clean. You got what it takes . . . I'd be right up there now, if I got an education."

Briefly, our lives ascend together. We exchange laurels. I recount the prizes that I win in school; he, a boss, tells stories about his men.

"What'd you do in school today? What's that you're reading?"

"French. I'm reading French."

"I'll be damned! Go on, say something in French for me."

"Ma plume est sur le bureau," I tell him, waiting until I make him ask for the translation, then: "My pen is on the desk."

"Me, I know some Polack and a lot of Eyetalian," he boasts. Then he says, "Eh! Ven'aca!" which means "Come over here," or "No capcesh?" for "Don't you get it?"

"You say it after me," he instructs, proud of my agile tongue and that textbook-stilted French, passwords into a world unlike his own, where he will not be welcome. Obeying him, I taste the flavor of my father's role at Work. The spoken phrases teach him to me. I see him merciful but just, commanding them in their homespoken tongues: *Come over here. Hey, buddy, don't you get it?*

"I got my men's respect," he always finishes.

They have simple, children's names, those men: Little, Big, Young, Old. Little Carl brings in the spring each Easter. He brings it tied up in a stout bag full of hard anise-seed cookies, the predictable chocolate rabbit that I am too old for now; a big bottle of bright red wine for my father, and a littler blue bottle of Evening

143

in Paris perfume for my smiling mother. My father laughs, holding the wine up to the light. "Dago red!" And Little Carl laughs at himself, too, while my father claps him on his rounded back. "He's a pain in the ass, that guy," my father says, but says it chuckling.

"Why don't you fire him? *I* would," my mother vows.

"Ah, he's all right," my father redetermines.

Then the war lets go of us, and one day—no holiday at all—little Carl runs shouting and weeping towards our house, waving the first telegram from a brother he had thought was dead. In our staid Northern European neighborhood, people come defensively to the railings of their porches, grimace at him, and go back inside. Final judgment. But, "Hey, buddy! Eh, paysan!" my father is already running out to meet him, infected with his joy. They embrace, Italians together, in the back yard, while indoors my mother hardly needs to ask, but does, "What will people think?"

I watch them through the glass. They are clasping and dancing their fellowship. "You get damned close to guys, workin' with 'em," he has often said. But men don't hug each other like that, do they? Do they? I ask myself if what I see is love, workborn. My mother, as if she has heard my silent question, states, "Blood is stronger," looking at them too. Jealous now, "Blood can't be broken," she reminds us both. "*His* men indeed!"

She herself maintains a distance which my French lessons have not yet taught me to name *noblesse oblige*.

"Wouldn't you like a nice cup of coffee?" she asks, moving already towards the speckled coffee pot on a back burner. "It's only this morning's heated up, but I think it's still O.K."

A bearish blond giant stands shy and huge against our kitchen door. One black-mittened hand wrings another, warming him against the late November cold. He has just delivered our winter kindling.

"No, t'ank you, missus," he says roundly and severely.

"Oh, dear! Well, at least sit down for a minute. You look chilled to the bone!"

Wearing a darker shadow even than my father's, he maintains his statue's pose against the yellow door.

"No, t'ank you, I get your floor all dirty. Anyway, got to get to another job." Only, "chob" he says.

"They sure keep you busy, don't they? What's the next one?"

The silence lengthens. I wonder whether his language or his wits can run so slowly. At last, "We dump barrels in that old canal," he remembers.

"Oh? What're they dumping?"

"They don't tell *me*, missus."

"Well. Well, I guess you've got to run, then," she dismisses him. "Now you tell 'the boss,' " my mother winks, "I said, 'Hello there!' " She thinks it is a joke that both of them work for the same boss. He does not.

"Be seein' you, missus," he tells her. Then, still unsmiling, he lifts his denim cap, work-blackened, to make a courtly gesture that starts me laughing inwardly. But my laughter dies unborn. I take in the strip of forehead underneath the brim: pure and white as day. Beneath the dusty skin, the shadow of his livelihood, another man is hiding, a man all pale and gold: a Viking or a lion.

Only one of the men, Shorty, ever stays. Anomalously black as a junebug, delicate and maimed, with a glass eye to match his equally freakish blue one, and one elegant leg made out of wood, he calls my mother "Miz Elizabeth." His stump is aching, he tells her, as she pours her coffee in his cup; he thinks that it will rain or snow, that's how he knows.

My mother bends, easy in her sure superiority. From below the cupboard she lifts up an almost-full bottle of brandy for emergencies. She adds a dollop to the black coffee in his cup. "Don't you tell a soul!"

One September afternoon, while my mother was taking down her steel-colored hair, the telephone rang. "Your father!" she knew, although he never called home.

For once she loved him, she rushed so quickly to the telephone. But she let it ring one more shrill time, while her hand endorsed her breastbone with the sign of the cross, as if she were putting on perfume.

"I just knew it was you! What's happened?" she spilled into the receiver. ". . .Oh, *no*! Who is it? . . . No, I didn't, *don't* . . . Just where is he now? Is he still. . .? Oh, Oh. . . . I see. And when are you coming home?" Just as I thought she was about to hang up, she added gently, "Honey," as if her love must make some kind of difference now.

"What is it? Is there a strike?" I asked excitedly.

"No, there's been an accident at Work. Oh, your father's O.K., just shook up," she said. "But one of his men got badly hurt."

"Which one?" I warmed to the drama, selecting a victim in my imagination. "Shorty? Little Carl?"

"No. His name is Stash, Stanley . . . Wuh . . . I don't know how to say it," She added, "Be awful good to your father when he gets home."

But I hardly had the chance. He walked in, giftless and mad, deliberately striding right onto the forbidden linoleum with his abrasive dust, then even into the hallway where my mother's sacred expanse of new carpet started. He moved tight and fast, dramatically ignoring us. Then, angrily too, he tore a number into the telephone dial.

"Hello, is Mrs. Wyczolaski there? . . . Oh. Well, this here's Herb O'Connor. I'm Stash's . . . Stash and me, we work together," he said. "You just tell Stella if there's anything she wants, *anything*, why, us boys'll give blood or whatever else. . .? I see. Yeah, I understand. I'd feel the same damned way. Well, like I said, *anything*. I'll call back later."

In the kitchen my mother was already sweeping up the fine black silt behind his rage. But she swept slowly and gently, so as not to anger him, I felt, or, perhaps, so as not to remind him that it was there. It made a dark and gritty sound in her dustpan.

"There's dirt all over here!" I imitated her.

But, "Never mind," she said. And when he returned to the kitchen, my mother did not mention it, only, "Tell me what happened," and a moment later, "Your paper's over there on the chair," as she always said, as it always was.

"Yes, tell us about it!" but I felt my enthusiasm for a story thrown back at me by their silence. Ashamed, I stopped, and heard my father speak only to my mother, to himself.

He documented it, how in the hot September afternoon, Stash and the other men were out in the yard, "sweatin' like pigs," he said. He would have called to them to quit work early, it was so damned hot, only a bigger boss walked through, inspecting. Just as the whistle blew, "Put 'er down!" he shouted. And Stash, tired, hot himself, carelessly leaned over the pallet of the forklift and pushed the release button. The whole load flattened him.

"Oh, Jesus," my father recalled. "Everybody's shoutin' and yellin', nobody even remembered to get that fuckin' thing off of

146

him. 'Herb, help me!' he's screamin'. I push this button and it lifts up in the air, takin' part of him with it, I swear to God. Joe Vetucci, he fainted. And there's this sound out of him when I did it, like a crunch, only. . ."

"Oh, don't!" my mother cried. "No, no, that's all right. No. Tell me."

"Softer," he said. "Like a deep breath when it goes out." His face sealed itself over the trace of the mystery, the failure of his own description of it.

My mother's hand reached out for him as over greater space, but his words bore him away, back to the yard, miles from us, back to quitting time, centuries ago.

"You couldn't tell his shirt from his chest. Blood everywhere. Mrs. Prince, she's the company nurse, she come runnin' from the clinic with her bag and give him oxygen. They called the ambulance. Then she started cuttin' his shirt away, and he was screamin'. No. It wasn't a *scream*," he corrected. "He couldn't scream. It was more. . . ." And his voice left off in a chugging sound as his own mouth filled up with vomit. Keeping it back with an unwashed hand, he rushed into the bathroom. We could hear him vomiting there, wildly trying to get rid of what he had seen that day, or saying it.

"Shouldn't we go in?" I asked.

"No, leave him alone," my mother said.

After a while the vomiting dried off into sobs. The sobs stopped too. Finally, he came out angry.

"I'm gettin' the hell outta here! I'm goin' for a ride!" he shouted in my mother's direction, as if she meant to stop him.

"Herb, be careful! Please!" Futile. The door slammed; he punished the car, its parts shrieking and grinding against each other; it squealed down the street, him in it.

In the silence that gathered thickly where he had stood, I asked, "Can't that man get better? Can't they fix him?"

"Now, what do you *think*!" I heard my mother cry. Then, seeing that my question had for once been almost innocent, she added more kindly, "Oh, I doubt it." She took my father's plate away from the table, heaping it with portions of dinner, then putting it in the oven to keep it warm. She glanced at the kitchen clock, adjusted a dial, then moved our two remaining plates side by side. "Why, it would be a miracle if that man got well!" she afterthought.

147

But I lived then in a climate of miracles as of dust. First there were the stained-glass cures that had entertained my Sundays since my babyhood: "Take up thy bed and walk." These, however, I had recently understood to be ancient, outgrown events, mere precursors of the newer miracles, which my century's god, science, was dispensing. Through science—they told me so at school—we were getting an edge on death and illiteracy: also on other kinds of darknesses, bigotry, for example, and communism. Surely one of these hoarded miracles could save Stash.

Out of the clustered silence, my mother's voice awoke me. "Of course, *his* wife'll get a bundle."

"What? Oh."

"Because he died on the job," she explained. "That's why."

"Even if it was an accident?"

"Why, that's true," she considered. "He was *careless*, after all. Maybe she won't get anything." And now her voice took on vindication. "After all, it was his own fault, he didn't look what he was doing." *Careless.* I startled into shame, I who was accused daily of negligence and a child's innocent amnesia before the world. She had called me by my own secret name. Was death a kind of carelessness too?

Eight o'clock. Nine. The night went on without my being sent to bed. My mother turned on the radio, sat sewing against its background of ventriloquists and organ chords. I, defying sleep, lay listening, raised my head to see her golden thimble twinkle as she stitched, magically recalling my father, thread by thread. At last her simple magic worked, and he came home.

The car gently ("Don't wake the neighbors") in the driveway; the careful clasping of the garage doors; the snap of the familiar lock. His older, lonelier steps came towards us.

"Are you feeling any better, Herb?" she asked.

"Oh, shit," he said. "Shit. I seen him. I went to the hospital and seen him."

"How . . uh, what hospital is he in?"

"Memorial. It was nearest. She wanted St. Catherine's 'cause they're Catholics. But they can't move him anyplace, shape he's in. I seen him. He's so bad off they got him strapped to the bed, tubes goin' in and out. Givin' him blood. . . . ." The uncaring tone began to take him away from us. Perhaps to prevent it, my mother cried too empathetically, *"Oh that poor man!"*

148

"He says to me, he says, 'Herb, I wanna die. Honest to God, I just wanna die,' is what he said. 'Just let me go.' Well, he mouthed it. I couldn't hardly make it out."

"Why, for heaven's sake!" My mother strung out her words like counted beads. "Didn't they give him something for the pain, those people?" An alert, outraged expression stuck to her face.

"Oh, sure, sure," my father answered bitterly. "But they can't give him enough, is all. I seen his doctor, I says to him, 'Doc, why the hell can't you people deaden this man's pain?' What were they there for, I asked him. And you know what? He told me they *would*, only that much pain-killer might kill Stash too. Dying anyway, I says. And the doctor just froze me out, said that's *different*, it's the *law*."

At the word "law" my mother faltered. "Well, maybe he's right, Herb. I mean, it probably *is* the law, isn't it?"

"The law can go fuck itself, far as I'm concerned."

"Now, Herb," my mother went on academically, "you have to see it from the doctor's side. . ."

"No, I don't. Why should I? Goddamned legalized thieves's all they are!"

My mother touched his arm. "Maybe he's got a chance, though . . . Stash, I mean."

"Oh, hell, Lizzie, you'd a seen him you wouldn't talk like that. The man's crushed to a pulp, that's what. A pulp." (The cliché tried to come alive in my mind, but didn't.) "And his wife's standin' out in the hall cryin', and his son . . . well, Jesus. 'I just wanna die,' he says to me."

"Son? I didn't know the . . . Wuh. . . ."

"Wyczolaski," he spat at her.

"I didn't know they had *two* children," my mother said almost brightly. "I thought there was only that one girl who goes to school with Annie. Annie, what's her name?"

"Wanda," I replied, disliking my mother. "Her name is Wanda."

"Of course," my mother acknowledged with the littlest of her smiles.

"Yeah, two kids. That poor woman. What's she gonna do now?"

My mother suppressed something sharper than she said. "Why, she's got Compensation coming, hasn't she? She'll do all right."

"Well, she gets it if I testify it happened on company time, before quitting," he said. "Or that the machine slipped."

149

In the length of silence my mother picked her way among the thickets where we lived. "A lot of people saw what happened, though," she finally ventured. "I mean, they'd know if you were lying, if you swore it happened on company time. Or was the equipment." His look, which I could not see from where I sat, must have embarrassed her. "Well, I *mean*, he *was* careless, really. It was his own fault."

"Own fault! Who the hell wouldn't get careless, all day in that heat?" He brought his fist down against the table. There was an interval of tiny chimes as her porcelain knick-knacks trembled against each other. "Anybody'd get 'careless,' that's all. That's *all*."

"But suppose you lose *your* job? You're not even in the union any more. There's witnesses."

"Now, Lizzie. . ."

"What about us? Have you ever thought of that? Oh, no; not you. And there's *witnesses*," she repeated, her voice rising. Her finger rose too and pointed him out, one red nail gleaming blood-drop pure.

"You make a better lawyer than a wife, Lizzie. Now shut up. It was on company time, and that's that."

"But it wasn't. . . ."

"I said shut up, Lizzie, and I meant it," he commanded in a stonedust voice. Then my father's eye caught sight of me. "What the hell are *you* doin' up? Ain't you got school tomorrow?"

"It's not her fault."

"Well, go on. Scoot. Go get your beauty sleep," my father said. As I escaped the room, his large hand lightly told me of the shape of my child's head.

Through my door, half open to let in the whisper of the cooler early autumn night, a long finger of light crossed the thin yellow varnished floorboards and pillared up the wall. There a wallpaper lattice lifted up its repeated clusters of white roses, stale and old.

I slept a white sleep.

Later in the night, half conscious and alone, I heard the customary thunder of their household quarrel. It no longer frightened me. I could identify their cadences like phrases in a symphony. Sometimes I even fell asleep, while they still raged, as constant and as changing as the sea, beneath my painted bed. This time, sitting up alive, I sorted out new and different sounds.

Against the rocking of their human voices, he was throwing

things. Their dense thuds declared them heavy, breakable. They rang out dully. They reverberated against the floor. Once, I remembered, he had gotten angry at my mother and had thrown his breakfast at the wall. The plate splintered. But the fried egg slid slowly downward to the baseboard, a cartoon sun. Watching its descent, I held back my laughter, lest I disrespect the enchantment of my father's violence. But fear brought more laughter bubbling to my nervous lips. He had only broken the plate that one time, though. This breakage went on and on.

Where usually my mother's voice climbed, sickening, to half-evasive pleas, it kept instead a low and reasonable horizon note, a stranger's tone. They walked the circle of the rooms below, my father pacing heavily, erratically, my mother keeping up while he shouted: "That goddamn bastard! Polack son-of-a-bitch!" Crash—an object seconded his rage. "Stupid fucking idiot! If I told him once, I told him a hundred times: *One slip* and it's curtains, buddy! Yeah, I told him. . . ." Something struck the floor. "You, you gold-crowned son-of-a-bitch . . ." (even my mother's voice protested it) "Be-all, know-all fucker of the rest of us! . . . No, no, I won't, I won't . . ." And his body bore his words away, stepping through the stairwell to the kitchen to the dining room, almost never used, then the circuit of the downstairs floor. His muffled voice remained; against it, my mother's preserving obbligato. From time to time he climbed above language, and then I heard another heavy thud, and tried to imagine what it was he threw.

Slowly the intervals lengthened. At last, exhausting things to throw, he broke himself and cried. I lay in my changed bed, shocked in my hearing and my heart, while the night air carried up to me his foreign male weeping, wholly of this earth. I felt that my father's sobs would go on unbearably forever, but he was diminished too. In astonished meditation on the edge of sleep, I knew that he was less my father than he had been before. Aware of his abandonment, I abandoned myself to dreams.

There was a next day, and on it, everything resumed functionally but awkwardly, like a broken machine. Breakfast brought gluey oatmeal, acid orange juice, and lukewarm milk in the old chipped cup with a hair-thin crack through its pale wall. A lump of breakfast in me, I underwent my regimented schoolday. But through getting dressed and the roll call, through the Products of Peru and our spiritless public school singing of "The Volga Boatman," I waited. Something else must happen, I assumed. Nothing did.

When I got home from school, home was still there, a semaphore of well-known laundry strung behind it. My mother, newly powdered, wearing the set, severe expression of a woman living out a holy but mistaken life, ran her finger over a few inches of windowsill: "Just look at that! Third time today I dusted it!" she said. Then, at four o'clock exactly, she disappeared to put on a fresh dress, to brush out her cold hair. Even her face in the center of it all was her old face, rigid and alone, the face I remember her by, even now: my mother.

"Wash your hands, Annie," she commanded absently." And put on another blouse; that one's just covered with ink. How do you ever do it?"

Coming in to us, me with my clean hands, my mother in her unmarked apron, my father made no jokes at all that night, but went downstairs at once to scrub himself. I could hear the water rushing into the washtub, could sense his muted gestures as he changed into clean clothes. I felt his feet, my father's feet, measuring the steps deliberately as he climbed, purified, to the kitchen. Only then did my mother look at him questioningly, gently.

He shook his head. No. And again, as she asked, "Is he. . .?" No, but only with his eyes.

"Is Stash dead?" I asked, voicing what I knew must be her question too.

"Mr. Wyczolaski," he corrected me. "No."

"I suppose he's in a coma," my mother said.

"Still conscious."

"Oh, that's good," I tried.

"It isn't good at all! What do *you* know . . . !" my mother scowled.

"Somebody oughta do something," my father said only to her.

"Well, they won't," she answered him. "You know it and I know it. Your paper's over there on the chair," she said.

Proving what nobody would do, they separated their lives from the dying man's. Humming a little, even, she set out dinner plates in their three places; we thanked our same God for her utilitarian food, which was not really the same every night, but seemed so. Only our voices, by an unspoken accord, stayed deep inside us, and we did not talk.

After dinner, while I laid out my assignment book and papers to do homework, my parents briefly whispered together in the kitchen, murmuring low enough for mourning in our altered house. ". . . a collection?" I caught, and then my father said, "Oh, flowers, sure," loud enough to carry easily to me. "Hey, Lizzie, did you know they put coins on their eyes, them Polacks? Honest to God. It's to pay their way into heaven."

In the outer room, always my room, with my books and my unbidden fear spread out around me, I felt myself only fraudulently theirs: my untapped excitement, my young urgency against their casual resumption of our life. A man was dying. And it was their fault, I decided. Too easily, too carelessly, they had let go of him, just as if they had let go of my hand in a crowd and I was lost forever. They had not kept him in their minds, they had excluded him. I felt a spirit sympathy between the man and myself; but even more warmly, a learned and rancid sense of drama took possession of my imagination, phrase by rehearsed phrase, as I tried to encompass him. "He's in God's hands now." "His life is hanging by a thread!" Where had I heard those words, those keys to my unwritten drama? Which would work, would open it? "Nothing tried, nothing gained. . ." "Perseverance wins the crown" (my mother's favorite). And "if at first you don't succeed. . . ." So that was it. They hadn't cared to try for the magical third time. And that was why he was dying so invisibly.

"Somebody should do something," my father had admitted. *I* would, I answered to myself.

I did. Leaving my homework and my parents' voices in the rooms below, I put my own small upstairs bedroom in close to perfect order. The rug, a worn pink pile, I placed equidistant from the headboard and the footboard of my narrow bed. I spat on a turned-up corner of the chenille bedspread for luck, as if it were my skirt hem, and then I smoothed it into place. The window-shades, I saw, jogged awkwardly, one up, one down: I evened them.

Then I took up my last thing, my prayerbook, white leather stamped with a delicate gold cross. A recent Christmas present, it smelled like nothing else in the house, papery and new. Its thin pages clung to my clumsy fingers, and its scarlet bookmark lay silkenly against last Sunday's portion of the Psalter, accusing me of the early place where I had let my attention wander from the text. I was sorry now that I did not pray every day. I promised myself and God that, starting now, I would. I would read the Bible too, each morning, if only—but even I stopped sort of bribery.

Almost at once, I turned to the right prayer, but, like any browser, kept my finger there to scan the nearby titles. "For Social Justice," I read, "For the Navy," "For Rain." And I kept on reading, delaying as long as possible the moment of what I now suddenly saw to be a test. At last nothing but the moment of my trial remained, and I resorted to my destined prayer: "For a Sick Person." Briefly its Renaissance cadences helped me on, but then I stumbled from the archaic words, falling back into my century and my place. Perhaps, I reconsidered, spontaneous prayer would be better? Yes.

Still I had to find the name of God.

I meant to choose a title which best suited my petition and my own unaccustomed voice, used only to a bedside "Our-Father-who-art-in-heaven" run off proudly and not even consciously, the same way I recited muliplication tables or conjugated French verbs. But by now my knees reminded me of time, and all the names of God began to sound ponderous and strange. I could not even repeat some of them without hearing, over mine, the priest's majestic voice drawing out vowels and clicking consonants shut to speak God's grandeur—or his own.

"Most Gracious God," I imitated. But I felt at once remoter from Him than I had ever known myself to be. "Our Heavenly Father," then. No. I was only one abashed person speaking, no "we" at all; and anyway, "heavenly" felt too distant, and "father" too close in. "Lord" avoided these degrees, but struck me as bare and abrupt, almost rude. And I passed over "God Almighty" embarrassedly. Except when a priest said it, it was a curse. In our household, where everyone but me blasphemed with Celtic latitude, I had often heard that title eased into a punctuating "Goddamighty!" I could not now make my own tongue disobey these family cadences, replace them with the unctious elevation of the priest's. They were in me, my people's voices. Hearing them, the others, I stopped altogether, afraid that my mouth might name God wrongly and undo my prayer.

Finally, on my numb knees and exhausting God's known names, I shifted my felt weight and got familiar: "God," I said, "please. . ." (minding my manners), "please take care of, of. . ." But here again I hesitated like a child in a spelling bee. I practiced the word in my head, then spoke, "Mr. Wyczolaski," out loud, fast and right. Borne on my confidence in the victim's name, and in my own power to pronounce it, I next told God why he should save Stash, "*Stanley*," I reminded God, although He would know a nickname, too, I reasoned to myself. "Save him for his daughter Wanda, who's the same age as me, and for his wife. . ." I had forgotten her name, but chanted bravely on, since God knew everything, "and for himself," I said. After a moment I added, "In Thy Infinite Mercy. . ." I felt the thrill of my translation. The extemporaneous prayer sounded almost like those in my book: I knew that it was good. But with this recognition of my composition's quality, I almost praised myself, the speaker: suddenly I knew that God must save Stash for my own sake most of all. It was for my words that I wanted the miracle to happen: to make them good. The prayer was for myself. Before this forbidden fact, I arrested: and the prayer's lost momentum fell away from me, inexorable as dust.

"Not just for *me*," I tried to get it back. "For everyone, O God." But I doubted that He would be taken in by this patchwork charity: I did not believe it myself. It opened falsely onto my new world, which was flat, not round, no matter what they said, and had an edge where heaven ought to be, and big deaths even for its smallest, most accidental men.

Almost dumb with loss, I waited out my first time of nothingness. It felt like death, that space between the outgrown child who had dared to pray and this self-conscious stranger who suddenly could not. Then the image of the careless, crushed man formed itself in my mind, textbook clear. I knew he must lay smashed— "like an egg," my father had described him—beneath a hospital sheet; and so I started there. I envisioned it whiter and coarser than my mother's sheets, decently containing him. The room around him smelled of purity and pain.

I drew nearer to that invented bed. But I did not open his eyes. They closed on his unimaginable expression, which I did not know how to see. His iconic head, I saw, resembled my father's, was not a young man's head; and his imagined features came to view both personal and sure, as if I had seen him many times before.

155

Then—even now—I knew I really saw Stanley Wyczolaski's face. Safe white bandages held back his damage, like the swaddling on the porcelain Della Robbia in my new classroom.

I wanted to know more. In my mind's chamber still, I folded the silver bandages aside, neat as a lifted page. Underneath, everything showed itself smooth and charted, the proud high cage of ribs, the shadow of male hair. "There, there, you'll be all right," I comforted. Then, for the first time, I heard my own voice say, "Darling," in a whisper. At the word his body, a lattice in a birthday card, answered me by opening up. I saw all the mysteries that I had only read of: this, the four-chambered heart, but still, so still; here the arteries and veins running blue into it and red away; there the lungs, pink as shell. They lay as real as my eye, but unreal, too.

By now I had forgotten God. My dreaming hands moved in circles over the dying man, and in my vision they restored his life. Veins and arteries, collapsed, sprang full and fresh as stems after rainfall. I bent to kiss him better, and my borrowed breath lifted new roundness in his flattened lungs. I gave him my voice, too. "There, you see," I proved to him out loud.

Then my real hands began to move tenderly over the chenille ridges of my bed's coverlet. I breathed faster, conscious of a drum of pulse, my own, and of my will contracted tightly to a concrete thing meant to uphold him. The unguessed power of my life ran free, and with it, sadness older than the earth.

I could not know yet that my caresses, my reverence, and—when I moved—my newfound exactitude of care, made me a lover. But I knew that everything I did was futile, that I could not really mend: only I made the gestures of the healer all the same, defiantly. I felt my own bones age against the hardness of the floor, and, breathing for us both, for myself and for the dying man, I tasted my own mystery. In that dark way, among my vanquished gods, I began my work in the world.

1981

HARMONY OF THE WORLD

by CHARLES BAXTER
from MICHIGAN QUARTERLY REVIEW

I

IN THE SMALL OHIO TOWN where I grew up, many homes had parlors that contained pianos, sideboards, and sofas, heavy objects signifying gentility. These pianos were rarely tuned. They went flat in summer around the fourth of July and sharp in winter at Christmas. Ours was a Story and Clark. On its music stand were copies of Stephen Foster and Ethelbert Nevin favorites, along with one Chopin prelude that my mother would practice for twenty minutes every three years. She had no patience, but since she thought Ohio — all of it, every scrap — made sense, she was happy and did not need to practice anything. Happiness is not infectious, but somehow her happiness infected my father, a pharmacist, and then spread through the rest of the household. My whole family was obstinately cheerful. I think of my two sisters, my brother, and my parents as having artificial pasted-on smiles, like circus clowns. They apparently thought cheer and good Christian words were universals, respected everywhere. The pianos were part of this cheer. They played for celebrations and moments of pleasant pain. Or rather: someone played them, but not too well, since excellent playing would have been faintly antisocial. "Chopin," my mother said, shaking her head as she stumbled through the prelude. "Why is he famous?"

When I was six, I received my first standing ovation. On the stage of the community auditorium, where the temperature was about 94°, sweat fell from my forehead onto the piano keys, making their ivory surfaces slippery. At the conclusion of the piece, when everyone stood up to applaud, I thought they were just being nice. My playing had been mediocre; only my sweating had been extraordinary. Two years later, they stood up again. When I was eleven, they cheered. By that time I was astonishing these small-town audiences with Chopin and Rachmaninoff recital chestnuts. I thought I was a genius and read biographies of Einstein. Already the townspeople were saying that I was the best thing Parkersville had ever seen, *that I would put the place on the map*. Mothers would send their children by to watch me practice. The kids sat with their mouths open while I polished off another classic.

Like many musicians, I cannot remember ever playing badly, in the sense of not knowing what I was doing. In high school, my identity was being sealed shut: my classmates called me "el señor longhair," even though I wore a crewcut, this being the 1950s. Whenever the town needed a demonstration of local genius, it called upon me. There were newspaper articles detailing my accomplishments, and I must have heard the phrase "future concert career" at least two hundred times. My parents smiled and smiled as I collected applause. My senior year, I gave a solo recital and was hired for umpteen weddings and funerals. I was good luck. On the fourth of July the townspeople brought out a piano to the city square so that I could improvise music between explosions at the fireworks display. Just before I left for college, I noticed that our neighbors wanted to come up to me ostensibly for small talk, but actually to touch me.

In college I made a shocking discovery: other people existed in the world who were as talented as I was. If I sat down to play a Debussy etude, they would sit down and play Beethoven, only louder and faster than I had. I felt their breath on my neck. Apparently there were other small towns. In each one of these small towns there was a genius. Perhaps some geniuses were not actually geniuses. I practiced constantly and began to specialize in the non-Germanic piano repertoire. I kept my eye out for students younger than I was, who might have flashier technique. At my senior recital I played Mozart, Chopin, Ravel, and Debussy, with encore pieces by Scriabin and Thomson. I managed to get the audience to stand up for the last time.

I was accepted into a large midwestern music school, famous for its high standards. Once there, I discovered that genius, to say nothing of talent, was a common commodity. Since I was only a middling composer, with no interesting musical ideas as such, I would have to make my career as a performer or teacher. But I didn't want to teach, and as a performer I lacked pizzazz. For the first time, it occurred to me that my life might be evolving into something unpleasant, something with the taste of stale bread.

I was beginning to meet performers with more confidence than I had, young musicians to whom doubt was as alien as proper etiquette. Often these people dressed like tramps, smelled, smoked constantly, were gay or sadistic. Whatever their imbalances, they were not genteel. *They did not represent small towns*. I was struck by their eyes. Their eyes seemed to proclaim, "The universe believes in me. It always has."

My piano teacher was a man I will call Luther Stecker. Every year he taught at the music school for six months. For the following six months he toured. He turned me away from the repertoire with which I was familiar and demanded that I learn several pieces by composers whom I had not often played, including Bach, Brahms, and Liszt. Each one of these composers discovered a weak point in me: I had trouble keeping up the consistent frenzy required by Liszt, the mathematical precision required by Bach, the unpianistic fingerings of Brahms.

I saw Stecker every week. While I played, he would doze off. When he woke, he would mumble some inaudible comment. He also coached a trio I participated in, and he spoke no more audibly then than he did during my private lesson.

I couldn't understand why, apart from his reputation, the school had hired him. Then I learned that in every Stecker-student's life, the time came when the Master collected his thoughts, became blunt, and told the student exactly what his future would be. For me, the moment arrived on the third of November, 1966. I was playing sections of the Brahms Paganini Variations, a fiendish piece on which I had spent many hours. When I finished, I saw him sit up.

"Very good," he said, squinting at me. "You have talents."

There was a pause. I waited. "Thank you," I said.

"You have a nice house?" he asked.

"A nice house? No."

"You should get a nice house somewhere," he said, taking his handkerchief out of his pocket and waving it at me. "With windows. Windows with a view."

I didn't like the drift of his remarks. "I can't afford a house," I said.

"You will. A nice house. For you and your family."

I resolved to get to the heart of this. "Professor," I asked, "what did you think of my playing?"

"Excellent," he said. "That piece is very difficult."

"Thank you."

"Yes, technically excellent," he said, and my heart began to pound. "Intelligent phrasing. Not much for me to say. Yes. That piece has many notes," he added, enjoying the *non sequitur*.

I nodded. "Many notes."

"And you hit all of them accurately. Good pedal and good discipline. I like how you hit the notes."

I was dangling on his string, a little puppet.

"Thousands of notes, I suppose," he said, staring at my forehead, which was beginning to get damp, "and you hit all of them. You only forgot one thing."

"What?"

"The passion!" he roared. "You forgot the passion! You always forget it! Where is it? Did you leave it at home? You never bring it with you! Never! I listen to you and think of a robot playing! A smart robot, but a robot! No passion! Never ever ever!" He stopped shouting long enough to sneeze. "You *should* buy a house. You know why?"

"Why?"

"Because the only way you will ever praise God is with a family, that's why! Not with this piano! You are a fine student," he wound up, "but you make me sick! Why do you make me sick?"

He waited for me to answer.

"Why do you make me sick?" he shouted. "Answer me!"

"How can I possibly answer you?"

"By articulating words in English! Be courageous! Offer a suggestion! Why do you make me sick?"

I waited for a minute, the longest minute my life has seen or will ever see. "Passion," I said at last. "You said there wasn't enough passion. I thought there was. Perhaps not."

He nodded. "No. You are right. No passion. A corruption of music itself. Your playing is too gentle, too much good taste. To play the piano like a genius, you must have a bit of the fanatic. Just a bit. But it is essential. You have stubbornness and talent but no fanaticism. You don't have the salt on the rice. Without salt, the rice is inedible, no matter what its quality otherwise." He stood up. "I tell you this because sooner or later someone else will. You will have a life of disappointments if you stay in music. You may find a teacher who likes you. Good, good. *But you will never be taken up! Never!* You should buy a house, young man. With a beautiful view. Move to it. Don't stay here. You are close to success, but it is the difference between leaping the chasm and falling into it, one inch short. You are an inch short. You could come back for more lessons. You could graduate from here. But if you are truly intelligent, you will say goodbye. Goodbye." He looked down at the floor and did not offer me his hand.

I stood up and walked out of the room.

Becalmed, I drifted down and up the hallways of the building for half an hour. Then a friend of mine, a student of conducting from Bolivia, a Marxist named Juan Valparaiso, approached, and, ignoring my shallow breathing and cold sweat, started talking at once.

"Terrible, furious day!" he said.

"Yes."

"I am conducting *Benvenuto Cellini* overture this morning! All is going well until difficult flute entry. I instruct, with force, flutists. Soon all woodwinds are ignoring me." He raised his eyebrows and stroked his huge gaucho mustache. "Always! Always there are fascists in the woodwinds!"

161

"Fascists everywhere," I said.

"Horns bad, woodwinds worse. Demands of breath made for insanes. Pedro," he said, "you are appearing irresoluted. Sick?"

"Yes," I nodded. "Sick. I just came from Stecker. My playing makes *him* sick."

"He said that? That you are making him sick?"

"That's right. I play like a robot, he says."

"What will you do?" Juan asked me. "Kill him?"

"No." And then I knew. "I'm leaving the school."

"What? Is impossible!" Tears leaped instantly into Juan's eyes. "Cannot, Pedro. After one whipping? No! Disappointments everywhere here. Also outside in world. Must stick to it." He grabbed me by the shoulders. "Fascists put here on earth to break our hearts! Must live through. You cannot go." He looked around wildly. "Where could you go anyway?"

"I'm not sure," I said. "He said I would never amount to anything. I think he's right. But I could do something else." To prove that I could imagine options, I said, "I could work for a newspaper. You know, music criticism."

"Caterpillars!" Juan shouted, his tears falling onto my shirt. "Failures! Pathetic lives! Cannot, cannot! Who would hire you?"

I couldn't tell him for six months, until I was given a job in Knoxville on a part-time trial basis. But by then I was no longer writing letters to my musician friends. I had become anonymous. I worked in Knoxville for two years, then in Louisville — a great city for music — until I moved here, to this city I shall never name, in the middle of New York state, where I bought a house with a beautiful view.

In my home town, they still wonder what happened to me, but my smiling parents refuse to reveal my whereabouts.

II

Every newspaper has a command structure. Within that command structure, editors assign certain stories, but the writers must be given some freedom to snoop around and discover newsworthy material themselves. In this anonymous city, I was hired to review all the concerts of the symphony orchestra and to provide some hype articles during the week to boost the ticket sales for Friday's program. Since the owner of the paper was on the symphony board of trustees, writing about the orchestra and its programs was necessarily part of good journalistic citizenship. On my own, though, I initiated certain projects, wrote book reviews for the Sunday section, interviewed famous visiting musicians — some of them my ex-classmates — and during the summer I could fill in on all sorts of assignments, as long as I cleared what I did with the feature editor, Morris Cascadilla.

"You're the first serious musician we've ever had on the staff here," he announced to me when I arrived, suspicion and hope fighting for control on his face. "Just remember this: be clear and concise. Assume they've got intelligence but no information. After that, you're on your own, except you should clear dicey stuff with me. And never forget the Maple Street angle."

The Maple Street angle was Cascadilla's equivalent to the Nixon Administration's "How will it play in Peoria?" No matter what subject I wrote about, I was expected to make it relevant to Maple Street, the newspaper's mythical locus of middle-class values. I could write about electronic, aleatory, or post-Boulez music *if* I suggested that the city's daughters might be corrupted by it. Sometimes I found the Maple Street angle, and sometimes I couldn't. When I failed, Cascadilla would call me in, scowl at my copy and mutter, "All the Juilliard graduates in town will love this." Nevertheless, the Maple Street angle was a spiritual exercise in humility, and I did my best to find it week after week.

When I first learned that the orchestra was scheduled to play Paul Hindemith's *Harmony of the World* symphony, I didn't think of Hindemith, but of Maple Street, that mythically harmonious piano and write reviews.

III

Working on the paper left me some time for other activities. Unfortunately, there was nothing I knew how to do except play the piano and write reviews.

Certain musicians are very practical. Trumpet players (who love valves) tend to be good mechanics, and I have met a few composers

163

who fly airplanes and can restore automobiles. Most performing violinists and pianists, however, are drained by the demands of their instruments and seldom learn how to do anything besides play. In daily life they are helpless and stricken. In midlife the smart ones force themselves to find hobbies. But the less fortunate come home to solitary apartments without pictures or other decorations, warm up their dinners in silence, read whatever books happen to be on the dinner table, and then go to bed.

I am speaking of myself here, of course. As time passed, and the vacuum of my life made it harder to breathe, I required more work. I fancied I was a tree, putting out additional leaves. I let it be known that I would play as an accompanist for voice students and other recitalists, if their schedules didn't interfere with my commitments for the paper.

One day I received a call at my desk. A quietly controlled female voice asked, "Is this Peter Jenkins?"

"Yes."

"Well," she said, pausing, as if she'd forgotten what she meant to tell me, "this is Karen Jensen. That's almost like Jenkins, isn't it?" I waited. "I'm a singer," she said, after a moment. "A soprano. I've just lost my accompanist and I'm planning on giving a recital in three months. They said you were available. Are you? What do you charge?"

I told her.

"Isn't that kind of steep? That's kind of steep. Well, I suppose . . . I can use somebody else until just before, and then I can use you. They say you're good. And I've read your reviews. I really admire the way you write!"

"Thank you."

"You get so much information into your reviews! Sometimes, when I read you, I imagine what you look like. Sometimes a person can make a mental picture. I just wish the paper would publish a photo or something of you."

"They want to," I said, "but I asked them to please don't."

"Even your voice sounds like your writing!" she said excitedly. "I can see you in front of me now. Can you play Fauré and Schubert? I mean, is there any composer or style you don't like and won't play?"

"No," I said. "I play anything."

"That's *wonderful!*" she said, as if I had confessed to a remarkable tolerance. "Some accompanists are so picky. 'I won't do this, I won't do that.' Well, *one* I know is like that. Anyhow, could we meet soon? Do you sightread? Can we meet at the music school downtown? In a practice room? When are you free?"

I set up an appointment.

She was almost beautiful. Her deep eyes were accented by depressive bowls in quarter-moon shadow under them. Though she was only in her late twenties, she seemed slightly scorched by anxiety. She couldn't keep still. Her hands fluttered as they fixed her hair; she scratched nervously at her cheeks; and her eyes jumped every few seconds. Soon, however, she calmed down and began to look me in the eye, evaluating me. Then *I* turned away.

She wanted to test me out and had brought along her recital numbers, mostly standard fare: a Handel aria, Mozart, Schubert, and Fauré. The last set of songs, *Nine Epitaphs*, by an American composer I had never heard of, Theodore Chanler, was the only novelty.

"Who is this Chanler?" I asked, looking through the sheet music.

"I . . . I found it in the music library," she said. "I looked him up. He was born in Boston and died in 1961. There's a recording by Phyllis Curtin. Virgil Thomson says these are maybe the best American art songs ever written."

"Oh."

"They're kind of, you know, lugubrious. I mean they're all epitaphs written supposedly on tombstones, set to music. They're like portraits. I love them. Is it all right? Do you mind?"

"No, I don't mind."

We started through her program, beginning with Handel's "*Un sospiretto d'un labbro pallido*" from *Il Pastor fido*. I could immediately see why she was still in central New York state and why she would always be a student. She had a fine voice, clear and distinct, somewhat styled after Victoria de los Angeles (I thought), and her articulation was superb. If these achievements had been the whole story, she might have been a professional. But her pitch wobbled on sustained notes in a maddening way; the effect was not comic and would probably have gone unnoticed by most non-musicians, but to me the result was harrowing. She could sing perfectly for several measures and then she would miss a note by a semi-tone, which drove an invisible fingernail into my scalp. It was as though a gypsy's curse descended every five or six seconds, throwing her off pitch; then she was allowed to be a great singer until the curse descended again. Her loss of pitch was so regularized that I could see it coming and squirmed in anticipation. I felt as though I were in the presence of one of God's more complicated pranks.

Her choice of songs highlighted her failings. Their delicate textures were constantly broken by her lapses. When we arrived at the Chanler pieces, I thought I was accustomed to her, but I found I wasn't. The first song begins with the following verse, written by Walter de la Mare, who had crafted all the poems in archaic epitaph style:

> Here lyeth our infant, Alice Rodd;
> > She were so small,
> > Scarce aught at all,
> But a mere breath of Sweetness sent from God.

The vocal line for "She were so small" consists of four notes, the last two rising a half-step from the two before them. To work, the passage requires a dead-eye accuracy of pitch:

Singing this line, Karen Jensen hit the D-sharp but missed the E and skidded up uncontrollably to F-sharp, which would sound all right to anyone who didn't have the music in front of his nose, as I did. Only a fellow-musician could be offended.

Infuriated, I began to feel that I could *not* participate in a recital with this woman. It would be humiliating to perform such lovely songs in this excruciating manner. I stopped playing, turned to her to tell her that I could not continue after all, and then I saw her bracelet.

I am not, on the whole, especially observant, a failing that probably accounts for my having missed the bracelet when we first met. But I saw it now: five silver canaries dangled down quietly from it, and as it slipped back and forth, I saw her wrist and what I suddenly realized *would* be there: the parallel lines of her madness, etched in scar tissue.

The epitaphs finished, she asked me to work with her, and I agreed. When we shook hands, the canaries shook in tiny vibrations, as if pleased with my dutiful kindness, my charity, toward their mad mistress.

IV

Though Paul Hindemith's reputation once equalled Stravinsky's and Bartók's, it suffered after his death in 1963 an almost complete collapse. Only two of his orchestral works, the *Symphonic Metamorphoses on Themes of Weber* and the *Mathis der Maler* symphony, are played with any frequency, thanks in part to their use of borrowed tunes. One hears his woodwind quintets and choral pieces now and again, but the works of which he was most proud — the ballet *Nobilissima Visione, Das Marienleben* (a song cycle), and the opera *Harmonie die Welt* — have fallen into total obscurity.

The reason for Hindemith's sudden loss of reputation was a mystery to me; I had always considered his craftsmanship if not his inspiration to be first-rate. When I saw that the *Harmony of the World* symphony, almost never played, would be performed in our anonymous city, I told Cascadilla that I wanted to write a story for that week on how fame was gained and lost in the world of music. He thought that subject might be racy enough to interest the tone-deaf citizens of leafy and peaceful Maple Street, where no one is famous, if I made sure the story contained "the human element."

I read up on Hindemith, played his piano music, and listened to the recordings. I slowly found the music to be technically astute but emotionally arid, as if some problem of purely local interest kept the composer's gaze safely below the horizon. Technocratic and oddly timid, his work reminded me of a model train chugging through a tiny town where only models of people actually lived. In fact, Hindemith did have a lifelong obsession with train sets: in Berlin, his took up three rooms, and the composer wrote elaborate timetables so that the toys wouldn't collide.

But if Hindemith had a technocrat's intelligence, he also believed in the necessity of universal participation in musical activities. Listening was not enough. Even non-musical citizens could learn to sing and play, and he wrote music expressly for this purpose. He seems to have known that passive, drugged listening was a side-effect of totalitarian environments and that elitist composers such as Schoenberg were engaged in antisocial Faustian projects that would bewilder and infuriate most audiences, leaving them isolated and thus eager to be drugged by a musical superman.

As the foremost anti-Nietzschean German composer of his day, therefore, Hindemith left Germany when his works could not be performed, thanks to the Third Reich; wrote textbooks with simple exercises; composed a requiem in memory of Franklin Roosevelt, set to words by Walt Whitman; and taught students, not all of them talented, in Ankara, New Haven, and Buffalo ("this caricature of a town"). As he passed through late middle age, he turned to a project he had contemplated all his life, an opera based on the career of the German astronomer Johannes Kepler, author of *De Harmonice Mundi*. This opera, a summary of Hindemith's ideas, would be called *Harmony of the World*. Hindemith worked out the themes first in a symphony, which bore the same title as the opera, and completed it in 1951. The more I thought about this project, the more it seemed anachronistic. Who believed in world harmony in 1951? Or thereafter? Such a symphony would have to pass beyond technical sophistication into divine inspiration, which Hindemith had never shown any evidence of possessing.

It occurred to me that Hindemith's lifelong sanity had perhaps given way in this case, toppled not by despair (as is conventional) but by faith in harmony.

For the next rehearsal, I drove to Karen Jensen's apartment, where there was, she said, a piano. I'd become curious about the styles of her insanity; I imagined a hamster cage in the kitchen, a doll-head mobile in the living room, and mottos written with different colored inks on memo pads tacked up everywhere on the walls.

She greeted me at the door without her bracelet. When I looked at her wrist, she said, "Hmmm. I see that you noticed. A memento of adolescent despair." She sighed. "But it does frighten people off. Once you've tried to do something like that, people don't really trust you. I don't know why exactly. Don't want your blood on their hands or something. Well, come on in."

I was struck first by her forthrightness and secondly by her tiny apartment. Its style was much like the style in my house. She owned an attactive but worn-down sofa, a sideboard that supported an antique clock, one chair, a glass-top dinner table, and one nondescript poster on the wall. Trying to keep my advantage, I looked hard for tell-tale signs of insanity but found none. The piano was off in the corner, almost hidden, unlike those in the parlors back home.

"Very nice," I said.

"Well, thanks," she said. "It's not much. I'd like something bigger, but . . . where I work, I'm an administrative assistant, and they don't pay me very much. So that's why I live like a snail here. It's hardly big enough to move around in, right?" She wasn't looking at me. "I mean, I could almost pick it up and carry it away."

I nodded. "You just don't think like a rich person," I said, trying to be hearty. "They like to expand. They need room. Big houses, big cars, fat bodies."

"Oh, I know!" she said, laughing. "My uncle . . . would *you* like to stay for dinner? You look like you need a good meal. I mean, after the rehearsal. You're just skin and bones, Pet — . . . may I call you Peter?"

"Sure." I sat down on the sofa and tried to think up an excuse. "I really can't stay, Miss Jensen. I have another rehearsal to go to later tonight. I wish I could."

"That's not it, is it?" she asked suddenly, looking down at me. "I don't believe you. I bet it's something else. I bet you're afraid of me."

"Why should I be afraid of you?"

She smiled and shrugged. "That's all right. You don't have to say anything. I know how it goes." She laughed once more, faintly. "I never found a man who could handle it. They want to show you *their* scars, you know? They don't want to see any on you, and if they discover any, they just run." She slapped her right hand into her forehead and then ran her fingers through her hair. "Well, shit. I didn't mean to do this *at all!* I mean, I admire you so much and everything, and here I am, running on like this. I guess we should get down to business, right? Since I'm paying you by the hour."

I smiled professionally and went to her piano.

Beneath the high culture atmosphere that surrounds them, art songs have one subject: love. The permutations of love (lust, solitude, and loss) are present in abundance, of course, but for the most part they are simple vehicles for the expression of that one emotion. I was reminded of this as I played through the piano parts. As much as I concentrated on the music in front of me, I couldn't help but notice that my employer stood next to the piano, singing the words sometimes toward me, sometimes away. She was rather courageously forcing eye-contact on me. She kept this up for an hour and a half until we came to the Chanler settings, when at last she turned slightly, singing to the walls.

As before, her voice broke out of control every five seconds, giving isolated words all the wrong shadings. The only way to endure it, I discovered, was to think of her singing as a post-modern phenomenon with its own conventions and rules. As the victim of necessity rather than accident, Karen Jensen was tolerable.

> Here sleep I,
> Susannah Fry,
> No one near me,
> No one nigh:
> Alone, alone
> Under my stone,
> Dreaming on,
> Still dreaming on:
> Grass for my valance

170

And coverlid,
Dreaming on
As I always did.
'Weak in the head?'
Maybe. Who knows?
Susannah Fry
Under the rose.

There she was, facing away from me, burying Susannah Fry, and probably her own past and career into the bargain.

When we were done, she asked, "Sure you won't stay?"

"No, I don't think so."

"You really haven't another engagement, do you?"

"No," I admitted.

"I didn't think so. You were scared of me the moment you walked in the door. You thought I'd be crazy." She waited. "After all, only ugly girls live alone, right? And I'm not ugly."

"No, you aren't," I said. "You're quite attractive."

"Do you think so?" she asked, brightening. "It's so nice to hear that from you, even if you're just paying a compliment. I mean, it still means *something*." Then she surprised me. As I stood in the doorway, she got down on her knees in front of me and bowed her head in the style of one of her songs. "Please stay," she asked. Immediately she stood up and laughed. "But don't feel obliged to."

"Oh, no," I said, returning to her living room. "I've just changed my mind. Dinner sounds like a good idea."

After she had served and we had started to eat, she looked up at me and said, "You know, I'm not completely good." She paused. "At singing."

"What?" I stopped chewing. "Yes, you are. You're all right."

"Don't lie. I know I'm not. You know I'm not. Come on: let's at least be honest. I think I have certain qualities of musicality, but my pitch is . . . you know. Uneven. You probably think it's awfully vain of me to put on these recitals like this. With nobody but friends and family coming."

"No, I don't."

"Well, I don't care what you say. It's . . . hmm, I don't know. People encourage me. And it's a discipline. Music's finally a discipline that rewards you. Privately, though. Well, that's what my mother says."

171

Carefully, I said, "She may be right."

"Who cares if she is?" she laughed, her mouth full of food. "I enjoy doing it. Like I enjoy doing this. Listen, I don't want to seem forward or anything, but are you married?"

"No."

"I didn't think so." She picked up a string bean and eyed it suspiciously. "Why aren't you? You're not ugly. In fact you're all right looking. You obviously haven't been crazy. Are you gay or something?"

"No."

"No," she agreed, "you don't look gay. You don't even look very happy. You don't look very anything. Why is that?"

"I should be offended by this line of questioning."

"But you're not. You know why? Because I'm interested in you. I hardly know you, but I like you, what I can see. Don't you have any trust?"

"Yes," I said, finally.

"So answer my question. Why don't you look very anything?"

"Do you want to hear what my piano teacher once said?" I asked. "He said I wasn't enough of a fanatic. He said that to be one of the great ones you have to be a tiny bit crazy. Touched. And he said I wasn't. And when he said it, I knew all along he was right. I was waiting for someone to say what I already knew, and he was the one. I was too much a good citizen, he said. I wasn't possessed."

She rose, walked around the table to where I was sitting, and stood in front of me, looking down at my face. I knew that whatever she was going to do had been picked up, in attitude, from one of her songs. She touched the back of my arm with two fingers on her right hand. "Well," she said, "maybe you aren't possessed, but what would you think of me as another possession?"

VI

In 1618 at the age of seventy, Katherine Kepler, the mother of Johannes Kepler, was put on trial for witchcraft. The records indicate that her personality was so deranged, so deeply offensive to all, that if she were alive today she would *still* be called a witch.

One of Kepler's biographers, Angus Armitage, notes that she was "evil-tempered" and possessed an interest in unnamed "outlandish things." Her trial lasted, on and off, for three years; by 1621, when she was acquitted, her personality had disintegrated completely. She died the following year.

At the age of six, Kepler's son Frederick died of smallpox. A few months later, Kepler's wife, Barbara, died of typhus. Two other children, Henry and Susanna, had died in infancy.

Like many another of his age, Kepler spent much of his adult life cultivating favor from the nobility. He was habitually penniless and was often reduced, as his correspondence shows, to begging for handouts. He was the victim of religious persecution, though luckier in this regard than some.

After he married for a second time, three more children died in infancy, a statistic that in theory carries less emotional weight than one might think, given the accepted levels of infant mortality for that era.

In 1619, despite the facts cited above, Kepler published *De Harmonice Mundi*, a text in which he set out to establish the correspondence between the laws of harmony and the disposition of planets in motion. In brief, Kepler argued that certain intervals, such as the octave, major and minor sixths, and major and minor thirds, were pleasurable, while other intervals were not. History indicated that mankind had always regarded certain intervals as unpleasant. Feeling that this set of universal tastes pointed to immutable laws, Kepler sought to map out the pleasurable intervals geometrically, and then to transfer that geometrical pattern to the order of the planets. The velocity of the planets, rather than their strict placement, constituted the harmony of the spheres. This velocity provided each planet with a note, what Armitage calls a "term in a mathematically determined relation."

> In fact, each planet performed a short musical scale, set down by Kepler in staff notation. The length of the scale depended upon the eccentricity of the orbit; and its limiting notes could generally be shown to form a concord (except for Venus and the Earth with their nearly circular orbits, whose scales were of very constricted range). . . . at the Creation . . . complete concord prevailed and the morning stars sang together.

VII

We began to eat dinner together. Accustomed to solitude, we did not always engage in conversation. I would read the newspaper or ink in letters on my geometrically patterned crossword puzzles at my end of the table, while Karen would read detective novels or *Time* at hers. If she had cooked, I would clear and wash the dishes; if I had cooked, she did the cleaning. Experience and disappointments had made us methodical. She told me that she had once despised structured experiences governed by timetables, but that after several manic-depressive episodes, she had learned to love regularity. This regularity included taking lithium at the same time — to the minute — each day.

The season being summer, we would pack towels and swimming suits after dinner and drive out to one of several public beaches, where we would swim until darkness came on. On calm evenings, Karen would drop her finger in the water and watch the waves lap outward. I favored immature splashing, or grabbing her by the arm and whirling her around me until I released her and she would spin back and fall into the water, laughing as she sank. One evening, we found a private beach, two hundred feet of sand all to ourselves, on a lake thirty miles out of town. Framed on both sides by woods and well-hidden from the highway, this beach had the additional advantage of being unpatrolled. We had no bathhouse in which to change, however, so Karen instructed me not to look as she walked about fifty feet away to a spot where she undressed and put on her suit.

Though we had been intimate for at least a week, I had still not seen her naked: like a good Victorian, she demanded the shades be drawn, the lights out, and the covers pulled discreetly over us. But now, with the same methodical thoroughness, she wanted me to see her, so I looked, despite her warnings. She was bent over, under the tree boughs, the evening light breaking through the leaves and casting broken gold bands on her body. Her arms were delicate, the arms of a schoolgirl, I thought, an impression heightened by the paleness of her skin, but her breasts were full, at first making me think of Rubens' women, then of Renoir's, then of nothing at all. Slowly, knowing I was watching her, she pinned her hair up. Not her breasts or arms, but that expression of vague contentment as she looked out toward the water away from me: *that* made me feel a tingling below my heart, somewhere in an emotional center near my stomach. I wanted to pick her up and carry her somewhere, but with my knees wobbly it was all I could do to make my way over to where she stood and take her in my arms before she cried out. "Jesus," she said, shivering, "you gave me a surprise." I kissed her, waiting for inspiration to direct me on what to do next: pick her up? Carry her? Make love to her on the sand? Wade into the water with her and swim out to the center of the bay, where we would drown together in a Lawrentian love-grip? But then we broke the kiss; she put on her swimsuit like a good citizen, and we swam for our usual fifteen minutes in silence. Afterwards, we changed back into our clothes and drove home, muttering smalltalk. Behavior inspired by and demonstrating love embarrassed both of us. When I told her that she was beautiful and that I loved her, she patted me on the cheek and said, "Aw, how nice. You always try to say the right thing."

VIII

The Maple Street angle for *Harmony of the World* ran as follows: SYMPHONY OF FAITH IN A FAITHLESS AGE. Hindemith, I said, wished to confound the skeptics by composing a monument of faith. In an age of organized disharmony, of political chaos, he stood at the barricades defending tonality and traditional musical form. I carefully avoided any specific discussion of the musical materials of the symphony, which in the Schott orchestral score looked over-complex and melodically ugly. From what I could tell without hearing the piece, Hindemith had employed stunning technique in order to disguise his lack of inspiration, though I did not say so in print. Instead, I wrote that the symphony's failure to win public support was probably the result of Hindemith's refusal to use musical gimmicks on the one hand and sticky sweet melodies on the other. I wrote that he had not been dismayed by the bad reviews *Harmony of the World* had received, which was untrue. I said he was a man of integrity. I did not say that men of integrity are often unable to express joy when the occasion demands. Cascadilla liked my article. "This guy sounds like me," he

175

said, reading my copy. "I respect him." The article ran five days before the concert and was two pages away from the religion-and-faith section. Not long after, the symphony ticket office called me to say that my piece had caused a rush of ticket orders from ordinary folk, non-concert types, who wanted to hear this "religious symphony." The woman from the business office thanked me for my trouble. "Let's hope they like it," I said.

"Of course they will," she assured me. "You've told them to."

But they didn't. Despite all the oratory in the symphony, it was spiritually as dead as a lampshade. I could see why Hindemith had been shocked by the public reaction. Our audience applauded politely in discouragement, and then I heard an unusual sound for this anonymous city: one man, full of fun and conviction, booing loudly from the balcony. Booing the harmony of the world! He must be a Satanist! Don't intentions mean anything? So what if the harmony and joy were all counterfeit? The conductor came out for a bow, smiled at the booing man, and very soon the applause died away. I left the hall, feeling responsible. Arriving at the paper, I wrote a review of crushing dullness that reeked of bad faith. Goddamn Hindemith! Here he was, claiming to have seen God's workings, and they sounded like the workings of a steam engine or a trolley car. A fake symphony, with optimism the composer did not feel! I decided (but did not write) that *Harmony of the World* was just possibly the largest, most misconceived fiasco in modern music's history. It was a symphony that historically could not be written by a man who was constitutionally not equipped to write it. In my review, I kept a civil pen: I said that the performance lacked "luster," "a certain necessary glow."

IX

"I'm worried about the recital tomorrow."

"Aw, don't worry. Here, kiss me. Right here."

"Aren't you listening? I'm worried."

"I'm singing. You're just accompanying me. Nobody's going to notice you. Move over a little, would you? Yeah, there. That pillow was forcing my head against the wall."

176

"Why aren't you worried?"

"Why should I be worried? I don't want to worry. I want to make love. Isn't that better than worrying?"

"Not if I'm worried."

"People won't notice *you*. By the way, have you noticed that when I kiss you on the stomach, you get goosebumps?"

"Yes. I think you're taking this pretty lightly. I mean, it's almost unprofessional."

"That's because I'm an amateur. A 100% amateur. Always and totally. Even at this. But that doesn't mean I don't have my moments. Mmmmmm. That's better."

"I thought it would maybe help. But listen. I'm still worried."

"Uhhhn. Oh, wait a minute. Wait a minute. Oh, I get it."

"What?"

"I get it. You aren't worried about yourself. You're worried about me."

X

Forty people attended her recital, which was sponsored by the city university's music school, in which Karen was a sometime student. Somehow we made our way through the program, but when we came to the Chanler settings, I suddenly wanted Karen to sing them perfectly. I wanted an angel to descend and to take away the gypsy's curse. But she sang as she always had — off pitch — and when she came to "Ann Poverty," I found myself in that odd region between rage and pity.

> Stranger, here lies
>   Ann Poverty;
> Such was her name
>   And such was she.
> May Jesu pity
>   Poverty.

But I was losing my capacity for pity.

In the green room, her forty friends came back to congratulate her. I met them. They were all very nice. She smiled and laughed:

there would be a party in an hour. Would I go? I declined. When we were alone, I said I was going back to my place.

"Why?" she asked. "Shouldn't you come to my party? You're my lover after all. That *is* the word."

"Yes. But I don't want to go with you."

"Why?"

"Because of tonight's concert, that's why."

"What about it?"

"It wasn't very good, was it? I mean, it just wasn't."

"I thought it was all right. A few slips. It was pretty much what I was capable of. All those people said they liked it."

"Those people don't matter!" I said, my eyes watering with anger. "Only the music matters. Only the music is betrayed, they aren't. They don't know about pitch, most of them. I mean, Jesus, they aren't genuine musicians, so how would they know? Do you really think what we did tonight was good? It wasn't! It was a travesty! We ruined those songs! How can you stand to do that?"

"I don't ruin them. I sing them adequately. I project feeling. People get pleasure from them. That's enough."

"It's awful," I said, feeling the ecstatic lift-off into rage. "You're so close to being good, but you *aren't* good. Who cares what those ignoramuses think? They don't know what notes you're *supposed* to hit. It's that goddamn slippery pitch of yours. You're killing those songs. You just *drop* them like watermelons on the stage! It makes me sick! I couldn't have gone on for another day listening to you and your warbling! I'd die first."

She looked at me and nodded, her mouth set in a half-moue, half-smile of non-surprise. There may have been tears in her eyes, but I didn't see them. She looked at me as if she were listening hard to a long-distance call. "You're tired of me," she said.

"I'm not tired of you. I'm tired of hearing you sing! Your voice makes my flesh crawl! Do you know why? Can you tell me why you make me sick? Why do you make me sick? Never mind. I'm just glad this is over."

"You don't look glad. You look angry."

"And you look smug. Listen, why don't you go off to your party? Maybe there'll be a talent scout there. Or roses flung riotously at you. But don't give a recital like this again, please, okay? It's a public disgrace. It offends music. It offends *me*."

I turned my back on her and walked out to my car.

XI

After the failure of *Harmony of the World,* Hindemith went on a strenuous tour that included Scandinavia. In Oslo, he was rehearsing the Philharmonic when he blinked his bright blue eyes twice, turned to the concertmaster, and said, "I don't know where I am." They took him away to a hospital; he had suffered a nervous breakdown.

XII

I slept until noon, having nothing to do at the paper and no reason to get up. At last, unable to sleep longer, I rose and walked to the kitchen to make coffee. I then took my cup to the picture window and looked down the hill to the trees of the conservation area, the view Stecker had once told me I should have.

The figure of a woman was hanging from one of the trees, a noose around her neck. I dropped my coffee cup and the hot coffee spilled out over my feet.

I ran out the back door in my pajamas and sprinted painfully down the hill's tall grass toward the tree. I was fifty feet away when I saw that it wasn't Karen, wasn't in fact a woman at all, but an effigy of sorts, with one of Karen's hats, a pillow head, and a dress hanging over a broomstick skeleton. Attached to the effigy was a note:

> In the old days, this might have been me. Not anymore. Still, I thought it'd make you think. And I'm not giving up singing, either. By the way, what your playing lacks is not fanaticism, but concentration. You can't seem to keep your mind on one thing for more than a minute at a time. *I* notice things, too. You aren't the only reviewer around here. Take good care of this doll, okay?
>
> XXXXX,
> Karen

I took the doll up and dropped it in the clothes closet, where it stands to this hour.

179

Hindemith's biographer, Geoffrey Skelton, writes, "[On the stage] the episodic scenes from Kepler's life fail to achieve immediate dramatic coherence, and the basic theme remains obscure. . . ."

She won't of course see me again. She won't talk to me on the phone, and she doesn't answer my letters. I am quite lucidly aware of what I have done. And I go on seeing doubles and reflections and wave motion everywhere. There is symmetry, harmony, after all. I suppose I should have been nice to her. That, too, is a discipline. I always tried to be nice to everyone else.

On his deathbed, Hindemith has Kepler sing:

> *Und muss sehn am End:*
> *Die grosse Harmonie, das is der Tod.*
> *Absterben ist, sie zu bewirken, not.*
> *Im Leben hat sie keine Statte.*

> Now, at the end, I see it:
> the great harmony: it is death.
> To find it, we must die.
> In life it has no place.

XIII

Hindemith's words may be correct. But Dante says that the residents of limbo, having never been baptised, will not see the face of God. This despite their having committed no sin, no active fault. In their fated locale, they sigh, which keeps the air "forever trembling." No harmony for them, these guiltless souls. Through eternity, the residents of limbo — where one can imagine oneself if one cannot stand to imagine any part of hell — experience one of the most shocking of all the emotions that Dante names: "duol senza martíri," grief without torment. These sighs are rather like the sounds one hears drifting from front porches in small towns on soft summer nights.

1982

180

A SMALL, GOOD THING

by RAYMOND CARVER

from PLOUGHSHARES

SATURDAY AFTERNOON she drove to the bakery in the shopping center. After looking through a loose-leaf binder with photographs of cakes taped onto the pages, she ordered chocolate, the child's favorite. The cake she chose was decorated with a space ship and launching pad under a sprinkling of white stars at one end of the cake, and a planet made of red frosting at the other end. His name, SCOTTY, would be in raised green letters beneath the planet. The baker, who was an older man with a thick neck, listened without saying anything when she told him the child would be eight years old next Monday. The baker wore a white apron that looked like a smock. Straps cut under his arms, went around in back and then to the front again where they were secured under his heavy waist. He wiped his hands on his apron as he listened to her. He kept his eyes down on the photographs and let her talk. He let her take her time. He'd just come to work and he'd be there all night, baking, and he was in no real hurry.

She gave the baker her name, Ann Weiss, and her telephone number. The cake would be ready on Monday morning, just out of the oven, in plenty of time for the child's party that afternoon. The baker was not jolly. There were no pleasantries between them, just the minimum exchange of words, the necessary information. He made her feel uncomfortable, and she didn't like that. While he was bent over the counter with the pencil in his hand, she studied his coarse features and wondered if he'd ever done anything else with his life besides be a baker. She was a mother and thirty-three years old, and it seemed to her that everyone, especially someone the baker's age—a man old enough to be her father—must have children who'd gone through this special time of cakes and birthday parties. There must be that between them, she thought. But he was abrupt with her, not rude, just abrupt. She gave up trying to make friends with him. She looked into the back of the bakery and coud see a long, heavy wooden table with aluminum pie pans stacked at one end, and beside the table a metal container filled with empty racks. There was an enormous oven. A radio was playing country-western music.

The baker finished printing the information on the special order card and closed up the binder. He looked at her and said, "Monday morning." She thanked him and drove home.

On Monday morning, the birthday boy was walking to school with another boy. They were passing a bag of potato chips back and forth and the birthday boy was trying to find out what his friend intended to give him for his birthday that afternoon. Without looking, he stepped off the curb at an intersection and was immediately knocked down by a car. He fell on his side with his head in the gutter and his legs out in the road. His eyes were closed, but his legs began to move back and forth as if he were trying to climb over something. His friend dropped the potato chips and started to cry. The car had gone a hundred feet or so and stopped in the middle of the road. A man in the driver's seat looked back over his shoulder. He waited until the boy got unsteadily to his feet. The boy wobbled a little. He looked dazed, but okay. The driver put the car into gear and drove away.

The birthday boy didn't cry, but he didn't have anything to say about anything either. He wouldn't answer when his friend asked him what it felt like to be hit by a car. He walked home, and his friend went on to school. But after the birthday boy was inside his house and was telling his mother about it, she sitting beside him on the sofa, holding his hands in her lap, saying, "Scotty, honey, are you sure you feel all right, baby?" thinking she would call the doctor anyway, he suddenly lay back on the sofa, closed his eyes, and went limp. When she couldn't wake him up, she hurried to the telephone and called her husband at work. Howard told her to remain calm, remain calm, and then he called an ambulance for the child and left for the hospital himself.

Of course, the birthday party was cancelled. The child was in the hospital with a mild concussion and suffering from shock. There'd been vomiting, and his lungs had taken in fluid which needed pumping out that afternoon. Now he simply seemed to be in a very deep sleep—but no coma, Doctor Francis had emphasized; no coma, when he saw the alarm in the parents' eyes. At eleven o'clock that Monday night when the boy seemed to be resting comfortably enough after the many X-rays and the lab work, and it was just a matter of his waking up and coming around, Howard left the hospital. He and Ann had been at the hospital with the child since that morning, and he was going home for a short while to bathe and to change clothes. "I'll be back in an hour," he said. She nodded. "It's fine," she said. "I'll be right here." He kissed her on the forehead, and they touched hands. She sat in a chair beside the bed and looked at the child. She was waiting for him to wake up and be all right. Then she could begin to relax.

Howard drove home from the hospital. He took the wet, dark streets very fast, then caught himself and slowed down. Until now, his life had gone smoothly and to his satisfaction—college, marriage, another year of college for the advanced degree in business, a junior partnership in an investment firm. Fatherhood. He was happy and, so far, lucky—he knew that. His parents were still living, his brothers and his sister were established, his friends from college had gone out to take their places in the world. So far he had kept away from any real harm, from those forces he knew existed and that could cripple or bring down a man, if the luck went bad, if things suddenly turned. He pulled into the driveway and parked. His left leg began to tremble. He sat in the car for a minute and tried to deal with the present situation in a rational manner. Scotty had been hit by a car and was in the hospital, but he was going to be all right. He closed his eyes and ran his hand over his face. In a minute, he got out of the car and went up to the front door. The dog was barking inside the house. The telephone rang and rang while he unlocked the door and fumbled for the light switch. He shouldn't have left the hospital, he shouldn't have. "God dammit!" he said. He picked up the receiver and said, "I just walked in the door!"

"There's a cake here that wasn't picked up," the voice on the other end of the line said.

"What are you saying?" Howard asked.

"A cake," the voice said. "A sixteen dollar cake."

Howard held the receiver against his ear, trying to understand. "I don't know anything about a cake," he said. "Jesus, what are you talking about?"

"Don't hand me that," the voice said.

Howard hung up the telephone. He went into the kitchen and poured himself some whiskey. He called the hospital. But the child's condition remained the same; he was still sleeping and nothing had changed there. While water poured into the tub, Howard lathered his face and shaved. He'd just stretched out in the tub and closed his eyes when the telephone began to ring. He hauled himself out, grabbed a towel, and hurried through the house, saying "Stupid, stupid," for having left the hospital. But when he picked up the receiver and shouted, "Hello!" there was no sound at the other end of the line. Then the caller hung up.

He arrived back at the hospital a little after midnight. Ann still sat in the chair beside the bed. She looked at Howard, and then she looked back at the child. The child's eyes stayed closed, the head was still wrapped in bandages. His breathing was quiet and regular. From an apparatus over the bed hung a bottle of glucose with a tube running from the bottle to the boy's arm.

"How is he?" Howard said. "What's all this?" waving at the glucose and the tube.

"Doctor Francis's orders," she said. "He needs nourishment. He needs to keep up his strength. Why doesn't he wake up, Howard? I don't understand, if he's all right."

Howard put his hand against the back of her head. He ran his fingers through her hair. "He's going to be all right. He'll wake up in a little while. Doctor Francis knows what's what."

After a time he said, "Maybe you should go home and get some rest. I'll stay here. Just don't put up with this creep who keeps calling. Hang up right away."

"Who's calling?" she asked.

"I don't know who, just somebody with nothing better to do than call up people. You go on now."

She shook her head. "No," she said, "I'm fine."

"Really," he said. "Go home for a while, and then come back and spell me in the morning. It'll be all right. What did Doctor Francis say? He said Scotty's going to be all right. We don't have to worry. He's just sleeping now, that's all."

A nurse pushed the door open. She nodded at them as she went to the bedside. She took the left arm out from under the covers and put her fingers on the wrist, found the pulse, and then consulted her watch. In a little while she put the arm back under the covers and moved to the foot of the bed where she wrote something on a clipboard attached to the bed.

"How is he?" Ann said. Howard's hand was a weight on her shoulder. She was aware of the pressure from his fingers.

"He's stable," the nurse said. Then she said, "Doctor will be in again shortly. Doctor's back in the hospital. He's making rounds right now."

"I was saying maybe she'd want to go home and get a little rest," Howard said. "After the doctor comes," he said.

"She could do that," the nurse said. "I think you should both feel free to do that, if you wish." The nurse was a big Scandinavian woman with blond hair. There was the trace of an accent in her speech.

"We'll see what the doctor says," Ann said. "I want to talk to the doctor. I don't think he should keep sleeping like this. I don't think that's a good sign." She brought her hand up to her eyes and let her head come forward a little. Howard's grip tightened on her shoulder, and then his hand moved to her neck where his fingers began to knead the muscles there.

"Doctor Francis will be here in a few minutes," the nurse said. Then she left the room.

Howard gazed at his son for a time, the small chest quietly rising and falling under the covers. For the first time since the terrible minutes after Ann's telephone call to him at his office, he felt a genuine fear starting in his limbs. He began shaking his head, trying to keep it away. Scotty was fine, but instead of sleeping at home in his own bed he was in a hospital bed with bandages around his head and a tube in his arm. But this help was what he needed right now.

Doctor Francis came in and shook hands with Howard, though they'd just seen each other a few hours before. Ann got up from the chair. "Doctor?"

"Ann," he said and nodded. "Let's just first see how he's doing," the doctor said. He moved to the side of the bed and took the boy's pulse. He peeled back one eyelid and then the other. Howard and Ann stood beside the doctor and watched. Then the doctor turned back the covers and listened to the boy's heart and lungs with his stethoscope. He pressed his fingers here and there on the abdomen. When he was finished he went to the end of the bed and studied the chart. He noted the time, scribbled something on the chart, and then looked at Howard and Ann.

"Doctor, how is he?" Howard said. "What's the matter with him exactly?"

"Why doesn't he wake up?" Ann said.

The doctor was a handsome, big-shouldered man with a tanned face. He wore a three-piece suit, a striped tie, and ivory cuff-links. His grey hair was combed along the sides of his head, and he looked as if he had just come from a concert. "He's all right," the doctor said. "Nothing to shout about, he could be better, I think. But he's all right. Still, I wish he'd wake up. He should wake up pretty soon." The doctor looked at the boy again. "We'll know some more in a couple of hours, after the results of a few more tests are in. But he's all right, believe me, except for that hair-line fracture of the skull. He does have that."

"Oh, no," Ann said.

"And a bit of a concussion, as I said before. Of course, you know he's in shock," the doctor said. "Sometimes you see this in shock cases."

"But he's out of any real danger?" Howard said. "You said before he's not in a coma. You wouldn't call this a coma then, would you, doctor?" Howard waited. He looked at the doctor.

"No, I don't want to call it a coma," the doctor said and glanced over at the boy once more. "He's just in a very deep sleep. It's a restorative, a measure the body is taking on its own. He's out of any real danger, I'd say that for certain, yes. But we'll know more when he wakes up and the other tests are in. Don't worry," the doctor said.

"It's a coma," Ann said. "Of sorts."

"It's not a coma yet, not exactly," the doctor said. "I wouldn't want to call it coma. Not yet anyway. He's suffered shock. In shock cases this kind of reaction is common enough; it's a temporary reaction to bodily trauma. Coma. Well, coma is a deep, prolonged unconsciousness that could go on for days, or weeks even. Scotty's

186

not in that area, not as far as we can tell anyway. I'm certain his condition will show improvement by morning. I'm betting that it will anyway. We'll know more when he wakes up, which shouldn't be long now. Of course, you may do as you like, stay here or go home for a time. But by all means feel free to leave the hospital for a while if you want. This is not easy, I know." The doctor gazed at the boy again, watching him, and then he turned to Ann and said, "You try not to worry, little mother. Believe me, we're doing all that can be done. It's just a question of a little more time now." He nodded at her, shook hands with Howard again, and then he left the room.

Ann put her hand over her child's forehead. "At least he doesn't have a fever," she said. Then she said, "My God, he feels so cold though. Howard? Is he supposed to feel like this. Feel his head."

Howard touched the child's temples. His own breathing had slowed. "I think he's supposed to feel this way right now," he said. "He's in shock, remember? That's what the doctor said. The doctor was just in here. He would have said something if Scotty wasn't okay."

Ann stood there a while longer, working her lip with her teeth. Then she moved over to her chair and sat down.

Howard sat in the chair next to her chair. They looked at each other. He wanted to say something else and reassure her, but he was afraid too. He took her hand and put it in his lap, and this made him feel better, her hand being there. He picked up her hand and squeezed it. Then he just held her hand. They sat like that for a while, watching the boy and not talking. From time to time he squeezed her hand. Finally, she took her hand away.

"I've been praying," she said.

He nodded.

She said, "I almost thought I'd forgotten how, but it came back to me. All I had to do was close my eyes and say, 'Please, God, help us, —help Scotty'; and then the rest was easy. The words were right there. Maybe if you prayed too," she said to him.

"I've already prayed," he said. "I prayed this afternoon, yesterday afternoon, I mean, after you called, while I was driving to the hospital. I've been praying," he said.

"That's good," she said. For the first time now, she felt they were together in it, this trouble. She realized with a start it had only been happening to her and to Scotty. She hadn't let Howard into it, though he was there and needed all along. She felt glad to be his wife.

The same nurse came in and took the boy's pulse again and checked the flow from the bottle hanging above the bed.

In an hour another doctor came in. He said his name was Parsons, from Radiology. He had a bushy moustache. He was wearing loafers, a western shirt, and a pair of jeans.

"We're going to take him downstairs for more pictures," he told them. "We need to do some more pictures, and we want to do a scan."

"What's that?" Ann said. "A scan?" She stood between this new doctor and the bed. "I thought you'd already taken all your X-rays."

"I'm afraid we need some more," he said. "Nothing to be alarmed about. We just need some more pictures, and we want to do a brain scan on him."

"My God," Ann said.

"It's perfectly normal procedure in cases like this," this new doctor said. "We just need to find out for sure why he isn't back awake yet. It's normal medical procedure, and nothing to be alarmed about. We'll be taking him down in a few minutes," this doctor said.

In a little while two orderlies came into the room with a gurney. They were black-haired, dark-complexioned men in white uniforms, and they said a few words to each other in a foreign tongue as they unhooked the boy from the tube and moved him from his bed to the gurney. Then they wheeled him from the room. Howard and Ann got on the same elevator. Ann stood beside the gurney and gazed at the child. She closed her eyes as the elevator began its descent. The orderlies stood at either end of the gurney without saying anything, though once one of the men made a comment to the other in their own language, and the other man nodded slowly in response.

Later that morning, just as the sun was beginning to lighten the windows in the waiting room outside the X-Ray department, they brought the boy out and moved him back up to his room. Howard and Ann rode up on the elevator with him once more, and once more they took up their places beside the bed.

They waited all day, but still the boy did not wake up. Occasionally one of them would leave the room to go downstairs to the cafeteria to drink coffee and then, as if suddenly remembering and feeling guilty, get up from the table and hurry back to the room. Doctor Francis came again that afternoon and examined the boy once more and then left after telling them he was coming along and could wake up any minute now. Nurses, different nurses than the night before, came in from time to time. Then a young woman from the lab knocked and entered the room. She wore white slacks and a white blouse and carried a little tray of things which she put on the stand beside the bed. Without a word to them, she took blood from the boy's arm. Howard closed his eyes as the woman found the right place on the boy's arm and pushed the needle in.

"I don't understand this," Ann said to the woman.

"Doctor's orders," the young woman said. "I do what I'm told to do. They say draw that one, I draw. What's wrong with him, anyway?" she said. "He's a sweetie."

"He was hit by a car," Howard said. "A hit and run."

The young woman shook her head and looked again at the boy. Then she took her tray and left the room.

"Why won't he wake up?" Ann said. "Howard? I want some answers from these people."

Howard didn't say anything. He sat down again in the chair and crossed one leg over the other. He rubbed his face. He looked at his son and then he settled back in the chair, closed his eyes, and went to sleep.

Ann walked to the window and looked out at the parking lot. It was night and cars were driving into and out of the parking lot with their lights on. She stood at the window with her hands gripping the sill and knew in her heart that they were into something now, something hard. She was afraid, and her teeth began to chatter until she tightened her jaws. She saw a big car stop in front of the hospital and someone, a woman in a long coat, got into the car. For a minute she wished she were that woman and somebody, any-body, was driving her away from here to somewhere else, a place where she would find Scotty waiting for her when she stepped out of the car, ready to say *Mom* and let her gather him in her arms.

In a little while Howard woke up. He looked at the boy again, and then he got up from the chair, stretched, and went over to stand beside her at the window. They both stared out at the parking lot. They didn't say anything. But they seemed to feel each other's insides now, as though the worry had made them transparent in a perfectly natural way.

The door opened and Doctor Francis came in. He was wearing a different suit and tie this time. His gray hair was combed along the sides of his head, and he looked as if he had just shaved. He went straight to the bed and examined the boy. "He ought to have come around by now. There's just no good reason for this," he said. "But I can tell you we're all convinced he's out of any danger. We'll just feel better when he wakes up. There's no reason, absolutely none, why he shouldn't come around. Very soon. Oh, he'll have himself a dilly of a headache when he does, you can count on that. But all of his signs are fine. They're as normal as can be."

"Is it a coma then?" Ann asked.

The doctor rubbed his smooth cheek. "We'll call it that for the time being, until he wakes up. But you must be worn out. This is hard. Feel free to go out for a bite," he said. "It would do you good. I'll put a nurse in here while you're gone, if you'll feel better about going. Go and have yourselves something to eat."

"I couldn't eat," Ann said. "I'm not hungry."

"Do what you need to do, of course," the doctor said. "Anyway, I wanted to tell you that all the signs are good, the tests are positive, nothing at all negative, and just as soon as he wakes up he'll be over the hill."

"Thank you, doctor," Howard said. He shook hands with the doctor again. The doctor patted Howard's shoulder and went out.

"I suppose one of us should go home and check things," Howard said. "Slug needs to be fed, for one thing."

"Call one of the neighbors," Ann said. "Call the Morgans. Anyone will feed a dog if you ask them to."

"All right," Howard said. After a while he said, "Honey why don't you do it? Why don't you go home and check on things, and then come back? It'll do you good. I'll be right here with him. Seriously," he said. "We need to keep up our strength on this. We'll want to be here for a while even after he wakes up."

"Why don't you go?" she said. "Feed Slug. Feed yourself."

"I already went," he said. "I was gone for exactly an hour and fifteen minutes. You go home for an hour and freshen up. Then come back. I'll stay here."

She tried to think about it, but she was too tired. She closed her eyes and tried to think about it again. After a time she said, "Maybe I will go home for a few minutes. Maybe if I'm not just sitting right here watching him every second he'll wake up and be all right. You know? Maybe he'll wake up if I'm not here. I'll go home and take a bath and put on clean clothes. I'll feed Slug. Then I'll come back."

"I'll be right here," he said. "You go on home, honey, and then come back. I'll be right here keeping an eye on things." His eyes were bloodshot and small, as if he'd been drinking for a long time. His clothes were rumpled. His beard had come out again. She touched his face, and then she took her hand back. She understood he wanted to be by himself for a while, to not have to talk or share his worry for a time. She picked up her purse from the nightstand, and he helped her into her coat.

"I won't be gone long," she said.

"Just sit and rest for a little while when you get home," he said. "Eat something. Take a bath. After you get out of the bath, just sit for a while and rest. It'll do you a world of good, you'll see. Then come back down here," he said. "Let's try not to worry. You heard what Doctor Francis said."

She stood in her coat for a minute trying to recall the doctor's exact words, looking for any nuances, any hint of something behind his words other than what he had said. She tried to remember if his expression had changed any when he bent over to examine the child. She remembered the way his features had composed themselves as he rolled back the child's eyelids and then listened to his breathing.

She went to the door where she turned and looked back. She looked at the child, and then she looked at the father. Howard nodded. She stepped out of the room and pulled the door closed behind her.

She went past the nurses' station and down to the end of the corridor, looking for the elevator. At the end of the corridor she turned to her right where she found a little waiting room where a Negro family sat in wicker chairs. There was a middle-aged man in a khaki shirt and pants, a baseball cap pushed back on his head. A large woman wearing a house dress and slippers was slumped in one of the chairs. A teenaged girl in jeans, hair done in dozens of little braids, lay stretched out in one of the chairs smoking a

191

cigarette, her legs crossed at the ankles. The family swung their eyes to her as she entered the room. The little table was littered with hamburger wrappers and styrofoam cups.

"Franklin," the large woman said as she roused herself. "Is about Franklin?" Her eyes widened. "Tell me now, lady," the woman said. "Is about Franklin?" She was trying to rise from her chair, but the man had closed his hand over her arm.

"Here, here," he said. "Evelyn."

"I'm sorry," Ann said. "I'm looking for the elevator. My son is in the hospital, and now I can't find the elevator."

"Elevator is down that way, turn left," the man said as he aimed a finger.

The girl drew on her cigarette and stared at Ann. Her eyes were narrowed to slits, and her broad lips parted slowly as she let the smoke escape. The Negro woman let her head fall on her shoulder and looked away from Ann, no longer interested.

"My son was hit by a car," Ann said to the man. She seemed to need to explain herself. "He has a concussion and a little skull fracture, but he's going to be all right. He's in shock now, but it might be some kind of coma too. That's what really worries us, the coma part. I'm going out for a little while, but my husband is with him. Maybe he'll wake up while I'm gone."

"That's too bad," the man said and shifted in the chair. He shook his head. He looked down at the table, and then he looked back at Ann. She was still standing there. He said, "Our Franklin, he's on the operating table. Somebody cut him. Tried to kill him. There was a fight where he was at. At this party. They say he was just standing and watching. Not bothering nobody. But that don't mean nothing these days. Now he's on the operating table. We're just hoping and praying, that's all we can do now." He gazed at her steadily.

Ann looked at the girl again, who was still watching her, and at the older woman who kept her head down, but whose eyes were now closed. Ann saw the lips moving silently, making words. She had an urge to ask what those words were. She wanted to talk more with these people who were in the same kind of waiting she was in. She was afraid, and they were afraid. They had that in common. She would have liked to have said something else about the accident, told them more about Scotty, that it had happened on the day of his birthday, Monday, and that he was still unconscious. Yet

192

she didn't know how to begin. She stood there looking at them without saying anything more.

She went down the corridor the man had indicated and found the elevator. She stood for a minute in front of the closed doors, still wondering if she was doing the right thing. Then she put out her finger and touched the button.

She pulled into the driveway and cut the engine. She closed her eyes and leaned her head against the wheel for a minute. She listened to the ticking sounds the engine made as it began to cool. Then she got out of the car. She could hear the dog barking inside the house. She went to the front door, which was unlocked. She went inside and turned on lights and put on a kettle of water for tea. She opened some dog food and fed Slug on the back porch. The dog ate in hungry little smacks. It kept running into the kitchen to see that she was going to stay. As she sat down on the sofa with her tea, the telephone rang.

"Yes!" she said as she answered. "Hello!"

"Mrs. Weiss," a man's voice said. It was five o'clock in the morning, and she thought she could hear machinery or equipment of some kind in the background.

"Yes, yes! What is it?" she said. "This is Mrs. Weiss. This is she. What is it, please?" She listened to whatever it was in the background. "Is it Scotty, for Christ's sake?"

"Scotty," the man's voice said. "It's about Scotty, yes. It has to do with Scotty, that problem. Have you forgotten about Scotty?" the man said. Then he hung up.

She dialed the hospital's number and asked for the third floor. She demanded information about her son from the nurse who answered the telephone. Then she asked to speak to her husband. It was, she said, an emergency.

She waited, turning the telephone cord in her fingers. She closed her eyes and felt sick to her stomach. She would have to make herself eat. Slug came in from the back porch and lay down near her feet. He wagged his tail. She pulled at his ear while he licked her fingers. Howard was on the line.

"Somebody just called here," she said. She twisted the telephone cord. "He said, he said it was about Scotty." She cried.

"Scotty's fine," Howard told her. "I mean he's still sleeping. There's been no change. The nurse has been in twice since you've been gone. They're in here every thirty minutes or so. A nurse or else a doctor. He's all right."

"Somebody called, he said it was about Scotty," she said.

"Honey, you rest for a little while, you need the rest. Then come back here. It must be that same caller I had. Just forget it. Come back down here after you've rested. Then we'll have breakfast or something."

"Breakfast," she said. "I don't want any breakfast."

"You know what I mean," he said. "Juice, something, I don't know. I don't know anything, Ann. Jesus, I'm not hungry either. Ann, it's hard to talk now. I'm standing here at the desk. Doctor Francis is coming again at eight o'clock this morning. He's going to have something to tell us then, something more definite. That's what one of the nurses said. She didn't know any more than that. Ann? Honey, maybe we'll know something more then. At eight o'clock. Come back here before eight. Meanwhile, I'm right here and Scotty's all right. He's still the same," he added.

"I was drinking a cup of tea," she said, "when the telephone rang. They said it was about Scotty. There was a noise in the background. Was there a noise in the background on that call you had, Howard?"

"I don't remember," he said. "Maybe the driver of the car, maybe he's a psychopath and found out about Scotty somehow. But I'm here with him. Just rest like you were going to do. Take a bath and come back by seven or so, and we'll talk to the doctor together when he gets here. It's going to be all right, honey. I'm here, and there are doctors and nurses around. They say his condition is stable."

"I'm scared to death," she said.

She ran water, undressed, and got into the tub. She washed and dried quickly, not taking the time to wash her hair. She put on clean underwear, wool slacks, and a sweater. She went into the living room where the dog looked up at her and let its tail thump once against the floor. It was just starting to get light outside when she went out to the car.

She drove into the parking lot of the hospital and found a space close to the front door. She felt she was in some obscure way responsible for what had happened to the child. She let her thoughts move to the Negro family. She remembered the name "Franklin" and the table that was covered with hamburger papers,

194

and the teenaged girl staring at her as she drew on her cigarette. "Don't have children," she told the girl's image as she entered the front door of the hospital. "For God's sake, don't."

She took the elevator up to the third floor with two nurses who were just going on duty. It was Wednesday morning, a few minutes before seven. There was a page for a Doctor Madison as the elevator doors slid open on the third floor. She got off behind the nurses, who turned in the other direction and continued the conversation she had interrupted when she'd gotten into the elevator. She walked down the corridor to the little alcove where the Negro family had been waiting. They were gone now, but the chairs were scattered in such a way that it looked as if people had just jumped from them the minute before. The table top cluttered with the same cups and papers, the ashtray was filled with cigarette butts.

She stopped at the nurses' station just down the corridor from the waiting room. A nurse was standing behind the counter, brushing her hair and yawning.

"There was a Negro man in surgery last night," Ann said. "Franklin was his name. His family was in the waiting room. I'd like to inquire about his condition."

A nurse who was sitting at a desk behind the counter looked up from a chart in front of her. The telephone buzzed and she picked up the receiver, but she kept her eyes on Ann.

"He passed away," said the nurse at the counter. The nurse held the hairbrush and kept on looking at her. "Are you a friend of the family or what?"

"I met the family last night," Ann said. "My own son is in the hospital. I guess he's in shock. We don't know for sure what's wrong. I just wondered about Mr. Franklin, that's all. Thank you." She moved down the corridor. Elevator doors the same color as the walls slid open and a gaunt, bald man in white pants and white canvas shoes pulled a heavy cart off the elevator. She hadn't noticed these doors last night. The man wheeled the cart out into the corridor and stopped in front of the room nearest the elevator and consulted a clipboard. Then he reached down and slid a tray out of the cart. He rapped lightly on the door and entered the room. She could smell the unpleasant odors of warm food as she passed the cart. She hurried past the other station without looking at any of the nurses and pushed open the door to the child's room.

Howard was standing at the window with his hands behind his back. He turned around as she came in.

"How is he?" she said. She went over to the bed. She dropped her purse on the floor beside the nightstand. She seemed to have been gone a long time. She touched the child's face. "Howard?"

"Doctor Francis was here a little while ago," Howard said. She looked at him closely and thought his shoulders were bunched a little.

"I thought he wasn't coming until eight o'clock this morning," she said quickly.

"There was another doctor with him. A neurologist."

"A neurologist," she said.

Howard nodded. His shoulders were bunching, she could see that. "What'd they say, Howard? For Christ's sake, what'd they say? What is it?"

"They said they're going to take him down and run more tests on him, Ann. They think they're going to operate, honey. Honey, they are going to operate. They can't figure out why he won't wake up. It's more than just shock or concussion, they know that much now. It's in his skull, the fracture, it has something, something to do with that, they think. So they're going to operate. I tried to call you, but I guess you'd already left the house."

"Oh, God," she said. "Oh, please, Howard, please," she said, taking his arms.

"Look!" Howard said then. "Scotty! Look, Ann!" He turned her toward the bed.

The boy had opened his eyes, then closed them. He opened them again now. The eyes stared straight ahead for a minute, then moved slowly in his head until they rested on Howard and Ann, then traveled away again.

"Scotty," his mother said, moving to the bed.

"Hey, Scott," his father said. "Hey, son."

They leaned over the bed. Howard took the child's hand in his hands and began to pat and squeeze the hand. Ann bent over the boy and kissed his forehead again and again. She put her hands on either side of his face. "Scotty, honey, it's mommy and daddy," she said. "Scotty?"

The boy looked at them, but without any sign of recognition. Then his eyes scrunched closed, his mouth opened, and he howled until he had no more air in his lungs. His face seemed to relax and soften then. His lips parted as his last breath was puffed through his throat and exhaled gently through the clenched teeth.

The doctors called it a hidden occlusion and said it was a one-in-a-million circumstance. Maybe if it could have been detected somehow and surgery undertaken immediately, it could have saved him. But more than likely not. In any case, what would they have been looking for? Nothing had shown up in the tests or in the X-rays. Doctor Francis was shaken. "I can't tell you how badly I feel. I'm so very sorry, I can't tell you," he said as he led them into the doctors' lounge. There was a doctor sitting in a chair with his legs hooked over the back of another chair, watching an early morning TV show. He was wearing a green delivery room outfit, loose green pants and green blouse, and a green cap that covered his hair. He looked at Howard and Ann and then looked at Doctor Francis. He got to his feet and turned off the set and went out of the room. Doctor Francis guided Ann to the sofa, sat down beside her and began to talk in a low, consoling voice. At one point he leaned over and embraced her. She could feel his chest rising and falling evenly against her shoulder. She kept her eyes open and let him hold her. Howard went into the bathroom, but he left the door open. After a violent fit of weeping, he ran water and washed his face. Then he came out and sat down at the little table that held a telephone. He looked at the telephone as though deciding what to do first. He made some calls. After a time, Doctor Francis used the telephone.

"Is there anything else I can do for the moment?" he asked them.

Howard shook his head. Ann stared at Doctor Francis as if unable to comprehend his words.

The doctor walked them to the hospital's front door. People were entering and leaving the hospital. It was eleven o'clock in the morning. Ann was aware of how slowly, almost reluctantly she moved her feet. It seemed to her that Doctor Francis was making them leave, when she felt they should stay, when it would be more the right thing to do, to stay. She gazed out into the parking lot and then turned around and looked back at the front of the hospital. She began shaking her head. "No, no," she said. "I can't leave him here, no." She heard herself say that and thought how unfair it was

197

that the only words that came out were the sort of words used on TV shows where people were stunned by violent or sudden deaths. She wanted her words to be her own. "No," she said, and for some reason the memory of the Negro woman's head lolling on the woman's shoulder came to her. "No," she said again.

"I'll be talking to you later in the day," the doctor was saying to Howard. "There are still some things that have to be done, things that have to be cleared up to our satisfaction. Some things that need explaining."

"An autopsy," Howard said.

Doctor Francis nodded.

"I understand," Howard said. Then he said, "Oh, Jesus. No, I don't understand, Doctor. I can't, I can't. I just can't."

Doctor Francis put his arm around Howard's shoulders. "I'm sorry. God, how I'm sorry." He let go of Howard's shoulders and held out his hand. Howard looked at the hand, and then he took it. Doctor Francis put his arms around Ann once more. He seemed full of some goodness she didn't understand. She let her head rest on his shoulder, but her eyes stayed open. She kept looking at the hospital. As they drove out of the parking lot, she looked back at the hospital once more.

At home, she sat on the sofa with her hands in her coat pockets. Howard closed the door to the child's room. He got the coffee maker going and then he found an empty box. He had thought to pick up some of the child's things. But instead he sat down beside her on the sofa, pushed the box to one side, and leaned forward, arms between his knees. He began to weep. She pulled his head over into her lap and patted his shoulder. "He's gone," she said. She kept patting his shoulder. Over his sobs she could hear the coffee maker hissing in the kitchen. "There, there," she said tenderly. "Howard, he's gone. He's gone and now we'll have to get used to that. To being alone."

In a little while Howard got up and began moving aimlessly around the room with the box, not putting anything into it, but collecting some things together on the floor at one end of the sofa. She continued to sit with her hands in her coat pockets. Howard put the box down and brought coffee into the living room. Later, Ann made calls to relatives. After each call had been placed and the party had answered, Ann would blurt out a few words and cry for a minute. Then she would quietly explain, in a measured voice, what had happened and tell them about arrangements. Howard took the box out to the garage where he saw the child's bicycle. He dropped the box and sat down on the pavement beside the bicycle. He took hold of the bicycle awkwardly so that it leaned against his chest. He held it, the rubber pedal sticking into his chest. He gave the wheel a turn.

Ann hung up the telephone after talking to her sister. She was looking up another number, when the telephone rang. She picked it up on the first ring.

"Hello," she said, and she heard something in the background, a humming noise. "Hello!" she said. "For God's sake," she said. "Who is this? What is it you want?"

"Your Scotty, I got him ready for you," the man's voice said. "Did you forget him?"

"You evil bastard!" she shouted into the receiver. "How can you do this, you evil son of a bitch?"

"Scotty," the man said. "Have you forgotten about Scotty?" Then the man hung up on her.

Howard heard the shouting and came in to find her with her head on her arms over the table, weeping. He picked up the receiver and listened to the dial tone.

Much later, just before midnight, after they had dealt with many things, the telphone rang again.

"You answer it," she said. "Howard, it's him, I know." They were sitting at the kitchen table with coffee in front of them. Howard had a small glass of whisky beside his cup. He answered on the third ring.

"Hello," he said. "Who is this? Hello! Hello!" The line went dead. "He hung up," Howard said. "Whoever it was."

"It was him," she said. "That bastard. I'd like to kill him," she said. "I'd like to shoot him and watch him kick," she said.

"Ann, my God," he said.

"Could you hear anything?" she said. "In the background? A noise, machinery, something humming?"

"Nothing, really. Nothing like that," he said. "There wasn't much time. I think there was some radio music. Yes, there was a radio going, that's all I could tell. I don't know what in God's name is going on," he said.

She shook her head. "If I could, could get, my hands, on him." It

199

came to her then. She knew who it was. Scotty, the cake, the telephone number. She pushed the chair away from the table and got up. "Drive me down to the shopping center," she said. "Howard."

"What are you saying?"

"The shopping center. I know who it is who's calling. I know who it is. It's the baker, the son-of-a-bitching baker, Howard. I had him bake a cake for Scotty's birthday. That's who's calling. That's who has the number and keeps calling us. To harass us about the cake. The baker, that bastard."

They drove out to the shopping center. The sky was clear and stars were out. It was cold, and they ran the heater in the car. They parked in front of the bakery. All of the shops and stores were closed, but there were cars at the far end of the lot in front of the cinema. The bakery windows were dark, but when they looked through the glass they could see a light in the back room and, now and then, a big man in an apron moving in and out of the white, even light. Through the glass she could see the display cases and some little tables with chairs. She tried the door. She rapped on the glass. But if the baker heard them he gave no sign. He didn't look in their direction.

They drove around behind the bakery and parked. They got out of the car. There was a lighted window too high up for them to see inside. A sign near the back door said, "The Pantry Bakery, Special Orders." She could hear faintly a radio playing inside and something—an oven door?—creak as it was pulled down. She knocked on the door and waited. Then she knocked again, louder. The radio was turned down and there was a scraping sound now, the distinct sound of something, a drawer, being pulled open and then closed.

Someone unlocked the door and opened it. The baker stood in the light and peered out at them. "I'm closed for business," he said. "What do you want at this hour? It's midnight. Are you drunk or something?"

She stepped into the light that fell through the open door. He blinked his heavy eyelids as he recognized her.

"It's you," he said.

"It's me," she said. "Scotty's mother. This is Scotty's father. We'd like to come in."

The baker said, "I'm busy now. I have work to do."

She had stepped inside the doorway anyway. Howard came in behind her. The baker moved back. "It smells like a bakery in here. Doesn't it smell like a bakery in here, Howard?"

"What do you want?" the baker said. "Maybe you want your cake? That's it, you decided you want your cake. You ordered a cake, didn't you?"

"You're pretty smart for a baker," she said. "Howard, this is the man who's been calling us. This is the baker man." She clenched her fists. She stared at him fiercely. There was a deep burning inside her, an anger that made her feel larger than herself, larger than either of these men.

"Just a minute here," the baker said. "You want to pick up your three day old cake? That it? I don't want to argue with you, lady. There it sits over there, getting stale. I'll give it to you for half of what I quoted you. No. You want it? You can have it. It's no good to me, no good to anyone now. It cost me time and money to make that cake. If you want it, okay, if you don't, that's okay too. I have to get back to work." He looked at them and rolled his tongue behind his teeth.

"More cakes," she said. She knew she was in control of it, of what was increasing her. She was calm.

"Lady, I work sixteen hours a day in this place to earn a living," the baker said. He wiped his hands on his apron. "I work night and day in here, trying to make ends meet." A look crossed Ann's face that made the baker move back and say, "No trouble now." He reached to the counter and picked up a rolling pin with his right hand and began to tap it against the palm of his other hand. "You want the cake or not? I have to get back to work. Bakers work at night," he said again. His eyes were small, mean-looking, she thought, nearly lost in the bristly flesh around his cheeks. His neck was thick with fat.

"We know bakers work at night," Ann said. "They make phone calls at night too. You bastard," she said.

The baker continued to tap the rolling pin against his hand. He glanced at Howard. "Careful, careful," he said to Howard.

"My son's dead," she said with a cold, even finality. "He was hit by a car Monday morning. We've been waiting with him until he died. But of course, you couldn't be expected to know that, could you? Bakers can't known everything. Can they, Mr. Baker? But he's dead. He's dead, you bastard!" Just as suddenly as it had welled in her the anger dwindled, gave way to something else, a dizzy feeling of nausea. She leaned against the wooden table that was sprinkled with flour, put her hands over her face and began to cry, her shoulders rocking back and forth. "It isn't fair," she said. "It isn't, isn't fair."

Howard put his hand at the small of her back and looked at the baker. "Shame on you," Howard said to him. "Shame."

The baker put the rolling pin back on the counter. He undid his apron and threw it on the counter. He looked at them, and then he shook his head slowly. He pulled a chair out from under a card table that held papers and receipts, an adding machine and a telephone directory. "Please sit down," he said. "Let me get you a chair," he said to Howard. "Sit down now, please." The baker went into the front of the shop and returned with two little wrought-iron chairs. "Please sit down you people."

Ann wiped her eyes and looked at the baker. "I wanted to kill you," she said. "I wanted you dead."

The baker had cleared a space for them at the table. He shoved the adding machine to one side, along with the stacks of note paper and receipts. He pushed the telephone directory onto the floor, where it landed with a thud. Howard and Ann sat down and pulled their chairs up to the table. The baker sat down too.

"I don't blame you," the baker said, putting his elbows on the table. "First. Let me say how sorry I am. God alone knows how sorry. Listen to me. I'm just a baker. I don't claim to be anything else. Maybe once, maybe years ago I was a different kind of human being, I've forgotten, I don't known for sure. But I'm not any longer, if I ever was. Now I'm just a baker. That don't excuse my offense, I know. But I'm deeply sorry. I'm sorry for your son, and I'm sorry for my part in this. Sweet, sweet Jesus," the baker said. He spread his hands out on the table and turned them over to reveal his palms. "I don't have any children myself, so I can only imagine what you must be feeling. All I can say to you now is that I'm sorry. Forgive me, if you can," the baker said. "I'm not an evil man, I don't think. Not evil, like you said on the phone. You got to understand that what it comes down to is I don't know how to act anymore, it would seem. Please," the man said, "let me ask you if you can find it in your hearts to forgive me?"

It was warm inside the bakery. In a minute, Howard stood up from the table and took off his coat. He helped Ann from her coat.

The baker looked at them for a minute and then nodded and got up from the table. He went to the oven and turned off some switches. He found cups and poured coffee from an electric coffee maker. He put a carton of cream on the table, and a bowl of sugar.

"You probably need to eat something," the baker said. "I hope you'll eat some of my hot rolls. You have to eat and keep going. Eating is a small, good thing in a time like this," he said.

He served them warm cinnamon rolls just out of the oven, the icing still runny. He put butter on the table and knives to spread the butter. Then the baker sat down at the table with them. He waited. He waited until they each took a roll from the platter and began to eat. "It's good to eat something," he said, watching them. "There's more. Eat up. Eat all you want. There's all the rolls in the world in here."

They ate rolls and drank coffee. Ann was suddenly hungry, and the rolls were warm and sweet. She ate three of them, which pleased the baker. Then he began to talk. They listened carefully. Although they were tired and in anguish, they listened to what the baker had to say. They nodded when the baker began to speak of loneliness, and the sense of doubt and limitation that had come to him in his middle years. He told them what it was like to be childless all these years. To repeat the days with the ovens endlessly full and endlessly empty. The party food, the celebrations he'd worked over. Icing knuckle-deep. The tiny wedding couples stuck into cakes. Hundreds of them, no, thousands by now. Birthdays. Just imagine all those candles burning. He had a necessary trade. He was a baker. He was glad he wasn't a florist. It was better to be feeding people. This was a better smell anytime than flowers.

"Smell this," the baker said, breaking open a dark loaf. "It's a heavy bread, but rich." They smelled it, then he had them taste it. It had the taste of molasses and coarse grains. They listened to him. They ate what they could. They swallowed the dark bread. It was like daylight under the fluorescent trays of light. They talked on into the early morning, the high pale cast of light in the windows, and they did not think of leaving.

1983

GRAVEYARD DAY

by BOBBIE ANN MASON

from ASCENT

Holly, SWINGING HER LEGS FROM THE KITCHEN STOOL, lectures her mother on natural foods. Holly is ten.

Waldeen says, "I'll have to give your teacher a talking-to. She's put notions in your head. You've got to have meat to grow."

Waldeen is tenderizing liver, beating it with the edge of a saucer. Her daughter insists that she is a vegetarian. If Holly had said Rosicrucian, it would have sounded just as strange to Waldeen. Holly wants to eat peanuts, soyburgers, and yogurt. Waldeen is sure this new fixation has something to do with Holly's father, Joe Murdock, although Holly rarely mentions him. After Waldeen and Joe were divorced last September, Joe moved to Arizona and got a construction job. Joe sends Holly letters occasionally, but Holly won't let Waldeen see them. At Christmas he sent Holly a copper Indian bracelet with unusual marks on it. It is Indian language, Holly tells her. Waldeen sees Holly polishing the bracelet while she is watching TV.

Walden shudders when she thinks of Joe Murdock. If he weren't Holly's father, she might be able to forget him. Waldeen was too young when she married him, and he had a reputation for being wild, which he did not outgrow. Now she could marry Joe McClain, who comes over for supper almost every night, always bringing something special, such as roast or dessert. He seems to be oblivious to what things cost, and he frequently brings Holly presents. If Waldeen married Joe, then Holly would have a stepfather—something like a sugar substitute, Waldeen imagines. Shifting relationships confuse her. She doesn't know what marriage means anymore. She tells Joe they must wait. Her ex-husband is still on her mind, like the lingering after-effects of an illness.

Joe McClain is punctual, considerate. Tonight he brings fudge ripple ice cream and a half-gallon of Coke in a plastic jug. He kisses Waldeen and hugs Holly.

Waldeen says, "We're having liver and onions, but Holly's mad 'cause I won't make Soybean Supreme."

"Soybean *Delight*," says Holly.

"Oh, excuse me!"

"Liver is full of poison. The poisons in the feed settle in the liver."

"Do you want to stunt your growth?" Joe asks, patting Holly on the head. He winks at Waldeen and waves his walking stick at her playfully, like a conductor. Joe collects walking sticks, and he has an antique one that belonged to Jefferson Davis. On a gold band, in italics, it says Jefferson Davis. Joe doesn't go anywhere without a walking stick, although he is only thirty. It embarrasses Waldeen to be seen with him.

"Sometimes a cow's liver just explodes from the poison," says Holly. "Poisons are *oozing* out."

"Oh, Holly, hush, that's disgusting." Waldeen plops the pieces of liver onto a plate of flour.

"There's this restaurant at the lake that has Liver Lovers' Night," Joe says to Holly. "Every Tuesday is Liver Lovers' Night."

"Really?" Holly is wide-eyed, as if Joe is about to tell a long story, but Waldeen suspects Joe is bringing up the restaurant— Sea's Breeze at Kentucky Lake—to remind her that it was the scene of his proposal. Waldeen, not accustomed to eating out, studied the menu carefully, wavering between pork chops and T-bone steak and then suddenly, without thinking, ordering catfish. She was disappointed to learn that the catfish was not even local, but frozen ocean cat. "Why would they do that," she kept saying, interrupting Joe, "when they've got all the fresh channel cat in the world right here at Kentucky Lake?"

During supper, Waldeen snaps at Holly for sneaking liver to the cat, but with Joe gently persuading her, Holly manages to eat three bites of liver without gagging. Holly is trying to please him, as though he were some TV game show host who happened to live in the neighborhood. In Waldeen's opinion, families shouldn't shift memberships, like clubs. But here they are, trying to be a family. Holly, Waldeen, Joe McClain. Sometimes Joe spends the weekend, but Holly prefers weekends at Joe's house because of his shiny wood floors and his parrot that tries to sing "Inka Dinka Doo." Holly likes the idea of packing an overnight bag.

Waldeen dishes out the ice cream. Suddenly inspired, she suggests a picnic Saturday. "The weather's fairing up," she says.

"I can't," says Joe. "Saturday's graveyard day."

"Graveyard day?" Holly and Waldeen say together.

"It's my turn to clean off the graveyard. Every spring and fall somebody has to rake it off." Joe explains that he is responsible for taking geraniums to his grandparents' graves. His grandmother always kept the pot in her basement during the winter, and in the spring she took it to her husband's grave, but she had died in November.

"Couldn't we have a picnic at the graveyard?" asks Waldeen.

"That's gruesome."

"We never get to go on picnics," says Holly. "Or anywhere." She gives Waldeen a look.

"Well, okay," Joe says. "But remember, it's serious. No fooling around."

"We'll be real quiet," says Holly.

"Far be it from me to disturb the dead," Waldeen says, wondering why she is speaking in a mocking tone.

After supper, Joe plays rummy with Holly while Waldeen cracks pecans for a cake. Pecan shells fly across the floor, and the cat pounces on them. Holly and Joe are laughing together, whooping loudly over the cards. They sound like contestants on "Let's Make a Deal." Joe Murdock wanted desperately to be on a game show and strike it rich. He wanted to go to California so he would have a chance to be on TV and so he could travel the freeways. He drove in the stock car races, and he had been drag racing since he learned to drive. Evel Knievel was his hero. Waldeen couldn't look when the TV showed Evel Knievel leaping over canyons. She told Joe many times, "He's nothing but a show-off. But if you want to break your fool neck, then go right ahead. Nobody's stopping you." She is better off without Joe Murdock. If he were still in town, he would do something to make her look foolish, such as paint her name on his car door. He once had WALDEEN painted in large red letters on the door of his LTD. It was like a tattoo. It is probably a good thing he is in Arizona. Still, she cannot really understand why he had to move so far away from home.

After Holly goes upstairs, carrying the cat, whose name is Mr. Spock, Waldeen says to Joe, "In China they have a law that the men have to help keep house." She is washing dishes.

Joe grins. "That's in China. This is *here*."

Waldeen slaps at him with the dish towel, and Joe jumps up and grabs her. "I'll do all the housework if you marry me," he says. "You can get the Chinese to arrest me if I don't."

"You sound just like my ex-husband. Full of promises."

"Guys named Joe are good at making promises." Joe laughs and hugs her.

"All the important men in my life were named Joe," says Waldeen, with pretended seriousness. "My first real boyfriend was named Joe. I was fourteen."

"You always bring that up," says Joe. "I wish you'd forget about them. You love *me*, don't you?"

"Of course, you idiot."

"Then why don't you marry me?"

"I just said I was going to think twice is all."

"But if you love me, what are you waiting for?"

"That's the easy part. Love is easy."

In the middle of "The Waltons," C. W. Redmon and Betty Mathis drop by. Betty, Waldeen's best friend, lives with C.W., who works with Joe on a construction crew. Waldeen turns off the TV and clears magazines from the couch. C. W. and Betty have just returned from Florida and they are full of news about Sea World. Betty shows Waldeen her new tote bag with a killer whale pictured on it.

"Guess who we saw at the Louisville airport," Betty says.

"I give up," says Waldeen.

"Colonel Sanders!"

"He's eighty-four if he's a day," C. W. adds.

"You couldn't miss him in that white suit," Betty says. "I'm sure it was him. Oh, Joe! He had a walking stick. He went strutting along—"

"No kidding!"

He probably beats chickens to death with it," says Holly, who is standing around.

"That would be something to have," says Joe. "Wow, one of the Colonel's walking sticks."

"Do you know what I read in a magazine?" says Betty. "That the Colonel Sanders outfit is trying to grow a three-legged chicken."

"No, a four-legged chicken," says C.W.

"Well, whatever."

Waldeen is startled by the conversation. She is rattling ice cubes, looking for glasses. She finds an opened Coke in the refrigerator, but it may have lost its fizz. Before she can decide whether to open the new one Joe brought, C. W. and Betty grab glasses of ice from her and hold them out. Waldeen pours the Coke. There is a little fizz.

"We went first class the whole way," says C.W. "I always say, what's vacation for if you don't splurge?"

"I thought we were going to buy *out* Florida," says Betty. "We spent a fortune. Plus, I gained a ton."

"Man, those jumbo jets are really nice," says C.W.

C.W. and Betty seem changed, exactly like all people who come back from Florida with tales of adventure and glowing tans, except that they did not get tans. It rained. Waldeen cannot imagine flying, or spending that much money. Her ex-husband tried to get her to go up in an airplane with him once—a $7.50 ride in a Cessna—but she refused. If Holly goes to Arizona to visit him, she will have to fly. Arizona is probably as far away as Florida.

When C.W. says he is going fishing on Saturday, Holly demands to go along. Waldeen reminds her about the picnic. "You're full of wants," she says.

"I just wanted to go somewhere."

"I'll take you fishing one of these days soon," says Joe.

"Joe's got to clean off his graveyard," says Waldeen. Before she realizes what she is saying, she has invited C.W. and Betty to come along on the picnic. She turns to Joe. "Is that okay?"

"I'll bring some beer," says C.W. "To hell with fishing."

"I never heard of a picnic at a graveyard," says Betty. "But it sounds neat."

Joe seems embarrassed. "I'll put you to work," he warns.

Later, in the kitchen, Waldeen pours more Coke for Betty. Holly is playing solitaire on the kitchen table. As Betty takes the

Coke, she says, "Let C.W. take Holly fishing if he wants a kid so bad." She has told Waldeen that she wants to marry C.W., but she does not want to ruin her figure by getting pregnant. Betty pets the cat. "Is this cat going to have kittens?"

Mr. Spock, sitting with his legs tucked under his stomach, is shaped somewhat like a turtle.

"Heavens, no," says Waldeen. "He's just fat because I had him nurtured."

"The word is *neutered!*" cries Holly, jumping up. She grabs Mr. Spock and marches up the stairs.

"That youngun," Waldeen says with a sigh. She feels suddenly afraid. Once, Holly's father, unemployed and drunk on whiskey and Seven-Up, snatched Holly from the school playground and took her on a wild ride around town, buying her ice cream at the Tastee-Freez, and stopping at Newberry's to buy her an "All in the Family" Joey doll, with correct private parts. Holly was eight. When Joe brought her home, both were tearful and quiet. The excitement had worn off, but Waldeen had vividly imagined how it was. She wouldn't be surprised if Joe tried the same trick again, this time carrying Holly off to Arizona. She has heard of divorced parents who kidnap their own children.

The next day Joe McClain brings a pizza at noon. He is working nearby and has a chance to eat lunch with Waldeen. The pizza is large enough for four people. Waldeen is not hungry.

"I'm afraid we'll end up horsing around and won't get the graveyard cleaned off," Joe says. "It's really a lot of work."

"Why's it so important, anyway?"

"It's a family thing."

"Family. Ha!"

"Why are you looking at me in that tone of voice?"

"I don't know what's what anymore," Waldeen wails. "I've got this kid that wants to live on peanuts and sleeps with a cat—and didn't even see her daddy at Christmas. And here *you* are, talking about family. What do you know about family? You don't know the half of it."

"What's got into you lately?"

Waldeen tries to explain. "Take Colonel Sanders, for instance. He was on 'I've Got A Secret' once, years ago, when nobody knew who he was. His secret was that he had a million-dollar check in his

209

pocket for selling Kentucky Fried Chicken to John Y. Brown. *Now* look what's happened. Colonel Sanders sold it but didn't get rid of it. He's still Colonel Sanders. John Y. sold it too and he can't get rid of it either. Everybody calls him the Chicken King, even though he's governor. That's not very dignified, if you ask me."

"What in Sam Hill are you talking about? What's that got to do with families?"

"Oh, Colonel Sanders just came to mind because C.W. and Betty saw him. What I mean is, you can't just do something by itself. Everything else drags along. It's all *involved*. I can't get rid of my ex-husband just by signing a paper. Even if he *is* in Arizona and I never lay eyes on him again."

Joe stands up, takes Waldeen by the hand, and leads her to the couch. They sit down and he holds her tightly for a moment. Waldeen has the strange impression that Joe is an old friend who moved away and returned, years later, radically changed. She doesn't understand the walking sticks, or why he would buy such an enormous pizza.

"One of these days you'll see," says Joe, kissing her.

"See what?" Waldeen mumbles.

"One of these days you'll see. I'm not such a bad catch."

Waldeen stares at a split in the wallpaper.

"Who would cut your hair if it wasn't for me?" he asks, rumpling her curls. "I should have gone to beauty school."

"I don't know."

"Nobody else can do Jimmy Durante imitations like I can."

"I wouldn't brag about it."

On Saturday Waldeen is still in bed when Joe arrives. He appears in the doorway of her bedroom, brandishing a shiny black walking stick. It looks like a stiffened black racer snake.

"I overslept," Waldeen says, rubbing her eyes. "First I had insomnia. Then I had bad dreams. Then—"

"You said you'd make a picnic."

"Just a minute. I'll go make it."

"There's not time now. We've got to pick up C.W. and Betty."

Waldeen pulls on her jeans and a shirt, then runs a brush through her hair. In the mirror she sees blue pouches under her eyes. She catches sight of Joe in the mirror. He looks like an actor in a vaudeville show.

They go into the kitchen, where Holly is eating granola. "She promised me she'd make carrot cake," Holly tells Joe.

"I get blamed for everything," says Waldeen. She is rushing around, not sure why. She is hardly awake.

"How could you forget?" asks Joe. "It was your idea in the first place."

"I didn't forget. I just overslept." Waldeen opens the refrigerator. She is looking for something. She stares at a ham.

When Holly leaves the kitchen, Waldeen asks Joe, "Are you mad at me?" Joe is thumping his stick on the floor.

"No. I just want to get this show on the road."

"My ex-husband always said I was never dependable, and he was right. But *he* was one to talk. He had his head in the clouds."

"Forget your ex-husband."

"His name is Joe. Do you want some juice?" Waldeen is looking for orange juice, but she cannot find it.

"No." Joe leans on his stick. "He's over and done with. Why don't you just cross him off your list?"

"Why do you think I had bad dreams? Answer me that. I must be afraid of *something*."

There is no juice. Waldeen closes the refrigerator door. Joe is smiling at her enigmatically. What she is really afraid of, she realizes, is that he will turn out to be just like Joe Murdock. But it must be only the names, she reminds herself. She hates the thought of a string of husbands, and the idea of a step-father is like a substitute host on a talk show. It makes her think of Johnny Carson's many substitute hosts.

"You're just afraid to do anything new, Waldeen," Joe says. "You're afraid to cross the street. Why don't you get your ears pierced? Why don't you adopt a refugee? Why don't you get a dog?"

"You're crazy. You say the weirdest things." Waldeen searches the refrigerator again. She pours a glass of Coke and watches it foam.

It is afternoon before they reach the graveyard. They had to wait for C.W. to finish painting his garage door, and Betty was in the shower. On the way, they bought a bucket of fried chicken. Joe said little on the drive into the country. When he gets quiet,

Waldeen can never figure out if he is angry or calm. When he put the beer cooler in the trunk, she caught a glimpse of the geraniums in an ornate concrete pot with a handle. It looked like a petrified Easter basket. On the drive, she closed her eyes and imagined that they were in a funeral procession.

The graveyard is next to the woods on a small rise fenced in with barbed wire. A herd of Holsteins grazes in the pasture nearby, and in the distance the smokestacks of the new industrial park send up lazy swirls of smoke. Waldeen spreads out a blanket, and Betty opens beers and hands them around. Holly sits down under a tree, her back to the gravestones, and opens a Vicki Barr flight steward-ess book.

Joe won't sit down to eat until he has unloaded the geraniums. He fusses over the heavy basket, trying to find a level spot. The flowers are not yet blooming.

"Wouldn't plastic flowers keep better?" asks Waldeen. "Then you wouldn't have to lug that thing back and forth." There are several bunches of plastic flowers on the graves. Most of them have fallen out of their containers.

"Plastic, yuck!" cries Holly.

"I should have known I'd say the wrong thing," says Waldeen.

"My grandmother liked geraniums," Joe says.

At the picnic, Holly eats only slaw and the crust from a drum-stick. Waldeen remarks, "Mr. Spock is going to have a feast."

"You've got a treasure, Waldeen," says C.W. "Most kids just want to load up on junk."

"Wonder how long a person can survive without meat," says Waldeen, somewhat breezily. Suddenly, she feels miserable about the way she treats Holly. Everything Waldeen does is so round-about, so devious, a habit she is sure she acquired from Joe Murdock. Disgusted, Waldeen flings a chicken bone out among the graves. Once, her ex-husband wouldn't bury the dog that was hit by a car. It lay in a ditch for over a week. She remembers Joe saying several times, "Wonder if the dog is still there?" He wouldn't admit that he didn't want to bury it. Waldeen wouldn't do it because he had said he would do it. It was a war of nerves. She finally called the Highway Department to pick it up. Joe McClain, at least, would never be that barbaric.

Joe pats Holly on the head and says, "My girl's stubborn, but she knows what she likes." He makes a Jimmy Durante face which

212

causes Holly to smile. Then he brings out a surprise for her, a bag of trail mix, which includes pecans and raisins. When Holly pounces on it, Waldeen notices that Holly is not wearing the Indian bracelet her father gave her. Waldeen wonders if there are vegetarians in Arizona.

Blue sky burns through the intricate spring leaves of the maples on the fence line. The light glances off the gravestones—a few thin slabs that date back to the last century and eleven sturdy blocks of marble and granite. Joe's grandmother's grave is a brown heap.

Waldeen opens another beer. She and Betty are stretched out under a maple tree and Holly is reading. Betty is talking idly about the diet she intends to go on. Waldeen feels too lazy to move. She watches the men work. While C.W. rakes leaves, Joe washes off the gravestones with water he brought in a camp carrier. He scrubs out the carvings with a brush. He seems as devoted as a man washing and polishing his car on a Saturday afternoon. Betty plays he-loves-me-he-loves-me-not with the fingers of a maple leaf. The fragments fly away in a soft breeze.

From her Sea World tote bag, Betty pulls out playing cards with Holly Hobbie pictures on them. The old-fashioned child with the bonnet hiding her face is just the opposite of Waldeen's own strange daughter. Waldeen sees Holly secretly watching the men. They pick up their beer cans from a pink, shiny tombstone and drink a toast to Joe's great-great-grandfather Joseph McClain, who was killed in the Civil War. His stone, almost hidden in dead grasses, says 1841-1862.

"When I die, they can burn me and dump the ashes in the lake," says C.W.

"Not me," says Joe. "I want to be buried right here."

"*Want* to be? You planning to die soon?"

Joe laughs. "No, but if it's my time, then it's my time. I wouldn't be afraid to go."

"I guess that's the right way to look at it."

Betty says to Waldeen, "He'd marry me if I'd have his kid."

"What made you decide you don't want a kid, anyhow?" Waldeen is shuffling the cards, fifty-two identical children in bonnets.

"Who says I decided? You just do whatever comes natural. Whatever's right for you." Betty has already had three beers and she looks sleepy.

"Most people do just the opposite. They have kids without thinking. Or get married."

"Talk about decisions," Betty goes on. "Did you see 'Sixty Minutes' when they were telling about Palm Springs? And how all those rich people live? One woman had hundreds of dresses and Morley Safer was asking her how she ever decided what on earth to wear. He was *strolling* through her closet. He could have played *golf* in her closet."

"Rich people don't know beans," says Waldeen. She drinks some beer, then deals out the cards for a game of hearts. Betty snatches each card eagerly. Waldeen does not look at her own cards right away. In the pasture, the cows are beginning to move. The sky is losing its blue. Holly seems lost in her book, and the men are laughing. C.W. stumbles over a footstone hidden in the grass and falls onto a grave. He rolls over, curled up with laughter.

"Y'all are going to kill yourselves," Waldeen says, calling to him across the graveyard.

Joe tells C.W. to shape up. "We've got work to do," he says.

Joe looks over at Waldeen and mouths something. "I love you"? Her ex-husband used to stand in front of the TV and pantomime singers. She suddenly remembers a Ku Klux Klansman she saw on TV. He was being arrested at a demonstration, and as he was led away in handcuffs, he spoke to someone off-camera, ending with a solemn message, "I *love* you." He was acting for the camera, as if to say, "Look what a nice guy I am." He gave Waldeen the creeps. That could have been Joe Murdock, Waldeen thinks. Not Joe McClain. Maybe she is beginning to get them straight in her mind. They have different ways of trying to get through to her. The differences are very subtle. Soon she will figure them out.

Waldeen and Betty play several hands of hearts and drink more beer. Betty is clumsy with the cards and loses three hands in a row. Waldeen cannot keep her mind on the cards either. She wins accidentally. She can't concentrate because of the graves, and Joe standing there saying "I love you." If she marries Joe, and doesn't get divorced again, they will be buried here together. She picks out a likely spot and imagines the headstone and the green carpet and the brown leaves that will someday cover the twin mounds. Joe and C.W. are bringing leaves to the center of the graveyard and piling them on the place she has chosen. Waldeen feels peculiar, as if the burial plot, not a diamond ring, symbolizes the

214

promise of marriage. But there is something comforting about the thought, which she tries to explain to Betty.

"Ooh, that's gross," says Betty. She slaps down a heart and takes the trick.

Waldeen shuffles the cards for a long time. The pile of leaves is growing dramatically. Joe and C.W. have each claimed a side of the graveyard, and they are racing. It occurs to Waldeen that she has spent half her life watching guys named Joe show off for her. Once, when Waldeen was fourteen, she went out onto the lake with Joe Suiter in a rented pedal-boat. When Waldeen sees him at the bank, where he works, she always remembers the pedal-boat and how they stayed out in the silver-blue lake all afternoon, ignoring the people waving them in from the shore. When they finally returned, Joe owed ten dollars in overtime on the boat, so he worked Saturdays, mowing yards, to pay for their spree. Only recently in the bank, when they laughed over the memory, he told her that it was worth it, for it was one of the great adventures of his life, going out in a pedal-boat with Waldeen, with nothing but the lake and time.

Betty is saying, "We could have a nice bon-fire and a wienie roast—what *are* you doing?"

Waldeen has pulled her shoes off. And she is taking a long, running start, like a pole vaulter, and then with a flying leap she lands in the immense pile of leaves, up to her elbows. Leaves are flying and everyone is standing around her, forming a stern circle, and Holly, with her book closed on her fist, is saying, "Don't you know *any*thing?"

1983

215

HIDING

by SUSAN MINOT

from GRAND STREET

O̲ur father doesn't go to church with us but we're all downstairs in the hall at the same time, bumbling, getting ready to go.
Mum knuckles the buttons of Chicky's snowsuit till he's knot-tight,
crouching, her heels lifted out of the backs of her shoes, her nylons
creased at the ankles. She wears a black lace veil that stays on her
hair like magic. Sherman ripples by, coat flapping, and Mum grabs
him by the hood, reeling him in, and zips him up with a pinch at
his chin. Gus stands there with his bottom lip out, waiting, looking
like someone's smacked him except not that hard. Even though
he's nine, he still wants Mum to do him up. Delilah comes half-
hurrying down the stairs, late, looking like a ragamuffin with her
skirt slid down to her hips and her hair all slept on wrong. Caitlin
says, "It's about time." Delilah sweeps along the curve of the
banister, looks at Caitlin who's all ready to go herself with her pea
jacket on and her loafers and bare legs, and tells her, "You're going
to freeze." Everyone's in a bad mood because we just woke up.

Dad's outside already on the other side of the French doors,
waiting for us to go. You can tell it's cold out there by his white
breath blowing by his cheek in spurts. He just stands on the porch,
hands shoved in his black parka, feet pressed together, looking at
the crusty snow on the lawn. He doesn't wear a hat but that's
because he barely feels the cold. Mum's the one who's warm-
blooded. At skiing, she'll take you in when your toes get numb.
You sit there with hot chocolate and a carton of french fries and the
other mothers and she rubs your foot to get the circulation back.
Down on the driveway the car is warming up and the exhaust goes
straight up, disappearing in thin white curls.

"Okay, Monkeys," says Mum, filing us out the door. Chicky starts down the steps one red boot at a time till Mum whisks him up under a wing. The driveway is wrinkled over with ice so we take little shuffle steps across it, blinking at how bright it is, still only half-awake. Only the station wagon can fit everybody. Gus and Sherman scamper in across the huge backseat. Caitlin's head is the only one that shows over the front. (Caitlin is the oldest and she's twelve. I'm next, then Delilah, then the boys.) Mum rubs her thumbs on the steering wheel so that her gloves are shiny and round at the knuckles. Dad is doing things like checking the gutters, waiting till we leave. When we finally barrel down the hill, he turns and goes back into the house which is big and empty now and quiet.

We keep our coats on in church. Except for the O'Shaunesseys, we have the most children in one pew. Dad only comes on Christmas and Easter, because he's not Catholic. A lot of times you only see the mothers there. When Dad stays at home, he does things like cuts prickles in the woods or tears up thorns, or rakes leaves for burning, or just stands around on the other side of the house by the lilacs, surveying his garden, wondering what to do next. We usually sit up near the front and there's a lot of kneeling near the end. One time Gus got his finger stuck in the diamond-shaped holes of the heating vent and Mum had to yank it out. When the man comes around for the collection, we each put in a nickel or a dime and the handle goes by like a rake. If Mum drops in a five-dollar bill, she'll pluck out a couple of bills for her change.

The church is huge. Out loud in the dead quiet, a baby blares out *DAH-DEE*. We giggle and Mum goes *Ssshhh* but smiles too. A baby always yells at the quietest part. Only the girls are old enough to go to Communion; you're not allowed to chew it. The priest's neck is peeling and I try not to look. "He leaves me cold," Mum says when we leave, touching her forehead with a fingertip after dipping it into the holy water.

On the way home, we pick up the paper at Cage's and a bag of eight lollipops—one for each of us, plus Mum and Dad, even though Dad never eats his. I choose root beer. Sherman crinkles his wrapper, flicking his eyes around to see if anyone's looking. Gus says, "Sherman, you have to wait till after breakfast." Sherman gives a fierce look and shoves it in his mouth. Up in front, Mum, flicking on the blinker, says, "Take that out," with eyes in the back of her head.

Depending on what time of year it is, we do different things on the weekends. In the fall we might go to Castle Hill and stop by the orchard in Ipswich for cider and apples and red licorice. Castle Hill is closed after the summer so there's nobody else there and it's all covered with leaves. Mum goes up to the windows on the terrace and tries to peer in, cupping her hands around her eyes and seeing curtains. We do things like roll down the hills, making our arms stiff like mummies, or climb around on the marble statues which are really cold, or balance along the edge of the fountains without falling. Mum says *Be careful* even though there's no water in them, just red leaves plastered against the sides. When Dad notices us he yells *Get down*.

One garden has a ghost, according to Mum. A lady used to sneak out and meet her lover in the garden behind the grape trellis. Or she'd hide in the garden somewhere and he'd look for her and find her. But one night she crept out and he didn't come and didn't come and finally when she couldn't stand it any longer, she went crazy and ran off the cliff and killed herself and now her ghost comes back and keeps waiting. We creep into the boxed-in place smelling the yellow berries and the wet bark and Delilah jumps— "What was that?"—trying to scare us. Dad shakes the wood to see if it's rotten. We run ahead and hide in a pile of leaves. Little twigs get in your mouth and your nostrils; we hold still underneath listening to the brittle ticking leaves. When we hear Mum and Dad get close, we burst up to surprise them, all the leaves fluttering down, sputtering from the dust and tiny grits that get all over your face like grey ash, like Ash Wednesday. Mum and Dad just keep walking. She brushes a pine needle from his collar and he jerks his head, thinking of something else, probably that it's a fly. We follow them back to the car in a line all scruffy with leaf scraps.

After church, we have breakfast because you're not allowed to eat before. Dad comes in for the paper or a sliver of bacon. One thing about Dad, he has the weirdest taste. Spam is his favorite thing or this cheese that no one can stand the smell of. He barely sits down at all, glancing at the paper with his feet flat down on either side of him, ready to get up any minute to go back outside and sprinkle white fertilizer on the lawn. After, it looks like frost.

This Sunday we get to go skating at Ice House Pond. Dad drives. "Pipe down," he says into the back seat. Mum faces him with white fur around her hood. She calls him Uncs, short for Uncle, a kind of joke, I guess, calling him Uncs while he calls her Mum, same as we do. We are making a racket.

"Will you quit it?" Caitlin elbows Gus.

"What? I'm not doing anything."

"Just taking up all the room."

Sherman's in the way back. "How come Chicky always gets the front?"

"Cause he's the baby." Delilah is always explaining everything.

"I en not a baby," says Chicky without turning around.

Caitlin frowns at me. "Who said you could wear my scarf?"

I ask into the front seat, "Can we go to the Fairy Garden?" even though I know we won't.

"Why couldn't Rummy come?"

Delilah says, "Because Dad didn't want him to."

Sherman wants to know how old Dad was when he learned how to skate.

Dad says, "About your age." He has a deep voice.

"Really?" I think about that for a minute, about Dad being Sherman's age.

"What about Mum?" says Caitlin.

This isn't his department so he just keeps driving. Mum shifts her shoulders more toward us but still looks at Dad.

"When I was a little girl on the Boston Common." Her teeth are white and she wears fuchsia lipstick. "We used to have skating parties."

Caitlin leans close to Mum's fur hood, crossing her arms into a pillow. "What? With dates?"

Mum bats her eyelashes. "Oh sure. Lots of beaux." She smiles, acting like a flirt. I look at Dad but he's concentrating on the road.

We saw one at a football game once. He had a huge mustard overcoat and bow tie and a pink face like a ham. He bent down to shake our tiny hands, half-looking at Mum the whole time. Dad was someplace else getting the tickets. His name was Hank. After he went, Mum put her sunglasses on her head and told us she used to watch him play football at BC. Dad never wears a tie except to work. One time Gus got lost. We waited until the last people had trickled out and the stadium was practically empty. It had started to get dark and the headlights were crisscrossing out of the parking field. Finally Dad came back carrying him, walking fast, Gus's head bobbing around and his face all blotchy. Dad rolled his eyes and made a kidding groan to Mum and we laughed because Gus was always getting lost. When Mum took him, he rammed his head onto her shoulder and hid his face while we walked back to the car, and under Mum's hand you could see his back twitching, trying to hide his crying.

We have Ice House Pond all to ourselves. In certain places the ice is bumpy and if you glide on it going *Aauuuuhhhh* in a low tone, your voice wobbles and vibrates. Every once in a while, a crack shoots across the pond, echoing just beneath the surface, and you feel something drop in the hollow of your back. It sounds like someone's jumped off a steel wire and left it twanging in the air.

I try to teach Delilah how to skate backwards but she's flopping all over the ice, making me laugh, with her hat lopsided and her mittens dangling out of her sleeves. When Gus falls, he just stays there, polishing the ice with his mitten. Dad sees him and says, "I don't care if my son is a violin player," kidding.

Dad played hockey in college and was so good his name is on a plaque that's right as you walk into the Harvard rink. He can go really fast. He takes off—*whooosh*—whizzing, circling at the edge of the pond, taking long strides, then gliding, chopping his skates, crossing over in little jumps. He goes zipping by and we watch him: his hands behind him in a tight clasp, his face as calm as if he were just walking along, only slightly forward. When he sweeps a corner, he tips in, then rolls into a hunch, and starts the long side-pushing again. After he stops, his face is red and the tears leak from the sides of his eyes and there's a white smudge around his mouth like frostbite. Sherman, copying, goes chopping forward on collapsed ankles and it sounds like someone sharpening knives.

Mum practices her 3s from when she used to figure skate. She pushes forward on one skate, turning in the middle like a petal flipped suddenly in the wind. We always make her do a spin. First she does backwards crossovers, holding her wrists like a tulip in her fluorescent pink parka, then stops straight up on her toes, sucking in her breath and dips, twisted, following her own tight circle, faster and faster, drawing her feet together. Whirring around, she lowers into a crouch, ventures out one balanced leg, a twirling whirlpool, hot pink, rises again, spinning, into a blurred

220

pillar or a tornado, her arms going above her head and her hands like the eye of a needle. Then suddenly: stop. Hiss of ice shavings, stopped. We clap our mittens. Her hood has slipped off and her hair is spread across her shoulders like when she's reading in bed, and she takes white breaths with her teeth showing and her pink mouth smiling. She squints over our heads. Dad is way off at the car, unlacing his skates on the tailgate but he doesn't turn. Mum's face means that it's time to go.

Chicky stands in the front seat leaning against Dad. Our parkas crinkle in the cold car. Sherman has been chewing on his thumb and it's a pointed black witch's hat. A rumble goes through the car like a monster growl and before we back up Dad lifts Chicky and sets him leaning against Mum instead.

The speed bumps are marked with yellow stripes and it's like sea serpents have crawled under the tar. When we bounce, Mum says, "Thank-you-Ma'am" with a lilt in her voice. If it was only Mum, the radio would be on and she'd turn it up on the good ones. Dad snaps it off because there's enough racket already. He used to listen to opera when he got home from work but not anymore. Now we give him hard hugs and he changes upstairs then goes into the TV room to the same place on the couch, propping his book on his crossed knees and reaching for his drink without looking up. At supper, he comes in for a handful of onion-flavored bacon crisps or a dish of miniature corn-on-the-cobs pickled. Mum keeps us in the kitchen longer so he can have a little peace and quiet. Ask him what he wants for Christmas and he'll say *No more arguing*. When Mum clears our plates, she takes a bite of someone's hot dog or a quick spoonful of peas before dumping the rest down the pig.

In the car, we ask Dad if we can stop at Shucker's for candy. When he doesn't answer, it means *No*. Mum's eyes mean *Not today*. She says, "It's treat night anyway." Treats are ginger ale and vanilla ice cream.

On Sunday nights we have treats and BLTs and get to watch Ted Mack and Ed Sullivan. There are circus people on almost every time, doing cartwheels or flips or balancing. We stand up in our socks and try some of it. Delilah does an imitation of Elvis by making jump rope handles into a microphone. Girls come on with silver shoes and their stomachs showing and do clappity tap dances. "That's a cinch," says Mum behind us.

"Let's see you then," we say and she goes over to the brick in

221

front of the fireplace to show us. She bangs the floor with her sneakers, pumping and kicking, thudding her heels in smacks, not like clicking at all, swinging her arms out in front of her like she's wading through the jungle. She speeds up, staring straight at Dad who's reading his book, making us laugh even harder. He's always like that. Sometimes for no reason, he'll snap out of it going, "What? What? What's all this? What's going on?" as if he's emerged from a dark tunnel, looking like he does when we wake him up and he hasn't put on his glasses yet, sort of angry. He sits there before dinner, popping black olives into his mouth one at a time, eyes never leaving his book. His huge glass mug is from college and in the lamplight you can see the liquid separate. One layer is beer, the rest is gin. Even smelling it makes you gag.

Dad would never take us to Shucker's for candy. With him, we do things outside. If there's a storm we go down to the rocks to see the waves—you have to yell—and get sopped. Or if Mum needs a nap, we go to the beach. In the spring it's wild and windy as anything, which I love. The wind presses against you and you kind of choke but in a good way. Sherman and I run, run, run! Couples at the end are so far away you can hardly tell they're moving. Rummy races around with other dogs, flipping his rear like a goldfish, snapping at the air, or careening in big looping circles across the beach. Caitlin jabs a stick into the wet part and draws flowers. Chicky smells the seaweed by smushing it all over his face. Delilah's dark bangs jitter across her forehead like magnets and she yells back to Gus lagging behind. Dad looks at things far away. He points out birds—a great blue heron near the breakers as thin as a safety pin or an osprey in the sky, tilting like a paper cutout. We collect little things. Delilah holds out a razor shell on one sandy palm for Dad to take and he says *Uh-huh* and calls Rummy. When Sherman, grinning, carries a dead seagull to him, Dad says, "Cut that out." Once in Maine, I found a triangle of blue and white china and showed it to Dad. "Ah, yes, a bit of crockery," he said.

"Do you think it's from the Indians?" I whispered. They had made the arrowheads we found on the beach.

"I think it's probably debris," he said and handed it back to me. According to Mum, debris is the same thing as litter, as in Don't Be a Litter Bug.

When we get home from skating, it's already started to get dark.

Sherman runs up first and beats us to the door but can't open it himself. We are all used to how warm it was in the car so everybody's going *Brrrr,* or *Hurry up,* banging our feet on the porch so it thunders. The sky is dark blue glass and the railing seems whiter and the fur on Mum's hood glows. From the driveway Dad yells, "I'm going downtown. Be right back," slamming the door and starting the car again.

Delilah yells, "Can I come?" and Gus goes, "Me too!" as we watch the car back up.

"Right back," says his deep voice through the crack in the window and he rounds the side of the house.

"How come he didn't stop on the way home?" asks Caitlin, sticking out her chin.

"Yah," says Delilah. "How come?" We look at Mum.

She kicks the door with her boot. "In we go, Totsies," she says instead of answering and drops someone's skate on the porch because she's carrying so much stuff.

Gus gets in a bad mood, standing by the door with his coat on, not moving a muscle. His hat has flaps over the ears. Delilah flops onto the hall sofa, her neck bent, ramming her chin into her chest. "Why don't you take off your coat and stay awhile?" she says, drumming her fingers as slow as a spider on her stomach.

"I don't have to."

"Yah," Sherman butts in. "Who says you're the boss?" He's lying on the marble tile with Rummy, scissor-kicking his legs like windshield wipers.

"No one," says Delilah, her fingers rippling along.

On the piano bench, Caitlin is picking at her split ends. We can hear Mum in the kitchen putting the dishes away.

Banging on the piano fast because she knows it by heart, Caitlin plays "Walking in a Winter Wonderland." Delilah sits up and imitates her behind her back, shifting her hips from side to side, making us all laugh. Caitlin whips around, "What?"

"Nothing." But we can't help laughing.

"Nothing what?" says Mum coming around the corner, picking up mittens and socks from the floor, snapping on the lights.

Delilah stiffens her legs. "We weren't doing anything," she says.

We make room for Mum on the couch and huddle. Gus perches at the edge, sideways.

"When's Dad coming back?" he says.

"You know your father," says Mum vaguely, smoothing Delilah's hair on her lap, daydreaming at the floor but thinking about something. When Dad goes to the store, he only gets one thing, like a can of black bean soup or watermelon rind.

"What shall we play?" says Sherman, strangling Rummy in a hug.

"Yah. Yah. Let's do something," we say and turn to Mum.

She narrows her eyes into spying slits. "All rightee. I might have a little idea."

"What?" we all shout, excited. "What?" Mum hardly ever plays with us because she has to do everything else.

She rises, slowly, lifting her eyebrows, hinting. "You'll see."

"What?" says Gus and his bottom lip loosens nervously.

Delilah's dark eyes flash like jumping beans. "Yah, Mum. What?"

"Just come with me," says Mum in a singsong and we scamper after her. At the bottom of the stairs, she crouches in the middle of us. Upstairs behind her, it's dark.

"Where are we going?" asks Caitlin and everybody watches Mum's face, thinking of the darkness up there.

"Hee hee hee," she says in her witch voice. "We're going to surprise your father, play a little trick."

"What?" asks Caitlin again, getting ready to worry but Mum's already creeping up the stairs so we follow, going one mile per hour like her, not making a peep even though there's no one in the house to hear us.

Suddenly she wheels around. "We're going to hide," she cackles.

"Where?" we all want to know, sneaking along like burglars.

Her voice is hushed. "Just come with me."

At the top of the stairs it is dark and we whisper.

"How about your room?" says Delilah. "Maybe under the bed."

"No," says Sherman breathlessly. "In the fireplace." We all laugh because we could never fit in there.

Standing in the hall, Mum opens the door to the linen closet and pulls the light string. "How about right here?" The light falls across our faces. On the shelves are stacks of bed covers and rolled puffs, red and white striped sheets and pink towels, everything clean and folded and smelling of soap.

All of a sudden Caitlin gasps, "Wait—I hear the car!"

Quickly we all jumble and scramble around, bumbling and

knocking and trying to cram ourselves inside. Sherman makes whimpering noises like an excited dog. *Sshhh,* we say or *Hurry Hurry,* or *Wait.* I knee up to a top shelf and Sherman gets a boost after me and then Delilah comes grunting up. We play in here sometimes. Gus and Chicky crawl into the shelf underneath, wedging themselves in sideways. Caitlin half-sits on molding with her legs dangling and one hand braced against the door frame. When the rushing settles, Mum pulls out the light and hikes herself up on the other ledge. Everyone is off the ground then, and quiet.

Delilah giggles. Caitlin says *Ssshhhh* and I say *Come on* in a whisper. Only when Mum says *Hush* do we all stop and listen. Everyone is breathing; a shelf creaks. Chicky knocks a towel off and it hits the ground like a pillow. Gus says, "I don't hear anything." *Sshhh,* we say. Mum touches the door and light widens and we listen. Nothing.

"False alarm," says Sherman.

Our eyes start to get used to the dark. Next to me Delilah gurgles her spit.

"What do you think he'll do?" whispers Caitlin. We all smile, curled up in the darkness with Mum thinking how fooled he'll be, coming back and not a soul anywhere, standing in the hall with all the lights glaring not hearing a sound.

"Where will he think we've gone?" We picture him looking around for a long time, till finally we all pour out of the closet.

"He'll find out," Mum whispers. Someone laughs at the back of his throat, like a cricket quietly ticking.

Delilah hisses, "Wait—"

"Forget it," says Caitlin who knows it's a false alarm.

"What will he do?" we ask Mum.

She's in the darkest part of the closet, on the other side of the light slant. We hear her voice. "We'll see."

"My foot's completely fallen asleep," says Caitlin.

"Kick it," says Mum's voice.

"Ssshhh," lisps Chicky and we laugh at him copying everybody.

Gus's muffled voice comes from under the shelf. "My head's getting squished."

"Move it," says Delilah.

"Quiet!"

And then we really do hear the car.

225

"Silence, Monkeys," says Mum and we all hush, holding our breaths. The car hums up the hill.

The motor dies and the car shuts off. We hear the door crack, then clip shut. Footsteps bang up the echoing porch, loud, toe-hard and scuffing. The glass panes rattle when the door opens, resounding in the empty hall, and then the door slams in the dead quiet, reverberating through the whole side of the house. Some-one in the closet squeaks like a hamster. Downstairs there isn't a sound.

"Anybody home?" he bellows, and we try not to giggle.

Now what will he do? He strides across the deep hall, going by the foot of the stairs, obviously wondering where everybody's gone, stopping at the hooks to hang up his parka.

"What's he doing?" whispers Caitlin to herself.

"He's by the mitten basket," says Sherman. We all have smiles, our teeth like watermelon wedges, grinning in the dark.

He yells toward the kitchen, "Hello?" and we hunch our shoulders to keep from laughing, holding onto something tight like our toes or the shelf, or biting the side of our mouths.

He starts back into the hall.

"He's getting warmer," whispers Mum's voice, far away. We all wait for his footsteps on the stairs.

But he stops by the TV room doorway. We hear him rustling something, a paper bag, taking out what he's bought, the bag crinkling, setting something down on the hall table, then crum-pling up the bag and pitching it in the wastebasket. Gus says, "Why doesn't he—?" *Ssshhh*, says Mum like spitting and we all freeze. He moves again—his footsteps turn and bang on the hollow threshold into the TV room where the rug pads the sound.

Next we hear the TV click on, the sound swelling and the dial switching *tick-ah tikka tikka tick* till it lands on a crowd roar, a football game. We can hear the announcer's voice and the hiss-breath behind it of cheering.

Then it's the only sound in the house.

"What do we do now?" says Delilah only half-whispering. Mum slips down from her shelf and her legs appear in the light, touching down.

Still hushed, Sherman goes, "Let's keep hiding."

The loud thud is from Caitlin jumping down. She uses her regular voice. "Forget it. I'm sick of this anyway." Everyone starts

226

to rustle. Chicky panics, "I can't get down" as if we're about to desert him.

"Stop being such a baby," says Delilah, disgusted.

Mum doesn't say anything, just opens the door all the way. Past the banister in the hall it is yellow and bright. We climb out of the closet, feet-feeling our way down backwards, bumping out one at a time, knocking down blankets and washcloths by mistake. Mum guides our backs and checks our landings. We don't leave the narrow hallway. The light from downstairs shines up through the railing and casts shadows on the wall—bars of light and dark like a fence. Standing in it we have stripes all over us. *Hey look*, we say whispering, with the football drone in the background, even though this isn't anything new—we always see this, holding out your arms and seeing the stripes. Lingering near the linen closet we wait. Mum picks up the tumbled things, restacking the stuff we knocked down, folding things, clinching a towel with her chin, smoothing it over her stomach and then matching the corners left and right, like crossing herself, patting everything into neat piles. The light gets like this every night after we've gone to bed and we creep into the hall to listen to Mum and Dad downstairs. The bands of shadows go across our nightgowns and pajamas and we press our foreheads against the railing trying to hear the mumbling of what Mum and Dad are saying down there. Then we hear the deep boom of Dad clearing his throat and look up at Mum. Though she is turned away, we can still see the wince on her face like when you are waiting to be hit or right after you have been. So we keep standing there, our hearts pounding, waving our hands through the flickered stripes, suddenly interested the way you get when it's time to take a bath and you are mesmerized by something. We're stalling, waiting for Mum to finish folding, waiting to see what she's going to do next because we don't want to go downstairs yet, where Dad is, without her.

1984

LAWNS

by MONA SIMPSON

from THE IOWA REVIEW

I STEAL. I've stolen books and money and even letters. Letters
are great. I can't tell you the feeling, walking down the street with
twenty dollars in my purse, stolen earrings in my pocket. I don't
get caught. That's the amazing thing. You're out on the sidewalk,
other people all around, shopping, walking, and you've got it.
You're out of the store, you've done this thing you're not supposed
to do, but no one stops you. At first it's a rush. Like you're even for
everything you didn't get before. But then you're left alone, no
one even notices you. Nothing changes.

I work in the mailroom of my dormitory, Saturday mornings. I
sort mail, put the letters in these long narrow cubbyholes. The
insides of mailboxes. It's cool there when I stick in my arm.

I've stolen cash—these crisp, crackling, brand new twenty-
dollar bills the fathers and grandmothers send, sealed up in sheets
of wax paper. Once I got a fifty. I've stolen presents, too. I got a
sweater and a football. I didn't want the football, but after the
package was messed up on the mail table, I had no choice, I had to
take the whole thing in my daypack and throw it out on the other
side of campus. I found a covered garbage can. It was miles away.
Brand new football.

Mostly, what I take are cookies. No evidence. They're edible. I
can spot the coffee cans of chocolate chip. You can smell it right
through the wrapping. A cool smell, like the inside of a pantry.
Sometimes I eat straight through a can during just my shift.

Tampering with the United States mail is a Federal Crime, I
know. Listen, let me tell you, I know. I got a summons in my

mailbox to go to the Employment Office next Wednesday. Sure I'm scared.

The University cops want to talk to me. Great. They think, suspect is the word they use, that one of us is throwing out mail instead of sorting it. Wonder who? Us is the others. I'm not the only sorter. I just work Saturdays, mail comes, you know, six days a week in this country. They'll never guess it's me.

They say this in the letter, they think it's out of LAZINESS. Wanting to hurry up and get done, not spend the time. But I don't hurry. I'm really patient on Saturday mornings. I leave my dorm early, while Lauren's still asleep, I open the mailroom—it's this heavy door and I have my own key. When I get there, two bags are already on the table, sagging, waiting for me. Two old ladies. One's packages, one's mail. There's a small key opens the bank of doors, the little boxes from the inside. Through the glass part of every mail slot, I can see. The astroturf field across the street over the parking lot, it's this light green. I watch the sky go from black to grey to blue while I'm there. Some days just stay foggy. Those are the best. I bring a cup of coffee in with me from the vending machine—don't want to wake Lauren up—and I get there at like seven-thirty or eight o'clock. I don't mind it then, my whole dorm's asleep. When I walk out it's as quiet as a football game day. It's eleven or twelve when you know everyone's up and walking that it gets bad being down there. That's why I start early. But I don't rush.

Once you open a letter, you can't just put it in a mailbox. The person's gonna say something. So I stash them in my pack and throw them out. Just people I know. Susan Brown, I open, Annie Larsen, Larry Helprin. All the popular kids from my high school. These are kids who drove places together, took vacations, they all ski, they went to the prom in one big group. At morning nutrition—nutrition, it's your break at ten o'clock for donuts and stuff. California State law, you have to have it.

They used to meet outside on the far end of the math patio, all in one group. Some of them smoked. I've seen them look at each other, concerned at ten in the morning. One touched the inside of another's wrist, like grown-ups in trouble.

And now I know. Everything I thought those three years, worst years of my life, turns out to be true. The ones here get letters. Keri's at Santa Cruz, Lilly's in San Diego, Kevin's at Harvard and

Beth's at Stanford. And like from families, their letters talk about problems. They're each other's main lives. You always knew, looking at them in high school, they weren't just kids who had fun. They cared. They cared about things.

They're all worried about Lilly now. Larry and Annie are flying down to talk her into staying at school.

I saw Glenn the day I came to Berkeley. I was all unpacked and I was standing there leaning into the window of my father's car, saying "Smile, Dad, jeez, at least try, would you?" He was crying because he was leaving. I'm thinking oh, my god, some of these other kids, carrying in their trunks and backpacks are gonna see him, and then finally, he drives away and I was sad. That was the moment I was waiting for, him gone and me alone and there it was and I was sad. I took a walk through campus and I'd been walking for almost an hour and then I see Glenn, coming down on a little hill by the infirmary, riding on one of those lawn mowers you sit on, with grass flying out of the side and he's smiling. Not at me but just smiling. Clouds and sky behind his hair, half of Tamalpais gone in fog. He was wearing this bright orange vest and I thought, fall's coming.

I saw him that night again in our dorm cafeteria. This's the first time I've been in love. I worry. I'm a bad person, but Glenn's the perfect guy, I mean for me at least, and he thinks he loves me and I've got to keep him from finding out about me. I'll die before I'll tell him. Glenn, OK, Glenn. He looks like Mick Jagger, but sweet, ten times sweeter. He looks like he's about ten years old. His father's a doctor over at UC Med. Gynecological surgeon.

First time we got together, a whole bunch of us were in Glenn's room drinking beer, Glenn and his roommate collect beer cans, they have them stacked up, we're watching TV and finally everybody else leaves. There's nothing on but those grey lines and Glenn turns over on his bed and asks me if I'd rub his back.

I couldn't believe this was happening to me. In high school, I was always ending up with the wrong guys, never the one I wanted. But I wanted it to be Glenn and I knew it was going to happen, I knew I didn't have to do anything. I just had to stay there. It would happen. I was sitting on his rear end, rubbing his back, going under his shirt with my hands. His back felt so good, it was smooth and warm, like cement around a pool.

All of a sudden, I was worried about my breath and what I

smelled like. When I turned fourteen or fifteen, my father told me once that I didn't smell good. I slugged him when he said that and didn't talk to him for days, not that I cared about what I smelled like with my father. He was happy, though, kind of, that he could hurt me. That was the last time, though, I'll tell you.

Glenn's face was down in the pillow. I tried to sniff myself but I couldn't tell anything. And it went all right anyway.

I don't open Glenn's letters but I touch them. I hold them and smell them—none of his mail has any smell.

He doesn't get many letters. His parents live across the Bay in Marin County, they don't write. He gets letters from his grandmother in Michigan, plain, even handwriting on regular envelopes, a sticker with her return address printed on it, Rural Route #3, Guns Street. See, I got it memorized.

And he gets letters from Diane, Di, they call her. High school girlfriend. Has a pushy mother, wants her to be a scientist, but she already got a C in Chem 1A. I got an A +, not to brag. He never slept with her, though, she wouldn't, she's still a virgin down in San Diego. With Lilly. Maybe they even know each other.

Glenn and Di were popular kids in their high school. Redwood High. Now I'm one because of Glenn, popular. Because I'm his girlfriend, I know that's why. Not 'cause of me. I just know, OK, I'm not going to start fooling myself now. Please.

Her letters I hold up to the light, they've got florescent lights in there. She's supposed to be blonde, you know, and pretty. Quiet. The soft type. And the envelopes. She writes on these sheer cream-colored envelopes and they get transparent and I can see her writing underneath, but not enough to read what it says, it's like those hockey lines painted under layers of ice.

I run my tongue along the place where his grandmother sealed the letter. A sharp, sweet gummy taste. Once I cut my tongue. That's what keeps me going to the bottom of the bag, I'm always wondering if there'll be a letter for Glenn. He doesn't get one every week. It's like a treasure. Cracker Jack prize. But I'd never open Glenn's mail. I kiss all four corners where his fingers will touch, opening it, before I put it in his box. Sometimes I hold them up and blow on it.

I brought home cookies for Lauren and me. Just a present. We'll eat 'em or Glenn'll eat 'em. I'll throw them out for all I care.

231

They're chocolate chip with pecans. This was one good mother. A lucky can. I brought us coffee, too. I *bought* it.

Yeah, OK, so I'm in trouble. Wednesday, at ten-thirty, I got this notice I was supposed to appear. I had a class, Chem 1C, pre-med staple. Your critical thing. I never missed it before. I told Glenn I had a doctor's appointment.

OK, so I skip it anyway and I walk into this room and there's these two other guys, all work in the mailroom doing what I do, sorting. And we all sit there on chairs on this green carpet. I was staring at everybody's shoes. And there's a cop. University cop, I don't know what's the difference. He had this sagging, pear-shaped body. Like what my dad would have if he were fat, but he's not, he's thin. He walks slowly on the carpeting, his fingers hooked in his belt loops. I was watching his hips.

Anyway, he's accusing us all and he's trying to get one of us to admit we did it. No way.

"I hope one of you will come to me and tell the truth. Not a one of you knows anything about this? Come on, now."

I shake my head no and stare down at the three pairs of shoes. He says they're not going to do anything to the person who did it, right, wanna make a bet, they say they just want to know, but they'll take it back as soon as you tell them.

I don't care why I don't believe him. I know one thing for sure and that's they're not going to do anything to me as long as I say, NO, I didn't do it. That's what I said, no, I didn't do it, I don't know a thing about it. I just can't imagine where those missing packages could have gone, how letters got into garbage cans. Awful. I just don't know.

The cop had a map with Xs on it every place they found mail. The garbage cans. He said there was a group of students trying to get an investigation. People's girlfriends sent cookies that never got here. Letters were missing. Money. These students put up xeroxed posters on bulletin boards showing a garbage can stuffed with letters.

Why should I tell them, so they can throw me in jail? And kick me out of school? Four-point-oh average and I'm going to let them kick me out of school? They're sitting there telling us it's a felony. A Federal Crime. No way, I'm gonna go to medical school.

This tall, skinny guy with a blonde mustache, Wallabees, looks kind of like a rabbit, he defended us. He's another sorter, works Monday/Wednesdays.

"We all do our jobs," he says. "None of us would do that." The rabbity guy looks at me and the other girl, for support. So we're going to stick together. The other girl, a dark blonde, chewing her lip, nodded. I loved that rabbity guy that second. I nodded too.

The cop looked down. Wide hips in the coffee-with-milk-colored pants. He sighed. I looked up at the rabbity guy. They let us all go.

I'm just going to keep saying no, not me, didn't do it and I just won't do it again. That's all. Won't do it anymore. So, this is Glenn's last chance for homemade cookies. I'm sure as hell not going to bake any.

I signed the form, said I didn't do it, I'm OK now. I'm safe. It turned out OK after all, it always does. I always think something terrible's going to happen and it doesn't. I'm lucky.

I'm afraid of cops. I was walking, just a little while ago, today, down Telegraph with Glenn, and these two policemen, not the one I'd met, other policemen, were coming in our direction. I started sweating a lot. I was sure until they passed us, I was sure it was all over, they were there for me. I always think that. But at the same time, I know it's just my imagination. I mean, I'm a four-point-oh student, I'm a nice girl just walking down the street with my boyfriend.

We were on our way to get Happy Burgers. When we turned the corner, about a block past the cops, I looked at Glenn and I was flooded with like this feeling. It was raining a little and we were by People's Park. The trees were blowing and I was looking at all those little gardens coming up, held together with stakes and white string.

I wanted to say something to Glenn, give him something. I wanted to tell him something about me.

"I'm bad in bed," that's what I said, I just blurted it out like that. He just kind of looked at me, he was nervous, he just giggled. He didn't know what to say, I guess, but he sort of slung his arm around me and I was so grateful and then we went in. He paid for my Happy Burger, I usually don't let him pay for me, but I did and it was the best goddamn hamburger I've ever eaten.

I want to tell him things.

I lie all the time, always have, but I keep track of each lie I've ever told Glenn and I'm always thinking of the things I can't tell him.

Glenn was a screwed up kid, kind of. He used to go in his

backyard, his parents were inside the house I guess, and he'd find this big stick and start twirling around with it. He'd dance, he called it dancing, until if you came up and clapped in front of him, he wouldn't see you. He'd spin around with that stick until he fell down dead on the grass, unconscious, he said he did it to see the sky break up in pieces and spin. He did it sometimes with a tire swing, too. He told me when he was spinning like that, it felt like he was just hearing the earth spinning, that it really went that fast all the time but we just don't feel it. When he was twelve years old or something, his parents took him in the city to a clinic t'see a psychologist. And then he stopped. See, maybe I should go to a psychologist. I'd get better, too. He told me about that in bed one night. The ground feels so good when you fall, he said to me. I loved him for that.

"Does anything feel that good now?" I said.

"Sex sometimes. Maybe dancing."

Know what else he told me that night? He said, right before we went to sleep, he wasn't looking at me, he said he'd been thinking what would happen if I died, he said he thought how he'd be at my funeral, all my family and my friends from high school and my little brother would all be around at the front and he'd be at the edge in the cemetery, nobody'd even know who he was.

I was in that crack, breathing the air between the bed and the wall. Cold and dusty. Yeah, we're having sex. I don't know. It's good. Sweet. He says he loves me. I have to remind myself. I talk to myself in my head while we're doing it. I have to say, it's OK, this is just Glenn, this is who I want it to be and it's just like rubbing next to someone. It's just like pushing two hands together, so there's no air in between.

I cry sometimes with Glenn, I'm so grateful.

My mother called and woke me up this morning. Ms. I'm-going-to-be-perfect. Ms. anything-wrong-is-your-own-fault. Ms. if-anything-bad-happens-you're-a-fool.

She says if she has time, she MIGHT come up and see my dorm room in the next few weeks. Help me organize my wardrobe, she says. She didn't bring me up here, my dad did. I wanted Danny to come along, I love Danny.

But my mother has NO pity. She thinks she's got the answers. She's the one who's a lawyer, she's the one who went back to law

234

school and stayed up late nights studying while she still made our lunch boxes. With gourmet cheese. She's proud of it, she tells you. She loves my dad, I guess. She thinks we're like this great family and she sits there at the dinner table bragging about us, to us. She xeroxed my grade card first quarter with my Chemistry A+ so she's got it in her office and she's got the copy up on the refrigerator at home. She's sitting there telling all her friends that and I'm thinking, you don't know it, but I'm not one of you.

These people across the street from us. Little girl, Sarah, eight years old. Maybe seven. Her dad, he worked for the army, some kind of researcher, he decides he wants to get a sex-change operation. And he goes and does it, over at Stanford. My mom goes out, takes the dog for a walk, right. The mother CONFIDES in her. Says the thing she regrets most is she wants to have more children. The little girl, Sarah, eight years old, looks up at my mom and says, "Daddy's going to be an aunt."

Now that's sad, I think that's really sad. My mom thinks it's a good dinner table story, proving how much better we are than them. Yeah, I remember exactly what she said that night. "That's all Sarah's mother's got to worry about now, is that she wants another child. Meanwhile, Daddy's becoming an aunt."

She should know about me.

So my dad comes to visit for the weekend. Glenn's dad came to speak at UC one night, he took Glenn out to dinner to a nice place, Glenn was glad to see him. Yeah, well. My dad. Comes to the dorm. Skulks around. This guy's a BUSINESSMAN, in a three-piece suit, and he acts inferior to the eighteen-year-old freshmen coming in the lobby. My dad. Makes me sick right now thinking of him standing there in the lobby and everybody seeing him. He was probably looking at the kids and looking jealous. Just standing there. Why? Don't ask me why, he's the one that's forty-two years old.

So he's standing there, nervous, probably sucking his hand, that's what he does when he's nervous, I'm always telling him not to. Finally, somebody takes him to my room. I'm not there, Lauren's gone, and he waits for I don't know how long.

When I come in he's standing with his back to the door looking out the window. I see him and right away I know it's him and I have this urge to tip-toe away and he'll never see me.

My pink sweater, a nice sweater, a sweater I wore a lot in high school was over my chair, hanging on the back of it and my father's got one hand on the sweater shoulder and he's like rubbing the other hand down an empty arm. He looks up at me, already scared and grateful when I walk into the room. I feel like smashing him with a baseball bat. Why can't he just stand up straight?

I drop my books on the bed and stand there while he hugs me.

"Hi, Daddy, what are you doing here?"

"I wanted to see you." He sits in my chair now, his legs crossed and big, too big for this room, and he's still fingering the arm of my pink sweater. "I missed you so I got away for the weekend," he says. "I have a room up here at the Claremont Hotel."

So he's here for the weekend. He's just sitting in my dorm room and I have to figure out what to do with him. He's not going to do anything. He'd just sit here. And Lauren's coming back soon so I've got to get him out. It's Friday afternoon and the weekend's shot. OK, so I'll go with him. I'll go with him and get it over with.

But I'm not going to miss my date with Glenn Saturday night. No way. I'd die before I'd cancel that. It's bad enough missing dinner in the cafeteria tonight. Friday's eggplant, my favorite, and Friday nights are usually easy, music on the stereos all down the hall. We usually work, but work slow and talk and then we all meet in Glenn's room around ten.

"Come, sit on my lap, honey." My dad like pulls me down and starts bouncing me. BOUNCING ME. I stand up. "OK, we can go somewhere tonight and tomorrow morning, but I have to be back for tomorrow night. I've got plans with people. And I've got to study, too."

"You can bring your books back to the hotel," he says. "I'm supposed to be at a convention in San Francisco, but I wanted to see you. I have work, too, we can call room service and both just work."

"I still have to be back by four tomorrow."

"All right."

"OK, just a minute." And he sat there in my chair while I called Glenn and told him I wouldn't be here for dinner. I pulled the phone out into the hall, it only stretches so far, and whispered. "Yeah, my father's here," I said, "he's got a conference in San Francisco. He just came by."

Glenn lowered his voice, sweet, and said, "Sounds fun."

My dad sat there, hunched over in my chair, while I changed my shirt and put on deodorant. I put a nightgown in my shoulder pack and my toothbrush and I took my chem book and we left. I knew I wouldn't be back for a whole day. I was trying to calm myself thinking, well, it's only one day, that's nothing in my life. The halls were empty, it was five o'clock, five-ten, everyone was down at dinner.

We walk outside and the cafeteria lights are on and I see everyone moving around with their trays. Then my dad picks up my hand.

I yank it out. "Dad," I say, really mean.

"Honey, I'm your father." His voice trails off. "Other girls hold their fathers' hands." It was dark enough for the lights to be on in the cafeteria, but it wasn't really dark out yet. The sky was blue. On the tennis courts on top of the garage, two Chinese guys were playing. I heard that thonk-pong and it sounded so carefree and I just wanted to be them. I'd have even given up Glenn, Glenn-that-I-love-more-than-anything, at that second, I would have given everything up just to be someone else, someone new. I got into the car and slammed the door shut and turned up the heat.

"Should we just go to the hotel and do our work? We can get a nice dinner in the room."

"I'd rather go out," I said, looking down at my hands. He went where I told him. I said the name of the restaurant and gave directions. Chez Panisse and we ordered the most expensive stuff. Appetizers and two desserts just for me. A hundred and twenty bucks for the two of us.

OK, this hotel room.

So, my dad's got the Bridal Suite. He claimed that was all they had. Fat chance. Two-hundred-eighty room hotel and all they've got left is this deal with the canopy bed, no way. It's in the tower, you can almost see it from the dorm. Makes me sick. From the bathroom, there's this window, shaped like an arch, and it looks over all of Berkeley. You can see the bridge lights. As soon as we got there, I locked myself in the bathroom, I was so mad about that canopy bed. I took a long bath and washed my hair. They had little soaps wrapped up there, shampoo, may as well use them, he's paying for it. It's this deep old bathtub and wind was coming in from outside and I felt like that window was just open, no glass, just a hole cut out in the stone.

237

I was thinking of when I was little and what they taught us in catechism. I thought a soul was inside your chest, this long horizontal triangle with rounded edges, made out of some kind of white fog, some kind of gas or vapor. I could be pregnant. I soaped myself all up and rinsed off with cold water. I'm lucky I never got pregnant, really lucky.

Other kids my age, Lauren, everybody, I know things they don't know. I know more for my age. Too much. Like I'm not a virgin. Lots of people are, you'd be surprised. I know about a lot things being wrong and unfair, all kinds of stuff. It's like seeing a UFO, if I ever saw something like that, I'd never tell, I'd wish I'd never seen it.

My dad knocks on the door.

"What do you want?"

"Let me just come in and talk to you while you're in there."

"I'm done, I'll be right out. Just a minute." I took a long time towelling. No hurry, believe me. So I got into bed, with my nightgown on and wet already from my hair. I turned away. Breathed against the wall. "Night."

My father hooks my hair over my ear and touches my shoulder. "Tired?"

I shrug.

"You really have to go back tomorrow? We could go to Marin or to the beach. Anything."

I hugged my knees up under my nightgown. "You should go to your conference, Dad."

I wake up in the middle of the night, I feel something's going on, and sure enough, my dad's down there, he's got my nightgown worked up to like a frill around my neck and my legs hooked over his shoulders.

"Dad, stop it."

"I just wanted to make you feel good," he says and looks up at me. "What's wrong? Don't you love me anymore?"

I never really told anybody. It's not exactly the kind of thing you can bring up over lunch. "So, I'm sleeping with my father. Oh, and let's split a dessert." Right.

I don't know, other people think my dad's handsome. They say he is. My mother thinks so, you should see her traipsing around the balcony when she gets in her romantic moods, which, on her professional lawyer schedule, are about once a year, thank god. It's pathetic. He thinks she's repulsive, though. I don't know that, that's what I think. But he loves me, that's for sure.

So next day, Saturday—that rabbity guy, Paul's his name, he did my shift for me—we go downtown and I got him to buy me this suit. Three hundred dollars from Saks. Oh, and I got shoes. So I stayed later with him because of the clothes, and I was a little happy because I thought at least now I'd have something good to wear with Glenn. My dad and I got brownie sundaes at Sweet Dreams and I got home by five. He was crying when he dropped me off.

"Don't cry, Dad. Please," I said. Jesus, how can you not hate someone who's always begging from you.

Lauren had Poly Styrene on the stereo and a candle lit in our room. I was never so glad to be home.

"Hey," Lauren said. She was on her bed, with her legs propped up on the wall. She'd just shaved. She was rubbing in cream.

I flopped down on my bed. "Ohhhh," I said, grabbing the sides of the mattress.

"Hey, can you keep a secret about what I did today?" Lauren said. "I went to that therapist, up at Cowell."

"You have the greatest legs," I said, quiet. "Why don't you ever wear skirts?"

She stopped what she was doing and stood up. "You think they're good? I don't like the way they look, except in jeans." She looked down at them. "They're crooked, see?" She shook her head. "I don't want to think about it."

Then she went to her dresser and started rolling a joint. "Want some?"

"A little."

She lit up, lay back on her bed and held her arm out for me to come take the joint.

"So, she was this really great woman. Warm, kind of chubby. She knew instantly what kind of man Brent was." Lauren snapped her fingers. "Like that." Brent was the pool man Lauren had an affair with, home in LA.

I'm back in the room maybe an hour, putting on mascara, my jeans are on the bed pressed, and the phone rings and it's my dad and I say, "Listen, just leave me alone."

"You don't care about me anymore."

239

"I just saw you. I have nothing to say. We just saw each other."

"What are you doing tonight?"

"Going out."

"Who are you seeing?"

"Glenn."

He sighs. "So you really like him, huh?"

"Yeah, I do and you should be glad. You should be glad I have a boyfriend." I pull the cord out into the hall and sit down on the floor there. There's this long pause.

"We're not going to end up together, are we?"

I felt like all the air's knocked out of me. I looked out the window and everything looked dead and still. The parked cars. The trees with pink toilet paper strung between the branches. The church all closed up across the street.

"No, we won't, Daddy."

He was crying. "I know, I know."

I hung up the phone and went back and sat in the hall. I'm scared, too. I don't know what'll happen.

I don't know. It's been going on I guess as long as I can remember. I mean, not the sex, but my father. When I was a little kid, tiny little kid, my dad came in before bed and said his prayers with me. He kneeled down by my bed and I was on my back. PRAYERS. He'd lift up my pajama top and put his hands on my breast. Little fried eggs, he said. One time with his tongue. Then one night, he pulled down the elastic of my pajama pants. He did it for an hour and then I came. Don't believe anything they ever tell you about kids not coming. That first time was the biggest I ever had and I didn't even know what it was then. It just kept going and going as if he was breaking me through layers and layers of glass and I felt like I'd slipped and let go and I didn't have myself anymore, he had me, and once I'd slipped like that I'd never be the same again.

We had this sprinkler in our back lawn, Danny and me used to run through it in summer and my dad'd be outside, working on the grass or the hedge or something and he'd squirt us with the hose. I used to wear a bathing suit bottom, no top—we were this modern family, our parents walked around the house naked after showers and then Danny and I ended up both being these modest kids, can't stand anyone to see us even in our underwear, I always dress facing the closet, Lauren teases me. We'd run through the sprinkler and my dad would come up and pat my bottom and the way he put his hand on my thigh, I felt like Danny could tell it was different than the way he touched him, I was like something he owned.

First time when I was nine, I remember, Dad and me were in the shower together. My mom might have even been in the house, they did that kind of stuff, it was supposed to be OK. Anyway, we're in the shower and I remember this look my dad had. Like he was daring me, knowing he knew more than I did. We're both under the shower. The water pasted his hair down on his head and he looked younger and weird. "Touch it. Don't be afraid of it," he says. And he grabs my thighs on the outside and pulls me close to him, pulling on my fat.

He waited till I was twelve to really do it. I don't know if you can call it rape, I was a good sport. The creepy thing is I know how it felt for him, I could see it on his face when he did it. He thought he was getting away with something. We were supposed to go hiking but right away that morning when we got into the car, he knew he was going to do it. He couldn't wait to get going. I said I didn't feel good, I had a cold, I wanted to stay home, but he made me go anyway and we hiked two miles and he set up the tent. He told me to take my clothes off and I undressed just like that, standing there in the woods. He's the one who was nervous and got us into the tent. I looked old for twelve, small but old. And right there on the ground, he spread my legs open and pulled my feet up and fucked me. I bled. I couldn't even breathe the tent was so small. He could have done anything. He could have killed me, he had me alone on this mountain.

I think about that sometimes when I'm alone with Glenn in my bed. It's so easy to hurt people. They just lie there and let you have them. I could reach out and choke Glenn to death, he'd be so shocked, he wouldn't stop me. You can just take what you want.

My dad thought he was getting away with something but he didn't. He was the one that fell in love, not me. And after that day, when we were back in the car, I was the one giving orders. From then on, I got what I wanted. He spent about twice as much money on me as on Danny and everyone knew it, Danny and my mom, too. How do you think I got good clothes and a good bike and a good stereo? My dad's not rich, you know. And I'm the one who got to go away to college even though it killed him. Says it's the saddest thing that ever happened in his life, me going away and leaving him. But when I was a little kid that day, he wasn't in love with me, not like he is now.

Only thing I'm sad about isn't either of my parents, it's Danny. Leaving Danny alone there with them. He used to send Danny out of the house. My mom'd be at work on a Saturday afternoon or something or even in the morning and my dad would kick my little brother out of his own house. Go out and play, Danny. Why doncha catch some rays. And Danny just went and got his glove and baseball from the closet and he'd go and throw it against the house, against the outside wall, in the driveway. I'd be in my room, I'd be like dead, I'd be wood, telling myself this doesn't count, no one has to know, I'll say I'm still a virgin, it's not really happening to me, I'm dead, I'm blank, I'm just letting time stop and pass, and then I'd hear the sock of the ball in the mitt and the slam of the screen door and I knew it was true, it was really happening.

Glenn's the one I want to tell. I can't ever tell Glenn.

I called my mom. Pay phone, collect, hour long call. I don't know, I got real mad last night and I just told her. I thought when I came here, it'd just go away. But it's not going away. It makes me weird with Glenn. In the morning, with Glenn, when it's time to get up, I can't get up. I cry.

I knew it'd be bad. Poor Danny. Well, my mom says she might leave our dad. She cried for an hour, no jokes, on the phone.

How could he DO this to me, she kept yelping. To her. Everything's always to her.

But then she called an hour later, she'd talked to a psychiatrist already, she's kicked Dad out, and she arrives, just arrives here at Berkeley. But she was good. She says she's on my side, she'll help me, I don't know, I felt OK. She stayed in a hotel and she wanted to know if I wanted to stay there with her but I said no, I'd see her more in a week or something, I just wanted to go back to my dorm. She found this group. She says, just in San Jose, there's hundreds of families like ours, yeah, great, that's what I said. But there's groups. She's going to a group of other thick-o mothers like her,

242

these wives who didn't catch on. She wanted me to go to a group of girls, yeah, molested girls, that's what they call them, but I said no, I have friends here already, she can do what she wants.

I talked to my dad, too, that's the sad thing, he feels like he's lost me and he wants to die and I don't know, he doesn't know what he's doing. He called in the middle of the night.

"Just tell me one thing, honey. Please tell me the truth. When did you stop?"

"Dad."

"Because I remember once you said I was the only person who ever understood you."

"I was ten years old."

"OK, OK. I'm sorry."

He didn't want to get off the phone. "You know, I love you, honey. I always will."

"Yeah, well."

My mom's got him lined up for a psychiatrist, too, she says he's lucky she's not sending him to jail. I *am* a lawyer, she keeps saying, as if we could forget. She'd pay for me to go to a shrink now, too, but I said no, forget it.

It's over. Glenn and I are, over. I feel like my dad's lost me everything. I sort of want to die now. I'm telling you I feel terrible. I told Glenn and that's it, it's over. I can't believe it either. Lauren says she's going to hit him.

I told him and we're not seeing each other anymore. Nope. He said he wanted to just think about everything for a few days. He said it had nothing to do with my father but he'd been feeling a little too settled lately. He said we don't have fun anymore, it's always so serious. That was Monday. So every meal after that, I sat with Lauren in the cafeteria and he's there on the other side, messing around with the guys. He sure didn't look like he was in any kind of agony. Wednesday, I saw Glenn over by the window in this food fight, slipping off his chair and I couldn't stand it, I got up and left and went to our room.

But I went and said I wanted to talk to Glenn that night, I didn't even have any dinner, and he said he wanted to be friends. He looked at me funny and I haven't heard from him. It's, I don't know, seven days, eight.

I know there are other guys. I live in a dorm full of them, or half-

243

full of them. Half girls. But I keep thinking of Glenn 'cause of happiness, that's what makes me want to hang onto him.

There was this one morning when we woke up in his room, it was light out already, white light all over the room. We were sticky and warm, the sheet was all tangled. His roommate, this little blonde boy, was still sleeping. I watched his eyes open and he smiled and then he went down the hall to take a shower. Glenn was hugging me and it was nothing unusual, nothing special. We didn't screw. We were just there. We kissed, but slow, the way it is when your mouth is still bad from sleep.

I was happy that morning. I didn't have to do anything. We got dressed, went to breakfast, I don't know. Took a walk. He had to go to work at a certain time and I had that sleepy feeling from waking up with the sun on my head and he said he didn't want to say good-bye to me. There was that pang. One of those looks like as if at that second, we both felt the same way.

I shrugged. I could afford to be casual then. We didn't say good-bye. I walked with him to the shed by the Eucalyptus Grove. That's where they keep all the gardening tools, the rakes, the hoes, the mowers, big bags of grass seed slumped against the wall. It smelled like hay in there. Glenn changed into his uniform and we went to the North Side, up in front of the Chancellor's manor, that thick perfect grass. And Glenn gave me a ride on the lawn mower, on the handlebars. It was bouncing over these little bumps in the lawn and I was hanging onto the handlebars, laughing. I couldn't see Glenn but I knew he was there behind me. I looked around at the buildings and the lawns, there's a fountain there, and one dog was drinking from it.

See, I can't help but remember things like that. Even now, I'd rather find some way, even though he's not asking for it, to forgive Glenn. I'd rather have it work out with him, because I want more days like that. I wish I could have a whole life like that. But I guess nobody does, not just me.

I saw him in the mailroom yesterday, we're both just standing there, each opening our little boxes, getting our mail—neither of us had any—I was hurt but I wanted to reach out and touch his face. He has this hard chin, it's pointy and all bone. Lauren says she wants to hit him.

I mean, I think of him spinning around in his backyard and that's why I love him and he should understand. I go over it all and think

I should have just looked at him and said I can't believe you're doing this to me. Right there in the mailroom. Now when I think that, I think maybe if I'd said that, in those words, maybe it would be different.

But then I think of my father—he feels like there was a time when we had fun, when we were happy together. I mean, I can remember being in my little bed with Dad and maybe cracking jokes, maybe laughing, but he probably never heard Danny's baseball in his mitt the way I did or I don't know. I remember late in the afternoon, wearing my dad's navy blue sweatshirt with a hood and riding bikes with him and Danny down to the diamond.

But that's over. I don't know if I'm sorry it happened. I mean I am, but it happened, that's all. It's just one of the things that happened to me in my life. But I would never go back, never. And what hurts so much is that maybe that's what Glenn is thinking about me.

I told Lauren last night. I had to. She kept asking me what happened with Glenn. She was so good, you couldn't believe it, she was great. We were talking late and this morning we drove down to go to House of Pancakes for breakfast, get something good instead of watery eggs for a change. And on the way, Lauren's driving, she just skids to a stop on this street, in front of this elementary school. "Come on," she says. It's early, but there's already people inside the windows.

We hooked our fingers in the metal fence. You know, one of those aluminum fences around a playground. There were pigeons standing on the painted game circles. Then a bell rang and all these kids came out, yelling, spilling into groups. This was a poor school, mostly black kids, Mexican kids, all in bright colors. There's a Nabisco factory nearby and the whole air smelled like blueberry muffins.

The girls were jumproping and the boys were shoving and running and hanging onto the monkey bars. Lauren pinched her fingers on the back of my neck and pushed my head against the fence.

"Eight years old. Look at them. They're eight years old. One of their fathers is sleeping with one of those girls. Look at her. Do you blame her? Can you blame her? Because if you can forgive her you can forgive yourself."

245

"I'll kill him," I said.

"And I'll kill Glenn," Lauren says.

So we went and got pancakes. And drank coffee until it was time for class.

I saw Glenn yesterday. It was so weird after all this time. I just had lunch with Lauren. We picked up tickets for Talking Heads and I wanted to get back to the lab before class and I'm walking along and Glenn was working, you know, on the lawn in front of the Mobi Building. He was still gorgeous. I was just going to walk, but he yelled over at me.

"Hey, Jenny."

"Hi, Glenn."

He congratulated me, he heard about the NSF thing. We stood there. He has another girlfriend now. I don't know, when I looked at him and stood there by the lawnmower, it's chugging away, I felt the same as I always used to, that I loved him and all that, but he might just be one of those things you can't have. Like I should have been for my father and look at him now. Oh, I think he's better, they're all better, but I'm gone, he'll never have me again.

I'm glad they're there and I'm here, but it's strange, I feel more alone now. Glenn looked down at the little pile of grass by the lawnmower and said, "Well, Kid, take care of yourself," and I said, "You too, bye," and started walking.

So, you know what's bad, though, I started taking stuff again. Little stuff from the mailroom. No packages and not people I know anymore.

But I take one letter a Saturday, I make it just one and someone I don't know. And I keep 'em and burn 'em with a match in the bathroom sink and wash the ashes down the drain. I wait until the end of the shift. I always expect it to be something exciting. The two so far were just everyday letters, just mundane, so that's all that's new, I-had-a-porkchop-for-dinner letters.

But something happened today. I was in 'the middle, three-quarters way down the bag, still looking, I hadn't picked my letter for the day, I'm being really stern, I really mean just one, no more, and there's this little white envelope addressed to me. I sit there, trembling with it in my hand. It's the first one I've gotten all year. It was my name and address, typed out, and I just stared at it. There's no address. I got so nervous, I thought maybe it was from

Glenn, of course. I wanted it to be from Glenn so bad, but then I knew it couldn't be, he's got that new girlfriend now, so I threw it in the garbage can right there, one of those with the swinging metal door and then I finished my shift. My hands were sweating, I smudged the writing on one of the envelopes.

So all the letters are in boxes, I clean off the table, fold the bags up neat and close the door, ready to go. And then I thought, I don't have to keep looking at the garbage can, I'm allowed to take it back, that's my letter. And I fished it out, the thing practically lopped my arm off. And I had it and I held it a few minutes, wondering who it was from. Then I put it in my mailbox so I can go like everybody else and get mail.

1986

COMMUNIST

by RICHARD FORD

from ANTAEUS

My mother once had a boyfriend named Glen Baxter. This was in 1961. We—my mother and I—were living in the little house my father had left her up the Sun River, near Victory, Montana, west of Great Falls. My mother was thirty-one at the time. I was sixteen. Glen Baxter was somewhere in the middle, between us, though I cannot be exact about it.

We were living then off the proceeds of my father's life insurance policies, with my mother doing some part-time waitressing work up in Great Falls and going to the bars in the evenings, which I know is where she met Glen Baxter. Sometimes he would come back with her and stay in her room at night, or she would call up from town and explain that she was staying with him in his little place on Lewis Street by the GN yards. She gave me his number every time, but I never called it. I think she probably thought that what she was doing was terrible, but simply couldn't help herself. I thought it was all right, though. Regular life it seemed and still does. She was young, and I knew that even then.

Glen Baxter was a Communist and liked hunting, which he talked about a lot. Pheasants. Ducks. Deer. He killed all of them, he said. He had been to Vietnam as far back as then, and when he was in our house he often talked about shooting the animals over there—monkeys and beautiful parrots—using military guns just for sport. We did not know what Vietnam was then, and Glen, when he talked about that, referred to it only as "the far east." I think now he must've been in the CIA and been disillusioned by something he saw or found out about and had been thrown out, but that kind of thing did not matter to us. He was a tall, dark-eyed man with thick black hair, and was usually in a good humor. He had gone halfway through college in Peoria, Illinois, he said, where he grew up. But when he was around our life he worked wheat farms as a ditcher, and stayed out of work winters and in the bars drinking with women like my mother, who had work and some money. It is not an uncommon life to lead in Montana.

What I want to explain happened in November. We had not been seeing Glen Baxter for some time. Two months had gone by. My mother knew other men, but she came home most days from work and stayed inside watching television in her bedroom and drinking beers. I asked about Glen once, and she said only that she didn't know where he was, and I assumed they had had a fight and that he was gone off on a flyer back to Illinois or Massachusetts, where he said he had relatives. I'll admit that I liked him. He had something on his mind always. He was a labor man as well as a Communist, and liked to say that the country was poisoned by the rich, and strong men would need to bring it to life again, and I liked that because my father had been a labor man, which was why we had a house to live in and money coming through. It was also true that I'd had a few boxing bouts by then—just with town boys and one with an Indian from Choteau—and there were some girlfriends I knew from that. I did not like my mother being around the house so much at night, and I wished Glen Baxter would come back, or that another man would come along and entertain her somewhere else.

At two o'clock on a Saturday, Glen drove up into our yard in a car. He had had a big brown Harley-Davidson that he rode most of the year, in his black-and-red irrigators and a baseball cap turned backwards. But this time he had a car, blue Nash Ambassador. My mother and I went out on the porch when he stopped inside the olive trees my father had planted as a shelter belt, and my mother had a look on her face of not much pleasure. It was starting to be cold in earnest by then. Snow was down already onto the Fairfield Bench, though on this day a chinook was blowing, and it could as easily have been spring, though the sky above the Divide was turning over in silver and blue clouds of winter.

"We haven't seen you in a long time, I guess," my mother said coldly.

"My little retarded sister died," Glen said, standing at the door of his old car. He was wearing his orange VFW jacket and canvas shoes we called wino shoes, something I had never seen him wear before. He seemed to be in a good humor. "We buried her in Florida near the home."

"That's a good place," my mother said in a voice that meant she was a wronged party in something.

"I want to take this boy hunting today, Aileen," Glen said. "There're snow geese down now. But we have to go right away or they'll be gone to Idaho by tomorrow."

"He doesn't care to go," my mother said.

"Yes I do," I said and looked at her.

My mother frowned at me. "Why do you?"

"Why does he need a reason?" Glen Baxter said and grinned.

"I want him to have one, that's why." She looked at me oddly. "I think Glen's drunk, Les."

"No, I'm not drinking," Glen said, which was hardly ever true. He looked at both of us, and my mother bit down on the side of her lower lip and stared at me in a way to make you think she thought something was being put over on her and she didn't like you for it. She was very pretty, though when she was mad her features were sharpened and less pretty by a long way. "All right then, I don't care," she said to no one in particular. "Hunt, kill, maim. Your father did that too." She turned to go back inside.

"Why don't you come with us, Aileen?" Glen was smiling still, pleased.

"To do what?" my mother said. She stopped and pulled a package of cigarettes out of her dress pocket and put one in her mouth.

"It's worth seeing."

"See dead animals?" my mother said.

"These geese are from Siberia, Aileen," Glen said. "They're not like a lot of geese. Maybe I'll buy us dinner later. What do you say?"

"Buy what with?" my mother said. To tell the truth, I didn't know why she was so mad at him. I would've thought she'd be glad to see him. But she just suddenly seemed to hate everything about him.

"I've got some money," Glen said. "Let me spend it on a pretty girl tonight."

250

"Find one of those and you're lucky," my mother said, turning away toward the front door.

"I already found one," Glen Baxter said. But the door slammed behind her, and he looked at me then with a look I think now was helplessness, though I could not see a way to change anything.

My mother sat in the back seat of Glen's Nash and looked out the window while we drove. My double gun was in the seat between us beside Glen's Belgian pump, which he kept loaded with five shells in case, he said, he saw something beside the road he wanted to shoot. I had hunted rabbits before, and had ground-sluiced pheasants and other birds, but I had never been on an actual hunt before, one where you drove out to some special place and did it formally. And I was excited. I had a feeling that something important was about to happen to me and that this would be a day I would always remember.

My mother did not say anything for a long time, and neither did I. We drove up through Great Falls and out the other side toward Fort Benton, which was on the benchland where wheat was grown.

"Geese mate for life," my mother said, just out of the blue, as we were driving. "I hope you know that. They're special birds."

"I know that," Glen said in the front seat. "I have every respect for them."

"So where were you for three months?" she said. "I'm only curious."

"I was in the Big Hole for a while," Glen said, "and after that I went over to Douglas, Wyoming."

"What were you planning to do there?" my mother asked.

"I wanted to find a job, but it didn't work out."

"I'm going to college," she said suddenly, and this was something I had never heard about before. I turned to look at her, but she was staring out her window and wouldn't see me.

"I knew French once," Glen said. "Rose's pink. Rouge's red." He glanced at me and smiled. "I think that's a wise idea, Aileen. When are you going to start?"

"I don't want Les to think he was raised by crazy people all his life," my mother said.

"Les ought to go himself," Glen said.

"After I go, he will."

251

"What do you say about that, Les?" Glen said, grinning.

"He says it's just fine," my mother said.

"It's just fine," I said.

Where Glen Baxter took us was out onto the high flat prairie that was disked for wheat and had high, high mountains out to the east, with lower heartbreak hills in between. It was, I remember, a day for blues in the sky, and down in the distance we could see the small town of Floweree and the state highway running past it toward Fort Benton and the high line. We drove out on top of the prairie on a muddy dirt road fenced on both sides, until we had gone about three miles, which is where Glen stopped.

"All right," he said, looking up in the rearview mirror at my mother. "You wouldn't think there was anything here, would you?"

"*We're* here," my mother said. "You brought us here."

"You'll be glad though," Glen said, and seemed confident to me. I had looked around myself but could not see anything. No water or trees, nothing that seemed like a good place to hunt anything. Just wasted land. "There's a big lake out there, Les," Glen said. "You can't see it now from here because it's low. But the geese are there. You'll see."

"It's like the moon out here, I recognize that," my mother said, "only it's worse." She was staring out at the flat, disked wheatland as if she could actually see something in particular and wanted to know more about it. "How'd you find this place?"

"I came once on the wheat push," Glen said.

"And I'm sure the owner told you just to come back and hunt any time you like and bring anybody you wanted. Come one, come all. Is that it?"

"People shouldn't own land anyway," Glen said. "Anybody should be able to use it."

"Les, Glen's going to poach here," my mother said. "I just want you to know that, because that's a crime and the law will get you for it. If you're a man now, you're going to have to face the consequences."

"That's not true," Glen Baxter said, and looked gloomily out over the steering wheel down the muddy road toward the mountains. Though for myself I believed it was true, and didn't care. I didn't care about anything at that moment except seeing geese fly over me and shooting them down.

"Well, I'm certainly not going out there," my mother said. "I like towns better, and I already have enough trouble."

"That's okay," Glen said. "When the geese lift up you'll get to see them. That's all I wanted. Les and me'll go shoot them, won't we, Les?"

"Yes," I said, and I put my hand on my shotgun, which had been my father's and was heavy as rocks.

"Then we should go on," Glen said, "or we'll waste our light."

We got out of the car with our guns. Glen took off his canvas shoes and put on his pair of black irrigators out of the trunk. Then we crossed the barbed-wire fence and walked out into the high, tilled field toward nothing. I looked back at my mother when we were still not so far away, but I could only see the small, dark top of her head, low in the back seat of the Nash, staring out and thinking what I could not then begin to say.

On the walk toward the lake, Glen began talking to me. I had never been alone with him and knew little about him except what my mother said—that he drank too much, or other times that he was the nicest man she had ever known in the world and that some day a woman would marry him, though she didn't think it would be her. Glen told me as we walked that he wished he had finished college, but that it was too late now, that his mind was too old. He said he had liked "the far east" very much, and that people there knew how to treat each other, and that he would go back some day but couldn't go now. He said also that he would like to live in Russia for a while and mentioned the names of people who had gone there, names I didn't know. He said it would be hard at first, because it was so different, but that pretty soon anyone would learn to like it and wouldn't want to live anywhere else, and that Russians treated Americans who came to live there like kings. There were Communists everywhere now, he said. You didn't know them, but they were there. Montana had a large number and he was in touch with all of them. He said that Communists were always in danger and that he had to protect himself all the time. And when he said that he pulled back his VFW jacket and showed me the butt of a pistol he had stuck under his shirt against his bare skin. "There are people who want to kill me right now," he said, "and I would kill a man myself if I thought I had to." And we kept walking. Though in a while he said, "I don't think I know much about you, Les. But I'd like to. What do you like to do?"

"I like to box," I said. "My father did it. It's a good thing to know."

"I suppose you have to protect yourself too," Glen said.

"I know how to," I said.

"Do you like to watch TV?" Glen said, and smiled.

"Not much."

"I love to," Glen said. "I could watch it instead of eating if I had one."

I looked out straight ahead over the green tops of sage that grew at the edge of the disked field, hoping to see the lake Glen said was there. There was an airishness and a sweet smell that I thought might be the place we were going, but I couldn't see it. "How will we hunt these geese?" I said.

"It won't be hard," Glen said. "Most hunting isn't even hunting. It's only shooting. And that's what this will be. In Illinois you would dig holes in the ground to hide in and set out your decoys. Then the geese come to you, over and over again. But we don't have time for that here." He glanced at me. "You have to be sure the first time here."

"How do you know they're here now?" I asked. And I looked toward the Highwood Mountains twenty miles away, half in snow and half dark blue at the bottom. I could see the little town of Floweree then, looking shabby and dimly lighted in the distance. A red bar sign shone. A car moved slowly away from the scattered buildings.

"They always come November first," Glen said.

"Are we going to poach them?"

"Does it make any difference to you?" Glen asked.

"No, it doesn't."

"Well then we aren't," he said.

We walked then for a while without talking. I looked back once to see the Nash far and small in the flat distance. I couldn't see my mother, and I thought that she must've turned on the radio and gone to sleep, which she always did, letting it play all night in her bedroom. Behind the car the sun was nearing the rounded mountains southwest of us, and I knew that when the sun was gone it would be cold. I wished my mother had decided to come along with us, and I thought for a moment of how little I really knew her at all.

Glen walked with me another quarter mile, crossed another barbed-wire fence where sage was growing, then went a hundred yards through wheatgrass and spurge until the ground went up and formed a kind of long hillock bunker built by a farmer against the wind. And I realized the lake was just beyond us. I could hear the sound of a car horn blowing and a dog barking all the way down in the town, then the wind seemed to move and all I could hear then and after then were geese. So many geese, from the sound of them, though I still could not see even one. I stood and listened to the high-pitched shouting sound, a sound I had never heard so close, a sound with size to it—though it was not loud. A sound that meant great numbers and that made your chest rise and your shoulders tighten with expectancy. It was a sound to make you feel separate from it and everything else, as if you were of no importance in the grand scheme of things.

"Do you hear them singing?" Glen asked. He held his hand up to make me stand still. And we both listened. "How many do you think, Les, just hearing?"

"A hundred," I said. "More than a hundred."

"Five thousand," Glen said. "More than you can believe when you see them. Go see."

I put down my gun and on my hands and knees crawled up the earthwork through the wheatgrass and thistle until I could see down to the lake and see the geese. And they were there, like a white bandage laid on the water, wide and long and continuous, a white expanse of snow geese, seventy yards from me, on the bank, but stretching onto the lake, which was large itself—a half mile across, with thick tules on the far side and wild plums farther and the blue mountain behind them.

"Do you see the big raft?" Glen said from below me, in a whisper.

"I see it," I said, still looking. It was such a thing to see, a view I had never seen and have not since.

"Are any on the land?" he said.

"Some are in the wheatgrass," I said, "but most are swimming."

"Good," Glen said. "They'll have to fly. But we can't wait for that now."

And I crawled backwards down the heel of land to where Glen was, and my gun. We were losing our light, and the air was purplish and cooling. I looked toward the car but couldn't see it, and I was no longer sure where it was below the lighted sky.

"Where do they fly to?" I said in a whisper, since I did not want anything to be ruined because of what I did or said. It was important to Glen to shoot the geese, and it was important to me.

"To the wheat," he said. "Or else they leave for good. I wish your mother had come, Les. Now she'll be sorry."

I could hear the geese quarreling and shouting on the lake surface. And I wondered if they knew we were here now. "She might be," I said with my heart pounding, but I didn't think she would be much.

It was a simple plan he had. I would stay behind the bunker, and he would crawl on his belly with his gun through the wheatgrass as near to the geese as he could. Then he would simply stand up and shoot all the ones he could close up, both in the air and on the ground. And when all the others flew up, with luck some would turn toward me as they came into the wind, and then I could shoot them and turn them back to him, and he would shoot them again. He could kill ten, he said, if he was lucky, and I might kill four. It didn't seem hard.

"Don't show them your face," Glen said. "Wait till you think you can touch them, then stand up and shoot. To hesitate is lost in this."

"All right," I said. "I'll try it."

"Shoot one in the head, and then shoot another one," Glen said. "It won't be hard." He patted me on the arm and smiled. Then he took off his VFW jacket and put it on the ground, climbed up the side of the bunker, cradling his shotgun in his arms, and slid on his belly into the dry stalks of yellow grass out of my sight.

Then for the first time in that entire day I was alone. And I didn't mind it. I sat squat down in the grass, loaded my double gun, and took my other two shells out of my pocket to hold. I pushed the safety off and on to see that it was right. The wind rose a little then, scuffed the grass and made me shiver. It was not the warm chinook now, but a wind out of the north, the one geese flew away from if they could.

Then I thought about my mother in the car alone, and how much longer I would stay with her, and what it might mean to her for me to leave. And I wondered when Glen Baxter would die and if someone would kill him, or whether my mother would marry him and how I would feel about it. And though I didn't know why, it occurred to me then that Glen Baxter and I would not be friends when all was said and done, since I didn't care if he ever married my mother or didn't.

Then I thought about boxing and what my father had taught me

256

about it. To tighten your fists hard. To strike out straight from the shoulder and never punch backing up. How to cut a punch by snapping your fist inwards, how to carry your chin low, and to step toward a man when he is falling so you can hit him again. And most important, to keep your eyes open when you are hitting in the face and causing damage, because you need to see what you're doing to encourage yourself, and because it is when you close your eyes that you stop hitting and get hurt badly. "Fly all over your man, Les," my father said. "When you see your chance, fly on him and hit him till he falls." That, I thought, would always be my attitude in things.

And then I heard the geese again, their voices in unison, louder and shouting, as if the wind had changed and put all new sounds in the cold air. And then a *boom*. And I knew Glen was in among them and had stood up to shoot. The noise of geese rose and grew worse, and my fingers burned where I held my gun too tight to the metal, and I put it down and opened my fist to make the burning stop so I could feel the trigger when the moment came. *Boom*, Glen shot again, and I heard him shuck a shell, and all the sounds out beyond the bunker seemed to be rising—the geese, the shots, the air itself going up. *Boom*, Glen shot another time, and I knew he was taking his careful time to make his shots good. And I held my gun and started to crawl up the bunker so as not to be surprised when the geese came over me and I could shoot.

From the top I saw Glen Baxter alone in the wheat field, shooting at a white goose with black tips of wings that was on the ground not far from him, but trying to run and pull into the air. He shot it once more, and it fell over dead with its wings flapping.

Glen looked back at me and his face was distorted and strange. The air around him was full of white rising geese and he seemed to want them all. "Behind you, Les," he yelled at me and pointed. "They're all behind you now." I looked behind me, and there were geese in the air as far as I could see, more than I knew how many, moving so slowly, their wings wide out and working calmly and filling the air with noise, though their voices were not as loud or as shrill as I had thought they would be. And they were so close! Forty feet, some of them. The air around me vibrated and I could feel the wind from their wings and it seemed to me I could kill as many as the times I could shoot—a hundred or a thousand—and I raised my gun, put the muzzle on the head of a white goose and fired. It shuddered in the air, its wide feet sank below its belly, its wings cradled out to hold back air, and it fell straight down and landed with an awful sound, a noise a human would make, a thick, soft, *hump* noise. I looked up again and shot another goose, could hear the pellets hit its chest, but it didn't fall or even break its pattern for flying. *Boom,* Glen shot again. And then again. "Hey," I heard him shout. "Hey, hey." And there were geese flying over me, flying in line after line. I broke my gun and reloaded, and thought to myself as I did: I need confidence here, I need to be sure with this. I pointed at another goose and shot it in the head, and it fell the way the first one had, wings out, its belly down, and with the same thick noise of hitting. Then I sat down in the grass on the bunker and let geese fly over me.

By now the whole raft was in the air, all of it moving in a slow swirl above me and the lake and everywhere, finding the wind and heading out south in long wavering lines that caught the last sun and turned to silver as they gained a distance. It was a thing to see, I will tell you now. Five thousand white geese all in the air around you, making a noise like you have never heard before. And I thought to myself then: This is something I will never see again. I will never forget this. And I was right.

Glen Baxter shot twice more. One shot missed, but with the other he hit a goose flying away from him and knocked it half-falling and flying into the empty lake not far from shore, where it began to swim as though it was fine and make its noise.

Glen stood in the stubbly grass, looking out at the goose, his gun lowered. "I didn't need to shoot that, did I, Les?"

"I don't know," I said, sitting on the little knoll of land, looking at the goose swimming in the water.

"I don't know why I shoot 'em. They're so beautiful." He looked at me.

"I don't know either," I said.

"Maybe there's nothing else to do with them." Glen stared at the goose again and shook his head. "Maybe this is exactly what they're put on earth for."

I did not know what to say because I did not know what he could mean by that, though what I felt was embarrassment at the great number of geese there were, and a dulled feeling like a hunger because the shooting had stopped and it was over for me now.

Glen began to pick up his geese, and I walked down to my two that had fallen close together and were dead. One had hit with such an impact that its stomach had split and some of its inward parts were knocked out. Though the other looked unhurt, its soft white belly turned up like a pillow, its head and jagged bill-teeth and its tiny black eyes looking as if it were alive.

"What's happened to the hunters out here?" I heard a voice speak. It was my mother, standing in her pink dress on the knoll above us, hugging her arms. She was smiling though she was cold. And I realized that I had lost all thought of her in the shooting. "Who did all this shooting? Is this your work, Les?"

"No," I said.

"Les is a hunter, though, Aileen," Glen said. "He takes his time." He was holding two white geese by their necks, one in each hand, and he was smiling. He and my mother seemed pleased.

"I see you didn't miss too many," my mother said and smiled. I could tell she admired Glen for his geese, and that she had done some thinking in the car alone. "It *was* wonderful, Glen," she said. "I've never seen anything like that. They were like snow."

"It's worth seeing once, isn't it?" Glen said. "I should've killed more, but I got excited."

My mother looked at me then. "Where's yours, Les?"

"Here," I said and pointed to my two geese on the ground beside me.

My mother nodded in a nice way, and I think she liked everything then and wanted the day to turn out right and for all of us to be happy. "Six, then. You've got six in all."

"One's still out there," I said and motioned where the one goose was swimming in circles on the water.

"Okay," my mother said and put her hand over her eyes to look. "Where is it?"

Glen Baxter looked at me then with a strange smile, a smile that said he wished I had never mentioned anything about the other goose. And I wished I hadn't either. I looked up in the sky and could see the lines of geese by the thousands shining silver in the light, and I wished we could just leave and go home.

"That one's my mistake there," Glen Baxter said and grinned. "I shouldn't have shot that one, Aileen. I got too excited."

My mother looked out on the lake for a minute, then looked at Glen and back again. "Poor goose." She shook her head. "How will you get it, Glen?"

"I can't get that one now," Glen said.

My mother looked at him. "What do you mean?" she said.

"I'm going to leave that one," Glen said.

"Well, no. You can't leave one," my mother said. "You shot it. You have to get it. Isn't that a rule?"

"No," Glen said.

And my mother looked from Glen to me. "Wade out and get it, Glen," she said, in a sweet way, and my mother looked young then for some reason, like a young girl, in her flimsy short-sleeved waitress dress, and her skinny, bare legs in the wheatgrass.

"No." Glen Baxter looked down at his gun and shook his head. And I didn't know why he wouldn't go, because it would've been easy. The lake was shallow. And you could tell that anyone could've walked out a long way before it got deep, and Glen had on his boots.

My mother looked at the white goose, which was not more than thirty yards from the shore, its head up, moving in slow circles, its wings settled and relaxed so you could see the black tips. "Wade out and get it, Glenny, won't you please?" she said. "They're special things."

"You don't understand the world, Aileen," Glen said. "This can happen. It doesn't matter."

"But that's so cruel, Glen," she said, and a sweet smile came on her lips.

"Raise up your own arms, Leeny," Glen said. "I can't see any angel's wings, can you Les?" He looked at me, but I looked away.

"Then you go on and get it, Les," my mother said. "You weren't raised by crazy people." I started to go, but Glen Baxter suddenly grabbed me by my shoulder and pulled me back hard, so hard his fingers made bruises in my skin that I saw later.

"Nobody's going," he said. "This is over with now."

And my mother gave Glen a cold look then. "You don't have a heart, Glen," she said. "There's nothing to love in you. You're just a son of a bitch, that's all."

And Glen Baxter nodded at my mother as if he understood something that he had not understood before, but something that he was willing to know. "Fine," he said, "that's fine." And he took his big pistol out from against his belly, the big blue revolver I had only seen part of before and that he said protected him, and he pointed it out at the goose on the water, his arm straight away from him, and shot and missed. And then he shot and missed again. The goose made its noise once. And then he hit it dead, because there was no splash. And then he shot it three times more until the gun was empty and the goose's head was down and it was floating toward the middle of the lake where it was empty and dark blue. "Now who has a heart?" Glen said. But my mother was not there when he turned around. She had already started back to the car and was almost lost from sight in the darkness. And Glen smiled at me then and his face had a wild look on it. "Okay, Les?" he said.

"Okay," I said.

"There're limits to everything, right?"

"I guess so," I said.

"Your mother's a beautiful woman, but she's not the only beautiful woman in Montana." I did not say anything. And Glen Baxter suddenly said, "Here," and he held the pistol out at me. "Don't you want this? Don't you want to shoot me? Nobody thinks they'll die. But I'm ready for it right now." And I did not know what to do then. Though it is true that what I wanted to do was to hit him, hit him as hard in the face as I could, and see him on the ground bleeding and crying and pleading for me to stop. Only at that moment he looked scared to me, and I had never seen a grown man scared before—though I have seen one since—and I felt sorry for him, as though he was already a dead man. And I did not end up hitting him at all.

A light can go out in the heart. All of this went on years ago, but I still can feel now how sad and remote the world was to me. Glen Baxter, I think now, was not a bad man, only a man scared of something he'd never seen before—something soft in himself—his life going a way he didn't like. A woman with a son. Who could blame him there? I don't know what makes people do what they do or call themselves what they call themselves, only that you have to live someone's life to be the expert.

My mother had tried to see the good side of things, tried to be hopeful in the situation she was handed, tried to look out for us both and it hadn't worked. It was a strange time in her life then and after that, a time when she had to adjust to being an adult just when she was on the thin edge of things. Too much awareness too early in life was her problem, I think.

And what I felt was only that I had somehow been pushed out into the world, into the real life then, the one I hadn't lived yet. In a year I was gone to hardrock mining and no-paycheck jobs and not to college. And I have thought more than once about my mother saying that I had not been raised by crazy people, and I don't know what that could mean or what difference it could make, unless it means that love is a reliable commodity, and even that is not always true, as I have found out.

Late on the night that all this took place I was in bed when I heard my mother say, "Come outside, Les. Come and hear this." And I went out onto the front porch barefoot and in my underwear, where it was warm like spring, and there was a spring mist in the air. I could see the lights of the Fairfield Coach in the distance on its way up to Great Falls.

And I could hear geese, white birds in the sky, flying. They made their high-pitched sound like angry yells, and though I couldn't see them high up, it seemed to me they were everywhere. And my mother looked up and said, "Hear them?" I could smell her hair wet from the shower. "They leave with the moon," she said. "It's still half wild out here."

And I said, "I hear them," and I felt a chill come over my bare chest, and the hair stood up on my arms the way it does before a storm. And for a while we listened.

"When I first married your father, you know, we lived on a street called Bluebird Canyon, in California. And I thought that was the prettiest street and the prettiest name. I suppose no one brings you up like your first love. You don't mind if I say that, do you?" She looked at me hopefully.

"No," I said.

"We have to keep civilization alive somehow." And she pulled her little housecoat together because there was a cold vein in the air, a part of the cold that would be on us the next day. "I don't feel part of things tonight, I guess."

"It's all right," I said.

"Do you know where I'd like to go?" she said.

"No," I said. And I suppose I knew she was angry then, angry with life but did not want to show me that.

"To the Straits of Juan de Fuca. Wouldn't that be something? Would you like that?"

"I'd like it," I said. And my mother looked off for a minute, as if she could see the Straits of Juan de Fuca out against the line of mountains, see the lights of things alive and a whole new world.

"I know you liked him," she said after a moment. "You and I both suffer fools too well."

"I didn't like him too much," I said. "I didn't really care."

"He'll fall on his face. I'm sure of that," she said. And I didn't say anything because I didn't care about Glen Baxter anymore, and was happy not to talk about him. "Would you tell me something if I asked you? Would you tell me the truth?"

"Yes," I said.

And my mother did not look at me. "Just tell the truth," she said.

"All right," I said.

"Do you think I'm still very feminine? I'm thirty-two years old now. You don't know what that means. But do you think I am?"

And I stood at the edge of the porch, with the olive trees before me, looking straight up into the mist where I could not see geese but could still hear them flying, could almost feel the air move below their white wings. And I felt the way you feel when you are on a trestle all alone and the train is coming, and you know you have to decide. And I said, "Yes, I do." Because that was the truth. And I tried to think of something else then and did not hear what my mother said after that.

And how old was I then? Sixteen. Sixteen is young, but it can also be a grown man. I am forty-one years old now, and I think about that time without regret, though my mother and I never talked in that way again, and I have not heard her voice now in a long, long time.

1986

263

THE FLOWERS
OF BERMUDA

by D. R. MACDONALD

from SEWANEE REVIEW

In memory of M. D. M.

Bilkie sutherland took the postcard from behind his rubber bib and slowly read the message one more time: "I'm going here soon. I hope your lobsters are plentiful. My best to Bella. God bless you. Yours, Gordon MacLean." Bilkie flipped it over: a washed out photograph in black and white. *The Holy Isle. Iona. Inner Hebrides.* On the land stood stone ruins, no man or woman anywhere, and grim fences of cloud shadowed a dark sea. So this was Iona.

"You want that engine looked at?" Angus Carmichael, in his deepwater boots, was standing on the wharf above Bilkie's boat.

"Not now. I heard from the minister."

"MacLean?"

"He's almost to Iona now."

Angus laughed, working a toothpick around in his teeth. "Man dear, *I've* been to Iona, was there last Sunday." Angus meant where his wife was from, a Cape Breton village with a Highland museum open in the summer.

"It's a very religious place," Bilkie said, ignoring him. "Very ancient, in that way."

"Like you, Bilkie."

"I'm the same as the rest of you."

"No, Bilkie. Sometimes you're not. And neither is your Reverend MacLean."

Angus's discarded toothpick fluttered down to the deck. Bilkie picked it up and dropped it over the side. Angus never cared whether his own deck was flecked with gurry and flies. Nor was he keen on Gordon MacLean. Said the man was after putting in a good word for the Catholics. But that wasn't the minister's point at all. "We're all one faith, if we go back to Iona," is what he'd said. And nothing much more than that.

As Bilkie laid out his gear for the next day's work, he heard singing. No one sang around here anymore. Radios took care of that. He stood up to listen. Ah! It was Johnny, Angus's only boy, home from Dalhousie for the summer. He had a good strong voice, that boy, one they could use over at the church. But you didn't see him there, not since college. No singer himself, Bilkie could appreciate a good tune. His grandfather had worked the schooners in the West Indies trade, and Johnny's song had the flavor of that, of those rolling vessels . . . " 'He could smell the flowers of Bermuda in the gale, when he died on the North Rock Shoal. . . . ' " Bilkie stared into the wet darkness underneath the wharf where pilings were studded with snails. Algae hung like slicked hair on the rocks. He had saved Gordon MacLean under that wharf, when the man was just a tyke. While hunting for eels, Gordon had slipped and fallen, and Bilkie heard his cries and came down along the rocks on the other side to pull him out, a desperate boy clutching for his hand.

Bilkie's car, a big salt-eaten Ford, was parked at the end of the wharf, and whenever he saw it he wished again for horses who could shuck salt like rain. At home the well pump had quit this morning and made him grumpy. He'd had to use the woods, squat out there under a fir, the birds barely stirring overhead, him staring at shoots of Indian Pipe wondering what in hell they lived on, leafless, white as wax, hardly a flower at all. Up by the roadside blue lupines were a little past their prime. What flowers, he wondered, grew on Iona?

The car swayed through rain ruts, past clumps of St. Johnswort (*allas Colmcille* his grandfather had called them) that gave a wild yellow border to the driveway. His house appeared slowly behind a corridor of tall maples. In their long shade red cows rested. Sometimes everything seemed fixed, for good. His animals, his life. But God had taken away his only boy, and Bilkie could not fathom that even yet. For a time he had kept sheep, but quit because killing the lambs bothered him.

Bella was waiting at the front door, not the back, her palm pressed to her face. He stopped shy of the porch, hoping it wasn't a new well-pump they needed.

"What's wrong?"

"Rev. MacLean's been stabbed in Oban," his wife said, her voice thin.

Bilkie repeated the words to himself. There was a swallow's nest above the door. The birds swooped and clamored. "Not there?" he said. "Not in Scotland?" A mist of respect, almost of reverence, hovered over the old country. You didn't get stabbed there.

"Jessie told me on the phone, not a minute ago. Oh, he'll live all right. He's living."

Over supper Bella related what she knew. Gordon MacLean had been walking in Oban, in the evening it was, a woman friend with him. Two young thugs up from Glasgow went for her handbag, right rough about it too. Gordon collared one but the other shoved a knife in his back.

"He's not a big man either," Bilkie said, returning a forkful of boiled potato to his plate. He had known Gordon as a child around the wharf, a little boy who asked hard questions. He had pulled him from the water. He'd seen him go off to seminary, thinking he would never come back to Cape Breton, not to this corner of it, but after awhile he did. To think of him lying in blood, on a sidewalk in Oban. "Did they catch the devils?"

"They did. He'll have to testify."

"What, go back there?"

"When he's able. Be a long time until the trial."

Bilkie felt betrayed. A big stone had slipped somehow out of place. Certain things did not go wrong there, not in the Islands where his people came from. Here, crime was up, too few caring about a day's work, kids scorning church. Greedier now, more for themselves, people were. But knives, what the hell. There in the Hebrides they'd worked things out, hadn't they, over a long span of time? It had seemed to him a place of hard wisdom, hard won. Not a definite place, for he had never been there, but something like stone about it: sea-washed, nicely worn, and high cliffs where waves whitened against the rocks. He knew about the Clearances, yes, about the bad laws that drove his grandfather out of Lewis where he'd lived in a turf house. But even then they weren't knifing people. Gordon MacLean, a minister of God, couldn't return there and come to no harm? To Mull first he'd been headed, to MacLean country. And then to Iona, across a strait not much wider than this one. But a knife stopped him in Oban, a nice sort of town by the sea.

From his parlor window Bilkie could see a bit of the church in the east, the dull white shingles of its steeple above the dark spruce. *We all have Iona inside us,* the man had said. *Our faith was lighted there.* Why then did this happen?

Bilkie had asked such a question before and found no answer. They'd had a son, he and Bella, so he knew about shock, and about grief. Even now, thinking of his son and the schoolhouse could suck the wind right out of him. The boy was born late in their lives anyway, and maybe Bilkie's hopes had come too much to rest in him. Was that the sin? Tormod they called him, an old name out of the Hebrides, after Bella's dad. But one October afternoon when the boy was nine, he left the schoolhouse and forgot his coat, a pea coat, new, with a big collar turned up like a sailor's. So he went back to get it, back to the old white schoolhouse where he was learning about the world. It was just a summer house now, owned by strangers. But that day it was locked tight, and the teacher gone home. A young woman. No blame to her. His boy jimmied open the window with his knife. They were big, double-hung windows, and you could see them open yet on a warm weekend, hear people drunk behind the screens. But Tormod had tried to hoist himself over the sill, and the upper half of the window unjammed then and came down on his neck. Late in the day it was they found him, searching last the grounds of the school. A time of day about now. The sash lay along his small shoulders like a yoke, that cruel piece of wood, blood in his nose like someone had punched him. . . .

Bilkie barely slept. He was chased by a misty street, black and wet, and harrowing cries that seemed one moment a man's, the next a beast's. He was not given to getting up in the night but he dressed and went outside to walk off the dreariness he'd woke to. A cold and brilliant moon brightened the ground fog which layered the pasture like a fallen cloud. The high ridge of hill behind his fields was ragged with wormshot spruce, wicks of branch against the sky. As a boy he'd walked those high woods with his grandfather who offered him the Gaelic names of things, most of them forgotten now, gone with the good trees. One day he'd told Bilkie about the words for heaven and hell, how they, Druid words, went

267

far back before the time of Christ. *Ifrinn,* the Isle of the Cold Clime, was a dark and frigid region of venomous reptiles and savage wolves. There the wicked were doomed to wander, chilled to their very bones and bereft even of the company of their fellow sinners. And the old heaven, though the Christians kept that name too, was also different: *Flathinnis,* the Isle of the Brave, a paradise full of light which lay far distant, somewhere in the Western Ocean. "I like that some better," his grandfather had said. "Just the going there would be good. As for hell, nothing's worse than cold and loneliness."

As he moved through the fog, it thinned like steam, but gathered again and closed in behind him. Suddenly he heard hoofbeats. Faintly at first, then louder. He turned in a circle, listening. Not a cow of his. They were well-fenced. Maybe the Dunlop's next door. But cow or horse it was coming toward him at a good clip and yet he couldn't make it out, strain as he might. Soon his heart picked up the quick, even thud of the hooves, and when in the pale fog a shape grew and darkened and then burst forth, a head shaggy as seaweed and cruelly horned, he raised his arms wildly in a shout of fear and confusion as the bull shied past him, a dark rush of heat and breath, staggering him like a blow. Aw, that goddamn Highland bull, that ugly bugger. Trembling with anger and surprise, he listened to it crash through thickets off up the hill, the fog eddying in its wake, until Bella called him and he turned back to the house.

On the porch of the manse Bilkie waited for Mrs. MacQueen to answer the door. The porch Rev. MacLean had built, but the white paint and black trim were Bilkie's work, donated last summer when his lobstering was done. He'd enjoyed those few days around the minister. One afternoon when Bilkie was on the ladder he thought he heard Gordon talking to himself, but no, he was looking up, shading his eyes. "It's only a mile from Mull, Iona," Gordon said to him. "Just across the Sound. So it's part of going home, really." Bilkie had said yes, he could see that. But he wasn't sure, even now, that he and the minister meant home in the same way. "Monks lived there, Bilkie. For a long, long time. They had a different view of the world, a different feel for it altogether. God was still *new* there, you see. Their faith was . . . robust."

Mrs. MacQueen, the housekeeper, filled the doorway and Bilkie told her what he would like.

"A book about Iona?" She was looking him up and down. She smelled of Joy, lemon-scented, the same stuff he used on his decks. "I don't read the man's books, dear, I dust them."

"He wouldn't mind me looking. Me and himself are friends." He rapped the trim of the door. "My paint."

"Well, he could have used some friends in Oban."

Mrs. MacQueen showed him into the minister's study, making it clear she would not leave. She turned the television on low, as if this were a sickroom, and sat down on a hassock, craning her ear to the screen.

Wine-colored drapes, half-drawn, gave the room a warm light. Bookshelves lined one wall, floor to ceiling, and Bilkie touched their bindings as he passed. He hadn't a clue where to begin or how to search in this hush: he only wanted to know more about that place, and maybe when the man returned they could talk about what went wrong there. But he felt shy with Mrs. Mac-Queen in the room. A map of Scotland was thumbtacked to the wall. The old clan territories were done in bright colors. Lewis he spotted easily, and Mull. And tiny Iona. On the desktop, under sprigs of lilac in a small vase, he saw a slim red book. In it were notes in Gordon's hand. With a quick glance at the housekeeper, he took it to the leather chair close by the north window, a good bright spot where Gordon must have sat many a time, binoculars propped on the sill. Bilkie put them to his eyes instinctively. Behind the manse a long meadow ran down to the shore. Across the half mile of water his boat rocked gently in the light swells. Strange to see his yellow slicker hanging by the wheel, emptied of him. Moving the glasses slightly he made out Angus standing over his boy, Johnny hunched down into some work or other. Good with engines, was Johnny. Suddenly Angus looked toward Bilkie. Of course his eyes would take in only the white manse on the hill, and the church beside it. Yet Bilkie felt seen in a peculiar way and he put down the binoculars.

Aware of the time, he turned pages, reading what he could grasp. That Iona's founder, St. Columba, had sailed there from Ireland to serve his kinsmen, the Scots of Dalriada. That he and his monks labored with their own hands, tilling and building, and that in their tiny boats they spread the faith into the remote and lesser isles, converting even the heathen Picts. That even before he was born, Columba's glory had been foretold to his mother in a dream:

269

"An angel of the Lord appeared to her, and brought her a beautiful robe—a robe which had all the colors of all the flowers of the world. Immediately it was rapt away from her, and she saw it spread across the heavens, stretched out over plains and woods and mountains. . . ." He read testaments to St. Columba's powers and example, how once in a great storm his ship met swelling waves that rose like mountains, but at his prayer they were stilled. He was a poet and loved singing, and songs praising Columba could keep you from harm. His bed was bare rock and his pillow a stone. During the three days and three nights of his funeral, a great wind blew, without rain, and no boat could reach or leave the island.

Bilkie was deep in the book when Mrs. MacQueen, exclaiming, "That's desperate, just desperate!", turned off the soap opera and came over to him.

"You'll have to go now," she said. "This isn't the public library, dear, and I have cleaning to do."

He would never talk himself past her again, not with Gordon away. He returned the book to the desk and followed her to the front door.

"Did you ever pray to a saint, Mrs. MacQueen?"

She crossed her arms. "I'm no R.C., Mr. Sutherland."

"I don't think that matters, Mrs. MacQueen. The minister has a terrible wound. Say a word to St. Columba."

"He's healing. He's getting better and soon might be coming home, is what I heard."

The next morning the sun glared up from a smooth sea as Bilkie hauled his traps, moving from one swing to another over the grounds his grandfather had claimed. By the time Bilkie was old enough to fish, there was a little money in it. But you had to work. Nobody ever gave it to you, and the season was short. He had started out young hauling by hand, setting out his swings in the old method, the backlines anchored with kellicks, and when he wasn't hauling he was rowing, and damned hard if a wind was on or the tide against you. He had always worked alone, rowed alone. Except when his boy was with him, and that seemed as brief now as a passing bird. He preferred it out here by himself, free of the land for awhile, the ocean at his back.

This season the water was so clear he could see ten fathoms, see

270

the yellow backline snaking down, the traps rising. His grandfather told him about the waters of the West Indies, the clear blue seas with the sun so far down in them it wouldn't seem like drowning at all, for the light there.

He gaffed a buoy and passed the line over the hauler, drawing the trap up to the washboard where he quickly culled the dripping, scurrying collection. He measured the lobsters, threw a berried one back. But after he dropped the trap and moved on, he knew he'd forgotten, for the second time that morning, to put in fresh bait. To hell with it. On the bleak rocks of the Bird Islands shags spread their dark wings to dry. A school of mackerel shimmered near the boat, an expanding and contracting disturbance just beneath the surface as they fed. He cut the engine, letting the boat drift like his mind. He hummed the song of Johnny Carmichael but stopped. Couldn't get the damn tune out of his head. Sick of it. He picked a mackerel out of the bait box and turned it over in his hands, stroking the luminous flow of stripes a kind of sky was named for: a beautiful fish, if you looked at it—the smooth skin, dark yet silvery. Gordon MacLean said from the pulpit that a man should find beauty in what's around him, for that too was God. But for Bilkie everything had been so familiar, everything he knew and saw and felt, until Tormod died. He took out his knife and slid it slowly into the dead fish: now, what might that be like, a piece of steel like that inside you? A feeling you'd carry a long while, there, under the scar.

Astern, the head of the cape rose behind buff-colored cliffs, up into the deep green nap of the mountain. He had no fears here, never in weather like this when the sea was barely breathing. Still, he missed the man, the sound of his voice on Sunday. The last service before he left for Iona, the minister had read Psalm 44, the one, he said, that St. Columba sang to win the Picts away from their magi, the Druids . . . *O God, our fathers have told us, what work thou didst in their days, in the times of old. . . .*

After Bilkie lost his son, he'd stayed away from church, from the mournful looks and explanations, why he should accept God's taking an innocent boy in such a way. His heart was sore, he told Bella, and had to heal up, and nothing in the church then could help it. But a few weeks after Rev. MacLean arrived, Bilkie went to hear him. Damn it, the man could preach. Not like those TV preachers who couldn't put out anything much but their palms and a phone number. A slender string it was that Gordon MacLean couldn't take a tune from. And only once had he mentioned Tormod, in a roundabout way, to show he was aware there'd been a boy, that he knew what a son could mean.

As Bilkie turned in toward the wharf that afternoon, he saw three boats in ahead of him. Above Angus's blue and white Cape Islander the men had gathered in a close circle, talking and nodding. Only Johnny Carmichael was still down below, sitting on the gunnels with his guitar. Bilkie approached the wharf in a wide arc, trying to discern what he saw in the huddled men and the boy off alone bent into his instrument. He brought his boat up into the lee and flung a line to Angus who was waving for it.

"Bilkie, you're late, boy!" he shouted.

"Aw, I was feeling slow today!"

When the lines were secured, Angus called down to him. "Did you hear about it?"

"About what?"

"The minister, Bilkie, for God's sake! He's passed away! It was sudden, you know. Complications. Not expected at all."

Bilkie's hands were pressed against a crate he'd been about to shift. He could feel the lobsters stirring under the wood. He looked up at Angus. "I knew that already," he said.

Instead of going home, Bilkie drove to a tavern fifteen miles away. He sat near a window at one of the many small tables. Complications. Lord. The sun felt warm on his hands and he watched bubbles rise in his glass of beer. The tavern was quiet but tonight it would be roaring. Peering into the dim interior he made out Jimmy Carey alone at a table. Jimmy was Irish and had acted cranky here more than once. But he seemed old and mild now, back there in the afternoon dark, not the hell-raiser he used to be. And wasn't St. Columba an Irishman, after all? Bilkie raised his glass and held it there until Jimmy, who looked as if he'd been hailed from across the world, noticed it and raised his own in return. Bilkie beckoned him over. They drank until well past supper, leaning over the little table and knocking glasses from time to time. Bilkie told him about St. Columba, about the monks in their frail vessels.

"You know about St. Brendan, of course," Jimmy said, his eyes fixing on Bilkie but looking nowhere. "They say he got as far as here even, and clear to Bermuda before he was done."

"Bermuda I know about." Bilkie tried to sing what he remembered. " 'Oh there be flowers in Bermuda, beauty lies on every hand . . . and there be laughter, ease and drink for every man. . . .' " He leaned close to Jimmy's face: " '. . . but there not be joy for *me.*' "

On the highway Bilkie focussed hard on the center line, thinking that Jimmy Carey might have bought one round at least, St. Brendan be damned. To the west the strait ran deep and dark, the sun just gone from it as he turned away toward home. Bad time to meet the mounties. He lurched to a stop by the roadside where a small waterfall lay hidden. He plunged through a line of alders into air immediately cool. The falls stepped gently through mossed granite, down to a wide, clear pool, and he remembered Bella bending her head into it years ago, her hair fanning out red there as she washed the salt away after swimming. He knelt and cupped the water, so cold he groaned, over his face again and again.

As he drove the curves the white church appeared and disappeared above the trees. When he came upon it, it seemed aloof, unattended. Cars were parked carelessly along the driveway to the manse, and Bilkie slowed down long enough to see a man and woman climbing the front steps, Mrs. MacQueen, in her flowered apron, waiting at the door. Oh, there'd be some coming and going today, the sharing of the hard news. When he felt the schoolhouse approaching, he vowed again not to look, not to bother what went on there. But he couldn't miss the blue tent in the front yard, and the life raft filled with water for a wading pool. This time he did not slow down. Too often he had wondered about that blow on the neck, about what his son had felt, and who, in that instant, he had blamed . . . something so simple as a window coming down on his bones. There. In a schoolhouse.

Bella had not seen Bilkie drunk like this in years, but she knew why and said nothing, not even about Rev. MacLean. She could not get him to come inside for supper. He reeled around angrily in the lower pasture, hieing cows away when they trotted toward the fence for handouts of fresh hay. He shouted up at the ridge. Finally he stalked to the back door.

"Gordon was going to Iona," he said to his wife. "He could check the fury of wild animals, that saint they had there. Did Gordon no damn good, eh?"

"You've had some drink, Bilkie, and I've had none. I'm tired now."

He stepped up close to her and took her face in his hands. "Ah, Bella. Your hair was so pretty."

She made him go to bed, but after dark he woke. He smelled of the boat and wanted to wash. Hearing a car, he went over to the window. Near his neighbor's upper pasture headlights bounced and staggered over the rough ground. They halted, backed up, then swept suddenly in another direction until the shaggy bull galloped across the beams. Loose again. A smallish, wild-looking beast they'd imported from Scotland. Could live out on its own in the dead of winter, that animal. You might see it way off in a clearing, quiet, shouldering snow like a monument. The headlights, off again in pursuit, captured the bull briefly but it careened away into the darkness, and the car—a Dunlop boy at the wheel no doubt—raked the field blindly. Complications. A stone for a pillow. His own boy would be a man now. Passed away, like a wave.

It was difficult for Bilkie to get up that day. He had always opened his eyes on the dark side of four a.m. but now Bella had to push and coax him. He sat on the edge of the bed for a long time staring at the half-model of a schooner mounted on the wall. His grandfather had worked her, the *Ocean Rose*, lost on Hogsty Reef in the Bahamas with his Uncle Bill aboard.

"You don't get up anymore. What's the matter with you?" Bella said. He took the cup of coffee she held out to him, nodding vaguely. Squalls had lashed the house all night and now a thick drizzle whispered over the roof. "You know Rev. MacLean is coming home this day, and tonight they'll wake him."

"I can't go," Bilkie said.

"What would he think, you not there at his wake with the others who loved him?"

"He's not thinking at all anymore. That's just a body there, coming back."

"Don't be terrible. Don't be the way you were after Tormod."

"They could have buried him over there. Couldn't they have? Near where he wanted to go?"

"He was born *here*, Bilkie. Nobody asked, I don't suppose, one way or the other."

He could see that she'd been crying. He put the coffee down carefully on the window sill and took her hands in his, still warm

274

from the cup. "Bella, dear," he said. "You washed your hair in that water. It must have hurt, eh? Water so cold as that?"

Gusts rocked the car as Bilkie crossed the bridge that joined the other island. He was determined to take himself out of the fuss, some of it from people who would never bestir themselves were Gordon MacLean here and breathing. Above him the weather moved fast. The sky would whiten in patches but all the while churn with clouds black as the cliffs by the lighthouse. There was a good lop on the water, looking east from the bridge, and when the strait opened out a few miles away the Atlantic flashed white against an ebbing tide.

In the lee of the wharf the lobster boats were surging like tethered horses. No one was around. The waves broke among the pilings beneath him and the timbers creaked. He walked to the seaward end where Angus had stacked his broken traps. Across the roughening water the manse looked small, the cars tiny around it. Every morning his grandfather would say, old as he was, *Dh'iarr am muir a thadhal*. The sea wants to be visited.

He threw off his lines and headed out into the strait, rounding up into the wind, battering the waves until he checked back on the throttle. In the turns of wind he smelled the mackerel in the bait box, the fumes of the engine. But as he drew abreast of Campbell Point, a gust of fragrance came off the land and he strained to see its source in the long, blowing grass of the point. It was quickly gone and there was nothing to account for it but what had been there all along—the thin line of beach, the grass thick as hay all the way back to the woods. To the west, on the New Skye Road, he glimpsed St. David's Church, a small white building behind a veil of rain, set in the dense spruce, no one there now but Bible Camp kids in the summer.

The sea was lively at the mouth of the strait where wind and tide met head to head. He bucked into the whitecaps, slashes of spray cracking over the bow. The waves deepened as the sea widened out but he'd ride better when he reached the deeper water where the breaking crests would cease. He had a notion of the West Indies, of his grandfather under sails, out there over the curve of the world and rolling along in worse weather than this. Hadn't the Irish monks set out in their currachs of wickerwork and hide, just for the love of God? They had survived. They reached those islands they sailed for, only dimly sure where they were. But maybe you could come by miracles easier then, when all of life was harder, and God closer to the sea than he was now. Now with no saints around, saints who could sow a field and sail a boat, you had to find your own miracles. You couldn't travel to them, could you, Gordon, boy?

He would have to go back. He would have to stand at the wake holding his hat like the rest of them, looking at Gordon who'd come dead such a distance. Bilkie watched the rhythm of the waves. He needed a break in them to bring his boat around and run with the sea. But then he wasn't hearing the engine anymore, and the boat was falling away, coming around slowly with no more sound than a sail would make. Columba. A dove. Strange name for a man. *Colmcille. Caoir gheal,* his grandfather called waves like these. A bright flaming of white. The sea had turned darker than the sky, and over the land the boat was swinging toward, clouds lay heavy and thick, eased along like stones, dark as dolmens. "Ah!" was all Bilkie said when the wave rose under him, lifting the boat high like an offering.

1986

276

THE LOVER OF HORSES

by TESS GALLAGHER

from ZYZZYVA

They say my great-grandfather was a gypsy, but the most popular explanation for his behavior was that he was a drunk. How else could the women have kept up the scourge of his memory all these years, had they not had the usual malady of our family to blame? Probably he was both a gypsy and a drunk.

Still, I have reason to believe the gypsy in him had more to do with the turn his life took than his drinking. I used to argue with my mother about this, even though most of the information I have about my great-grandfather came from my mother, who got it from her mother. A drunk, I kept telling her, would have had no initiative. He would simply have gone down with his failures and had nothing to show for it. But my great-grandfather had eleven children, surely a sign of industry, and he was a lover of horses. He had so many horses he was what people called "horse poor."

I did not learn, until I traveled to where my family originated at Collenamore in the west of Ireland, that my great-grandfather had most likely been a "whisperer," a breed of men among the gypsies who were said to possess the power of talking sense into horses. These men had no fear of even the most malicious and dangerous horses. In fact, they would often take the wild animal into a closed stall in order to perform their skills.

Whether a certain intimacy was needed or whether the whisperers simply wanted to protect their secret conversations with horses is not known. One thing was certain—that such men gained power over horses by whispering. What they whispered no one knew. But the effectiveness of their methods was renowned, and anyone for counties around who had an unruly horse could send for a whisperer and be sure that the horse would take to heart whatever was said and reform his behavior from that day forth.

By all accounts, my great-grandfather was like a huge stallion himself, and when he went into a field where a herd of horses was grazing, the horses would suddenly lift their heads and call to him. Then his bearded mouth would move, and though he was making sounds that could have been words, which no horse would have had reason to understand, the horses would want to hear; and one by one they would move toward him across the open space of the field. He could turn his back and walk down the road, and they would follow him. He was probably drunk my mother said, because he was swaying and mumbling all the while. Sometimes he would stop deadstill in the road and the horses would press up against him and raise and lower their heads as he moved his lips. But because these things were only seen from a distance, and because they have eroded in the telling, it is now impossible to know whether my great-grandfather said anything of importance to the horses. Or even if it was his whispering that had brought about their good behavior. Nor was it clear, when he left them in some barnyard as suddenly as he'd come to them, whether they had arrived at some new understanding of the difficult and complex relationship between men and horses.

Only the aberrations of my great-grandfather's relationship with horses have survived—as when he would bathe in the river with his favorite horse or when, as my grandmother told my mother, he insisted on conceiving his ninth child in the stall of a bay mare named Redwing. Not until I was grown and going through the family Bible did I discover that my grandmother had been this ninth child, and so must have known something about the matter.

These oddities in behavior lead me to believe that when my great-grandfather, at the age of fifty-two, abandoned his wife and family to join a circus that was passing through the area, it was not simply drunken bravado, nor even the understandable wish to escape family obligations. I believe the gypsy in him finally got the upper hand, and it led to such a remarkable happening that no one in the family has so far been willing to admit it: not the obvious transgression—that he had run away to join the circus—but that he was in all likelihood a man who had been stolen by a horse.

This is not an easy view to sustain in the society we live in. But I have not come to it frivolously, and have some basis for my belief. For although I have heard the story of my great-grandfather's defection time and again since childhood, the one image which prevails in all versions is that of a dappled gray stallion that had been trained to dance a variation of the mazurka. So impressive was this animal that he mesmerized crowds with his sliding step-and-hop to the side through the complicated figures of the dance, which he performed, not in the way of Lippizaners—with other horses and their riders—but riderless and with the men of the circus company as his partners.

It is known that my great-grandfather became one of these dancers. After that he was reputed, in my mother's words, to have gone "completely to ruin." The fact that he walked from the house with only the clothes on his back, leaving behind his own beloved horses (twenty-nine of them to be exact), further supports my idea that a powerful force must have held sway over him, something more profound than the miseries of drink or the harsh imaginings of his abandoned wife.

Not even the fact that seven years later he returned and knocked on his wife's door, asking to be taken back, could exonerate him from what he had done, even though his wife did take him in and looked after him until he died some years later. But the detail that no one takes note of in the account is that when my great-grandfather returned, he was carrying a saddle blanket and the black plumes from the headgear of one of the circus horses. This passes by even my mother as simply a sign of the ridiculousness of my great-grandfather's plight—for after all, he was homeless and heading for old age as a "good for nothing drunk" and a "fool for horses."

No one has bothered to conjecture what these curious emblems—saddle blanket and plumes—must have meant to my great-grandfather. But he hung them over the foot of his bed—"like a fool," my mother said. And sometimes when he got very drunk he would take up the blanket and, wrapping it like a shawl over his shoulders, he would grasp the plumes. Then he would dance the mazurka. He did not dance in the living room but took himself out into the field, where the horses stood at attention and watched as if suddenly experiencing the smell of the sea or a change of wind in the valley. "Drunks don't care what they do," my mother would say as she finished her story about my great-grandfather. "Talking to a drunk is like talking to a stump."

Ever since my great-grandfather's outbreaks of gypsy necessity, members of my family have been stolen by things—by mad ambitions, by musical instruments, by otherwise harmless pursuits from mushroom hunting to childbearing or, as was my father's case, by the more easily recognized and popular obsession with card playing. To some extent, I still think it was failure of imagination in this respect that brought about his diminished prospects in the life of our family.

But even my mother had been powerless against the attraction of a man so convincingly driven. When she met him at a birthday dance held at the country house of one of her young friends, she asked him what he did for a living. My father pointed to a deck of cards in his shirt pocket and said, "I play cards." But love is such as it is, and although my mother was otherwise a deadly practical woman, it seemed she could fall in love with no man but my father.

So it is possible that the propensity to be stolen is somewhat contagious when ordinary people come into contact with people such as my father. Though my mother loved him at the time of the marriage, she soon began to behave as if she had been stolen from a more fruitful and upright life which she was always imagining might have been hers.

My father's card playing was accompanied, to no one's surprise, by bouts of drinking. The only thing that may have saved our family from a life of poverty was the fact that my father seldom gambled with money. Such were his charm and powers of persuasion that he was able to convince other players to accept his notes on everything from the fish he intended to catch next season to the sale of his daughter's hair.

I know about this last wager because I remember the day he came to me with a pair of scissors and said it was time to cut my hair. Two snips and it was done. I cannot forget the way he wept onto the backs of his hands and held the braids together like a broken noose from which a life had suddenly slipped. I was thirteen at the time and my hair had never been cut. It was his pride and joy that I had such hair. But for me it was only a burdensome difference between me and my classmates, so I was glad to be rid of it. What anyone else could have wanted with my long shiny braids is still a mystery to me.

When my father was seventy-three he fell ill and the doctors gave him only a few weeks to live. My father was convinced that his illness had come on him because he'd hit a particularly bad losing streak at cards. He had lost heavily the previous month, and items of value, mostly belonging to my mother, had disappeared from the house. He developed the strange idea that if he could win at cards he could cheat the prediction of the doctors and live at least into his eighties.

By this time I had moved away from home and made a life for myself in an attempt to follow the reasonable dictates of my mother, who had counseled her children severely against all manner of rash ambition and foolhardiness. Her entreaties were leveled especially in my direction since I had shown a suspect enthusiasm for a certain pony at around the age of five. And it is true I felt I had lost a dear friend when my mother saw to it that the neighbors who owned this pony moved it to pasture elsewhere.

But there were other signs that I might wander off into unpredictable pursuits. The most telling of these was that I refused to speak aloud to anyone until the age of eleven. I whispered everything, as if my mind were a repository of secrets which could only be divulged in this intimate manner. If anyone asked me a question, I was always polite about answering, but I had to do it by putting my mouth near the head of my inquisitor and using only my breath and lips to make my reply.

My teachers put my whispering down to shyness and made special accommodations for me. When it came time for recitations I would accompany the teacher into the cloakroom and there whisper to her the memorized verses or the speech I was to have prepared. God knows, I might have continued on like this into the present if my mother hadn't plotted with some neighborhood boys to put burrs into my long hair. She knew by other signs that I had a terrible temper, and she was counting on that to deliver me into the world where people shouted and railed at one another and talked in an audible fashion about things both common and sacred.

When the boys shut me into a shed, according to plan, there was nothing for me to do but to cry out for help and to curse them in a torrent of words I had only heard used by adults. When my mother heard this she rejoiced, thinking that at last she had broken the treacherous hold of the past over me, of my great-grandfather's gypsy blood and the fear that against all her efforts I might be stolen away, as she had been, and as my father had, by some as yet unforeseen predilection. Had I not already experienced the consequences of such a life in our household, I doubt she would have been successful, but the advantages of an ordinary existence among people of a less volatile nature had begun to appeal to me.

It was strange, then, that after all the care my mother had taken for me in this regard, when my father's illness came on him, my mother brought her appeal to me. "Can you do something?" she wrote, in her cramped, left-handed scrawl. "He's been drinking and playing cards for three days and nights. I am at my wit's end. Come home at once."

Somehow I knew this was a message addressed to the very part of me that most baffled and frightened my mother—the part that belonged exclusively to my father and his family's inexplicable manias.

When I arrived home my father was not there.

"He's at the tavern. In the back room," my mother said. "He hasn't eaten for days. And if he's slept, he hasn't done it here."

I made up a strong broth, and as I poured the steaming liquid into a Thermos I heard myself utter syllables and other vestiges of language which I could not reproduce if I wanted to. "What do you mean by that?" my mother demanded, as if a demon had leapt out of me. "What did you say?" I didn't—I couldn't—answer her. But suddenly I felt that an unsuspected network of sympathies and distant connections had begun to reveal itself to me in my father's behalf.

There is a saying that when lovers have need of moonlight, it is there. So it seemed, as I made my way through the deserted town toward the tavern and card room, that all nature had been given notice of my father's predicament, and that the response I was waiting for would not be far off.

But when I arrived at the tavern and had talked my way past the barman and into the card room itself, I saw that my father had an enormous pile of blue chips at his elbow. Several players had fallen out to watch, heavy-lidded and smoking their cigarettes like weary gangsters. Others were slumped on folding chairs near the coffee urn with its empty "Pay Here" styrofoam cup.

My father's cap was pushed to the back of his head so that his forehead shone in the dim light, and he grinned over his cigarette at me with the serious preoccupation of a child who has no intention of obeying anyone. And why should he, I thought as I sat down just behind him and loosened the stopper on the Thermos.

The five or six players still at the table casually appraised my presence to see if it had tipped the scales of their luck in an even more unfavorable direction. Then they tossed their cards aside, drew fresh cards, or folded.

In the center of the table were more blue chips, and poking out from my father's coat pocket I recognized the promissory slips he must have redeemed, for he leaned to me and in a low voice, without taking his eyes from his cards, said, "I'm having a hell of a good time. The time of my life."

He was winning. His face seemed ravaged by the effort, but he was clearly playing on a level that had carried the game far beyond the realm of mere card playing and everyone seemed to know it. The dealer cocked an eyebrow as I poured broth into the plastic Thermos cup and handed it to my father, who slurped from it noisily, then set it down.

"Tell the old kettle she's got to put up with me a few more years," he said, and lit up a fresh cigarette. His eyes as he looked at me, however, seemed over-brilliant, as if doubt, despite all his efforts, had gained a permanent seat at his table. I squeezed his shoulder and kissed him hurriedly on his forehead. The men kept their eyes down, and as I paused at the door, there was a shifting of chairs and a clearing of throats. Just outside the room I nearly collided with the barman, who was carrying in a fresh round of beer. His heavy jowls waggled as he recovered himself and looked hard at me over the icy bottles. Then he disappeared into the card room with his provisions.

I took the long way home, finding pleasure in the fact that at this hour all the stoplights had switched onto a flashing-yellow caution cycle. Even the teenagers who usually cruised the town had gone home or to more secluded spots. *Doubt*, I kept thinking as I drove with my father's face before me, that's the real thief. And I knew my mother had brought me home because of it, because she knew that once again a member of our family was about to be stolen.

Two more days and nights I ministered to my father at the card room. I would never stay long because I had the fear myself that I might spoil his luck. But many unspoken tendernesses passed between us in those brief appearances as he accepted the nourishment I offered, or when he looked up and handed me his beer bottle to take a swig from—a ritual we'd shared since my childhood.

My father continued to win—to the amazement of the local barflies who poked their faces in and out of the card room and gave the dwindling three or four stalwarts who remained at the table a commiserating shake of their heads. There had never been a winning streak like it in the history of the tavern, and indeed, we heard later that the man who owned the card room and tavern had to sell out and open a fruit stand on the edge of town as a result of my father's extraordinary good luck.

Twice during this period my mother urged the doctor to order my father home. She was sure my father would, at some fateful moment, risk the entire winnings in some mad rush toward oblivion. But his doctor spoke of a new "gaming therapy" for the terminally ill, based on my father's surge of energies in the pursuit of his gambling. Little did he know that my father was, by that stage, oblivious to even his winning, he had gone so far into exhaustion.

Luckily for my father, the hour came when, for lack of players, the game folded. Two old friends drove him home and helped him down from the pickup. They paused in the driveway, one on either side of him, letting him steady himself. When the card playing had ended there had been nothing for my father to do but to get drunk.

My mother and I watched from the window as the men steered my father toward the hydrangea bush at the side of the house, where he relieved himself with perfect precision on one mammoth blossom. Then they hoisted him up the stairs and into the entryway. My mother and I took over from there.

"Give 'em hell, boys," my father shouted after the men, concluding some conversation he was having with himself.

"You betcha," the driver called back, laughing. Then he climbed with his companion into the cab of his truck and roared away.

Tied around my father's waist was a cloth sack full of bills and coins which flapped and jingled against his knees as we bore his weight between us up the next flight of stairs and into the living room. There we deposited him on the couch, where he took up residence, refusing to sleep in his bed—for fear, my mother claimed, that death would know where to find him. But I preferred to think he enjoyed the rhythms of the household; from where he lay at the center of the house, he could overhear all conversations that took place and add his opinions when he felt like it.

My mother was so stricken by the signs of his further decline

284

that she did everything he asked, instead of arguing with him or simply refusing. Instead of taking his winnings straight to the bank so as not to miss a day's interest, she washed an old goldfish bowl and dumped all the money into it, most of it in twenty-dollar bills. Then she placed it on the coffee table near his head so he could run his hand through it at will, or let his visitors do the same.

"Money feels good on your elbow," he would say to them. "I played them under the table for that. Yes sir, take a feel of that!" Then he would lean back on his pillows and tell my mother to bring his guests a shot of whiskey. "Make sure she fills my glass up," he'd say to me so that my mother was certain to overhear. And my mother, who'd never allowed a bottle of whiskey to be brought into her house before now, would look at me as if the two of us were more than any woman should have to bear.

"If you'd only brought him home from that card room," she said again and again. "Maybe it wouldn't have come to this."

This included the fact that my father had radically altered his diet. He lived only on greens. If it was green he would eat it. By my mother's reckoning, the reason for his change of diet was that if he stopped eating what he usually ate, death would think it wasn't him and go look for somebody else.

Another request my father made was asking my mother to sweep the doorway after anyone came in or went out.

"To make sure death wasn't on their heels; to make sure death didn't slip in as they left." This was my mother's reasoning. But my father didn't give any reasons. Nor did he tell us finally why he wanted all the furniture moved out of the room except for the couch where he lay. And the money, they could take that away too.

But soon his strength began to ebb, and more and more family and friends crowded into the vacant room to pass the time with him, to laugh about stories remembered from his childhood or from his nights as a young man at the country dances when he and his older brother would work all day in the cotton fields, hop a freight train to town and dance all night. Then they would have to walk home, getting there just at daybreak in time to go straight to work again in the cotton fields.

"We were like bulls then," my father would say in a burst of the old vigor, then close his eyes suddenly as if he hadn't said anything at all.

As long as he spoke to us, the inevitability of his condition seemed easier to bear. But when, at the last, he simply opened his mouth for food or stared silently toward the far wall, no one knew what to do with themselves.

My own part in that uncertain time came to me accidentally. I found myself in the yard sitting on a stone bench under a little cedar tree my father loved because he liked to sit there and stare at the ocean. The tree whispered, he said. He said it had a way of knowing what your troubles were. Suddenly a craving came over me. I wanted a cigarette, even though I don't smoke, hate smoking, in fact. I was sitting where my father had sat, and to smoke seemed a part of some rightness that had begun to work its way within me. I went into the house and bummed a pack of cigarettes from my brother. For the rest of the morning I sat under the cedar tree and smoked. My thoughts drifted with its shifting and murmurings, and it struck me what a wonderful thing nature is because it knows the value of silence, the innuendos of silence and what they could mean for a word-bound creature such as I was.

I passed the rest of the day in a trance of silences, moving from place to place, revisiting the sites I knew my father loved—the "dragon tree," a hemlock which stood at the far end of the orchard, so named for how the wind tossed its triangular head; the rose arbor where he and my mother had courted; the little marina where I sat in his fishing boat and dutifully smoked the hated cigarettes, flinging them one by one into the brackish water.

I was waiting to know what to do for him, he who would soon be a piece of useless matter of no more consequence than the cigarette butts that floated and washed against the side of his boat. I could feel some action accumulating in me through the steadiness of water raising and lowering the boat, through the sad petal-fall of roses in the arbor and the tossing of the dragon tree.

That night when I walked from the house I was full of purpose. I headed toward the little cedar tree. Without stopping to question the necessity of what I was doing, I began to break off the boughs I could reach and to pile them on the ground.

"What are you doing?" my brother's children wanted to know, crowding around me as if I might be inventing some new game for them.

"What does it look like?" I said.

"Pulling limbs off the tree," the oldest said. Then they dashed away in a pack under the orchard trees, giggling and shrieking.

As I pulled the boughs from the trunk I felt a painful permission, as when two silences, tired of holding back, give over to each other some shared regret. I made my bed on the boughs and resolved to spend the night there in the yard, under the stars, with the hiss of the ocean in my ear, and the maimed cedar tree standing over me like a gift torn out of its wrappings.

My brothers, their wives and my sister had now begun their nightly vigil near my father, taking turns at staying awake. The windows were open for the breeze and I heard my mother trying to answer the question of why I was sleeping outside on the ground—"like a damned fool" I knew they wanted to add.

"She doesn't want to be here when death comes for him" my mother said, with an air of clairvoyance she had developed from a lifetime with my father. "They're too much alike," she said.

The ritual of night games played by the children went on and on past their bedtimes. Inside the house, the kerosene lantern, saved from my father's childhood home, had been lit—another of his strange requests during the time before his silence. He liked the shadows it made and the sweet smell of the kerosene. I watched the darkness as the shapes of my brothers and sister passed near it, gigantic and misshapen where they bent or raised themselves or crossed the room.

Out on the water the wind had come up. In the orchard the children were spinning around in a circle, faster and faster until they were giddy and reeling with speed and darkness. Then they would stop, rest a moment, taking quick ecstatic breaths before plunging again into the opposite direction, swirling round and round in the circle until the excitement could rise no higher, their laughter and cries brimming over, then scattering as they flung one another by the arms or chased each other toward the house as if their lives depended on it.

I lay awake for a long while after their footsteps had died away and the car doors had slammed over the goodbyes of the children being taken home to bed and the last of the others had been bedded down in the house while the adults went on waiting.

It was important to be out there alone and close to the ground. The pungent smell of the cedar boughs was around me, rising up in the crisp night air toward the tree, whose turnings and swayings had altered, as they had to, in order to accompany the changes about to overtake my father and me. I thought of my great-grandfather bathing with his horse in the river, and of my father who had just passed through the longest period in his life without the clean feel of cards falling through his hands as he shuffled or dealt them. He was too weak now even to hold a cigarette; there was a burn mark on the hardwood floor where his last cigarette had fallen. His winnings were safely in the bank and the luck that was to have saved him had gone back to that place luck goes to when it is finished with us.

So this is what it comes to, I thought, and listened to the wind as it mixed gradually with the memory of children's voices which still seemed to rise and fall in the orchard. There was a soft crooning of syllables that was satisfying to my ears, but ultimately useless and absurd. Then it came to me that I was the author of those unwieldy sounds, and that my lips had begun to work of themselves.

In a raw pulsing of language I could not account for, I lay awake through the long night and spoke to my father as one might speak to an ocean or the wind, letting him know by that threadbare accompaniment that the vastness he was about to enter had its rhythms in me also. And that he was not forsaken. And that I was letting him go. That so far I had denied the disreputable world of dancers and drunkards, gamblers and lovers of horses to which I most surely belonged. But from that night forward I vowed to be filled with the first unsavory desire that would have me. To plunge myself into the heart of my life and be ruthlessly lost forever.

1987

ISLAND

by ALISTAIR MACLEOD

from THE ONTARIO REVIEW

A$_{LL}$ DAY THE RAIN FELL upon the island and she waited. Sometimes it slanted against her window with a pinging sound which meant it was close to hail, and then it was visible as tiny pellets for a moment on the pane before the pellets vanished and rolled quietly down the glass, each drop leaving its own delicate trickle. At other times it fell straight down, hardly touching the window at all, but still there beyond the glass, like a delicate, beaded curtain at the entrance to another room.

She poked the fire within the stove, turning the half-burned lengths of wood so that they would burn more evenly. Some of the wood lengths were old fence posts or timbers which had been hauled from the shore before being cut into sizes which would fit the stove. Some of them contained ancient nails which were bent and twisted deep into the wood's core. When the fire was very hot, they glowed to a cherry red, reminiscent of a blacksmith's shop or, perhaps, their earliest casting. They would glow in the intense heat while the wood was consumed around them and, in the morning, they would be shaken down with the ashes, black and twisted but still there in the grayness of the ashpan. On days when the fire burned with less intensity because the wood was damp or the drafts poor, they remained a rusted brown while the damp wood sputtered and hissed reluctantly before releasing them from the coffins in which they were confined. Today was such a day.

She went to the window and looked out once more. Beneath the table the three black and white dogs followed her with their eyes but made no other movement. They had been outside several times during the day and the wetness of their coats gave off the odor of damp woolen garments which have been hung to dry. When they came in, they shook themselves vigorously beside the stove, causing a further sputtering and hissing, as the water droplets fell against the heated steel.

Through the window and the beaded sheets of rain she could see the gray shape of *tir mòr*, the mainland, more than two miles away. Because of her failing sight and the nature of the weather she was not sure if she could really see it. But she had seen it in all weathers and over so many decades that the image of it was clearly in her mind, and whether she actually saw it or remembered it, now, seemed to make no difference.

The mainland was itself but another large island although most people did not think of it in that way. It was, as many said, larger than the province of Prince Edward Island and even some European countries and it had paved roads and cars and now even shopping centers and a fairly large population.

On rainy or foggy evenings such as this, it was always hard to see and to understand the mainland but when the sun shone it was clearly visible with its white houses and red or gray barns, and with the green lawns and fields surrounding the houses while the rolling mountains of dark green spruce rose behind them. At night the individual houses, and the communities they formed, seemed to be magnified because of the lights. In the daytime if you looked at a certain spot you might see only one house and, perhaps, a barn, but at night there might be several lights shining from the different windows of the house, and perhaps a light at the barn and other lights shining from hydro poles in the yard, or in the driveway or along the road. And there were the moving lights caused by the headlights of the travelling cars. It all seemed more glamorous at night, perhaps because of what you could not see, and conversely a bit more disappointing in the day.

She had been born on the island at a time so long ago that there was now nobody living who could remember it. The event no longer lived in anybody's mind nor was it recorded with accuracy anywhere on paper. She had been born a month prematurely at the beginning of the spring breakup when crossing from the island to the mainland was impossible.

290

At other times her mother had tried to reach the mainland before her children were born. Sometimes she would cross almost a month before the expected delivery because the weather and the water in all seasons, except summer, could never be depended upon. She had planned to do so this time as well but the ice that covered the channel during the winter months began to decay earlier than usual. It would not bear the weight of a horse and sleigh or even a person on foot and there were visible channels of open water running like eager rivers across what seemed like the gray-white landscape of the rotting ice. It was too late for foot travel and too early for a boat because there was not, as yet, enough open water. And then too she was born a month earlier than expected. All of this she was, of course, told much later. She was also told that when the winter began her parents did not realize that her mother was pregnant. Her father was sixty at the time and her mother close to fifty and they were already grandparents. They had not had any children for five years and had thought their child-bearing years were past and the usual signs were no longer there or at least not recognized until later in the season. So her birth, as her father said, was "unexpected" in more ways than one.

She was the first person ever born on the island as far as anybody knew.

Later she was brought across to the mainland to be christened. And still later when the clergyman was sending his baptismal records to the provincial capitol he included hers along with those of the children who had been born on the mainland. And perhaps to simplify matters he recorded her birthplace as being the same as that of the other children and of her brothers and sisters or if he did not intend to simplify perhaps he had merely forgotten. He also had the birthdate wrong and it was thought that perhaps he had forgotten to ask the parents or had forgotten what they had told him and by the time he was ready to send in his records they had already gone back to the island and he could not contact them. So he seemed to have counted back a number of days before the christening and selected his own date. Her middle name was wrong too. Her parents had called her Agnes but he had somehow copied it down as Angus. Again perhaps he had forgotten or was preoccupied and he was a very old man at the time, as evidenced by his shaky, spidery handwriting. And, it was pointed out, his own middle name was Angus. She did not know any of this until years later when she

291

sent for her official birth certificate in anticipation of her own marriage. Everyone was surprised that a single document could contain so many errors and by that time the old clergyman had died.

Although hers was thought to be the only birth to have occurred on the island there had been a number of deaths. One of them was that of her own grandfather who died one November from "a pain in the side" after pulling up his boat for the winter—thinking there would be no further need for a boat until the spring. He was only forty when it happened, the death occurring only two weeks after his birthday. His widow and children did not know what to do as there was no adequate radio communication and they were not strong enough to get the boat he had so recently hauled up, back into the water. They waited for two days hoping the sullen gray waves would subside, and stretching his body out on the kitchen table and covering it with white sheets—afraid to put too much fire in the kitchen stove lest it might hasten the body's decay.

On the third day they launched a small skiff and tried to row across to the mainland. They did not know if they would be strong enough to make it so they gathered large numbers of dried cattails and reeds from one of the island's marshes and placed them in a metal washtub and doused them with the oil used for the lamp at the lighthouse. They placed the tub in the prow of the skiff and when they rowed out beyond the shape of the island they set the contents of the tub on fire hoping that it might act as a signal and a sign. On the mainland someone saw the rising funnel of gray-black smoke and the shooting flames at its base and then the skiff moving erratically—rowed by the desperate hands of the woman and her children. Most of the mainland boats had already been pulled up for the winter but one was launched and the men went out to what looked like a burning boat and tossed a line to it and towed it in to the wharf after first taking off the woman and her children and comforting them and listening to their story. Later the men went out to the island and brought the man's body over to the mainland so that although he died on the island, he was not buried there. And still later that evening someone went over to light the lamp in the lighthouse so that it might send out its flashing warning to possible travellers on the nighttime sea. Even in the face of her husband's death, the woman, as well as her family, harbored fears that they might lose the job if the Government realized the lightkeeper was dead. They had already purchased their supplies for the winter and there was no other place to go so late in the season, so they decided to say nothing until the spring and returned to the island after the funeral accompanied by the woman's brother.

The original family had gone to the island because of death or rather to aid in death's reduction. The lighthouse was established in the previous century because of the danger the island represented to ships travelling in darkness or in uncertain weather. It was thought that the light would warn sea travellers of the danger of the island or, conversely, that it might represent hope to those already at the sea's mercy and who yearned so much to reach its rocky shore. Before the establishment of the light there had been a number of wrecks which might or might not have been avoided had there been a light. What was known with certainty was that survivors had landed on the island only to die from exposure and starvation because no one knew that they were there. Their skeletons being found, accidently by fishermen in the spring—huddled under trees or outcrops of rock in the positions of their deaths. Some still had the remains of their arms around one another. Some still with tattered, flapping clothes covering their bones although the flesh between the clothing and the bones was no longer there.

When the family first went they were told that their job was to keep the light and to offer salvation to any of those who might come ashore. The Government erected buildings for them which were better than those of their relatives on the mainland and helped them with the purchase of livestock and original supplies. To some it seemed they had a good job—a Government job. In answer to the question of the isolation, they told themselves they would get used to it. They told themselves they were already used to it, coming as they did from a people in the far north of Scotland who had for generations been used to the sea and the sleet and the wind and the rocky outcrops at the edge of their part of Europe. Used to the long nights when no one spoke and to the isolation of islands. Used to seeing their men going to work for the Hudson's Bay Company and the North West Company and not expecting them back for years. Used to seeing their men going to the vast ocean-like tracts of prairie in places like Montana and Wyoming to work as sheepherders. Spending months that sometimes stretched into years, talking only to dogs or to themselves or to imaginary people who blended into ghosts. Startled by the response to their own voices when they appeared, strange and unexpectedly, at the camp or at the store or

293

at the rural trading post. In demand as sheepherders, because it was believed, and because they had been told, that they did not mind the isolation. "Of course I spoke to ghosts," a man was supposed to have said once upon his returning. "Wouldn't you if there was no one else to speak to?"

In the early days on the island, there was no adequate radio communication and if they were in trouble and unable to get across they would light fires on the shore in the hope that such signs would be visible on the mainland. In the hope that they who had gone to the island as part of the business of salvation, might they themselves be saved. And when the Great War was declared, it was said, they did not know of it for weeks, coming ashore to be told the news by their relatives, coming ashore to a world which would be forever changed.

Gradually, with the passage of the years, the family's name as well as their identity became entwined with that of the island. So that although the island had an official name on the marine and nautical charts it became known generally as MacPhedran's Island while they themselves became known less as MacPhedrans than as people "of the island." Being identified as "John the Island," "James the Island," "Mary of the Island," "Theresa of the Island." As if in giving their name to the island they had received its own lonely designation in return.

All of this was already history by the time she was born and she had no choice in any of it. Not choosing, for herself, to be born on the island (although the records said she was not) and not choosing the rather surprised individuals who became her parents after they had already become the grandparents of others. For by the time she was born the intertwined history of her family and the island was already far advanced. And when she was later told the story of the man who died from the pain in his side, it seemed very far away to her although it was not so for her father who had been one of the children in the skiff, rowing with small desperate freezing hands at the bidding of his mother. By the time of her early memories, the Government had already built a wharf at the island which was superior to any on the mainland. The wharf was built "to service" the lighthouse but it also attracted mainland fishermen who were drawn to its superior facilities. Especially during the lobster season months of May and June, men came to live in the shacks and shanties they erected along the shore. Leaving their shanties at four in the morning and returning in the early afternoon to sell their catches to the buyers who came in their big boats from far away. And returning to their mainland homes on Saturday and coming back again on Sunday, late in the afternoon or in the early evening, their weekly supplies of bread and provisions in burlap bags lying at the bottom of their boats. Sometimes lying in the bottoms of the boats there were also yearling calves with trussed feet and eyes bulging with fear who were brought to the island for summer pasturage and would be taken off half-wild in the cold, gray months of fall. Later in the summer the energetic, stifled rams would be brought in the same way, to spend monastic, frustrated months in all-male company before returning to the mainland and the fall fury of the breeding season.

He came to the island the summer she was seventeen. Came before the rams or the young cattle or the buyers' boats. Came at the end of April when there were still white cakes of ice floating in the ocean and when the family's dogs still ran down to the wharf to bark at the approaching boats and to snarl at the men who got out of them. In the time before such boats and men became familiar sights and sounds and odors. Yet even as the boat came into the wharf the dogs seemed to make less fuss than was usual and whatever he said quietened them and caused them to be still. She saw all this from the window of the kitchen. She was drying the dishes for her mother at the time and she wrapped the damp dish towel around her hand as if it were a bandage and then she as quickly unwrapped it again. As he bent to loop the boat's rope to the wharf, his cap fell off and she saw the redness of his hair. It seemed to flash and reflect in the April sun like the sudden and different energy of spring. She and most of her people were dark-haired and had dark eyes as well.

He had come, she learned, to fish for the season with one of the regular men from the mainland. He was the nephew of the man's wife and came from a place located over the mountain. From a distance of some twenty-five miles which was a long distance at the time. He had come early to make preparations for the season. To work on the shanty and repair the winter's damages, to repair the man's lobster traps and to make a few new ones. He told them all of this in the evening when he came up to the lighthouse to borrow oil for his lamp. He brought them bits and scraps of news from the mainland as well although they did not have that many people in common. He spoke in both Gaelic and English although his accent was different from theirs. He seemed about twenty years of age and his eyes were very blue.

They looked at one another often. They were the youngest people in the room.

In the early madness of the lobster season they did not speak to one another although they saw each other almost every day. The men were often up at three in the morning brewing their tea by the flickering lamps, casting their large shadows eerily upon the shanties' walls as they moved about in the semi-darkness. At night they sometimes fell asleep by eight. Sometimes still sitting on their chairs, their heads tilting suddenly forward or backward and their mouths dropping open. She worked with her mother, planting the garden and the potatoes. Sometimes in the evening she would walk down by the shanties but not very often. Not because her parents openly disapproved but because she felt uncomfortable walking so close to so many men. Sometimes they nodded and smiled as all of them knew her name and who she was and some of them were her distant relatives. But at other times she felt uneasy, hearing only bits of the comments and remarks exchanged among them as they stood in their doorways or sat on their homemade chairs or overturned lobster crates. The remarks seemed mainly for themselves, to demonstrate their wit and masculinity to each other. As if they were young schoolboys instead of being mostly beyond middle age. Sometimes they reminded her of the late summer rams, playful and friendly and generally grazing contentedly in *achadh nan caoraich*, the field of the sheep, although sometimes given to spontaneous rages against those who would trespass into their territory or sometimes unleashing their suppressed fury against one another. Rearing and smashing against one another until their skulls thundered and reverberated like the growling icebergs of spring and their pent-up semen ejaculated in spurting jets, leaving them stunned and weak in the knees.

She and her mother were the only women on the island.

One evening she walked to the back of the island, down to the far shore which did not face the mainland but only the open sea. There was a small cove there which was known as *bagh na long bhriseadh*, bay of the shipwreck, because there were timbers found there in the long ago time before the lighthouse was established. She sat on *creig a bhoird*, the table rock which was called so because of its shape, and looked out across the seeming infinity of the sea. And then he was standing beside her. He made no sound in coming and the dog which had accompanied her gave no signal of his approach.

"Oh," she said, on realizing him so unexpectedly close. She stood up quickly.

"Do you come here often?" he said.

"No," she said. "Well yes, sometimes."

The ocean stretched out flat and far before them.

"Were you born here?" he asked.

"Yes," she said. "I guess so."

"Do you stay here all the time? Even in the winter?"

"Yes," she said, "most of the time."

She was defensive, like most of her family, on the subject of the island. Knowing that they were often regarded as slightly eccentric because of how and where they lived. Always anticipating questions about the island's loneliness.

"Some people are lonely no matter where they are," he said as if he were reading her mind.

"Oh," she said. She had never heard anyone say anything quite like that before.

"Would you like to live somewhere else?" he asked.

"I don't know," she said. "Maybe."

"I have to go now," he said. "I'll see you later. I'll come back."

And then he was gone. As suddenly as he had come. Seeming to vanish behind the table rock and the water's edge. She waited for a while, sitting down once more upon the rock to compose herself and then walking up the island's rise towards the lighthouse. Later when she looked down from the kitchen window towards the shanties, she could see him hammering lathes onto a broken lobster trap and readying the bait buckets for the morning. His cap was pushed back upon his head and the evening sun caught the golden highlights of his burnished hair. He looked up once and her hand tightened upon the cloth she was holding. Her mother asked her if she would like some tea.

It was into the next week before she again walked down by the shanties. He was sitting on a lobster crate splicing rope. As she went by she thought she heard him say *Àite na cruinneachadh*. She quickened her step as she felt her color rise, hoping or perhaps imagining that he had said "the meeting place." She went there immediately, down to the bay of shipwrecks and the table rock and waited. She faced out to the sea and sat in such a way that she could

297

not see him *not* coming if that was the way it was supposed to be. The dog sat at her feet and neither of them moved when he came to stand beside them.

"I told you I'd come back," he said.

"Oh," she said. "Oh yes. You did."

In the weeks that followed they went more frequently to the meeting place. Standing and later sitting on the table rock and looking out across the vastness of the sea. Talking more and sometimes laughing and, in retrospect, she could not remember when he asked her to marry him but only that she had burst into tears when she said "Oh yes" and they joined their hands on the flatness of the table rock which was still warm from the retained heat of the descending sun. "Oh yes," she had said. "Oh yes. Oh yes."

He planned to work in a sawmill, he said, after the lobster season was done; and then in the fall or early winter, after the snows began to fall and the ground became frozen, he would go to work in the winter woods of Maine. He would return to fish with the same man the next spring and then in the summer they would marry. They would go then, he said, "to live somewhere else."

"Oh yes," she said. "Oh yes, we will."

It was in the late fall, on the night following a day of cold and slanting rain that she was awakened by the dog pulling at the blankets that lay so heavily upon her bed. She sat up, even as she shivered and pulled the blankets about her shoulders, and tried to adjust her eyes to the darkness of the room. The rain slanted against the window with a pinging sound which meant that it was close to hail and even in the darkness she could see the near-white pellets visible for a moment before they vanished on the pane. The eyes of the dog seemed to glow in the dark and she felt the cold wetness of its nose when she extended her hand beyond the boundary of the bed. She could smell the wetness of its coat and when she moved her hand across its head and down its neck the water filmed upon her palm. She got up then, throwing on what clothes she could find in the darkness of the room, and followed the clacking nails of the dog as it moved down the hallway and past the closed door behind which her parents snored, sometimes snoring regularly and at other times with fitful catches in their sound. She went down through the kitchen and through the tiny puddles caused by the rain slanting through the opened door. Outside it was wet and windy although nothing like a gale and she followed the dog down the darkened path. And then in the revolving cycle of the high lighthouse light the pale beam shone in a straight but moving path. In a single white instant she saw the dark shape of the boat bobbing at the wharf and his straight but dripping form by the corner of the shanties.

The creaky door of the summer shanty yielded easily to his familiar shoulder. Inside it was slightly musty although the wind persisted through some of the unsealed cracks. Their eyes adjusted to the gloom and the few sticks of basic furniture that still remained. The primitive mattresses had been stored away to protect them from mice and the dampness of the sea. They held one another in their urgency and lay upon the floor fumbling with the encumbrances of their clothes. She felt the wet burden of his garments almost heavy upon her although the length of his body seemed light within them.

"Oh," she said, digging her fingers into the dampness of his neck, "when we are married we can do this all the time."

At the moment of explosion their breaths bonded into a single gasp that bordered on a cry.

She thought of this later as she passed the closed door of her parents' room. Thought of how her breath and his had become one and contrasted it with the irregular individual snoring which came from beyond her parents' door. She could not imagine them ever being young.

The same wonder was there the next morning as she watched her father in his undershirt preparing the fire and later going to polish the thick glass of the lighthouse lamp. She watched her mother washing the dishes and then reaching for her knitting needles and the always present ball of yarn.

She went outside and walked down towards the shanties. The door was pulled tight and she had a hard time getting it to move. Inside it all seemed different, probably, she thought, because of the daylight. She looked at the gray boards of the floor thinking she might see the outline of their bodies or even a spot of dampness but there was nothing. She went outside and walked to the wharf, to the spot where the dark boat was moored, but again there was no sign. He had "borrowed" the boat of the man he had fished with and had to have it back before dawn.

The wind was rising as the temperature was dropping. The hail-like rain had given way to stinging snow and the ground was beginning to freeze. She touched her body to see if it had been a dream.

As the winter began she was alive with the prospect of marriage. She sent for her birth certificate without ever revealing why and helped her mother with the knitting. As the winter deepened she looked at the calendar more often.

When the ice began to rot and break in the spring she looked out the window more frequently. It seemed like a later spring than usual although her father said there was nothing unusual about it. One day the channel would be clear of ice but the next day it would again be solid. The wind shifted and blew from inconsistent directions. On the mainland they could see, or imagined they could see, men moving about and readying their gear for the opening of the season. Because of the ice they were still afraid to launch their boats into the water. They all looked very small and far away.

When the first boats finally came, the dogs ran down to the wharf barking and snarling and her father went down also, calling to the dogs and welcoming the men and telling them not to be afraid. She looked out the window but did not see him in the boats or on the wharf nor moving about the familiar shanties. But neither did she see the mainland man he fished with nor his boat.

When her father came in he was filled with news and carried some fresh supplies and a bundle of newspapers and a bag of mail.

In the midst of all the newness it was a long time before he mentioned the mainland fisherman's name and added, almost as an afterthought, "That young man who fished with him last year was killed in the woods this winter. Went to Maine and was killed on a skidway. He's looking for another man right now."

When her father spoke he was already looking at a marine catalogue and had put on his glasses. He raised his eyes above the rims of his spectacles as he lowered the catalogue and looked towards them. "You remember him," he said without emotion, "the young fellow with the red hair."

"Oh poor fellow," said her mother. "God have mercy on his soul."

"Oh," was all she could say. Her hands tightened so whitely on the metal knitting needles that the point of one pierced and penetrated the ball of her thumb.

"Your hand is bleeding," said her mother. "What happened? You'll have to be more careful or you'll get blood on your knitting and everything will be ruined. What happened?" she asked again. "You'll have to be more careful."

"Nothing," she said, rising quickly and going to the door. "Nothing at all. Yes I'll have to be more careful."

She went outside and looked down towards the shanties where the newly arrived men were busy preparing for the new spring season. The banter of their voices seemed to float on the current of the wind. Sometimes she could hear their actual words but at other times they were lost and unknown. She could not believe the magnitude and suddenness of change. Could not believe the content of the news nor the method of its arrival. Could not believe that news of such outstanding impact could arrive in such a casual manner and mean so little to all of those around her.

She looked down at her bloodied hand. "Why didn't he write?" she asked herself and considered going back in to recheck the contents of the mailbag. But then she thought that both of them were beyond letters and that in the instant of his death it was already too late for that. She did not even know if he could read or write. She had never thought to ask. It had not seemed important at the time. The blood was beginning to darken and dry upon her palm and between her fingers. Suddenly last winter, although it was barely over, seemed like a long, long time ago. She pressed her hand against her stomach and turned her face away from the mainland and the sea.

When it became obvious that she was expecting a child there was great wonder as to how it came to be. She herself was rather surprised that no one had ever seen them together. It was true that she had always walked "over" or "across" the island while he had walked "around": seeming to emerge suddenly and unexpectedly out of the sea by the table rock of their meeting place. Still the island was small and, especially during the fishing season, there was little opportunity for privacy. Perhaps, she thought, they had been more successful, in some ways, than they planned. It was as if he had been invisible to everyone but herself. She was struck by this and tried to relive over and over again their last damp meeting in the dark. Only the single instant of his dark silhouette in the lighthouse beam was recallable to vision. All the rest of it had been touching in the dark. She remembered the lightness of his body in his dark, wet clothes but it was a memory of feeling rather than of sight. She had never seen him with all his clothes off. Had never slept with him in a bed. She had no photograph to emphasize reality. It was as if in

301

vanishing from her future he had also vanished from her past. It was almost as if he had been a ghost, and as she advanced in her pregnancy she found the idea strangely attractive.

"No," she kept saying to the pressure of their questions. "I don't know. I can't say. No, I can't tell you what he looked like."

She wavered only twice. The first time was a week before her delivery at a time when the approximate date of the conception was more than obvious. They were all on the mainland and the late August heat shimmered in layers above the clear deep water. The shape of the island loomed gray and blue and green across the channel and she who had wished to leave it now wished she might return. They were at her aunt's house and she would remain there until her baby would be born. She and her aunt had never liked each other and it bothered her now to be dependent upon her. Before her parents left to return to the island they came into her room accompanied by the aunt who turned to her father and said, "Well go ahead. Tell her what people are saying."

She was shocked to see the pained embarrassment on his face as he twisted his cloth cap and looked out the window in the direction of the island.

"It is just the way we live," he said. "Some say there was no other man."

She remembered the erratic snoring coming from her parents' room and how she could not imagine that they ever had been young.

"Oh," she said. "I'm sorry."

"Is that all you have to say for yourself?" said her aunt.

She wavered a moment. "Yes," she said. "That's all. That's all I have to say."

After the birth of her daughter, with the jet black hair, she received a visit from the clergyman. He was an old man although not as old as she imagined the one who had confused her own birth records, it seemed to her, so very long ago.

At that time it was in the power of clergymen to refuse to christen children unless they knew the identities of both parents. In cases such as hers the identities could be kept as confidential.

"Well," he said. "Can you tell me who the father is?"

"No," she said. "I can't say."

He looked at her as if he had heard it all before. And as if it were an aspect of his job he did not greatly like. He looked at her daughter and back at her. "We wouldn't want innocent people to burn in hell because of the willfulness of others," he said.

She was startled and frightened and looked towards the window.

"Tell me," he said quietly. "Is it your father?"

She thought for a flash of her own unexpected birth and of how her father was surprised again although the situation was so very much different.

"No," she said firmly. "It isn't him."

He seemed vastly relieved. "Good," he said. "I didn't think he would ever do anything like that. I will stop the rumors."

He moved towards the door as if one answer were all answers but then he hesitated with his hand upon the knob. "Tell me then," he said, "one more thing. Do I know him? Is he from around here?"

"No," she said, gaining confidence from seeing his hand upon the knob. "He isn't from around here at all."

That fall she stayed on the mainland until quite late in the season. It seemed as if her daughter were constantly sick and each time the journey was planned a new variation of illness appeared to stifle the departure. Out on the island her parents seemed to grow old all at once or maybe it was just that she saw them in a different light. Of course they had always seemed old to her and she had often thought of having grandparents for parents. But now they seemed for the first time to be almost afraid of the island and the coming of winter. Never since the first year of their marriage had they been there without a child. When her father fell from the ladder leading up to the lighthouse lamp it was almost as if the fall and the resulting broken arm had been expected.

Ever since her grandfather's death from "a pain in the side," the Government had more or less left them alone. It was as if the officials had been embarrassed by the widow's reluctance to tell them of her husband's death and by her fear that she might lose, in addition to her husband, the only income the family possessed. It was as if the officials had understood that "some MacPhedran" would always be on the island that bore the name and that no further questions ever would be asked. The check always arrived and the light always shone.

But when her father fell it brought a deeper seriousness. He could neither climb to the light nor navigate the boat across the channel, nor manage, quite, to look after the house and buildings

303

and the animals. It seemed best that they should all try to stay on the mainland for the winter.

Her brother came home from Halifax, reluctantly, and manned the light deep into fall. He was a single man who worked on construction crews and who drank quite heavily at times and was given to moods of deep depression. He was uneasy about the island although he understood it and was regarded as "an excellent man in a boat." At the beginning of the winter he said to his father who stood in the departing boat, "I don't want to stay here. I don't want to stay here at all."

"Oh," said his father, "you'll get used to it," which was what they had always said to one another.

But it seemed he did not get used to it. Deep in the blizzards of February one of the island dogs crossed on the ice to the mainland and came to a familiar door. It was impossible to see or move for three days because of the severe temperatures and the force of the wind-driven snow. Impossible for a man to stand upright in the wind or, as they said, for one "to see the palm of his hand in front of his face." When the storm abated four men started across the vast white landscape of the ice. They could feel parts of their exposed faces freezing and the exhaled moisture of their breath froze upon their eyebrows and they could see their eyelashes drooping heavily with ice. As they neared the island's wharf they could see that it was almost buried under gigantic pans of ice. Some of the pans had been pushed so far up on the shore that they almost tilted against the doors of the summer shanties. There was no smoke from the chimney of the house. The dogs came down snarling and circling at first, but the one who had crossed to the mainland had returned and had a calming effect upon the others. The door of the house was open and the stove was cold. The water in the crockery teapot had frozen causing the teapot itself to split into two delicate halves. There was nobody in any of the rooms and no answer to their calls. Outside, the barn doors were open and swinging in the wind. The animals were all dead, still tied and frozen in their stalls. The frozen flesh of some of them had been gnawed on by the dogs.

It seemed his coat and cap and winter mitts were missing but that was all. A loaded rifle and a shotgun were hanging in the porch. The men started a fire in the stove and made themselves something to eat from the store of winter provisions. Later they went outside again. Some walked across the island and some walked around it.

They found no tracks other than their own. They looked at the dogs for a signal or a sign. They even spoke to them and asked them questions but they received nothing in return. He had vanished like his tracks beneath the winter snow.

The men remained for the night and the next day crossed back to the mainland. They told what they had found and not found. The sun shone and although it was a weak February sun it was stronger than it had been a week earlier. It melted the ice upon the window panes and someone pointed out that the days were getting longer and that the winter was more than half way over.

Under the circumstances they decided to go back but to leave the baby behind.

"There seems almost more reason to go back now," said her father, looking through the melting ice on the windows. His broken arm had healed although he knew it would never be the same.

She was often to think of why she went back although at the time there seemed little conscious thought surrounding the decision. While her parents were willing to leave the island to the care of their son they were not willing to abandon it to others. They had found life on the mainland not as attractive as it sometimes seemed when viewed from across the water. They also seemed bothered by complicated shafts of guilt concerning their lost son and their head-strong daughter and while these shafts might persist on the island there would be no people to emphasize and expose them. She, herself, as the child of their advanced years seemed suddenly willing to consider herself old also and to identify with the past now that her future seemed to point in that direction.

She went back with almost a bitter gladness. Glad to leave her carping aunt and her mainland family behind although worried about leaving her sickly daughter in their care. Still, she knew they were right to say that the winter island was no place for a sick child and she felt also that if she did not go her parents could not manage.

"Who will climb up to the light?" asked her father simply. They viewed her youth as their immediate salvation and thought of her as their child rather than as someone else's mother.

It seemed a long time since the red-haired man had asked her to marry him and to share his life in the magical region of "somewhere else." In her persistent refusal to identify him she had pushed him so far back into the recesses of her mind that he seemed even more ghostly than before. She thought sometimes of his body in the dark

305

and of his silhouette by the sea. She was struck by the mystery of his age—if he had an age she thought it had suddenly "stopped" and he had become part of a kind of timelessness—unlike the visible deterioration she witnessed in her father.

In the winter cold of February they returned with a certain sense of relief, each harboring individual reasons. Because of her youth she did most of the work, dressing in her father's heavy, shapeless clothes and following easily the rituals and routines that had become part of her since childhood. More and more her parents remained close to the stove, talking in Gaelic and sometimes playing cards or

When March came in with its howling blizzards it seemed that they had been betrayed by the fickle promise of the February sun and although her father's will was strong his aging body seemed also to contribute to a pattern of betrayal. He was close to eighty and it seemed that each day there was another function which his body refused to perform. It was as if it had suddenly grown tired and was in the process of forgetting.

One day when there was a lull in the storms some of their relatives crossed the ice with a horse and sleigh. They were shocked at the condition and appearance of her father, seeing him changed "suddenly" after an absence of weeks while those who were with him had seen him change but gradually. They insisted that he return with them while the weather was good and the ice still strong. Reluctantly he agreed on the condition that his wife go with him.

After years of isolated permanence he was aware of all the questionable movement.

"Sometimes life is like that," he said to his daughter as he sat bundled in the sleigh at the moment before departure. "It goes on and on at a certain level and then there comes a year when everything changes."

Suddenly a gust of wind passed between them, whipping their faces with fine, sharp granules of snow. And suddenly she knew in that instant that she would never ever see him again. She wanted to tell him, to thank him or perhaps confess now that their time was vanishing between them. The secret of her own loneliness came down upon her and she reached towards his bundled body and his face which was muffled in scarves except for his eyes which were filled with water converting to ice.

"It was," she said, "the red-haired man."

"Oh yes," he said but she did not know with what degree of comprehension he said it. And then the sleigh moved off with its runners squeaking on the winter snow.

Although she was prepared for the death of her father she had not anticipated the loss of her mother who died ten days behind her husband. There was no physical explanation for her death and it seemed not unlike that of certain animals who pine away without their mates or who are unwilling or unable to adjust to new surroundings. As wild birds die in captivity or those who have been caged die from the shock of unexpected freedom or the loss of familiar boundaries.

Because of the spring breakup she was unable to attend either of their funerals and on the respective days she looked across the high gray waves and the grotesque icebergs that rolled between. From the edge of the island she saw the long funeral processions following the horse-drawn coffins along the muddy roads to the graveyard by the mainland church. She turned her face into the wind and climbed up towards the light.

That spring and summer she continued to tend the light although she had little to do with the mainland fishermen and never walked down by the shanties. She began to sign the requisition slips for government supplies with the name "A. MacPhedran" because her initial and that of her father were the same. After a while the checks came in the name of "A. MacPhedran" and she had no trouble cashing any of them. No one came to question the keeper of the light, and the sex of A. MacPhedran seemed ambiguously unimportant. After all, she told herself, wryly, her official birth certificate stated that her given name was Angus.

When the fall came she decided to remain on the island for the winter. Some of her relatives approved because they wanted "some MacPhedran" to remain on the island and they cited her youth and the fact that she was "used to it" as part of their reasoning. They were interested in "maintaining tradition" as long as they were not the ones to maintain that specific part of it. Others disapproved and towards them she was, secretly, most defiant. Her aunt and her aunt's family had grown attached to her daughter, had "gotten used to her" as they said and regarded the child as their own. When she visited them she experienced a certain fearful hostility on their part, as if they feared that she might snatch the child and flee while they were busy in another room.

307

Most of her relatives, however, either willingly or unwillingly, agreed to help her with the island, by assisting her with supplies, by doing some of the heavier autumn work or even by visiting occasionally. She settled into the life with a sort of willful determination tempered by the fact that she was still waiting for something to happen and to bring about the change.

Two years later on a hot summer afternoon, she was in the lighthouse tower when she saw the boat approaching. She had been restless all day and had walked the length and width of the island twice. She had gone to its edge as if testing the boundaries, somewhat as a restless animal might explore the limitations of its cage. She had walked out into the cold salt water feeling it move gradually up and through and under the legs of her father's coveralls which had become, for her, a sort of uniform. She walked farther out feeling the water rise as she felt the rocks turning beneath her feet. She looked downward and saw her coveralled limbs distorted in the green water, shot through by the summer sun. They seemed not to be a part of her but to have become disembodied and convoluted and to be almost floating away from her at a horizontal level. When she closed her eyes she could feel them intensely but when she looked at them they did not appear the way they felt. The dogs lay on the shore, just above the water line, and watched her. They were panting in the summer heat and drops of water fell from the extended redness of their tongues.

She returned to the shore, still dripping, and walked among the shanties. The lobster fishermen had departed at the end of the season leaving very little of themselves behind. She walked among the deserted buildings looking at the few discarded objects, sometimes touching and turning them with her toes: a worn woolen sock, a length of spliced and twisted rope, a rusted knife with a broken blade, tobacco packages with bleached and faded lettering, a rubber boot with a hole in it. It was as if she were walking through the masculine remnants of an abandoned and vanished civilization. She went back to the house to put on dry coveralls and to hang the wet ones on the outside clothesline. As she left to climb to the lighthouse she looked over her shoulder and was startled by the sight of the vertical coveralls. Their dangling legs rasped together with the gentlest of frictions and the moisture had changed their color up to the waist. Droplets dripped from them onto the summer grass which was visibly distorted by their own moving shadow.

There were four men in the approaching boat and she realized that they were mackerel fishing and did not have the island in mind as a specific destination. The boat zigzagged back and forth across the stillness of the blue-green water stopping frequently while the men tossed their weighted lines overboard. They jerked their lines up and down rhythmically hoping to attract the fish by the movement of the lures. Sometimes they dipped their hands into pails or tubs of *gruth,* dried cottage cheese, and flung the white handfuls onto the surface of the water, waiting and hoping for the unseen fish to strike. She turned her head and looked towards the back of the island. From her high vantage point she could see, or thought she could see, pods or schools of mackerel breaking the surface, beyond the meeting place and the table rock, and beyond the bay of the shipwreck. They seemed like moving, floating islands, changing the clear, flat surface into agitated areas that resembled boiling water.

She hurried down from the lighthouse and shouted and gestured to the men in the boat. They were still far offshore and, perhaps, saw her before they heard her but were still unable to comprehend her message. They directed the boat towards the island. As they approached she realized that the movement of her arm, which was intended as a pointing gesture to the back of the island, was also a beckoning gesture, as they might understand it.

When they were within earshot she shouted to them, "The mackerel. At the back of the island. Go around."

They stopped the boat and leaned forward trying to catch the meaning of her words. One of the younger men, probably the one with the best hearing, understood her first and relayed the message to the others.

"Behind the island?" shouted the oldest man, cupping his hands to his mouth.

"Yes," she shouted back. "By the bay of the shipwreck."

She almost added, "By the meeting place" before realizing that the phrase would be meaningless to them.

"Thank you," shouted the oldest man. He took off his cap and tipped it to her and she could see the whiteness of his hair. "Thank you," he repeated. "We'll go around."

They changed the course of the boat and began to go around the island.

She rushed up to the house and changed out of her coveralls and put on a summer dress which she found in the back of a closet. She walked across the island accompanied by the dogs and went down to the meeting place where she sat on the table rock and waited. The rock was hot from the heat of the day's sun and burned her thighs and the backs of her legs. She could see the floating islands of frenzied mackerel beyond the mouth of the bay. They were deep into their spawning season and she hoped they would still be there when the men in the boat arrived.

"They seem to be taking an awfully long time," she said to no one in particular. And then she saw the prow of the boat rounding the island's end.

She stood up and pointed to the boiling, bubbling mackerel but they had already seen them and even as they waved back they were in the process of readying all their available lines. The boat glided silently towards the fish and by the time the first one struck it was almost completely stilled. The mackerel seemed to surround the boat, changing the water to black by their own density. Their snapping mouths fastened on anything thrown their way and when the men jerked up their lines there were sometimes two or three fish on a single hook. Sometimes they broke the surface as if they would jump into the boat and sometimes their bodies were so densely packed that they became "snagged" as the hooks went into their bellies or their eyes or their backs or their tails. The scent of their own blood spreading within the water spurred them to an even greater frenzy and they fell upon their mutilated fellows, snapping the still living flesh from the moving bones. The men moved in their own frenzy as if to keep pace. Hooks snagged in their thumbs and the singing, sizzling lines burned through the calluses on their hands. The fish filled the bottom of the boat and began to rise in a blue-green, flopping, snapping mass to the level of the men's knees. And then, suddenly, they were gone. The hooks brought back nothing but clear drops of water or shreds of mutilated seaweed. There was no indication of them anywhere either on the surface of the sea or beneath. It was as if they had never been, apart from the heaving weight which caused the boat to ride so low within the water. The men wiped the sweat from their foreheads with swollen hands, sometimes leaving other streaks behind. Some of the streaks contained a mixture of fishblood and their own.

The men looked towards the shore and saw her rise from the table rock and come towards them until she reached the water's edge. They guided the boat across the glass-like sea until its prow grounded heavily on the gravelly shore. They tossed the painter rope to her and she caught it with willing hands.

All afternoon they lay on the table rock. At first they seemed driven by the frenzy of all that had happened and not happened to them. By all the heat and the loneliness and the waiting and all the varied events that had conspired to create their day. The clothes of the men were sprinkled with blackening clots of blood and the golden spawn of the female fish and the milky white semen of the male. She had never seen fully aroused men before, having known only one man at one time, and having experienced in that damp darkness more of feeling than of sight.

She was to remember, for the rest of her life, the oldest man with the white hair. How he took off his cap and then pulled his heavy navy-blue jersey over his shoulders and folded it neatly and placed it on the rock beside her. She was to remember the whiteness of his skin and arms compared with the bronzed redness of his face and neck and that of his bleeding and swollen hands. As if, without clothes, his upper body was still clothed in a costume made of two different materials. The whiteness of his skin and the whiteness of his hair were the same color but totally different as well. After he had folded his jersey he placed his cap neatly upon it. It was as if he were doing it out of long habit and was preparing to lie down with his wife. She almost expected him to brush his teeth.

After the first frenzy they were quieter, lying stretched beneath the sun. Sometimes one of the younger men got up and skipped flat stones across the surface of the sea. The dogs lay above the waterline panting and watching everything. She was later to think how often she had watched them in the fury of their own mating. And how she had seen their surplus young placed in burlap bags, weighted down with rocks, and tossed over the boat's side into the sea.

The sun began to decline and the tide began to fall, the water receding from the heavy boat which was in danger of becoming beached. The men got up and adjusted their clothes. Some walked some distance away to urinate. They came back and all four of them put their shoulders to the prow and prepared to push the boat back into the water.

"One, two, three, heave!" they said, moving in concentrated unison on the last syllable. Their bodies were stretched out almost horizontally as they pushed, the toes of their rubber boots scrabbling in the loose beach gravel. The boat began to move, grudgingly

311

at first, and then more rapidly as the water took its weight. The men scrambled over the prow and over the sides. Most of them were wet up to their waists. They seized their oars to push the boat farther out so there would be room to turn it around and face it towards home.

She watched them leave, standing on the shore. As the boat moved out, she noticed her undergarment crumpled and discarded by the edge of the table rock. The boat moved farther out and farther away and the men waved to her. She felt her arm rising in a similar gesture, almost without her willing it. The man with the white hair tipped his cap. She knew in one of those intuitive flashes that they would never say anything to anyone or scarcely mention the events of the day among themselves. She also knew that they would never be back. As the boat rounded the island's end, she scrunched up her undergarment and threw it into the sea. She began to walk up towards the lighthouse. She touched her body. It was sticky with blood and fishspawn and human seed. "It will have to happen this time," she thought, "because there was so much of it and it went on so long." Comparing the afternoon to her one previous brief encounter in the dark.

When she reached the lighthouse she heard the cries of the scavenging gulls. She looked in the direction of the sound and saw the boat cutting a "v" in the placid water on its way to the mainland. The men were bent double grasping their fishforks and throwing the dead mackerel back into the sea. The gulls swooped and screamed in a whitened noisy cloud.

Two years later she was in a mainland store ordering supplies to take back to the island. Usually she made arrangements with one of her relatives to take the supplies from the store to the water's edge and then ferry them across to the island but on this day she could not find the particular young man. One of the items was a bag of flour. As she stood paying her bill and looking out the door in some agitation, she saw, out of the corner of her eye, the white-haired man in the navy-blue jersey.

"This is too heavy for you," he said. "Let me help," and he bent down and picked up the hundred pound flour sack and threw it easily onto his shoulder. When it landed some of the flour puffed out, sprinkling his blue jersey and his cap and his hair with its fine white powder. She remembered the whiteness of his body beneath the blue jersey and the frenzied afternoon beneath the summer sun. As they were going out the door they met her young relative.

"Here, I'll take that," he said, relieving the man of the bag of flour.

"Thank you," she said to the man.

"My pleasure," he said and tipped his cap towards her. The flour dust fell from his cap onto the floor between them.

"He is a real nice fellow," said her young relative as they moved towards the shore. "But of course you don't know him the way we do."

"No," she said. "Of course I don't." She looked across the channel to the stillness of the island. Her expected child had never arrived.

The years of the next decade passed by in a blur of monotonous sameness. She realized that she was becoming more careless of her appearance and that such carelessness was regarded as further evidence of eccentricity. She came ashore less frequently preferring to try to understand the world through radio. She found her teen-age daughter to be foreign and aloof and embarrassed by her presence. Her aunt's family harbored doubts about their decision to rear the girl and, one day, when she was visiting, suggested that she might want to live on the island with her "real mother." The girl laughed and walked into another room.

Gradually during the next years things changed even more, but so quietly that, in retrospect, she could not link the specific events to the specific years. Many of them had to do with changes on the mainland. The Government built a splendid new wharf and the spring fishermen no longer came to inhabit the shanties which began to fall into disrepair, their doors banging in the wind and the shingles flying from their roofs. Sometimes she looked at the initials carved by the absent men on the shanties' walls but his, as she knew, would never be among them.

Community pastures were established, with regular attendants, and the bound young cattle and the lusty rams no longer came to the summer pasturage. The sweeping headlights of cars became a regular feature of her night vision, mirroring in a myriad manner the beam from her solitary lighthouse. One night after a quarrel with her aunt's family, her daughter left in such a car, and vanished into the mystery of Toronto. She did not know of it until weeks later when she came ashore for the purchase of supplies.

The wharf at the island began to deteriorate and the visitors came less often. She found herself often dealing with members of a newer

313

generation. Many of them were sulky and contributed to the maintaining of island tradition with the utmost reluctance and only because of the badgering of their parents.

Yet the light still shone and the various missives to and from "A. MacPhedran" continued to travel through the mails. The nature of such missives also changed, however gradually. When the first generation of her family went to the island it had been close to the age of sail when captains were at the mercies of the winds. In her own time she had seen the coming of the larger ships and the increasing sophistication of their technology. There had not been a wreck upon the island in all her time of habitation and no freezing, ice-caked travellers had ever knocked upon her midnight door. The "emergency chest" and its store of supplies remained unopened from one inspection to the next.

One summer she realized with a shock that her child-bearing years were over and that that part of her life was past.

Mainland boat operators began to offer "trips around the island," taking tourists on circumnavigational voyages. Very often because of time limitations they did not land but merely circled or anchored briefly offshore. When the boats approached the dogs barked, bringing her to her door or sometimes to the water's edge. At first she was not aware of the image she presented to the tourists with their binoculars or their cameras. Nor was she aware of how she was described by the operators of the boats. Standing at the edge of the sea in her dishevelled men's clothing and surrounded by her snarling dogs, she later realized, she had passed into folklore. She had, without realizing it, become "the mad woman of the island."

It was on a hot summer's day, some years later when, in answer to the barking of the dogs, she looked out the window and saw the big boat approaching. The men wore tan-colored uniforms and the Canadian flag flew from the mast. They tied the boat to the remnants of the wharf and began to climb towards the house as she called off the dogs. The decision had been made, they told her quietly, while sitting in the kitchen, to close the lighthouse officially. The light would still shine but it would be maintained by "modern technology." It would operate automatically and be serviced by supply boats which would come at certain times of the year or, in emergency, they added, by helicopter. It would, however, be maintained in its present state for approximately a year and a half. After that, they said, she would have "to live somewhere else." They got up to leave and thanked her for her decades of fine service.

After they had gone she walked the length and width of the island. She repeated all the place names, many of them in Gaelic, and marvelled that the places would remain but the names would vanish. "Who would know?" she wondered that this spot had once been called *achadh nan caoraich,* or that another was called *creig a bhoird.* And who she thought, with a catch in her heart, would ever know of *Àite na cruinneachadh* and of what had transpired there. She looked across the landscape repeating the phrases of the place-names as if they were those of children about to be abandoned without knowledge of their names. She felt like whispering their names to them so they would not forget.

She realized with a type of shock that in spite of generations of being people "of the island" they had never really owned it in any legal sense. There was nothing physical of it that was, in strict reality, formally theirs.

That autumn and winter her rituals seemed without meaning. There was no need of so many supplies because the future was shorter and she approached each winter task with the knowledge that it would be her last. She approached spring with a longing born of confused emotions. She who had wanted to leave and wanted to return and wanted to stay felt the approaching ache of those who leave the familiar behind. She felt, perhaps, as those who leave bad places or bad situations or bad marriages behind them. As those who must look over their shoulders one last time and who say quietly to themselves, "Oh I have given a lot of my life to this, such as it was, and such was I. And no matter where I go I will never be the same."

That April as the ice broke, for her the final time, she was drying the dishes and looking through the window. Because of her failing eyesight she did not see the boat until it was almost at the remains of the wharf and the dogs did not make their usual sound. She saw the man bending to loop the boat's rope to the wharf and as he did so his cap fell off and she saw the redness of his hair. It seemed to flash and reflect in the April sun like the sudden and different energy of spring. She wrapped the damp dish towel around her hand as if it were a bandage and then she as quickly unwrapped it again.

315

He started up the path towards the house and the dogs ran happily beside him. She stood in the doorway uncertainly. As he approached she realized that he was talking to the dogs and his accent was slightly unfamiliar. He seemed about twenty years of age and his eyes were very blue. He had an earring in his ear.

"Hello," he said, extending his hand. "I don't know if you recognize me."

It had been so long and so much had happened that she did not know what to say. Her hand tightened on the cloth she was still holding. She stepped aside to let him enter the house and watched as he sat on a chair.

"Do you stay here all the time?" he asked, looking around the kitchen, "even in the winter?"

"Yes," she said. "Most of the time."

"Were you born here?"

"Yes," she said. "I guess so."

"It must be lonely," he said, "but I guess some people are lonely no matter where they are."

She looked at him as if he were a ghost.

"Would you like to live somewhere else?" he asked.

"I don't know," she said. "Maybe."

He raised his hand and touched the earring as if to make certain it was still there. His glance travelled about the kitchen, seeming to rest lightly on each of the familiar objects. She realized that the kitchen had hardly changed since that other April visit so long ago. She could not think of what to say.

"Would you like some tea?" she asked after a moment of awkward silence.

"No thank you," he said. "I'm pressed for time right now but perhaps we'll have it later."

She nodded although she was not certain of his meaning. The dogs lay under the table, now and then thumping the floor with their tails. Through the window she could see the white gulls hanging over the ocean which was still dotted with cakes of floating ice.

He looked at her carefully, as if remembering, and he smiled. Neither of them seemed to know just what to say.

"Well," he said getting up suddenly. "I have to go now. I'll see you later. I'll come back."

"Wait," she said rising as quickly, "please don't go," and she almost added the word "again."

"I'll be back," he said, "in the fall. And then I will take you with me. We will go and live somewhere else."

"Yes," she said and then added almost as an afterthought, "Where have you been?"

"In Toronto," he said. "I was born there. They told me on the mainland that you are my grandmother."

She looked at him as if he were a genetic wonder which indeed he seemed to be.

"Oh," she said.

"I have to go now," he repeated, "but I'll see you later. I'll come back."

"Oh yes," she said. "Oh yes we will."

And then he was gone. She sat transfixed not daring to move. Part of her felt that she should rush and call him back and another fearful part told her she should not know what she might see. Finally she went to the window. Halfway across to the mainland there was a single man in a boat but she could make no clear identification. She did not say anything to anyone about the visit. She could think of no way she could tactfully introduce it. After years of secrecy it seemed a dangerous time to bring up the subject of the red-haired man. Perhaps, again, no one else had seen him? She did not wish to add further evidence to her designation as "the mad woman of the island." She scanned the faces of her relatives carefully but could find nothing. Perhaps he had visited them, she thought, and they had told him not to come. Perhaps they considered themselves in the business of not disturbing the disturbed.

Now as the October rain fell she added yet another stick to the fire. She was no longer bothered by the declining stock of wood because she would not need it for the winter. The rain fell turning more to the consistency of hail and she knew this by its sound as well as by her sight. She looked away from the door as she had so many years ago, the first time at the table rock. Deliberately not looking in the direction of his possible coming so that she could not see him *not* coming if that was the way it was supposed to be. She waited, listening to the regular pattern of the rain, and wondered if she were on the verge of sleep. Suddenly the door blew open and the hail-like rain skittered across the floor. The wet dogs moved from beneath the table and she heard them rather than saw. Perhaps she should mop the wet floor she thought but then she remembered that they planned to tear the house down anyway and its cleanliness seemed like a minor virtue. The water rippled across the floor in rolling little wind-driven waves. The dog came in, its nails clacking across the floor even as little spurts of water rose from beneath its padded paws. It came and lay its head upon her lap. She got up not daring to believe. Outside it was wet and windy and she followed the dog down the darkened path. And then in the revolving cycle of the high lighthouse light she saw in a single white instant the dark shape of the boat bobbing at the wharf and his straight but dripping form by the corner of the shanties.

They moved towards each other.

"Oh," she said, digging her fingers into the dampness of his neck.

"I told you I'd come back," he said.

"Oh," she said. "Oh yes. You did."

She ran her fingers over his face in the darkness and when the light revolved again she saw the blueness of his eyes and his red hair darkened by the dripping water. He was not wearing any earring.

"How old are you?" she asked, embarrassed by the girlish triviality of the question which had bothered her all these years.

"Twenty-one," he said. "I thought I told you."

He took her hands and walked backwards while facing her, down to the darkness of the bobbing boat and the rolling sea.

"Come," he said. "Come with me. It is time we went to live somewhere else."

"Oh yes," she said. "Oh yes we will."

She dug her nails into the palms of his hands as he guided her over the spume-drenched rocks.

"This boat," he said, "has to be back before dawn."

The wind was rising as the temperature was dropping. The hail-like rain had given way to stinging snow and the ground they left behind was beginning to freeze.

A dog barked once. And when the light revolved, its solitary beam found no MacPhedrans on the island or the sea.

1989

318

TYPICAL

by PADGETT POWELL

from GRAND STREET

Yesterday a few things happened. Every day a few do. My dog beat up another dog. He does this when he can. It's his living, more or less, though I've never let him make money doing it. He could. Beating up other dogs is his thing. He means no harm by it, expects other dogs to beat him up—no anxiety about it. If anything makes him nervous, it's that he won't get a chance to beat up or be beaten up. He's healthy. I don't think I am.

For one thing, after some dog-beating-up, I think I feel better than even the dog. It's an occasion calls for drinking. I have gotten a pain in the liver zone, which it is supposed to be impossible to feel. My doctor won't say I can't feel anything, outright, but he does say *he* can't feel anything. He figures I'll feel myself into quitting if he doesn't say I'm nuts. Not that I see any reason he'd particularly cry if I drank myself into the laundry bag.

I drank so much once, came home, announced to my wife it was high time I went out, got me a black woman. A friend of mine, well before this, got in the laundry bag and suddenly screamed at his wife to keep away from him because she had *turned* black, but I don't think there's a connection. I just told mine I was heading for some black women pronto, and I knew where the best ones were, they were clearly in Beaumont. The next day she was not speaking, little rough on pots and pans, so I had to begin the drunk detective game and open the box of bad breath no drunk ever wants to open. That let out the black women of Beaumont, who were not so attractive in the shaky light of day with your wife standing there pink-eyed holding her lips still with little inside bites. I sympathized fully with her, fully.

I'm not nice, not too smart, don't see too much point in pretending to be either. Why I am telling anyone this trash is a good question, and it's stuff it obviously doesn't need me to tell myself. Hell, I know it, it's mine. It would be like the retired justice of the peace that married me and my wife.

We took a witness which it turned out we didn't need him, all a retired JP needs to marry is a $20 tip, and he'd gotten two thousand of those tips in his twenty years retired, cash. Anyway, he came to the part asks did anyone present object to our holy union please speak up now or forever shut up, looked up at the useless witness, said, "Well, hell, he's the only one here, and *y'all* brought him, so let's get on with it." Which we did.

This was in Sealy, Texas. We crossed the town square, my wife feeling very married, proper and weepy, not knowing yet I was the kind to talk of shagging black whores, and we went into a nice bar with a marble bartop and good stools and geezers at dominoes in the back, and we drank all afternoon on one ten-dollar bill from large frozen goblet-steins of some lousy Texas beer we're supposed to be so proud of and this once it wasn't actually terribly bad beer. There was our bouquet of flowers on the bar and my wife was in a dressy dress and looked younger and more innocent than she really was. The flowers were yellow, as I recall, the marble white with a blue vein, and her dress a light, flowery blue. Light was coming into the bar from high transomlike windows making glary edges and silhouettes—the pool players were on fire, but the table was a black hole. All the stuff in the air was visible, smoke and dust and tiny webs. The brass nails in the old floor looked like stars. And the beer was 50 cents. What else? It was pretty.

She's not so innocent as it looked that day because she had a husband for about ten years who basically wouldn't sleep with her. That tends to reduce innocence about marriage. So she was game for a higher stepper like me, but maybe thinks about the cold frying pan she quit when I volunteer to liberate the dark women of the world.

I probably mean no harm, to her or to black women, probably am like my dog, nervous I won't get *the chance.* I might fold up at the first shot. I regret knowing I'll never have a date with Candice Bergen, this is in the same line of thought. Candice Bergen is my pick for the most good to look at and probably kiss and maybe all-you-could-do woman in the world. All fools have their whims. Should an ordinary, daily kind of regular person carry around desire like this? Why do people do this? Of course a lot of money is made on fools with pinups in the backs of their heads, but why do we continue to buy? We'd be better off with movie stars what look like the girls from high school that had to have sex to get any attention at all. You put Juicy Lucy Spoonts on the silver screen and everybody'd be happy to go home to his faithful, hopeful wife. I don't know what they do in Russia, on film, but if the street women are any clue, they're on to a way of reducing foolish desire. They look like good soup-makers, and no head problems, but they look like potatoes, I'm sorry. They've done something over there that prevents a common man from wanting the women of Beaumont.

There are many mysteries in this world. I should be a better person, I know I should, but I don't see that finally being up to choice. If it were, I would not stop at being a better person. Who would? The girls what could not get dates in high school, for example, are my kind of people now, but *then* they weren't. I was like everybody else.

I thought I was the first piece of sliced bread to come wrapped in plastic, then. Who didn't. To me it is really comical, how people come to realize they are really a piece of shit. More or less. Not everybody's the Candy Man or a dog poisoner. I don't mean that. But a whole lot of folk who once thought otherwise of themself come to see they're just not that hot. That is something to think on, if you ask me, but you don't, and you shouldn't, which it proves my point. I'm a fellow discovers he's nearly worth disappearing without a difference to anyone or anything, no one to be listened to, trying to say that not being worth being listened to is the discovery we make in our life that then immediately, sort of, ends the life and its feedbag of self-serious and importance.

I used to think niggers were the worst. First they were loud as Zulus at bus stations and their own bars and then they started walking around with radio stations with jive jamming up the entire air. Then I realized you get the same who-the-hell-asked-for-it noise off half, more than half, the white fools everywhere you are. Go to the ice house: noise. Rodeo: Jesus. Had to quit football games. There's a million hot shots in this world wearing shorts and loud socks won't take no for an answer.

And un*like* high school, you can't make them go home, quit coming. You can't make them quit playing life. I'd like to put up a cut-list on the locker-room door to the world itself. Don't suit up today, the following:

And I'm saying I'd be in the cut myself. Check your pads in, sell your shoes if you haven't fucked them up. I did get cut once, and a nigger who was going to play for UT down the road wouldn't buy my shoes because he said they stank—a nigger now. He was goddamned right about the toe jam which a pint of foo foo water had made worse, but the hair on his ass to say something like that to me. I must say he was nice about it, and I'm kind of proud to tell it was Earl Campbell wouldn't wear a stink shoe off me.

Hell, just take what I'm saying right here in that deal. *I'm* better than a nigger who breaks all the rushing records they had at UT twice and then pro records and on bad teams, when I get *cut* from a bad team that names itself after a tree. Or something, I've forgotten. We might have been the Tyler Rosebuds. That's the lunacy I'm saying. People have to *wake up*. Some do. Some don't. I have: I'm nobody. A many hasn't. Go to the ice house and hold your ears.

This is not that important. It just surprised me when I came to it, is all. You're a boob, a boob for life, I realized one day. Oh, I got Stetsons, a Silverado doolie, ten years at ARMCO, played poker with Mickey Gilley, shit, and my girlfriends I don't keep in a little black book but on candy wrappers flying around loose in the truck. One flies out, so what? More candy, more wrappers at the store. But one day, for no reason, or no reason I know it or can remember anything happening which it meant anything, I stopped at what I was doing and said, John Payne, you are a piece of crud. You are a common, long-term drut. *Look* at it.

It's not like this upset me or anything, why would it? It's part of the truth to what I'm saying. You can't disturb a nobody with evidence he's a nobody. A nobody is not disturbed by anything significant. It's like trying to disturb a bum by yelling *poor fuck* at him. What's new? he says. So when I said, John Payne, you final asshole, I just kept on riding. But the moment stuck. I began watching myself. I watched and proved I was an asshole.

This does not give you a really good feeling, unless you are drunk, which is when you do a good part of the proving.

I've been seeing things out of the corners of my eyes and feeling like I have worms since this piece-of crud thing. It works like this. I'm in a ice house out Almeda, about to Alvin in fact, and I see this pretty cowboy type must work for Nolan Ryan's ranch or something start to come up to me to ask for a light. That's what I *would* have seen, before. But now it works like this: before he gets to me, before he even starts coming over, see, because I'm legged up in a strange bar thinking I'm a piece of shit and a out-of-work beer at three in the afternoon in a dump in Alvin it proves it, I see out the corner of my eye this guy put his hand in his pants and give a little wink to his buddies as he starts to come over. That's enough, whatever it means, he may think I'm a fag, or he may be one himself, but he thinks you're enough a piece of shit he can touch his dick and wink about you, only he don't know that he is winking about a known piece of shit, and winking about a known piece of shit is a dangerous thing to do.

Using the mirror over the bar about like Annie Oakley shooting backwards, I spot his head and turn and slap him in the temple hard enough to get the paint to fall off a fender. He goes down. His buddies start to push back their chairs and I step one step up and they stop.

"What's all the dick and grinning about, boys?"

On the floor says, "I cain't *see.*"

"He cain't see," I tell the boys.

I walk out.

Outside it's some kind of dream. There's ten Hell's Angel things running around a pickup in the highway like a Chinese fire drill, whatever that is. In the middle by the truck is a by-God muscle man out of Charles Atlas swinging chains. He's *whipping* the bikers with their own motorcycle chains. He's got all of the leather hogs bent over and whining where he's stung them. He picks up a bike and drops it headfirst on the rakes. Standing there with a hot Bud, the only guy other than Tarzan not bent over and crying, I get the feeling we're some kind of tag team. I drive off.

That's how it works. Start out a piece of shit, slap some queer-bait blind, watch a wrestling match in the middle of Almeda Road, drive home a piece of shit, spill the hot beer I forgot about all over the seat and my leg.

I didn't always feel this way, who could afford to? When I was fifteen, my uncle, who was always kind of my real dad, gave me brand new Stetson boots and a hundred-dollar bill on a street corner in Galveston and said spend it all and spend it all on whores. It was my birthday. I remember being afraid of the black whores and the ones with big tits, black or white, otherwise I was a ace. In those days a hundred dollars went a long way with ladies in Galveston. I got home very tired a fifteen-year-old *king* with new boots and a wet dick.

That's what you do with the world before you doubt yourself. You buy it, dress up in it, fuck it. Then, somehow, it starts fucking back. A Galveston whore you'd touch now costs the whole hundred dollars, for example, in other words. I don't know. Today I would rather just *talk* to a girl on the street than fuck one, and I damn sure don't want to talk to one. There's no point. I need some kind of pills or something. There must be ways which it will get you out of feeling like this.

For a while I thought about having a baby. But Brillo Tucker thought this up about fifteen years ago, and two years ago his boy whips his ass. When I heard about that I refigured. I don't need a boy whipping my ass, mine or anybody else's. That would just about bind the tit. And they'll do that, you know, because like I say they come out *kings* for a while. Then the crown slips and pretty soon the king can't get a opera ticket, or something, I don't know anything about kings.

This reminds me of playing poker with Mickey Gilley, stud. First he brings ten times as much money as anyone, sits down in new boots, creaking, and hums all his hit songs so nobody can think. He wins a hand, which it is rare, and makes this touchdown kind of move and comes down slowly and rakes the pot to his little pile. During the touchdown, we all look at this dry-cleaning tag stapled to the armpit of his vest. That's the Pasadena crooner.

I was at ARMCO Steel for ten years, the largest integrated steel mill west of the Mississippi, a word we use having nothing to do with niggers for once. It means we could take ore and make it all the way to steel. Good steel. However, I admit that with everybody standing around eating candy bars in their new Levis, it cost more than Jap steel. I have never seen a Japanese eating a candy bar or dipping Skoal showing off his clothes. They wear lab coats, like they're all dentists. We weren't dentists.

We were, by 1980, out of a job, is what we were. It goes without saying it, that is life. They were some old-timers that just moped about it, and some middle-lifer types that had new jobs in seconds, and then us young turks that moped *mad*. We'd filler up and drive around all day bitching about the capitalist system, whatever that is, and counting ice houses. We discovered new things, like Foosball. Foosball was one of the big discoveries. Pool we knew about, shuffleboard we knew about, Star Wars pinball we knew about, but Foosball was a kick.

For a while we bitched as a club. We were on the icehouse frontier, tent-city bums with trucks. Then a truckload of us—not me, but come to think of it, Brillo Tucker was with them, which is perfect—get in it on the Southwest Freeway with a truckload of niggers and they all pull over outside the *Post* building and the niggers whip their *ass*. They're masons or something, plumbers. A photographer at the *Post* sees it all and takes pictures. The next day a thousand ARMCO steel workers out of a job read about themselves whipped by employed niggers on the freeway. This lowered our sail. We got to be less of a club, quick. I don't know what any of my buddies are doing now and I don't care. ARMCO was ARMCO. It was along about in here I told my wife I was off to Beaumont for black chicks, and there could be a connection, but I doubt it.

As far as I can really tell, I'm still scared of them in the plain light of day. At a red light on Jensen Drive one day, a big one in a fur coat says to me, "Come here, Sugar, I got something for you," and opens her coat on a pair of purple hot pants and a yellow bra.

I say, "I know you do," and step on it. Why in hell I'd go home and pick on a perfectly innocent wife about it is the kind of evidence it convinces you you're not a prince in life.

Another guy I knew in the ARMCO club had a brother who *was* a dentist, and this guy tells him not to worry about losing his job, to come out with him golfing on Thursdays and *relax*. Our guy starts going—can't remember his name—and he can't hit the ball for shit. It's out of bounds or it's still on the tee. And the dentist who wants him to relax starts ribbing him until our guy says if you don't shut the fuck up I'm going to put this ball down and aim it at *you*. The dentist laughs. So Warren—that's his name—puts the ball down and aims at the dentist who's standing there like William Tell giggling and swings and hits his brother, the laughing dentist who wants him to relax, square in the forehead. End of relaxing golf.

Another guy's brother, a yacht broker, whatever that is, became a flat *hero* when we got laid off because he found his brother the steel worker in the shower with his shotgun and took it away from him. Which it wasn't hard to do, because he'd been drinking four days and it wasn't loaded.

Come to look at it, *we* all sort of disappeared and all these Samaritans *with* jobs creamed to the top and took the headlines, except for the freeway. The whole world loves a job holder.

One day I drove out to the Highway 90 bridge over the San Jacinto and visited Tent City, which was a bunch of pure bums pretending to be unfortunate. There were honest-to-God river rats down there, never lived anywhere but on a river in a tent, claiming to be victims of the economy. They had elected themselves a mayor, who it turns out the day I got there was up for re-election. But he wasn't going to run again because God had called him to a higher cause, preaching. He announced this with shaking hands and wearing white shoes and a white belt and a maroon leisure suit. Out the back of his tent was a pyramid of beer cans all the way to the river, looked like a mud slide in Colombia. People took me around because they thought I was out there to *hire* someone.

I met the new mayor-to-be, who was a Yankee down here on some scam that busted, had left a lifelong position in dry cleaning, had a wife who swept their little camp to where it was smoother and cleaner than concrete. I told him to call Mickey Gilley. He was a nice guy, they both were, makes you think a little more softly about the joint. How a white woman from Michigan, I think, knew how to sweep dirt like a Indian I'll never know. Maybe it's natural. I don't think it's typical though.

This one dude, older dude, they called Mr. C, was walking around asking everybody if this stick of wood he was carrying belonged to them. He had this giant blue and orange thing coming off his nose, about *like* an orange, which it is why they called him Mr. C, I guess. A kid who was very pretty, built well—could of made a fortune in Montrose—ran to him with a bigger log and took him by the arm all the way back to his spot, some hanging builder's plastic and a chair, and set a fire for him. It's corny as hell, but I started liking the place. It was like a pilgrim place for pieces of shit, pieces of crud.

Then a couple gets me, tells me their life story if I'll drink instant coffee with them. The guy rescued the girl from some kind of mess in Arkansas that makes Tent City look like Paradise. He's about six eight with mostly black teeth and sideburns growing into his mouth, and she's about four foot flat with a nice ass and all I can think of is how can they fuck and why would she let him. For some reason I asked him if he played basketball, and the *girl* pipes up, "I played basketball."

"Where?"

"In high school."

"Then what did you do?" I meant by this, how is it Yardog here has you and I don't.

"Nothing," she says.

"What do you mean, nothing?"

"I ain't done *nuttin.*" That's the way she said it, too.

It was okay by me, but if she had fucked somebody other than the buzzard, it would have been *something*.

I was just kind of cruising there at this point, about like leg-up in Alvin, ready to buy them all a case of beer and talk about hard luck the way they wanted to, when something happened. This gleaming, purring, fully restored, *immaculate* as Brillo Tucker would say, '57 Chevy two-door pulls in and eases around Tent City and up to us, and out from behind the mirrored windshield, wearing sunglasses to match it, steps this nigger who was a kind of shiny, shoe-polish brown, an *exact* color and finish of the car. The next thing you saw was that his hair was black and oily and so were the black sidewalls of his car. Everything had dressing on it.

The nigger comes up all smiles and takes cards out of a special little pocket in his same brown suit as the car and himself. The card says something about community development.

"I am prepared to offer all of you, if we have enough, a seminar in job-skills acquistion and full-employment methodology." This comes out of the gleaming nigger beside his purring '57 Chevy.

The girl with the nice butt who's done nothing but fuck a turkey vulture says, "Do what?"

Then the nigger starts on a roll about the seminar, about the only thing which in it people can catch is it will take six hours. That is longer than most of these people want to *hold* a job, including me at this point. I want to steal his car.

"Six hours?" the girl repeats. "For *what?*"

"Well, there are a lot of tricks to getting a job."

I say, "Like what?"

"Well, like shaking hands."

"Shaking hands." I remember Earl Campbell not buying my stinky shoes. That was okay. This is too far.

"Do you know how to shake hands?" the gleaming nigger asks. Out of the corner of my eye I see the turkey buzzard looking at his girl with a look that is like they're in high school and in love.

"Let's find out," I say. I grab him and crush him one, he winces.

"You know how to shake hands."

"I thought I did."

Who the fuck taught *him* how? Maybe Lyndon Johnson.

He purrs off to find a hall for the seminar and the group at Tent City proposes putting a gas cylinder in the river and shooting it with a .22.

I've got my own brother to contend with, but we got over it a long time ago. He was long gone when ARMCO troubles let everybody else's brother loose on him. He, *my* brother, goes off to college, which I don't, which it pissed me off at the time, but not so much now. Anyway, he goes off and comes back with half-ass long hair talking *Russian*. Saying, *Goveryou po rooskie* in my face. It's about the time Earl Campbell has told me he won't wear my cleats because they stink, so I take all my brother's college crap laying down.

Then he says, "I study Russian with an old woman who escaped the revolution with nothing. There's only one person in the

328

class, so we meet at her house. Actually, we meet in her back-yard, in a hole."

"You what?"

"We sit in a hole she dug and study Russian. All I lack being Dostoevsky's underground man is more time." He laughed.

"All I lack being a gigolo," I said, "is having a twelve-inch dick." And hit him, which is why he doesn't talk to me today, and I don't care. If he found out I was in the shower with my shotgun he'd pass in a box of shells. Underground man. What a piece of shit.

That's about it. Thinking of my brother, now, I don't feel so hot about running at the mouth. I'm not feeling so hot about living, so what? What call is it to drill people in their ears? I'm typical.

1990

ASTRONAUTS

by WALLY LAMB

from THE MISSOURI REVIEW

"NEXT SLIDE," THE astronaut says. For a second, the auditorium is as void and dark as space itself. Then a curve of the earth's ulcerated surface flashes on the screen and the students' silhouettes return, bathed in tones of green. This is the third hour in a row Duncan Foley has seen this picture and heard the smiling public relations astronaut, sent, in the wake of the Challenger disaster, to the high school where Duncan teaches. It's September; attendance at the assembly is mandatory.

A hand goes up.

"Yes?" the astronaut says.

"What did it feel like out there from so far away?"

"Well, it was exhilarating. A whole different perspective. I felt privileged to be a part of a great program."

"But was it scary?"

"I'm not sure I know what you mean?"

"Could you sleep?"

The astronaut's smile, which has lasted for three periods, slackens. He squints outward; his hands are visors over his yes. "Truthfully?" he says. "No one's ever asked me that one. I didn't sleep very well, no."

"What were you afraid of?" another voice asks. "Crashing?"

"No," the astronaut says. He has walked in front of the screen so that the earth's crust is his skin, his slacks and shirt. "It's hard to explain. Let's call it indifference. The absolute blackness of it. Life looks pretty far away from out there."

For five seconds longer than is comfortable, no one moves. Then ten seconds. "So, no," the astronaut repeats. "I didn't sleep well."

A student stands, his auditorium seat flapping up behind him, raising a welcome clatter. "How do you go to the bathroom in a space suit?"

There is laughter and applause. Relief. The astronaut grins, returning to his mission. He's had the same question in the first two sessions. "I knew *some*body was going to ask me that," he says.

Scanning his juniors in the middle rows, Duncan spots James Bocheko, his worst student. Jimmy's boots are wedged up against the back of the seat in front of him, his knees gaping out of twin rips in his jeans. There's a magazine in his lap, a wire to his ear. He's shut out the school and the astronaut's message from space. Duncan leans past two girls and taps Jimmy's shoulder.

"Let's have it," he says.

The boy looks up—a confused child being called out of a nap rather than a troublemaker. His red bangs are an awning over large, dark eyes. He remembers to scowl.

"What?"

"The Walkman. You know they're not allowed. Let's have it."

Jimmy shakes his head. Students around them are losing interest in the astronaut. Duncan snatches up the recorder.

"Hey!" Jimmy says out loud. Other teachers are watching.

"Get out," Duncan whispers.

"Get laid," the boy says. Then he unfolds himself, standing and stretching. His boots clomp a racket up the aisle. He's swaggering, smiling. "Later, Space Cadets!" he shouts to all of them just before he gives the door a slam.

On stage, the astronaut has stopped to listen. Duncan feels the blood in his face. His hand is clamped around the Walkman, the thin wire rocking back and forth in front of him.

Stacie Vars can't stand this bus driver. She liked the one they had last year—that real skinny woman with braids who let them smoke. Linda something—she used to play all those Willie Nelson songs on her boombox. Stacie saw Willie Nelson in a cowboy movie on Cinemax last night. It was boring. He wears braids, too, come to think of it. This new bus driver thinks her shit don't flush.

Nobody at school knows Stacie is pregnant yet, not even the kids in Fire Queens. She's not sure if they'll let her stay in the drum corps or not. She doesn't really care about marching; maybe she could hold kids' jackets and purses or something. Ever since she got pregnant, she has to go the bathroom all the time. Which is a pain, because whenever you ask those teachers for the lav pass, it's like a personal insult or something. She couldn't believe that geeky kid who asked the astronaut today about taking a crap. God. That whole assembly was boring. Except when Jimmy got kicked out by her homeroom teacher. She's not sure if Jimmy saw her or not when he passed her. He gets mad if she speaks to him at school. He's so moody. She doesn't want to take any chances.

The bus jerks and slows. Up ahead Stacie can see the blue winking lights of an accident. The kids all run over to that side of the bus, gawking. Not her; she doesn't like to look at that kind of thing. Jimmy says there's this movie at the video store where they show you actual deaths from real life. Firing squads and people getting knifed, shit like that. He hasn't seen it yet; it's always out. "Maybe it's fake," she told him. He laughed at her and said she was a retard—that if it was fake, then you could rent it whenever you wanted to. She hates when he calls her that. She's got feelings, too. Last week Mrs. Roberge called Stacie's whole science class "brain dead." Stacie doesn't think that's right. Somebody ought to report that bitch. Those police car lights are the same color of the shaving lotion her father used to keep on top of the toilet. Ice Blue Aqua Velva. She wonders if he still uses that stuff. Not that it's important. It's just something she'd like to know.

Duncan is eating a cheese omelet from the frying pan, not really tasting it. He's worried what to do about Jimmy Bocheko's hatred; he wishes he didn't have all those essays to grade. Duncan replays the scene from two days ago when he'd had the class write on their strengths and weaknesses. Bocheko had done his best to disrupt the class. "Is this going to count? . . . What do we have to write on something so stupid for? . . . "

"Just do it!" Duncan shouted.

The boy reddened, balled up the paper he'd just barely started, and threw it on the floor. Then he walked out.

The other students, boisterous and itchy, were suddenly still, awaiting Duncan's move.

"Okay, now," he said in a shaky voice. "Let's get back to work." For the rest of the period, Duncan's eyes kept bouncing back to the paper ball on the floor. The astronaut's assembly today was *supposed* to have given them distance from that confrontation.

At the sink of his efficiency apartment, Duncan scrapes dried egg off the frying pan with his fingernails. This past week when he did the grocery shopping (he uses one of those plastic baskets now, instead of a wheel-around cart), he forgot the S.O.S. Yesterday he forgot to go to a faculty meeting. He was halfway home before he remembered Mrs. Shefflot, his carpooler, whose husband was already there picking her up by the time Duncan got back to school. He knows three people his age whose parents have Alzheimer's. He wonders if it ever skips a generation—plays a double dirty trick on aging parents.

When the phone rings, Duncan tucks the receiver under his chin and continues his chores. The cord is ridiculously long; he can navigate his entire residence while tethered to the phone.

The caller is Rona, a hostess at the racquetball club Duncan joined as part of his divorce therapy. Rona is divorced, too, but twenty-three, eleven years younger than Duncan—young enough to have been his student, though she wasn't. She grew up near Chicago.

"What's worse than getting AIDS on a blind date?" Rona asks in her cheerful rasp. At the club, she is known as a hot shit. Kevin, Duncan's racquetball partner, thinks she's desperate, would screw anything.

Duncan doesn't know.

She is giggling; he has missed the punchline. This is the second AIDS joke he's heard this week. Duncan waters his plant and puts a bag of garbage on the back porch while Rona complains about her boss.

" . . . to get you and me over the mid-week slump," she is saying. She may have just asked him out for a drink. There is a pause. Then she adds, "My treat."

Duncan has had one date with Rona. More or less at her insistence, he cooked dinner at his apartment. She arrived with two gifts: a bottle of Peachtree schnapps and a copy of *People* magazine. All evening she made jokes about his kitchen curtains being

333

too short. Fingering through his record collection, she told him it was "real vintage." (Her favorite group is Whitesnake, plus she likes jazz.) After dinner they smoked dope, hers, and settled for James Taylor's Greatest Hits. She didn't leave until twelve thirty, two hours after the sex. This struck Duncan as inconsiderate; it was a school night.

"I think I'd better beg off," Duncan says. "I've got essays to correct tonight." He holds them to the phone as if to prove it's the truth. Kevin is probably right about her. He's glad he used that rubber she had in her purse, embarrassing as that was.

"Oh wow," she says. "I'm being shot down for 'What I Did Over Summer Vacation.' " Duncan tells her he'll see her at the club.

Duncan's ex-wife used to love to read his students' work. She always argued there was a certain nobility amidst all the grammatical errors and inarticulateness. Kids being confessional, kids struggling for truth. After they separated, Duncan kept dropping by unannounced with half-gallons of ice cream and papers he thought might interest her. Then, when she had her brother change all the locks, Duncan would sit on the front porch step like Lassie, waiting for her to relent. Once she stood at the picture window with a sheet of notebook paper pressed against the glass. *Cut this shit out*, it said in Magic Marker capitals. *Grow up!* Duncan assumes he will love her forever.

Wearing underpants, sweatshirt, and gym socks, Duncan crawls between his chilly sheets. He snaps on his clock radio and fans out the essays before him. He'll do the worst ones first. The disc jockey has free movie tickets for the first person who can tell him who sang "If You're Going to San Francisco, Be Sure To Wear Some Flowers in Your Hair."

"Scott MacKenzie," Duncan says out loud. He owns the album.

Halfway through his third paper, he looks up at the radio. The announcer has just mentioned James Bocheko.

"Bocheko, a local youth, was dead on arrival at Twin Districts Hospital after the car he was driving . . . "

When the music starts again, Duncan turns off the radio and lies perfectly still, confused by his own giddy feeling. He leans over and picks up James Bocheko's paper which he took from the floor that afternoon and flattened with the palm of his hand. The wrinkled yellow paper is smudgy with fingerprints, the penmanship as large and deliberate as a young child's.

Strength's: I am HONEST. Not a wimp.

Weakness's: Not enouf upper body strength.

Duncan drinks bourbon from a jelly jar until the shivering stops. Then he dials his old telephone number. "Listen," he says to his ex-wife. "Can I talk to you for a minute? Something awful happened. One of my kids got killed."

At two, he awakens totally cold, knowing that's it for the night's sleep. When he rolls over, his students' papers crinkle in the folds of the quilt.

Stacie sits with her hands on the table, waiting for her mother to go to work.

"You ought to eat something besides this crap," her mother tells her, picking up the large box of Little Debbie cakes. She blows a cone of cigarette smoke at Stacie. "A fried egg or something."

It's the second morning since Stacie's felt like eating, but the thought of an egg puckering in a frying pan gives her a queasy feeling. She's eaten three of the cakes and torn the cellophane packaging into strips.

"Mrs. Faola's knitting a sweater and booties for the baby," she says, trying to change the subject. "Pale pink."

"Well, that'll look pretty g.d. foolish if you end up with a boy, won't it?"

"Mrs. Faola says if I wear something pink every day for a month, it will be a girl."

Her mother takes a deep drag on her cigarette and exhales. "If that wasn't so pathetic, it'd be hilarious, Stacie. Real scientific. I don't suppose you told the mystery man the good news yet."

Stacie picks at a ball of lint on the sleeve of her pink sweater. "You better get going," she says. "You'll be late for work."

"Have you?"

"What?"

"Told him yet?"

Stacie's cuticles go white against the table top. "I *told* you I was telling him when the time is right, Mommy. Get off my fucking case."

Linda snatches up her car keys and gives her daughter a long, hard stare. "Nice way for a new mother to talk," she says. Stacie stares back for as long as she can, then looks away. A ripple of nausea passes through her.

Her mother leaves without another word. Stacie watches the door's Venetian blind swing back and forth. God, she hates her mother. That woman is so intense.

If it's a girl, Stacie's decided to name her Desiree. Desiree Dawne Bocheko. Stacie's going to decorate her little room with Rainbow Brite stuff. Mrs. Faola says they sell scented wallpaper now. Scratch'n'sniff—she seen it in a magazine. Stacie might get that, too. She's not sure yet.

Everything is finally falling into place, in a way. At least she can eat again. This weekend, Stacie's going to tell him. "Jimmy," she'll say, "Guess what? I'm having your baby." She hopes they're both buzzed. She could very well be a married woman by Halloween; it could happen. God. She already feels older than the kids in Fire Queens. Maybe they'll give her a surprise baby shower. She imagines herself walking into a room filled with balloons, her hands over her face.

When the phone rings, it embarrasses her. "Oh, hi, Mrs. Faola. No, she left about ten minutes ago. Yeah, my pink sweater and pink underpants. No, I'm going to school today."

Mrs. Faola lives in Building J. She watches for Stacie's mother's car to leave, then calls and bribes Stacie to skip school and visit. Today she has cheese popcorn. Oprah Winfrey's guests are soap stars.

"Nah, I really think I should go today," Stacie repeats. She loves to see Jimmy in the hall, even though she can't talk to him. No one's supposed to know they're semi-going out. "When *can* I tell people," she asked him once. "When you lose about half a ton," he said. She's *going* to lose weight, right after the baby. Mrs. Faola says Stacie better get used to having her feelings hurt—that that's just the way men are. Stacie would die for Jimmy. Mrs. Faola had an unmarried sister that died having a baby. Stacie's seen her picture.

"Tomorrow I'm staying home," she promises Mrs. Faola. "Gym on Friday."

She guesses most people would find it weird, her friendship with Mrs. Faola, but she don't care. Last week they played slapjack and Mrs. Faola gave her a crocheting lesson. She's going to give her a home perm when Stacie gets a little farther along, too. In her mind, Stacie's got this picture of herself sitting up in a hospital bed wearing a French braid like Kayla Brady on *Days of Our Lives*. Desiree is holding on to her little finger. They're waiting for Jimmy to visit the hospital. He's bringing a teddy bear and roses for Stacie. The baby has made him wicked happy.

Mrs. Faola is right about abortion being a fancy name for murder. Stacie won't even say the word out loud. At least her mother's off her case about that.

She stands up quick and gets that queasy feeling again, but it passes. She coats her mouth with cherry lip gloss and picks up her notebook. On the cover she's drawn a marijuana leaf and surrounded it with the names of rock groups in fancy letters. She keeps forgetting to erase BonJovi. Jimmy says they're a real suck group, and now that she thinks about it, they aren't that good.

On her way out, she looks at the cowgirl on the Little Debbie box. She's so cute. Maybe Desiree will look something like her.

Unable to sleep, Duncan has dressed and walked, ending not by design at an early morning mass at the church of his childhood. In the unlit back pew he sits like a one-man audience, watching uniformed workers and old people—variations on his parents—huddled together, making their peace. They seem further away than the length of the church. In his coat pocket Duncan fingers James Bocheko's list of strengths and weaknesses. The priest is no one he knows. His hair is an elaborate silver pompadour. From the lectern he smiles like a game show host, coaxing parishioners to be ready for their moment of grace when it comes hurling toward them. Duncan thinks of spiraling missiles, whizzing meteors. He imagines the priest naked with a blow-dryer, vainly arranging that hair. He leaves before communion.

This early, the teachers' room is more quiet than Duncan is used to. He listens to the sputter of a fluorescent light, the gurgle of the coffee maker. Jimmy Bocheko stares back at him indifferently, his eyes blank and wide-set. A grammar school picture. Duncan draws the newspaper close to his face and listens to his own breathing against the paper. The boy dissolves into a series of black dots.

337

At 8:15, Duncan is seated at his desk, eavesdropping. His homeroom students are wide-eyed, animated.

"My brother-in-law's on the rescue squad. The dude's head was ripped right off."

" . . . No, that red-haired kid in our health class last year, the one with the earring."

"Head-on collision, man. He bought it."

A girl in the front row asks Duncan if he knew a boy named Jim Bocheko.

"Yes," Duncan says. "Awful." The girl seems disappointed not to be the one breaking the news. Then she is looking at his reaction. He thinks foolishly of handing her Jimmy's list.

The restless liquor night has already settled in Duncan's stomach, behind the lids of his eyes. The P.A. hums on. "All right, quiet now," Duncan says, pointing half-heartedly toward the box on the wall.

" . . . a boy whose tragic death robs us just as his life enriched us." The principal's mouth is too close to the microphone; his words explode at them. "Would you all please rise and observe a moment of silence in memory of your fellow student and friend, James Bocheko?"

Chairs scrape along the floor. The students' heads are bowed uneasily. They wait out the P.A.'s blank hum.

Duncan notices the fat girl, Stacie, the chronic absentee, still in her seat. Those around her give her quick, disapproving glances. Should he say something? Make her stand?

The girl's head begins to bob up and down, puppet-like; she is grunting rhythmically. "Gag reflex," Duncan thinks objectively.

Yellow liquid spills out of her mouth and onto the shiny desktop. "Oh Christ, get the wastebasket!" someone calls. "Je-sus!" The vomit splatters onto the floor. Those nearby force themselves to look, then jerk their heads away. Two boys begin to laugh uncontrollably.

A gangly boy volunteers to run for the janitor and Duncan assigns the front row girl to walk Stacie to the nurse's office. "Come on," the girl says to her, pinching a little corner of the pink sweater, unwilling to get closer. Stacie obeys her, bland and sheep-dazed, her chin still dribbling.

Jimmy Bocheko's moment of silence has ended but nobody notices. The vomit's sweet vinegar has pervaded the classroom.

338

Windows are thrown open to the cold. Everyone is giggling or complaining.

" . . . And to the republic for which it stands, one nation under God, indivisible . . . " the P.A. announcer chants.

The first period bell rings and they shove out loudly into the hall. Duncan listens to the random hoots and obscenities and details of the accident. "If he gives us a quiz today, I'll kill myself," a girl says.

Duncan turns a piece of chalk end over end. He wonders if the decapitation is fact or some ghoulish embellishment.

A freshman thumps into the room, skids his gym bag across the floor toward his seat. "Hey, Mr. Foley, did you know that kid that got wasted yesterday? He lives next door to my cousin," he says proudly. "Whoa, what stinks in here?"

Stacie keeps pushing the remote control but everything on is boring. That Willie Nelson movie is on Cinemax for the one zillionth time. She wishes she could just talk to someone like that last year's bus driver—someone who could make it clear. Only what's she supposed to do—call up every Linda in the stupid phone book? It's *weird*; he never even knew. Unless he's somewhere watching her. Like a spirit or something. Like one of those shoplifting cameras at Cumberland Farms. She lies down on the rug and covers herself with the afghan. Her stone-washed jeans are only three months old and they're already too tight. She undoes the top button and her fat flops out. She can feel it there, soft and dead against the scratchy carpet and she lets herself admit something: she didn't tell him because she was afraid to. Afraid to wreck that hospital picture she wanted. Her whole life sucks. She could care less about this stupid baby . . .

She wakes with the sound of footsteps on the porch, then the abrupt light. She clamps her eyes shut again. Her mother's shadow is by the light switch. The rug has made marks in her cheek.

"What time is it?"

"Five after seven. Get up. I'll make supper. You should eat."

Stacie begins quietly when the macaroni and cheese is on the table. "I got something to tell you," she says. "Don't get mad."

Her mother looks disgustedly at something—a gummy strand

of hair hanging down in Stacie's plate. Stacie wipes her hair with a napkin.

"There's this kid I know, Jimmy Bocheko. He got killed yesterday. In an accident."

"I know. I saw it in the paper."

"He's the one."

"The one what?"

"The father."

Stacie's mother is chewing a forkful of food and thinking hard. "Are you telling me the truth?" she says.

Stacie nods and looks away. She hates it that she's crying.

"Well, Stacie, you sure know how to pick them, don't you?" her mother says. "Jesus Christ, you're just a regular genius."

Stacie slams both fists on the table, surprising herself and her mother, who jumps. "You could at least be a little nice to me," she shouts. "I puked at school today when I found out. It's practically like I'm a widow."

This makes her mother hitting mad. She is on her feet, shoving her, slapping. Stacie covers her face. "Stop it. Mommy! Stop it!"

"Widow? I'll tell you what you are. You're just a stupid girl living in a big fat dream world. And now you've played with fire and got yourself good and burnt, didn't you?"

"Stop it!"

"Didn't you? Answer me! Didn't you?"

"The jade plant looks nice over there," Duncan says. His ex-wife has rearranged the living room. It looks more angular, less comfortable without his clutter.

"It's got aphids," she says.

He remembers the presents out on his back seat. "Be right back," he says. When he returns, he hands her a small bag of the raw cashews she loves, and a jazz album. His ex-wife looks at the album cover, her face forming a question. "I've been getting into jazz a little," he explains, shrugging.

Although he would have preferred the kitchen, she has set the dining room table. The meal is neutral; chicken, baked potatoes, salad.

After dinner, he wipes the dishes while she washes. She's bought a wok and hung it on the kitchen wall. Duncan's eyes keep landing on it. "What's the difference between oral sex and oral hygiene?" he asks abruptly after an uncomfortable silence. It's one Rona has told him.

"Oh, Duncan, how am I supposed to know? How's your family?"

"Okay, I guess. My sister is pregnant again."

"I know," she says. "I saw your father at Stop and Shop. Did he mention it?" She hands him the gleaming broiler pan. "He was wearing a jogging suit. Gee, he looked old. He was mad at your mother. She sent him to the store for yeast and birthday candles and he couldn't find the yeast. Then there I am, the ex-daughter-in-law. He was having trouble handling eye contact."

"Did you tell him where the yeast was?"

"Yeah, then he thanked a pile of apples over my left shoulder and walked up the aisle." She turns to Duncan with a worried look. "How come he's limping?"

"Arthritis. It's weird, Ruthie. He and my mother are turning into little cartoon senior citizens. They go out to lunch every day and find fault. Last week I got stuck in a line of traffic; there's some slowpoke holding everybody up. It turns out to be my father. They're, I don't know, shrinking or something. She has a jogging suit, too. They wear them because they're warm. I can't help seeing them from a distance. It's bizarre."

Two years ago, when the specialist confirmed that his wife had indeed finally conceived, Duncan drove to his parents' house to break the news. His mother was out, his father in the back yard pruning a bush. "See what a little prayer can get you, Mr. Big Deal Atheist?" his father said, jabbing Duncan in the stomach with the butt of the clippers, harping all the way back to an argument they'd had when Duncan was still in college. When he went to hug him, Duncan drew back, resentful of his father's claiming credit for himself and his god. They'd been putting up with those fertility treatments for two years.

Duncan's ex-wife begins to munch on the cashews. "These are stale," she says. "Good. Now I won't pig out."

"I'm going out with somebody. She's divorced. Somebody from racquetball."

There is a pause. She pops more nuts into her mouth and chews. "Well," she says, "that's allowed."

341

"So when did you take up Chinese cooking?" he asks, pointing to the wok. He means to be nonchalant but is sounding like Perry Mason grilling a guilty woman. The wok is a damning piece of evidence.

"I'm taking one of those night courses at the community college. With a friend of mine from work."

"Male or female?"

She clangs the broiler pan back into the bottom drawer of the stove. "An androgyn, okay? A hermaphrodite. I thought you wanted to talk about this kid who got killed."

He takes Bocheko's paper out of his wallet and unfolds it for her. "Oh, Duncan," his ex-wife sighs. "Oh, shit."

"The kids were high on the death thing all day, exchanging gruesome rumors. Nobody wanted to talk about anything else. Do you think I should write them a letter or something?"

"Who?"

"His parents."

"I don't know," she says. "Do what you need to do."

On TV, James Taylor is singing "Don't Let Me Be Lonely Tonight." On their honeymoon, Duncan and his ex-wife sat near James Taylor at a Chinese restaurant in Soho. Duncan and he ordered the exact same meal. Duncan is dismayed to see James Taylor so bald.

"You know my record collection?" Duncan says to his ex-wife. "Do you think it's real 'vintage'?"

"Real what?" she asks in a nasal voice. He realizes suddenly that she's been crying. But when he presses her, she refuses to say why.

Yellow leaves are smashed against the sidewalk. Duncan collapses his black umbrella and feels the cold drizzle on the back of his neck. An undertaker holds open the door. Duncan nods a thank you and sees that the man is in his twenties. This has been happening more and more: people his father's age have retired, leaving in charge people younger than Duncan.

He signs a book on a lighted podium and takes a holy picture, a souvenir. On the front is a sad-eyed Jesus, his sacred heart exposed. On the back, James Bocheko's name is printed in elegant script. Duncan thinks of the boy's signature, those fat, loopy letters.

342

In the main room, it's that pompadour priest before the casket, leading a rosary. Duncan slips quietly past and sits in a cushioned folding chair, breathing in the aroma of carnations. Someone taps his arm and Duncan sees he has sat next to one of his students, a loud-mouthed boy in James' class.

"Hi, Mr. Foley," the boy whispers hoarsely. Duncan is surprised to see him fingering rosary beads.

James Bocheko's family is in a row of high-backed chairs at a right angle to the closed casket. They look ill at ease in their roles as the designated royalty of this occasion. A younger brother pumps his leg up and down and wanders the room. An older sister rhythmically squeezes a Kleenex. Their father, a scruffy man with a bristly crewcut and a loud plaid sports jacket, looks sadly out at nothing.

Only James Bocheko's mother seems to be concentrating on the rosary. Her prayer carries over the hushed responses of the others. "Blessed art thou who art in heaven and blessed is the fruit of thy womb."

When the prayers are finished, the priest takes Mrs. Bocheko's wrists, whispers something to her. Others shuffle to the front, forming an obedient line. Duncan heads for the foyer. They will see his signature in the book. Mrs. Bocheko will remember him from the conference. "I know he's no angel," she said specifically to Duncan that afternoon, locking her face into a defense against the teachers and counselors around the table. Only now does he have the full impact of how alone she must have felt.

He sees that girl, Stacie, at the rear of the room. She is wearing a low-cut blouse and corduroy pants; her feet are hooked around the legs of the chair in front of her.

"How are you feeling?" Duncan whispers to her.

"Okay." she says, looking away.

"Were you a friend of his?"

"Kind of." She says it to her lap.

In the vestibule, the undertaker is helping the priest into his raincoat. "So who's your money on for the Series this year, Father?" he asks him over his shoulder.

Stacie walks past two other girls, representatives from the student council who stare after her and smirk.

The door is opened again for Duncan. The drizzle has turned to slanted rain.

343

Stacie is lying on her bed, wondering what happened to her notebook. She hasn't been back to school in over a month, since the day she found out about Jimmy—that day she threw up. She's not going back, either, especially now that she's showing. Let the school send all the letters they want. She'll just burn them all up and flush the ashes down the toilet. She's quitting as soon as she turns sixteen anyways. What does she care?

That Mr. Foley probably has her notebook. She's pretty sure she left it in his room that morning. Of all his teachers, Jimmy hated Mr. Foley's guts the most. He was always trying to get them to write stuff, Jimmy said, stuff that wasn't any of his fucking business. What she can't figure out is why he was at Jimmy's wake—unless he was just snooping around. By now, he's probably looked through her notebook, seen the pages where she's written "Mrs. Stacie Bocheko" and "Property of Jimmy B." and the other private stuff.

Being pregnant is boring. There's nothing good on TV and nothing around to eat. She wishes she and Mrs. Faola didn't have that fight. She still wants to get that perm.

She reaches back for her pillow. Drawing it close to her face, she pokes her tongue out and gives it a shy lick. She remembers the feel of Jimmy's tongue flicking nervously all over the insides of her mouth. She remembers the part just before he finished—when he'd reach out for her like some little boy. She gives the pillow several more little cat licks. She likes doing it. It feels funny.

Then she's aware of something else funny, down there. It feels like a little butterfly bumping up against her stomach, trying to get out. It makes her laugh. She kisses the pillow and feels it again. She begins either to giggle or to cry. She can't tell which. She can't stop.

"Why don't you ever make us write *good* stuff?" they wanted to know.

Duncan turned from the chalkboard and faced them. "Like what?" he asked.

"Like stories and stuff. You know."

So he gave them what they wanted and on Friday every student had a story to hand in. He has read them over and over again, all weekend, but has not been able to grade them. Each of the stories ends in death; sentimentally tragic death, the death of a thousand bad television plots. Not knowing where to put the anxiety with which James Bocheko's death has left them, they have put it down on paper, locked it into decorous penmanship, self-conscious sentences they feel are works of art. How can he affix a grade?

The newspapers are full of fatal accidents. A bride has shot her husband. A girl choked to death in a restaurant. On the hour, Duncan's clock radio warns parents against maniacs, purveyors of tainted Halloween candy.

His wife is not safe. She could die in a hundred random ways: a skidding truck, faulty wiring, some guy with AIDS.

It was in a Howard Johnson's ladies' room that she first noticed she was spotting. "It's as if her body's played a joke on itself," the gynecologist explained to Duncan the next afternoon while his wife stared angrily into her hospital sheets, tapping her fist against her lip. "The amniotic sac had begun to form itself, just *as if* fertilization had occurred. But there was no evidence of an egg inside." Duncan recalls how she spent the next several weeks slamming things, how he rushed up to the attic to cry. There was no death to mourn—only the absence of life, the joke.

When he hears the knocking, he is sure it's his ex-wife, wearing her jeans and her maroon sweater, answering his need for her. But it is Rona, shivering in a belly dancer's costume. "Trick or treat," she says, holding out a tiny vial of coke. "We deliver." Inside, she lifts her coat off her shoulders and her costume jangles. She runs her chilled fingers over the stubble of Duncan's jaw.

* * *

The janitors have taken over the school, rigging the country western station through the PA system and shouting back and forth from opposite ends of the corridor as they repair the year's damages. It's the beginning of summer vacation. Duncan sits in his classroom, surrounded by the open drawers of his desk. He's in a throwing away mood.

What he should do is make plans—get to the beach more, visit someone far away. He should spend more time with his father, who is hurting so badly. Sick with grief: that phrase taking on new meaning. "You're not alone, I know what it's like," Duncan

345

told him last week. The two of them were fumbling with supper preparations in Duncan's mother's kitchen, self-consciously intent on doing things the way she'd always done them. "When Ruthie got remarried this spring, it was like she died to me, too."

"Bullshit!" his father snapped. His grip tightened around a fistful of silverware. "That divorce was *your* doing, the two of you. Don't you *dare* compare your mother's death to that. Don't you *dare* say you know what it's like for me." That was six days ago. Duncan hasn't called since.

He's saved the bottom right desk drawer for last, avoiding it as if there's something in there—a homemade bomb or a snake. But it's the confiscated Walkman, buried under piles of notices and tests. Duncan sees again James Bocheko, crouched in the dark auditorium.

Tentatively, Duncan fixes the headphones to his ears and finds the button. He's expecting screaming guitars, a taunting vocal, but it's electronic music—waves of blips and notes that may or may not mean anything. After awhile the music lulls him, makes him feel removed and afloat. He closes his eyes and sees black.

The janitor makes him jump.

"What?" Duncan says. He yanks off the earphones to hear the sound that goes with the moving lips.

"I said, we're going now. We're locking up."

He drives to the mall for no good reason. It's becoming a pattern: tiptoeing in and out of the bright stores, making small purchases because he feels watched. At the K-Mart register, he places his lightbulbs and sale shampoo before the clerk like an offering.

Exiting, he passes the revolving pretzels, the rolling hot dogs, a snack bar customer and a baby amidst the empty orange tables.

"Hey!" she says. "Wait."

He moves toward them, questioning. Then he knows her.

"You're a teacher, ain't you?" She's flustered for having spoken. "I had you for homeroom this year. For a while."

Bocheko's wake. The one who vomited—Stacie something. It's her hair that's different—shorter, close cropped.

"Hello," he says. It scares her when he sits down.

The baby has glossy cheeks and fuzzy red hair that makes Duncan smile. He pushes the infant seat away from the edge of the table.

"Did you find a notebook in your class? It's green and it's got writing on the front."

The baby's arms are flailing like a conductor's. "What did you say?"

"My notebook. I lost it in your room and I kind of still want it."

There's a large soda on the table and a cardboard french fry container brimming with cigarette butts. Behind her, the unoccupied arcade games are registering small explosions. "I don't remember it. But I'll look."

"I thought maybe you were saving it or something."

Duncan shrugs. "Cute baby," he smiles. "Boy or girl?"

"Boy." She blushes, picks him up so abruptly that he begins to cry.

"How old?"

"Stop it," she tells the baby. She hooks a strand of hair behind her ear with her free hand.

"*How* old is he?"

"Almost three months. Shut up, will you? God," Her clutch is too tight. The crying has turned him red. "Could you hold him for a second?" she says.

Duncan receives the baby—tense and bucking—with a nervous laugh. "Like this?" he asks.

Stacie dunks her finger into her soda and sticks it, dripping, into his mouth. "This sometimes works," she says. The crying subsides. The baby begins to suck.

"Uh, what is it?" Duncan asks.

"Diet Pepsi, It's okay. He ain't really getting any. It's just to soothe him down." The baby's shoulders against Duncan's chest relax. "You have to trick them," she says. Then she smiles at the baby. "Don't you?" she asks him.

"What's his name?"

"Jesse," she says. "Jesse James Bocheko."

Her eyes are gray and marbled, non-committal. He looks away from them, down. "I'm sorry," he says.

It's she who breaks the silence. "Could you do me a favor? Could you just watch him for a couple of seconds so's I can go to the ladies' room?"

He nods eagerly. "Yes," he says. "You go."

The soft spot on the baby's head indents with each breath. Duncan *sees* his own thighs against the plastic chair, his shoes on the floor, but can't *feel* them. He's weightless, connected only to this warm, small body.

"Baby . . . " he whispers. He closes his eyes and puts two fingertips to the spot, feeling both the strength and the frailty, the gap and pulse together.

1990

MY LORD BAG OF RICE

by CAROL BLY

from THE LAUREL REVIEW

WHEN VIRGIL HAD been healthy and mean, Eleanor had loved him; now that he was dying, in his pain grinding shoulders and hips into the bed, she sometimes found herself daydreaming, *If Virgil died this week instead of next, I could start everything that much sooner.* "Do you feel guilty?" B. J. at the Women's Support Group asked. "You have a right to your own life." It sounded nineteen-eighties-OK to have a right to your own life; it did not sound so good to say, If Virgil Grummel would only die this week instead of next, or tonight instead of tomorrow night, she could inherit the farm and the engine repair service all the sooner. She could sell it all and take the $183,000 cash which their neighbor, Almendus Leitz, said it was probably worth. She would start a boarding house in St. Paul and never, never again hear cruel language around her. *Never,* she thought, patting Virgil's ankle skin.

It was three in the morning, the hour when she usually visited Virgil at Masonic Hospital because then the drugs didn't cover the pain. She drove over from St. Paul twice a day. Sometimes, like tonight, when she walked right into the hot, wide doorway of the hospital, no one sat guard at Reception. The flowers leaned on their stems in the shadowy glass cooler. The crossword puzzle kits waited motionless in the gift case. Someone could perfectly well walk in and hurt people, and steal things, and trot back out into the August night. Eleanor always walked past the dark counters to the elevator and came up to Three.

Despite his morphine Virgil was awake and in pain. He wanted to talk about the good old days. His agonized, liquid eyes

349

watched her as she cut in half each sock of a new woolen pair. Then she slipped the toe-half over his icy feet. Whole socks didn't work because of the styrofoam packed around Virgil's insteps to prevent bedsores.

He pled with her to mention the good old days. In his wispy, throttled voice he said, "Do you remember how we went to Monte to get you your stone?" Dawson was their town, but Montevideo was the town that counted, the place for buying major things like wall-to-wall carpeting and diamond rings. Eleanor smiled down at Virgil's face in the shadowy hospital room, but she was thinking how he had never called the ring an engagement ring: he called it a "stone," just as meals were "chow" and love was "your medicine." One day their older neighbor lady, Mrs. Almendus Leitz, had come over and told Eleanor how Almendus was always telling her to "just roll over and take your medicine." Mrs. Leitz was sick of it. She and Eleanor stood on the stoop, both of them with their work-strong arms folded, squinting out over Virgil's steaming acreage of corn and beans. It crossed Eleanor's mind at the time that all over the whole breathless prairie, with farm places at half-mile intervals, men were telling women to roll over and take their medicine, but she decided not to think about it.

"Yes, but you *should* have been thinking about it," they all said firmly, down at the Women's Support Group which she now belonged to in Minneapolis. Not just B.J. said so. All of them. B.J. said she fervently hoped that now Eleanor was in the Twin Cities she would become sexually active. Eleanor let her talk.

As soon as they were married, Virgil put in a bid for the old District 73 Country School and won it; he dragged it over to their place on the flatbed, laid down a concrete floor for it, and set it down. He never yanked the old school cupboards and bookshelves off the walls. There were dozens of Elson-Gray Readers and some children's books. There was a book of Japanese fairy tales which Eleanor took up whenever she had a moment.

Now Virgil wanted her to recall how he'd be repairing machinery out there in the shop, and he'd call her on the two-way to come out, and how they worked together out there. "Do you remember," he whispered, "how you'd quit whatever you was doing in the house and come on out and help me in the shop?" She remembered: the two-way crackled and growled all the time in the kitchen. She could hear the field hands from Almendus's west half-section swearing because they'd dropped a furrow wheel or a lunchbox out in the plowing somewhere. Then, very loud and close, Virgil's voice would cut in, "Hey, Little Girl, this is Big Red Chief, get your butt out here a minute," and he would go off without waiting for her to answer. He had fixed up both the laundry area and the kitchen for radio reception, so he knew she'd hear him, wherever she was, canning or what. She would go out to the shop, arms crossed across her breasts if it was cold, running if it was summer, looking out over the fields past Almendus's place towards Dawson Mills. Virgil was fond of the radio. Sometimes he wanted to make love in the shop; he would lay out the hood dropcloth on the station wagon back seat which he never did get back into the station wagon. When the wagon finally threw a rod, the backseat stayed in the shop. Each time he was through making love, he said, "This is Big Red Chief, over and out," and gave her a little slap on the temple.

Eleanor knew she was lucky. All her childhood her father had gone on every-six-months beating binges. He beat up her mother and then he forced her sister. "You don't have to look so owlly," he told Eleanor when she stood dumb, watching, "your big sister is a real princess." She was so lucky to be married to a good man like Virgil, who didn't drink much. It was boring helping a man in the shop, though. Much of the time he would say, "Don't go away, Little Girl, I might need you." He didn't care whether she had quart jars boiling in the processor. So she would give his feet a glance (he had dollied himself underneath someone's Buick now) and she carried the Japanese fairy tale book over to one of the old schoolroom windows. Virgil's FARM AND ENGINE RE-PAIRS sign creaked outside, the corn tattered in the wind, and Eleanor found a story that she read over and over.

"Hey," Virgil shouted from under the Buick he was fixing. "Get that V-belt and hand it to me." Then he said, "No, dang it all, not that one—the other one!" Then she would open the book again.

"Hey, get your ass over here," Virgil cried. "Hand me all this stuff when I tell you, one by one in order."

She wiped the grease off her hands and went back to the story. A young Japanese hero had a retinue of servants. Watercolor illustrations showed him mustachioed, with slant eyes and nearly white skin. All his servants wore sashes with thin swords tucked into them. They looked a little like middle-aged, effeminate Americans in dressing gowns who had chosen to arm themselves. Eleanor couldn't keep her eyes off the pictures. The hero was travelling through Japan, looking for adventure, when he came to a high, rounded bridge over a river which ran to the sea. As he began to cross it, he saw that a frightful dragon slept at the top of its arch. The dragon's scales and horns and raised back ridge were everything a child would count on when it came to dragons. No one was around to sneer at a grown woman reading a child's book when she was supposed to be helping her husband.

The young Japanese started to step right across the dragon, and it suddenly reared up. His servants dropped back, aghast, but the hero held his ground. Then the dragon took the form of a beautiful woman, who explained that she was ruler of a sea kingdom under the bridge. Each night a centipede of gigantic size slid down from the mountain to the north (she pointed) and ate dozens of her subjects, who were fishes and sea-animals. They realized they needed a man—but not an ordinary man. "You can imagine what fright an ordinary man would feel," the sea princess said.

Dusk was falling. She pointed again to the mountain, which now showed only its black profile before the green, darkening sky. Some sort of procession of people carrying lanterns seemed to descend the near slope of the mountain. "Those are not people," the sea princess said. "Those are the eyes of the centipede."

"I will kill it," the young Japanese said simply.

"I think you are brave enough," the princess said. "I took the form of a dragon and placed myself on this bridge, pretending to sleep. You are the only man who hasn't fled at the sight of me."

The hero drew a light green arrow from the quiver on his shoulder. He sent it at one of the centipede's eyes. That eye went out, but the monster kept coming. He took another arrow—a pale pink one this time—but it only put out another eye. Then he recalled a proverb of the Japanese people: human saliva is poison to magical enemies. He licked the tip of an arrow the color of a bird's egg and sent it off into the thick dusk. It went true. It put out the creature's foremost eye—and then the princess and the hero were joyous to see all the eyes darken to red, then grey, like worn coals.

The princess clapped. "Wait, O hero!" she cried. She clapped again. Fishes dressed in silk robes rose from the river. They carried gigantic vases from earlier, greater times. They brought hundreds of yards of hand-embroidered silks and linens. They handed everything to the hero's servants to carry.

Finally, a sea serpent brought a large plain bag. In the water-color illustration it was light brown like a gunnysack gone pale. The sea princess said, "The other gifts are for you and your court, since obviously you are a prince. But this bag is for your people. Even if famine comes to your country, your people will never be hungry. This bag full of rice will never empty."

"Then I will carry it myself," he told her. But before raising it to his shoulder, he bowed very low, and the sea princess bowed low back to him. Then she faded.

In his own country, the young man was forever after known as My Lord Bag of Rice.

In the first year of her marriage, Eleanor Grummel read through all the books left in the District 73 schoolhouse. She would hand Virgil what he needed—the snowblower sprocket, the fan belt, the lag-screw, or the color-coded vacuum tubing—and then lean against the wall or sometimes sit on the old station wagon back seat and read. She read all the books, but returned over and over to My Lord Bag of Rice.

Now, eighteen years later, she held Virgil's hand while he whispered to her, his memories blurred by drugs, getting the times wrong, getting the occasions wrong, his eyes weeping from illness and recollection. Eleanor saw herself again standing at the old schoolhouse window, sometimes glancing out at the fields, sometimes studying the illustrations in the fairy tale book. Now she thought that she read in an enchanted way, because she had been too unconscious to know she lived in misery.

Twice each day, throughout Virgil's dying, Eleanor drove happily from Masonic, a building of the University of Minnesota hospital system, back to Mrs. Zenobie's boarding house in St. Paul. On her night run, generally at about three in the morning, Eleanor recited aloud in the car whole passages from the King James translation. Aloud she cried, "And the darkness comprehendeth it not!" or she shouted in the car, "And none shall prevent Him!" She remembered to add "Saith the Lord" after any pronouncements she could remember from Genesis.

August changed to early fall; she still drove with the windows open. The air was dusty and smooth, its blackness so thorough she felt as if it lay all over the Middle West—as if even the Twin Cities, a polite place, hardly made a pinprick of light in all the blackness. Of course the Twin Cities were not really a polite place: Mrs. Zenobie, the landlady at her boarding house, was not polite—but in the Twin Cities politeness was possible.

In the normal course Eleanor would have lodged nearer the hospital where Virgil was dying. The University people explained that all the special housing for people like Eleanor happened to be full. Mrs. Zenobie was not the greatest, they explained, and Eleanor would have to drive across to St. Paul, but she was reasonable. They gave her a map and highlighted her route from I-94 to Newell Avenue, St. Paul. They urged her to join a certain Women's Support Group, since she was under stress and was new in the city. They told her she could visit her husband any hour of the night or day she liked.

The night runs brought her back to Mrs. Zenobie's at about four in the morning. No matter how quietly Eleanor turned the key and tiptoed past the roomers' coat hooks, Mrs. Zenobie always woke and came out from behind the Japanese room divider. She slept downstairs, she told Eleanor, because of the crime. If crooks ever realized no one was on the ground floor, especially when it was a woman who ran the household, they would take advantage. And once they robbed a woman they'd rob her again. The police right now were looking for LeRoy Beske, the low-life who had owned 1785 Newell, three houses over, and then sold it to someone who never moved in. "You got to learn these things," Mrs. Zenobie told Eleanor, "if you're serious about wanting to start a rooming house. Also I wanted to say I'd be the last not to be grateful you have brought us so many doughnuts from the bakery, but I can't give you anything off the rent for that."

"I didn't expect it," Eleanor said.

"It doesn't matter how many men boarders you got," Mrs. Zenobie said. "It doesn't do any good. Crime is crime."

Mrs. Zenobie had five elderly male boarders, four of whom were not so polite as Eleanor hoped to find for clientele whenever she finally got her own house. Her idea was to have a five o'clock social hour: they would all gather in the living room before dinner and she would give each boarder some wine or cider, so it would be like home. Eleanor herself had never seen a home like the one she had in mind, but the image was clear to her.

Eleanor started up the staircase, exhausted.

"If you're serious about wanting a house," Mrs. Zenobie whispered fiercely up after her, "I heard that 1785 is for sale again now. It'd be big enough." Mrs. Zenobie's eyes glared up as steady as bathroom nightlights. "I wouldn't feel you were cutting into my prospects," she said. "There's so many people wanting boarding houses these days there's enough for everyone."

Eleanor slept well all that late August and early September. She felt the grateful passion for sleep of people whose lives are a shambles. Only sleep was completely reliable. She dreamed. Every morning she woke up haunted and mystified by the dreams.

In the mornings Alicia Fowler, a realtor recommended by B.J. at the Support Group, picked her up. Eleanor felt cared for in Alicia's car. They ignored the big sun-dried thoroughfares— Snelling, Cleveland, Randolph. Alicia knew every house in St. Paul or Minneapolis and what it likely was worth. Eleanor said, "My idea is three stories, homey, decently built. I can't afford Summit Avenue, but I don't want a dangerous part of town."

After the morning's searches with Alicia, Eleanor took her own (or still Virgil's) car over to the hospital for an hour or so. If Virgil was sleeping, she daydreamed beside his tubings. Once a technician came in to get Virgil ready to wheel down for X-rays. Eleanor realized that, whatever the X-rays would teach Virgil's doctor, these trips were not for Virgil's sake but for other patients after Virgil's death. They were making a lab rat out of Virgil. She pointed out that it was painful for Virgil to be moved onto the stretcher table and off again. The technician said he was only following orders. Eleanor did not dare oppose the doctor's orders. After they wheeled Virgil down, she thought of how she should have protected him from that extra pain. Her fist shook as she held his drip stand.

After an hour she left and drove courteously home on Oak and Fulton streets, onto 94, and east towards St. Paul. She waved to drivers backed up at Erie Street and let them onto the road in front of her. They waved back. She waved to let people from parking lots enter the column of cars. She was delighted to be courteous to strangers. For eighteen years she had shrunk in her seat while Virgil gave the finger to anyone who honked when Virgil crossed lanes. On their few Twin Cities junkets, he would pull ahead two feet into the pedestrian crossing when he had to wait for a stoplight. It forced pedestrians to walk around the front of the car. When a pedestrian gave Virgil a hostile glance Virgil would gun the engine, which made the pedestrian jump. Eleanor always looked out the right-hand window in order not to see Virgil smile. When Virgil was caught speeding, he would not look up as he passed his driver's license out the window to the officer. While the man asked him a question or told Virgil his computer reading, Virgil stared steadily at the steering wheel and kept both hands on it, as if to drive off. His face looked full and stung with blood. The moment the officer turned away, initialed the citation, and wound up the invariably courteous request to keep it down, Virgil came to life: he snarled, "I took your number, fellow! If you ever, like *ever*, try to drive through Chippewa or Lac Qui Parle County, I know the right people that'll put you up so high by the time you hit the ground eagles will have made a nest in your ass!"

Now Eleanor enjoyed driving under the speed limit: she played at imagining other drivers having their lives saved by her carefulness. She even formed a mental image of those in the oncoming traffic saying to themselves, "At least *there's* a car not driven by some natural killer!" as they whipped past on their side of the white line.

On Tuesdays she went to St. Swithin's Episcopal Church confirmation class for instruction. There were three men in the group, and an innumerable, changing roster of women—all of them older than Eleanor. One of the youngish men spoke wrathfully and weakly about one issue or another. Two of the women kept saying, "I'm not sure this is relevant," a remark that caused the young priest to tremble. Eleanor felt at odds with all of them since her aim in church instruction was not relevance but beauty. She wanted to learn polite ideas, whatever they were. She memorized a good deal of what Father said. Once—only once—she repeated one of the phrases she had memorized. The group looked astonished and then disgusted. She stayed on but only because the group met in a room called the Lady Chapel where the royal and navy blue stained-glass windows pleased her.

356

On Thursdays she had the Women's Support Group. They were people so different from herself that she didn't like to think about it. B.J.—all of them—had been sympathetic when she told them about her father's abuse. When her thoughts grew more and more centered around getting a boarding house, they turned indifferent. Anyone in pain was a priority. In October a recently sexually-assaulted woman joined them. After that, Eleanor felt unseen. She knew these women were more intelligent than she was; on the other hand, she felt stung when they wouldn't rejoice with her over having found a house she could buy.

In the week of Virgil's death and the weeks following it, Eleanor had so much to think of that she forgot to tell B.J. and the others that she was widowed at last. When they found out, B.J. threw her arms around Eleanor, crying "You are so wonderfully centered!"

Eleanor blushed. She felt stupid. People had emotions which meant nothing to her; they used words she never used— "centered" and "on top of your shit."

Eleanor stayed on at Mrs. Zenobie's. There was no social hour before dinner, as Eleanor planned for her own boarding house, but now and then Mrs. Zenobie's niece brought in a group of Sunday school students for what was announced as a very, very special occasion. One October Saturday, the children came to explain some small kits to Mrs. Zenobie's boarders. If the boarders would be good enough to assemble these kits, the children would pick them up on St. Andrew's Day.

Eleanor perked up a little at hearing "St. Andrew's Feast," since memorizing trivia about saints was a favorite part of her new church life. Each kit was a plastic sandwich bag in which lay two tongue depressors, a plastic twister, and a plastic baby poinsettia. The idea was to use the twister to attach the tongue depressors at right angles to make a cross, then jam the poinsettia's stem into the twist as well. While it made a good Christmas present for shut-ins, you could trade the poinsettia for a lily and, presto, you had an Easter symbol, too, which was the kind of thing that shut-ins could relate to.

Eleanor backed around the room divider as discreetly as possible and made for the staircase.

Suddenly a man's voice said, "Oh, no, you don't, Eleanor! No one gets out of this!"—with a laugh. He came out to the hallway where she hovered. "I have seen many cultural atrocities in my life," he said to her, not only not lowering his voice but raising it slightly, and even, as she had heard him do any number of times at the dinner table, adding a slight British inflection—"but I think this one surpasses them all!" It was Jack Lackie, the retired Episcopal priest, a mysterious member of Mrs. Zenobie's household.

"The mystery is, what was he really?" Mrs. Zenobie later said, gouging a used kleenex into her apron pocket. "Janitor, maybe. Not a priest. You get wise to what people used to be and what they say they used to be. To hear it, I've had boarders who invented the atom bomb and I've had CIA operatives and I've had three hundred of President Kennedy's cousins. He wasn't all *that* Catholic."

Eleanor felt endeared to Jack Lackie because he never once lifted his trouser cuff to show the ribbing of long underwear. Mrs. Zenobie's other men liked to explain that now winter had set in they put on their long underwear and that was it until spring. Two of them shoved their wooden chairs back, bent over and lifted the bottoms of their trouser legs in case Eleanor didn't believe them. Jack Lackie was the only man not to do it, and Eleanor had made up her mind that she would have him for a boarder in her home when she got it.

Now she smiled at him. It would give such a classy tone to the place if someone spoke of "cultural atrocities!"

She lay on her bed upstairs, hearing the children's voices singing from below. Under the house the ground throbbed from the parked Amtrak train on Transfer Street, throbbing gently through the concrete basement and wooden studs. Eleanor smiled in the dark: this was her favorite mood. She felt simple, full of plans, and not confused. It was true that nearly everyone she talked to that day was so different from her that they could never be friends. She passed quickly over the idea that she might be lonely the rest of her life. She raced to make image after image of her boarding house. There would never, never be any church groups allowed into it. There would be a wood-burning stove in the living room. There would be a wine and cider hour before dinner each night. If anyone sneered or shouted, she would ask them to leave. There would be an outside barbeque. There would be climbing roses. She would tell Alicia the realtor that she definitely wanted 1785 Newell Avenue.

It seemed like a million years since Big Red Chief's voice crackled at her from the speakers in the farmhouse kitchen. Was it true that you needed to be widowed in order to lead a courteous life? She didn't pause to think that idea through but happily imagined the stained-glass window at 1785 and thought how holy it looked even if what it lighted was a staircase, not a church. It made her feel holy and unconfused. Months ago Father said, "It is always a risk to take your soul into real life!" The others nodded, as if wakened and strengthened by his remark. Eleanor made nothing of it but she memorized it, another graceful phrase, even if "risk" to her meant only the risk of borrowing against her inheritance to buy a three-story house. Her mind drifted back to the house.

On the third Sunday in November, Alicia hurried Eleanor to an office building in downtown St. Paul, where they crowded into a small room with a conference table and vinyl chairs. There were four other people. Alicia sat close by Eleanor, bending right over the papers in front of Eleanor, making sure she signed nothing that wasn't right. A man at the opposite end of the crowded table, presumably the owner of 1785 Newell Avenue, was being similarly coached by his real estate agent. Eleanor supposed she would shake hands with him at the end, but for now each avoided the other's eyes. The closing agent's dull energetic voice kept explaining terms. There was some cloud on the title, but it was cleared. The police had asked that if Ms. Grummel ever saw LeRoy Beske to call them immediately: he had been seen hanging around several times since he sold the house.

Eleanor was in a dream. She looked affectionately at Alicia's permanented head: it was back-combed and sprayed as stiff as a howitzer shell. If you touched it surely your hand would come away with tiny cuts. Eleanor had two feelings: affection for this tough person who had helped her get her life's dream, and the memory of her mother, who wore dark glasses when she went to the beauty parlor for a permanent. Even if she had to cover bruises with pancake, she never missed a hair setting: the time she had three stitches in her right cheek, she postponed her hairdo by two hours. Eleanor kept signing in exactly the places where Alicia pointed a Lee's press-on nail to show her.

Keys tinkled across the table. Smiles. The men stood up: people's hands reached across to shake. Then they were back out into the cold street. Alicia said, "Come on. We'll drive to Mrs. Zenobie's and walk to your new house."

Eleanor was learning the small graces of the rich. They brought each other small but ceremonial presents. Women brought just a few rosebuds for other women when they had a meeting together; the Support Group people sometimes arrived with newspaper cones full of flowers, to celebrate someone getting their shit together. At instruction classes, Father kept a good sherry for the confirmands. Women drank with women. No one talked about "hen parties." Now Eleanor opened a bottle of champagne.

The previous owners had left a dining room table and two chairs. Alicia held two styrofoam cups securely, as Eleanor poured. Then they both heard scrabbling below them.

"Not rats," Alicia said quickly and firmly. "I checked that out before. Everything else, of course—but not rats."

"I'm not afraid of rats," Eleanor said. "I'm a farm girl." She was about to tell Alicia about how Virgil would lift up a bale of hay, sometimes, and when the rats burst out she whacked as many as she could.

"Down we go," Alicia said, rising.

As they moved through the fine old kitchen, Eleanor realized with surprise that she had paid no attention to the basement. It was the third floor that had fascinated her: one finished room, church-like, with steep eaves going up to the ridge-pole and a charming dilapidated balcony at the peak-end. The other half of the third floor was not finished. Boarders could store their luggage there. The second floor was like all second floors of abused houses: radiators with paint chipped off, smudgy windows, deeply checked sills and mullions.

Alicia turned on the basement light. They trotted about the basement, between the abandoned coal room and the laundry room, around the monstrous octopus of a furnace spray-painted aluminum like ship's equipment. Behind the worktable there sat against the wall a very thin, old, dirty woman. Her awful eyes gleamed. One skinny hand plucked at her blouse buttons.

Alicia said, "OK, both together . . . . " They raised the woman up. "Nope—she's too weak to stand." Alicia paused.

"Here," Eleanor said. She bent down, her back to Alicia. All that farm work. "Just put her on my back." They got the woman upstairs and laid her on the floor in the living room, which had carpet.

"Police first," Alicia said.

"I'll run to Mrs. Zenobie's," Eleanor said.

Mrs. Zenobie herself frankly listened while Eleanor called 911. She rubbed an elbow and smiled. "You're getting into the problems of running a rooming house even faster than I did! You haven't been there even one night and already you got a nonpaying-type tenant hiding in the basement! Karsh!"

Eleanor riffled through Mrs. Zenobie's directory. She ordered one chicken-onions-snowpeas and rice and gave the address.

"Unsuitable tenants is the second greatest pain next to taxes," Mrs. Zenobie offered.

The police car was already parked at 1785 when Eleanor ran back.

"It's Sunday, so the only social workers on are the primary-interventions. We'll just take her to jail for the night," one of the two young men explained.

Alicia said she had to beat it, since the situation seemed to be under control.

Eleanor said, "I'll keep her for the night." She added, "I run a boarding house."

"Doesn't look like one yet," the other young cop said. "We've been kind of keeping a watch on this house. There was a real bad-news type here. This lady probably needs a doctor. We'll take her, and we'll get a social worker around to you tomorrow."

The policeman looked down at the old woman. "Can you talk, lady?" he said gently.

He waited a second. "OK, we'll wait for the ambulance." One of them went out to radio.

"This the kind of customer you going to have in this house?" the remaining policeman asked with a grin.

There was a knock. Eleanor paid the oriental foods delivery man and brought in her little white paper buckets with their wire handles.

The policeman got the idea. He and Eleanor both knelt on the floor. "If you can eat, lady, it's the best thing you can do," the officer said. He said to Eleanor, "Show it to her."

Eleanor said, "We're going to help you lean up against the wall." She opened one of the packets, and the old woman suddenly dug her whole hand into the rice. She put a palm full of it into her own face and began to chew slowly. She reached in again and again.

"She needs chopsticks like I need chopsticks," the young officer said comfortably. Eleanor leaned on her heels. The woman finished all the rice. Eleanor offered her the chicken. "This is going to be a mess," the policeman said. He stood up and ambled into the kitchen. "Someone at least left you some paper towels." Together they wiped the woman's face. Then Eleanor wiped her neck where the Cantonese sauce and a few onions had run down. The ambulance came. The policeman left a number to call if there was any trouble. Eleanor walked over to Mrs. Zenobie's for the last time. *Tomorrow night I'll homestead,* she thought.

When the social worker came the next day, he explained that he was Rex, from Primary Intervention. He told Eleanor that none of the women's shelters had any room for a new person. Eleanor and he sat at the dining room table together, while he told her that there used to be an office especially for cases like this woman's. Now there wasn't the dollars. He told Eleanor that he thought this woman was named Eunice something. She was a victim of the second-to-last owner here, this LeRoy Beske, who'd run a racket of diverting old people's welfare checks to himself. Then Rex looked at his hands.

"I don't know how you'd feel about this," he said. "I don't know what kind of house you want to have, but if you could take care of Eunice on a temporary basis, we could offer you the Difficult Care rate. That is, we'd pay you $22 a day to feed and shelter her. The hospital says she is OK. She's just in shock and can't talk. They don't think there is anything organically wrong except she's nearly starved to death. If you wanted to take her in four or five days . . . ."

Eleanor said to herself fast, *I could still get five or six courteous people who would have polite conversations at the table. It shouldn't be too hard: it'd still be a house where no one told anyone else to get their butt over here or there.*

The truck finally came from Dawson with the furniture. Eleanor bought three more beds from Montgomery Ward. She interviewed prospective tenants. She put Mercein, Mrs. Sol-

362

strom, Dick, Carolyn, and George on the second floor. She put Eunice in the room she had imagined for herself, behind the kitchen on the ground floor. She slept on the sofa for several weeks. She kept the third floor bedroom untenanted until the second floor was filled.

"Here," Mrs. Zenobie said. "They've got that racket on the TV so loud I can't hear myself think. Come in the kitchen."

She watched Eleanor with eyes blazing.

"Have I got this straight?" she said finally. "You want to trade one of your tenants for one of mine? What kind of crap is that?" She paused. "I don't want to get tough with you. I know you are mourning your husband. But you're in business, too, and you and I are doing business on the same street. So naturally I am looking at everything carefully. Let me just give this back to you and you tell *me*. You want me to take someone named Mrs. Joanne Solstrom into my house and then you want Mr. Jack Lackie to move to your house? You're going to pay them $100 each for the inconvenience?"

Eleanor nodded.

Mrs. Zenobie looked at her fingernails with the finesse of an actress. Since they were cut to just above the quick, there couldn't be much to discover about them. "I never paid any money to have some man move into any house of mine," she remarked.

There are some things you can't explain to some people, Eleanor thought. You can't tell the Support Group that you're *not* going through "the grief process" for your husband but you are furious at the State of Minnesota for chipping tax out of your late husband's engine repair service inventory before you inherited it. You couldn't tell Mrs. Zenobie that you wanted a retired Episcopal priest in your boarding house because he talked about history and culture and that you did *not* want a perfectly nice woman named Mrs. Solstrom because she constantly sneered. On Sundays, during wine and cider hour, she sneered that if Tommy Kramer couldn't learn to move his butt out of the pocket, he deserved every sack he got.

"I don't get it," Mrs. Zenobie said. "She pays her rent? She's clean? OK. But if you think you're going to get any help out of that Lackie, think again. He's retired. He never picked up a leaf in the yard, not around this place, he didn't."

363

Their lives went smoothly through the winter. Eunice still didn't speak, but everyone fed her. Mercein and Dick brought her Whopper Burgers, Carolyn brought her doughnuts, George brought her take-out Italian food from a place near his plant. Jack brought her cans of Dinty Moore Beef Stew and helped her stack them up in the unfinished part of the attic. She grew fat. Rex, the cordial social worker, thought it might be months before Eunice could speak again.

She followed Jack everywhere; he talked to her all the time. Eleanor began to feel happy. She moved Eunice to the north end of the second floor; she herself took the downstairs bedroom. Jack arranged his few possessions—his oddly old-fashioned clothes, his set of Will and Ariel Durant—in the third-floor room. Jack took over laying and lighting the fire in the living room stove which Eleanor bought at an auction on Fulton Street. Each late afternoon, they all watched the dull, comfortable flame through the isinglass while Jack served the wine and cider. Whenever he rose to refill someone's glass, Eunice stood up too. If he left the room, she followed him. He had to turn directly to her and say, "No," when he wanted to be alone.

The other tenants were grateful that she followed Jack instead of driving them crazy. Eleanor was glad because she needed the hour before dinner to cook, she needed the hour after dinner to plan the next day's work, and she liked to sit alone in the kitchen at night. The dishwasher chugged through its hissing cycles. Eleanor wrote out lists of repairs needed, hardware to buy, meals for the rest of the week. She could hear Jack's voice rising and falling in the living room. He was apparently telling Eunice everything that ever happened in human history.

As the weather warmed, Jack took on some outside chores. He renailed the rose trellis to the house while Eunice passed nails up to him. He sorted through the loose bricks lying in the back-yard, dividing wholes from brokens. Whenever he lifted a brick, Eunice picked one up, watching his face. When he set his down, she set hers down. When her hands were free, she ate. There was always food in her jacket pockets—a wrapped ham-and-cheese or Mushroom and Swiss from Hardee's. Sometimes Jack let her into the third-floor storage area to count her cans of stew and soup. Eunice arranged and rearranged them into pyramids, straight walls, squares. Her eyes lost the terrible glint they

364

had at first. The boarders decided that probably she was only sixty or sixty-five, not eighty or ninety. She bathed, dressed, cleaned her teeth, and followed Jack everywhere.

In March, on a Saturday, it was Eleanor's turn to manage the food shelves at St. Swithin's. By now she was a confirmed church member.

Just before she left home, someone outside threw something through the first-floor stained-glass window. Glass and wood splinters scattered all over the base of the stairs. Sharp, normal sunlight broke in. George, Eunice, and Jack had been clearing the breakfast table. Now they stood still. Then Eunice moved towards the mess of glass and smashed sash-work: she bent and picked up a brick. Jack immediately took it from her, in case there were glass shards stuck to it. Eleanor called the police.

"Go on to church," Jack told her. "I'll sweep this up and George can go outside to see if he can see anybody."

Like most people who have done plain work in their lives, Eleanor could separate events at home from the job. All day she worked hard, instructing volunteers, making quick judgments about clients. She knew now who were the few people who picked up food and sold it later. When they showed up and explained what they wanted, Eleanor looked them right in the face, with a deliberate smile, and said, "I'm so sorry, we're fresh out of that." If the person pointed angrily to where that very item stood on the shelf, Eleanor smiled and said, "I know it looks as if we have it. The funny thing is we're out of it."

She was happy to get out of her car and start up the sidewalk to her boarding house. Since it was still March, Jack would have lighted a fire, and they could all gather as usual and speculate about who had broken their stained-glass window.

Her neighbor from across the street called, "Big trouble, huh, Eleanor?"

He was coming after her to talk. "In a way I'm glad that happened, Eleanor," he said in a kind tone. "I know it doesn't seem like the right thing to say, but at least now that guy'll get what's coming to him."

Eleanor said slowly, "LeRoy Beske you mean."

"That creep," the neighbor said. "Hanging around here. Trouble whenever he shows up. I'm sorry it had to happen at your place, Eleanor, but all of us along the street feel relieved." He paused. "Cops came of course," he said. "They wanted to talk to you and said they'd be back around now or so."

Then a last word from the neighbor: "That Jack Lackie, that tenant of yours! I'll say one thing for him! If a job needs doing, he does it!"

Eleanor looked and saw that the paper towelling she had suggested Jack stuff into the broken window wasn't there: the whole window was reglazed, although only in clear glass now.

Inside the house the living room was empty and dark.

"Hello?" Eleanor called up the staircase.

"Hello!" Jack called down in an odd tone.

Eleanor turned back to the door, since someone had rung the bell. It was the two policemen Eleanor remembered from months ago.

"Finally you got home," one of them said. "We've knocked and rung your bell—but no one would let us in."

"It's never locked!" Eleanor said.

"Locked today, Ms. Grummel," the other policeman said. As soon as Eleanor straightened from putting her key in, both policemen were right in the doorway.

"I hated losing that stained-glass window," Eleanor told them.

"That's the last window Beske'll bust in a long time," one man told her. The other loped over to the staircase and called upstairs, "Everybody down! Police!"

"Well," Eleanor said, preening a little, "I think it is very nice of you men to be so concerned about it."

Then they told her what had happened. LeRoy Beske had thrown the brick through her window, all right. Then he had hung around and the boarders had seen him in the yard. He went around to the side of the house. They heard a sharp cry: Dick and George ran outside and found Beske bleeding severely from a head wound. A blood-splashed brick lay near him. They glanced around a little—and then upward at the little balcony off Jack's third-story room. There was no one there. Both men hurried into the house to call the police. They both noticed that neither Jack nor Eunice was in the living room, where the other boarders began to huddle, overhearing the telephone call to 911.

Eleanor said to herself that her boarding house, her polite structure, had fallen into violence just as quickly as any other

366

household in a crime-filled country. The man she had designated to be the cultural leader had assaulted someone right in her own side yard.

One after another the boarders denied any knowledge. Jack's turn came. Eleanor nearly shuddered. His voice denied knowledge just as flatly as the others had.

"Now this lady: your name is?" The policemen were now looking at Eunice. She was forty pounds heavier than when they had seen her three months ago.

George said, "That's Eunice. We can pretty much answer for her, officer."

The officer said, "She'll have to speak for herself. Eunice," he said, "what did you see and where were you?"

Eunice opened her mouth. Her voice croaked and squealed like equipment long unused; phlegm caught in her throat and stopped a vowel now and then, but Eunice talked. When she started in, Eleanor remembered My Lord Bag of Rice and how the hero helped the sea princess. For the moment, Eleanor forgot that her reason for having Jack in her boarding house was that he should provide cultivated conversation. Now she believed that she had intuitively spotted Jack as a kind figure who would stand guard when they needed him. She thought, *well—Well!—now he'd done it,* so she had been canny. Her mind felt large and nervous.

Eunice was not ratting on Jack. Eunice said, "In the beginning the human race needed strong leaders. The Jews in Egypt needed a leader to get them out. When medieval farmers had their lands stolen by the church or the state or by their landlords, they needed brave people to get them their freeholds."

She kept talking. When Eunice got to the Reformation, she switched to Chinese history. She explained that the Chinese invented watertight doors for ships, so that no enemy could rake through the entire hold and sink a ship. Any leader knew it was devastating for a man to be trapped in a watertight compartment with the sea pouring in. Nonetheless, a leader told men on the other sides to turn the battens on the watertight doors. They heard the doomed man's screams, but the leader could save the whole. A leader could do desperate acts while others froze.

Then there was a brief pause in which Eleanor could see that Eunice was going to switch to another culture. She explained how

367

painful it was to learn that the world was not terracentric—so painful a truth thousands couldn't bear it.

"OK, lady, OK," one policeman said.

"For now, that's enough," the other said to Eleanor. "You all have your dinner. We'll come back tomorrow, and anyway, they will know by then if LeRoy Beske is going to live or not."

Before the door had closed behind the policeman, Eunice began again. She explained that in every age of bullies, a leader shows up to give the people respite. She told them about John Ball, a sixteenth-century agricultural reformer. She explained the Odal Law of Norway. Jack declined to have wine with the others, and Eunice followed him upstairs, telling him about how Captain Cook used psychology to induce his men to eat sauerkraut. It saved them from scurvy.

Those down below could still hear her hoarse, unaccustomed voice, less distinct, as she and Jack rounded the landing and started up the reverse flight. They heard her close the door of her room. Jack's steps continued up on the third-floor stairs. Then they heard Eunice speaking to herself in her room.

Eleanor lighted the stove, listening to the boarders' various exclamations. Gradually they told each other their versions over and over, more and more quietly. After a while, Eleanor put the crock pot of stew onto the dining room table. She called to Jack and Eunice. Everyone sat quietly, whispering now and then, "Would you please pass the rolls?" "Would you send the carrot sticks down here?"—with a good deal of glancing at Eunice.

Her face was full of color. She looked fifty now, not sixty. She kept facing Jack and she kept talking. She had got to the nineteenth century. Chinese grandmothers were certainly sorry to see their granddaughters' feet bound the first time. Eunice described how the mothers and daughters cried as they removed their clogs at night, unwinding the bloodied cloths from their toes—yet, they, more than the men, made certain the practice was kept up.

One by one the boarders finished eating, nodded to Eleanor, and left the table. Eleanor and Jack and Eunice remained at the strewn tablecloth.

At last Jack rose. Eunice followed him immediately, in her usual way. She was explaining what the Marines did in Mexico in 1916. Eleanor set the dishwasher growling over its first load.

When she went upstairs, she could hear Eunice, alone in her room behind her door, saying that the Michigan National Guard helped Fisher Body Plant #1 defeat union workers in 1937. Eunice's voice, getting exercise, was sounding smoother now. Eleanor paused on the landing, decided to go back downstairs to bed, then noticed Jack sitting on a stair on the flight above.

"You're listening," she whispered to him, going up a few steps. They regarded each other in the weak night light.

"How can I help it!" he said in a whispered laugh. "Amazing! Amazing!"

Eleanor said, "She's not so amazing! It isn't her! *You're* the one that's amazing!" She didn't mind if her enormous happiness showed in her whisper. She felt out of her class, somehow—but this much she knew: it is amazing when a man uses all that violence that's in men to help people instead of just pushing people around! Virgil would never drop a brick on a friend's enemy. Her father never defended anyone. She realized that some time between dinner and this minute she had decided to lie for Jack if she had to. She would say what was necessary to keep the police from cornering him. It would be something new for her: she had not even been able to prevail on the X-ray technicians to leave poor Virgil in peace. She had underestimated Jack, admiring only his ability to talk courteously.

Now she whispered, "You have actually saved her life!"

He said, "You don't even know what happened."

Eleanor ignored that idiotic modesty and whispered, "What's more, she half-saved yours, too. When she rattled on and on all that history to the police, they obviously decided she was out of her head and they got up and went home! Of course, " Eleanor added, feeling very sage the way bystanders do when they double-guess the police, "they had been looking for that awful LeRoy Beske for a long time anyway."

"She didn't save my life, either," Jack now said.

Behind her door Eunice was moving away from Max Planck and introducing Marilyn French and Ruth Bleier.

Jack said from his stair slightly above Eleanor's: "I want you to listen now. I did not, repeat, did *not* drop or throw a brick onto LeRoy Beske from that balcony. You know who goes around this house carrying cans of beef stew and books and bricks."

Eleanor was still. "I don't believe you," she said then.

Jack said, "LeRoy Beske swiped her welfare check for over two years. At the end he hid her and then nearly starved her to death and dumped her in your basement when he couldn't figure out anything more convenient. She was mad at him. Then he made a mistake. He was drunk when he came around here this morning. For the fun of it he tossed a brick through your window. He didn't figure Eunice right: she was on the balcony when he ambled by a few hours later. He shouted, 'Hi, little girl!' to her when he saw her. People on the other side of the house heard him. He probably didn't recognize her. He shouted, 'Hi, princess!' Her rage made her very clean-cut. She had a brick with her because she and I were going to build the barbeque today. Anyway," Jack finished up in a satisfied, brutal way, "she got him good."

He whispered down at Eleanor, "Another thing. You had better know. I am not a retired priest. I am a retired janitor. What you have here is a retired janitor who has read a lot of history."

By now Eunice's voice had almost the lilt and ease of ordinary women's voices. She described the hole widening in the Antarctic ozone. Then she said that Eskimos' teeth had caries from eating American-made candy bars. She said Eskimos were listening to reggae, on the ice floes.

Eleanor and Jack lingered on the staircase. Eleanor imagined the Eskimos looking out over the ice-filled water. But she also remembered the watercolor illustration of the hero with his huge bag of rice: he was looking out over water; his robe was painted in baby colors—pink and light-blue—his quiver dusty-yellow, and the Sea of Japan was pale green, a shade you might choose for a child's nursery.

1990

GLOSSOLALIA

by DAVID JAUSS

from SHENANDOAH

THAT WINTER, LIKE every winter before it, my father woke early each day and turned up the thermostat so the house would be warm by the time my mother and I got out of bed. Sometimes I'd hear the furnace kick in and the shower come on down the hall and I'd wake just long enough to be angry that he'd wakened me. But usually I slept until my mother had finished making our breakfast. By then, my father was already at Goodyear, opening the service bay for the customers who had to drop their cars off before going to work themselves. Sitting in the sunny kitchen, warmed by the heat from the register and the smell of my mother's coffee, I never thought about him dressing in the cold dark or shoveling out the driveway by porchlight. If I thought of him at all, it was only to feel glad he was not there. In those days my father and I fought a lot, though probably not much more than most fathers and sons. I was sixteen then, a tough age. And he was forty, an age I've since learned is even tougher.

But that winter I was too concerned with my own problems to think about my father's. I was a skinny, unathletic, sorrowful boy who had few friends, and I was in love with Molly Rasmussen, one of the prettiest girls in Glencoe and the daughter of a man who had stopped my father on Main Street that fall, called him a "goddamned debt-dodger," and threatened to break his face. My father had bought a used Ford Galaxie from Mr. Rasmussen's lot, but he hadn't been able to make the payments and eventually Mr. Rasmussen repossessed it. Without a second car my mother couldn't get to work—she had taken a job at the school lunch-room, scooping out servings of mashed potatoes and green beans—so we drove our aging Chevy to Minneapolis, where no one knew my father, and bought a rust-pitted yellow Studebaker. A few days later Molly Rasmussen passed me in the hall at school and said, "I see you've got a new car," then laughed. I was so mortified I hurried into a restroom, locked myself in a stall, and stood there for several minutes, breathing hard. Even after the bell rang for the next class, I didn't move. I was furious at my father. I blamed him for the fact that Molly despised me, just as I had for some time blamed him for everything else that was wrong with my life—my gawky looks, my discount-store clothes, my lack of friends.

That night, and others like it, I lay in bed and imagined who I'd be if my mother had married someone handsome and popular like Dick Moore, the PE teacher, or Smiley Swenson, who drove stock cars at the county fair, or even Mr. Rasmussen. Years before, my mother had told me how she met my father. A girl who worked with her at Woolworth's had asked her if she wanted to go out with a friend of her boyfriend's, an Army man just back from the war. My mother had never agreed to a blind date be-fore, or dated an older man, but for some reason this time she said yes. Lying there, I thought about that fateful moment. It seemed so fragile—she could as easily have said no and changed everything—and I wished, then, that she had said no, I wished she'd said she didn't date strangers or she already had a date or she was going out of town—anything to alter the chance conjunc-tion that would eventually produce me.

I know now that there was something suicidal about my desire to undo my parentage, but then I knew only that I wanted to be someone else. And I blamed my father for that wish. If I'd had a different father, I reasoned, I would be better-looking, happier, more popular. When I looked in the mirror and saw my father's thin face, his rust-red hair, downturned mouth, and bulging Ad-am's apple, I didn't know who I hated more, him or me. That winter I began parting my hair on the right instead of the left, as my father did, and whenever the house was empty I worked on changing my voice, practicing the inflections and accents of my classmates' fathers as if they were clues to a new life. I even practiced one's walk, another's crooked smile, a third's wink. I did not think, then, that my father knew how I felt about him, but now that I have a son of my own, a son almost as old as I was then, I know different.

If I had known what my father was going through that winter, maybe I wouldn't have treated him so badly. But I didn't know anything until the January morning of his breakdown. I woke that morning to the sound of voices downstairs in the kitchen. At first I thought the sound was the wind rasping in the bare branches of the cottonwood outside my window, then I thought it was the radio. But after I lay there a moment I recognized my parents' voices. I couldn't tell what they were saying, but I knew they were arguing. They'd been arguing more than usual lately, and I hated it—not so much because I wanted them to be happy, though I did, but because I knew they'd take their anger out on me, snapping at me, telling me to chew with my mouth closed, asking me who gave me permission to put my feet up on the coffee table, ordering me to clean my room. I buried one ear in my pillow and covered the other with my blankets, but I could still hear them. They sounded distant, yet somehow close, like the sea crashing in a shell held to the ear. But after a while I couldn't hear even the muffled sound of their voices, and I sat up in the bars of gray light slanting through the blinds and listened to the quiet. I didn't know what was worse: their arguments or their silences. I sat there, barely breathing, waiting for some noise.

Finally I heard the back door bang shut and, a moment later, the Chevy cough to life. Only then did I dare get out of bed. Crossing to the window, I lowered one of the slats in the blinds with a finger and saw, in the dim light, the driveway drifted shut with snow. Then my father came out of the garage and began shoveling, scooping the snow furiously and flinging it over his shoulder, as if each shovelful were a continuation of the argument. I couldn't see his face, but I knew that it was red and that he was probably cursing under his breath. As he shoveled, the wind scuffed the drifts around him, swirling the snow into his eyes, but he didn't stop or set his back to the wind. He just kept shoveling fiercely, and suddenly it occurred to me that he might have a heart attack, just as my friend Rob's father had the winter before. For an instant I saw him slump over his shovel, then collapse face-first into the snow. As soon as this thought came to me, I did my best to make myself think it arose from love and terror, but even then I knew part of me wished his death, and that knowledge went through me like a chill.

I lowered the slat on the blinds and got back into bed. The house was quiet but not peaceful. I knew that somewhere in the silence my mother was crying and I thought about going to comfort her, but I didn't. After a while I heard my father rev the engine and back the Chevy down the driveway. Still I didn't get up. And when my mother finally came to tell me it was time to get ready, her eyes and nose red and puffy, I told her I wasn't feeling well and wanted to stay home. Normally, she would have felt my forehead and cross-examined me about my symptoms, but that day I knew she'd be too upset to bother. "Okay, Danny," she said. "Call me if you think you need to see a doctor." And that was it. She shut my door and a few minutes later I heard the whine of the Studebaker's cold engine, and then she was gone.

It wasn't long after my mother left that my father came home. I was lying on the couch in the living room, trying to figure out the hidden puzzle on "Concentration," when I heard a car pull into the driveway. At first I thought my mother had changed her mind and come back to take me to school. But then the back door sprang open and I heard him. It was a sound I had never heard before and since have heard only in my dreams, a sound that will make me sit up in the thick dark, my eyes open to nothing, and my breath panting. I don't know how to explain it, other than to say it was a kind of crazy language, like speaking in tongues. It sounded as if he was crying and talking at the same time, and in some strange way his words had become half-sobs and his sobs something more than words—or words turned inside out, so that only their emotion and not their meaning came through. It scared me. I knew something terrible had happened, and I didn't know what to do. I wanted to go to him and ask him what was wrong, but I didn't dare. I switched off the sound on the TV so he wouldn't know I was home and sat there staring at Hugh Downs' smiling face. But then I couldn't stand it anymore and I got up and ran down the hall to the kitchen. There, in the middle of the room, wearing his Goodyear jacket and work-clothes, was my father. He was on his hands and knees, his head hanging as though it were too heavy to support, and he was rocking back and forth and babbling in a rhythmical stutter. It's funny, but the first thing I thought when I saw him like that was the way he used to let me ride on his back, when I was little, bucking and neighing like a horse. And as soon as I thought it, I felt my heart lurch in my chest. "Dad?" I said. "What's wrong?" But he didn't hear me. I went over to him then. "Dad?" I said again and touched him on the shoulder. He jerked at the touch and looked up at me, his lips moving but no sounds coming out of them now. His forehead was knotted and his eyes were red, almost raw-looking. He swallowed hard and for the first time spoke words I could recognize, though I did not understand them until years later, when I was myself a father.

"Danny," he said. "Save me."

Before I could finish dialing the school lunchroom's number, my mother pulled into the driveway. Looking out the window, I saw her jump out of the car and run up the slick sidewalk, her camel-colored overcoat open and flapping in the wind. For a moment I was confused. Had I already called and told her what had happened? How much time had passed since I found my father on the kitchen floor? A minute? An hour? Then I realized someone else must have told her something was wrong.

She burst in the back door then and called out, "Bill? Bill? Are you here?"

"Mom," I said, "Dad's—" and then I didn't know how to finish the sentence.

She came in the kitchen without stopping to remove her galoshes. "Oh, Bill," she said when she saw us, "are you all right?"

My father was sitting at the kitchen table now, his hands fluttering in his lap. A few moments before, I had helped him to his feet and, draping his arm over my shoulders, led him to the table like a wounded man.

"Helen," he said. "It's you." He said it like he hadn't seen her for years.

My mother went over and knelt beside him. "I'm so sorry," she said, but whether that statement was born of sorrow over something she had said or done or whether she just simply and guiltlessly wished he weren't suffering, I never knew. Taking his hands in hers, she added, "There's nothing to worry about. Everything's going to be fine." Then she turned to me. Her brown

375

hair was wind-blown, and her face was so pale the smudges of rouge on her cheeks looked like bruises. "Danny, I want you to leave us alone for a few minutes."

I looked at her red-rimmed eyes and tight lips. "Okay," I said, and went back to the living room. There, I sat on the sagging couch and stared at the television, the contestants' mouths moving wordlessly, their laughs eerily silent. I could hear my parents talking, their steady murmur broken from time to time by my father sobbing and my mother saying "Bill" over and over, in the tone mothers use to calm their babies, but I couldn't hear enough of what they said to know what had happened. And I didn't want to know either. I wanted them to be as silent as the people on the TV, I wanted all the words to stop, all the crying.

I lay down and closed my eyes, trying to drive the picture of my father on the kitchen floor out of my head. My heart was beating so hard I could feel my pulse tick in my throat. I was worried about my father but I was also angry that he was acting so strange. It didn't seem fair that I had to have a father like that. I'd never seen anybody else's father act that way, not even in a movie.

Outside, the wind shook the evergreens and every now and then a gust would rattle the windowpane. I lay there a long time, listening to the wind, until my heart stopped beating so hard.

Some time later, my mother came into the room and sat on the edge of the chair under the sunburst mirror. Her forehead was creased, and there were black mascara streaks on her cheeks. Leaning toward me, her hands clasped, she asked me how I was feeling.

"What do you mean?" I wasn't sure if she was asking if I was still feeling sick or if she meant something else.

She bit her lip. "I just wanted to tell you not to worry," she said. "Everything's going to be all right." Her breath snagged on the last word, and I could hear her swallowing.

"What's wrong?" I asked.

She opened her mouth, as if she were about to answer, but suddenly her eyes began to tear. "We'll talk about it later," she said. "After the doctor's come. Just don't worry, okay? I'll explain everything."

"The doctor?" I said.

"I'll explain later," she answered.

Then she left and I didn't hear anything more until ten or fifteen minutes had passed and the doorbell rang. My mother ran to the door and opened it, and I heard her say, "Thank you for coming so quickly" and "He's in the kitchen." As they hurried down the hall past the living room, I caught a glimpse of Dr. Lewis and his black leather bag. It had been years since the doctors in our town, small as it was, made house calls, so I knew now that my father's problem was something truly serious. The word *emergency* came into my mind, and though I tried to push it out, it kept coming back.

For the next half-hour or so, I stayed in the living room, listening to the droning sound of Dr. Lewis and my parents talking. I still didn't know what had happened or why. All I knew was that my father was somebody else now, somebody I didn't know. I tried to reconcile the father who used to read to me at night when my mother was too tired, the man who patiently taught me how to measure and cut plywood for a birdhouse, even the man whose cheeks twitched when he was angry at me and whose silences were suffocating, with the man I had just seen crouched like an animal on the kitchen floor babbling some incomprehensible language. But I couldn't. And though I felt sorry for him and his suffering, I felt as much shame as sympathy. *This is your father,* I told myself. *This is you when you're older.*

It wasn't until after Dr. Lewis had left and my father had taken the tranquilizers and gone upstairs to bed that my mother came back into the living room, sat down on the couch beside me, and told me what had happened. "Your father," she began, and her voice cracked. Then she controlled herself and said, "Your father has been fired from his job."

I looked at her. "Is that it?" I said. "That's what all this fuss is about?" I couldn't believe he'd put us through all this for something so unimportant. All he had to do was get a new job. What was the big deal?

"Let me explain," my mother said. "He was fired some time ago. Eight days ago, to be exact. But he hadn't said anything to me about it, and he just kept on getting up and going down to work every morning, like nothing had happened. And every day Mr. Siverhus told him to leave, and after arguing a while, he'd go. Then he'd spend the rest of the day driving around until quitting time, when he'd finally come home. But Mr. Siverhus got

377

fed up and changed the locks, and when your father came to work today he couldn't get in. He tried all three entrances, and when he found his key didn't work in any of them well, he threw a trash barrel through the showroom window and went inside."

She paused for a moment, I think to see how I was taking this. I was trying to picture my father throwing a barrel through that huge, expensive window. It wasn't easy to imagine. Even at his most angry, he had never been violent. He had never even threatened to hit me or my mother. But now he'd broken a window, and the law.

My mother went on. "Then when he was inside, he found that Mr. Siverhus had changed the lock on his office too, so he kicked the door in. When Mr. Siverhus came to work, he found your dad sitting at his desk, going over service accounts." Her lips started to tremble. "He could have called the police," she said, "but he called me instead. We owe him for that."

That's the story my mother told me. Though I was to find out later that she hadn't told me the entire truth, she had told me enough of it to make me realize that my father had gone crazy. Something in him—whatever slender idea or feeling it is that connects us to the world and makes us feel a part of it—had broken, and he was not in the world anymore, he was outside it, horribly outside it, and could not get back in no matter how he tried. Somehow I knew this, even then. And I wondered if some day the same thing would happen to me.

The rest of that day, I stayed downstairs, watching TV or reading *Sports Illustrated* or *Life*, while my father slept or rested. My mother sat beside his bed, reading her ladies magazines while he slept and talking to him whenever he woke, and every now and then she came downstairs to tell me he was doing fine. She spoke as if he had some temporary fever, some twenty-four hour virus, that would be gone by morning.

But the next morning, a Saturday, my father was still not himself. He didn't feel like coming down for breakfast, so she made him scrambled eggs, sausage, and toast and took it up to him on a tray. He hadn't eaten since the previous morning, but when she came back down a while later all the food was still on the tray. She didn't say anything about the untouched meal; she just said my father wanted to talk to me.

"I can't," I said. "I'm eating." I had one sausage patty and a few bites of scrambled egg left on my plate.

"Not this minute," she said. "When you're done."

I looked out the window. It had been snowing all morning, and the evergreens in the back yard looked like flocked Christmas trees waiting for strings of colored lights. Some sparrows were flying in and out of the branches, chirping, and others were lined up on the crossbars of the clothesline poles, their feathers fluffed out and blowing in the wind.

"I'm supposed to meet Rob at his house," I lied. "I'll be late."

"Danny," she said, in a way that warned me not to make her say any more.

"All right," I said, and I shoved my plate aside and got up. "But I don't have much time."

Upstairs, I stopped at my father's closed door. Normally I would have walked right in, but that day I felt I should knock. I felt as if I were visiting a stranger. Even his room—I didn't think of it as belonging to my mother anymore—seemed strange, somehow separate from the rest of the house.

When I knocked, my father said, "Is that you, Danny?" and I stepped inside. All the blinds were shut, and the dim air smelled like a thick, musty mixture of hair tonic and Aqua Velva. My father was sitting on the edge of his unmade bed, wearing his old brown robe, nubbled from years of washings, and maroon corduroy slippers. His face was blotchy, and his eyes were dark and pouched.

"Mom said you wanted to talk to me," I said.

He touched a spot next to him on the unmade bed. "Here. Sit down."

I didn't move. "I've got to go to Rob's," I said.

He cleared his throat and looked away. For a moment we were silent, and I could hear the heat register ticking.

"I just wanted to tell you to take good care of your mother," he said then.

I shifted my weight from one foot to the other. "What do you mean?"

He looked back at me, his gaze steady and empty, and I wondered how much of the way he was that moment was his medication and how much himself. "She needs someone to take care of her. That's all."

"What about you? Aren't you going to take care of her any-more?"

He cleared his throat again. "If I can."

"I don't get it," I said. "Why are you doing this to us? What's going on?"

"Nothing's going on," he answered. "That the problem. Not a thing is going on."

"I don't know what you mean. I don't like it when you say things I can't understand."

"I don't like it either," he said. Then: "That wasn't me yester-day. I want you to know that."

"It sure looked like you. If it wasn't you, who was it then?"

He stood up and walked across the carpet to the window. But he didn't open the blinds; he just stood there, his back to me. "It's all right for you to be mad," he said.

"I'm not mad."

"Don't lie."

"I'm not lying. I just like my father to use the English language when he talks to me, that's all."

For a long moment he was quiet. It seemed almost as if he'd forgotten I was in the room. Then he said, "My grandmother used to tell me there were exactly as many stars in the sky as there were people. If someone was born, there'd be a new star in the sky that night, and you could find it if you looked hard enough. And if someone died, you'd see that person's star fall."

"What are you talking about?" I asked.

"People," he answered. "Stars."

Then he just stood there, staring at the blinds. I wondered if he was seeing stars there, or his grandmother, or what. And all of a sudden I felt my eyes start to sting. I was surprised—a moment before I'd been so angry, but now I was almost crying.

I tried to swallow, but I couldn't. I wanted to know what was wrong, so I could know how to feel about it; I wanted to be sad or angry, either one, but not both at the same time. "What *happened?*" I finally said. "*Tell* me."

He turned, but I wasn't sure he'd heard me, because he didn't answer for a long time. And when he did, he seemed to be an-swering some other question, one I hadn't asked.

"I was so arrogant," he said. "I thought my life would work out."

I stood there looking at him. "I don't understand."

"I hope you never do," he said. "I hope to God you never do."

"Quit talking like that."

"Like what?"

"Like you're so *smart* and everything. Like you're above all of this when it's you that's causing it all."

He looked down at the floor and shook his head slowly.

"Well?" I said. "Aren't you going to say something?"

He looked up. "You're a good boy, Danny. I'm proud of you. I wish I could be a better father for you."

I hesitate now to say what I said next. But then I didn't hesitate.

"So do I," I said bitterly. "So the hell do I." And I turned to leave.

"Danny, wait," my father said.

But I didn't wait. And when I shut the door, I shut it hard.

Two days later, after he took to fits of weeping and laughing, we drove my father to the VA hospital in Minneapolis. Dr. Lewis had already called the hospital and made arrangements for his admission, so we were quickly escorted to his room on the seventh floor, where the psychiatric patients were kept. I had expected the psych ward to be a dreary, prison-like place with barred doors and gray, windowless walls, but if anything, it was cheerier than the rest of the hospital. There were sky-blue walls in the hallway, hung here and there with watercolor landscapes the patients had painted, and sunny yellow walls in the rooms, and there was a brightly lit lounge with a TV, card tables, and a shelf full of board games, and even a crafts center where the patients could do decoupage, leatherwork, mosaics and macramé. And the patients we saw looked so normal that I almost wondered whether we were in the right place. Most of them were older, probably veterans of the First World War, but a few were my father's age or younger. The old ones were the friendliest, nodding their bald heads or waving their liver-spotted hands as we passed, but even those who only looked at us seemed pleasant or, at the least, not hostile.

I was relieved by what I saw but evidently my father was not, for his eyes still had the quicksilver shimmer of fear they'd had all during the drive from Glencoe. He sat stiffly in the wheelchair and looked at the floor passing between his feet as the big-boned nurse pushed him down the hall toward his room.

We were lucky, the nurse told us, chatting away in a strange accent, which I later learned was Czech. There had been only one private room left, and my father had gotten it. And it had a *lovely* view of the hospital grounds. Sometimes she herself would stand in front of that window and watch the snow fall on the birches and park benches. It was such a beautiful sight. She asked my father if that didn't sound nice, but he didn't answer.

Then she wheeled him into the room and parked the chair beside the white, starched-looking bed. My father hadn't wanted to sit in the chair when we checked him in at the admissions desk, but now he didn't show any desire to get out of it.

"Well, what do you think of your room, Mr. Conroy?" the nurse asked. My mother stood beside her, a handkerchief squeezed in her hand.

My father looked at the chrome railing on the bed, the stainless steel tray beside it, and the plastic-sealed water glasses on the tray. Then he looked at my mother and me.

"I suppose it's where I should be," he said.

During the five weeks my father was in the hospital, my mother drove to Minneapolis twice a week to visit him. Despite her urgings, I refused to go with her. I wanted to forget about my father, to erase him from my life. But I didn't tell her that. I told her I couldn't stand to see him in that awful place, and she felt sorry for me and let me stay home. But almost every time she came back, she'd have a gift for me from him: a postcard of Minnehaha Falls decoupaged onto a walnut plaque, a leather billfold with my initials burned into the cover, a belt decorated with turquoise and white beads. And a request: would I come see him that weekend? But I never went.

Glencoe was a small town, and like all small towns it was devoted to gossip. I knew my classmates had heard about my father—many of them had probably even driven past Goodyear to see the broken window the way they'd drive past a body shop to see a car that had been totaled—but only Rob and a couple of other friends said anything. When they asked what had happened, I told them what Dr. Lewis had told me, that my father was just overworked and exhausted. They didn't believe me any more than I believed Dr. Lewis, but they pretended to accept that explanation. I wasn't sure if I liked them more for that pretense, or less.

It took a couple of weeks for the gossip to reach me. One day during lunch Rob told me that Todd Knutson, whose father was a mechanic at Goodyear, was telling everybody my father had been fired for embezzling. "I know it's a dirty lie," Rob kept saying, "but some kids think he's telling the truth, so you'd better do something."

"Like what?" I said.

"Tell them the truth. Set the record straight."

I looked at my friend's earnest, acne-scarred face. As soon as he'd told me the rumor, I'd known it was true, and in my heart I had already convicted my father. But I didn't want my best friend to know that. Perhaps I was worried that he would turn against me too and I'd be even more alone.

"You bet I will," I said. "I'll make him eat those words."

But I had no intention of defending my father. I was already planning to go see Mr. Siverhus right after school and ask him, straight out, for the truth, so I could confront my father with the evidence and shame him the way he had shamed me. I was furious with him for making me even more of an outcast than I had been—I was the son of a *criminal* now—and I wanted to make him pay for it. All during my afternoon classes, I imagined going to see him at the hospital and telling him I knew his secret. He'd deny it at first, I was sure, but as soon as he saw I knew everything, he'd confess. He'd beg my forgiveness, swearing he'd never do anything to embarrass me or my mother again, but nothing he would say would make any difference—I'd just turn and walk away. And if I were called into court to testify against him, I'd take the stand and swear to tell the whole truth and nothing but the truth, my eyes steady on him all the while, watching him sit there beside his lawyer, his head hung, speechless.

I was angry at my mother too, because she hadn't told me the whole truth. But I didn't realize until that afternoon, when I drove down to Goodyear to see Mr. Siverhus, just how much she hadn't told me.

383

Mr. Siverhus was a tall, silver-haired man who looked more like a banker than the manager of a tire store. He was wearing a starched white shirt, a blue and gray striped tie with a silver tie tack, and iridescent sharkskin trousers, and when he shook my hand he smiled so hard his crow's feet almost hid his pale watery eyes. He led me into his small but meticulous office, closing the door on the smell of grease and the noise of impact wrenches removing lugs from wheels, and I blurted out my question before either of us even sat down.

"Who told you that?" he asked.

"My mother," I answered. I figured he wouldn't try to lie to me if he thought my mother had already told me the truth. Then I asked him again: "Is it true?" But Mr. Siverhus didn't answer right away. Instead, he gestured toward a chair opposite his gray metal desk and waited until I sat in it. Then he pushed some carefully stacked papers aside, sat on the edge of the desk, and asked me how my father was doing. I didn't really know—my mother kept saying he was getting better all the time, but I wasn't sure I could believe her. Still, I said, "Fine."

He nodded. "I'm glad to hear that," he said. "I'm really terribly sorry about everything that's happened. I hope you and your mother know that."

He wanted me to say something, but I didn't. Standing up, he wandered over to the gray file cabinet and looked out the window at the showroom, where the new tires and batteries were on display. He sighed, and I knew he didn't want to be having this conversation.

"What your mother told you is true," he said then. "Bill was taking money. Not much, you understand, but enough that it soon became obvious we had a problem. After some investigating, we found out he was the one. I couldn't have been more surprised. Your father had been a loyal and hardworking employee for years—we never would have put him in charge of the service department otherwise—and he was the last person I would have expected to be stealing from us. But when we confronted him with it, he admitted it. He'd been having trouble meeting his mortgage payments, he said, and in a weak moment he'd taken some money and, later on, a little more. He seemed genuinely sorry about it and he swore he'd pay back every cent, so we gave him another chance."

"But he did it again, didn't he?" I said.

I don't know if Mr. Siverhus noticed the anger shaking my voice or not. He just looked at me and let out a slow breath. "Yes," he said sadly. "He did. And so I had to fire him. I told him we wouldn't prosecute if he returned the money, and he promised he would."

Then he went behind his desk and sat down heavily in his chair. "I hope you understand."

"I'm not blaming you," I said. "You didn't do anything wrong."

He leaned over the desk toward me. "I appreciate that," he said. "You don't know how badly I've felt about all of this. I keep thinking that maybe I should have handled it differently. I don't know, when I think that he might have taken his life because of this, well, I—"

"Taken his life?" I interrupted.

Mr. Siverhus sat back in his chair. "Your mother didn't tell you?"

I shook my head and closed my eyes for a second. I felt as if something had broken loose in my chest and risen into my throat, making it hard to breathe, to think.

"I assumed you knew," he said. "I'm sorry, I shouldn't have said anything."

"Tell me," I said.

"I think you'd better talk to your mother about this, Danny. I don't think I should be the one to tell you."

"I need to know," I said.

Mr. Siverhus looked at me for a long moment. Then he said, "Very well. But you have to realize that your father was under a lot of stress. I'm sure that by the time he gets out of the hospital, he'll be back to normal, and you won't ever have to worry about him getting like that again."

I nodded. I didn't believe him, but I wanted him to go on.

Mr. Siverhus took a deep breath and let it out slowly. "When I came to work that morning and found your father in his office, he had a gun in his hand. A revolver. At first, I thought he was going to shoot me. But then he put it up to his own head. I tell you, I was scared. 'Bill,' I said, 'that's not the answer.' And then I just kept talking. It took me ten or fifteen minutes to get him to put the gun down. Then he left, and that's when I called your mother."

385

I must have had a strange look on my face because the next thing he said was, "Are you all right?"

I nodded, but I wasn't all right. I felt woozy, as if I'd just discovered another world inside this one, a world that made this one false. I wanted to leave, but I wasn't sure I could stand up. Then I did.

"Thank you, Mr. Siverhus," I said, and reached out to shake his hand. I wanted to say more but there was nothing to say. I turned and left.

Outside in the parking lot, I stood beside the Chevy, looking at the new showroom window and breathing in the cold. I was thinking how, only a few months before, I had been looking through my father's dresser for his old Army uniform, which I wanted to wear to Rob's Halloween party, and I'd found the revolver tucked under his dress khakis in the bottom drawer. My father had always been full of warnings—don't mow the lawn barefoot, never go swimming in a river, always drive defensively—but he had never even mentioned he owned this gun, much less warned me not to touch it. I wondered why, and I held the gun up to the light, as if I could somehow see through it to an understanding of its meaning. But I couldn't—or at least I refused to believe that I could—and I put it back exactly where I found it and never mentioned it to anyone.

Now, standing there in the bitter cold, I saw my father sitting at a desk that was no longer his and holding that same gun to his head. And I realized that if he had killed himself with it, the police would have found my fingerprints on its black handle.

I didn't tell my mother what I had learned from Mr. Siverhus, and I didn't tell anyone else either. After dinner that night I went straight to my room and stayed there. I wanted to be alone, to figure things out, but the more I thought, the more I didn't know what to think. I wondered if it was starting already, if I was already going crazy like my father, because I wasn't sure who I was or what I felt. It had been a long time since I'd prayed, but that night I prayed that when I woke the next day everything would make sense again.

But the next morning I was still in a daze. Everything seemed so false, so disconnected from the real world I had glimpsed the day before, that I felt disoriented, almost dizzy. At school, the chatter of my classmates sounded as meaningless as my father's babble, and everything I saw seemed out of focus, distorted, the way things do just before you faint. Walking down the hall, I saw Todd Knutson standing by his locker, talking with Bonnie Kahlstrom, a friend of Molly Rasmussen's, and suddenly I found myself walking up to them. I didn't know what I was going to say or do, I hadn't planned anything, and when I shoved Todd against his locker, it surprised me as much as it did him.

"I hope you're happy now," I said to him. "My father *died* last night." I'm not sure I can explain it now, but in a way I believed what I was saying, and my voice shook with a genuine grief.

Todd slowly lowered his fists. "What?" he said, and looked quickly at Bonnie's startled, open face.

"He had *cancer*," I said, biting down on the word to keep my mind from whirling. "A tumor on his brain. That's why he did the things he did, taking that money and breaking that window and everything. He couldn't help it."

And then my grief was too much for me, and I turned and strode down the hall, tears coming into my eyes. As soon as I was around the corner and out of their sight, I broke into a run. Only then did I come back into the world and wonder what I had done.

That afternoon, my mother appeared at the door of my algebra class in her blue uniform and black hair net. At first I thought she was going to embarrass me by waving at me, as she often did when she happened to pass one of my classrooms, but then I saw the look on her face. "Excuse me, Mr. Laughlin," she said grimly, "I'm sorry to interrupt your class but I need to speak with my son for a moment."

Mr. Laughlin turned his dour face from the blackboard, his stick of chalk suspended in mid-calculation, and said, "Certainly, Mrs. Conroy. I hope there's nothing the matter."

"No," she said. "It's nothing to worry about."

But out in the hall, she slapped my face hard.

"How *dare* you say your father is dead," she said through clenched teeth. Her gray eyes were flinty and narrow.

"I didn't," I answered.

She raised her hand and slapped me again, even harder this time.

"Don't you lie to me, Daniel."

I started to cry. "Well, I wish he *was*," I said. "I wish he was dead, so all of this could be over."

My mother raised her hand again, but then she let it fall. She didn't have enough left in her to hit me again. "Go," she said. "Get away from me. I can't bear to look at you another minute."

I went back into the classroom and sat down. I felt awful about hurting my mother, but not so awful that I wasn't worried whether my classmates had heard her slap me or noticed my burning cheek. I saw them looking at me and shaking their heads, heard them whispering and laughing under their breath, and I felt humiliation rise in me like nausea. I stood up, my head roiling, and asked if I could be excused.

Mr. Laughlin looked at me, then without even asking what was wrong, wrote out a pass to the nurse's office and handed it to me. As I left the room, I heard him say to the class, "That's enough. If I hear one more remark . . . "

Later, lying on a cot in the nurse's office, my hands folded over my chest, I closed my eyes and imagined I was dead, and my parents and classmates were kneeling before my open coffin, their heads bowed in mourning.

After that day, my mother scheduled meetings for me with Father Ondahl, our priest, and Mr. Jenseth, the school counselor. She said she hoped they could help me through this difficult time, then added, "Obviously, I can't." I saw Father Ondahl two or three times, and as soon as I assured him that I still had my faith, though I did not, he said I'd be better off just seeing Mr. Jenseth from then on. I saw Mr. Jenseth three times a week for the next month, then once a week for the rest of the school year. I'm not sure how these meetings helped, or even if they did. All I know is that, in time, my feelings about my father, and about myself, changed.

My mother continued her visits to my father, but she no longer asked me to go along with her, and when she came home from seeing him, she waited until I asked before she'd tell me how he was. I wondered whether she'd told him I was seeing a counselor, and why, but I didn't dare ask. And I wondered if she'd ever forgive me for my terrible lie.

Then one day, without telling me beforehand, she returned from Minneapolis with my father. "Danny," she called, and I came out of the living room and saw them in the entryway. My father was stamping the snow off his black wingtips, and he had his suitcase in one hand and a watercolor of our house in the other, the windows yellow with light and a thin swirl of gray smoke rising from the red brick chimney. He looked pale and even thinner than I remembered. I was so surprised to see him, all I could say was, "You're home."

"That's right," he said, and put down the suitcase and painting. "The old man's back." Then he tried to smile, but it came out more like a wince. I knew he wanted me to hug him and say how happy I was to see him, and part of me wanted to do that, too. But I didn't. I just shook his hand as I would have an uncle's or a stranger's, then picked up the painting and looked at it.

"This is nice," I said. "Real nice."

"I'm glad you like it," he answered.

And then we just stood there until my mother said, "Well, let's get you unpacked, dear, and then we can all sit down and talk."

Despite everything that had happened, our life together after that winter was relatively peaceful. My father got a job at Firestone, and though for years he barely made enough to meet expenses, eventually he worked his way up to assistant manager and earned a good living. He occasionally lost his temper and succumbed to self-pity as he always had, but for the rest of his life he was as normal and sane as anybody. Perhaps Dr. Lewis had been right after all, and all my father had needed was a good rest. In any case, by the time I was grown and married myself, his breakdown seemed a strange and impossible dream and I wondered, as I watched him play with my infant son, if I hadn't imagined some of it. It amazed me that a life could break so utterly, then mend itself.

But of course it had not mended entirely, as my life had also not mended entirely. There was a barrier between us, the thin but impenetrable memory of what we had been to each other that winter. I was never sure just how much he knew about the way I'd felt about him then, or even whether my mother had told him my lie about his death, but I knew he was aware that I hadn't been a good son. Perhaps the barrier between us could have been broken with a single word—the word "love" or its synonym "forgive"—but as if by mutual pact we never spoke of that difficult winter or its consequences.

Only once did we come close to discussing it. He and my mother had come to visit me and my family in Minneapolis, and we had just finished our Sunday dinner. Caroline and my mother were clearing the table, Sam was playing on the kitchen floor with the dump truck my parents had bought him for his birthday, and my father and I were sitting in the living room watching "60 Minutes." The black pastor of a Pentecostal church in Texas was talking to Morley Safer about "the Spirit that descends on us and inhabits us." Then the camera cut to a black woman standing in the midst of a clapping congregation, her eyes tightly closed and her face glowing with sweat as she rocked back and forth, speaking the incoherent language of angels or demons. Her syllables rose and fell, then mounted in a syntax of spiraling rapture until finally, overcome by the voice that had spoken through her, she sank to her knees, trembling, her eyes open and glistening. The congregation clapped harder then, some of them leaping and dancing as if their bodies were lifted by the collapse of hers, and they yelled, "Praise God!" and "Praise the Lord God Almighty!"

I glanced at my father, who sat watching this with a blank face, and wondered what he was thinking. Then, when the camera moved to another Pentecostal minister discussing a transcript of the woman's speech, a transcript which he claimed contained variations on ancient Hebrew and Aramaic words she couldn't possibly have known, I turned to him and asked, in a hesitant way, whether he wanted to keep watching or switch channels.

My father's milky blue eyes looked blurred, as if he were looking at something a long way off, and he cleared his throat before he spoke. "It's up to you," he said. "Do you want to watch it?"

I paused. Then I said, "No" and got up to change the channel.

Perhaps if I had said yes, we might have talked about that terrible day he put a gun to his head and I could have told him what I had since grown to realize—that I loved him. That I had always loved him, though behind his back, without letting him know it. And, in a way, behind my back too. But I didn't say yes, and in the seven years that remained of his life, we never came as close to ending the winter that was always, for us, an unspoken but living part of our present.

That night, though, unable to sleep, I got up and went into my son's room. Standing there in the wan glow of his night light, I listened to him breathe for a while, then quietly took down the railing we'd put on his bed to keep him from rolling off and hurting himself. I sat on the edge of his bed and began to stroke his soft, reddish blond hair. At first he didn't wake, but his forehead wrinkled and he mumbled a little dream-sound.

I am not a religious man. I believe, as my father must have, the day he asked me to save him, that our children are our only salvation, their love our only redemption. And that night, when my son woke, frightened by the dark figure leaning over him, and started to cry, I picked him up and rocked him in my arms, comforting him as I would after a nightmare. "Don't worry," I told him over and over, until the words sounded as incomprehensible to me as they must have to him, "it's only a dream. Everything's going to be all right. Don't worry."

1991

THE HAIR

by JOYCE CAROL OATES

from PARTISAN REVIEW

THE COUPLES FELL in love but not at the same time, and not evenly.

There was perceived to be, from the start, an imbalance of power. The less dominant couple, the Carsons, feared social disadvantage. They feared being hopeful of a friendship that would dissolve before consummation. They feared seeming eager.

Said Charlotte Carson, hanging up the phone, "The Riegels have invited us for dinner on New Year's," her voice level, revealing none of the childlike exultation she felt, nor did she look up to see the expression on her husband's face as he murmured, "Who? The Riegels?" pausing before adding, "That's very nice of them."

Once or twice, the Carsons had invited the Riegels to their home, but for one or another reason the Riegels had declined the invitation.

New Year's Eve went very well indeed and shortly thereafter—though not too shortly—Charlotte Carson telephoned to invite the Riegels back.

The friendship between the couples blossomed. In a relatively small community like the one in which the couples lived, such a new, quick, galloping sort of alliance cannot go unnoticed.

So it was noted by mutual friends who felt some surprise, and perhaps some envy. For the Riegels were a golden couple, newcomers to the area who, not employed locally, had about them the glamour of temporary visitors.

392

In high school, Charlotte Carson thought with a stab of satisfaction, the Riegels would have snubbed me.

Old friends and acquaintances of the Carsons began to observe that Charlotte and Barry were often busy on Saturday evenings, their calendar seemingly marked for weeks in advance. And when a date did not appear to be explicitly set Charlotte would so clearly—insultingly—hesitate, not wanting to surrender a prime weekend evening only to discover belatedly that the Riegels would call them at the last minute and ask them over. Charlotte Carson, gentlest, most tactful of women, in her mid-thirties, shy at times as a schoolgirl of another era, was forced repeatedly to say, "I'm sorry—I'm afraid we can't." And insincerely.

Paul Riegel, whose name everyone knew, was in his early forties: he was a travel writer; he had adventures of a public sort. He published articles and books, he was often to be seen on television, he was tall, handsome, tanned, gregarious, his graying hair springy at the sides of his head and retreating rather wistfully at the crown of his head. "Your husband seems to bear the gift of happiness," Charlotte Carson told Ceci Riegel. Charlotte sometimes spoke too emotionally and wondered now if she had too clearly exposed her heart. But Ceci simply smiled one of her mysterious smiles. "Yes. He tries."

In any social gathering the Riegels were likely to be, without visible effort, the cynosure of attention. When Paul Riegel strode into a crowded room wearing one of his bright ties, or his familiar sports-coat-sports-shirt-open-collar with well-laundered jeans, people looked immediately to him and smiled. There's Paul Riegel! He bore his minor celebrity with grace and even a kind of aristocratic humility, shrugging off questions in pursuit of the public side of his life. If, from time to time, having had a few drinks, he told wildly amusing exaggerated tales, even, riskily, outrageous ethnic or dialect jokes, he told them with such zest and childlike self-delight his listeners were convulsed with laughter.

Never, or almost never, did he forget names.

And his wife, Ceci—petite, ash-blond, impeccably dressed, with a delicate classically proportioned face like an old-fashioned cameo—was surely his ideal mate. She was inclined at times to be fey but she was really very smart. She had a lovely whitely glistening smile as dazzling as her husband's and as seemingly sincere. For years she had been an interior designer in New York

City and since moving to the country was a consultant to her former firm; it was rumored that her family had money and that she had either inherited a small fortune or spurned a small fortune at about the time of her marriage to Paul Riegel.

It was rumored too that the Riegels ran through people quickly, used up friends. That they had affairs.

Or perhaps it was only Paul who had affairs.

Or Ceci.

Imperceptibly, it seemed, the Carsons and the Riegels passed from being friendly acquaintances who saw each other once or twice a month to being friends who saw each other every week, or more. There were formal dinners, and there were cocktail parties, and there were Sunday brunches—the social staples of suburban life. There were newly acquired favorite restaurants to patronize and, under Ceci's guidance, outings to New York City to see plays, ballet, opera. There were even picnics from which bicycle rides and canoe excursions were launched—not without comical misadventures. In August when the Riegels rented a house on Nantucket Island they invited the Carsons to visit; when the Riegels had houseguests the Carsons were almost always invited to meet them; soon the men were playing squash together on a regular basis. (Paul won three games out of five, which seemed just right. But he did not win easily.) In time Charlotte Carson overcame her shyness about telephoning Ceci as if on the spur of the moment—"Just to say hello!"

Ceci Riegel had no such scruples, nor did Paul, who thought nothing of telephoning friends—everywhere in the world; he knew so many people—at virtually any time of the day or night, simply to say hello.

The confidence born of never having been rejected.

Late one evening the Carsons were delighted to hear from Paul in Bangkok, of all places, where he was on assignment with a *Life* photographer.

Another time, sounding dazed and not quite himself, he telephoned them at 7:30 A.M. from John F. Kennedy Airport, newly arrived in the States and homesick for the sound of "familiar" voices. He hadn't been able to get hold of Ceci, he complained, but they were next on his list.

Which was enormously flattering.

Sometimes when Paul was away on one of his extended trips, Ceci was, as she said, morbidly lonely, so the three of them went out for Chinese food and a movie or watched videos late into the night; or impulsively, rather recklessly, Ceci got on the phone and invited a dozen friends over, and neighbors too, though always, first, Charlotte and Barry—"Just to feel I *exist*."

The couples were each childless.

Barry had not had a male friend whom he saw so regularly since college, and the nature of his work—he was an executive with Bell Labs—seemed to preclude camaraderie. Charlotte was his closest friend but he rarely confided in her all that was in his heart: this wasn't his nature.

Unlike his friend Paul he preferred the ragged edges of gatherings, not their quicksilver centers. He was big-boned with heavy-lidded quizzical eyes, a shadowy beard like shot, deep in the pores of his skin, wide nostrils, a handsome sensual mouth. He'd been an all-A student once and carried still that air of tension and precariousness strung tight as a bow. Did he take himself too seriously? Or not seriously enough? Wild moods swung in him, rarely surfacing. When his wife asked him why was he so quiet, what was he thinking, he replied, smiling, "Nothing important, honey," though resenting the question, the intrusion. The implied assertion: *I have a right to your secrets.*

His heart pained him when Ceci Riegel greeted him with a hearty little spasm of an embrace and a perfumy kiss alongside his cheek, but he was not the kind of man to fall sentimentally in love with a friend's wife. Nor was he the kind of man, aged forty and wondering when his life would begin, to fall in love with his friend.

The men played squash daily when Paul was in town. Sometimes, afterward, they had lunch together, and a few beers, and talked about their families: their fathers, mainly. Barry drifted back to his office pale and shaken and that evening might complain vaguely to Charlotte that Paul Riegel came on a little too strong for him, "As if it's always the squash court, and he's always the star."

Charlotte said quickly, "He means well. And so does Ceci. But they're aggressive people." She paused, wondering what she was saying. "Not like us."

When Barry and Paul played doubles with other friends, other men, they nearly always won. Which pleased Barry more than he would have wished anyone to know.

And Paul's praise: it burned in his heart with a luminosity that endured for hours and days and all in secret.

The Carsons were childless but had two cats. The Riegels were childless but had a red setter bitch, no longer young.

The Carsons lived in a small mock-Georgian house in town; the Riegels lived in a glass, stone, and redwood house, custom-designed, three miles out in the country. The Carsons' house was one of many attractive houses of its kind in their quiet residential neighborhood and had no distinctive features except an aged enormous plane tree in the front which would probably have to be dismantled soon—"It will break our hearts," Charlotte said. The Carsons' house was fully exposed to the street; the Riegels' house was hidden from the narrow gravel road that ran past it by a seemingly untended meadow of juniper pines, weeping willows, grasses, wildflowers.

Early on in their friendship, a tall cool summer drink in hand, Barry Carson almost walked through a plate glass door at the Riegels'—beyond it was the redwood deck, Ceci in a silk floral-printed dress with numberless pleats.

Ceci was happy and buoyant and confident always. For a petite woman—size five, it was more than once announced—she had a shapely body, breasts, hips, strong-calved legs. When she and Charlotte Carson played tennis, Ceci was all over the court, laughing and exclaiming, while slow-moving premeditated Charlotte, poor Charlotte, who felt, in her friend's company, ostrich-tall and ungainly, missed all but the easy shots. "You need to be more aggressive, Char!" Paul Riegel called out. "Need to be *murderous!*"

The late-night drive back to town from the Riegels' along narrow twisty country roads, Barry behind the wheel, sleepy with drink yet excited too, vaguely sweetly aching, Charlotte yawning and sighing, and there was the danger of white-tailed deer so plentiful in this part of the state leaping in front of the car; but they returned home safely, suddenly they were home, and, inside, one of them would observe that their house was so lacking in imagination, wasn't it? So exposed to the neighbors? "Yes, but you wanted this house." "No, you were the one who wanted this house." "Not *this* house—but this was the most feasible." Though sometimes one would observe that the Riegels' house had flaws: so much glass and it's drafty in the winter, so many queer elevated decks and flights of stairs, wall-less rooms, sparsely furnished rooms like designers' showcases, and the cool chaste neutral colors that Ceci evidently favored: "It's beautiful, yes, but a bit sterile."

In bed exhausted they would drift to sleep, separately wandering the corridors of an unknown building, opening one door after another in dread and fascination. Charlotte, who should not have had more than two or three glasses of wine—but it was an anniversary of the Riegels: they'd uncorked bottles of champagne—slept fitfully, waking often dry-mouthed and frightened not knowing where she was. A flood of hypnagogic images raced in her brain; the faces of strangers never before glimpsed by her thrummed beneath her eyelids. In that state of consciousness that is neither sleep nor waking Charlotte had the volition to will, ah, how passionately, how despairingly, that Paul Riegel would comfort her: slip his arm around her shoulders, nudge his jaw against her cheek, whisper in her ear as he'd done once or twice that evening in play but now in seriousness. Beside her someone stirred and groaned in his sleep and kicked at the covers.

Paul Riegel entranced listeners with lurid tales of starving Cambodian refugees, starving Ethiopian children, starving Mexican beggars. His eyes shone with angry tears one moment and with mischief the next, for he could not resist mocking his own sobriety. The laughter he aroused at such times had an air of bafflement, shock.

Ceci came to him to slip an arm through his as if to comfort or to quiet, and there were times when quite perceptibly Paul shook off her arm, stepped away, stared down at her with a look as if he'd never seen the woman before.

When the Carsons did not see or hear from the Riegels for several days their loneliness was almost palpable: a thickness in the chest, a density of being, to which either might allude knowing the other would immediately understand. If the Riegels were actually away that made the separation oddly more bearable than if they were in fact in their house amid the trees but not seeing the Carsons that weekend or mysteriously incommunicado with their telephone answering tape switched on. When Charlotte called, got the tape, heard the familiar static-y overture, then Paul Riegel's cool almost hostile voice that did not identify itself but merely stated *No one is here right now; should you like to leave a message please wait for the sound of the bleep,* she felt a loss too profound to be named and often hung up in silence.

It had happened as the Carsons feared—the Riegels were dominant. So fully in control.

For there was a terrible period, several months in all, when for no reason the Carsons could discover—and they discussed the subject endlessly, obsessively—the Riegels seemed to have little time for them. Or saw them with batches of others in which their particular friendship could not be readily discerned. Paul was a man of quick enthusiasms, and Ceci was a woman of abrupt shifts of allegiance; thus there was logic of sorts to their cruelty in elevating for a while a new couple in the area who were both theoretical mathematicians, and a neighbor's houseguest who'd known Paul in college and was now in the diplomatic service, and a cousin of Ceci's, a male model in his late twenties who was staying with the Riegels for weeks and weeks and weeks, taking up every spare minute of their time, it seemed, so when Charlotte called, baffled and hurt, Ceci murmured in an undertone, "I can't talk now, can I call you back in the morning?" and failed to call for days, days, days.

One night when Charlotte would have thought Barry was asleep he shocked her by saying, "I never liked her, much. Hotshit little Ceci." She had never heard her husband utter such words before and did not know how to reply.

They went away on a trip. Three weeks in the Caribbean, and only in the third week did Charlotte scribble a postcard for the Riegels—a quick scribbled little note as if one of many.

One night she said, "*He's* the dangerous one. He always tries to get people to drink too much, to keep him company."

They came back, and not long afterward Ceci called, and the friendship was resumed precisely as it had been—the same breathless pace, the same dazzling intensity—though now Paul had a new book coming out and there were parties in the city, book signings at bookstores, an interview on a morning news program. The Carsons gave a party for him, inviting virtually everyone they knew locally, and the party was a great success and in a corner of the house Paul Riegel hugged Charlotte Carson so hard she laughed, protesting her ribs would crack, but when she drew back to look at her friend's face she saw it was damp with tears.

Later, Paul told a joke about Reverend Jesse Jackson that was a masterpiece of mimicry though possibly in questionable taste. In the general hilarity no one noticed, or at least objected. In any case there were no blacks present.

The Riegels were childless but would not have defined their condition in those terms: as a lack, a loss, a negative. Before marrying they had discussed the subject of children thoroughly, Paul said, and came to the conclusion *no*.

The Carsons too were childless but would perhaps have defined their condition in those terms, in weak moods at least. Hearing Paul speak so indifferently of children, the Carsons exchanged a glance almost of embarrassment.

Each hoped the other would not disclose any intimacy.

Ceci sipped at her drink and said, "I'd have been willing."

Paul said, "*I* wouldn't."

There was a brief nervous pause. The couples were sitting on the Riegels' redwood deck in the gathering dusk.

Paul then astonished the Carsons by speaking in a bitter impassioned voice of families, children, parents, the "politics" of intimacy. In any intimate group, he said, the struggle to be independent, to define oneself as an individual, is so fierce it creates terrible waves of tension, a field of psychic warfare. He'd endured it as a child and young adolescent in his parents' home, and as an adult he didn't think he could bear to bring up a child—"especially a son"—knowing of the doubleness and secrecy of the child's life.

"There is the group life, which is presumably open and observable," he said, "and there is the secret inner real life no one can penetrate." He spoke with such uncharacteristic vehemence that neither of the Carsons would have dared to challenge him or even to question him in the usual conversational vein.

Ceci sat silent, drink in hand, staring impassively out into the shadows.

After a while conversation resumed again and they spoke softly, laughed softly. The handsome white wrought-iron furniture on which they were sitting took on an eerie solidity even as the human figures seemed to fade: losing outline and contour, blending into the night and into one another.

Charlotte Carson lifted her hand, registering a small chill spasm of fear that she was dissolving, but it was only a drunken notion of course.

For days afterward Paul Riegel's disquieting words echoed in her head. She tasted something black, and her heart beat in anger like a cheated child's. *Don't you love me then? Don't any of us love any of us?* To Barry she said, "That was certainly an awkward moment, wasn't it? When Paul started his monologue about family life, intimacy, all that. What did you make of it?"

Barry murmured something evasive and backed off.

The Carsons owned two beautiful Siamese cats, neutered male and neutered female, and the Riegels owned a skittish Irish setter named Rusty. When the Riegels came to visit Ceci always made a fuss over one or the other of the cats, insisting it sit in her lap, sometimes even at the dinner table, where she'd feed it on the sly. When the Carsons came to visit, the damned dog as Barry spoke of it went into a frenzy of barking and greeted them at the front door as if it had never seen them before. "Nice dog! Good dog! Sweet Rusty!" the Carsons would cry in unison.

The setter was rheumy-eyed and thick-bodied and arthritic. If every year of a dog's age is approximately seven years in human terms, poor Rusty was almost eighty years old. She managed to shuffle to the front door to bark at visitors but then lacked the strength or motor coordination to reverse herself and return to the interior of the house so Paul had to carry her, one arm under her bony chest and forelegs, the other firmly under her hindquarters, an expression of vexed tenderness in his face.

Dryly he said, "I hope someone will do as much for me someday."

One rainy May afternoon when Paul was in Berlin and Barry was in Virginia visiting his family, Ceci impulsively invited Charlotte to come for a drink and meet her friend Nils Larson—or was the name Lasson? Lawson?—an old old dear friend. Nils was short, squat-bodied, energetic, with a gnomish head and bright malicious eyes, linked to Ceci, it appeared, in a way that allowed him to be both slavish and condescending. He was a "theater person"; his bubbly talk was studded with names of the famous and near-famous. Never once did he mention Paul Riegel's name, though certain of his mannerisms—head thrown back in laughter, hands gesticulating as he spoke—reminded Charlotte of certain of Paul's mannerisms. The man was Paul's elder by perhaps a decade.

Charlotte stayed only an hour, then made her excuses and slipped away. She had seen Ceci's friend draw his pudgy forefinger across the nape of Ceci's neck in a gesture that signaled intimacy or the arrogant pretense of intimacy, and the sight offended her. But she never told Barry and resolved not to think of it and of whether Nils spent the night at the Riegels' and whether Paul knew anything of him or of the visit. Nor did Ceci ask Charlotte what she had thought of Nils Larson—Lasson? Lawson?—the next time the women spoke.

Barry returned from Virginia with droll tales of family squabbling: his brother and his sister-in-law, their children, the network of aunts, uncles, nieces, nephews, grandparents, ailing elderly relatives whose savings were being eaten up—invariably the expression was "eaten up"—by hospital and nursing home expenses. Barry's father, severely crippled from a stroke, was himself in a nursing home from which he would never be discharged, and all his conversation turned upon this fact, which others systematically denied, including, in the exigency of the moment, Barry. He had not, he said, really recognized his father. It was as if another man—aged, shrunken, querulous, sly—had taken his place.

The elderly Mr. Carson had affixed to a wall of his room a small white card on which he'd written some Greek symbols, an inscription he claimed to have treasured all his life. Barry asked what the Greek meant and was told, *When my ship sank, the others sailed on.*

Paul Riegel returned from Berlin exhausted and depressed despite the fact, a happy one to his wife and friends, that a book of his was on the paperback bestseller list published by *The New York Times*. When Charlotte Carson suggested with uncharacteristic gaiety that they celebrate, Paul looked at her with a mild quizzical smile and asked, "Why, exactly?"

The men played squash, the women played tennis.

The Carsons had other friends, of course. Older and more reliable friends. They did not need the Riegels. Except they were in love with the Riegels.

401

Did the Riegels love them? Ceci telephoned one evening and Barry happened to answer and they talked together for an hour, and afterward, when Charlotte asked Barry what they'd talked about, careful to keep all signs of jealousy and excitement out of her voice, Barry said evasively, "A friend of theirs is dying. Of AIDS. Ceci says he weighs only ninety pounds and has withdrawn from everyone: 'slunk off to die like a sick animal.' And Paul doesn't care. Or won't talk about it." Barry paused, aware that Charlotte was looking at him closely. A light film of perspiration covered his face; his nostrils appeared unusually dark, dilated. "He's no one we know, honey. The dying man, I mean."

When Paul Riegel emerged from a sustained bout of writing the first people he wanted to see were the Carsons of course, so the couples went out for Chinese food—"a banquet, no less!"—at their favorite Chinese restaurant in a shopping mall. The Dragon Inn had no liquor license so they brought bottles of wine and six-packs of beer. They were the last customers to leave, and by the end waiters and kitchen help were standing around or prowling restlessly at the rear of the restaurant. There was a minor disagreement over the check, which Paul Riegel insisted had not been added up "strictly correctly." He and the manager discussed the problem and since the others were within earshot he couldn't resist clowning for their amusement, slipping into a comical Chinese (unless it was Japanese?) accent. In the parking lot the couples laughed helplessly, gasping for breath and bent double, and in the car driving home—Barry drove: they'd taken the Carsons' Honda Accord, and Barry was seemingly the most sober of the four of them—they kept bursting into peals of laughter like naughty children.

They never returned to the Dragon Inn.

The men played squash together but their most rewarding games were doubles in which they played, and routed, another pair of men.

As if grudgingly, Paul Riegel would tell Barry Carson he was a "damned good player." To Charlotte he would say, "Your husband is a damned good player but if only he could be a bit more *murderous!*"

Barry Carson's handsome heavy face darkened with pleasure when he heard such praise, exaggerated as it was. Though afterward, regarding himself in a mirror, he felt shame: he was forty years old, he had a very good job in a highly competitive field, he had a very good marriage with a woman he both loved and respected, he believed he was leading, on the whole, a very good life, yet none of this meant as much to him as Paul Riegel carelessly complimenting him on his squash game.

How has my life come to this?

Rusty developed cataracts on both eyes and then tumorous growths in her neck. The Riegels took her to the vet and had her put to sleep, and Ceci had what was reported to the Carsons as a breakdown of a kind: wept and wept and wept. Paul too was shaken by the ordeal but managed to joke over the phone about the dog's ashes. When Charlotte told Barry of the dog's death she saw Barry's eyes narrow as he resisted saying Thank God! and said instead, gravely, as if it would be a problem of his own, "Poor Ceci will be inconsolable."

For weeks it wasn't clear to the Carsons that they would be invited to visit the Riegels on Nantucket; then, shortly before the Riegels left, Ceci said as if casually, "We did set a date, didn't we? For you two to come visit?"

On their way up—it was a seven-hour drive to the ferry at Woods Hole—Charlotte said to Barry, "Promise you won't drink so much this year." Offended, Barry said, "I won't monitor your behavior, honey, if you won't monitor mine."

From the first, the Nantucket visit went awkwardly. Paul wasn't home and his whereabouts weren't explained, though Ceci chattered brightly and effusively, carrying her drink with her as she escorted the Carsons to their room and watched them unpack. Her shoulder-length hair was graying and disheveled; her face was heavily made up, especially about the eyes. Several times she said, "Paul will be so happy to see you," as if Paul had not known they were invited; or, knowing, like Ceci herself, had perhaps forgotten. An east wind fanned drizzle and soft gray mist against the windows.

Paul returned looking fit and tanned and startled about the eyes; in his walnut-brown face the whites glared. Toward dusk the sky lightened and the couples sat on the beach with their drinks. Ceci continued to chatter while Paul smiled, vague and distracted, looking out at the surf. The air was chilly and damp but wonderfully fresh. The Carsons drew deep breaths and spoke admiringly of the view. And the house. And the location. They were wondering had the Riegels been quarreling? Was something wrong? Had they themselves come on the wrong day or at the wrong time? Paul had been effusive too in his greetings but had not seemed to see them and had scarcely looked at them since.

Before they sat down to dinner the telephone began to ring. Ceci in the kitchen (with Charlotte who was helping her) and Paul in the living room (with Barry; the men were watching a televised tennis tournament) made no move to answer it. The ringing continued for what seemed like a long time, then stopped and resumed again while they were having dinner, and again neither of the Riegels made a move to answer it. Paul grinned, running both hands roughly through the bushy patches of hair at the sides of his head, and said, "When the world beats a path to your doorstep, beat it back, friends! *Beat it back for fuck's sake!*"

His extravagant words were meant to be funny of course but would have required another atmosphere altogether to be so. As it was, the Carsons could only stare and smile in embarrassment.

Ceci filled the silence by saying loudly, "Life's little ironies! You spend a lifetime making yourself famous, then you try to back off and dismantle it. But it won't dismantle! It's a mummy and you're inside it!"

"Not *in* a mummy," Paul said, staring smiling at the lobster on his plate, which he'd barely eaten, "you *are* a mummy." He had been drinking steadily, Scotch on the rocks and now wine, since arriving home.

Ceci laughed sharply. " 'In,' 'are,' what's the difference?" she said, appealing to the Carsons. She reached out to squeeze Barry's hand, hard. "In any case you're a goner, right?"

Paul said, "No, *you're* a goner."

The evening continued in this vein. The Carsons sent despairing glances at each other.

The telephone began to ring, and this time Paul rose to answer it. He walked stiffly and took his glass of wine with him. He took the call not in the kitchen but in another room at the rear of the house, and he was gone so long that Charlotte felt moved to ask if something was wrong. Ceci Riegel stared at her coldly. The whites of Ceci's eyes too showed above the rims of the iris, giving her a fey festive party look at odds with her carelessly combed hair and the tiredness deep in her face. "With the meal?" she asked. "With the house? With us? With *you?* I don't know of anything wrong."

Charlotte had never been so rebuffed in her adult life. Barry too felt the force of the insult. After a long stunned moment Charlotte murmured an apology, and Barry too murmured something vague, placating, embarrassed.

They sat in suspension, not speaking, scarcely moving, until at last Paul returned. His cheeks were ruddy as if they'd been heartily slapped and his eyes were bright. He carried a bottle of his favorite Napa Valley wine, which he'd been saving, he said, just for tonight. "This is a truly special occasion! We've really missed you guys!"

They were up until two, drinking. Repeatedly Paul used the odd expression "guys" as if its sound, its grating musicality, had imprinted itself in his brain. "OK, guys, how's about another drink?" he would say, rubbing his hands together. "OK, guys, how the hell have you been?"

Next morning, a brilliantly sunny morning, no one was up before eleven. Paul appeared in swimming trunks and T-shirt in the kitchen around noon, boisterous, swaggering, unshaven, in much the mood of the night before—remarkable! The Riegels had hired a local handyman to shore up some rotting steps and the handyman was an oldish gray-grizzled black and after the man was paid and departed Paul spoke in an exaggerated comical black accent, hugging Ceci and Charlotte around their waists until Charlotte pushed him away stiffly, saying, "I don't think you're being funny, Paul." There was a moment's startled silence; then she repeated, vehemently, *"I don't think that's funny, Paul."*

As if on cue Ceci turned on her heel and walked out of the room.

But Paul continued his clowning. He blundered about in the kitchen, pleading with "white missus": bowing, shuffling, tugging what remained of his forelock, kneeling to pluck at Charlotte's denim skirt. His flushed face seemed to have turned to rubber, his lips red, moist, turned obscenely inside out. "Beg pardon, white missus! Oh, white missus, beg pardon!"

Charlotte said, "I think we should leave."

Barry, who had been staring appalled at his friend, as if he'd never seen him before, said quickly, "Yes. I think we should leave."

They went to their room at the rear of the house, leaving Paul behind, and in a numbed stricken silence packed their things, each of them badly trembling. They anticipated one or both of the Riegels following them but neither did, and as Charlotte yanked sheets off the bed, towels off the towel rack in the bathroom, to fold and pile them neatly at the foot of the bed, she could not believe that their friends would allow them to leave without protest.

With a wad of toilet paper she cleaned the bathroom sink as Barry called to her to please hurry. She examined the claw-footed tub—she and Barry had each showered that morning—and saw near the drain a tiny curly dark hair, hers or Barry's, indistinguishable, and this hair she leaned over to snatch up but her fingers closed in air and she tried another time, still failing to grasp it, then finally she picked it up and flushed it down the toilet. Her face was burning and her heart knocking so hard in her chest she could scarcely breathe.

The Carsons left the Riegels' cottage in Nantucket shortly after noon of the day following their arrival.

They drove seven hours back to their home with a single stop, silent much of the time but excited, nervously elated. When he drove Barry kept glancing in the rearview mirror. One of his eyelids had developed a tic.

He said, "We should have done this long ago."

"Yes," Charlotte said, staring ahead at dry sunlit rushing pavement. "Long ago."

That night in their own bed they made love for the first time in weeks, or months. "I love you," Barry murmured, as if making a vow. "No one but you."

Tears started out of the corners of Charlotte's tightly shut eyes.

Afterward Barry slept heavily, sweating through the night. From time to time he kicked at the covers, but he never woke. Beside him Charlotte lay staring into the dark. What would become of them now? Something tickled her lips, a bit of lint, a hair, and though she brushed it irritably away the tingling sensation remained. What would become of them, now?

1991

NOSOTROS

by JANET PEERY

from SHENANDOAH

Iᴛ ᴡᴀꜱ ᴀʟᴡᴀʏꜱ hot in the little house, her mother's house, even in December. Licha, lying on the floor, arms above her head and braced against the mirrored bedroom door, thought how cool it was here, in Madama's house where the big air conditioners hummed, pumping cold air through all the louvered vents in the spacious rooms. Madama's son Raleigh strained above her, drops of his sweat pooling on her breasts and belly like warm coins, his movements grinding her hips into the wool carpet until they stung, but it was cooler. Licha drew up her knees and curled her toes; even the carpet was cool, and she wondered how far down the coolness went.

All the houses in the Valley were slab houses, built on concrete. There were no basements; hurricanes came this far inland. Few peaked roofs: there was no snow here. Ever. Under the slab, Licha knew, and in the space between the walls, lived thousands of lizards: stripebacks, *chalotes,* green anoles. They came out to bask on the hot packed dirt around the foundation, to crawl up the screens. Madama hated them. If she saw too many she called the exterminators down from McAllen. Then Licha's mother Camarena was set to draping the furniture in sheeting, removing dishes, food and clothing from the house so the pesticide wouldn't contaminate Madama and Raleigh. When the exterminator's immense plastic tent was pulled from the house and all the lizard carcasses were shoveled into bushel baskets, her mother would come back in to give the house a thorough cleaning:

407

Pine-Sol the terrazzo, scrub the pecky cypress walls, shampoo the carpets. Then she would move everything back in, washing each dish and glass and fork in hot detergent water while Madama supervised, giving orders in her tight rough voice.

At the little house behind Madama's, her mother's house, lizards entered and departed through the gap between the screen door and the flagstone sill, unremarked. Geckos made their way around the walls, eating insects, spatulate toepads mocking gravity. But it was so hot there. Licha thought about the house she and Raleigh could have when she finished high school and moved from the Valley, a little college house with a peaked roof and an air conditioner in the window, a Boston fern hanging above the table, her biology texts and notes spread out beneath it.

"Squeeze your titties together," Raleigh said. "I want to see them that way."

She braced her feet against the floor and took her hands from the door. She tried to place them on the sides of her breasts, but his movements inched her too far up. "I can't. I'll hit my head."

Raleigh balanced on one arm, pushing his glasses farther up on his nose. She didn't understand how he could sweat so, when it was as cool in the room as it was in the stores downtown. The lenses of his glasses were fogged. She wondered why he wore them, what he saw as he watched, if he saw the two of them as a watery image, the edges of their bodies blurred and running together. She wondered what it was he wanted to see in the mirror, with his glasses. She looked up at him, under the rims, at his eyes, and their blue startled her. It was an uncommon color, she thought, a surprise of a color, a color she marveled the human body, with its browns and tans and pinks, could produce. She couldn't look at it long without imagining it was from another place—foreign, vaguely holy, like the blue of the Blessed Virgin's mantle at the church of San Benito; cool and infinite, like the blue of the sky when the heat lifted and the haze that sealed the Valley blew away in the wind of a norther. It was a blue like ice and snow.

It snowed sometimes in Austin, even in San Antonio. Where her brother Tavo had gone—to Fort Dix, New Jersey—it was probably snowing now, great fat flakes floating and floating, covering the barracks until they looked like rows of sugared cakes, and Tavo, inside with other soldiers, maybe some from other warm places, laughed from the surprise of it. As much as she hoped Tavo wouldn't have to go to Vietnam, she envied him his chance to be away, to open a window and draw the coolness in. She closed her eyes and imagined she could smell the snow. It must be sweet and powdery, she thought, like coconut. She looked again at Raleigh, his neck cords straining, watching in the mirror. "Have you ever seen snow?"

"Don't talk," he said. "I'm almost there." He clenched his jaw, and Licha knew her question had irritated him.

Raleigh went to school in Tennessee, to Vanderbilt. He was home for winter break. Madama had picked him up at the Brownsville airport, taking the yardman Perfilio along to drive the big car. She refused to drive the road alone. Raleigh's father, called Papa by everyone in the little towns along the highway, had been killed on this road, on an inspection tour of his groves. As he pulled out of the Donna off-ramp, he was struck by one of his own trucks, the driver drunk and running with no lights, a load of stolen television sets concealed by cotton bales in the truck bed. On the day of Raleigh's return Licha had seen Perfilio pull the car into the driveway, Raleigh and Madama in the back seat. When Perfilio piled Raleigh's red plaid luggage on the *porche* beside the tall white poinsettias, Licha thought they looked like Christmas packages from another country, from England or Scotland, not like they should belong to Raleigh, whom Licha and Tavo had grown up with, the three of them playing in the shell-flecked dirt around the roots of the live oaks in the backyard, none of them wearing a shirt, Raleigh's hair bleached almost white with the sun, tanned until he was nearly as brown as Licha and Tavo.

Licha was nine when she overheard Madama's order: the children were not to play together any longer. Madama stood by the laundry shed, her mother at the clothesline. "Camarena," she said, "that girl of yours isn't mine to boss, but she's about to bust out of herself."

Her mother pretended she didn't understand Madama's English, and it irritated Licha; her mother smiling, nodding, an impassive, half-comprehending look in her eyes, wiping her hands on a dish towel or patting little balls of dough into flat round tortillas: pat-pat-pat, smile, nod, shuffle around the big *cocina* in her starched blue work dress and apron, her backless sandals.

She had lived in the little house eleven years, since Licha was five, but still she pretended she didn't understand, or understood only dimly, forcing Madama into a fractured mixture of languages: "Camarena, *deja* all that laundry *sucio en el* whatchamacallit."

Licha and Tavo had laughed about it, about their mother getting the best of bossy Madama in such a sly, funny way, but it made Licha angry that her mother could let Madama think she was stupid; her mother understood everything Madama said. After Madama's bridge-club meetings she entertained Tavo and Licha with stories and imitations until they collapsed on their beds in the little house, wrung out from laughing at the dressed-up stupidity of Madama and her henna-rinsed friends. On the day of Madama's order, she had pretended not to understand, but she complied, keeping Tavo and Licha from Raleigh. Licha remembered how unfair it seemed, and that Madama saw it as her fault: *that girl.*

"Hurry, Raleigh," she said. "They'll be back."

"Maybe if you did something more than lie there," he said. "Move a little."

She tried moving her hips in a small circle. She wasn't sure if it was the right way, the way he expected or was used to, or if there was a right way. Their first time, two days before, when they stood behind the closed door of Raleigh's bedroom, she hadn't had to move at all, and it had been over sooner. Madama and her mother had gone to the grocery store. Raleigh came around the side of the big house to the clothesline where Licha was hanging towels. He held a radio to her ear, as though the years they spent avoiding each other had been no more than a few weeks. She heard a raspy female voice.

"Janis Joplin," he said. "Great, isn't she?"

He lowered the radio when Licha nodded. "Bobby McGee," she said. "I heard it at school."

Raleigh looked the same as he had in high school, when Licha would see him in the halls or at a football game, surrounded by other boys in the same kind of clothing: madras shirts, wheat jeans, loafers they wore without socks. They dressed as if they were already in college, and everyone knew it was where they would end up. The other Anglo boys—those who would stay in the Valley to work and marry, to hunt whitewing dove in the fall, *javelinas* and coyote the rest of the year—wore blue jeans and white T-shirts. Raleigh's hair was still cut in Beatle bangs, but he had grown sideburns, the earpieces of his new wire-rim glasses cutting into them. "Are you at Consolidated?" he asked.

She looked at him, trying to decide if he was joking. She reached for a clothespin to clip the corner of a towel over the line. He should know she wouldn't be at Blessed Sacrament; she was the daughter of a maid, and the public high school was her only choice. When she nodded, he asked her what she was taking.

She wanted to tell him about the frog dissection they had done the week before in biology, how she had cut into the pale, pearlescent belly to expose the first layer of organs, the ventral abdominal vein like a tiny, delicately branching river, the torsion of the small intestine giving way to the bulk of the large intestine and how both of them, when held aside, revealed the deeper viscera, the long posterior vena cava, the testes, kidneys and adrenal bodies; how the heart and lungs lay over the perfect fork of the aortic arch; how surprisingly large the liver was, its curves, its fluted edges, and how she could hardly catch her breath, not because of the formaldehyde or out of revulsion, like some of the other students, but from awe, for joy at the synchrony and mystery of the workings of the body laid out before her, its legs splayed on the cutting table, the fragile mandible upturned and yielding to her touch. She wanted to tell him how she felt as her probe and scalpel moved through the frog's body, about the sacred, almost heartbreaking invitation of it, but she couldn't. "I'm taking biology," she said.

"Does Mohesky still teach it?"

She nodded. "I really like him." She became aware of Raleigh looking at her breasts, and when she stooped to pick up another towel from the basket she checked the buttons of her blouse. She hoped he didn't notice the downward glance that meant she knew he was looking at her.

"Come in the house a minute," he said. "I want to show you something."

When they were just inside his bedroom he closed the door, telling her how beautiful she was, how sweet. She was all he thought about his first semester away at school. Her breasts were beautiful; titties, he called them, and he'd bet they'd grown— would she show him? She was surprised to feel her nipple tighten when he took it into his mouth, the whole breast seem to swell around it. He lifted her skirt and eased his fingers past her panties until the middle one was inside her. "You know all about it," he said. He unzipped his pants.

"It hurts," she said, and he stopped moving his fingers. "A little."

"You don't act like it," he said. He slid his fingers out and guided himself into her, knees bent, his hand pressing against her hip.

"That doesn't mean it doesn't."

"You like it, though." It wasn't a question, and Licha didn't bother to answer. She did like it. She liked it that he wanted her. She liked the push of it, the tip of him pushing past the part of her that felt like a small, rugate tunnel into a bigger part that had less feeling, more like a liquid cave that seemed to swallow him. She worried that she was too big. Anglo boys said Mexican girls were built for breeding. She wondered if Raleigh was small. She had seen other men; several times she had surprised Tavo, and she had seen *braceros* relieving themselves in the groves after *siesta*. She hadn't looked closely, but it seemed that most of these were more substantial, their color fuller, more nearly like the rest of their skin. Raleigh's was the color of sunburn, almost purple at the tip.

When it was over he had gone into the bathroom. She heard the tap running, a flush. She cleaned herself with her panties, not wanting to use the lacquered box of tissues beside Raleigh's bed. She noticed only a slight pink tinge, no more blood than from a paper cut. She tucked the panties into the waistband of her skirt and pulled down her blouse to conceal them.

Now, two days later, he had come up behind her as she emptied trash from the little house onto the burn pile at the back of the property. "*Nalgas*," he said, patting her bottom. She laughed at the *pachuco* word for buttocks, at the growling, mock-salacious way he said it, the furtive waggle of his eyebrows behind his glasses, and she had gone with him again to the big house, this time to Madama's bedroom where he locked the door and showed her the full-length mirror behind it. Facing it, with Raleigh behind her, Licha watched his hands, nervous and more intent this time, move up her body, the tips of his fingers tapered, almost delicate, nails bitten to the quick. She could see ragged cuticles and dark flecks of dried blood as his fingers

412

worked at buttons, at the elastic of her shorts. He pressed himself closer, sweating already, his breathing shallow and uneven, and when they were on the floor, Licha on her hands and knees, Raleigh upright, kneeling behind her, she looked at their image in the mirror, at Raleigh watching, his head thrown back and arms extended so his hands grasped her hips, his movements regular and insistent. She thought of the mice they had mated in biology lab, of the male, a solid black, his motions powerful and concentrated in mount, of the female, a pink-eyed white, hunched and holding her ground to help him, her neck at an angle of submission, and she knew they were more alike than different, the mating mice, herself and Raleigh; that this impulse shot through all of life, through male and female, and made them do the things they did, made men and women lie down together. We are mating, she marveled.

He seemed to go deeper this time, deeper than when they stood against his bedroom wall. She felt her belly swell from him, a soft, cramping fullness like her menstrual cycle, pleasant at first, then almost painful. She asked him to stop, and he had waited while she turned over to face him, her arms braced against the door. Then he had continued. Again she tried to hold her breasts for him and to move her hips at the same time. "You have to take it out," she said. "Before." She had forgotten to tell him the first time.

He said nothing, concentrating on their image in the mirror. Finally he moaned, withdrawing, and Licha felt slow, warm spurts against her thigh. She squirmed beneath his weight, and when he rolled over she got up. "We'll leave a spot."

She went into the bathroom, looking for a cloth for the carpet. She didn't want to use the pale yellow towels folded in a complicated way across the bar, so she tore a length of paper, setting the roller spinning, and hurried to dab at the wetness where they had lain. The paper pilled and shed, leaving lint on the close shear of the wool. She tried to pick it off with her fingers, but it stuck here, too. Raleigh laughed and got up to go to the bathroom. "Don't worry so much," he said. He closed the door. "Camarena will get it."

His mention of her mother startled Licha; she and Madama would be back soon from McAllen. She dressed quickly, tucking the wad of paper into her pocket. She was halfway down the *galería* to the stairs when she heard the bathroom door click open and Raleigh call out, but she didn't want to risk the time to answer.

The little house felt hot and close after the expanse of the big rooms. Even before she opened the door she smelled the heat inside, the dust, warm *cominos* simmering into the beans in the big cast-iron *olla* on the hot plate. As she crossed the room to her bed she compared what she had seen upstairs in the big house with her mother's attempts to brighten things: a scattering of secondhand bathroom rugs across the dull linoleum, knickknacks cast off from Madama, paper flowers at the single window. Licha's bed was the lower bunk of a government-issue set, curtained with a sheet tucked under the mattress of Tavo's top bunk where boxes of clothing and household things were stored now that Tavo had gone. The beds were white, but the paint had chipped, exposing leopard-spots of army green. At the head and foot the letters US were carved into the wood. When Licha was learning to read, she thought the letters meant herself and Tavo; us, *nosotros*, and she felt special, good, tracing the letters with her fingers, with a purple crayon, lucky: no one else had a bed that told of herself and her brother, of their place in the world. She didn't want to believe Tavo when he laughed and told her what the letters stood for. Her mother slept on a daybed in the opposite corner, behind a partition made of crates and a blue shower curtain with a picture of an egret wading among green rushes. Licha lifted her sheet curtain and lay down, letting the heat and dimness envelop her.

She heard the car pull into the driveway, the sound of its doors closing and Madama's voice telling Perfilio to wash the car. She heard the slap of her mother's sandals on the flagstone path, coming toward the little house. She wished she had washed; the girls at school said other people could tell by your smell if you had been with a boy. In the stuffiness of the room her mother would notice it. She lay still and hoped her mother would think she was asleep.

Through the thin sheet Licha saw her come in, silhouetted in the light streaming through the doorway. She could see well enough to tell her mother still wore her apron. Madama insisted on it, especially when they went to town. Licha watched as she

414

took it off and folded it over a wooden chair, then began taking dishes and pots and pans from the crates stacked to form shelves, wisps of hair springing from the bun at the back of her neck.

She tried to remember how her mother looked when her skin wasn't glistening with sweat, when her hair wasn't escaping from the bun: Saturday before church, sometimes for whole days in winter if a norther came in and work at the house was light. Even through the screen of the sheet Licha could see the patches of darker blue under her mother's arms, around her waist, between her shoulder blades. They were as much a part of her mother as the starched workdress, as the apron, as the low song she sang while she worked, a song that irritated Licha for its persistence, its quality of being a song yet not a song, more a droning, melodic murmur made low in the throat that had the power to remove her mother, lift her beyond Licha's reach and back into the time before Licha, a song from her mother's earlier life in the *barrancas* of the East Sierra Madre, the place she had left to come here, first to work for Papa in the fields, then for Madama in the house, a place she never talked about.

When Tavo and Licha asked about it she said little. All they knew was that Papa had found her walking along the road, fifteen, pregnant with Tavo, on one of his trips below the border to find workers. He didn't like the migrant teams, preferring whole families who wanted to come across, to live in the block houses at the bend in the levee until they found something better, or even asked about something better, and then he would help them, with papers, by getting their children into school, with medicine and food. Her mother had been alone on the road, in the last months of pregnancy, but Papa had idled the truck alongside her, asking questions in Spanish, inviting her to join the families in the truck bed. Tavo had been born in the block house by the levee. Licha was born three years later. Her father was a *Latino* from Las Cruces working a few months with the Army Corps of Engineers on an irrigation project before he moved on. This was all she knew. She and Tavo had stopped asking; their mother didn't welcome questions about the other life.

A stack of Melmac plates clattered to the floor, causing Licha to jump. Her mother stooped to pick them up, her eyes on Licha's curtain. "*¿Estás aquí?*"

415

Licha swung her legs over the edge of the bed. "I'm here, Mama." She made it a practice to answer her mother's Spanish with English, as though she were talking to a toddler just learning the words for things. "What are you doing?"

Her mother ignored her and continued picking up the scattered plates. Licha sighed and repeated the question in Spanish. Her mother was stubborn enough to ignore the question all day if it was a matter of will.

Her mother smiled at her, setting the stack of plates on the wooden table. She told Licha she and Madama had gone to an appliance store in McAllen. She described the shining rows of silver and white, and a new color for stoves and refrigerators called avocado green. They had picked out a new stove for the *cocina* in the big house. It was to be delivered tomorrow. And guess who, as a gift for Christmas, was to have the old one? Licha smiled in spite of herself. "We are!"

Her mother crossed the room and stood behind the big chair next to the window. "*Ayudame, chica.*"

Licha helped her move the chair. They placed it at an angle by Licha's bed, then lifted the table from the corner where the new stove would go. They put it by the window. While her mother dusted the tabletop, Licha went outside to get one of the potted aloes that lined the step. She arranged it in the center of the table.

"*Mira*, Mama," she said, gesturing grandly toward the plant. "*Better Homes and Gardens.*" They laughed, and Licha felt good, good and happy, like Licha-nine-years-old, Licha-of-no-secrets, her mother's *chula niña* in a ruffled skirt and braids stretched tight for church. She watched her mother poke the broom into the cleared corner and shoo a lizard along the baseboard toward the door, her throaty song rising in the heat, happy with so little, and suddenly she was angry.

"A stove," she said. "An old stove. How much did the new one cost?"

Her mother continued sweeping, the hem of her work dress swaying stiffly with the motions of the broom. "*No importa.*"

She felt like grabbing the broom away and forcing her mother to listen. "We don't need a stove. Let her sell the old one and give us the money. Let her buy us an air conditioner. She has enough. She has everything." She thought of nights in the little

416

house, trying to sleep with only the old black fan to cool her, its woven cord stretched from chair to chair, tripping her if she got up to get a drink of water, the frayed fabric encasing it reticulated like the backs of the water snakes she sometimes saw in the arroyo. "It will only make it hotter in this place!" She pushed against the screen door hard enough to wedge the flimsy frame against the bump on the far edge of the step and walked out.

She cut through the live oaks, through the rows of oleander set out like railroad tracks to shield the little house from view, around to the back of the property to the overgrown area she and Tavo and Raleigh had called the jungle when they were little. It was mostly scrub pecan choked with ololiuque vines, avocado trees, crotons and yucca, but a few banana and papaya trees survived, making it seem exotic and lush. Saw palmetto slashed her legs as she ran past the boundaries. She looked down to see the thin lines like razor cuts across her thighs. She darted through the algarroba thicket and came out on the other side, to Grand Texas Boulevard. A fine name, she thought, for the rutted road that led to the highway toward Reynosa.

She slowed down, thinking about what had just happened, thinking that she now knew what made people run away. It wasn't a simple matter of not liking home, it was far more complicated than that, and at the point when things became too complicated to even think about any longer, people ran away. For whatever reasons they had that were too entwined to sort out. She imagined her mother, a pregnant girl from the *barrancas*, walking along a road, and she imagined a man in a truck, a man in khaki workpants and a Panama hat, a smiling, red-mustached man. She would have climbed inside the truck bed, too. She saw herself riding away from the Valley to a different place, any place, maybe a place with snow. To Fort Dix where Tavo was, a soldier in uniform, able to be what he was without people thinking they *knew* what he was just by looking at him, by knowing where he came from, where there was more to get excited about than avocado appliances, where he made his own money and didn't have to depend on a bossy old woman like Madama, where he didn't have to care what such a woman thought of anything he did. Tavo would understand how she felt. He had been glad to leave the Valley.

417

She picked up a stone and threw it at an irrigation pump. She knew what Tavo would think of what she and Raleigh did. He would spit, and make the jerking, upward jab with his wrist, like stabbing. He would stab Raleigh if he knew. He wouldn't see that Raleigh wasn't like the others; he was more like Papa. Tavo would see only his side of it, the *pachuco* side that hated all Anglos. He wouldn't see that it was different with Raleigh, that they were what they were, male and female, Licha and Raleigh. He wanted her, he found her beautiful. The feeling made her stomach tighten as she walked along, slower now. She held her shoulders straighter and began to sway her hips the way she had seen other girls do, feeling the heads of her femurs articulating deep in her pelvis. She knew now why those girls walked like this: a man wanted them.

She stopped to watch the sun go down behind a grove of Valencias. The heavy fruit hung full and brilliant, orange as the sun, as the bright new tennis balls Madama kept in canisters on the laundry-shed shelf. She heard the big trucks start up, loading *braceros* for the trip back to the *colonia*. Traffic on the highway quickened and Licha turned to go home, the trucks rumbling by. When she heard the clicking noises the men made, their high-pitched yips of appreciation, she toned down her walk, but she thought: let them look, let them want.

He didn't come for her the next day, or the next, though she made many trips between the house and the laundry shed, the laundry shed and the burn pile, watching the back door of the big house. She began to think she had been a fool, that Tavo's version of the way things were with Anglo boys and Mexican girls might be right. She could hardly bear her mother's excitement about the stove, and she snapped at her to stop polishing it so often—she'd polished it every day for eleven years—to speak English, to pick up her feet when she walked and stop shuffling around like a cow. Her mother stared at her when she said this, and Licha had seen her face close down.

On Saturday Perfilio brought two chickens and her mother baked them, filling the house with a rich yellow smell that made Licha queasy. She couldn't touch the chicken and she didn't go with her mother to church. She knew it was far too early, improbable, given the dates of her cycle, but she began to worry beyond reason that she was pregnant.

At sundown Saturday a norther blew in, rattling the rickety door and filling the house with random pockets of cold air. Licha pulled a sweater from the box under her bed and put it on. She slid the shutter panel across the window and shut the heavy storm door. She sat at the table in the dark, not bothering to pull the string on the overhead light. When the first knock came she thought it was the wind, but it kept up and finally she opened the door.

Raleigh wore a zippered red windbreaker and his hair blew up behind his head like a rooster's tail. He was smiling. "Did you miss me?"

She wanted to slap his glasses away so they skittered across the flagstone into the potted plants and he would never find them. She wanted to tear off her blouse and sweater and show him her breasts, press them into his chest so hard they burned him. "No," she said.

"You're mad at me." He tried to look around her to see inside the house. "Can I come in?"

She looked behind her into the dark room, at the silly rugs and the shower curtain and the stove in its corner like a squat white ghost. "I'll come out.

They walked around the house to the jungle, Licha with her arms folded across her chest, her hands tucked into the sweater sleeves, Raleigh with his hands jammed into the pockets of his windbreaker, neither of them speaking. Licha sat on the rim of a discarded tractor tire where Tavo had once found a coral snake. She shivered, glad it was too cold for snakes. Raleigh sat beside her, quiet. He bent to flick an oleander leaf from the toe of his loafer.

Alarm surged through her. He had found someone else, she wasn't good enough. Madama had found out. She wanted Licha gone—that girl, her mother, gone.

"I'm busted at Vanderbilt," he said. He looked at her. "Kicked out."

Licha hoped she kept a straight face, kept from smiling: this is *all?*

"Mother's been hauling me all over south Texas for the last two days, throwing her weight around." He laughed, but Licha could tell he didn't think it was funny. "She thinks she can get me into

San Marcos or Pan American. They're piss-poor schools, but I guess it's better than getting drafted." He laughed again.

Licha waited to see if he had anything else to say, but he was quiet, drumming his knuckles on the thick black tread of the tire. "Maybe it's not so bad," she said. She thought about telling him what Mr. Mohesky had told her—that if she continued to work hard he would help her apply for a scholarship to San Marcos— but she didn't.

He shrugged, then pulled a jeweler's box from his pocket. "Anyway, I got you these." He handed her the box. "For Christmas."

"Not yet," she said.

"You don't want it?"

"I mean, it's not Christmas yet." She held the box, stroking the nap of the black velveteen.

"Soon enough," he said. "Open it."

Inside was a pair of earrings, tiny gold chains with filigree hummingbirds at the ends, red stones for each eye. In the moonlight she could make out the store name on the inner lid: Didde's of San Marcos. She imagined him on the streets of the college town, going into the jewelry store while Madama waited in the car, poring over hundreds of boxes until he chose these, for her. "Thank you," she said, and when he stood and held his hand for her she went with him through the jungle to the laundry shed. He waited while she removed the silver hoops she wore, then he inserted the posts of the new earrings into her lobes. She tilted her head to each side to help him, and she was reminded of the female mouse. The thought came to her that staying still was just as powerful an act as moving, just as necessary, and she again felt linked to the everlasting, perfect cycle of things.

They made love on the floor of the laundry shed, her hips lifted, supported by a pile of towels. They were damp against her skin and smelled of Lifebuoy soap and Clorox. Her carotid artery throbbed from the rush of blood to her head, but she didn't complain, and she didn't tell him to withdraw. She wanted to give him this, a sign of trust, of utter welcome. It would be all right, no matter what. What they were doing, this act, was a promise of that, a pact. She felt the earrings slide back and forth against her neck.

She made it back to the little house and into bed before her mother returned from church, and when she woke up Sunday morning, the first things she felt were the hummingbird earrings. She thought of Raleigh. Was he waking up just now in his room in the big house, remembering what they had done? She moved her hands down her body to the warm pocket between her legs and wondered how she felt to him. How could they ever know, male and female, what each felt like to the other? She heard her mother stirring and she sat up to part the curtain. Her mother was tying her apron on over her work dress.

"¿Café?"

"Coffee," Licha repeated automatically. Sunday mornings they usually sat at the table drinking coffee. It was her mother's day off. "Why are you wearing that?"

There was no answer. Licha sighed, repeating the question in Spanish. Her mother explained that Madama needed her to help with a party. She had to clean, prepare food, set things up. She would come home in the middle of the afternoon to rest, then she would go back in the evening to serve.

"On Sunday?" Licha pulled out a chair and sat down at the table, pouring coffee into a Melmac cup, adding sugar.

Her mother shrugged, and the helpless gesture irritated Licha.

"Why didn't you tell her no? You always do everything she says. 'Sí, Madama, no, Madama, ¿algo más, Madama?'" She rose from her chair and went to the small refrigerator for the milk.

Her mother stood at the sink, calmly tucking wisps of hair into her bun with bobby pins, her back to Licha, saying nothing. Licha thought she may as well have been talking to the stove, for all the effect it had. Even her mother's back looked obstinate, her hips wide and stolid, square and stupid, the apron bow at her back as ridiculous as the daisy garland around the ear of the cow on the milk carton she took from its shelf. She stirred the milk into her coffee and looked at the older woman. She knew her mother's life would always be the same, shuffling back and forth between houses, going to church, easing her knees and elbows with salve she made from Vaseline and aloe, waiting on others, obsequious, stubborn in her obsequiousness, forcing Madama into pidgin silliness, and all of it because of stubbornness, because she wanted nothing more, because she thought no further

421

than the day after tomorrow. Licha banged her cup onto the table, sloshing coffee over the edge and onto her cotton shift. "Why didn't you get papers when Papa offered? You could get a better job."

Her mother turned, and Licha saw her face, hurt, defiant.

"You could *learn* to read, Mama." She felt suddenly defeated; there was nothing she could do. "It's your only day off," she said weakly.

She watched her mother rinse her own cup and dry it; she took it with her to work because Madama believed disease was spread by sharing dishes with the help. She left the house, closing the screen door gently, leaving Licha alone at the table sipping coffee she could barely swallow for her welling sense of injustice. Licha got up and ran after her mother, catching up with her along the flagstone path. "Don't do it, Mama. Say no. Say it for once in your life. Show her what you think of her."

Her mother shook her head. "I think nothing. I only work." She resumed her walk.

"You work for nothing. For a house too little and too hot. For a stove!" She grabbed her mother's arm and shook it. Her mother looked away, across the yard toward the laundry shed.

"*Dejame en paz.*"

"English, Mama, your English is good. Use it. Make her *see* you!"

Her mother looked at her hard, and Licha felt suddenly exposed in her cotton shift, as though she was standing naked on the path. Her mother shook off Licha's hand. "No."

Perfilio came around the corner of the house with a wheelbarrow full of sand and a box of candles. He began placing the *luminarias* around the patio. Licha stood still, watching her mother walk toward the service entrance. Her mother had almost reached the door when she whirled, throwing her coffee cup to the ground. She started back down the path toward Licha, her face dark and angry. She reached out and with a violent flick at Licha's ear set one earring spinning wildly. "*Éstos son de Madama!*"

Licha's hand flew to her ear, to the sting. She was dumbfounded by her mother's anger until she realized she thought Licha had stolen the earrings from the big house. "They are mine," she said, proud that they were, glad her mother was wrong. "Raleigh gave them to me."

Her mother's eyes widened. Licha watched as she took in the information, as she looked at her daughter for clues. She felt her mother's eyes on her body, looking through the thin shift at her breasts which seemed in that moment huge and bobbing, giving away her secret. Her mother slapped her.

"Fool!" She slapped her again and Licha reeled. "It is worse!"

Licha ran to the little house, to her bed, where she cried until her eyes were red and swollen and her throat was raw. She got up to dress. Her hands felt limp as she pulled her skirt up over her hips. She didn't want to be home when her mother returned for her nap, but she didn't know where to go. She didn't want to go for a walk, and the few girls at school she could call her friends were just that, school friends; they rarely saw each other outside, and if they did they only teased Licha about studying so hard and taking everything so seriously. When she opened the refrigerator to look for something to eat she realized it was Raleigh she wanted to talk to. She sat at the table most of the afternoon, pushing cold rice around her plate with the tines of a fork, watching the activity at the big house, Perfilio arranging the *luminarias*, raking palm trash from the drive, pulling the car around. When she saw her mother come out the service entrance, she left the house and hurried to the laundry shed.

The pile of towels was still on the floor, flattened slightly from the weight of her body and Raleigh's. She fluffed them up with her foot to make them look more natural. She looked out the window to see her mother going into their house, then she took a tennis ball from the shelf. She planned to stand behind the poinsettia bush outside Raleigh's window and throw the ball against the screen.

Her first throw fell short of the window, and her second, thumping against the wire mesh, was louder than she imagined it would be. The ball bounced into a plot of white azaleas. Its presence there looked miraculous and unreal, like one fully ripened orange in a grove of trees still in blossom. Licha thought of leaving it there and giving up, but she wanted to see Raleigh. As she crossed the front yard to retrieve the ball, she heard the heavy, carved door swing open on its wrought-iron hinges.

Raleigh stood on the *porche*, the fingers of his right hand kneading his left bicep, the blue stone in his class ring glinting in the sun. He stepped from the *porche* and walked toward her. His face looked fuller, younger, somehow; he had shaved his sideburns. She remembered her mother's slap. She couldn't make herself meet his eyes.

"What's the matter?"

She still couldn't look at him. "My mother knows," she said. She felt bad and stupid, as though she alone was responsible for what they had done. It was her fault her mother knew. "I'm sorry." She hoped he would tell her it was all right, that he didn't care, that he was glad: now they could be together.

He laughed. "Is that all?"

She looked at him, relieved beyond words.

"It's not like she hasn't done the same thing," he said. "She's been around the block."

She was puzzled. "What?"

He waved his hand, dismissing it. "It was a long time ago." He winked at her. "You know. When we were kids."

Licha never thought of her mother in that way. Her mother was just what she was—aproned, blue-dressed, patting tortillas, sweeping: working. She started to ask him what he meant, but all of a sudden she knew. She remembered when they had first come to live in the little house, her mother—younger, thinner—had sat on the floor with them, showing them how to cut circles of colored paper and twist them into the shapes of bougainvillea, oleander, the blue trumpets of jacaranda, her hair loose and fragrant from the Castile shampoo she kept on the shelf above the sink. Laughing, she had tucked one of Licha's flowers behind her ear, and in the hollow of her throat a small vein pulsed. Licha had reached up to place her fingers on it, moved to joy, to longing at the happy mystery of her mother's beauty. Her mother had scooped her up and hugged her with a strength that surprised her. In the hot still nights after she and Tavo were in bed, her mother would leave the house. Just for a walk, she said, just to cool off. Licha would try to stay awake until she came back in, but the hum of the fan would always put her to sleep. In the morning her mother would be at the sink, running water for coffee, draining the soak water from the beans, and Licha would forget. But it was Papa who brought the fan, Papa with the red mustache that fascinated her, taking off his Panama before he entered the little house, patting the top of her head, *"Qué chula niña."* Papa who brought the beds.

"Come inside," Raleigh said. "You can see the preparations for Mother's big to-do." From his tone Licha could tell what he thought of Madama's party, but she hesitated.

"She's not here. She's at the club getting a bag on."

She followed him into the house. As they passed through the big hall she caught a glimpse of the *sala* with the grand Spanish windows she had seen only from the outside. At the far end of the room stood an enormous fir, its branches flocked with white, shimmering with gold and silver birds. She thought of the plastic Santas she and her mother would hang on the potted Norfolk pine they brought in from its place among the other plants that rimmed the little house, the red suits nearly pink from sun and age, the white of the beards and fur trim gone yellow.

"She's got it all decked out," he said, starting up the stairs to the *galería*. Licha followed him. She nodded though she knew he couldn't see her. When they were inside his bedroom he locked the door and took a mirror from the wall. He propped it on the floor against the bed. He fingered one of her earrings. "Beautiful," he said.

She pushed his hand away, but then stood still, her arms lifted as he pulled her blouse over her head. He kissed her, unhooking her bra. She felt her nipples draw and tighten. "My mother isn't what you think," she said. The words surprised her; she felt her knees weaken, almost buckle.

He eased himself down and took her nipple in his mouth, but she drew it back. "She speaks English. She only pretends she doesn't so your mother will look like a fool." She felt the beating of her heart, shuddering and rapid, almost hot, astonishing as sudden anger.

He laughed, nuzzling her, pulling at the elastic of her skirt. "I know," he said. "It's been a joke for years. I used to spy on Mother's bridge club just to hear her do the Camarena imitation."

Licha stared at him as he unbuckled his belt and stepped out of his jeans. "Lie down, *chula.*" His hands on her shoulders, he pressed her down with him until they were kneeling beside the

mirror. She looked at him, at the dark triangle of pubic escutch-
eon against his pale skin, at his penis rising, then to the mirror
where she saw the flexion at the side of his buttock where the
gluteus inserted, where she saw herself, smaller, a fool looking up
at him, a fool somehow more beautifully made, browner, smoother,
more round. She tried to meet his eyes, fixed on his own, but
couldn't, and she had the feeling each of them was seeing something different in the framed rectangle, like two people looking at
the same slide under a microscope, trying to adjust the focus to
accommodate both their visions, failing. She removed his hands
from her shoulders and stood up, gathering her clothes. "I have
to go," she said.

She walked out into the early dark of December. Light shone
from the little house, and as she got closer she saw her mother's
form moving back and forth against it. Licha knew she would be
eating her supper, standing over the *olla* eating beans rolled into
a flour tortilla, alternating beans with bites of pepper, waiting to
go back to work. She looked up when Licha entered, but didn't
meet her eyes.

"Café," she said, gesturing toward the pot on the stove. Licha
saw that the light came from behind the pot, from a small bulb
under the hood of the stove that cast the shadows of the *olla* and
the coffee pot onto the floor. She sat down at the table. Her
mother took cups from their hooks, poured them full and placed
them on the table. She sat down across from Licha, and Licha
looked at her, at the crease from her nap across the smooth
brown of her cheek, her hair freshly brushed and fastened back,
in her eyes the sleepy distance of the saints, the prophets. Her
mother lifted the lid of the sugar bowl. "¿*Azúcar?*"

Licha nodded. Her mother spooned the sugar into their cups.
They were small things—not objecting to her Spanish, letting her
mother serve her—but Licha could tell they pleased her. The low
song began in her throat, obscuring for a while the faint metallic
buzz of the stove light rattling under its enameled hood. Then it
trailed away. They sat for a long time at the table, speechless,
beyond apology. Even the presence of a small green anole emerging from behind the stove to skitter across the top and bask
briefly in the harsh white glare, the ruby throat it expanded
when threatened now a flaccid sac, was not enough to disturb the

426

silence between them. When her mother scraped her chair back on the linoleum and left for work Licha sat for a long time afterward, drained and still, stunned by the complex living heart of grace.

1991

THE COLUMBUS SCHOOL FOR GIRLS

by LIZA WIELAND

from THE GEORGIA REVIEW

"IT'S THE OLDEST story in America," Mr. Jerman says, "only no one seems to know it. When Christopher Columbus went to ask Queen Isabella to bankroll his voyage to the east, she just laughed at him, and she told him it was about as likely he could make that trip as it was that he could make an egg stand on its end. But that Columbus, he said, okay Isabella, watch closely. And he took out an egg—the one he always carried for state occasions just like this—and tapped it ever so gently on one end, not enough to shatter it, but enough to flatten that end just slightly, and there the egg stood, and Isabella gave Columbus the dough, and the rest is history."

We love this story, and we love the teacher who tells it to us and girls like us, year after year at The Columbus School for Girls. We love the way he stands over the lectern at Chapel, right in front of the red-and-white banner that says *Explore thyself!* below the headmaster's favorite words of wisdom, copied from money, IN GOD WE TRUST. We like to sit left of center and close one eye. Half-blind we see Mr. Jerman's face like a hieroglyph in the midst of wisdom, a blessed interruption, and the words say IN GOD WE RUST.

We don't care much for the other teachers, the ones who tell us to spit out our chewing gum, pull up our knee socks, and button our blouses all the way up, the ones who warn us we'll never amount to anything. We know how they fear us—we're walking danger to them, the way we whoop in the halls, the way we dance in slow circles to no music—but still they dream of having us for their daughters, of taking us home and seeing what, given the proper tools and rules, we might become. We smoke cigarettes in the bathroom. We've been known to carry gin in vanilla bottles and have a swig or two after lunch.

Mr. Jerman, though, we would be his daughters in a heartbeat. We would change our names, we would all become Jermans. We would let his wife, Emily Jerman, be the mother of us all. We see her rarely, at wind-ensemble concerts, at dances, and at field-hockey games, standing on the sidelines behind the opposing team. Tiny thin Emily Jerman, always so cold that we'd like to build a fire right at her feet. Emily Jerman, always wearing one of her husband's sweaters, smiling at us, leaning her thin bones against her husband's arm and talking into his ear in a voice we've never heard but guess must sound like baby birds. We want to be like her, so we steal our fathers' sweaters, our brothers' sweaters, our boyfriends'. We let ourselves grow thin. Emily Jerman and Bryan Jerman—we say their names over and over at night into the darkness of the Upper Five Dormitory where the air is already hazy with girls' breath. We pass his name between the beds—*have you had Bryan Jerman yet?*—like he's something you could catch.

In the morning when we wake up, their names are still hanging over us, and it's still November, always November. November is by far the cruelest month at The Columbus School for Girls. By then nothing is new anymore, not the teachers, not the books, not the rules and the bravest ways to break them. November is Indian summer, and then it's rain. November, Mr. Jerman says, is longing, and we agree. We long for Thanksgiving, but we don't know why, because it will only lead to real winter, killer winter when nothing moves. All month, we long to go back to the days when our school uniforms were new and tight across our hips, when our notebooks were empty, when no one had discovered us yet.

"Girls," Mr. Jerman says in the middle of this cruel November, "I have been thinking about you."

We could say the same thing, especially since he has been reading us Emily Dickinson these past weeks. We have come to think of Emily Dickinson as Emily Jerman and vice versa. We whisper about Emily Jerman's closet full of white dresses and her strange ideas about certain birds and flowers and angleworms. We think this must be what Emily Jerman does all day in the bungalow behind Lower Four Dormitory: she writes hundreds of poems on the backs of school memoranda that Mr. Jerman has folded and torn in quarters, just the right size for one of her poems about yellow daisies beheaded by winter, that white assassin.

"I have been thinking," Mr. Jerman says again, "that we need to do a little more exploring. We have been sitting like bumps on logs reading these poems when we could do so much more."

We look at him, making our smiles bright and trusting the way we think he must like them, letting him lead us on.

"I could take you to Emily Dickinson's house," Mr. Jerman says, and we lean forward over our desks. It feels like he's invited us into his own home. "If you're interested, I can call up there this afternoon. We can take one of the school vans. I'm sure my wife would love to come along too. She's always wanted to go there."

We can imagine. We can imagine Emily Jerman going to the home of her namesake, her other, her true self. We can imagine our own selves being the Jermans' daughters for a whole weekend, far away from The Columbus School for Girls, deep in what we think must be the savage jungle of western Massachusetts.

*

Mr. Jerman has a hard time convincing the headmaster to let us go. We listen to them discuss it late the next afternoon while we're waiting for tardy slips.

"Bryan," the headmaster is saying, "think about it. All of *them*. And just you and Emily. What if something happens? What if one of them goes berserk? Or gets arrested? Or smuggles along contraband?"

"Leo," Mr. Jerman says, "nonsense. The girls will be perfect ladies. It will be good for them to get out, see some more of the world. And Emily will be along to take care of any, you know, girl problems."

"I just don't think so," the headmaster says. "I'm not sure these are girls you can trust."

"Rust," we say.

"Of course I can trust them," Mr. Jerman says. "That gin at lunchtime business is all a made-up story. They're chafing at the bit a little, that's all. This trip will be just the thing. I've told their parents to call you about it."

"Oh God, Bryan," the headmaster says.

"Oh God," we say.

"Girls," the headmaster's secretary says, "you know there's none of that on school grounds."

The telephone on the secretary's desk rings in a stifled *brrrr*. We're sure it's our parents—all of them making one huge impossible conference call to tell the headmaster to keep us at this school forever, until we grow old and die. We can't stand it anymore. We forge the signatures on our tardy slips and beat it to smoke cigarettes behind Lower Four. From there we can see the Jermans' bungalow, and we keep smoking until Mr. Jerman comes home. We think his shoulders look awfully slumped, and we notice, too, the way the fiery late-afternoon light seems to have taken all the color out of his face. The front door opens, and Emily Jerman is standing there, a yellow halo surrounding her whole tiny body from head to toe. When she reaches up to touch Mr. Jerman's face, we try to look away but we can't. Our eyes have become hard cold points of darkness fixed on them, on their tenderness, and learning it. Emily and Bryan Jerman go inside their bungalow and the door closes. We watch them move from room to room past the windows until it's so dark we have to feel our way back to Upper Five, crawling on our hands and knees, lighting matches to see what little of the way we know.

At night we dream Emily Jerman has come to stand at our bedside. She is putting small pieces of paper under our pillow— Columbus School for Girls memoranda, torn in quarters. *Lie still*, she commands. *If you move, they will explode.*

The next day is Saturday, when we always have detention, and then Sunday, when we have Chapel. The opening hymn is "A Mighty Fortress Is Our God." Mr. Jerman has told us you can sing most of Emily Dickinson's poems to the tune of "A Mighty Fortress Is Our God," so we try it. The headmaster glares at us, but we stare at the word RUST beside his head, rising like the balloon of talk in a comic strip. We sing to him, enunciating like there's no tomorrow, and he watches our mouths move, trying to

431

discover our blasphemies, the mystery of us. Was there ever one of us he understood, he must be asking himself; was there ever one of us who did not have a black heart and carry a knife in her teeth?

*

"Girls," Mr. Jerman says on Monday morning, "grab your coats and hats, pack your bags. It's all set. We leave Friday afternoon. Friday night in Pennsylvania. Saturday at the Emily Dickinson Homestead."

We're stunned, and then we cheer until Mr. Jerman's eyes move from our faces and out to the middle distance. We turn in our desks to see Emily Jerman standing at the window. She waves to us and moves off across the garden.

"She wanted to get a look at you," Mr. Jerman says, his voice strangling in his throat.

We watch her as she gathers wood for kindling: birch, alder, even green pine. Her arms are full of wood and purple thistles, her red hair falling forward to cover her face and throat.

Oh Emily Jerman! Her name rises, almost to our lips. We burn for her, all day long, wherever she goes—our long hair fallen like hers, in flames.

*

By the time we're ready to leave Friday afternoon, it's getting dark. The Jermans are going to drive three hours apiece to get us as far as Harrisburg, Pennsylvania, where we've got rooms in a motel. We look out the windows and watch the back of Emily Jerman's head. She has said hello to us, but nothing after that. She rides up in front next to her husband, and sometimes their arms touch, his right and her left across the space between the seats. We stare at them when this happens, our eyes glittering and hungry, and we play charades. By the time we get an hour out of town, all we can see is night rising on the soft shoulders of the road and our own faces reflected in the windows. The highway is our own hair streaming behind us, and the moon is our eye. For miles and miles, there haven't been any lights. We're all there is in this world, just us and the Jermans.

432

In Zanesville, we stop for supper. Mr. Jerman drives off the highway and through a web of back streets to a Chinese restaurant—the "Imperious Wok," he calls it, glancing over at his wife, who turns to him and smiles. When we get to the parking lot, the marquee says, "The Imperial Wok," and we laugh, even though we don't get the joke and we don't like them having secrets between themselves, a whole history we can never know. Inside, Mr. Jerman explains the menu and shows us how to use chopsticks. He is amazed that we've never had Chinese food before. He toasts us with his tiny bowl of tea.

When the waiter comes, Emily Jerman orders a cocktail. Mr. Jerman looks at her and raises his blonde eyebrows, but doesn't say anything. We realize this is the first whole sentence we have ever heard Emily Jerman say: *I would like a double vodka on the rocks.* Her voice is surprisingly low and sweet. We have always thought she should have a high voice to go with her tiny frail body, but instead it's a voice like being wrapped in a smoky blanket. We hope she'll keep on talking. Right now we want to be Emily Jerman's daughters more than anything else in the world.

The waiter brings our food, announcing each dish quietly, with a question, like he's trying to remind himself what it is. After each name, Mr. Jerman says "ah" and his wife laughs, a low, thrilling laugh, and we know we're going to have to spend all night in our motel room trying to imitate it exactly. She orders another double vodka.

"Dear," Mr. Jerman says, "who's going to help me drive for the next four hours?"

"We will," we say, reaching into our coat pockets for our driver's licenses. We hand them over to Emily Jerman, who looks at the pictures and then up at us, squinting her eyes to get the true likeness.

"Seventeen," she says, "Damn. I remember that." Then she laughs her low laugh—like a car's engine, we think, finely tuned.

Mr. Jerman hands around the dishes of steaming food. We still don't know what any of it is, but the strange new smells are making us not care. We feel a little drunk now, chasing gobbets of meat and snaking onion around on our plates with these wooden knitting needles. A triangle of something bright red flies from someone's plate and lands in Mr. Jerman's tea bowl, and grains of rice ring our placemats where we've let them fall. We lean our heads back and drip noodles into our mouths, noodles that taste like peanut butter. We lick the plum sauce spoon. We take tiny little sips of tea. We watch Emily Jerman get looped.

"Seventeen. Oh God, do I remember seventeen. It was before you," she says to her husband, leaning against him in that way that makes us stare at them with hard bright eyes. "I was at The Columbus School for Girls, can you imagine? Things were by the book then, no drinking gin at lunch, no blouses open down to here, no overnight trips. The goddamn earth was flat then. That's why it's called The Columbus School for Girls, to show how far you could go in the wrong direction."

"Emily," Mr. Jerman says, exactly the way he says the name in class, like he's a little afraid of it.

"Oh don't Emily me, sweetheart," she says thrillingly, her low laugh like a runaway vehicle. "I'm just giving your girls some true history, that's all."

"What was it like?" we ask.

"The same, really. We read Emily Dickinson, too. Or some of us did, 'A narrow fellow in the grass,' " she says, to prove it.

"What house did you live in?" we want to know.

"Cobalt," she says, naming a dormitory we've never heard of. "But the boiler exploded and it burnt to the ground ten years ago. Nobody likes to talk about it."

We glance over at Mr. Jerman, who seems lost to us, shaking his head.

"A girl nearly died," Emily Jerman says, looking us straight in the eye. "And the gardener did die. They were, you know, in her room. It was a big scandal. Hoo boy."

"Emily," Mr. Jerman says in a way that lets us know everything his wife is saying is true.

"He loved Emily Dickinson," Emily Jerman tells us.

"Who did?" her husband says. But we already know who she means.

"The gardener. He'd been to see her house. He had postcards. He gave me one."

"You never told me that." Bryan Jerman stares at his wife. Already we're miles ahead of him, and we can see it all: the girl who is Emily Jerman grown young, and the gardener there beside us, then the two bodies tangled together, singed, blackened by smoke.

"Fortune cookies!" Emily Jerman cries, clapping her hands. "We'll play fortune-cookie charades. It's just like regular charades, only when you get to the part about movie, book, or play, you do this."

She brings the palms of her hands together, pulls them in close to her chest, and bows from the waist. Mr. Jerman is smiling again, looking at his wife like he can't believe how clever she is. The fire, the girl, and the gardener drift from the table, guests taking their leave.

"A bit of mysterious East for you," the waiter says. "Many happy fortunes."

Look below the surface, truth lies within. Unusual experience will enrich your life. Positive attitude will bring desired result. Time is in your favor, be patient. The rare privilege of being pampered will delight you. The fun is just beginning, take it as it comes. Beware of those who stir the waters to suggest they are deep.

Our charades make Emily Jerman laugh until tears come to her eyes and run down her cheeks into her mouth. We watch her taste them and she watches us back, holding our eyes just as long as we hold hers. Then Mr. Jerman tells us it's time to get *on the road again*, singing it like Willie Nelson. Out in the parking lot, he takes his wife's hand and presses it to his heart. Light from the Imperial Wok falls on their coats, turning black to tender purple.

"See?" he says, and together they look east to where the lights of Zanesville die away and there's only stars and West Virginia and Pennsylvania and finally the great darkness of western Massachusetts. We stare at them, our eyes going clean through their bodies. Then we look east too, but we can't for the life of us tell what they're seeing.

Hours later, we wake to hear Emily Jerman singing along with the radio. "And when the birds fly south for a while," she sings, "oh I wish that I could go. Someone there might warm this cold heart, oh someone there might know." Her voice breaks on the last line, and we close our eyes again.

At the Holiday Inn in Harrisburg, the Jermans unload us one by one, right into our rooms, right into bed. We stay awake as long as we can listening to Emily and Bryan Jerman in the next

435

room, imagining we can hear the words and other sounds that pass between them when they're all alone.

In the morning, it's Scranton, New York City, Hartford, and on into Amherst. Emily Jerman looks terrible, her hair hanging loose, her skin the color of old snow, but she drives first and Mr. Jerman takes over after lunch. Then she stares out the window. We think something has happened to her during the night. At first we believe it has to do with love, but soon we see how wrong we are, how lost, and for a split second we wish we'd never left The Columbus School for Girls. We've been moving east with Emily Jerman, weightless, like swimmers, but now she's holding on to our uniform skirts, and she's dragging us under. When we get to the Dickinson Homestead in the middle of the afternoon, the air is so wet with snow that we're having to breathe water, like the nearly drowned.

Emily Jerman hasn't said a word all day, but when we're all out of the van, she tells us she's going to stay put. She's been moving too fast, she says, and now she needs to sit for a while. Mr. Jerman hands her the keys, squeezes her knee, and leads us inside the house. We try to catch a glimpse of her out the window as we're standing beside Emily Dickinson's piano, listening to Mr. Jerman make introductions.

The tour guide tell us she is the wife of an English professor who studies Emily Dickinson, and for a whole year when they were first married, he would talk about her in his sleep. That, she explains, is how she learned most of what she knows about the poet, by listening in on her husband's dreams. She looks straight at Mr. Jerman.

"It's how most husbands and wives come to know anything at all," she says.

He stares back at her out of his great blue unblinking eyes, and for the first time ever, we think he looks bullish and stupid. It unhinges us, and we have to sit down on Emily Dickinson's chintz sofa.

The professor's wife keeps talking. She tells us what belongs to Emily Dickinson and what doesn't. She lets us touch a teacup and hold a pair of wine glasses the color of fresh blood. We feel as though they want to leap out of our hands and smash on the floor. We almost want to throw them down to get it over with— the same way we think about standing up in Chapel and shouting

436

out something terrible. Then we wonder if we haven't already done it. At that moment, the back door opens and Emily Jerman walks into the hall. The professor's wife drops the guest book and its spine breaks. Pages and pages of visitors wash over the floor.

"See Bryan," Emily Jerman says to her husband, "I told you I shouldn't have come." As we pick up the pages of the guest book, she walks over to the piano. She stays there with her back to us for a long time, and we can tell that she is crying. We want Mr. Jerman to do something, but he stays with us, listening to the tour guide wander through all her dreamed facts, and we hate him for that.

Upstairs we see the dress and the bed, the writing table, the window that looks out over Main Street, the basket used to lower gingerbread down to children in the garden. We stick our noses inside like dogs and sniff to see if the smell of gingerbread is still there, and we tell each other that it is. When the guide's back is turned, we touch everything: the bed, the shawl, the hatbox, the dress, even the glass over the poet's soft silhouette.

We watch Emily Jerman move down the hall and into this room like she's walking in a trance. We see her eyes are red and her face is swollen. The professor's wife is talking about incontinence, and then about the Civil War, but we don't know how she got there. We watch Emily Jerman, more whisper than woman's body, a sensation in this house, a hot spirit distant from her husband and from us. We stare at the two of them, and all at once we know we will never remember anything Mr. Jerman has taught us, except this: that the world is a blind knot of electric and unspeakable desires, burning itself to nothing.

*

As we're leaving, the professor's wife makes us promise not to miss the graveyard, and we assure her that we won't. We tell her that we have already dreamed of it, just like her husband, and she tells us to button up our blouses. It's cold out, she says.

"We'll save that for tomorrow," Mr. Jerman says. "It's too dark now."

"Oh no," Emily Jerman tells him, the light beginning to come back into her voice, "it's perfect now, perfect for a graveyard."

437

She takes the keys out of her coat pocket, unlocks the van for the rest of us, and gets in behind the wheel.

"I know the way," she says. "I already looked on the map."

Emily Jerman makes three left turns and we're in West Cemetery where it's pitch dark. Mr. Jerman asks if she knows where the grave is and she nods, but then she drives us once around all the graves anyway. When we come back to the entrance road, she pulls a hard left and drives up on the grass. There in front of the van's lights are three headstones behind a black wrought-iron fence.

Emily Jerman climbs down quickly and opens the van doors from the outside. We're surprised at how strong she is, how determined she is for us to be here. She leads us to the graves, pushing us a little from behind, pointing to the marker in the middle. "Called Back," it says. She shows us all the offerings there—dried flowers, coins, somebody's ballpoint pen with its red barrel looking like a swipe of blood.

" 'Just lost when I was found,' " Emily Jerman says behind us, " 'just felt the world go by, just girt me for the onset with eternity when breath blew black and on the other side I heard recede the disappointed tide.' "

"Saved," Mr. Jerman says. "It's *saved*."

"Just lost when I was fucking *saved* then," his wife calls back. " 'Therefore as one returned I feel odd secrets of the line to tell. Some sailor skirting foreign shores.' "

We've turned around to look for her, for Emily Jerman, but she's standing in between the van's headlights, leaning back and against the grille, so we can't see her, only the smoky mist her breath makes in the cold as she speaks.

"Do another one," we say, but she won't.

"That's my favorite," she says. "It's the only one." She tells us to leave something at the grave. She says it doesn't matter what.

There's nothing in our coat pockets but spare change, wrappers from starlight mints, and our driver's licenses. We don't know what to do. We can feel panic beginning to take fire under our ribs, and we look up first at the evening sky, clear and blue-black, then across the street to the 7-Eleven, where the smell of chili dogs is billowing out the doors. We lean over and take hold of the hems of our Columbus School for Girls skirts. We find the

438

seam and pull sharply upward, and then down, tearing a rough triangle out of the bottom of the cloth. Cold air rushes in at our thighs and between our legs.

"Girls!" Mr. Jerman says, but his voice gets lost in the sound of his wife's laughter.

"What a waste," he says, but we tell him it isn't. At school, sewing is compulsory, and we know that with an extra tuck and the letting out of one pleat at the other seam, our skirts will look exactly the same again.

*

At dinner, Mr. Jerman hardly says a word while his wife orders double vodkas and tells us more about her days at The Columbus School for Girls.

"Those graduation dresses you have now," she says, "they were my idea."

We look at Mr. Jerman, who nods his head.

"I just couldn't stand the thought of black robes, and so I drew up a pattern and took it into the headmaster—who's dead now, by the way, and what a blessing *that* is."

"What did he say?" we ask.

"He said absolutely no, he wasn't going to have a bunch of girls traipsing around in their nighties. He wanted us fully covered. But I went ahead and made one dress and wore it every day. Every day for all of March and most of April. I got detention every day, too, and served them all, and finally he gave in."

We wonder why Emily Jerman would now be passing the rest of her life at a place that had treated her so badly. We think she must love Bryan Jerman beyond reason. We can't imagine that she wants to go back tomorrow, not any more than we do.

"It was a beautiful place then," she says. "The gardens were kept up. Outside was like Eden. The gardener could do anything, bring anything back to life. He was a genius."

"Emily," Mr. Jerman says, "I believe you had a crush on that gardener."

"Darling," she says, "we thought you'd never guess—didn't we, girls?"

His laugh dies to a choking sound as his wife stares at him, breathing hard and smiling like she's just won a race. The silence is terrible, beating between them, but we won't break it. We want to watch and see how it will break itself.

"To the new girls," Emily Jerman says finally, toasting us with her third vodka. We can see how, inside the glass, our own faces look back at us for a split second before they shatter into light and fire and gluey vodka running into Emily Jerman's mouth.

*

We don't know how long we've been asleep when Mr. Jerman comes in to wake us up. It's still dark outside. We have been dreaming but we couldn't say about what. Mr. Jerman stands beside our beds and reaches out to turn on the lamp. When he can't find the switch, he takes a book of matches from his pocket, lights one, and holds it over our heads. We think maybe we have been dreaming about that, a tongue of flame hissing above us, or about everything that is going to happen now.

Mr. Jerman tells us to put on our shoes and socks, our coats over our nightgowns, and then he leads us outside, down to the parking lot where the motel's airport van is waiting. The heat inside is on high, so we can barely hear what passes between Mr. Jerman and the driver, except when he says he couldn't very well leave young girls alone in a motel, now could he?

We know they're taking us back to Amherst, and when we pull into West Cemetery, we know why. There, exactly where Emily Jerman had parked it in the early evening, is our school van, the lights on, shining on the wrought-iron fence and the three headstones behind it. Emily Jerman is standing behind the fence, her right hand curled around one of the thin black posts rising up to shoulder height.

Two West Cemetery guards stand off to her left, motionless, watching, their bodies balanced slightly ahead of their feet and their heads hung down as if they had been running and then had to stop suddenly to keep from going over the edge of the world.

"Girls," Emily Jerman says when she sees us standing with her husband. "Look at you, traipsing around in your nighties. How far do you think you're going to get in this world dressed like that? You have to learn how to keep warm. When I was your age, I learned how. When I was your age, I was on fire. On *fire*, do you understand?"

440

We do. We see the two bodies pressed close, Emily Jerman and the gardener who could bring almost anything back to life. We hear his whispering and smell her hair in flames.

Mist rises in front of the van's headlights. The cemetery ground between us and Mr. Jerman looks like it's burning, but this does not surprise us. It only makes us curious, like the night birds that rise now from the leaves to ask *whose fire? whose fire?* and then drop back to sleep.

We know what will happen next. Mr. Jerman will walk through this fire and it won't consume him. He will move past us toward his wife, and we'll feel his breath as he passes, sweet and dangerously cold. This time, we'll look away when they touch. We won't have to see how they do it, or hear what words they use. We know what we need to know. This is the new world.

1993

FOUR STORIES

by LYDIA DAVIS

from CONJUNCTIONS

THE ACTORS

In our town there is an actor, H.—a tall, bold, feverish sort of
man—who easily fills the theater when he plays Othello, and
about whom the women here become very excited. He is handsome enough compared to the other men, though his nose is
somewhat thick and his torso rather short for his height. His acting is stiff and inflexible, his gestures obviously memorized and
mechanical, and yet his voice is strong enough to make one forget
all that. On the nights when he is unable to leave his bed because of illness or intoxication—and this happens more often than
one would imagine—the part is taken by J., his understudy. Now
J. is pale and small, completely unsuitable for the part of the
Moor; his legs tremble as he comes on stage and faces the many
empty seats. His voice hardly carries beyond the first few rows,
and his small hands flap uselessly in the smoky air. We feel only
pity and irritation as we watch him, and yet by the end of the
play we find ourselves unaccountably moved, as though he had
managed to convey something timid or sad in Othello's nature.
But the mannerisms and skill of H. and J.—which we analyze
minutely when we visit together in the afternoons and continue
to contemplate even once we are alone after dinner—seem suddenly insignificant when the great Sparr comes down from the
city and gives us a real performance of Othello. Then we are so
carried away, so exhausted with emotion, that it is impossible to
speak of what we feel. We are almost grateful when he is gone

and we are left with H. and J., imperfect as they are, for they are familiar to us and comfortable, like our own people.

TRYING TO LEARN

I am trying to learn that this playful man who teases me is the same as that serious man talking money to me so seriously he does not even see me anymore and that patient man offering me advice in times of trouble and that angry man slamming the door as he leaves the house. I have often wanted the playful man to be more serious, and the serious man to be less serious, and the patient man to be more playful. As for the angry man, he is a stranger to me and I do not feel it is wrong to hate him. Now I am learning that if I say bitter words to the angry man as he leaves the house, I am at the same time wounding the others, the ones I do not want to wound, the playful man teasing, the serious man talking money, and the patient man offering advice. Yet I look at the patient man, for instance, whom I would want above all to protect from such bitter words as mine, and though I tell myself he is the same man as the others, I can only believe I said those words, not to him, but to another, my enemy, who deserved all my anger.

THERAPISTS

A friend of mine goes with her three-year-old girl to a family therapist. This therapist has guided her in her troubles with the child's bed-wetting, fear of the dark, and dependence on the bottle. One by one these problems are solved. The mother, acting on the advice of the therapist, is careful to avoid attempting to solve more than one problem at a time. The child is unhappy and nervous and holds her body in a cramped position, as though protecting herself. Her mother is also nervous, and is never still: her hands flutter and her eyebrows fly up into her forehead. There is a dark brown mole on her cheek, and this dark point is the only color in her face.

Another friend calls her husband's therapist and tells him she is going to ask her husband to move out. Naturally, the therapist has to report this to his patient. The husband is hurt and indignant. My friend is adamant. Her own therapist thinks she must now be under great pressure from her husband, and this is true. Encouraged by her therapist, however, she persists in asking her husband to leave. At last he does. He now sees his children in his own apartment several times a week, including all day Sunday. Insulted by his wife's behavior, he tries to complain only to his therapist, as his therapist has advised, but he cannot help complaining to everyone—his therapist, his friends, his lawyer, his wife, and even his children. The older boy comes home angry at his mother because he does not know what is the truth anymore. He breaks two of the dining-room chairs. His mother, a frail and small woman, sits on him for several hours before he is calm enough to tell her what he is feeling.

WHAT I FEEL

These days I try to tell myself that what I feel is not very important. I've read this in several books now: that what I feel is important but not the center of everything. Maybe I do believe this, but not enough to act on it. I would like to believe it more deeply.

What a relief that would be. I wouldn't have to think about what I felt all the time, and try to control it, with all its complications and all its consequences. I wouldn't have to try to feel better all the time. In fact, if I didn't believe what I felt was so important, I probably wouldn't even feel so bad, and it wouldn't be so hard to feel better. I wouldn't have to say, Oh I feel so awful, this is like the end for me here, in this dark living-room late at night, with the dark street outside under the streetlamps, I am so very alone, everyone else in the house asleep, there is no comfort anywhere, just me alone down here, I will never calm myself enough to sleep, never sleep, never be able to go on to the next day, I can't possibly go on, I can't live, even through the next minute.

If I didn't believe what I felt was the center of everything, then it wouldn't be the center of everything, but just something off to the side, one of many things, and I would be able to see

444

and pay attention to those other things that are equally important, and in this way I would have some relief.

But it is curious how you can believe an idea is absolutely true and correct and yet not believe it deeply enough to act on it. So I still act as though my feelings were the center of everything, and they still cause me to end up alone by the livingroom window late at night. What is different now is that I have this idea: I have the idea that soon I will no longer believe that my feelings are the center of everything. This is a comfort to me, because if you despair of going on, but at the same time tell yourself that what you feel may not be very important, then either you may no longer despair of going on, or you may still despair of going on but not quite believe it anymore.

1992

MY BEST SOLDIER

by HA JIN

from AGNI

I COULDN'T BELIEVE it when I saw that the photograph sent over by the Regimental Political Department was Liu Fu's. How clumsy he looked in it: a submachine gun slanted before his chest; above his army fur hat, at the right corner, stretched a line of characters—"Defend My Motherland"; his smile was still a country boy's smile lacking the sternness of a soldier's face. He had been in my platoon for only about ten months. How could he, a new soldier, have become a secret customer of Little White Fairy in Hutou Town so soon?

Our political instructor, the Party secretary of our company, interrupted my thought, "I have already talked with him, and he admitted he had gone to that woman six times this year."

"Six times?" Again I was surprised. "He is new. How could he get to know her so quickly?"

"I've asked the same question." Instructor Chang tapped his cigarette lightly over an ashtray and raised his head, looking across the small room in which we were sitting. He wanted to make sure that the orderly was not in the next room. "I think there must have been a pimp, but Liu Fu insisted he got to know the Fairy by himself when he had his hair cut in her barbershop. Obviously, he is a novice in this business. No old hand would leave his picture with that weasel."

"You're right." I remembered last year a bulletin issued by the Regimental Political Department had carried a report on this young woman. After having been caught in bed with an officer,

446

Little White Fairy was brought to the Regimental Headquarters, where she confessed that many soldiers and officers had visited her. Once she had received six army men in a single night, but she didn't know any of their names. Each man would give her a two *yuan* bill and then go to bed with her. That was all. Regimental Commissar Feng swore to have those men found out, as they must have belonged to our Fifth Regiment, the only army unit in Hutou. But those were old dogs and would never leave any traces.

"You should also talk with him." Secretary Chang exhaled a small cloud in the air and continued, "Comrade Wang Hu, your platoon has done everything well this year except this Liu Fu matter. Don't get lost in doing military exercises and in improving fighting skills. Mind modeling is more important. You see whenever we slacken a little in ideological education, serious problems emerge among our men."

"Secretary Chang, I will talk with him immediately. From now on I will pay more attention to ideological education."

"That's good."

It seemed he didn't want to continue the talk, so I left the company headquarters to rejoin my platoon.

I was somewhat upset by Liu Fu's case. What a shame! I had always considered him as a potential successor of a squad leader. His squad leader, Li Yaoping, was going to be demobilized next year, and I had planned to promote Liu Fu to take over. To be fair, Liu was in every way an excellent soldier. He surpassed all my men in hand-grenade throwing. He could throw a grenade seventy-two meters. In our last practice with live ammunition, he scored eighty-four points with nine shots, which was higher than everybody except me. I got eighty-six. If we had a contest with the other three platoons, I would certainly place him as our first man.

Needless to say, I liked him, not only for his ability and skills but also for his person. He was a big fellow, over a hundred and eighty centimeters tall and a little heavily built but very nimble. His wide eyes reminded me of a small pony in my home village. His square mouth and bushy brows resembled those of the ancient generals in Spring Festival pictures. All the other soldiers liked him a lot too, and it seemed he had quite a few friends in our Ninth Company.

447

I can never forget how he became a figure of poetry. That spring when we sowed soybeans, I assigned the Third Squad to pull a plough, since we didn't have enough horses and oxen. On the first day the men were soaked with sweat and complained that it was animal's work. But the next day was different. Liu Fu and two other boys in the Third Squad appeared with bald heads. They said a bald head would make the sweating more endurable and the washing easier after the work. The atmosphere in the field came alive, because the three shining round heads were wavering about like balloons in the team pulling the plough. Everyone wanted to get some fun out of it. As Liu Fu was taller and had a bigger head, he became the main butt. By and by a poem was composed in his honor, and soon the whole company chanted:

When Big Liu takes off his hat
The county magistrate shakes his head:
"Such a vast piece of alkaline land,
How can the grain yield reach the Plan!"

When Big Liu takes off his hat,
The hardware store is so glad:
"With such a big shining bulb,
How many customers can we attract!"

When Big Liu takes off his hat,
The saleswoman is scared out of breath:
"Having sold condoms for so many years,
I've never seen such a length and breadth!"

Big Liu was never offended by the doggerel. He even chanted it with others, but he would replace the name "Big Liu" with "Small Wang," "Old Meng," and so forth. As his popularity increased he was welcomed everywhere in the company. A boy like him could be a very able leader of a squad or a platoon. This was why I had planned to promote him to be a squad leader the next year. But who knew he was a "Flowery Fox"!

Our Party Secretary was right: there must have been somebody who introduced him to Little White Fairy. Hutou was over fifty *li* away from Mati Mountain where we garrisoned; at most

448

Liu Fu had gone to the county town seven or eight times on Sundays. He had seen the White Fairy six times? Almost every time he went there? It was impossible, unless at the very beginning somebody took him directly to the woman. I remembered Li Dong had gone with him for his first visit to the town, and the second time Zhao Yiming had accompanied him. Both of the older soldiers were pretty reliable; it was unlikely that either of them could be a pimp. But to know a man's face is not to know his heart. I must question Liu Fu about this.

Our talk did not take long. He looked crestfallen and deeply ashamed, but he denied there had been somebody else involved and insisted, "A good man must shoulder the outcome of his own action."

In a way, I appreciated his only blaming himself for the whoring, because if another whoremonger was found in my platoon, I would have trouble clearing our name. People would chuckle and say: the First Platoon has a whoring gang. Besides, that would give Liu Fu himself a hard time too, as he would surely be treated by the other men as a sort of traitor.

But I took this case seriously, for I had to stop it. We garrisoned the border line to defend our country, and we must not lose our fighting spirit by chasing women. Unlike the Russians on the other side, we Chinese were revolutionary soldiers, and we must not rely upon women to keep up our morale. Every Saturday night we saw from our lookout tower the Russians having many college girls over in their barracks. They would sing and dance around bonfires, kiss and embrace each other in the open air, roll and fuck in the woods. They were barbarians and Revisionists, whereas we were Chinese and true Revolutionaries.

So I ordered Liu Fu to write out his self-criticism, examining the elements of bourgeois ideology in his brain and getting a clear understanding of the nature of his offense. He wept and begged me not to take disciplinary action against him, for his family would know it and he would carry the stain all his life. I told him a disciplinary action would have to be taken, and I was unable to help him with that. It was better to tell him the truth.

"So I am done for?" His dimmed horsy eyes watched my mouth expectantly.

"Your case was sent down by the Regimental Political Department, and you know our company cannot interfere with a decision from above. Usually, an offender like you *is* punished with a disciplinary action. But this doesn't mean you will have to carry it for the rest of your life. It depends on your own behavior. Say from now on if you behave well in every way, you may have it taken out of your file when you are demobilized."

He opened his big square mouth, but he didn't say anything, as if he swallowed down some words that had been stuck in his throat. The word "demobilized" must have struck him hard, since a soldier like him from the countryside would work diligently in order to be promoted to be an officer. It would be a misfortune for him to return to his poor home village, where no job waited for him, and without a job no girl would marry him. But with such a stigma in his record, Liu Fu's future in the army had been fixed: he would never be an officer.

Two days later he turned in his self-criticism. On eight white sheets were lines of big, heavily scrawled words and a few ink stains. A country boy certainly couldn't say extraordinary things. His language was plain, and many sentences were broken. The gist of his self-criticism was that he had not worked hard enough to purge the bourgeois ideology from his head and he had contracted the disease of bourgeois liberalism. The Seventh Rule for the Army stated clearly: "Nobody is allowed to take liberties with women," but he had forgotten Chairman Mao's instruction and violated the rule. He also had forgotten his duty as a soldier staying on the Northern Frontier: when the enemies were sharpening their teeth and grinding their sabers at the other side, he was indulging himself in sexual pleasure. He was unworthy of the nurture of the Party, unworthy of the Motherland's expectation, unworthy of his parents' efforts to raise him, unworthy of the gun that the people had entrusted to his hands, unworthy of the new green uniform . . .

I knew he was not a verbal person, so I spared him the trouble of putting more self-scathing and remorseful words in the writing. His attitude was sincere; this alone counted.

He looked a little comforted when I told him that I would try to persuade Secretary Chang to ask the Regimental Political Department to administer less severe punishment to him. "This is not over yet," I warned him. "But you must not take it as a heavy burden. Try to turn over a new leaf and work hard to make up for it."

He said he was grateful and would never forget my help.

Two weeks passed. We had not heard anything from the Political Department about the decision on Liu Fu's case. Neither our Party secretary nor our company commander ever requested an action. It would be unwise to do that, for the longer we waited the more lenient the punishment would be. Time would take away the interest and the urgency of the case. In fact, none of our company leaders would welcome a severe action against Liu Fu. Liu was their man, and no good leader would like to see his own man being punished.

A month passed. Still nothing happened. Liu Fu seemed very patient and was quieter than before. In order to prevent him from being involved with Little White Fairy again, we kept him at Mati Mountain on weekends. We also became very strict about permitting other men, especially new soldiers, to visit Hutou Town.

One night it was my turn to make the round through all our sentry posts, checking the men on duty and making sure they did not doze off. We had five posts, including the new one at the storehouse where we kept our food and a portion of our ammunition. I hated to do it at midnight when you had to jump out of your bed and pretend to be as awake as a cat. If you didn't look spirited in front of them, the men on duty would feel doubly sleepy.

I went to the parking yard first, where our trucks and mortars stood, and caught the sentry smoking in the dark. I ordered him to put out his cigarette. The boy complained it was too cold and he couldn't keep his eyelids apart if he had nothing to to. I told him everybody had to stand his hours on cold nights. Nobody but the Lord of Heaven was to blame for the cold. As for his sleepiness, he'd better bear in mind that we were merely four *li* away from the Russians. If he didn't stay alert, he put his own neck at risk. The Russians often sent over their agents to find out our sentry positions and our deployment. They would get rid of a sentry if they found it necessary and convenient. So for his own safety, he'd better keep his eyes open and not show them where he was.

Then I went to the gate post and our headquarters. Everything was fine at those two places. I chatted with each of the men for a few minutes and gave them some roasted sunflower seeds. Then I left for the storehouse.

The post was empty there, so I waited inside the house, believing the sentry must have been urinating or emptying his bowels somewhere outside.

After ten minutes nobody showed up. I began to worry and was afraid that something unusual might have happened. I couldn't shout to summon the sentry over. This was the last thing you would do at night, for it would wake up the whole company, and the Russians might hear it as well. But I had to find out where the sentry had hidden himself. He must have been dozing away somewhere. There were no disordered footprints in the snow; it was unlikely that the sentry had been kidnapped or murdered. I picked up a line of footprints that looked new and followed it for a little distance. They were heading towards our stable. I raised my eyes and saw a dim light at the skylight on the stable's roof. Somebody has to be there. What's he up to in the stable? Who is on duty now? I looked at my luminous watch—1:30—and couldn't recall who was the sentry.

Getting close to the door I heard some noise inside, so I hastened my steps. With my rifle I raised a little the cotton door-curtain to have a view inside and to make sure that nobody was hiding behind the door waiting to knock me down.

It was Liu Fu! He was standing beside our gray mule, buckling the belt around his pants. His gun leaned against the long manger, and his fur hat hung on its muzzle. Beyond the mule stood a dozen horses asleep with downcast heads. So he is the sentry. The rascal, he's using the stable as a latrine. How luxurious, keeping his butt warm here!

No, I noticed something unusual, for behind the gray mule's hindquarters was a bench. On the bench there were some particles of snow and some wet smudges. The beast! He has been screwing the mule! Looking at him, I found his sweating blood-stained face distorted with an awkward but clear expression, as if saying to me: *I can't help it, please I can't help it!*

I sprang at him and grabbed him by the front of his jacket. Though he was much bigger and stronger than I was, I felt he went limp in my hand. Of course, a spent beast! I started slapping him on the face and cursing, "You—mule-fucker! You never give your cock a break! I will geld you today and throw your itchy balls to the dogs!"

He didn't resist at all and merely moaned, as if my cursing and slapping made him feel better. He looked so ashamed. Not encountering any resistance, I soon cooled down. You couldn't go on for long beating a man who didn't even raise his hands to defend himself. I let him go and ordered, "Back to the storehouse. We'll settle it tomorrow."

He picked up his gun, wiped away the tears on his cheeks with his hat, and went out quietly. In the stable all the animals were out of sleep now, their eyes open and their ears cocked up. One horse snorted.

I couldn't wait for tomorrow, so I had Li Yaoping, his squad leader, awakened. We had to talk before I reported it to our Party secretary. I must know more about Liu Fu. It was understandable if a long-deprived monk screwed a girl in the town, since there was no woman on the mountain. But to screw a dumb animal like that, who could imagine it! It nauseated me.

Li was not completely awake when he came into my room. I gave him a cigarette and struck a match for him. "Sit down. I want to talk with you."

He sat on a stool and began smoking. "What do you want to talk about on a dark—" He looked at his watch. "It's already half past two in the morning."

"I want to talk about Liu Fu. Just now I found him in the stable fooling around with the gray mule." I wouldn't say: "He screwed the mule," since I didn't see him do it. But I was sure of it, as Liu Fu himself did not deny it when I cursed him, so I was ready to explain further to Li what I meant.

"Oh no, you mean he did it again?" Li shook his freckled face.

"Yes. So you knew everything already?" I was surprised.

"Ye—yes." He nodded

"Why didn't you inform me of that before? Who gave you the right to hide it from me?" I was angry and would have yelled at him if some of my men were not sleeping in the adjacent room.

"He promised me he would never do it again." Li looked worried. "I thought I should give him a chance."

"A chance? Didn't we give him one already when he was caught with Little White Fairy?" I felt outraged. Apparently this thing had been going on in my platoon for quite a while, but I had never got a whiff of it. "Tell me when did you see him do it and how many times."

"I saw him with the mule just once. It was last Saturday night. I saw him standing on a bench and hanging on to the mule's hindquarters. I watched for a while through the back window of the stable, then I coughed. He was scared and immediately fell off. When he saw me come in, he knelt down begging me to forgive him and not to tell on him. He looked so piteous, a big fellow like that, so I told him I wouldn't tell. But I did criticize him."

"What did you say? How did you conduct your ideological instruction, Comrade Squad Leader?" I felt it strange—he sounded as if he might have sold his sister if he took pity on a man.

"I asked him why he had to screw the mule." Li looked rather cheerful.

"What a stupid question. How did he answer it?"

"He said, 'You know, Squad Leader, only—only mules don't foal. I promise, I'll never touch any—any of these mares.'" Li started tittering.

"What? It's absurd. You mean he thought he could have got those mares with babies? What a silly fellow! So moral, he's afraid of being a father of horsy bastards!" I couldn't help laughing, and Li's tittering turned into loud laughter too.

"Sh—," I reminded him of the sleepers.

"I told him even the mule must not be 'touched,' and he promised not to do it again." Li winked at me.

"Old Li, you're an old fox."

"Don't be so hard on me, my platoon leader. To be fair, he is a good boy in every way except that he can't control his lust. I don't know why. If you say he has too much bourgeois stuff in his head, that won't fit. He is from a pure poor peasant family, a healthy seedling upon a red root—"

"I don't want you to work out a theory, Old Li," I interrupted him. "I want to know how we should handle him now. This morning, in a few hours, I will report it to our Company Headquarters. What should we say and how should we say it?"

"Well, do you want to get rid of him or keep him?"

This was indeed the crucial question, but I didn't know the answer. Liu Fu was my best man and I would need him in the future. "What's your opinion then? At least, we must not cover it up this time." I had realized that Old Li didn't tell on Liu Fu because he wanted to keep him in his squad.

"Certainly, he had his chance already, How about—"

The door burst open and somebody rushed in. It was Ma Pingli, our youngest boy, who was to stand the three o'clock shift at the storehouse. "Platoon Leader," he took the fur mask off his nose, panting hard, "Liu Fu is not—not at the post, and all the telephone wires are cut. We can't call anywhere."

"Did you go around and look for him?"

"Yes, everywhere."

"Where's his gun?"

"The gun is still there, in the post, but his person's gone."

"Hurry up! Bring over the horses!" I ordered. "We'll go and get him." Ma started running to the stable.

I glanced at Old Li. His looks showed he understood what was happening. "Take this with you." I handed him a semi-automatic rifle, which he accepted mechanically, and I picked up another one for myself. In an uneasy silence, we went out waiting for Ma.

The horses sweated all over, climbing towards the border line. I calculated that we would have enough time to stop him before he could get across. He had to climb a long way from the southern side of the mountain in order to avoid being spotted by our lookout tower. But when we three reached the Wusuli, a line of fresh footprints stretched in front of us, winding across the snow-covered surface of the river, extending itself into the other side, and gradually losing its trail in the bluish whiteness of the vast Russian territory.

"The beast, stronger than a horse and faster than a hound," I cursed. It was unimaginable that he could run so fast in the deep snow.

455

"He's there!" Ma Pingli pointed to a small slope partly covered by gray bushes.

Indeed, I saw a dark dot moving towards the edge of the thicket, which was about five hundred meters away from us. Impossible. Surely he was too smart not to put on his white camouflage cape. I raised my binoculars, and saw him carrying a big stuffed gunnysack on his right shoulder and running desperately for the shelter of the bushes, a camouflage cape secured around his neck flapping behind him like a huge butterfly. I gave the binoculars to Old Li.

Li watched. "He's taking a sack of *Forwards* with him!" he said with amazement.

"He stole it from the kitchen. I saw the kitchen door broken," Ma reported. We all knew our cooks stored *Forwards*, the newspaper of Shenyang Military Region, in gunny sacks as kindling. We had been told not to toss around the paper, because the Russians tried to get every issue of it in Hong Kong and would pay more than ten dollars for it.

"The Russians may not need those back issues at all," I explained. "They've already got them. They only want recent ones. He's dumb."

Suddenly a yellow light pierced the sky over the slope. The Russians' lookout tower must have spotted him; their Jeep was coming to pick him up.

Old Li and I looked at each other. We knew what we had to do. No time to waste. "We have no choice," I muttered, putting a sighting glass onto my rifle. "He had betrayed our country, and he is our enemy now."

I raised the rifle and aimed at him steadily. A burst of fire fixed him there. He collapsed in the distant snow, and the big sack fell off his shoulder and rolled down the slope.

"You got him!" Ma shouted.

"Yes, I got him," I replied. "Let's go back."

We mounted on the saddles; the horses immediately galloped down the mountain. They were eager to get out of the cold wind and return to their stable

All the way back, none of us said another word.

1992

MARIE

by EDWARD P. JONES

from THE PARIS REVIEW

Every now and again, as if on a whim, the Federal government people would write to Marie Delaveaux Wilson in one of those white, stampless envelopes and tell her to come in to their place so they could take another look at her. They, the Social Security people, wrote to her in a foreign language that she had learned to translate over the years, and for all of the years she had been receiving the letters the same man had been signing them. Once, because she had something important to tell him, Marie called the number the man always put at the top of the letters, but a woman answered Mr. Smith's telephone and told Marie he was in an all-day meeting. Another time she called and a man said Mr. Smith was on vacation. And finally one day a woman answered and told Marie that Mr. Smith was deceased. The woman told her to wait and she would get someone new to talk to her about her case, but Marie thought it bad luck to have telephoned a dead man and she hung up.

Now, years after the woman had told her Mr. Smith was no more, the letters were still being signed by John Smith. Come into our office at Twenty-first and M Streets, Northwest, the letters said in that foreign language. Come in so we can see if you are still blind in one eye. Come in so we can see if you are still old and getting older. Come in so we can see if you still deserve to get Supplemental Security Income payments.

She always obeyed the letters, even if the order now came from a dead man, for she knew people who had been temporarily

457

cut off from SSI for not showing up or even for being late. And once cut off, you had to move heaven and earth to get back on.

So on a not unpleasant day in March, she rose in the morning, even before the day had any sort of character, to give herself plenty of time to bathe, eat, lay out money for the bus, dress, listen to the spirituals on the radio. She was eighty-six years old and had learned that life was all chaos and painful uncertainty and that the only way to get through it was to expect chaos even in the most innocent of moments. Offer a crust of bread to a sick bird and you often draw back a bloody finger.

John Smith's letter had told her to come in at eleven o'clock, his favorite time, and by nine that morning she had had her bath and had eaten. Dressed by 9:30. The walk from Claridge Towers at Twelfth and M down to the bus stop at Fourteenth and K took her about ten minutes, more or less. There was a bus at about 10:30, her schedule told her, but she preferred the one that came a half hour earlier, lest there be trouble with the 10:30 bus. After she dressed, she sat at her dining room table and went over yet again what papers and all else she needed to take. Given the nature of life—particularly the questions asked by the Social Security people—she always took more than they might ask for: her birth certificate, her husband's death certificate, doctors' letters.

One of the last things she put in her pocketbook was a knife that she had, about seven inches long, which she had serrated on both edges with the use of a small saw borrowed from a neighbor. The knife, she was convinced now, had saved her life about two weeks before. Before then she had often been careless about when she took the knife out with her, and she had never taken it out in daylight, but now she never left her apartment without it, even when going down the hall to the trash drop.

She had gone out to buy a simple box of oatmeal, no more, no less. It was about seven in the evening, the streets with enough commuters driving up Thirteenth Street to make her feel safe. Several yards before she reached the store, the young man came from behind her and tried to rip off her coat pocket where he thought she kept her money, for she carried no purse or pocketbook after five o'clock. The money was in the other pocket with the knife, and his hand was caught in the empty pocket long enough for her to reach around with the knife and cut his hand as it came out of her pocket.

He screamed and called her an old bitch. He took a few steps up Thirteenth Street and stood in front of Emerson's Market, examining the hand and shaking off blood. Except for the cars passing up and down Thirteenth Street, they were alone, and she began to pray.

"You cut me," he said, as if he had only been minding his own business when she cut him. "Just look what you done to my hand," he said and looked around as if for some witness to her crime. There was not a great amount of blood, but there was enough for her to see it dripping to the pavement. He seemed to be about twenty, no more than twenty-five, dressed the way they were all dressed nowadays, as if a blind man had matched up their colors. It occurred to her to say that she had seven grandchildren about his age, that telling him this would make him leave her alone. But the more filth he spoke, the more she wanted him only to come toward her again.

"You done crippled me, you old bitch."

"I sure did," she said, without malice, without triumph, but simply the way she would have told him the time of day had he asked and had she known. She gripped the knife tighter, and as she did, she turned her body ever so slightly so that her good eye lined up with him. Her heart was making an awful racket, wanting to be away from him, wanting to be safe at home. I will not be moved, some organ in the neighborhood of the heart told the heart. "And I got plenty more where that come from."

The last words seemed to bring him down some and, still shaking the blood from his hand, he took a step or two back, which disappointed her. I will not be moved, that other organ kept telling her heart. "You just crazy, thas all," he said. "Just a crazy old hag." Then he turned and lumbered up toward Logan Circle, and several times he looked back over his shoulder as if afraid she might be following. A man came out of Emerson's, then a woman with two little boys. She wanted to grab each of them by the arm and tell them she had come close to losing her life. "I saved myself with this here thing," she would have said. She forgot about the oatmeal and took her raging heart back to the apartment. She told herself that she should, but she never washed the fellow's blood off the knife, and over the next few days it dried and then it began to flake off.

Toward ten o'clock that morning Wilamena Mason knocked and let herself in with a key Marie had given her.

"I see you all ready," Wilamena said.

"With the help of the Lord," Marie said. "Want a spot a coffee?"

"No thanks," Wilamena said, and dropped into a chair at the table. "Been drinkin' so much coffee lately, I'm gonna turn into coffee. Was up all night with Calhoun."

"How he doin'?"

Wilamena told her Calhoun was better that morning, his first good morning in over a week. Calhoun Lambeth was Wilamena's boyfriend, a seventy-five-year-old man she had taken up with six or so months before, not long after he moved in. He was the best-dressed old man Marie had ever known, but he had always appeared to be sickly, even while strutting about with his gold-tipped cane. And seeing that she could count his days on the fingers of her hands, Marie had avoided getting to know him. She could not understand why Wilamena, who could have had any man in Claridge Towers or any other senior citizen building for that matter, would take such a man into her bed. "True love," Wilamena had explained. "Avoid heartache," Marie had said, trying to be kind.

They left the apartment. Marie sought help from no one, lest she come to depend on a person too much. But since the encounter with the young man, Wilamena had insisted on escorting her. Marie, to avoid arguments, allowed Wilamena to walk with her from time to time to the bus stop, but no farther.

Nothing fit Marie's theory about life like the weather in Washington. Two days before, the temperature had been in the forties, and yesterday it had dropped to the low twenties, then warmed up a bit with the afternoon, bringing on snow flurries. Today the weather people on the radio had said it would warm enough to wear just a sweater, but Marie was wearing her coat. And tomorrow, the weather people said, it would be in the thirties, with maybe an inch or so of snow.

Appointments near twelve o'clock were always risky, because the Social Security people often took off for lunch long before

460

noon and returned sometime after one. And except for a few employees who seemed to work through their lunch hours, the place shut down. Marie had never been interviewed by someone willing to work through the lunch hour. Today, though the appointment was for eleven, she waited until 1:30 before the woman at the front of the waiting room told her she would have to come back another day, because the woman who handled her case was not in.

"You put my name down when I came in like everything was all right," Marie said after she had been called up to the woman's desk.

"I know," the woman said, "but I thought that Mrs. Brown was in. They told me she was in. I'm sorry." The woman began writing in a logbook that rested between her telephone and a triptych of photographs. She handed Marie a slip and told her again she was sorry.

"Why you have me wait so long if she whatn't here?" She did not want to say too much, appear too upset, for the Social Security people could be unforgiving. And though she was used to waiting three and four hours, she found it especially unfair to wait when there was no one for her at all behind those panels the Social Security people used for offices. "I been here since before eleven."

"I know," the woman behind the desk said. "I know. I saw you there, ma'am, but I really didn't know Mrs. Brown wasn't here." There was a nameplate at the front of the woman's desk and it said Vernelle Wise. The name was surrounded by little hearts, the kind a child might have drawn.

Marie said nothing more and left.

The next appointment was two weeks later, 8:30, a good hour, and the day before a letter signed by John Smith arrived to remind her. She expected to be out at least by twelve. Three minutes before eleven o'clock Marie asked Vernelle Wise if the man, Mr. Green, who was handling her case, was in that day, and each time the woman assured her that he was. At twelve, Marie ate one of the two oranges and three of the five slices of cheese she had brought. At one, she asked again if Mr. Green was indeed in that day and politely reminded Vernelle Wise that she had been

461

waiting since about eight that morning. Vernelle was just as polite and told her the wait would soon be over.

At 1:15, Marie began to watch the clock hands creep around the dial. She had not paid much attention to the people about her, but more and more it seemed that others were being waited on who had arrived long after she had gotten there. After asking about Mr. Green at one, she had taken a seat near the front and, as more time went by, she found herself forced to listen to the conversation that Vernelle was having with the other receptionist next to her.

"I told him . . . I told him . . . I said just get your things and leave," said the other receptionist, who didn't have a nameplate.

"Did he leave?" Vernelle wanted to know.

"Oh, no," the other woman said. "Not at first. But I picked up some of his stuff, that Christian Dior jacket he worships. I picked up my cigarette lighter and that jacket, just like I was gonna do something bad to it, and he started movin' then."

Vernelle began laughing. "I wish I was there to see that." She was filing her fingernails. Now and again she would look at her fingernails to inspect her work, and if it was satisfactory, she would blow on the nails and on the file. "He back?" Vernelle asked.

The other receptionist eyed her. "What you think?" and they both laughed.

Along about two o'clock Marie became hungry again, but she did not want to eat the rest of her food because she did not know how much longer she would be there. There was a soda machine in the corner, but all sodas gave her gas.

"You-know-who gonna call you again?" the other receptionist was asking Vernelle.

"I hope so," Vernelle said. "He pretty fly. Seemed decent too. It kinda put me off when he said he was a car mechanic. I kinda like kept tryin' to take a peek at his fingernails and everything the whole evenin'. See if they was dirty or what."

"Well, that mechanic stuff might be good when you get your car back. My cousin's boyfriend used to do that kinda work and he made good money, girl. I mean real good money."

"Hmmmm," Vernelle said. "Anyway, the kids like him, and you know how peculiar they can be."

"Tell me 'bout it. They do the job your mother and father used to do, huh? Only on another level."

"You can say that again," Vernelle said.

Marie went to her and told her how long she had been waiting.

"Listen," Vernelle said, pointing her fingernail file at Marie. "I told you you'll be waited on as soon as possible. This is a busy day. So I think you should just go back to your seat until we call your name." The other receptionist began to giggle.

Marie reached across the desk and slapped Vernelle Wise with all her might. Vernelle dropped the file, which made a cheap, tinny sound when it hit the plastic board her chair was on. But no one heard the file because she had begun to cry right away. She looked at Marie as if, in the moment of her greatest need, Marie had denied her. "Oh, oh," Vernelle Wise said through the tears. "Oh, my dear God. . ."

The other receptionist, in her chair on casters, rolled over to Vernelle and put her arm around her. "Security!" the other receptionist hollered. "We need security here!"

The guard at the front door came quickly around the corner, one hand on his holstered gun and the other pointing accusingly at the people seated in the waiting area. Marie had sat down and was looking at the two women almost sympathetically, as if a stranger had come in, hit Vernelle Wise, and fled.

"She slapped Vernelle!" said the other receptionist.

"Who did it?" the guard said, reaching for the man who was sitting beside Marie. But when the other receptionist said it was the old lady in the blue coat, the guard held back for the longest time, as if to grab her would be like arresting his own grandmother. He stood blinking and he would have gone on blinking had Marie not stood up.

She was too flustered to wait for the bus and so took a cab home. With both chains, she locked herself in the apartment, refusing to answer the door or the telephone the rest of the day and most of the next. But she knew that if her family or friends received no answer at the door or on the telephone, they would think something had happened to her. So the next afternoon, she began answering the phone and spoke with the chain on, telling Wilamena and others that she had a toothache.

For days and days after the incident she ate very little and asked God to forgive her. She was haunted by the way Vernelle's cheek had felt, by what it was like to invade and actually touch the flesh of another person. And when she thought too hard, she imagined that she was slicing through the woman's cheek, the way she had sliced through the young man's hand. But as time went on she began to remember the man's curses and the purplish color of Vernelle's fingernails, and all remorse would momentarily take flight. Finally, one morning nearly two weeks after she slapped the woman, she woke with a phrase she had not used or heard since her children were small: You whatn't raised that way.

It was the next morning that the thin young man in the suit knocked and asked through the door chains if he could speak with her. She thought that he was a Social Security man come to tear up her card and papers and tell her that they would send her no more checks. Even when he pulled out an identification card showing that he was a Howard University student, she did not believe.

In the end, she told him she didn't want to buy anything, not magazines, not candy, not anything.

"No, no," he said. "I just want to talk to you for a bit. About your life and everything. It's for a project for my folklore course. I'm talking to everyone in the building who'll let me. Please . . . I won't be a bother. Just a little bit of your time."

"I don't have anything worth talkin' about," she said. "And I don't keep well these days."

"Oh, ma'am, I'm sorry. But we all got something to say. I promise I won't be a bother."

After fifteen minutes of his pleas, she opened the door to him because of his suit and his tie and his tie clip with a bird in flight, and because his long, dark brown fingers reminded her of delicate twigs. But had he turned out to be death with a gun or a knife or fingers to crush her neck, she would not have been surprised. "My name's George. George Carter. Like the president." He had the kind of voice that old people in her young days would have called womanish. "But I was born right here in D.C. Born, bred and buttered, my mother used to say."

He stayed the rest of the day and she fixed him dinner. It scared her to be able to talk so freely with him, and at first she thought that at long last, as she had always feared, senility had taken hold of her. A few hours after he left, she looked his name up in the telephone book, and when a man who sounded like him answered, she hung up immediately. And the next day she did the same thing. He came back at least twice a week for many weeks and would set his cassette recorder on her coffee table. "He's takin' down my whole life," she told Wilamena, almost the way a woman might speak in awe of a new boyfriend.

One day he played back for the first time some of what she told the recorder:

> . . . My father would be sittin' there readin' the paper. He'd say whenever they put in a new president, "Look like he got the chair for four years." And it got so that's what I saw—this poor man sittin' in that chair for four long years while the rest of the world went on about its business. I don't know if I thought he ever did anything, the president. I just knew that he had to sit in that chair for four years. Maybe I thought that by his sittin' in that chair and doin' nothin' else for four years he made the country what it was and that without him sittin' there the country wouldn't be what it was. Maybe thas what I got from listenin' to father readin' and to my mother askin' him questions 'bout what he was readin'. They was like that, you see. . . .

George stopped the tape and was about to put the other side in when she touched his hand.

"No more, George," she said. "I can't listen to no more. Please . . . please, no more." She had never in her whole life heard her own voice. Nothing had been so stunning in a long, long while, and for a few moments before she found herself, her world turned upside down. There, rising from a machine no bigger than her Bible, was a voice frighteningly familiar and yet unfamiliar, talking about a man whom she knew as well as her husbands and her sons, a man dead and buried sixty years. She reached across to George and he handed her the tape. She turned it over and over, as if the mystery of everything could be discerned if she turned it enough times. She began to cry, and with her other hand she lightly touched the buttons of the machine.

465

Between the time Marie slapped the woman in the Social Security office and the day she heard her voice for the first time, Calhoun Lambeth, Wilamena's boyfriend, had been in and out of the hospital three times. Most evenings when Calhoun's son stayed the night with him, Wilamena would come up to Marie's and spend most of the evening sitting on the couch that was catty-corner to the easy chair facing the big window. She said very little, which was unlike her, a woman with more friends than hairs on her head and who, at sixty-eight, loved a good party. The most attractive woman Marie knew would only curl her legs up under herself and sip whatever Marie put in her hand. She looked out at the city until she took herself to her apartment or went back down to Calhoun's place. In the beginning, after he returned from the hospital the first time, there was the desire in Marie to remind her friend that she wasn't married to Calhoun, that she should just get up and walk away, something Marie had seen her do with other men she had grown tired of.

Late one night, Wilamena called and asked her to come down to the man's apartment, for the man's son had had to work that night and she was there alone with him and she did not want to be alone with him. "Sit with me a spell," Wilamena said. Marie did not protest, even though she had not said more than ten words to the man in all the time she knew him. She threw on her bathrobe, picked up her keys and serrated knife and went down to the second floor.

He was propped up in bed, surprisingly alert, and spoke to Marie with an unforced friendliness. She had seen this in other dying people—a kindness and gentleness came over them that was often embarrassing for those around them. Wilamena sat on the side of the bed. Calhoun asked Marie to sit in a chair beside the bed and then he took her hand and held it for the rest of the night. He talked on throughout the night, not always understandable. Wilamena, exhausted, eventually lay across the foot of the bed. Almost everything the man had to say was about a time when he was young and was married for a year or so to a woman in Nicodemus, Kansas, a town where there were only black people. Whether the woman had died or whether he had left her, Marie could not make out. She only knew that the woman and Nicodemus seemed to have marked him for life.

"You should go to Nicodemus," he said at one point, as if the town was only around the corner. "I stumbled into the place by accident. But you should go on purpose. There ain't much to see, but you should go there and spend some time there."

Toward four o'clock that morning, he stopped talking and moments later he went home to his God. Marie continued holding the dead man's hand and she said the Lord's Prayer over and over until it no longer made sense to her. She did not wake Wilamena. Eventually the sun came through the man's venetian blinds, and she heard the croaking of the pigeons congregating on the window ledge. When she finally placed his hand on his chest, the dead man expelled a burst of air that sounded to Marie like a sigh. It occurred to her that she, a complete stranger, was the last thing he had known in the world and that now that he was no longer in the world. All she knew of him was that Nicodemus place and a lovesick woman slept at the foot of his bed. She thought that she was hungry and thirsty, but the more she looked at the dead man and the sleeping woman, the more she realized that what she felt was a sense of loss.

Two days later, the Social Security people sent her a letter, again signed by John Smith, telling her to come to them one week hence. There was nothing in the letter about the slap, no threat to cut off her SSI payments because of what she had done. Indeed, it was the same sort of letter John Smith usually sent. She called the number at the top of the letter, and the woman who handled her case told her that Mr. White would be expecting her on the day and time stated in the letter. Still, she suspected the Social Security people were planning something for her, something at the very least that would be humiliating. And, right until the day before the appointment, she continued calling to confirm that it was okay to come in. Often, the person she spoke to after the switchboard woman and before the woman handling her case was Vernelle. "Social Security Administration. This is Vernelle Wise. May I help you?" And each time Marie heard the receptionist identify herself she wanted to apologize. "I whatn't raised that way," she wanted to tell the woman.

George Carter came the day she got the letter to present her with a cassette machine and copies of the tapes they had made about her life. It took quite some time for him to teach her how to use the machine, and after he was gone, she was certain it took so long because she really did not want to know how to use it. That evening, after her dinner, she steeled herself and put a tape marked "Parents/Early Childhood" in the machine.

> . . . My mother had this idea that everything could be done in Washington, that a human bein' could take all they troubles to Washington and things would be set right. I think that was all wrapped up with her notion of the gov'ment, the Supreme Court and the president and the like. "Up there," she would say, "things can be made right." "Up there" was her only words for Washington. All them other cities had names, but Washington didn't need a name. It was just called "up there." I was real small and didn't know any better, so somehow I got to thinkin' since things were on the perfect side in Washington, that maybe God lived there. God and his people. . . . When I went back home to visit that first time and told my mother all about my livin' in Washington, she fell into such a cry, like maybe I had managed to make it to heaven without dyin'. Thas how people was back in those days. . . .

The next morning she looked for Vernelle Wise's name in the telephone book. And for several evenings she would call the number and hang up before the phone had rung three times. Finally, on a Sunday, two days before the appointment, she let it ring and what may have been a little boy answered. She could tell he was very young because he said hello in a too loud voice, as if he was not used to talking on the telephone.

"Hello," he said. "Hello, who this? Granddaddy, that you? Hello. Hello. I can see you."

Marie heard Vernelle tell him to put down the telephone, then another child, perhaps a girl somewhat older than the boy, came on the line. "Hello. Hello. Who is this?" she said with authority. The boy began to cry, apparently because he did not want the girl to talk if he couldn't. "Don't touch it," the girl said. "Leave it alone." The boy cried louder and only stopped when Vernelle came to the telephone.

"Yes?" Vernelle said. "Yes." Then she went off the line to calm the boy who had begun to cry again. "Loretta," she said, "go get his bottle. . . . Well, look for it. What you got eyes for?"

There seemed to be a second boy, because Vernelle told him to help Loretta look for the bottle. "He always losin' things," Marie heard the second boy say. "You should tie everything to his arms." "Don't tell me what to do," Vernelle said. "Just look for that damn bottle."

"I don't lose noffin'. I don't," the first boy said. "You got snot in your nose."

"Don't say that," Vernelle said before she came back on the line. "I'm sorry," she said to Marie. "Who is this? . . . Don't you dare touch it if you know what's good for you!" she said. "I wanna talk to granddaddy," the first boy said. "Loretta, get me that bottle!"

Marie hung up. She washed her dinner dishes. She called Wilamena because she had not seen her all day, and Wilamena told her that she would be up later. The cassette tapes were on the coffee table beside the machine, and she began picking them up, one by one. She read the labels: Husband No. 1, Working, Husband No. 2, Children, Race Relations, Early D.C. Experiences, Husband No. 3. She had not played another tape since the one about her mother's idea of what Washington was like, but she could still hear the voice, her voice. Without reading its label, she put a tape in the machine.

> . . . I never planned to live in Washington, had no idea I would ever even step one foot in this city. This white family my mother worked for, they had a son married and gone to live in Baltimore. He wanted a maid, somebody to take care of his children. So he wrote to his mother and she asked my mother and my mother asked me about goin' to live in Baltimore. Well, I was young. I guess I wanted to see the world, and Baltimore was as good a place to start as anywhere. This man sent me a train ticket and I went off to Baltimore. Hadn't ever been kissed, hadn't ever been anything, but here I was goin' farther from home than my mother and father put together. . . . Well, sir, the train stopped in Washington, and I thought I heard

469

the conductor say we would be stoppin' a bit there, so I got off. I knew I probably wouldn't see no more than that Union Station, but I wanted to be able to say I'd done that, that I step foot in the capital of the United States. I walked down to the end of the platform and looked around, then I peeked into the station. Then I went in. And when I got back, the train and my suitcase was gone. Everything I had in the world on the way to Baltimore . . .

. . . I couldn't calm myself down enough to listen to when the redcap said another train would be leavin' for Baltimore, I was just that upset. I had a buncha addresses of people we knew all the way from home up to Boston, and I used one precious nickel to call a woman I hadn't seen in years, cause I didn't have the white people in Baltimore number. This woman come and got me, took me to her place. I 'member like it was yesterday that we got on this streetcar marked 13TH AND D NE. The more I rode, the more brighter things got. You ain't lived till you been on a streetcar. The further we went on that streetcar—dead down in the middle of the street—the more I knowed I could never go live in Baltimore. I knowed I could never live in a place that didn't have that streetcar and them clackety clack tracks. . . .

She wrapped the tapes in two plastic bags and put them in the dresser drawer that contained all that was valuable to her: birth and death certificates, silver dollars, life insurance policies, pictures of her husbands and the children they had given each other and the grandchildren those children had given her and the great-grands whose names she had trouble remembering. She set the tapes in a back corner of the drawer, away from the things she needed to get her hands on regularly. She knew that however long she lived, she would not ever again listen to them, for in the end, despite all that was on the tapes, she could not stand the sound of her own voice.

1993

THE LIFE OF THE BODY

by TOBIAS WOLFF

from TRIQUARTERLY

WILEY GOT LONELY one night and drove to a bar in North Beach owned by a guy he used to teach with. He watched a basketball game and afterwards fell into conversation with the woman sitting next to him. She was a veterinarian. Her name was Kathleen. When Wiley said her name he laid on a bit of the Irish and she smiled at him. She had freckles and very green eyes, "Green as the fields of Erin," he told her, and she laughed, holding her head back and deciding—he could tell, he could see it happen—to let things take their course. She was a little drunk. She touched him as she talked, his wrist, his hand, once even his thigh, to drive a point home. Wiley agreed but he didn't hear what she was saying. There was a rushing sound in his ears.

The man Kathleen had come in with, a short, redfaced, bearded man in a safari jacket, held his glass with both hands and pondered it. He sometimes looked over at Kathleen, at her back. Then he looked at his glass again. Wiley wanted to keep everything friendly, so he leaned forward and stared at him until their eyes met, and then he lifted his glass in salute. The man gaped like a fish. He jabbed his finger at Wiley and yelled something unintelligible. Kathleen turned and took his arm. Then the bartender joined them. He was wiping his hands with a towel. He leaned over the bar and spoke to Kathleen and the short man in a soft voice while Wiley looked on encouragingly.

"That's the ticket," Wiley said. "Talk him down."

The short man jerked his arm away from Kathleen. Kathleen looked around at Wiley and said, "You keep your mouth shut."

471

The bartender nodded. "Please be quiet," he said.

"Now just a minute," Wiley said.

The bartender ignored him. He went on talking in that soft voice of his. Wiley couldn't follow everything he said, but he did hear words to the effect that he, Wiley, had been drinking hard all night and that they shouldn't take him too seriously.

"Whoa!" Wiley said. "Just hold on a second. I'm having a quiet conversation with my neighbor here, and all of a sudden Napoleon declares war. Why is that my fault?"

"Sir, I asked you to be quiet."

"You ought to cut him off," the short man said.

"I was about to."

"I don't believe this," Wiley said. "For your information, I happen to be a very old friend of Bob's."

"Mr. Lundgren isn't here tonight."

"I can see that. I have eyes. My point is, if Bob were here. . ." Wiley stopped. The three of them were looking at him as if he were a complete asshole, the little guy so superior he wasn't even mad anymore. Wiley had to admit, he sounded like one—dropping the name of a publican, for Christ's sake. A former algebra teacher. He said, "I have many friends in high places," trying to make a joke of it, but they didn't laugh or even smile, they thought he was serious. "Oh, relax," he said.

"I'm sure Mr. Lundgren will be happy to take care of your tab," the bartender said. "If you want to make a complaint he'll be in tomorrow afternoon."

"You can't be serious. Are you actually throwing me out?"

The bartender considered the question. Then he said, "Right now we're at the request stage."

"But this is ridiculous."

"You're free to leave under your own steam, sir, and I'd be much obliged if you did."

"This is absolutely incredible," Wiley said, more to himself than the bartender, in whose studied courtesy he did not fail to hear the possibility of competent violence. But he was damned if he was going to be hurried. He finished his drink and set the glass down. He slid off his stool, inclined his head toward Kathleen, gravely thanked her for the pleasure of her company. He crossed the room with perfect dignity and stepped outside, taking care that the door should not slam behind him.

472

A cold light rain was falling. Wiley stood under the awning and hopelessly waited for it to stop. From the place across the street he heard a woman laugh loudly; he thought of lipstick-stained teeth, a pink tongue licking off the creamy mustache left by a White Russian. He leaned in that direction, thrusting his head forward as he did when he caught certain smells in the breeze, curry, roasting coffee, baking bread. Wiley raised his jacket collar and pushed off up the hill, toward the garage where he'd left his car. When he reached the corner he stopped. He could not go home now, not like this. He could not allow this absurd picture of himself to survive in Kathleen's mind. It was important that she know the truth about him, and not go through life believing that he was some kind of mouthy lush who got tossed out of bars. Because he wasn't. Nothing like this had ever happened to him before.

He crossed the street and walked back downhill to the other bar. Two women were sitting in the corner with three men. The one Wiley had heard laughing was still at it. Whenever anybody said anything she cracked up. They were all in their fifties, tourists from the look of them, the only customers in the place. Wiley bought a whiskey and carried it to a table by the window where he could keep an eye on the bar he'd just been asked to leave.

Nothing like this had ever happened to him. He was an English teacher in a private high school. He lived alone. He didn't go to bars much and almost never drank whiskey. He liked good wine, knew something about it, but was wary of knowing too much. At night, after he'd prepared his classes, he drank wine and read nineteenth-century novels. He didn't like modern fiction, its narcissism, its moral timidity, its silence in the face of great wrongs. Wiley had started teaching to support himself while he wrote his doctoral thesis on Dickens, and then lost interest in scholarship as he began to sense the power he had over his students. They were still young enough that they had no investment in the lies the world told about itself; he could make a difference in the way they saw things.

Wiley read thick books late into the night and sometimes got only a few hours' sleep, but in nine years he had never missed a day of work; come morning he pushed himself out of bed just in time and drove to school still fumbling with his buttons, stomach empty, coffee sloshing in the cup between his knees.

Wiley didn't like living alone. He wanted to get married, had always assumed he would be married by now, but he'd had bad luck with women. The last one brushed him off after four months. Her name was Monique. She was a French teacher on exchange, a tall jaunty Parisian who humiliated the boys in her class by mimicking their oafish accents, and the girls by rendering them invisible to the boys. She wore dark glasses even when she went to movies. Her full red lips were habitually pursed. Wiley learned they were held thus in readiness not for passion, but scorn, at least where he was concerned. After Monique read *Catcher in the Rye* her dissatisfaction found a home in the word "phony." He never understood why she'd settled on him in the first place. Sometimes he thought it was for his language—he liked to talk, and talked well, and Monique was in the States to polish her English. But her reasons were a mystery; she dropped him cold without ever making them clear.

Wiley had finished two whiskeys and had just bought a third when Kathleen and the little guy came out of the bar. They stopped in the doorway and watched the rain, which was falling harder now. They stood well apart, not speaking, and watched the rain drip off the awning. After a time she looked into her purse, said something to him. He patted his jacket pockets. She rummaged in her purse again and then the two of them ducked their heads and set off up the hill. Wiley stood suddenly, knocking his chair over. He picked it up and left the bar.

He had to walk fast. It was an effort. His feet kept taking him from side to side. He bent forward, compelling them to follow. He reached the corner and shouted, "Kathleen!"

She was on the opposite corner. The man was a few steps ahead of her, leaning into the rain. They both stopped and looked over at Wiley. Wiley walked into the street and came toward them. He said, "I love you, Kathleen." He was surprised to hear himself say this, and then to say, as he stepped up on the curb, "Come home with me." She didn't look the way he remembered her, she looked older and very tired. He barely recognized her. He understood that he had no idea who she was. She put her hand to her mouth. Wiley couldn't tell whether she was shocked or afraid or what. Maybe she was laughing. He smiled foolishly, confused by his own presence here and by what he'd said, not

474

sure what to say next. Then the little guy came past her and Wiley felt a blow on his cheek and his head snapped back, and right after that the wind went out of him in a whoosh and he folded up, clutching his stomach, unable to breathe or speak. There was another blow at the back of his knees and he fell forward onto the sidewalk. He saw a shoe coming at his face and tried to jerk his head away but it caught him just above the eye. He heard Kathleen screaming and the shoe hit him again on the mouth. He rolled away and covered his face with his hands. Kathleen kept screaming, *No Mike No Mike No Mike No.* Wiley could feel himself being kicked on his shoulders and back. It was a dull, faraway pain. It went on for a while, and then it stopped.

He lay where he was, not trusting the silence, afraid that by moving he would make it all start again. Finally he raised himself to his hands and knees. There was broken glass in the street, glittering on the wet asphalt, and to see it at just this angle, so close, so familiar, so perfectly a part of everything that had happened to him, was to feel utterly reduced; and he knew that he would never forget this, being on his knees with broken glass all around. The rain fell softly. He heard himself weeping, and stopped; it was a stagey, dishonest sound. His lower lip throbbed. He licked it; it was swollen, and tasted of salt and leather.

Wiley stood up. He steadied himself against the wall of a building. Two men came toward him, talking excitedly. He was afraid that they would stop to help him, ask him questions. What if they called the police? He had no excuse for his condition, no explanation. Wiley turned his face. The men walked past him as if he wasn't there, or as if he belonged there, in exactly that pose, as part of what they expected a street to look like.

Home. He had to get home. Wiley pushed away from the wall and started walking. He was surprised at how well he walked; his head was clear, his feet steady. He felt exuberant, even exultant, as if he'd gotten away with something. Light and easy. The feeling lasted through most of the drive home, and then it broke; by the time Wiley reached his apartment he was weak and cold, shaken with feverish trembling.

He went straight to the bathroom and turned on the light. His lower lip was split and bleeding, purplish in color, puffed up like a sausage. He had a cut over his left eyebrow and the skin above it was scraped raw all the way to his hairline. His chin was also scraped raw, and flecked with dirt. He could see a bruise beginning on his cheekbone. My God, he thought, looking at himself. He felt great tenderness for the person behind this lurid mask, as if it were not his face at all, but the face of a beaten child. He touched the hurt places. The raw skin clung to his fingertips.

Wiley took a long bath and tried to sleep, but whenever he closed his eyes he felt a malign presence in the room. In spite of the bath he still felt cold. He got up and looked at himself in the mirror again, hoping to find some change for the better. He inspected his face, then brewed a pot of coffee and spent the rest of the night at the kitchen table, staring blindly at a book and finally sleeping, slumped sideways in the chair, chin on his chest.

When the alarm went off Wiley roused himself and got ready for school. He couldn't think of a reason not to go except for embarrassment; given that others would have to cover his classes during their free time, this did not seem a very good reason. But he gave no consideration to what it would mean. When the first students saw him in the hallway and started quizzing him, he had no answers ready. One boy asked if he'd been mugged.

Wiley nodded, thinking that was basically true.

"Must have been a whole shitload of them."

"Well, not that many," Wiley said, and walked on. He went straight to his classroom instead of stopping off in the teachers' lounge, but he hadn't been at his desk five minutes before the principal came in. "Mr. Wiley," he said, "let's have a look at you." He walked up close and peered at Wiley's face. Students were filing in behind him, trying not to stare at Wiley as they took their seats. "What exactly happened?" the principal asked.

"I got mugged."

"Have you seen a doctor?"

"Not yet."

"You should. That's a prize set of bruises you've got there. Very nasty. Call the police?"

"No. I'm still in sort of a daze." Wiley said this in a low voice so the students wouldn't hear him.

Wiley's friend Mac stuck his head in the door. When he saw the principal he nodded coolly. "You O.K.?" he said to Wiley.

"I guess."

"I heard there were eight of them. Is that right, eight?"

"No." Wiley tried to smile but his face wouldn't let him. "Just two," he said. He couldn't admit to one, not with all this damage, but eight sounded like a movie.

"Two's enough," Mac said. "You O.K.?"

The principal said, "Just let me know if you want to go home. Seriously, now, Mr. Wiley—no heroics. I'm touched that you came in at all." He stopped at the door on his way out and turned to the students. "Be warned, ladies and gentlemen. What happened to Mr. Wiley is going to happen to your children. It will be a common occurrence. That's the kind of world they're going to live in if you don't do something to change it." He let his eyes pass slowly around the room the way he did at school assemblies. "The choice is yours," he said.

Mac applauded silently behind him.

After Mac and the principal left two boys got up and pretended to attack each other with kicks and chops, crying *Hai! Hai! Hai!* One of them drove the other to the back of the class, where he crashed to the floor and lay with his arms and legs twitching. Then the bell rang and they both went back to their desks.

This was a senior honors class. The students had been reading "Benito Cereno," one of Wiley's favorite stories, but he had trouble getting a discussion started because of the way they were looking at him. Finally he decided to give a straight lecture. He talked about Melville's exposure of the contradictions in human law, which claims to serve justice while it strengthens the hand of the property owner, even when that property is human. This was one of Wiley's pet subjects, the commodification of humanity. As he warmed to it he forgot the condition of his face and assumed his habitual patrol in front of the class, head bent, hands in his pockets, one eye cocked in a squint. He related this story to the last one they'd read, "Bartleby, the Scrivener," quoting with derisory, operatic exaggeration the well-intentioned narrator who cannot understand the truculence of a human being whom he has tried to turn into a Xerox machine. And this was not the voice of some reactionary fascist beast, Wiley said, jingling his keys and change as he paced the room—this was the voice of modern man; modern, enlightened, liberal man.

He had worked himself into that pitch of indignation where everything seemed clear to him, evil and good and all the sly imitations of good that lay in wait for the unwary pilgrim. At such moments he forgot himself entirely. He became Scott Fitzgerald denouncing the foul dust that floated in Gatsby's wake, Jonathan Swift laying waste to bourgeois complacency by suggesting a crime so obscene it took your breath away, yet was still less obscene than the crimes ordinary people tolerated without a second thought.

And what happened to Bartleby, Wiley said, was only a hint of things to come. "Look at the multinationals!" he said. And then, not for the first time, he described the evolution of business-school theory to its logical conclusion, high-tech factories in the middle of foreign jungles where, behind razor-wire fences guarded by soldiers and dogs, tribesmen who had never seen a flush toilet were made to assemble fax machines and laptop computers. A million Bartlebys, a billion Bartlebys!

Wiley didn't have the documentation on these factories in the jungle, it was something someone had told him, but it made sense and was right in tune with the spirit of late twentieth-century capitalism; it sounded true enough to make him furious whenever he talked about it. He finished his lecture with only a few minutes to go before the bell. He felt very professional. It was no mean feat, getting his ass kicked at two in the morning and giving a dynamite lecture at nine. He asked his students if they had any questions. None of them did, at first. Wiley heard whispers. Then a girl raised her hand, shyly, almost as if she hoped he wouldn't notice. When Wiley called on her she looked at the boy across the aisle, Robbins, and said, "What color were they?"

Wiley did not understand the question. She looked over at Robbins again. Robbins said, "They were black, right?"

"Who?"

"The guys that jumped you."

Wiley felt his throat tighten. He'd always liked this boy and expected him to learn something in here, to think better thoughts than his FBI-agent father who griped to the principal about Wiley's reading list. Wiley leaned against the blackboard. "I don't know," he said.

"Yeah, right," Robbins said.

"I really don't think so," Wiley said. This sounded improbably vague even to him, so he added, "It was dark. I couldn't see them."

478

Robbins gave a great bark of laughter. Some of the other students laughed too, and then one of them hit a wild note and it sent everyone into a kind of fit. "Quiet!" Wiley said, but they kept laughing. They were beyond his reach, all he could do was stand there and wait for them to stop. Wiley had three black students in this class, two girls and a boy. They stared at their desks in exactly the same way, as if by agreement, though they were sitting in different parts of the room. At the beginning of the year they'd always sat together, but now they drifted from place to place like everyone else. They seemed to feel at home in his class. And that was what he wanted, he wanted this room to be a sanctuary, a place the rest of the world should be like. There was no other reason for him to be here.

The bell rang. Wiley sat down and rustled through some papers as the students, suddenly and strangely quiet, walked past his desk. Then he went to the office and told the principal he was going home after all. He was feeling terrible, he said.

He slept for a few hours. After he got up he looked through the veterinarians' listings in the yellow pages and found a Dr. Kathleen Newman on the staff of a clinic specializing in surgery on exotic pets. He called the clinic and asked for Dr. Newman. The man who answered said she was in a meeting, asked if it was an emergency.

"I'm afraid so," Wiley said. "It is sort of an emergency. Tell her," he said, "that Mr. Melville's cetacean has distemper."

Wiley spelled out cetacean for him.

And then a woman's voice was on the line. "Who is this, please?" It was her. But sharp, no fooling around. Wiley couldn't answer, he'd expected her to pick up his joke and now he didn't know how to begin. "Hello? Hello? Damn," she said, and hung up.

Wiley turned to the white pages. There was a Dr. K. P. Newman on Filbert Street. He wrote down the number and address.

Mac's wife Alice stopped by that afternoon with bread and salad. She had been a student in Wiley's honors class, and one of his favorites, a pale, slow-moving, thoughtful girl he would never have suspected of carrying on with a teacher, which showed how much he knew; she and Mac had been going strong ever since her junior year. They got married right after she graduated.

There was a scandal, and Mac almost lost his job, but somehow it never came to that. Wiley found the whole thing very confusing. He disapproved and was jealous; he felt as if Mac had made a fool of him somehow. But six years had passed since then.

Alice stopped inside the door and looked at Wiley's face. He saw that she was shocked to the point of tears.

"It'll mend," he told her.

"But why would anyone do that to you?"

"These things happen," he said.

"Well, they shouldn't."

She sent him back to the living room. Wiley lay on the couch and watched her through the kitchen doorway while she set the table and made lunch. He was happy having her to himself in his apartment, it was a wish of his. Alice didn't know he felt that way. When they went to bars she sat beside him and leaned her head on his shoulder. She took sips from his drinks. She liked to dance, and when she danced with Wiley she moved right up close, talking all the while about everyday things that somehow made their closeness respectable. At the end of a night out, when Mac and Alice drove Wiley home and came inside to call their sitter and drink a glass of wine, and then another, and Wiley began to read to them some high-minded passage from whatever novel he was caught up in, she would stretch out on the couch and rest her head in Wiley's lap while Mac looked on benignly from the easy chair. Wiley knew that he was supposed to feel honored by all this faith, but he resented it. Faith had become an imposition. It made light of his capacity for desire. Still, he put up with it because he didn't know what else to do.

Now Alice was slicing tomatoes at his kitchen counter. She had a flat-footed way of standing. Her hair was gathered in a bun, but loose strands of it hung in her face; she blew them away as she worked. She had gained weight over the years. She had gained too much weight, but Wiley liked the little tuck of flesh under her chin, and the plumpness of her hands.

She called him to the table. She was quiet and when she looked at him she looked quickly down again. Wiley did not think it was because of his banged-up face, but because they had never been alone before. In all her playfulness with him there was an element of performance, and now she didn't have Mac here to give it irony and keep it safe.

480

Finally she said, "Do you want some wine with this?"

"No. Thanks."

"Sure?"

He nodded.

She pointed her fork at the empty bottles lined against the wall. "Did you drink all those?"

"Over a period of time."

"Oh, great. I'm glad you didn't drink them all at once. Like what period of time are we talking about?"

Wiley thought about it. "I don't know. I don't keep track of every drink."

"That's the trouble with living alone," she said, as if she knew.

"I guess."

"So how come you didn't marry Monique, anyway?" She gave him a quick sidelong look.

"Monique? Come on. She would have laughed me out of town if I'd even mentioned the subject."

"I thought she was nuts about you."

He shook his head.

"Well, I sure thought she was."

"She wasn't."

"O.K., then, what about Lynn?"

"That was crazy, that whole thing with Lynn. I don't even want to talk about Lynn."

"She was pretty spoiled."

"It wasn't her fault. It just got crazy."

"I didn't like her. She was so sarcastic. I was glad when you split up." Alice bit into a piece of bread. "So who are you seeing now? Some married woman, I bet."

"Why would you think that?"

"We haven't met anyone since Monique. So. You must have somebody under wraps. The Dark Lady."

"I wish you wouldn't try to act sophisticated."

She colored but said nothing.

"Do you really think I'm conducting some great love affair?"

"I figured you must have somebody." She sounded bored. She was studying his face. "Boy, those guys really did a job on you, didn't they?"

Wiley moved his plate to one side. "There was just one," he said. "Short fellow. No bigger than a minute."

481

"Oh. Mac told me two. 'Two of our dusky brethren,' was what he said. Where did he get that stuff?"

"From me," Wiley said.

And then, because he trusted her and felt the need, he began to tell her what had really happened to him the night before. Alice listened without any disgust or pity that he could see. She seemed purely interested. Now and then she laughed, because in talking about it Wiley could not help but make his little disaster into a story, and telling stories, even those about loneliness and humiliation, naturally brought out the hambone and wag in him. He could see she was having a good time listening to him, that this was something different for her, and not what she'd expected when Mac asked her to look in on him. And she was hearing some straight talk. She didn't get that at home. Mac was good-hearted, but he was also a tomcat and a liar.

Wiley's way of telling stories about himself was to tell them as if they'd happened to someone else. And from that distance he could see that there was something to be laughed at in the spectacle of a man who energetically professed the examined life, the life of the spirit and the mind, getting drunk and brawling over strange women. Well, the body had a mind of its own. He told it like that, like his body had abducted him for its own low purposes, like he'd been lashed to the back of a foaming runaway horse hell-bent on dragging him through every degradation.

But it was not on the whole a funny story. When he told Alice what went on in his class that morning she shook her head and looked down at the table.

"I was speechless," he said. "I couldn't say a thing. We do *Native Son*, we do *Invisible Man*, I get them really talking, really thinking about all this stuff, and then I start a race riot in my own classroom."

"Maybe you should tell them the truth."

"Are you serious?"

"They'd respect you for it."

"Hah!"

"Well, they should."

"Come on, Alice."

"Some of them would. And they'd be the right ones."

Wiley shook his head. "It would get all over school. I'd get fired."

"That's true," Alice said. She rested her cheek on her hand. "Still."

"Still what?" When she didn't answer, he said, "All right, let's say I don't care about getting fired. I do, but let's just hypothetically say I go in there tomorrow and tell them everything, the works. You know what they'll think? They'll think I'm making it up—the second story, not the first. You know, out of bleeding-heart sentimentality, to make the black kids feel better. But what'll really happen, they'll end up feeling worse. Condescended to. Insulted. They'll think I'm lying to protect them, as if they were guilty. Everyone will think I'm lying."

Wiley could see her hesitate. Then she said, "But you won't be lying. You'll be telling the truth."

"Yes, but no one will know it!"

"You will. You will know it."

"Look. Alice." Wiley was angry now and impatient. He waited, and then spoke so that his anger would not show. He said, "I feel terrible. I can't even count all the things I've done wrong today. But I did them. They're done. If I try to undo them I'm going to make them worse. Not only for me, for those kids." This seemed logical to Wiley, and well and reasonably said.

"Maybe so." She was turning one of her rings nervously. She looked over at him and said, "Maybe I'm being simplistic, but I just don't see where telling the truth can be wrong. I always thought that's what you were there for."

Wiley had other arguments to make. That he was a teacher, and could not afford to gamble with his moral authority. That when the truth did more harm than a lie, you had to give the lie its due. That if other people had to suffer just so you could have a clean conscience you should accept your fallen condition and get on with it. They were good arguments, the very oil of adult life, but he said nothing. He was no fool, he knew what her answers would be, because after all they were his answers too. He simply couldn't act on them.

They sat there unhappily and then Alice got up and cleared the table. Wiley followed her to the kitchen. He stood in the doorway and watched her rinse the plates and stack them in the sink. When she finished she stayed leaning against the counter with her back to him. "Alice," he said. "Are you listening?"

She nodded.

"I shouldn't have dropped all this stuff on you. It's pretty confusing."

"I'm not confused."

He didn't answer.

"I have to go," she said.

He walked her to the door.

"I won't say anything to Mac," she told him.

"I know that. I trust you."

"What, trust me to keep secrets from my husband?" She laughed, not pleasantly. "Don't worry," she said. "I know how he is."

Wiley corrected essays the rest of the afternoon. He broke for dinner and then finished them off. It was a good batch, the best he'd had all year. They were on "Bartleby, the Scrivener." One of his students, a girl, had compared the situation to a marriage, with the narrator as the husband and Bartleby as the wife: "He looks at Bartleby the way men look at women, as if Bartleby has no other purpose on earth than to be of use to him." She bent the story around to fit her argument, but Wiley didn't mind. The essay was fresh and passionate. This particular girl wouldn't have thought to take such a view at the beginning of the year. Wiley was moved, and proud of her.

He recorded the grades in his book and then called the Filbert Street number of Dr. K. P. Newman. When she answered, he said, "It's me, Kathleen. From last night," he added.

"You," she said. "Where did you get my number?"

"Out of the phone book. I just wanted to set things straight."

"You called me before, didn't you?" she said. "You called me at work."

"Yes."

"I knew it. You didn't even say anything. You didn't even have the balls to give your own name."

"That was a joke," Wiley said.

"You're crazy. You call me again and I'll have the police on you."

"Wait, Kathleen. I need to see you."

"I don't need to see you."

"Wait. Please. Listen, Kathleen. I'm not like that, not like I seemed last night. Really, Kathleen. Last night was a series of misunderstandings. I just want to stop by for a minute or two, straighten everything out."

"What, you have my *address?*"

"It's in the book."

"Christ! I can't believe this! Don't even think about coming here. Mike's here," she said. "This time I won't stop him. I mean it."

"You aren't married to Mike."

"Who said?"

"You would have said if you were."

"So? What difference does that make?"

"It makes a difference."

"You're crazy."

"All I need is a few minutes to talk things over."

"I'm hanging up."

"Just a few minutes, Kathleen. That's all I'm asking. Then I'll leave, if you still want me to."

"Mike's here," she said. She was silent. Then, just before she hung up, she said, "Don't you ever call me at work again."

Wiley liked the sound of that; it meant she assumed a future for them.

Before he went out he looked himself over in the mirror. He wasn't pretty. But he could still talk. All he had to do was get her to listen. He'd keep saying her name. Kathleen. Say it in that moony broguish way she liked. Said that way, almost sung, her name had power over her; he had seen it last night, the willing girl blooming on the face of the woman, the girl ready for love. He would hit that note, and once he got her listening there was no telling what might happen, because all he really needed was words, and of words, Wiley knew, there was no end.

1993

485

TELL ME EVERYTHING

by LEONARD MICHAELS

from THE THREEPENNY REVIEW

CLAUDE RUE had a wide face with yellow-green eyes and a long aristocratic nose. The mouth was a line, pointed in the center, lifted slightly at the ends, curving in a faint smile, almost cruelly sensual. He dragged his right foot like a stone, and used a cane, digging it into the floor as he walked. His dark blue suit, cut in the French style, arm holes up near the neck, made him look small in the shoulder, and made his head look too big. I liked nothing about the man that I could see.

"What a face," I whispered to Margaret, "Who would take anything he says seriously?"

She said, "Who wouldn't? Gorgeous. Just gorgeous. And the way he dresses. Such style."

After that, I didn't say much. I hadn't really wanted to go to the lecture in the first place.

Every seat in the auditorium was taken long before Rue appeared on stage. People must have come in from San Francisco, Oakland, Marin, and beyond. There were even sad creatures from the Berkeley streets, some loonies among them, in filthy clothes, open sores on their faces like badges. I supposed few in the audience knew that Claude Rue was a professor of Chinese history who taught at the Sorbonne, but everyone knew he'd written *The Mists of Shanghai,* a thousand-page, best-selling novel.

On stage, Rue looked lonely and baffled. Did all these people actually care to hear his lecture on the loss of classical Chinese?

He glanced about, as if there had been a mistake and he was searching for his replacement, the star of the show, the real Claude Rue. I approved of his modesty, and I might have enjoyed listening to him. But then, as if seized by an irrational impulse, Rue lifted the pages of his lectures for all to witness, and ripped them in half. "I will speak from my heart," he said.

The crowd gasped. I groaned. Margaret leaned toward him, straining, as if to pick up his odor. She squeezed my hand and checked my eyes to see whether I understood her feelings. She needed a reference point, a consciousness aside from her own to slow the rush of her being toward Rue.

"You're terrible," I said.

"Don't spoil my fantasy. Be quiet, O.K.?"

She then flattened her thigh against mine, holding me there while she joined him in her feelings, on stage, fifty feet away. Rue began his speech without pages or notes. The crowd grew still. Many who couldn't find seats stood in the aisles, some with bowed heads, staring at the floor as if they'd been beaten on the shoulders into penitential silence. For me it was also penitential. I work nights. I didn't like wasting a free evening in a crowded lecture hall when I could have been alone with Margaret.

I showed up at her loft an hour before the lecture. She said to her face in the bathroom mirror, "I can hardly wait to see the man. How do I look?"

"Chinese." I put the lid down on the toilet seat, sat on it.

"Answer me. Do I look all right, Herman?"

"You know what the ancient Greeks said about perfume?"

"I'm about to find out."

"To smell sweet is to stink."

"I use very little perfume. There's a reception afterwards, a party. It's in honor of the novel. A thousand pages and I could have kept reading it for another week. I didn't want it to end. I'll tell you the story later."

"Maybe I'll read it, too," I said, trying not to sound the way I felt. "But why must you see what the man looks like? I couldn't care less."

"You won't go with me?" She turned from the mirror, as if, at last, I'd provoked her into full attention.

"I'm not saying I won't."

"What are you saying?"

"Nothing. I asked a question, that's all. It isn't important. Forget it."

"Don't slither. You have another plan for the evening? You'd rather be somewhere else?"

"I have no other plan. I'm asking why should anyone care what an author looks like."

"I'm interested. I have been for months."

"Why?"

"Why not? He made me feel something. His book was an experience. Everybody wants to see him. Besides, my sister met him in Beijing. She knows him. Didn't I read you her letter?"

"I still don't see why. . ."

"Herman, what do you want me to say? I'm interested, I'm curious. I'm going to his lecture. If you don't want to go, don't go."

That is, leave the bathroom. Shut the door. Get out of sight.

Margaret can be too abrupt, too decisive. It's her business style carried into personal life. She buys buildings, has them fixed up, then rents or sells, and buys again. She has supported herself this way since her divorce from Sloan Pierson, professor of linguistics. He told her about Claude Rue's lecture, invited her to the reception afterwards, and put my name on the guest list. Their divorce, compared to some, wasn't bad. No lingering bitterness. They have remained connected—not quite friends— through small courtesies, like the invitation; also, of course, through their daughter, Gracie, ten years old. She lives with Sloan except when Margaret wants her, which is often. Margaret's business won't allow a strict schedule of visits. She has sometimes appeared without notice. "I need her," she says. Gracie scampers to her room, collects school books for the next day, and packs a duffle bag with clothes and woolly animals.

Sloan sighs, shakes his head. "Really, Margaret. Gracie has needs, too. She needs a predictable, daily life." Margaret says, "I'll phone you later. We'll discuss our needs."

She comes out of the house with Gracie. Sloan shouts, "Wait. Gracie's pills."

There's always one more word, one more thing to collect. "Goodbye. Wait." I wait. We all wait. Margaret and Gracie go back inside. I wait just outside. I am uncomfortable inside the house, around Sloan. He's friendly, but I know too much about him. I can't help thinking things, making judgments, and then I feel guilty. He's a fussy type, does everything right. If he'd only fight Margaret, not be so good, so right. Sloan could make trouble about Margaret's unscheduled appearances, even go to court, but he thinks, if Margaret doesn't have her way, Gracie will have no mother. Above all things, Sloan fears chaos. Gracie senses her daddy's fear, shares it. Margaret would die for Gracie, but it's a difficult love, measured by intensities. Would Margaret remember, in such love, about the pills?

Sloan finds the pills, brings them to the foyer, hands them to Margaret. There. He did another right thing. She and Gracie leave the house. We start down the path to the sidewalk. Gracie hands me her books and duffle bag, gives me a kiss, and says, "Hi, Herman German. I have an ear infection. I have to take pills four times a day." She's instructing Margaret, indirectly.

Margaret glares at me to show that she's angry. Her ten-year-old giving her instructions. I pretend not to understand. Gracie is a little version of Margaret, not much like Sloan. Chinese chemistry is dominant. Sloan thinks Gracie is lucky. "That's what I call a face," he says. He thinks he looks like his name—much too white.

I say, "Hi, Gracie Spacey." We get into my Volvo. I drive us away.

Gracie sits in back. Margaret, sitting beside me, stares straight ahead, silent, still pissed, but after awhile she turns, looks at Gracie. Gracie reads her mind, gives her a hug. Margaret feels better, everyone feels better.

While Margaret's houses are being fixed up, she lives in one, part of which becomes her studio where she does her painting. Years ago, at the university, studying with the wonderful painters Joan Brown and Elmer Bischoff, Margaret never discovered a serious commitment in herself. Later, when she married and had Gracie, and her time was limited, seriousness arrived. Then came the divorce, the real estate business, and she had even less time. She paints whenever she can, and she reads fifty or sixty novels a year; also what she calls "philosophy," which is religious literature. Her imagery in paintings comes from mythic, visionary works. From the *Kumulipo*, the Hawaiian cosmological chant, she took visions of land and sea, where creatures of the different realms are mysteriously related. Margaret doesn't own a television set or go to movies. She denies herself common entertainment for the same reason that Rilke refused to be analyzed by Freud. "I don't want my soul diluted," she says.

Sometimes, I sit with her in her loft in Emeryville—in a four-story brick building, her latest purchase—while she paints. "Are you bored?" she asks.

I'm never bored. I like being with her. I like the painting odors, the drag and scratch of brush against canvas. She applies color, I feel it in my eyes. Tingling starts along my forearms, hairs lift and stiffen. We don't talk. Sometimes not a word for hours, yet the time lacks nothing.

I say, "Let's get married."

She says, "We are married."

Another hour goes by.

She asks, "Is that a painting?"

I make a sound to suggest it is.

"Is it good?"

She knows.

When one of her paintings, hanging in a corner of a New York gallery owned by a friend, sold—without a formal show, and without reviews—I became upset. She'll soon be famous, I thought.

"I'll lose you," I said.

She gave me nine paintings, all she had in the loft. "Take this one, this one, this one. . ."

"Why?"

"Take them, take them."

She wanted to prove, maybe, that our friendship is inviolable; she had no ambition to succeed, only to be good. I took the paintings grudgingly, as if I were doing her a favor. In fact, that's how I felt. I was doing her a favor. But I wanted the paintings. They were compensations for her future disappearance from my life. We're best friends, very close. I have no vocation. She owed me the paintings.

I quit graduate school twenty years ago, and began waiting table at Gemma's, a San Francisco restaurant. From year to year, I expected to find other work or to write professionally. My one book, *Local Greens*, which is about salads, was published by a small press in San Francisco. Not a best seller, but it made money. Margaret told me to invest in a condominium and she found one for me, the top floor of a brown shingle house, architect unknown, in the Berkeley hills. I'd been living in Oakland, in a one-room apartment on Harrison Street, near the freeway. I have a sedentary nature. I'd never have moved out. Never really have known, if not for Margaret, that I could have a nicer place, be happier. "I'm happy," I said. "This place is fine." She said my room was squalid. She said the street was noisy and dangerous. She insisted that I talk to a realtor or check the newspapers for another place, exert myself, do something. Suddenly, it seemed, I had two bedrooms, living room, new kitchen, hardwood floors, a deck, a bay view, monthly payments—property.

It didn't seem. I actually lived in a new place, nicer than anything I'd ever known.

My partner, so to speak, lives downstairs. Eighty-year-old Belinda Forster. She gardens once a week by instructing Pilar, a silent Mexican woman who lives with Belinda, where to put the different new plants, where to prune the apple trees. Belinda also lunches with a church group, reviews her will, smokes cigarettes. She told me, if I find her unconscious in the garden, or in the driveway, or wherever, to do nothing to revive her. She looks not very shrunken, not extremely frail. Her eyes are beautifully clear. Her skin is without the soft, puffy surface you often see in old people.

Belinda's husband, a professor of plant pathology, died about fifteen years ago, shortly after his retirement. Belinda talks about his work, their travels in Asia, and his mother. Not a word about herself. She might consider that impolite, or boastful, claiming she too had a life, or a self. She has qualities of reserve, much out of style these days, which I admire greatly, but I become awkward talking to her. I don't quite feel that I say what I mean. Does she intend this effect? Is she protecting herself against the assertions, the assault, of younger energies?

Upstairs, from the deck of my apartment, I see sailboats tilted in the wind. Oil tankers go sliding slowly by Alcatraz Island.

491

Hovering in the fuchsias, I see hummingbirds. Squirrels fly through the black, light-streaked canopies of Monterey pines. If my temperament were religious, I'd believe there had to be a cause, a divinity in the fantastic theater of clouds above San Francisco Bay.

Rue spoke with urgency, his head and upper body lifting and settling to the rhythm of his sentences. His straight, blond hair, combed straight back, fell toward his eyes. He swept it aside. It fell. He swept it aside, a bravely feminine gesture, vain, distracting. I sighed.

Margaret pinched my elbow. "I want to hear him, not your opinions."

"I only sighed."

"That's an opinion."

I sat quietly. Rue carried on. His subject was the loss to the Chinese people, and to the world, of the classical Chinese language. "I am saying that, after the revolution, the ancients, the great Chinese dead, were torn from their graves. I am saying they have been murdered word by word. And this in the name of nationhood, and a social justice which annihilates language, as well as justice, and anything the world has known as social."

End.

The image of ancient corpses, torn from their graves and murdered, aroused loonies in the audience. They whistled and cried out. Others applauded for a whole minute. Rue had said nothing subversive of America. Even so, Berkeley adored him. Really because of the novel, not the lecture. On the way to the lecture, Margaret talked about the novel, giving me the whole story, not merely the gist, as if to defend it against my negative opinion. She was also apologizing, I think, by talking so much, for having been angry and abrupt earlier. Couldn't just say "I'm sorry." Not Margaret. I drove and said nothing, still slightly injured, but soothed by her voice, giving me the story; giving a good deal, really, more than the story.

She said *The Mists of Shanghai* takes place in nineteenth-century China during the opium wars, when high-quality opium, harvested from British poppy fields in India, was thrust upon the Chinese people. "Isn't that interesting?" she said. "A novel should teach you something. I learned that the production, transportation, and distribution of opium, just as today, was controlled by western military and intelligence agencies, there were black slaves in Macao, and eunuchs were very powerful figures in government."

The central story of the novel, said Margaret, which is told by an evil eunuch named Jujuzi, who is an addict and a dealer, is about two lovers—a woman named Neiping and a man named Goo. First we hear about Neiping's childhood. She is the youngest in a large, very poor family. Her parents sell her to an elegant brothel in Shanghai, where the madam buys little girls, selected for brains and beauty. She tells Neiping that she will be taught to read, and, eventually, she will participate in conversation with patrons. Though only eight years old, Neiping has strong character, learns quickly and becomes psychologically mature. One day a new girl arrives and refuses to talk to anyone. She cries quietly to herself at night. Neiping listens to her crying and she begins to feel sorry for herself. But she refuses to cry. She leaves her bed and crawls into bed with the crying girl who then grows quiet. Neiping hugs her and says, "I am Neiping. What's your name?"

She says, "Dulu."

They talk for hours until they both fall asleep. She and Neiping become dear friends.

It happens that a man named Kang, a longtime patron of the brothel, arrives one evening. He is a Shanghai businessman, dealing in Mexican silver. He also owns an ironworks, and has initiated a lucrative trade in persons, sending laborers to a hellish life in the cane fields of Pacific islands and Cuba. Kang confesses to the madam that he is very unhappy. He can't find anyone to replace his recently deceased wife as his opponent in the ancient game of wei-ch'i. The madam tells Kang not to be unhappy. She has purchased a clever girl who will make a good replacement. Kang can come to the brothel and play wei-ch'i. She brings little Neiping into the room, sits her at a table with Kang, a playing board between them. Kang has a blind eye that looks smokey and gray. He is unashamedly flatulent, and he is garishly tattooed. All in all, rather a monster. Pretty little Neiping is terrified. She nods yes, yes, yes as he tells her the rules of the game, and he explains how one surrounds the opponent's pieces and holds territory on the board. When he asks if she has understood everything, she nods yes again. He says to Neiping, "If you lose, I will eat you the way a snake eats a monkey."

Margaret said, "This is supposed to be a little joke, see? But, since Kang looks sort of like a snake, it's frightening."

Kang takes the black stones and makes the first move. Neiping, in a trance of fear, recalls his explanation of the rules, then places a white stone on the board far from his black stone. They play until Kang becomes sleepy. He goes home. The game resumes the next night and the next. In the end, Kang counts the captured stones, white and black. It appears that Neiping has captured more than he. The madam says, "Let me count them." It also appears Neiping controls more territory than Kang. The madam counts, then looks almost frightened. She twitters apologies, and she coos, begging Kang to forgive Neiping for taking advantage of his kindness, his willingness to let Neiping seem to have done well in the first game. Kang says, "This is how it was with my wife. Sometimes she seemed to win. I will buy this girl."

The madam had been saving Neiping for a courtier, highly placed, close to the emperor, but Kang is a powerful man. She doesn't dare reject the sale. "The potential value of Neiping is immeasurable," she says. Kang says Neiping will cost a great deal before she returns a profit. "The price I am willing to pay is exceptionally good."

The madam says, "In silver?"

Kang says, "Mexican coins."

She bows to Kang, then tells Neiping to say goodbye to the other girls.

Margaret said, "I'll never forget how the madam bows to Kang."

Neiping and Dulu embrace. Dulu cries. Neiping says they will meet again someday. Neiping returns to Kang. He takes her hand. The monster and Neiping walk through the nighttime streets of Shanghai to Kang's house.

For the next seven years, Neiping plays wei-ch'i with Kang. He has her educated by monks, and she is taught to play musical instruments by the evil eunuch, Jujuzi, the one who is telling the story. Kang gives Neiping privileges of a daughter. She learns how he runs his businesses. He discusses problems with her. "If somebody were in my position how might such a person reflect on the matters I have described?" While they talk, Kang asks Neiping to comb his hair. He never touches her. His manner is formal and gentle. He gives everything. Neiping asks for nothing. Kang is a happy monster, but then Neiping falls in love with Goo, the son of a business associate of Kang. Kang discovers this love and he threatens to undo Neiping, sell her back to the brothel, or send her to work in the cane fields at the end of the world. Neiping flees Kang's house that night with Goo. Kang then wanders the streets of Shanghai in a stupor of misery, looking for Neiping.

Years pass. Unable to find a way to live, Goo and Neiping fall in with a guerilla triad. Neiping becomes its leader. Inspired by Neiping, who'd become expert in metals while living with Kang, the triad undertakes to study British war technology. Neiping says they can produce cannons, which could be used against opium merchants. The emperor will be pleased. In fact, he will someday have tons of opium seized and destroyed. But there is no way to approach the emperor until Neiping learns that Dulu, her dear friend in the brothel, is now the emperor's consort. Neiping goes to Dulu.

"The recognition scene," said Margaret, "is heartbreaking. Dulu has become an icy woman who moves slowly beneath layers of silk. But she remembers herself as the little girl who once cried in the arms of Neiping. She and Neiping are now about twenty-three."

Through Dulu's help, Neiping gains the emperor's support. This enrages Jujuzi, the evil eunuch. Opium trade is in his interest, since he is an addict and a dealer. Everything is threatened by Neiping's cannons which are superior to the originals, but the triad's military strategy is betrayed by Jujuzi. Neiping and Goo are captured by British sailors and jailed.

Margaret said, "Guess what happens next. Kang appears. He has vanished for three hundred pages, but he's back in the action."

The British allow Kang to speak to Neiping. He offers to buy her freedom. Neiping says he must also buy Goo's freedom. Kang says she has no right to ask him to buy her lover's freedom. Neiping accepts Kang's offer, and she is freed from jail. She then goes to Dulu and appeals for the emperor's help in freeing Goo. Jujuzi, frustrated by Neiping's escape, demands justice for Goo. The British, who are in debt to Jujuzi, look the other way while he tortures Goo to death.

The emperor, who has heard Neiping's appeal through Dulu, asks to see Neiping. The emperor knows Goo is dead. He was told by Jujuzi. But the emperor is moved by Neiping's beauty and her poignant concern to save the already dead Goo. The emperor tells her that he will save him, but she must forget Goo. Then he says that Neiping, like Dulu, will be his consort. In the final chapter, Neiping is heavy with the emperor's child. She and Dulu wander in the palace gardens. Jujuzi watches the lovely consorts passing amid flowers, and he remembers in slow, microscopic detail the execution of Neiping's lover.

"What a story."

"I left most of it out."

"Is that so?"

"You think it's boring."

"No."

"You do."

"Don't tell me what I think. That's annoying."

"Do you think it's boring?"

"Yes, but how can I know unless I read the book?"

"Well, I liked it a lot. The last chapter is horribly dazzling and so beautiful. Jujuzi watches Neiping and Dulu stroll in the garden, and he remembers Goo in chains, bleeding from the hundred knives Jujuzi stuck in him. To Jujuzi, everything is aesthetic, knives, consorts, even feelings. He has no balls so he collects feelings. You see? Like jewels in a box."

Lights went up in the midst of the applause. Margaret said, "Aren't you glad you came?" Claude Rue bowed. Waves of praise poured onto his head. I applauded, too, a concession to the community. Besides, Margaret loved the lecture. She watched me from the corners of her eyes, suspicious of my enthusiasm. I nodded, as if to say yes, yes. Mainly, I needed to go to the toilet, but I didn't want to do anything that might look like a negative comment on the lecture. I'd go when we arrived at the reception for Rue. This decision was fateful. At the reception, in the Faculty Club, I carried a glass of white wine from the bar to Margaret,

496

then went to the men's room. I stood beside a man who had leaned his cane against the urinal. He patted his straight blond hair with one hand, holding his cock with the other, shaking it. The man was, I suddenly realized, himself, Claude Rue. Surprised into speech, I said I loved his lecture. He said, "You work here?"

Things now seemed to be happening quickly, making thought impossible. I was unable to answer. Exactly what was Rue asking—was I a professor? a men's room attendant? a toilet cruiser? Not waiting for my answer, he said he'd been promised a certain figure for the lecture. A check, made out to him from the regents of the university had been delivered to his hotel room. The check shocked him. He'd almost cancelled the lecture. He was still distressed, unable to contain himself. He'd hurried to the men's room, after the lecture, to look at his check again. The figure was less than promised. I was the first to hear about it. Me. A stranger. He was hysterical, maybe, but I felt very privileged. Money talk is personal, especially in a toilet. "You follow me?" he said.

"Yes. You were promised a certain figure. They gave you a check. It was delivered to your hotel room."

"Precisely. But the figure inscribed on the check is less than promised."

"Somebody made a mistake."

"No mistake. Taxes have been deducted. But I came from Paris with a certain understanding. I was to be paid a certain figure. I have the letter of agreement, and the contract." His green stare, fraught with helpless reproach, held me as he zipped up. He felt that he'd been cheated. He dragged to a sink. His cane, lacquered mahogany, with a black, iron ferrule, clacked the tile floor. He washed his hands. Water raged in the sink.

"It's a mistake, and it can be easily corrected," I said, speaking to his face in the mirror above the sink. "Don't worry, Mr. Rue. You'll get every penny they promised."

"Will you speak to somebody?" he said, taking his cane. "I'm very upset."

"Count on it, Mr. Rue."

"But will you speak to somebody about this matter?"

"Before the evening is over, I'll have their attention."

"But will you speak to a person?"

497

"Definitely."

I could see, standing close to him, that his teeth were heavily stained by cigarette smoke. They looked rotten. I asked if I might introduce him to a friend of mine. Margaret would get a kick out of meeting Claude Rue, I figured, but I mainly wanted her to see his teeth. He seemed thrown off balance, reluctant to meet someone described as a friend. "My time is heavily scheduled," he muttered; but, since he'd just asked me for a favor, he shrugged, shouldering obligation. I led him to Margaret. Rue's green eyes gained brightness. Margaret quickened within, but offered a mere "Hello," no more, not even the wisp of a smile. She didn't say she loved his lecture. Was she overwhelmed, having Claude Rue thrust at her like this? The silence was difficult for me, if not for them. Lacking anything else to say, I started to tell Margaret about Rue's problem with the university check. "It wasn't the promised amount." Rue cut me off:

"Money is offal. Not to be discussed."

His voice was unnaturally high, operatic and crowing at once. He told Margaret, speaking to her eyes—as if I'd ceased to exist—that he would spend the next three days in Berkeley. He was expected at lunches, cocktail parties, and dinner parties. He'd been invited to conduct a seminar, and to address a small gathering at the Asian Art museum.

"But my lecture is over. I have fulfilled my contract. I owe nothing to anybody."

Margaret said, "No point, then, cheapening yourself, is there?"

"I will cancel every engagement."

"How convenient," she said, hesitated, then gambled, adding, "for us."

Her voice was flat and black as an ice slick on asphalt, but I could hear, beneath the surface, a faint trembling. I prayed that she would look at Rue's teeth, which were practically biting her face. She seemed not to notice.

"Do you drive a car?"

She said, "Yes," holding her hand out to the side, toward me, blindly. I slipped the keys to my Volvo into her palm. Tomorrow, I'd ride to her place on my bike and retrieve the car. Margaret wouldn't remember that she'd taken it. She and Rue walked away, but I felt it was I who grew smaller in the gathering dis-

498

tance. Margaret glanced back at me to say goodbye. Rue, staring at Margaret, lost peripheral vision, thus annihilating me. I might have felt insulted, but he'd been seized by hormonal ferocity, and was focused on a woman. I'd have treated him similarly.

Months earlier, I'd heard about Rue from Margaret. She'd heard about him from her sister May who had a PhD in library science from Berkeley, and worked at the university library in Beijing. In a letter to Margaret, May said she'd met Professor Claude Rue, the linguistic historian. He was known in academic circles, but not yet an international celebrity. Rue was in Beijing completing his research for *The Mists of Shanghai*. May said, in her letter, that Rue was a "womanizer." He had bastard children in France and Tahiti. She didn't find him attractive, but other women might. "If you said Claude Rue is charming or has pretty green eyes, I wouldn't disagree, but, as I write to you, I have trouble remembering what he looks like."

Margaret said the word "womanizer" tells more about May than Rue. "She's jealous. She thinks Rue is fucking every woman except her."

"She says she doesn't find him attractive, and she knows what he looks like, what he sounds like, smells like, feels like. May has no respect for personal space. She touches people when she talks to them. She's a shark, with taste sensors in her skin. When May takes your hand, or brushes up against you, she's tasting you. Nobody but sharks and cannibals can do that. She shakes somebody's hand, then tells me, 'Needs salt and a little curry.' "

"All right. Maybe 'womanizer' says something about May, but the word has a meaning. Regardless of May, 'womanizer' means something."

"What?"

"You kidding?"

"Tell me. What does it mean?"

"What do you think? It means a man who sits on the side of the bed at two in the morning, putting on his shoes."

"What do you call women who do that? Don't patronize me, Herman. Don't you tell me what 'womanizer' means."

"Why did you ask?"

499

"To see if you'd tell me. So patronizing. I know exactly what the word means. 'Womanizer' means my sister May wants Claude Rue to fuck her."

"Get a dictionary. I want to see where it mentions your sister and Claude Rue."

"The dictionary is a cemetery of dead words. All words are dead until somebody uses them. 'Womanizer' is dead. If you use it, it lives, uses you."

"Nonsense."

"People once talked about nymphomaniacs, right? Remember that word? Would you ever use it without feeling it said something embarrassing about you? Get real, Herman. Everyone is constantly on the make—even May. Even you."

"Not me."

"Maybe that's because you're old-fashioned, which is to say narrow-minded. Self-righteous. Incapable of seeing yourself. You disappoint me, Herman. You really do. What about famous men who had bastards? Rousseau, Byron, Shelley, Wordsworth, the Earl of Gloucester, Edward VII."

"I don't care who had bastards. That isn't pertinent. You're trying to make a case for bad behavior."

"Rodin, Hegel, Marx, Castro—they all had bastards. If they are all bad, that's pertinent. My uncle Chan wasn't famous, but he had two families. God knows what else he had. Neither family knew of the other until he died. Then it became pertinent, everyone squabbling over property."

"What's your point, if you have one, which I seriously doubt?"

"And what about Kafka, Camus, Sartre, Picasso, Charlie Chaplin, Charlie Parker, JFK, MLK? What about Chinese emperors and warlords, Arab sheiks, movie actors, thousands of Mormons? Everybody collects women. That's why there are prostitutes, whores, courtesans, consorts, concubines, bimbos, mistresses, wives, flirts, hussies, sluts, etc., etc. How many words are there for man? Not one equivalent for 'cunt,' which can mean a woman. 'Prick' means some kind of jerk. Look at magazine covers, month after month. They're selling clothes and cosmetics? They sell women, stupid. You know you're stupid. Stupid Herman, that's you."

"They're selling happiness, not women."

"It's the same thing. Lions, monkeys, horses, goats, people . . . Many, many, many animals collect women animals. When they stop, they become unhappy and they die. Married men live longer than single men. This has long been true. The truth is the truth. What am I talking about? Hug me, please."

"The truth is you're madly in love with Claude Rue."

"I've never met the man. Don't depress me."

"Your sister mentions him in a letter, you imagine she wants him. She wants him, you want him. You're in love, you're jealous."

"You're more jealous."

"You admit it? You never before conceded anything in an argument. I feel like running in the streets, shrieking the news."

"I admit nothing. After reading my sister May's gossipy, puritanical letter, I find that I dislike Claude Rue intensely."

"You never met the man."

"How can that have any bearing on the matter?"

As for the people in the large reception room at the Faculty Club—deans, department heads, assistant professors, students, wives, husbands—gathered to honor Claude Rue—he'd flicked us off like a light. I admired Rue for that, and I wished his plane back to Paris would crash. Behind me, a woman whispered in the exact tone Margaret had used, "I dislike him intensely."

A second woman said, "You know him?"

"Of course not. I've heard things, and this novel is very sexist."

"You read the novel. Good for you."

"I haven't read it. I saw a review in a magazine at my hairdresser's. I have the magazine. I'll look for it tonight when I get home."

"Sexist?" said the first woman. "Odd. I heard he's gay."

"Gay?" said a man. "How interesting. I suppose one can be gay and sexist, but I'd never have guessed he was gay. He looks straight to me. Who told you he's gay? Someone who knows him?"

"Well, not with a capital K, if that's what you mean by 'knows,' but he was told by a friend of Rue's, that he agreed to fly here and give his lecture only because of the Sanfran bath houses. That's what he was told. Gossip in this town spreads quick as genital warts."

501

"Ho, ho, ho. People are so dreadfully bored. Can you blame them? They have no lives, just careers and Volvos."

"That's good. I intend to use it. Do look for conversational citations in the near future. But who is the Chinese thing? I'll die if I don't find out. She's somebody, isn't she? Ask him."

"Who?"

"Him, him. That man. He was standing with her." Someone plucked my jacket sleeve. I turned. A face desiccated by propriety, leaned close, old eyes, shimmering liquid gray, bulging, rims hanging open with thin crimson labia. It spoke:

"Pardon me, sir. Could you please tell us the name of the Chinese woman who, it now seems, is leaving the reception with Professor Rue?"

"Go fuck yourself."

Margaret said the success of his lecture left Rue giddily deranged, expecting something more palpable from the night. He said, she said, that he couldn't have returned to his hotel room, watched TV, and gone to sleep. " 'Why is it like this for me, do you think?' " he said, she said. " 'It would have no style. You were loved,' " she said, she said, sensing his need to be reminded of the blatant sycophancy of his herdlike audience. " 'Then you appeared,' " he said, she said. " 'You were magnificently cold.' "

Voila! Margaret. She is cold. She is attentive. She is determined to fuck him. He likes her quickness, and her legs. He says that to her. He also likes the way she drives, and her hair—the familiar black Asian kind, but which, because of its dim coppery strain, is rather unusual. He likes her eyes, too. I said: "Margaret, let me. Your gray-tinted glasses give a sensuous glow to your sharply tipped Chinese eyes, which are like precious black glittering pebbles washed by the Yangtze. Also the Yalu."

Margaret said, "Please shut up, dog-eyed white devil. I'm in no mood for jokes."

Her eyes want never to leave Rue's face, she said, but she must concentrate on the road as she drives. The thing is underway for them. I could feel it as she talked, how she was thrilled by the momentum, the invincible rush, the necessity. Resentment built in my sad heart. I thought, 'Margaret is over thirty years old. She has been around the block. But it's never enough. Once more around the block, up the stairs, into the room, and there lies happiness.'

" 'Why shouldn't I have abandoned the party for you?' " he said, she said, imitating his tone, plaintive and arrogant. " 'I wrote a novel.' " He laughs at himself. Margaret laughs, imitating him, an ironic self-deprecatory laugh. The moment seemed to her phony and real at once, said Margaret. He was nervous, as he'd been on stage, unsure of his stardom, unconvinced even by the flood of abject adoration. " 'Would a man write a novel except for love?' " he said, she said, as if he didn't really know. He was sincerely diffident, she said, an amazing quality considering that he'd slept with every woman in the world. But what the hell, he was human. With Margaret, sex will be more meaningful. " 'Except for love?' " she said, she said, gayly, wondering if he slept with her sister. " 'How about your check from the university?' "

" 'You think I'm inconsistent?' " He'd laughed. Spittle shot from his lips and rotten teeth. She saw everything except the trouble, what lay deep in the psychic plasma that rushed between them.

She drove him to her loft, in the warehouse and small factory district of Emeryville, near the bay, where she lived and worked, and bought and sold. Canvases, drawings, clothes—everything was flung about. She apologized.

He said, " 'A great disorder is an order.' ' "

"Did you make that up?"

He kissed her. She kissed him.

" 'Yes,' " he said. Margaret stared at me, begging for pity. He didn't make that up. A bit of an ass, then, but really, who isn't? She expected Rue to get right down to love. He wanted a drink first. He wanted to look at her paintings, wanted to use the bathroom and stayed inside a long time, wanted something to eat, then wanted to read poetry. It was close to midnight. He was reading poems aloud, ravished by beauties of phrasing, shaken by their music. He'd done graduate work at Oxford. Hours passed. Margaret sat on the couch, her legs folded under her. She thought it wasn't going to happen, after all. Ten feet away, he watched her from a low slung, leather chair. The frame was a steel tube bent to form legs, arms, and back-rest. A book of modern poetry lay open in his lap. He was about to read another poem when Margaret said, in the flat black voice. " 'Do you want me to drive you to your hotel?' "

He let the book slide to the floor. Stood up slowly, struggling with leather-wheezing-ass-adhesive chair seat, then came toward her, pulling stone foot. Leaning down to where she sat on the couch, he kissed her. Her hand went up, lightly, slowly, between his legs.

"He wasn't a very great lover," she said.

She had to make him stop, give her time to regather powers of feeling and smoke a joint before trying again. Then, him inside, "working on me," she said, she fingered her clitoris to make herself come. "There would have been no payoff otherwise," she said. "He'd talked too much, maybe. Then he was a tourist looking for sensations in the landscape. He couldn't give. It was like he had a camera. Collecting memories. Savoring the sex, you know what I mean? I could have been in another city." Finally, Margaret said, she screamed, " 'What keeps you from loving me?' " He fell away, damaged.

" 'You didn't enjoy it'?" he said, she said.

She turned on the lamp to roll another joint, and told him to lie still while she studied his cock, which was oddly discolored and twisted left. In the next three days, the sex got better, not great. She'd say, " 'You're losing me.' " He'd moan.

When she left him at the airport, she felt relieved, but, driving back to town, she began to miss him. She thought to phone her psychotherapist, but this wasn't a medical problem. The pain surprised her and it wouldn't quit. She couldn't work, couldn't think. Despite strong reservations—he hadn't been very nice to her—she was in love, had been since she saw him on stage. Yes; definitely love. Now he was gone. She was alone. In the supermarket, she wandered the aisles, unable to remember what she needed. She was disoriented—her books, her plants, her clothes, her hands—nothing seemed really hers. At night, the loneliness was very bad. Sexual. Hurt terribly. She cried herself to sleep.

"Why didn't you phone me?"

"I knew you weren't too sympathetic. I couldn't talk to you. I took Gracie out of school. She'd been here for the last couple of days."

"She likes school."

"That's just what you'd say, isn't it? You know, Herman, you are a kind of person who makes me feel like shit. If Gracie misses a couple of days it is no big deal. She's got a lot of high Q's. I

504

found out she also has head lice. Her father doesn't notice anything. Gracie would have to have convulsions before he'd notice. Too busy advancing himself, writing another ten books that nobody will read, except his pathetic graduate students."

"That isn't fair."

"Yes, it is. It's fair."

"No, it isn't."

"You defending Sloan? Whose friend are you?"

"Talking to you is like cracking nuts with my teeth."

She told me Rue had asked if she knew Chinese. She said she didn't. He proposed to teach her, and said, " 'The emperor forbid foreigners to learn Chinese, except imperfectly, only for purposes of trade. Did you know that?' "

" 'No. Let's begin.' "

Minutes into the lesson, he said, " 'You're pretending not to know Chinese. I am a serious person. Deceive your American lovers. Not me.' "

She said, "Nobody ever talked to me like that. He was furious."

"Didn't you tell him to go to hell?"

"I felt sorry for him."

She told him that she really didn't know a word of Chinese. Her family had lived in America for over a hundred years. She was raised in Sacramento. Her parents spoke only English. All her friends had been white. Her father was a partner in a construction firm. His associates were white. When the Asian population of the Bay Area greatly increased, she saw herself, for the first time, as distinctly Chinese. She thought of joining Chinese cultural organizations, but was too busy. She sent money.

" 'You don't know who you are,' " said Rue.

" 'But that's who I am. What do you mean?' "

" 'Where are my cigarettes?' "

"Arrogant bastard. Did you?"

"What I did is irrelevant. He felt ridiculed. He thought I was being contemptuous. I was in love. I could have learned anything. Chinese is only a language. It didn't occur to me to act stupid."

"What you did is relevant. Did you get his cigarettes?"

"He has a bald spot in the middle of his head."

"Is there anything really interesting about Rue?"

"There's a small blue tattoo on his right shoulder. I liked it. Black moles are scattered on his back like buckshot. The tattoo is an ideograph. I saw him minutely, you know what I mean? I was on the verge of hatred, really in love. But you wouldn't understand. I won't tell you anymore."

"Answer my question."

She didn't.

"You felt sorry for him. I feel sorry for you. Is it over now?"

"Did it begin? I don't really know. Anyhow, so what?"

"Don't you want to tell me? I want to know. Tell me everything."

"I must keep a little for myself. Do you mind? It's my life. I want to keep my feelings. You can be slightly insensitive, Herman."

"I never dumped YOU at a party in front of the whole town. You want to keep your feelings? Good. If you talk, you'll remember feelings you don't know you had. It's the way to keep them."

"No, it isn't. They go out of you. Then they're not even feelings anymore. They're chit-chat commodities. Some asshole like Claude will stick them in a novel."

"Why don't you just fly to Paris? Live with him."

"He's married. I liked him for not saying that he doesn't get along with his wife, or they're separated. I asked if he had an open marriage."

"What did he say?"

"He said, 'Of course not.' "

Margaret spoke more ill than good of Rue. Nevertheless, she was in love. Felt it every minute, she said, and wanted to phone him, but his wife might answer. He'd promised to write a letter, telling her where they would meet. There were going to be publication parties for his book in Rome and Madrid. He said that his letter would contain airline tickets and notification about her hotel.

"Then you pack a bag? You run out the door?"

"And up into the sky. To Rome. To Madrid."

"Just like that? What about your work? What about Gracie?"

"Just like that."

I bought a copy of *The Mists of Shanghai,* and began reading with primitive, fiendish curiosity. Who the hell was Claude Rue? The morning passed, then the afternoon. I quit reading at twilight, when I had to leave for work. I'd reached the point where Dulu comes to the brothel. It was an old-fashioned novel, something like Dickens, lots of characters and sentimental situations, but carefully written to seem mindless, and so clear that you hardly feel you're reading. Jujuzi's voice gives a weird edge to the story. Neiping suffers terribly, he says, but she imagines life in the brothel is not real, and that someday she will go home and her mother will be happy to see her. Just as I began to think Rue was a nitwit, Jujuzi reflects on Neiping's pain. He says she will never go home, and a child's pain is more terrible than an adult's, but it is the nourishment of sublime dreaming. When Dulu arrives, Neiping wishes the new girl would stop crying. It makes Neiping sad. She can't sleep. She stands beside the new girl, staring down through the dark, listening to her sob, wanting to smack her, make her be quiet. But then Neiping slides under the blanket and hugs the new girl. They tell each other their names. They talk. Dulu begins slowly to turn. She hugs Neiping. The little bodies lie in each other's arms, face to face. They talk until they fall asleep.

Did Claude Rue imagine himself as Neiping? Considering Rue's limp, he'd known pain. But maybe pain made him cold, like Jujuzi, master of sentimental feelings, master of cruelty. Was Claude Rue like Jujuzi?

A week passed. Margaret called, told me to come to her loft. She sounded low. I didn't ask why. When I arrived, she gave me a brutal greeting. "How come you and me never happened?"

"What do you mean?"

"How come we never fucked?"

She had a torn-looking smile.

"We're best friends, aren't we?"

I sat on the couch. She followed, plopped beside me. We sat beside each other, beside ourselves. Dumb. She leaned against me, put her head on my shoulder. I loved her so much it hurt my teeth. Light went down in the tall, steel-mullioned, factory windows. The air of the loft grew chilly.

"Why did you phone?" I asked.

"I needed you to be here."

"Do you want to talk?"

"No."

The perfume of her dark hair came to me. I saw dents on the side of her nose, left by her eyeglasses. They made her eyes look naked, vulnerable. She'd removed her glasses to see less clearly. Twisted the ends of her hair. Chewed her lip. I stood up, unable to continue doing nothing, crossed to a lamp, then didn't turn it on. Electric light was violent. Besides, it wasn't very dark in the loft, and the shadows were pleasant. I looked back. Her eyes had followed me. She asked what I'd like to drink.

"What do you have?"

"Black tea?"

"All right."

She put on her glasses and walked to the kitchen area. The cup and saucer rattled as she set them on the low table. I took her hands. "Sit," I said. "Talk."

She sat, but said nothing.

"Do you want to go out somewhere? Take a walk, maybe."

"We were together for three days," she said.

"Did he write to you?"

"We were together for hours and hours. There was so much feeling. Then I get this letter."

"What does he say? Rome? Barcelona?"

"He says I stole his watch. He says I behaved like a whore, going through his pockets when he was asleep."

"Literally, he says that?"

"Read it yourself."

"It's in French." I handed it back to her.

"An heirloom, he says. His most precious material possession, he says. He understands my motive, and finds it contemptible. He wants his watch back. He'll pay. How much am I asking?"

"You have his heirloom?"

"I never saw it."

"Let's look."

"Please, Herman, don't be tedious. There is no watch."

With the chaos of art materials scattered on the vast floor, and on table tops, dressers, chairs, and couch, it took twenty minutes before she found Claude Rue's watch jammed between a bedpost and the wall.

I laughed. She didn't laugh. I wished I could redeem the moment. Her fist closed around the watch, then opened slowly. She said, "Why did he write that letter?"

"Send him the watch and forget it."

"He'll believe he was right about me."

"Who cares what he believes?"

"He hurt me."

"Oh, just send him the watch."

"He hurt me, really hurt me. Three days of feeling, then that letter."

"Send it to him," I said.

But there was a set look in Margaret's eyes. She seemed to hear nothing.

1993

HONEY IN THE CARCASE

by JOSIP NOVAKOVICH

from THE THREEPENNY REVIEW

IVAN MEDVEDICH was washing his silvery mustache after eating a slice of dark bread with honey when a whistle cut through the air, deepened in frequency, and sank into an explosion that shook the house so that a bar of soap slid from the mirror ledge into the sink.

"Lord have mercy!" his wife Estera said. "What was that?"

"The *chetniks*, what else."

Soon, another whistle, and another explosion.

"Run for cover!" Estera shouted.

"What cover? This is the safest place in the house." Ivan had built the house alone—actually, with a little help from his oldest flat-footed son, Daniel, who had groaned more than he had worked. It took Ivan twenty years of careful labor to finish the house, but one thing he had skipped, a cellar, perhaps because snakes had nested and floods crept in the cellar of his childhood home. *God is my fortress and my strength* was his motto. But now, in addition to God, a cellar would help.

He turned off the lights and prayed, and after his last Amen, no bombs fell for the rest of the night.

Next morning Estera walked to the bakery, early, because after six o'clock, the dark whole-wheat disappeared, and only milky white, soft, cake-like, as expensive as sin, remained. The old baker's wife said nothing, handing her a two-kilo loaf as usual. When Estera exited, she heard a dog howl and then a high-pitched whistle. A bomb fell in a ditch ten yards away from her, exploding with a terrible blast. Shrapnel flew over her head, shattered the bakery attic windows and riddled the tops of the faces of the nearby houses, which now looked like lepers' foreheads. She walked home hurriedly.

If the bomb had fallen outside the ditch, the shrapnel would have flown low and struck her. She and Ivan concluded that God had saved her. Still, as Estera peeled onions that day, her neck twitched, jerking her head to one side. Estera had borne Ivan five sons. The youngest, whom she'd had at the age of forty-six, died several years before because the wall between the chambers of his heart had collapsed. Since his death silver streaked her hair.

Ivan played the violin by heart. Estera still chopped onions. Tears, from the onion fumes, glazed their eyes. They grieved so that salty water flowed, as though their swollen eyes, like balloons, needed to drop sand to gain in altitude; tears slid down their cheeks like little eyes, mirroring knives and violins.

Ivan walked out to the rabbit cages. Rabbits' split lips quickly drew grass into their mouths. He took a white rabbit by its long ears and held it in the air. He had often petted the rabbit, so the rabbit was not scared, not even as his fist went down and hit the neck. The rabbit twitched several times and went limp. He shuddered and walked into the house and lay the rabbit on the table to cool. "You skin it this time," he said.

That day he could not eat rabbit, his favorite meat, for the first time in his life; he ate more bread with honey, old honey that had crystallized into white grains.

At dusk, more whistles, and about a dozen blasts, all in the near neighborhood. It went on like that for a week—blasts at dusk and at twilight. A large crater loomed in their street between two shattered houses.

When he cautioned Estera not to go early in the morning to buy bread, she said, "I am used to explosions."

He said nothing to that, but hummed a tune, sounding like a buzz of bees, and bees it was that he was thinking about. It was the time to collect honey in his apiary, ten miles east, on a meadow of wild flowers near an acacia grove. He drove his old pick-up, put on a bee-keeper's hat and gloves, and opened the hives. His bees were so ardent that they had made honeycombs even outside of the frames; Ivan carved these additions out, and without draining honey, stored them. He placed framed honey-combs in a circular barrel, a separator. Turning the wheel, he listened to honey fall out of their hexagonal wax trenches and hit the metal wall, sticking to it and dripping. He did not mind bee stings—he'd got more than a dozen that day—because he believed they benefited his heart.

He harvested alone. His sons used to help him, dancing around the honey separator like Joseph's brothers around the grains of Egypt. But now, one of his sons was in Australia, another, Daniel, his first-born, worked as a doctor, the third one, Jakov, worked as a carpenter in Germany, and the youngest, Branko, stayed at home, studying for his entrance exams at the school of agricultural engineering.

When Ivan returned home with three barrels of honey and saw his son Daniel, he rolled up his sleeve because Daniel always took his blood pressure—especially after Ivan's heart-attack. (Ivan still suffered from angina pectoris but could not get a retirement settlement because his Communist boss hated him and, he suspected, wanted him to die at the factory.)

Daniel talked about how in the village where he doctored, chetniks went door to door, beating up old Croatian men, as though these men had been *ustashas.* "The chetniks with skulls and crossed bones painted on their caps drove people out of their homes, stole TV sets, burned haystacks. They cut off three old men's testicles and forced them to eat them. One bled to death, the others I stitched up as best I could."

"You should leave the village," said Ivan, "because of your young wife and child."

"That's right. A colleague of mine has invited me to work in the Osijek hospital."

"Are they going to have enough work for you there?"

"More than enough! Thousands will be wounded." He waved his hand as though to chase away a slow and fat fly.

Before his parents and brother could react, he was out, in his wobbly Citroen. This was the first time in five years that Daniel had visited without taking his father's blood pressure. Ivan rolled down his sleeve and turned on the radio.

The announcer said that Vinkovci was eerily quiet. Eerily quiet was a cliché in a newscaster's voice, but not so through the window when Estera opened it. No machine-gun fire, no cars, not even birds singing; only a woman's wailing far away.

"Estie," Ivan said, "We must take care of the honey. You know how the Montenegrin poet says, *A glass of honey asks for a glass of spleen, together they are easiest to drink.*"

"What kind of poetry is it if it doesn't even rhyme? Besides, give me no Montenegrin junk when you know that Montenegrin chetniks are bombing us."

Ivan let the honey sit in the barrels for several days, and then he scooped the creamy top—foamy, white, and exceedingly sweet. He was certain that this was ambrosia, the drink of Greek gods. He and Estera poured honey all evening long into glass bottles. Ivan looked back at the filled larder shelves and said, "It's good, isn't it?"

Just then a bomb fell at the edge of their garden so that the floor-boards shook and squeaked and the tiles on the roof quivered and slid, like teeth grinding. But the honey stayed calm in the bottles. Soon another bomb fell to the same spot. Ivan and Estera stayed in the larder, the safest room in the house because it had no windows.

Next day a couple of Federal MiG jets flew low, sharding people's windows, but no window burst on Medvedich's house. At night light from houses on fire flickered through the shades that could not be quite shut; red light on the wall seemed to be painting a message. The following morning, despite continuous mortar explosions, Estera wrapped a scarf under her chin and walked out.

"Where are you going, old woman?" Ivan asked.

"To buy bread."

"I think you shouldn't."

She walked out, proud of her courage.

Half an hour later, when she was not back, he stood on the threshold, and chewed a honeycomb with fresh honey. Chewing the wax calmed him better than chewing tobacco could. The phone rang; it was the baker. On the bakery steps, mortar shrapnel had struck and wounded Estera.

Ivan picked up Estera—unconscious, her abdomen torn—and drove to the hospital. A doctor took a quick X-ray and found that shrapnel had penetrated her liver. He dug in with his scalpel and gloved fingers, saying, "Too bad that we're out of anesthetics." As he fished for the metal Estera came to and swooned again. Just as the doctor tossed the bit of iron in the garbage bin, mortar hit the hospital, setting the roof on fire. Electricity went out. The doctor sewed up the wound with Ivan holding up a flashlight. They carried Estera to the basement, where the stench of crap and vomit hung about mustily.

For several days Estera lay half-dead, half-alive, green in the face, unable to sleep, too weak to be awake.

Ivan spent many hours with her but more at home lest brigands should break in, steal, and burn the house. He prayed but lost the meanings of his words in reveries and forgot to say his Amens. *Words without thoughts to heaven do not go.*

He missed his bees, abandoned behind the enemy lines. As he drank his ambrosia, he decided that next morning he'd drive into the eastern fields—no matter what, even through the hail of bullets—to his apiary. But next dawn a bomb fell in front of his house, shattering the windows and digging holes in the stuccoed bricks. The gate collapsed. Another bomb fell in the backyard, and demolished his pick-up. The shrapnel pierced through the house windows. Luckily, his son, trembling on the floor, was not injured.

A pharaoh did not weep when Persians slew his sons and raped his daughters because his sorrow was too deep for tears, but he did weep when after it all his ex-minister came by in rags and begged him for silver. Just so, Ivan had not wept when his wife bled in dirty hospitals, when his house had been nearly demolished, and when the truck he had saved for, for fifteen years, burst into pieces and shriveled in fire. But that he could not go out into the fields and take care of his bees, that made the cup— not of honey—overflow. He wept in his armchair, in his wooden shoes, will-less, nearly motionless, and daydreamed.

And reminisced. As a child he saw on the outskirts of his village Croatian peasants, dead, their eyes plucked out. His father had forbidden him to talk about it since this part of history was politically incorrect—*am strengstens verboten*—to recount.

One noon four Croatian soldiers walked in and asked for Branko. He was in the bathroom, but Ivan said he'd gone to the university library. He was surprised to hear himself lie, but then he remembered that Abraham lied that his sister was his wife so he would save her from a marriage in a foreign land. That Branko should be a soldier struck him as absurd. Ivan had raised him on "Turn the other cheek." For years boys beat him, broke his nose, yet he would not fight back even when Ivan told him to. Ivan had complained to the school president, who asked, "Is your son gay?" That was all he offered in the way of help, so Ivan had to protect Branko, giving him a beekeeper's mask to save his face, and walking him home while boys threw stones and shouted, "Baptists, Claptists." Branko, who had grown up as a theological experiment, without a malice in his head, spent his days developing landscape photographs in the darkroom, a shed, so that his eyes stayed watery and bloodshot.

Estera began to improve and her son Daniel took her to Osijek, together with Branko (to hide him from the draft), but Ivan would not leave his house, as though it was his skin. Now, on his block there were fewer than a dozen people left, and in the city, out of forty thousand, perhaps three thousand had remained. Neither phone or electricity worked anymore. He lived on water from a hand-pump in his yard and on honey.

He had been a corpulent, double-chinned man, but in a month in which it was all the same to him whether he was alive or dead, he became a thin man with sharp pentagonal jaws, overgrown in a Mosaic beard. Perhaps he would not have eaten honey either if it had not reminded him of his bees; he ate it in their remembrance, a sacrament to the little striped and winged tigresses.

One crisp morning Ivan felt tremendously alert. He wondered whether he was about to die, since before death one could get a moment of lucidity, to summon one's family and deliver blessings—that lucidity was a *sine qua non* in a Biblical death, and he, a father of several sons, would of course have a Biblical death. Or had his diet cleared his coronary arteries? The following day, since he still felt lucid, he concluded that honey had healed his heart and saved his life.

He biked to his brother David, the carpenter, in Andriasevci, in their father's house, ten miles away. On the way he saw starved shaggy cattle roaming, masterless. Horses rotted in dried-up sunflower fields. Blind dogs stumbled into trees. Cats

515

with red eyes purred so loudly that he could hear them even as he rode over cracking branches. Heads of wheat bent in the fields like contrite sinners; nobody harvested them.

David and Ivan hugged and kissed as brothers. After they had slurped rosehip tea, David said, "I have presents for you: one coffin for Estera and one for you. Come, take a look!"

"What? But Estera is alive. And I am all right."

"Of course. But in case you get killed, you won't be dumped in a mass grave if you have a coffin with your name."

Next morning Ivan decided to go back to Vinkovci. Not that he had not thought about death enough, or seen it enough—but that his young brother, who used to spend most of his time making tambourines and singing, should see the world as a plantation of coffins, incensed him against the invading armies. He rode through the groaning countryside.

From the edge of the village a black German shepherd followed him all the way to Ivan's home. There he wagged his tail, licked Ivan's shoe, and did all he could to endear himself to Ivan. Ivan gave him an old slice of bread and honey. The dog loved that.

Ivan stood on his threshold and stared at the cloudy horizon, with dark blue clouds. The stink of putrid animals, borne on an unusually warm wind, continued to hit his nostrils. Smoke and gangrene.

And when the rains began, a ghost crept along the surface of the earth, not as an image, white and gray, but as a stench of wet smoke and pus. The muddy soul of the Panonian valley sought fire to solidify into bricks of a tower of Babel, in which all languages would merge into one, Serbian. *Govori Srpski da te ceo svet razume.* Speak Serbian so the whole world could understand you, the Serb folk saying went.

He rode his bike to a foundry converted into a bomb factory and volunteered to make bombs for the under-armed Croatian soldiers. At the end of his shift, he always found the German shepherd, waiting for him.

One dawn MiG jets bombed the factory, mostly missing and hitting people's houses nearby, but they did damage it enough to shut it.

Ivan could finally take it no more, so he dragged a cart east, through Mirkovci. Now and then he stopped and scratched his dog's fur. He ran into a checkpoint made of stacked beer cases in the middle of the road. A chetnik asked him, "Where the hell are you going?"

"I need to take back my bees from the fields."

"Bees?" The chetnik pulled out a knife. "Your ID?"

"I have none."

"I'm gonna tattoo you so we can recognize you next time." He pushed his knife against Ivan's face. The dog growled, ready to pounce. A chetnik grabbed his comrade's arm. "Don't be crazy. Don't you see *he's* crazy. Let him get his bees." And turning to Ivan, he winked, and said, "God protects the crazy ones. I like that, bees. Bees!" When Ivan was at a fair distance, they shot at the German shepherd but missed.

That he had managed to pass surprised him. Perhaps the brigands had understood his beard as an emblem of Serbdom.

Ivan waxed entrances to ten beehives and stacked them on his cart. When he passed by the chetniks, they again shot at his dog, and this time they killed him. Ivan turned soil on the side of the road with a shovel and buried his friend.

It took him five trips—and a dozen kilos of honey as the "road tax" to the brigands—to take back all his bee-hives.

Ivan built a brick wall around the hives. He melted sugar for his friends so they would survive the winter. Since he had seen a sign that the winter would be a long one, Polish geese migrating south, he thoroughly filled the cracks in the hives with frame-wax.

For hours he listened to the congregation of bees. They were his revelation. *For the invisible things of him from the creation of the world are clearly seen, being understood by the things that are made, even his eternal power and Godhead . . .* Yes, the invisible Godhead and his plan are revealed in bees. Bees fulfill the Old Testament through the perfection of their laws and the New Testament through the perfection of their love for the Queen bee, for whom every bee is willing to die. Ivan thought that even if he had never read the Bible, from studying his bees, he'd conclude that a rational God existed.

After thinking so, he'd bring the bees several pounds of honey, apologizing for having taken it in the summer. He admired the heaven on earth, the earth in heaven.

His son Daniel visited and told him that Estera, although anemic, had nearly fully recovered. When asked to join her in Osijek, Ivan said, "Somebody has to stay here and protect the church and the bees."

The shack where his son had developed photographs had served as a chapel ever since Ivan had excommunicated himself from the Baptist church. Like-minded Baptists and Pentecostals, for whom their churches had not been pious enough, used to worship in the shack with Ivan and his family, until they discovered that they were not like-minded. Nobody came now, but still, it used to be—and it would continue to be—God's space.

Ivan played the violin in his chapel and studied scripture. He was disappointed that scripture mentioned bees only a few times and lions many times. It consoled him that in one verse bees got the better of the lion: *There was a swarm of bees and honey in the carcase of the lion.*

One passage intrigued Ivan: *And it shall come to pass in that day, that the Lord shall hiss for the fly that is in the uttermost part of the river of Egypt, and for the bee that is on the land of Assyria.*

He whistled and hissed to call out his bees, and none came out. Then he made a flute from a wet willow branch, with a low note, and found a hiss that indeed excited the bees so that they came out and criss-crossed the sky into a mighty net. When they came back, they tossed out their drones, and they kept tossing them for days. A peculiar fratricide—that aspect of bees theologically troubled Ivan. Some kind of wrath of God built in the natural order of things? In front of the beehives fat drones with stunted wings curled atop each other and shrank; the ditch filled up with drones. On a sunny day so many crows flew over Ivan's head, to feast on the drones, that it grew dark.

After a prolonged bombardment, a band of chetniks came to Ivan's street. He was now the only person living on his block. When he saw them coming, he unplugged the bee-hive entrances and hissed on his flute. At the same time a bomb flew, with a low whistle, fell in the street, and did not go off. Bees from several beehives grew agitated and flew out into the street where several sweaty chetniks, having loaded his neighbor's furniture on a truck, turned their eyes to Ivan's house.

Thousands of bees covered each brigand, giving him the appearance of an armored medieval knight. The brigands ran, helter-skelter, dropping their weapons. One of them staggered in circles and fell dead in front of Ivan's house; he kept swelling even after the rigor mortis gripped him.

1994

PARADISE PARK

by STEVEN MILLHAUSER

from GRAND STREET

Paradise park, which was destroyed by fire on May 31, 1924, except for a number of steel and concrete structures that rose eerily from the blackened ruins until they were torn down the following year, first opened its gates on June 1, 1912, on eight and two-thirds acres of the former site of Dreamland, across Surf Avenue from Luna Park. In an era noted for the brilliance and extravagance of its amusement parks, the new park seemed to be presenting itself as a culmination. Even the diminished acreage, with its mere 652 feet of ocean frontage, proved responsible for many of the park's most striking features, for it was immediately clear that Paradise Park was striving to overcome the limitations of space by a certain flamboyance or excess that pushed it in directions never before undertaken in the architecture of amusement parks.

The first sign that the new owner was prepared to respond boldly to the challenge of his rivals was the four-hundred-foot-high white wall that rose about the newly acquired property, dwarfing Luna's main tower, casting its late-afternoon shadow all the way to Steeplechase, and surpassing even the legendary tower of Dreamland, which was said to have been illuminated by one hundred thousand electric lights. In that early era of enclosed amusement parks, Paradise Park was the most visibly and radically enclosed of all. The soaring white wall, composed of staff over a lath-and-iron frame, suggested on the one hand a defiant act of exclusion, an outrageous assertion of privacy, and on the other an invitation, a deliberate titillation or provocation—the latter most clearly in evidence at the towering top of the unadorned wall, which only there, high in the sky, broke into a profusion of colorful towers, minarets, domes, and spires.

Two openings pierced the mystery of the great wall: an ocean entrance, across an iron pier and through the grimacing mouth of an immense clown's face, and the Surf Avenue entrance, through a soaring arch flanked by sixty-foot dragons. The openings did not reveal the inside of the park but ushered visitors into a broad, meandering tunnel that wound its way parallel to the wall for hundreds of feet before turning abruptly inward to the park itself. Lit with red, blue, and yellow electric lights, the winding tunnel was lined on both sides with ball-and-milkbottle booths, carnival wheels, Moxie stands, curtained freak shows, gypsy palmist tents, hot roasted corn stalls, phrenology shops displaying maps of skulls divided into zones, tattoo parlors, penny arcades, shooting galleries—all of it ringing with the mingled din of tumbling bottles, rattling balls, Graphophone music, the shouts of barkers ("And a jaunt for joy it is, ladies and gentlemen!"), and the muffled clatter of unseen rides. Scattered among the familiar pleasures of Paradise Alley, as the entrance tunnel came to be called, were a number of new and exciting ones that proved immediately popular, such as Sky Cars, small electric-traction elevators lined with black velvet and operated by masked female attendants in scarlet livery who took customers up to the top of the wall for a sudden, magnificent view of the park.

Since secrecy was part of the allure of Paradise Park, the elusive creator-manager, who from the beginning surrounded himself with a certain mystery, permitted no publicity photos in the course of an otherwise vigorous promotional campaign. The historian must therefore rely on a scattering of amateur photographs that focus on particular attractions but give no reliable view of the whole. Despite the absence of a definitive map or plan, it is nevertheless possible to reconstruct the early form of the park in some detail from the many reports, sometimes conflicting, of early witnesses.

What struck the first visitors, as they emerged from Paradise Alley into the park itself, was the powerful upward or vertical thrust. In the bewildering assault of first impressions it was immediately apparent that the park consisted of several levels, to which access was had by numerous stairways, escalators, and electric elevators. Each of the two upper levels was a system of wide iron bridges that intersected at one or more points to form broad plazas, large enough to house booths, cafés, brass bands, and mechanical rides, as well as a variety of exotic attractions: a Zulu village, a Chinese temple, a Javanese puppet theater, a replica of the marketplace of Marrakech, and a reconstructed village of Mbuti pygmies from the Ituri Forest, including forty-five Mbuti tribesmen living in reassembled native huts. The bridges were supported by a system of openwork iron towers, many of which were supplied with stairways and elevators; the entire structure of bridges and supports left a feeling of openness, so that at any point on the ground one could see big slices of blue sky. Fifty-five elevator shafts in the inner walls gave access to every bridge at both levels, and all around the inner wall rose the spiral of an immense railed stairway, which quickly became known as Paradise Road and led to the top of the wall. There people could walk four abreast along a balustrade lined with game booths and food stands and look down at Paradise Park itself, with its crisscrossing bridges, its festive plazas, its roller coaster and Ferris wheel, its exotic villages, its enticing spectacles with casts of thousands, such as the Destruction of Carthage and the Burning Skyscraper; or they could gaze outward at the great beach stretching east and west with its domed and towering hotels, its doubled-decked iron piers, its bathing pavilions—out beyond the lighthouse at Sea Gate in one direction and the sailboats on Sheepshead Bay in the other, and farther still, much farther, for it was said that on a clear day you could see sixty miles in any direction.

Although from the beginning there were critics of the new park, who argued that the vertical emphasis was reminiscent of the world of skyscrapers and elevated railroads from which the urban visitor longed to escape, the response of the public was decisively enthusiastic. Those who frequented the park began to say they could no longer enjoy single-level parks, which seemed too close to the ground; and so successful was the park that a single ride called the Sidewinder, which cost $86,000 to build, drew $375,000 in receipts in the first three seasons.

If the most striking and immediate fact about Paradise Park was its multilevel verticality, its continual invitation to half-glimpsed excitements high overhead, the crowds soon noticed that the park offered, along with familiar amusements, a number of new attractions. One sensation of the opening season was a brand-new mechanical ride called the Nightmare Railway, a development of the scenic railway and Old Mill in the direction of the House of Horrors. Delighted visitors discovered that the great white wall contained an elaborate set of tracks that rose and fell sharply along a dark, twisting tunnel which presented a series of frights: the car, which held twelve people on six benches, went rushing toward immense boulders that collapsed upon contact, approached another car that suddenly swooped overhead on a second set of tracks, experienced a landslide, a flood, an avalanche, and a raging fire, passed through a dragon's den, a mummy's crypt, a haunted graveyard, a cave of malignant dwarfs, and a vampire's castle, and emerged at last in a bright opening two hundred feet above the ground of Paradise Park.

Even more popular than the new mechanical rides was an entirely new group of amusements called Adventures. An Adventure, according to the promotional material, was not a ride but a carefully re-created real-life experience: for ten cents one could enter the Dark Forest and be attacked by a gang of bandits, or step into the Streets of Lisbon and experience the famous earthquake, or wander through Old Algeria and experience the thrill of being surrounded by angry Moslems, tied up in a burlap sack, carried off on the back of a camel, and dangled over a cliff above crashing waves. One of the more popular Adventures was Lovers' Leap, a three hundred-foot-high rocky cliff (staff over lath and iron) that rose at one corner of the park and offered to daredevil couples a fearful ledge jutting over a thundering waterfall that threw up great clouds of spray; the sound of the roaring water was produced by machines concealed in the artificial cliff and the thick spray was sent up through dozens of holes in the staff. The couples who jumped shrieking into the thundering mist were caught ten feet below in a concealed net that broke their fall lightly and carried them eighty feet down into the swirling mist, where muscular attendants released them and guided them into a descending elevator.

But the single most popular attraction of the 1912 season proved rather surprisingly to be an immense model of the resort itself, done in precise scale and measuring thirty by twenty-five feet. Located on a plaza of the third level and surrounded by roped pedestrian walks supplied with coin-operated telescopes, the model showed Coney Island in May of 1911, just before the fire that destroyed Dreamland. In brilliant detail it replicated the heart of Coney Island from Steeplechase Park to Dreamland, including Surf Avenue, Mermaid Avenue, the host of side streets with their saloons and music halls, their dance pavilions and hotels, their shooting galleries and souvenir shops, and the beach itself with its double-decked iron piers and its bathhouses, all populated by tiny automatons (the brass band played, the man in the straw boater shot the tin duck in the row of moving ducks, the girl on the roller coaster opened her mouth and rolled her eyes). The detail was so scrupulous that the model was said to duplicate every tie in every track of every roller coaster, every waxwork in the Eden Musée, including the pastework pearls of Jenny Lind, and every slat in every rocking chair on the porch of every hotel; and it was rumored that with the aid of a penny-in-the-slot telescope you could see not only the precise replication of every ornate machine in every penny arcade and the minuscule letters of every peepshow entertainment (*Actors and Models, After the Bath, Bare in the Bear Skin, What the Book Agent Saw*), but, through the elegantly duplicated peepshow viewer, the flickering, teasingly vague black-and-white pictures themselves. The highly popular model was the work of Otis Stilwell, a carver of carousel horses who as a hobby made lovingly detailed miniature merry-go-rounds, roller coasters, and funhouses that he sold in a shop on Surf Avenue and who, along with the inventor Otto Danziker, was to prove one of the owner-manager's closest advisers. The miniature Coney Island, which attracted amazed attention as a kind of wondrous toy, served a deeper purpose: by reducing the entire resort to a miniature within his amusement park, the manager was enhancing the size and power of his park, which became a gigantic and marvelous structure stretching away in every direction; at the same time he was inviting the admiring crowds to experience a subtle condescension toward all rival attractions, which were reduced to charming toys.

Like other amusement park entrepreneurs at the turn of the century, the owner-manager of Paradise Park was confronted by the problem of attracting a mass audience hungry for pleasure and excitement while excluding any threat to the supposed values of that audience, such as the prostitutes, gamblers, and gangsters who flourished on every Coney Island side street. By enclosing their parks and hiring enforcement squads, the entrepreneurs were able to exercise unprecedented control, but the astute manager noted a new problem: the new, safe pleasures of the enclosed parks threatened to make them too tame and predictable, to push them in the unfortunate direction of the genteel beer garden. This problem he solved brilliantly by hiring a troupe of eighteen hundred specially trained actors to imitate the rowdiness and vice whose exclusion had left a secret yearning. Hence the park included among its attractions a number of dark saloons, seedy roadhouses, and crooked alleys lined by dubious shops, in which customers could mingle with prostitutes, pickpockets, cutthroats, drunken sailors, pimps, con men, and gangland thugs, assured that the racy language, the shocking costumes, and the terrifying fights which periodically erupted were part of the show. Actresses playing the part of prostitutes were particularly admired by the male and female visitors, who enjoyed seeing at close range the disturbing, thrilling streetwalkers with their invitation to forbidden pleasures that were strictly and safely imaginary. Patrons who themselves became rowdy or offensive were swiftly removed by the very efficient park police, who roamed the grounds in uniform or in disguise. Because the distinction was not always clear between an actor dressed like a sailor with a false tattoo on his forearm and a real sailor with a real tattoo, or an actress with rouged cheeks and brazen eyes strutting along the booth-lined alleys and a factory girl from Brooklyn wearing a new chinchilla coat and a straw hat with a willow plume, a certain heady confusion was experienced by the park's patrons, who began to feel that they too were actors and actresses disguised as seamstresses, schoolteachers, department store clerks, typists, and shopkeepers—roles that they no longer took as seriously as they did in that other world of tiredness.

Among the many disguises in Paradise Park were those of the owner-manager himself, for it quickly became known that the secretive proprietor liked to mingle unseen with the crowds in order to observe the operation of his park at close range, overhear responses to his amusements, and imagine rearrangements and improvements. Disguised as a park workman in cap, shirtsleeves, and vest, an Irish shopkeeper in his Sunday bowler, a uniformed trombone player in epaulets, a city swell in striped pants, bow tie, and straw boater, a bearded Jew in a long coat of black gabardine, the manager would make the rounds of his park, studying the crowd and devising ways to improve congested areas. Once, overhearing a couple complain that the Lovers' Leap was disappointing because the concealed net broke the fall too soon, he had the net lowered by ten feet and discovered that revenues increased. As rumors of his presence persisted, visitors began to search for the disguised owner-manager among the throngs; and people began to wonder a little about the man who walked among them unseen, listening to them, observing them, and seeking to increase their delight.

They knew only that he was an outsider, from Manhattan, who had come late to the amusement-park business and who, it was said, had money to burn. Then a journalist named Warren Burchard wrote a long article that appeared in a special Coney Island supplement of the *Brooklyn Eagle* (August 10, 1912). In the course of analyzing Coney Island amusements, calculating trends, reporting revenues, and discussing patterns of crowd behavior, Burchard devoted several paragraphs to the latest proprietor of "marvelous Coney," Charles Sarabee. Sarabee, Burchard reported, was a native New Yorker who was yet another instance of that peculiarly American phenomenon, the self-made man. Sarabee's father had sold cigars in the shop of a small Manhattan hotel. As a boy Charles had worked long hours in the cigar shop, where by the age of nine he had not only mastered the bewildering array of names, prices, and cedarwood boxcovers, but had begun to arrange cigars in eye-catching displays, the most successful of which was a three-foot-high wire tree hung with Christmas ornaments and high-priced Havanas. At thirteen he went to work as a bellhop at the hotel. There his efficiency, industry, and cleverness endeared him to the manager and earned him a series of promotions starting with desk clerk and ending, when Charles was twenty-one, with the post of assistant manager, in which capacity he introduced a wide variety of improvements, including fruit trees in every lobby and, in every bathroom, up-to-date fixtures in stylish settings: mahogany-hooded shower-baths, heated brass towel-rails, and Ionic pilasters of Siena marble. His big break came several years later when as manager-owner of the hotel he decided to enter a partnership in a new downtown department store. He soon had the controlling interest in three other department stores, but his fortune was made at the age of thirty, when he introduced in his stores a revolutionary idea called the "leisure spot." Sarabee had always had a sharp eye for the behavior of customers, and he had noticed that many of them grew tired and irritable after an hour or two of strolling from department to department and riding elevators and escalators in search of something they thought they wanted but probably didn't need. He knew it was important to keep his customers cheerful and in a free-spending mood, but even more important than this was simply to keep them in the store for as long as possible. Thus arose the idea of leisure spots: small oases of comfort located on every floor, where customers could relax in pleasant surroundings and recover from the tremendous assault on the nervous system represented by the modern department store with its countless treasures temptingly displayed. The leisure spots would attempt to simulate the atmosphere of a cozy living room, with thick armchairs and couches, crocheted pillows, lace antimacassars, mahogany lamp tables on which stood porcelain lamps with tasseled shades, and in one corner a smiling, apple-cheeked young woman in a crisp blue uniform who sold steaming cups of tea and coffee and a variety of tarts, cakes, cookies, and gingerbread. Although the leisure spots took up valuable floor space and proved forbiddingly expensive to install, they turned out to be immensely popular, and after a month it was clear that customers were staying longer and spending more. Rival stores quickly imitated the new device, but Sarabee's leisure spots were always more appealing, and he took care to vary them in order to overcome monotony; in quick succession he introduced leisure spots in the style of an English pub, a Dutch cottage, a Victorian parlor, a Japanese tearoom, and an Alpine chalet. Inspired by his successes, he soon began to introduce more fanciful decors, such as the Amazon jungle, the Italian plaza, the Puritan village, and the hold of a whaling ship, all designed with extreme fidelity, if not to History herself, then to the public's romantic idea of each exotic place. His search for new ideas led him to visit world's fairs and expositions, where the reproduction of exotic places had become fashionable, as well as the big Eastern pleasure resorts that borrowed themes and purchased properties from defunct expositions; and in 1908, on a trip to Coney Island, which he had not visited since his childhood, and where he attempted without success to purchase the old three-hundred-foot-high Iron Tower that had once been the showpiece of the Philadelphia Centennial Exposition of 1876, he was struck by the festive architecture of the three new amusement parks—Steeplechase, Luna, and Dreamland—as well as by the immense, lively, and free-spending crowds. He had been growing a little stale in the department-store business; he needed a new outlet for his energies; the destruction of Dreamland Park by fire in the spring of 1911 was decisive. As the city hesitated to purchase the ruined grounds put up for sale by the Dreamland Corporation, who proposed that the fifteen acres of Dreamland and the fifteen additional acres destroyed by fire should be turned into a public park, Sarabee was able to arrange for the lease of eight and two-thirds acres of the former amusement park, with the stipulation that the lease would be terminated when public development began, an event that was delayed until the administration of Fiorello La-Guardia in 1934, while the remaining acres, during the intervening years, were operated as a parking lot.

With the instinct of a true showman, Sarabee understood that the fatal enemy of amusement is boredom, and he was tireless in his search for new mechanical rides, new spectacles, new thrills and excitements. Working closely with the inventor Otto Danziker, who had designed the Nightmare Railway, Sarabee introduced at least five major rides each season, dismantling any that failed to prove successful. Of the thirteen new rides presented at Paradise Park in the second two seasons (1913 and 1914) before the breakthrough of 1915, one of the most popular was the Swizzler, a three-hundred-foot-high openwork iron column containing a spiral track down which cars holding ten people rushed at terrifying speeds, only to crash through a floor straight into a twisting black tunnel that suddenly burst into light around a bend and revealed that the car was about to rush into a brick wall. At the last second a door in the wall sprung open to reveal a track plunging into a lake, which proved to be an optical illusion projected by tilted mirrors reflecting a movie of rippling lakewater; at the bottom of the track the car slowed and entered a small room that rose into the air—the room was a hydraulic elevator—and released the car into a tunnel that led through suddenly opened doors into a sunny opening at the base of the column. Other successful rides created by Danziker were the Tumbler, the Spider, the Whim-Wham, the Flip, the Lightnin' Lizzie, and the Crazy Wheel—this last a gigantic horizontal ring of steel over one hundred feet in diameter, balanced on a pivot with hanging, swinging seats on the inner and outer rims. Danziker also designed a special Ferris wheel that slowly rotated like a top while turning vertically, and he placed a medium-sized roller coaster on a plaza of the second level, some three hundred feet in the air, which Sarabee promptly advertised as the world's largest roller coaster.

By the end of the third season the box-office take made it clear that Paradise Park had achieved an unprecedented success and had begun to attract a significant portion of the Steeplechase and Luna crowds. The exciting new rides, the lure of the upper levels, the eighteen hundred actors, the sense of being in a place that was unlike any other place on earth but also reassuringly familiar, all this promised a triumphant future, and the outbreak of the European war, which some had feared might harm the amusement business, proved only a further impetus to pleasure. People speculated on the rides already said to be under construction for next season, and a journalist reported, on dubious evidence, that Sarabee was going to unveil an entirely new kind of ride. The rumor was in fact mistaken, for Sarabee and Danziker were planning a number of sophisticated mechanical rides that broke no new technological ground; but in a broad sense the rumor proved to be true, for it was during the last week of the 1914 season that a small incident occurred which led to a startling new development in Paradise Park.

A workman called Ed O'Hearn, who had been sent into the tunnel beneath the Swizzler on a routine check of the track, pulled a handkerchief out of his pocket to wipe some dirt from his face. He dislodged a dime, which began rolling down a packed-earth incline beside the track. O'Hearn had been planning to spend his dime on a hot dog with mustard and sauerkraut, and he hurried after it with his electric lantern. He saw the dime come to a stop some fifteen feet below him, but when he reached the spot, the dime had disappeared. O'Hearn crawled about on his knees and patted the hard earth with his palm. As he did so he was surprised to feel a current of cool air streaming upward. He lowered the lantern and saw a fissure in the earth about two feet long and the width of a finger. When he dropped a flat stone sideways into the crack he counted to twenty before he heard a faint sound. He immediately returned above ground to report to his boss, who sent a message to Sarabee.

An hour later a team of three engineers investigated the crevice and determined that a small limestone cavity existed far beneath the Swizzler but posed no danger to the ride or to the park itself. Sarabee, disguised as one of the engineers, withdrew into a kind of somber brooding. When one of his men tried to reassure him that the park was perfectly safe, Sarabee is reported to have said: "It's all clear now. What'd you say?"

Thus was born the idea that was to give to the history of the amusement park a certain swerve that some found dubious but that no one was able to ignore. All fall and winter the great plans were laid; in his park office on Surf Avenue, Sarabee met daily with Otto Danziker, Otis Stilwell, and the engineer William Engelstein. The project was carried forward with characteristic secrecy, and indeed it remains one of the remarkable facts about Sarabee that he was able to elicit from everyone who worked for him an unfailing loyalty. Two weeks before the start of the new season, red-and-black posters appeared in the windows of restaurants and dance halls, on hoardings and telephone poles, on hotel notice-boards and the walls of bathhouses, announcing a NEW PARADISE PARK: *You Have to See It to Believe It*. On opening day the great entrance remained closed; a barker with cane and striped derby announced from a platform sixty feet high that the park would open one week later, on May 29. Rumor had it that the delay was a promotional gimmick aimed at increasing the air of mystery that surrounded the park; there was talk of a new kind of roller coaster, a more thrilling funhouse; and some said that Sarabee himself, with cane and striped derby, had announced the delay from the platform between the heads of the great dragons that flanked the closed entrance.

The gates opened on May 29, 1915, at eight in the morning; by noon the crowd had exceeded one hundred thousand. People who had visited the park before were puzzled and disappointed. Apart from three new rides, including a splendid Haunted Mountain, a new sideshow consisting entirely of midgets (a midget Fat Lady, a midget Ossified Man, a midget Wild Man of Borneo, a midget Bearded Lady, a pair of midget Siamese twins), nothing about the park seemed new enough to merit the publicity campaign. Visitors did, however, notice a number of odd-looking structures scattered about. Each structure was a rotunda composed of columns with grotesque capitals—grimacing devils, weeping clown faces, winged lions and horses, struggling mermaids fondled by hairy monkeys, three-headed chickens—roofed with a gilt dome, on top of which sat a miniature Danziker merry-go-round turning to barrel-organ melodies. Each of the dozen rotundas contained a central pole, a circle of wooden benches, and a uniformed attendant. When people were seated on the benches, which held as many as forty, the attendant pulled a lever in the pole, causing the platform to descend rapidly through a cylindrical shaft. At the bottom of the shaft the benches suddenly flattened out, the floor began to turn, and whirling, laughing, frightened people began spinning off the edge down any of fourteen chutes that led to a red curtain—and as they passed through the curtain they saw, all around them, as an attendant helped them to their feet at the bottom of the slide, a vast underground amusement park.

This immense subterranean project, with its roller coaster and funhouse, its tents and pavilions, its spires and domes and minarets, all lit by electric lights and alive with carousel music, the shouts of barkers, the rattle of rides, and even the smell of the sea, had been designed by Engelstein with the help of engineers who had worked on the Boston and New York City subway systems, and had been carried out by a force of nearly two thousand Irish, Italian, and Polish immigrant laborers lowered into shafts with pickaxes, shovels, and wheelbarrows, as well as by teams of trained workers who laid charges of dynamite to blast through boulders or operated a hydraulic tunnel-shield designed by Danziker for boring through clay and quicksand. In the course of excavation workmen discovered the jaw of a mastodon, a casket of seventeenth-century Dutch coins, and the rusty anchor of a Dutch merchant ship. The final structure appears to have been a skillful mixture of broad tunnels serving as fairground midways and high, open stretches roofed in reinforced concrete lined with dark blue tiles to resemble a night sky in summer. The completed park included at one end a great beach of white sand and an artificial ocean—in reality a great shallow basin filled with ocean water and containing Danziker's wave machine, which caused long, perfectly breaking waves to fall on the flawless beach. Two immense hotels, a band pavilion, and half a dozen bathhouses lined the beach, and a great iron pier with shops and restaurants under its wooden roof stretched twelve hundred feet into the water. Five hundred seagulls brought down from the upper shore added a realistic touch, though later it was discovered that the birds did not prosper in the subterranean world and gave birth to sickly offspring with wobbly walks and crazed flight patterns, who frightened children and had to be replaced by fresh gulls and hand-painted balsa wood models. High above the beach, and the piers, and the park, and the always burning electric lights stretched the night sky of blueblack tiles, supplied with thousands of twinkling artificial stars and a brilliant moon emerging from and disappearing behind slow-moving clouds beamed up by hidden projectors.

The creation of an underground amusement park with an ocean setting may have been a triumph of engineering, but Sarabee was too shrewd to rely solely on first impressions. His underground park had features that distinguished it clearly from his upper park, so that customers, after the first shock of delight or admiration, did not grow impatient, did not feel cheated. In addition to four new rides, including the wildly popular Yo-Yo, an immense steel yo-yo suspended by a thick cable from a tower and supplied with seats, visitors to Sarabee's Bargain Basement, as the new park good-naturedly came to be called, discovered that many rides and attractions were playful or fiendish variations of familiar amusement park pleasures. Thus the merry-go-round included an all-white horse that turned out to be a bucking bronco, around a high curve the roller coaster left the tracks and soared over a twenty-foot gap to another set of tracks (such at least was the thrilling sensation, although in fact the cars were supported from beneath by hinged beams attached to the coaster frame), the funhouse mirrors turned people into hideous, frightening monsters, and the Ferris wheel, at the climax of the ride, dropped slowly from its stationary supports and rolled back and forth along a track that left room for the bottommost cars to pass unharmed. In the same spirit the architecture was more extravagant—the front roller-coaster cars were supplied with carved dragon's heads, the Old Mill began in the sneering mouth of an ogre, a papier-mâché mountain called the Haunted Grotto opened at a cave flanked by thirty-foot naked giantesses whose legs and arms were encircled by giant snakes—and the stage properties for the actors were more sinister, the actor-drunks rowdier, the false prostitutes more brazen, some going so far as to lure customers into back rooms that turned out to be part of the House of Mirth. The sense that the rides were, in a controlled way, out of control, that they were exceeding bounds, that they were imitating nightmarish breakdowns while remaining perfectly safe, all this proved intoxicating to the crowds, who at the same time were urged to a feverish carnival spirit by the winking electric lights, the artificial night sky, the crash of artificial waves, the sense of a vast underground adventure not bound by the rules of ordinary parks.

Despite the enthusiastic reception of Sarabee's New Paradise Park by Coney Island pleasure-seekers, by journalists, and by a number of distinguished foreign visitors, several critical voices were raised during the first months, and not only from the ranks of observers who might be expected to cast doubt on the new institutions of mass pleasure such as the dance hall, the vaudeville theater, the movie house, and the amusement park. An article in the August 1915 issue of *Munsey's Magazine* praised New Paradise Park for the boldness of its design and the ingenuity of its rides but paused to question whether Sarabee had not pushed the amusement park beyond its proper limit. Such developments as the leaping roller coaster and the rolling Ferris wheel, though of undoubted technological interest, threatened to make people bored with traditional rides and to encourage in them an unhealthy appetite for more extreme and dangerous sensations. It was in this sense that technology and morality became related issues, for a mass audience accustomed to violent mechanical pleasures was in danger of growing dissatisfied with the routines of everyday life and especially with their jobs, a dissatisfaction that in turn was bound to lead to a desire for more extreme forms of release. For finally the carefully engineered mechanical excitements and sensual stimulations of Sarabee's park were not and could not be satisfying, but were in the nature of a cheat, an ingenious illusion that left people secretly restless and unappeased. The unsigned article concluded by wondering whether this abiding restlessness was not the true aim of the great amusement-park showman, in whose interest it was to create an audience perpetually hungry for the unfruitful pleasures he knew so well how to provide.

Even as such questions were being raised by voices skeptical of the new mass culture in general and of New Paradise Park in particular, it was rumored that Sarabee and his staff were at work on new plans, and there were those who said that Sarabee would never rest until he had carried the amusement park to its farthest limit of expression.

The new stage in the evolution of Paradise Park was not completed for two years, during which attendance increased even as war threatened. Unlike the upper park, the underground park was not required to close after the summer season, and Sarabee was able to run it at a profit through mid-November, after which the thinning crowds forced him to close for the winter. In the profitable season of 1916 three new rides appeared in the underground park, including a Ferris wheel supplied with paired carousel horses instead of seats, while in the upper park small signs of a disturbing development first became noticeable. The rides, although still in operation, were no longer replaced by new ones; the high roller coaster suffered a mechanical breakdown and was shut down; here and there a booth stood empty. Although the lawns and paths around the famous rotundas were kept clean and neat, grass grew wild in far corners of the park, and occasional patches of rust appeared on brightly painted steel frames.

It was in the expanded park of 1917 that Sarabee achieved what many called the fulfillment of his dream, although a few voices were raised in dissent. Visitors to the famous underground park discovered, in scattered and unlikely locations—on the beach, in bathhouses, behind game booths, under the roller coaster—some two dozen escalators leading down. The simple escalators led to a second underground level where a puzzling new park had been created—a pastoral park of oak and beech woodlands, winding paths, peaceful lakes, rolling hills, flowering meadows, babbling brooks, wooden footbridges, and soothing waterfalls: a detailed artificial landscape composed entirely of plaster and pasteboard (except for an occasional actor-shepherd with his herd of real sheep), illuminated by the light of electric lanterns with colored glass panes, and inviting the tired reveler to solitude and meditation. This deliberate emphasis on pleasures opposed to those of the amusement park was not lost upon visitors, who savored the contrast but could not overcome a sense of disappointment. That carefully arranged dissatisfaction was in turn overcome when the visitor on his ramble discovered an opening in a hill, or a doorway in an old oak, or a tunnel in a riverbank, all of which contained stone steps that led down to another level, where at the end of rocky passageways with mossy mouths a brilliant new amusement park stretched away.

Here in a masterful mingling of attractions visitors were invited to ride the world's first spherical Ferris wheel; experience the thrilling sensation of being buried alive in a coffin in the Old Graveyard; visit a Turkish palace, including the secret rooms of the seraglio with over six hundred concubines; ride the exciting new Wild Wheel Coaster; visit an exact reproduction of the Alhambra with all its pillars, arches, courtyards, and gardens, including the seventy-five-foot-high dome of the Salo de los Embajadores and the Patio de los Leones with its alabaster fountain supported by twelve white marble lions; enter the world's most frightening House of Horrors with its unforgettable hall of Rats; witness the demonic possession of the girls at the witch trials of Salem; fly through the trees on the backs of mechanical monster-birds in the Forest of Night; ride a real burro down a replicated Grand Canyon trail; visit a bustling harbor containing reconstructions of a Nantucket whaling ship, a Spanish galleon, Darwin's *Beagle*, a Viking long ship, Oliver Hazard Perry's flagship *Lawrence*, a Phoenician trireme, a Chinese junk, and Old Ironsides; see a departed dear one during a seance in the Medium's Mansion; ride the sensational triple-decker merry-go-round; visit a medieval torture chamber and see actor-victims broken on the rack, crushed in the iron boot, and hoisted on the strappado; descend into a replica of the labyrinthine salt mines of Hallstatt, Austria; ride the death-defying Barrel, a padded iron barrel guided by cables along a white-water rapids and down a reconstruction of the Horseshoe Falls composed of real Niagara water; ride the Swirl-a-Whirl, the Hootchie-Kootchie, and the Coney Island Sling; and pay a heartwarming visit to the Old Plantation, where seventy-five genuine southern darkies (actually white actors in blackface) strummed banjos, danced breakdowns, ate watermelons, picked cotton, and sang spirituals in four-part harmony while a benign Master sat on a veranda between his blond-ringleted daughter and a faithful black mammy who from time to time said "Lawdee!"

This continually changing landscape of rides, spectacles, exotic places, and reconstructed cultural wonders was connected by an intricate system of cable cars designed by Danziker, which criss-crossed the entire park and permitted visitors to gain an overview of the multitude of attractions and travel conveniently from one section to another. Danziker had also designed a scale-model sub-way, consisting of roofless cars the size of scenic-railway cars, driven by real engines and underlying the entire park, with twenty-four stations indicated by small kiosks in twenty-four dif-ferent styles, including a circus tent, a Gothic cathedral, a tepee, a Persian summerhouse, a log cabin, and a Moorish palace.

In addition to the striking transportation system, certain fea-tures of the new park drew attention in the popular press, in particular the group of sixteen new mechanical rides invented by Danziker, of which the most successful was the Chute Ball: an openwork iron sphere twenty feet in diameter that rolled along a steep, curving chute while riders inside were seated on twelve benches attached in such a way that they remained upright while revolving on a spindle. It was noted that most of the traditional rides had been carried to further degrees of evolution: in the Double Coaster, specially built roller-coaster cars rounding a turn suddenly rushed from the track and soared unsupported over dangerous gaps onto the track of a second roller coaster, and an immense and swiftly turning Airplane Swing released its planes one by one to fly through the air to a powerful plane-catching machine that resembled an iron octopus. The popular Wild Wheel was seen as a combination of roller coaster and Ferris wheel: along a sinuous coasterlike track rolled a great iron wheel, forty feet in diameter; the wheel's two grooved rims turned along a pair of steel cables that had been suspended at intervals from wrought-iron posts and ran like telephone wires above the entire length of the dipping and rising track; up to one hundred riders sat strapped into wire cages on the inside of the wheel and turned as the wheel turned. But technological process was less evident in the mechanical rides, which at best were clever varia-tions of familiar rides, than in the methods of transportation, in the advanced plumbing system in the public bathrooms, and in minor effects, such as the much-praised pack of mechanical rats in the House of Horrors.

The new park was also praised for its many meticulous reconstructions of cultural landmarks and natural wonders, all of which made the similar attractions of Luna and the expositions seem crude and childish. Sarabee's customers were invited to visit not only the Alhambra, but also the Porcelain Tower of Nanking, the catacombs of Alexandria, the Inca ruins of Cuzco, the hanging gardens of Babylon, and the palace of Kubla Khan, as well as an alp, a fjord, a stalactite cavern, a desert containing an oasis, a redwood forest, an iceberg, a sea grotto, and a bamboo grove inhabited by real pandas. One of the most admired replicas was that of the Edison Laboratory at West Orange, New Jersey, with its three-story main building that contained machine shops, experimental rooms, and rooms for glassblowing and electrical testing, as well as the famous forty-foot-high library with its great fireplace and its displays of thousands of ores and minerals in glass-fronted cabinets, the whole building and its four outbuildings enclosed by a high fence with a guard at the entrance gate; the laboratory was supplied with a staff of sixty actor-assistants, and Edison himself was played by the Shakespearean actor Howard Ford, who was particularly good at imitating Edison's famous naps—after which he would spring up refreshed and invent the phonograph or the electric light. But Sarabee's mania for replication reached its culmination in an immense project that he designed with Otis Stilwell: a sixty-by-forty-foot model in wood and pasteboard of Paris, France, including over eighty thousand buildings and thirty thousand trees (representing thirty-six different species), the precise furnishings of every apartment, shop, church, café, and department store, all the fruits and vegetables in Les Halles and all the fishing nets in the Seine, all the horse-drawn carriages, motorcars, bicycles, fiacres, motor omnibuses, and electric streetcars, every tombstone in Pére Lachaise cemetery and every plant in the Jardin des Plantes, over two hundred thousand miniature waxwork figures representing all social classes and occupations, and at the heart of the little city, an exact scale model of the Louvre, including not only every gallery, every staircase, every window mullion and ceiling decoration, but a precise miniature reproduction of every painting (oil on copper)

537

and its frame (beechwood), every statue (ivory), and every artifact, from Egyptian sarcophagi to richly detailed eighteenth-century spoons so minuscule that they were invisible to the naked eye and had to be viewed through magnifying lenses.

The 1917 park was widely regarded as the most complete, most successful form of the modern amusement park, its final and classic expression, which might be varied and expanded but never surpassed; and the sole question that remained was where Sarabee would go from here.

Even as the classic park was being hailed in the press, Sarabee was said to be planning another park, about which he was more than usually secretive. At about the same time he began to lose interest in his older parks, which were placed under the management of a five-man board who were required to report to Sarabee only twice a year and who concentrated their attention on the first two underground parks and the pastoral park between them, while largely neglecting the aboveground park, which continued to decline. Patches of rust spread on the bridge-braces, paint peeled on the carousels, weeds grew under the roller coaster and between lanes of booths; and there were signs of deeper neglect. In certain stretches of the upper park, guards were removed and brought below; the remaining guards grew less vigilant, so that a dangerous element began to assert itself. A gang of actors, who seemed to have grown into their roles, prowled the darkened alleyways, where shanty brothels were said to spring up; and complaints were made against a gang of dwarf thugs who quit the Nightmare Railway and took up residence in a dark corner of the park called Dwarftown, where no one ventured after dusk.

Sarabee's new park, which opened in 1920 beneath the classic park of 1917, puzzled his admirers and caused lengthy reassessments of the showman's career. Here at one blow he did away with the four central features of the modern amusement park—the mechanical ride (roller coaster, Swizzler), the exotic attraction (replicated village, market, garden, temple), the spectacle (Destruction of Carthage), and the carnival amusement (freak show, game booth)—and replaced them with an entirely new realm of pleasures. In a dramatic turn away from meticulous replication, Sarabee presented to customers in his new underground level a scrupulously fantastic world. And here it becomes difficult to be precise, for Sarabee banned photographs and the historian is forced to rely on often contradictory eyewitness accounts, tainted at times by rumor and exaggeration. We hear of dream-landscapes with gigantic nightmare flowers and imaginary flying animals, of impalpable pillars and edible disks of light. There are reports of sudden stairways leading to underwater kingdoms, of disappearing towns, of vast complex structures that resemble nothing ever seen before. Illusionary effects appear to have been widely used, for we hear of high walls that suddenly melt away, of metamorphoses and vanishings, and of a device that made a strong impression: a springing monster suddenly stops in midair, as if frozen, and then dissolves. This last suggests that Sarabee made use of hidden movie projectors to enhance his other effects. The entire park appeared to have been a thorough rejection not only of the replica, the reconstruction, the exotic imitation, which had haunted amusement parks from the beginning, but also of the mechanical ride, which by its very nature proclaimed its kinship with the real world of steel, dynamos, and electrical power even while turning that world into play. Sarabee's new park seized instead on the unreality and otherworldliness of amusement parks and carried fantastic effects to an unprecedented development. But Sarabee was careful to avoid certain traditional elements of fantasy that had become familiar and cozy. We therefore never hear of comfortable creatures like dragons, witches, ghosts, and Martians, or even of familiar elements of fantasy architecture such as pinnacles, towers, and battlements. Everything is strange, unsettling, even shifting—for we hear of lighting effects that cause entire structures to be viewed differently, of uncanny replacements and transformations that resemble scene-shifting in a theater. Machinery appears to have been used solely in a disguised, invisible way; for only the presence of hidden machinery can explain certain repeatedly mentioned phenomena, such as solid islands floating in the air and a mysteriously sinking hill.

The response by the public to Sarabee's new park was curious: people descended, roamed about, uttered admiring sounds, felt a little puzzled, and finally returned to one of the higher parks. The opening-day attendance was the highest ever—over sixty-three thousand in the first two hours—but it quickly became apparent that crowds were not staying. By the second month receipts were far below those of even the uppermost park, in its state of increasing neglect. People seemed to admire the new park but not really to like it very much; they preferred the mechanical rides, the replicas, the booths, the barkers, the hot-dog stands, all of which had been rigorously banished from the new park. Sarabee, always alert to the mood of the crowds, did what he had never done before: instead of making alterations, he launched a mid-season promotional campaign. Attendance rose for one week, then took a dramatic plunge, and long before the end of the season it was clear that the new park was a resounding failure.

Sarabee met with his staff of advisers, who recommended three kinds of remedy: the addition of exciting new rides to enliven the somewhat inert park; the construction of a huge domed amphitheater in the center of the park, to contain twelve tiers of game booths, food stands, shops, restaurants, and penny arcades surrounding three revolving stages on which would be presented, respectively, a funhouse, an old-fashioned amusement park, and a three-ring circus; and the razing of the park and its replacement by an entirely new one on more conventional lines but with brand-new rides. Sarabee listened attentively, rejected all three recommendations, and shut himself up with Danziker and Stilwell to consider improvements that would enhance rather than alter the nature of the park. In an interview given in 1927, Danziker said that Sarabee had never seemed surer of himself than in this matter of the new park; and despite his own conviction that the park was a failure and that Sarabee should listen to the voice of the people, Danziker had laid his doubts aside and thrown himself willingly into Sarabee's effort to save the park, which had already begun to be known as Sarabee's Folly.

The enhanced park opened the next season, to a massive publicity campaign that promised people thrills and pleasures of a kind they had never experienced before; a journalist writing in the *New York Herald* called the new park the most brilliant revolution in the history of the amusement park, with effects so extraordinary that they were worthy of the name of art. The next day a journalist on a rival paper asked scornfully: It may be art, but is it fun? He granted the superiority, even the brilliance, of Sarabee's latest devices, but felt that Sarabee had lost touch with the amusement park spirit, which after all was a popular spirit and thrived on noise, laughter, and rough-and-tumble effects. Within a month it was obvious that the refurbished park was not a success. Sarabee continued to run it at a loss, refused to alter it in any way, and began to spend several hours a day walking in the shifting dream-perspectives of his nearly empty park, which still drew a small number of visitors, some of whom came solely in the hope of catching a glimpse of the famous entrepreneur. And a rumor began to grow that Sarabee was already making plans for an entirely new park, which would surpass his own most stunning creations and restore him to his rightful place as the Edison of amusement-park impresarios.

In the world of commercial amusement, success is measured in profit; but it is also measured in something less tangible, which may be called approval, or esteem, or fame, but which is really a measure of the world's compliance in permitting a private dream to become a public fact. Sarabee, who had made his fortune in department stores and had since made it many times over in his series of unrivaled parks, had always enjoyed the pleasurable sense that his dreams and inspirations were encouraged by the outer world, were so to speak confirmed and made possible by something outside himself that was greater than himself— namely, the mass of other people who recognized in his embodied dream their own vague dreams, who showered him with money as a sign of their pleasure, and for whom he was, in a way, dreaming. His newest park was Sarabee's first experience of commercial failure—his first experience, that is, of losing the world's approval, of dreaming the wrong dream. His peculiar stubbornness may be explained in many ways, but one way is simply this, that he refused to believe what had happened. He kept expecting the crowds to come round. When it became clear they wouldn't, he was already so soaked in his dream that he could not undream it. This is only another way of suggesting that Sarabee, whatever he was, was not cynical; his showmanship, his shrewd sense of what was pleasing to crowds, his painstaking efforts to adjust his inventions in the direction of wider and wider audiences, were only the practical and necessary expression of a cause he thoroughly believed in.

Admirers of Sarabee praised the failed park as a sign of his originality and of his growing independence from the corruptions of mass taste; critics regretted it as a sign of decline, of increasing remoteness from common humanity; but both camps agreed that the failure was a crucial moment in Sarabee's career, a moment that whetted their appetite for his next advance. For there was never any question of that. As Sarabee wandered the shifting illusions of his nearly deserted park, disguised as a weeping clown, or a journalist, or an old man with a cane, who dared to imagine that he hadn't already begun to plan another park?

It was about this time that the board of managers made an effort to save the declining upper park, if only because it served as entrance to the lower levels. Guards in maroon jackets were posted along the paths leading to the rotundas. The high grass was trimmed at the base of the openwork iron towers and under the roller coaster, bare patches were seeded and paths newtarred, booths cleaned and painted, rust on bridge-braces removed, roller-coaster tracks repaired and old cars replaced with shiny new ones. Only at the far corners of the park, in the dark, twisting alleys of Dwarftown or the decaying lanes inhabited by unsavory actors, did the board abandon its efforts at restoring order and permit a shantytown to flourish among the weeds, the refuse, the broken lights.

Eyewitness accounts of the new park, which opened on May 19, 1923, contradict themselves so sharply that it is difficult to know what was imagined and what was actually there, but the reports all suggest that Sarabee's new level had a deliberately provocative air, as if he had set out to construct a sinister amusement park, an inverted park of dark pleasures. We know that visitors were given a choice: either to pass through the other parks or to descend directly in any of the thirty-six elevators that had been installed on the outside of the great upper wall. Those who chose the new elevators found themselves in large, lanternlit elevator cars operated by masked attendants costumed like devils. We do not know exactly where the Costume Pavilions were located, although it appears that visitors were urged to assume a disguise before passing through red-curtained archways into an almost dark world. The park was lit only by red and ocher lights that dimly illuminated the midnight towers, the looming buildings and black alleys, where whispers of barkers in dark doorways and bursts of honky-tonk music were punctuated with darker noises—howls, harsh voices, clashes of glass. It was a world both alluring and disturbing, a dark underworld of uncertain pleasures that made people hesitate on the threshold before deciding to lose themselves in the dark.

However exaggerated some of the accounts may be, or confused by the presence of actors and stunt men, it is clear that the park was intended to startle and shock. Many visitors simply left in anger and disgust. But large numbers remained to stroll about uneasily, peering into archways, lingering in the dark alleys, looking about as if fearful of being caught, while still others abandoned themselves utterly to the extreme and dubious pleasures of the park. Such abandonment, such release from the constraints of the upper parks, is precisely what the park seems actively to have encouraged—hence the importance of the Costume Pavilions, which, apart from adding color and humor, served the more serious purpose of encouraging people to assume new identities. The park appears to have deliberately offered itself as a series of temptations; the crowds were continually invited to step over the very line carefully drawn in Sarabee's other parks. The complaints of scandalized visitors resulted in two separate police investigations, each of which turned up nothing, although critics of the investigation pointed out that Sarabee was more than capable of disguising the true nature of his amusements and that in any case the head of the investigations was a former roller-coaster operator in the upper park—a charge that was never substantiated.

In the face of questionable and conflicting evidence it is difficult to know how to assess the many eyewitness reports, which include disturbing accounts of a House of Horrors so frightening that visitors are reduced to fits of hysterical weeping, of funhouse mirrors that show back naked bodies in obscene postures. We hear of smoky sideshows in which the knife-thrower pierces the wrists of the spangled woman on the turning wheel and the sword-swallower draws from his throat a sword red with blood. We hear of rides so violent that people are rendered unconscious or insane, of a House of Eros filled with cries of terror and ecstasy. There are reports of troubling erotic displays in a Palace of Pleasure, where female visitors fitted with special harnesses are said to drop through trapdoors into transparent pillars of glass sixty feet high, which stand in a great hall filled with masked men and women who shout and cheer at the swift but harness-controlled falls that send skirts and dresses swirling high above the hips—an erotic display that is said to take on an eerie beauty as twenty or thirty women fall screaming in the great hall lit by red, blue, and green electric lights. We hear of a Lovers' Leap in which unhappy lovers chain their wrists together and jump to their deaths before crowds standing behind velvet ropes, of a Suicide Coaster built to leave the track at its highest curve and plunge to destruction in a dark field. There is talk of a Palace of Statues divided into a labyrinth of small rooms, in which replicas of famous classical statues are said to satisfy unspeakable desires. We hear of disturbing prodigies of scale-model art, such as an Oriental palace the size of a child's building block, filled with hundreds upon hundreds of chambers, corridors, stairways, dungeons, and curtained recesses, and containing over five thousand figures visible only with the aid of a magnifying lens, who exhibit over three thousand varieties of sexual appetite, and there are reports of a masterful miniature of Paradise Park itself, carved out of beechwood and revealing every level in rigorous detail, from the festive upper bridges with their rides, brass bands, and exotic villages to the most secret rooms of the darkest pleasure palaces in the blackest depths of the lowest level, containing over thirty thousand figures in sharply caught attitudes, the whole concealed under a silver thimble. Even taking exaggeration into account, what are we to make of a Children's Castle in which girls ten and eleven years old are said to prowl the corridors costumed as Turkish concubines, Parisian streetwalkers, and famous courtesans and lure small boys and girls into hidden rooms? What are we to think of deep pleasure-pits into which visitors are encouraged to leap by howling, writhing devils, or of a Tunnel of Ecstasy, a House of Blood, a Voyage of Unearthly Delights? From these and similar reports, however unreliable, it seems clear that the new park invited violations of an extreme kind, and carried certain themes to a dark fulfillment. But the park seems never to have been intrinsically unsafe; rather, the dangers lay in the rides and pleasure palaces themselves, and not in the promenades and alleys, where the costumed crowds were never violent and where serious troublemakers were led away by masked guards and dropped into straw-filled dungeons.

One of the more disturbing features of the new level, which quickly became known as Devil's Park, was the public suicides, which many visitors claimed to have witnessed, although among the witnesses were those who said it was all a hoax performed by specially trained actors. Even the majority who believed the suicides to be real were divided among themselves, some expressing moral outrage and others asserting what they called a right to suicide. The issue was brought to a head by the spectacular death of sixteen-year-old Anna Stanski, a high-school student from Brooklyn who disguised herself as a man in a porkpie hat, pushed her way through the turnstile at the top of the new Lovers' Leap, tore off her hat and set fire to her hair, and leaped flaming from the ledge before anyone could stop her—this at the very moment when a woman in her twenties and a man with wavy gray hair were having their wrists chained together by an attendant. Anna Stanski's fiery death was witnessed by hundreds of visitors, many of whom saw her lying in a field with twisted arms and a broken neck, and it was reported the next day in major newspapers across the country. The park management, forced to defend itself, pointed out that Anna Stanski was a troubled teenager with a history of depression, that those who accused the park of promoting public suicides were now in the odd position of having to admit that Anna Stanski's suicide actually saved two lives, since it discouraged the chained lovers from pursuing their leap, and that the park was no more responsible for her death than the city of New York was responsible for the deaths of those who leaped almost daily from its bridges and skyscrapers. Critics were quick to point out that there was a sharp distinction to be made between the city of New York and an immoral "amusement" that actively encouraged suicide, while others, scornful of the claim that lives had been saved, questioned whether the two so-called lovers were not rather actors hired to stir the passions of the crowd. Their scorn was turned against them by the park's defenders, who argued that if in fact the lovers were actors, then the park could not be accused of encouraging suicide; and they argued further that, in comparison with the number of accidental deaths that occur in all amusement parks and are accepted in good faith as part of the risk, the number of suicides in Sarabee's park, whether staged or real, was trivial and negligible, despite the grotesque attention paid to them by antagonists whose real enemy was not suicide at all but freedom pure and simple. The episode was soon overshadowed by a hotel fire in Brighton, in which fourteen people died, and the murder of minor racketeer Giambattista Salerno in a Surf Avenue seafood restaurant.

Responses to the new park were sharply divided, but even outraged critics who considered the park a moral disgrace admitted that Sarabee, while forfeiting the respect he had earned with his earlier parks, was a shrewd showman who knew how to appeal to the debased tastes of the urban masses. Several commentators made an effort to connect the park with the new postwar freedom, the collapse of middle-class morality, the indiscriminate rush toward pleasure—in short, the collective frenzy of which Devil's Park was but the latest symptom. In an attempt to assess the park and place it in Sarabee's career, one critic argued that it was the embittered showman's cynical response to his failed park: thoroughly disillusioned by failure, Sarabee had created an anti-park, a deliberately crude and savage park pandering to the most despicable instincts of the crowd. This interpretation, which attracted a good deal of attention, was answered incisively in a long article by Warren Burchard, who after an eleven-year silence on the subject of amusement parks returned to the charge and argued that Devil's Park, far from being an exception in Sarabee's career, was the latest expression of an unbroken line of development. Each park, the argument ran, carried the idea of the amusement park to a greater extreme. This remained true even of the failed park, which, despite its rejection of the mechanical ride, moved in the direction of newer and more intense pleasures. The ten-year history of Sarabee's parks, Burchard argued, was nothing less than an uninterrupted movement in a single direction, of which Devil's Park was not simply the latest but also the final development. For here Sarabee had dared to incorporate into his park an element that threatened the very existence of that curious institution of mass pleasure known as the amusement park: namely, an absence of limits. After this there could be no further parks, but only acts of refinement and elaboration, since any imaginable step forward could result only in the complete elimination of the idea of an amusement park. Burchard's argument was taken up and modified by a number of other critics, but it remained the classic defense of Devil's Park, against which opponents of Sarabee were forced to shape their counterarguments.

The moral outrage directed against the new park, the conflicting reports, the rumors and exaggerations, the death of Anna Stanski, all served to pique the public's curiosity and increase attendance, despite the many people who declared they would never return; and such evidence as we have suggests that many of Sarabee's most outspoken opponents did in fact return, again and again, lured by forbidden pleasures, by the protection of masks and disguises, by sheer curiosity.

Even as controversy raged, and investigation threatened, and attendance rose, rumor had it that Sarabee was planning still another park. It was said that Sarabee was working on a ride so extraordinary that to go on it would be to change your life forever. It was said that Sarabee was developing a magical or mystical park from which the unwary visitor would never return. It was said that Sarabee was creating a park consisting of small, separate booths in which, by means of a special machine attached to the head, each immobile visitor would experience the entire range of human sensation. It was said that Sarabee was creating an invisible park, an infinite park, a park on the head of a pin. The intense and often irresponsible speculation of that winter was a clear sign that Sarabee had touched a nerve; and as the new season drew near and the last mounds of snow melted in the shadows of the bathhouses, small weekend crowds began to arrive in order to walk around the famous white wall, to stare at the great gates, the high towers, the covered elevator booths, to hover about the closed park in the hope of piercing its newest secret.

The opening was set for Saturday, June 1, 1924, at 9 A.M.; as early as Friday evening a line began to form. By 6:30 the following morning the crowd was so dense that mounted police were called in to keep order. The eyewitness reports differ in important details, but most agree that shouts were heard from inside the park at about seven o'clock. A few minutes later the gates opened to let out a stream of workmen, concessionaires, actors, spielers, Mbuti tribesmen, ride operators, dwarfs, and maroon-jacketed guards, all of whom were gesticulating and shouting. The first alarm was sounded shortly thereafter, and witnesses claimed to see a thin trail of smoke at the top of the wall. Within twenty minutes the entire park was in flames. The great white wall, a highly flammable structure of lath and staff that had cost a small fortune to insure, quickly became a vast ring of fire; policemen cleared the streets as chunks of flaming wall fell like meteors and threw up showers of sparks. By the third alarm, fire engines were arriving from every firehouse in Brooklyn. As part of the wall collapsed, spectators could see the flaming rides within: the merry-go-round with its fiery roof and its circle of burning horses, the hellish Ferris wheel turning in a sheet of fire, the collapsing bridges, the blackened roller coaster with its blazing wooden struts, the fiery booths and falling towers. Suddenly a cry went up: from one of the rotundas leading to the first underground park, there rose a flock of flaming seagulls, crying a high, pained cry. Some of them flew in crazed circles directly into the crowd, where people screamed and covered their faces and beat the air with their hands.

By nine in the morning firemen were fighting only to contain the raging fire and save neighboring property; hoses poured water on the blistering facades of side-street boarding houses, and a police launch was sent to rescue nine fishermen trapped at the end of a blazing pier. Suddenly a sideshow lion, its mane on fire, leaped over a flaming section of wall and ran screaming in pain into the street. Three policeman with drawn revolvers chased it into a parking lot, where it sprang onto the hood of a parked car. They shot it twenty times in the head and then smashed its skull with an ax. By ten o'clock a portion of ground caved in and fell to the park below, which was also in flames; spectators from the tops of nearby buildings could see down into a pit of fire, which was consuming the two hotels, the six bathhouses, the shops, the restaurants, the underground roller coaster and House of Mirth. The fiery lower pier fell hissing into the artificial ocean, throwing up dark clouds of acrid smoke; and from the flames there rose again a flock of crazed and shrieking gulls, their backs and wings on fire, turning and spinning through the smoke and flames, until at last, one by one, they plunged down like stones.

By noon the fire was under control, although it continued to rage on every level all afternoon and far into the night. By the following morning Paradise Park was a smoking field of rubble and wet ashes. Here and there rose a few blackened and stunted structures: the melted metal housing of a Ferris-wheel motor, the broken concrete pediment of some vanished ride, clumps of curled iron. Somehow—the papers called it a miracle—only a single human life was lost, although innumerable lions, tigers, monkeys, pumas, elephants, and camels perished in the fire, as well as the seagulls of the first underground level. The single body, discovered in the debris of the deepest level and damaged beyond recognition, was assumed by many to be Sarabee himself, an assumption that seemed confirmed by the disappearance of the showman and the discovery, in his Surf Avenue office, of a signed letter transferring ownership of the park to Danziker in the event of Sarabee's death. Some, it is true, insisted that the evidence was by no means conclusive and that Sarabee had simply slipped away in another disguise. Although the cause of the fire was never determined, a strong suspicious of arson was never put to rest; reports from inside the park suggested that the fire had not spread from one level to another but had broken out on all levels simultaneously. The papers vied with one another in proclaiming it Sarabee's Greatest Show, or Another Sarabee Spectacular; the crude headlines may have contained a secret truth. For as Warren Burchard expressed it in a memorable obituary article, the fiery destruction of Paradise Park was the "logical last step" in a series of increasingly violent pleasures: after the extreme inventions of Devil's Park, only the dubious thrill of total destruction remained. Sarabee, the article continued, recognizing the inevitability of the next step, had designed the fire and arranged his own death, since to survive the completed circle of his parks was unthinkable. The historian can only note that such arguments, however attractive, however irrefutable, are not subject to the laws of evidence; and that we know as fact only that Paradise Park was utterly destroyed in a conflagration that lasted some twenty-six hours and cost an estimated eight million dollars in property damage.

It is nevertheless true that the brief history of Paradise Park, when separated from legend, may lead even the most cautious historian to wonder whether certain kinds of pleasure, by their very nature, do not seek more and more extreme forms until, utterly exhausted but unable to rest, they culminate in the black ecstasy of annihilation.

The ruined park was repossessed by the City of New York, which filled in the underground levels and turned the upper level into an extension of the parking lot that covered the remainder of the old Dreamland property; the enlarged parking lot became a public park in 1934 under the administration of Fiorello LaGuardia and has remained a park to this day. Here and there in shady corners of the park, on hot summer afternoons, it is said that you can feel the earth move slightly and hear, far below, the faint sound of subterranean merry-go-rounds and the cries of perishing animals.

In 1926 a paper presented by Coney Island historian John Carter Dixon to the Brooklyn Historical Society revealed that no one called Warren Burchard had ever worked for the *Brooklyn Eagle*. Later evidence uncovered by Dixon showed that the name had been invented by Sarabee as part of a promotional campaign. Although the author of the Burchard articles is unknown, Dixon suggests that they were written by one of Sarabee's press agents and touched up by Sarabee himself, who appears to have had a hand in his own obituary notice.

Nearly seventy years after the destruction of Paradise Park, Sarabee's legacy remains an ambiguous one. His most daring innovations have been ignored by later amusement-park entrepreneurs, who have been content to move in the direction of the safe, wholesome, family park. Sarabee, himself the inventor of a classic park, was driven by some dark necessity to push beyond all reasonable limits to more dangerous and disturbing inventions. He comes at the end of the era of the first great American amusements parks, which he carried to technological and imaginative limits unsurpassed in his time, and he set an example of restless invention that has remained unmatched in the history of popular pleasure.

A book of photographs called *Old New York*, published by Arc Books in 1957 and long out of print, contains fourteen views of Paradise Park: nine pictures of the upper level, including two of Paradise Alley, and five of the first underground level. The one most evocative of a vanished era shows a group of male bathers in sleeveless dark bathing costumes standing with their hands on their hips in the artificial surf before the crisscross iron braces of the underground pier, with its gabled wooden roof, its arches and turrets, its flying flags: some of the men stare boldly and even sternly at the camera, while others, with powerful shoulders and thick mustaches, are smiling in an easy, boyish-manly, innocent way that seems at one with the knee-high water, the pier, the ocean air, the unseen festive park.

1994

CAMO, DOPE & VIDEOTAPE

by HAROLD JAFFE

from FICTION INTERNATIONAL

"*SLEEP IS LOVELY, death is better still,*
Not to have been born is of course the miracle."
"Sylvia Plath?" Shirl says.
"Naw," Earl says.
"Shirley MacLaine?"
"Sorry."
"Pound? Ezra Pound?"
"You've got to be kidding."
"This game gets on my nerves," Shirl says. "Let's cut."
"Where to?"
"There's a rave down on Mombasa. Dance your blues away."
"Lovely, except I don't have a thing to wear."
"Wear what you're wearing."
"Tenement T and jockeys?"
"Sure."
"The jocks aren't that, uh, fresh."
"Be a funky honky, Earl."
They go out, Earl in his funky jocks, tenement T and yellow patent leather mules, Shirl in her tattoos, black leather mini and Chicago Bulls cap turned sideways. He carries the Sony vidcam on a strap on his shoulder. On the way to the rave they run into a riot of cops working over a man they pulled from a Hyundai.

The man is brown. The 17 cops (Shirl counts them) are white. The cops are whacking him with their batons, kicking and stomping him with their black, thick cop shoes. Rockports, the majority of them. Rockport made a bid the NYPD couldn't resist. Plus, they're made in the USA.

When the beaten brown man's blood starts to spurt the assaulting cops skip away. See, if that spurting infected blood finds a cut or nick in an assaulting cop's neck, glove, or tricep and gets into his circuitry—forget it.

Four cops are confiscating the vidcams of anyone who videotapes the assault. Fuck that shit.

Shirl and Earl continue to walk, traipse, saunter, prance to the dance, or rave, on Mombasa.

Every once in a while Earl pauses to shoot vid. Shoots a seagull jabbing at the remains of a pigeon, flattened by a bus or truck in the middle of the street.

The gull jabs vigorously, looking up and around after every jab.

Shirl bites into a Baby Ruth.

Earl shoots a pair walking in their direction. The doll wears an olive drab bulletproof vest over a fuchsia silk sleeveless nightgown. Her head is shaved, she wears a gold ring in her nose and white Reebok shitkickers. The dude, barechested, is wearing Rolex tit clamps, baggy camo fatigues, mirror shades, a red stetson, and lilac high-heeled mules. He has delicate feet and knows it.

Earl shoots gutted buildings and a monster graffito which says: **LOVE OF CUNT.** He shoots a doll shooting vid. The doll is shooting a knot of near-naked homeless squatting around a rubbish fire.

One of the homeless plays the concertina.

Hey, look what's coming. A phalanx of vicious skinheads on rollerblades coursing through the street. They're barechested and tattooed and carry heavy chains and baseball bats. Their steel-tipped Doc Martens are tied around their necks. One of the skating skins, rear left, is shooting the others.

Earl, squatting, shoots the whole deal.

They get to the rave on Mombasa. It's in a warehouse, what used to be a warehouse. The music is loud, pulsing, percussive, lots of bass.

The theme of the rave is **Black Hole,** so most of the dancers are bare-assed, bending, thrusting, jiggling, spreading.

Earl takes off his funky jocks and flips them to the underwear dude.

Shirl takes off her panties and flips them to the underwear dude.

553

Shirl doesn't remove her black leather mini. Forms a line with other assfrees, dolls and dudes. They do a can-can routine.

An assfree standing on his head is selling Ecstasy.

Earl buys four hits, swallows two, hands the others to Shirl.

This is fast-acting, fast-fading X, and pretty soon the dancers are sexing: squatting, stretching, pumping on the filthy cement floor. Earl and Shirl do some muck in a X chain, which is a daisy chain fueled by Ecstasy.

What about zafe zex?

Yo, what they're doing is safe, Counselor. Low risk, maybe a little bit of medium risk. Fact is each and every strung-out assfree funk-punk at the Mombasa rave is intimately familiar with the Surgeon General's white paper on *AIDS and Abstinence*. Some even have key passages of the white paper inscribed on the inside of their eyelids. It's the last jolly news they see before falling asleep.

Later an assfree climbs onto one of the stanchions which support the strobe lights and pees on the dancers. A second assfree climbs onto another stanchion and pees down on the dancers. Soon whacked-out assfrees are climbing all over the warehouse, peeing on the dancers.

Well, the rave ends, as all delirium must, or so they say.

And now the underwear dude can't come up with Earl's jocks.

He's an old dude with a hearing device behind his ear.

Earl cuffs him across the brow, the hearing device pops free and skitters along the filthy cement floor.

"Sorry about that," Earl says. "But I get mad when old dudes lose my jocks."

The old dude hands Earl someone else's jocks.

Back at the condo, Shirl recites:
"The criminal injustice that deceives
And rules us, lays our corpses end on end."
"Poe?" Earl says.
"No."
"Rimbaud?"
"Who?"
"Rimbaud. Real name: Sly Stallone. He's a writer and philosopher besides being an actor and superstar."
"No."
"The X wore off," Earl says. "I'm not up anymore. You up?"

"No."

"Let's get up."

"Blue or pink?" Shirl says.

"Either. Both."

Shirl shakes some pills out of a container into her mouth, swigs Diet Pepsi from the bottle. Then she shakes some pills into Earl's fist and hands him the plastic bottle of Diet Pepsi.

They stick the vid he shot in the streets into the VCR and watch it while waiting for the up.

"Look at that doll shooting those near-naked homeless," Shirl says.

"Look at that near-naked homeless dude playing the concertina," Earl says.

"Isn't that a doll?"

"Yeah, you're right. She can really play that concertina."

"Isn't that an accordion?" Shirl says.

"No. Accordion is larger."

"I thought accordion was smaller."

"Hey, look at that vicious barechested, tattooed, skating skinhead shooting those vicious, barechested, tattooed, skating skinheads."

"What's he shooting, Earl?"

"Sony. KDX. Top of the line."

They watch the tape of the assfrees peeing down at the dancers in the Mombasa rave.

"Look at the equipment on that dude," Earl says.

"That's a doll with a garden hose tied to her hips, Earl."

"You're right. I think it's coming on, Shirl."

"Me too," Shirl says. "What do you want to do?"

"Dunno. We screw already?"

"Yeah. No. I can't remember."

"Let's spiff up and cut."

Over the funky jockeys that aren't his, Earl puts on Shirl's black leather mini. Removes his tenement T exposing his Rolex tit clamps. Puts on a Banana Republic stonewashed denim jacket braided with gull feathers, pigeon feathers, human hair, snakeskin, shell casings.

Shirl puts on a dyed-camo horsetail hairpiece, purple latex jump suit and yellow high-top canvas Nikes. Snatches the vidcam.

"How you feelin', Shirl?"

"Hot to trot. What's that noise?"

"That's the highpitched, dissonant whine of law and order, Shirl."

Earl's right. Halfway down the block from their condo is a zig-zag of cop cars, strobes rotating. Looks like they're working over someone on the pavement.

"I bet they're brutalizing a black or Latino gang member," Shirl says.

"Those gangs are real bad," Earl says. "With their drive-by shootings, drugging, pimping, they louse things up for the rest of us."

"They don't obey the English-only statute of this great state," Shirl says.

"They talk inner-city-jive-cholo talk," Earl says.

Shirl and Earl traipse away from the cop cars.

"Is that rain?" from Shirl.

"Naw. I just spit up in the air."

"Do it again, I'll shoot it."

Earl spits up in the air. Does it several times while Shirl, crouched on one knee, shoots it with the Sony.

They walk again. I mean: traipse.

"You up, Earl?"

"Kinda. I think I'm good for another twenty minutes, maybe."

"We need stronger shit."

"Hey, Shirl, look at the old doll."

An old woman with her drawers around her knees is squatting against a gutted building, hanging on to a rusted railing to keep from falling in her dung.

"Shoot her, Shirl."

Hell, Shirl is already on one knee shooting the squatting old woman. Walking again.

"We need stronger shit," Shirl says.

"I hear you," Earl says. " 'Cept where we gonna cop?"

"Good question."

"They don't mind us doin' weak and medium-weak shit," Earl says. "But we cop some good shit they'll bust us. Which means the joint. You know what the joint means, Shirl."

"Joint means heavy-duty time with zero parole."

"Why's that, Shirl?"

" 'Cause they privatized prisons, right?"

"Exactly. Your penal institution is the biggest growth industry there is. Hey, catch that tall dude, Shirl."

"Where?"

"Leaning against that yield sign. He's a long drink of water, ain't he? Looks like he's shooting ice."

Shirl turns, squats and shoots the dude leaning against the yield sign shooting ice.

Sudden loud whirring of choppers overhead. Two of them, sweeping low and someone yelling down through a bullhorn.

"They yelling at us, Earl?"

"I thing they're yelling at that dude shooting ice."

Sure enough, one chopper sweeps real low, drops a rope ladder and two chopper cops scamper down and leap into the street right near the dude shooting ice. Weird thing is the dude don't even seem to notice. Cops wearing rubber riot-gear snatch the dude, take his works, work him over a little bit, push him up the street. The choppers meanwhile have moved north toward Khartoum.

Shirl, squatting, is shooting the whole deal with her vidcam.

When it's over Earl and Shirl exchange a high five.

"Good shoot, Shirl."

"Yeah."

Walking again, they turn west at the pier fronting the lordly Hudson. The pier is boarded up, the sign says **No Entry—Danger,** but fuck that shit. Earl and Shirl slip through a gap in the fence and hear music, a banjo. Walk onto the crumbling pier where a cluster of young men are square dancing. When they get closer they see that the men aren't young but middle-aged and older. One is playing the banjo and six are gracefully do-si-do-ing. The men are all gay, and each has approximately the same fused expression on his face: wry irony, defiant pride, resignation.

Or so it seems to Earl who, grinning, watched them, and Shirl, who, kneeling, shot them.

Back at the condo, Shirl recites:
*"A virus eats the heart out of our sides,
digs in and multiplies on our lost blood."*

"Allen Ginsberg?" Earl says.

"Nope."

"Baudelaire?"

"Who?"

"Charles Baudelaire. French."

"No," Shirl says.

"Hang on," Earl says. "I think I can identify your quote. It was that Disney executive, at the site of the opening of that billion-dollar-plus Disney theme park near Paris. I caught this on CNN business news.

The Disney guy was a Rob Lowe lookalike with pulsing cheekbones. He was into this deal about how faggoty AIDS is destroying the virtuous lust for leisure."

"Did you say Rob Lowe lookalike?"

"Right."

"Did you say virtuous lust for leisure?"

"Right. Well, did I identify your quote?" Earl says. "And if I did, what do I get?"

"You identified my quote," Shirl says. "And what you're about to get is a face full of funk."

1997

COURTING A MONK

by KATHERINE MIN

from TRIQUARTERLY

W<small>HEN</small> I <small>FIRST SAW</small> my husband he was sitting cross-legged under a tree on the quad, his hair as short as peach fuzz, large blue eyes staring upward, the smile on his face so wide and undirected as to seem moronic. I went flying by him every minute or two, guarding man-to-man, or chasing down a pass, and out of the corner of my eye I would see him watching and smiling. What I noticed about him most was his tremendous capacity for stillness. His hands were like still-life objects resting on his knees; his posture was impeccable. He looked so rooted there, like some cheerful, exotic mushroom, that I began to feel awkward in my exertion. Sweat funneled into the valley of my back, cooling and sticking when I stopped, hands on knees, to regain my breath. I tried to stop my gape-mouthed panting, refashioned my ponytail, and wiped my hands on the soft front of my sweatpants.

He was still there two plays later when my team was down by one. Sully stole a pass and flipped to Graham. Graham threw me a long bomb that sailed wide and I leapt for it, sailing with the Frisbee for a moment in a parallel line—floating, flying, reaching—before coming down whap! against the ground. I groaned. I'd taken a tree root in the solar plexus. The wind was knocked out of me. I lay there, the taste of dry leaves in my mouth.

"Sorry, Gina. Lousy pass," Graham said, coming over. "You O.K.?"

"Fine," I gasped, fingering my ribs. "Just let me sit out for a while."

I sat down in the leaves, breathing carefully as I watched them play. The day was growing dark and the Frisbee was hard to see.

Everyone was tired and played in a sloppy rhythm of errant throws and dropped passes.

Beside me on the grass crept the guy from under the tree. I had forgotten about him. He crouched shyly next to me, leaves cracking under his feet, and, when I looked up, he whispered, "You were magnificent," and walked away smiling.

I spotted him the next day in the vegetarian dining hall. I was passing through with my plate of veal cordon bleu when I saw him sitting by himself next to the window. He took a pair of wooden chopsticks out of the breast pocket of his shirt and poked halfheartedly at his tofu and wilted mung beans. I sat down across from him and demanded his life story.

It turned out he wanted to be a monk. Not the Chaucerian kind, bald-pated and stout, with a hooded robe, ribald humor and penchant for wine. Something even more baffling—a Buddhist. He had just returned from a semester in Nepal, studying in a monastery in the Himalayas. His hair was coming back in in soft spikes across his head and he had a watchful manner—not cautious but receptive, waiting.

He was from King of Prussia, off the Philadelphia Main Line, and this made me mistrust the depth of his beliefs. I have discovered that a fascination for the East is often a prelude to a pass, a romantic overture set in motion by an "I think Oriental girls are so beautiful," and a vise-like grip on the upper thigh. But Micah was different. He understood I was not impressed by his belief, and he did not aim to impress.

"My father was raised Buddhist," I told him. "But he's a scientist now."
"Oh," said Micah. "So, he's not spiritual."
"Spirit's insubstantial," I said. "He doesn't hold with intangibility."
"Well, you can't hold atoms in your hand," Micah pointed out.
"Ah," I said, smiling, "But you can count them."

* * *

I told Micah my father was a man of science, and this was true. He was a man, also, of silence. Unlike Micah, whose reticence seemed calming, so undisturbed, like a pool of light on still water, my father's silence was like the lid on a pot, sealing off some steaming, inner pressure.

Words were not my father's medium. "Language," my father liked to say, "is an imprecise instrument." (For though he said little, when he hit upon a phrase he liked, he said it many times.) He was fond of Greek letters and numerals set together in intricate equations, sym-

560

bolizing a certain physical law or experimental hypothesis. He filled yellow legal pads in a strong, vertical hand, writing these beauties down in black, indelible felt-tip pen. I think it was a source of tremendous irritation to him that he could not communicate with other people in so ordered a fashion, that he could not simply draw an equals sign after something he'd said, have them solve for x or y.

That my father's English was not fluent was only part of it. He was not a garrulous man, even in Korean, among visiting relatives, or alone with my mother. And with me, his only child—who could speak neither of his preferred languages, Korean or science—my father had conspicuously little to say. "Pick up this mess," he would tell me, returning from work in the evening. "Homework finished?" he would inquire, raising an eyebrow over his rice bowl as I excused myself to go watch television.

He limited himself to the imperative mood, the realm of injunction and command; the kinds of statement that required no answer, that left no opening for discussion or rejoinder. These communications were my father's verbal equivalent to his neat numerical equations. They were hermetically sealed.

When I went away to college, my father's parting words constituted one of the longest speeches I'd heard him make. Surrounded by station wagons packed with suitcases, crates of books and study lamps, amid the excited chattering and calling out of students, among the adults with their nervous, parental surveillance of the scene, my father leaned awkwardly forward with his hands in his pockets, looking at me intently. He said, "Study hard. Go to bed early. Do not goof off. And do not let the American boys take advantages."

This was the same campus my father had set foot on twenty years before, when he was a young veteran of the Korean War, with fifty dollars in his pocket and about that many words of English. Stories of his college years constituted family legend and, growing up, I had heard them so often they were as vivid and dream-like as my own memories. My father in the dorm bathroom over Christmas, vainly trying to hard-boil an egg in a sock by running it under hot water; his triumph in the physics lab where his ability with the new language did not impede him, and where his maturity and keen scientific mind garnered him highest marks and the top physics prize in his senior year—these were events I felt I'd witnessed, like some obscure, envious ghost.

In the shadow of my father's achievements then, on the same campus where he had first bowed his head to a microscope, lost in a

561

chalk-dust mathematical dream, I pursued words. English words. I committed myself to expertise. I studied Shakespeare and Eliot, Hardy and Conrad, Joyce and Lawrence and Hemingway and Fitzgerald. It was important to get it right, every word, every nuance, to fill in my father's immigrant silences, the gaps he had left for me.

Other gaps he'd left. Staying up late and studying little, I did things my father would have been too shocked to merely disapprove. As for American boys, I heeded my father's advice and did not let them take advantage. Instead I took advantage of them, of their proximity, their good looks, and the amiable way they would fall into bed with you if you gave them the slightest encouragement. I liked the way they moved in proud possession of their bodies, the rough feel of their unshaven cheeks, their shoulders and smooth, hairless chests, the curve of their backs like burnished wood. I liked the way I could look up at them, or down, feeling their shuddering climax like a distant earthquake; I could make it happen, moving in undulant circles from above or below, watching them, holding them, making them happy. I collected boys like baubles, like objects not particularly valued, which you stash away in the back of some drawer. It was the pleasant interchangeability of their bodies I liked. They were all white boys.

Micah refused to have sex with me. It became a matter of intellectual disagreement between us. "Sex saps the will," he said.

"Not necessarily," I argued. "Just reroutes it."

"There are higher forms of union," he said.

"Not with your clothes off," I replied.

"Gina," he said, looking at me with kindness, a concern that made me flush with anger. "What need do you have that sex must fill?"

"Fuck you, Micah," I said. "Be a monk, not a psychologist."

He laughed. His laughter was always a surprise to me, like a small disturbance to the universe. I wanted to seduce him, this was true. I considered Micah the only real challenge among an easy field. But more than seduction, I wanted to rattle him, to get under that sense of peace, that inward contentment. No one my age, I reasoned, had the right to such self-possession.

We went for walks in the bird sanctuary, rustling along the paths slowly, discussing Emily Dickinson or maple syrup-making, but always I brought the subject around.

"What a waste of a life," I said once. "Such indulgence. All that monkly devotion and quest for inner peace. Big deal. It's selfish. Not only is it selfish, it's a cop-out. An escape from this world and its messes."

Micah listened, a narrow smile on his lips, shaking his head regretfully. "You're so wonderfully passionate, Gina, so alive and in the world. I can't make you see. Maybe it is a cop-out, as you say, but Buddhism makes no distinction between the world outside or the world within the monastery. And historically, monks have been in the middle of political protest and persecution. Look at Tibet."

"I was thinking about, ahem, something more basic," I said.

Micah laughed. "Of course," he said. "You don't seem to understand, Gina, Buddhism is all about the renunciation of desire."

I sniffed. "What's wrong with desire? Without desire, you might as well not be alive."

The truth was that I was fascinated by this idea, the renunciation of desire. My life was fueled by longing, by vast and clamorous desires; a striving toward things I did not have and, perhaps, had no hope of having. I could vaguely imagine an end, some point past desiring, of satiety, but I could not fathom the laying down of desire, walking away in full appetite.

"The desire to renounce desire," I said now, "is still desire, isn't it?"

Micah sunk his hands into his pockets and smiled. "It's not," he said, walking ahead of me. "It's a conscious choice."

We came to a pond, sun-dappled in a clearing, bordered by white birch and maples with the bright leaves of mid-autumn. A fluttering of leaves blew from the trees, landing on the water as gently as if they'd been placed. The color of the pond was a deep canvas green; glints of light snapped like sparks above the surface. There was the lyric coo of a mourning dove, the chitter-chitter of late-season insects. Micah's capacity for appreciation was vast. Whether this had anything to do with Buddhism, I didn't know, but watching him stand on the edge of the pond, his head thrown back, his eyes eagerly taking in the light, I felt his peace and also his sense of wonder. He stood motionless for a long time.

I pulled at ferns, weaved their narrow leaves in irregular samplers, braided tendrils together, while Micah sat on a large rock and, taking his chopsticks from his breast pocket, began to tap them lightly against one another in a solemn rhythm.

"Every morning in the monastery," he said, "we woke to the prayer drum. Four o'clock and the sky would be dark and you'd hear the hollow wooden sound—plock, plock, plock—summoning you to meditation." He smiled dreamily. The chopsticks made a somewhat less effectual sound, a sort of ta ta ta. I imagined sunrise across a Himalayan valley—the wisps of pink-tinged cloud on a cold spring morning, the austerity of a monk's chamber.

Micah had his eyes closed, face to the sun. He continued to tap the chopsticks together slowly. He looked singular and new, sitting on that rock, like an advance scout for some new tribe, with his crest of hair and calm, and the attentiveness of his body to his surroundings.

I think it was then I fell in love with him, or, it was in that moment that my longing for him became so great that it was no longer a matter of simple gratification. I needed his response. I understood what desire was then, the disturbance of a perfect moment in anticipation of another.

"Wake-up call," I said. I peeled off my turtleneck and sweater in one clever motion and tossed them at Micah's feet. Micah opened his eyes. I pulled my pants off and my underwear and stood naked. "Plock, plock, who's there?"

Micah did not turn away. He looked at me, his chopsticks poised in the air. He raised one toward me and held it, as though he were an artist with a paintbrush raised for a proportion, or a conductor ready to lead an orchestra. He held the chopstick suspended in the space between us, and it was as though I couldn't move for as long as he held it. His eyes were fathomless blue. My nipples constricted with the cold. Around us leaves fell in shimmering lights to the water, making a soft rustling sound like the rub of stiff fabric. He brought his hand down and I was released. I turned and leapt into the water.

A few nights later I bought a bottle of cheap wine and goaded Micah into drinking it with me. We started out on the steps of the library after it had closed for the night, taking sloppy swigs from a brown paper bag. The lights of the Holyoke range blinked in the distance, across the velvet black of the freshman quad. From there we wandered the campus, sprawling on the tennis courts, bracing a stiff wind from the terrace of the science center, sedately rolling down Memorial Hill like a pair of tumbleweeds.

"J'a know what a koan is?" he asked me, when we were perched at the top of the bleachers behind home plate. We unsteadily contemplated the steep drop off the back side.

"You mean like ice cream?" I said.

564

"No, a ko-an. In Buddhism."

"Nope."

"It's a question that has no answer, sort of like a riddle. You know, like 'What is the sound of one hand clapping?' Or 'What was your face before you were born?'"

"'What was my face before it was born?' That makes no sense."

"Exactly. You're supposed to contemplate the koan until you achieve a greater awareness."

"Of what?"

"Of life, of meaning."

"Oh, O.K.," I said, "I've got it." I was facing backwards, the bag with the bottle in both my hands. "How 'bout, 'What's the sound of one cheek farting?'"

He laughed for a long time, then retched off the side of the bleachers. I got him home and put him to bed; his forehead was feverish, his eyes glassy with sickness.

"Sorry," I said. "I'm a bad influence." I kissed him. His lips were hot and slack.

"Don't mind," he murmured, half-asleep.

The next night we slept in the same bed together for the first time. He kept his underwear on and his hands pressed firmly to his sides, like Gandhi among his young virgins. I was determined to make it difficult for him. I kept brushing my naked body against him, draping a leg across his waist, stroking his narrow chest with my fingertips. He wiggled and pushed away, feigning sleep. When I woke in the morning, he was gone and the *Ode to Joy* was blasting from my stereo.

Graham said he missed me. We'd slept together a few times before I met Micah, enjoying the warm, healthful feeling we got from running or playing Ultimate, taking a quick sauna and falling into bed. He was good-looking, dark and broad, with sinewy arms and a tight chest. He made love to a woman like he was lifting Nautilus, all grim purpose and timing. It was hard to believe that had ever been appealing. I told him I was seeing someone else.

"Not the guy with the crew cut?" he said. "The one who looks like a baby seal?"

I shrugged.

Graham looked at me skeptically. "He doesn't seem like your type," he said.

"No," I agreed. "But at least he's not yours."

Meanwhile I stepped up my attack. I asked endless questions about Buddhist teaching. Micah talked about *dukkha;* the four noble truths; the five aggregates of attachment; the noble eightfold path to enlightenment. I listened dutifully, willing to acknowledge that it all sounded nice, that the goal of perfect awareness and peace seemed worth attaining. While he talked, I stretched my feet out until my toes touched his thigh; I slid my hand along his back; or leaned way over so he could see down my loose, barely-buttoned blouse.

"Too bad you aren't Tantric," I said. I'd been doing research.

Micah scoffed. "Hollywood Buddhism," he said. "Heavy breathing and theatrics."

"They believe in physical desire," I said. "They have sex."

"Buddha believes in physical desire," Micah said. "It's impermanent, that's all. Something to get beyond."

"To get beyond it," I said petulantly, "you have to do it."

Micah sighed. "Gina," he said, "you are beautiful, but I can't. There are a lot of guys who will."

"A lot of them do."

He smiled a bit sadly. "Well, then . . . "

I leaned down to undo his shoelaces. I tied them together in double knots. "But I want you," I said.

My parents lived thirty miles from campus and my mother frequently asked me to come home for dinner. I went only once that year, and that was with Micah. My parents were not the kind of people who enjoyed the company of strangers. They were insular people who did not like to socialize much or go out—or anyway, my father was that way, and my mother accommodated herself to his preferences.

My mother had set the table in the dining room with blue linen. There were crystal wine glasses and silver utensils in floral patterns. She had made some dry baked chicken with overcooked peas and carrots—the meal she reserved for when Americans came to dinner. When it came to Korean cooking, my mother was a master. She made fabulous marinated short ribs and sautéed transparent bean noodles with vegetables and beef, pork dumplings and batter-fried shrimp, and cucumber and turnip kimchis which she made herself and fermented in brown earthenware jars. But American cuisine eluded her; it bored her. I think she thought it was meant to be tasteless.

"Just make Korean," I had urged her on the phone. "He'll like that."

My mother was skeptical. "Too spicy," she said. "I know what Americans like."

"Not the chicken dish," I pleaded. "He's a vegetarian."

"We'll see," said my mother, conceding nothing.

Micah stared down at his plate. My mother smiled serenely. Micah nodded. He ate a forkful of vegetables, took a bite of bread. His Adam's apple seemed to be doing a lot of work. My father, too, was busy chewing, his Adam's apple moving up and down his throat like the ratchets of a tire jack. No one had said a thing since my father had uncorked the Chardonnay and read to us the description from his well-creased paperback edition of *The New York Times Guide to Wine*.

The sound of silverware scraping on ceramic plates seemed amplified. I was aware of my own prolonged chewing. My father cleared his throat. My mother looked at him expectantly. He coughed.

"Micah studied Buddhism in Nepal," I offered into the silence.

"Oh!" my mother exclaimed. She giggled.

My father kept eating. He swallowed exaggeratedly and looked up. "That so?" he said, sounding almost interested.

Micah nodded. "I was only there four months," he said. "Gina tells me you were brought up Buddhist."

My father grunted. "Well, of course," he said, "in Korea in those days, our families were all Buddhist. I do not consider myself a Buddhist now."

Micah and I exchanged a look.

"It's become quite fashionable, I understand," my father went on. "With you American college kids. Buddhism has become fad."

I saw Micah wince.

"I think it is wonderful, Hi Joon," my mother interceded, "for Americans to learn about Asian religion and philosophy. I was a philosophy major in college, Micah. I studied Whitehead, American pragmatism."

My father leaned back in his chair and watched, frowning, while my mother and Micah talked. It was like he was trying to analyze Micah, not as a psychiatrist analyzes—my father held a dim view of psychology—but as a chemist would, breaking him down to his basic elements, the simple chemical formula that would define his makeup.

Micah was talking about the aggregates of matter, sensation, perception, mental formations, and consciousness that comprise being in Buddhist teaching. "It's a different sense of self than in Christian religions," he explained, looking at my mother.

"Nonsense," my father interrupted. "There is no self in Buddhist doctrine. . . . "

My mother and I watched helplessly as they launched into discussion. I was surprised that my father seemed to know so much about it, and by how much he was carrying forth. I was surprised also by Micah's deference. He seemed to have lost all his sureness, the walls of his conviction. He kept nodding and conceding to my father certain points that he had rigorously defended to me before. "I guess I don't know as much about it," he said more than once, and "Yes, I see what you mean" several times, with a sickening air of humility.

I turned from my father's glinting, pitiless intelligence, to Micah's respectfulness, his timid manner, and felt a rising irritation I could not place, anger at my father's belligerence, at Micah's backing down, at my own strange motives for having brought them together. Had I really expected them to get along? And yet, my father was concentrating on Micah with such an intensity— almost as though he were a rival—in a way in which he never focused on me.

When the dialogue lapsed, and after we had consumed as much of the food as we deemed polite, my mother took the dishes away and brought in a bowl of rice with kimchi for my father. Micah's eyes lit up. "May I have some of that, too, Mrs. Kim?"

My mother looked doubtful. "Too spicy," she said.

"Oh, I love spicy food," Micah assured her. My mother went to get him a bowl.

"You can use chopsticks?" my mother said, as Micah began eating with them.

"Mom, it's no big deal," I said.

My father looked up from his bowl. Together, my parents watched while Micah ate a large piece of cabbage kimchi.

"Hah!" my father said, suddenly smiling. "Gina doesn't like kimchi," he said. He looked at me. "Gina," he said. "This boy more Korean than you."

"Doesn't take much," I said.

My father ignored me. "Gina always want to be American," he told Micah. "Since she was little girl, she want blue eyes, yellow hair." He stabbed a chopstick toward Micah's face. "Like yours."

"If I had hair," said Micah, grinning, rubbing a hand across his head.

My father stared into his bowl. "She doesn't want to be Korean girl. She thinks she can be 100 percent American, but she cannot. She has Korean blood—100 percent. Doesn't matter where you grow up— blood is most important. What is in the blood." He gave Micah a severe look. "You think you can become Buddhist. Same way. But it is not in your blood. You cannot know real Buddha's teaching. You should study Bible."

"God, Dad!" I said. "You sound like a Nazi!"

"Gina!" my mother warned.

"You're embarrassing me," I said. "Being rude to my guest. Discussing me as if I wasn't here. You can say what you want, Dad, I'm American whether you like it or not. Blood's got nothing to do with it. It's what's up here." I tapped my finger to my temple.

"It's not Nazi," my father said. "Is fact! What you have here," he pointed to his forehead, "is all from blood, from genetics. You got from me!"

"Heaven help me," I said.

"Gina!" my mother implored.

"Mr. Kim—" Micah began.

"You just like American girl in one thing," my father shouted. "You have no respect for father. In Korea, daughters do not talk back to their parents, is big shame!"

"In Korea, girls are supposed to be submissive doormats for fathers to wipe their feet on!" I shouted back.

"What do you know about Korea? You went there only once when you were six years old."

"It's in my blood," I said. I stood up. "I'm not going to stay here for this. Come on, Micah."

Micah looked at me uncertainly, then turned to my father.

My father was eating again, slowly levering rice to his mouth with his chopsticks. He paused. "She was always this way," he said, seeming to address the table. "So angry. Even as a little girl."

"Mr. Kim," Micah said, "Um, thank you very much. We're . . . I think we're heading out now."

My father chewed ruminatively. "I should never have left Korea," he said quietly, with utter conviction.

"Gina," my mother said. "Sit down. Hi Joon, please!"

"Micah," I said. "You coming?"

We left my father alone at the dining-room table.

"I should have sent you to live with Auntie Soo!" he called after me.

My mother followed us out to the driveway with a Tupperware container of chicken Micah hadn't eaten.

On the way home we stopped for ice cream. Koans, I told Micah. "What is the sound of Swiss chocolate almond melting?" I asked him. "What was the vanilla before it was born?"

Inside the ice-cream parlor the light was too strong, a ticking fluorescence bleaching everything bone-white. Micah leaned down to survey the cardboard barrels of ice cream in their plastic cases. He looked shrunken, subdued. He ordered a scoop of mint chocolate chip and one of black cherry on a sugar cone and ate it with the long, regretful licks of a child who'd spent the last nickel of his allowance. There was a ruefulness to his movements, a sense of apology. He had lost his monk-like stillness and seemed suddenly adrift.

The cold of the ice cream gave me a headache, all the blood vessels in my temples seemed strung out and tight. I shivered and the cold was like fury, spreading through me with the chill.

Micah rubbed my back.

"You're hard on your father," he said. "He's not a bad guy."

"Forget it," I said. "Let's go."

We walked from the dorm parking lot in silence. There were lights going on across the quad and music spilling from the windows out into the cool air. What few stars there were seemed too distant to wage a constant light.

Back in my room, I put on the Rolling Stones at full blast. Mick Jagger's voice was taunting and cruel. I turned out the lights and lit a red candle.

"O.K., this is going to stop," I said. I felt myself trembling. I pushed Micah back on the bed. I was furious. He had ruined it for me, the lightness, the skimming quality of my life. It had seemed easy, with the boys, the glib words and feelings, the simple heat and surface pleasures. It was like the sensation of flying, leaping for the Frisbee and sailing through the air. For a moment you lose a feeling for gravity, for the consciousness of your own skin or species. For a moment you are free.

I started to dance, fast, swinging and swaying in front of the bed. I closed my eyes and twirled wildly, bouncing off the walls like a pinball, stumbling on my own stockings. I danced so hard the stereo skipped, Jagger forced to stutter in throaty monosyllables, gulping repetitions.

I whirled and circled, threw my head from side to side until I could feel the baffled blood, brought my hair up off my neck and held it with both hands.

Micah watched me dance. His body made an inverted-S upon my bed, his head propped by the pillar of his own arm. The expression on his face was the same as he'd had talking with my father, that look of deference, of fawn-eyed yielding. But I could see there was something hidden.

With white-knuckled fingers, I undid the buttons of my sweater and ripped my shirt lifting it off my head. I danced out of my skirt and underthings, kicking them into the corner, danced until the song was over, until I was soaked with sweat and burning—and then I jumped him.

It was like the taste of food after a day's starvation—unexpectedly strong and substantial. Micah responded to my fury, met it with his own mysterious passion; it was like a brawl, a fight, with something at stake that neither of us wanted to lose. Afterward we sat up in bed and listened to *Ode to Joy* while Micah, who had a surplus supply of chopsticks lying around the room, did his Leonard Bernstein impersonation. Later, we went out for a late-night snack to All-Star Dairy and Micah admitted to me that he was in love.

*   *   *

My father refused to attend the wedding. He liked Micah, but he did not want me to marry a Caucasian. It became a joke I would tell people. Korean custom, I said, to give the bride away four months before the ceremony.

Micah became a high-school biology teacher. I am an associate dean of students at the local college. We have two children. When Micah tells the story of our courtship, he tells it with great self-deprecation and humor. He makes it sound as though he were crazy to ever consider becoming a monk. "Think of it," he tells our kids. "Your dad."

Lately I've taken to reading books about Buddhism. Siddhartha Gotama was thirty-five years old when he sat under the Bodhi-tree on the bank of the river Neranjara and gained Enlightenment. Sometimes, when I see my husband looking at me across the breakfast table, or walking toward me from the other side of a room, I catch a look of distress on his face, a blinking confusion, as though he cannot remember who I am. I have happened on him a few times, on a Sunday

571

when he has disappeared from the house, sitting on a bench with the newspaper in his lap staring across the town common, so immersed in his thoughts that he is not roused by my calling of his name.

I remember the first time I saw him, that tremendous stillness he carried, the contentment in his face. I remember how he looked on the rocks by that pond, like a pioneer in a new land, and I wonder if he regrets, as I do, the loss of his implausible faith. Does he miss the sound of the prayer drum, the call to an inner life without the configuration of desire? I think of my father, running a sock under heated water thousands of miles from home, as yet unaware of the daughter he will raise with the same hopeful, determined, and ultimately futile, effort. I remember the way I used to play around with koans, and I wonder, "What is the sound of a life not lived?"

1998

INVIERNO

by JUNOT DÍAZ

from GLIMMER TRAIN

FROM THE TOP OF Westminister, our main strip, you could see the thinnest sliver of ocean cresting the horizon to the east. My father had been shown that sight—the management showed everyone—but as he drove us in from JFK he didn't stop to point it out. The ocean might have made us feel better, considering what else there was to see. London Terrace itself was a mess; half the buildings still needed their wiring and in the evening light these structures sprawled about the landscape like ships of brick that had run aground. Mud followed gravel everywhere and the grass, planted late in fall, poked out of the snow in dead tufts.

Each building has its own laundry room, Papi said. Mami looked vaguely out of the snout of her parka and nodded. That's wonderful, she said. I was watching the snow sift over itself and my brother was cracking his knuckles. This was our first day in the States. The world was frozen solid.

Our apartment seemed huge to us. Rafa and I had a room to ourselves and the kitchen, with its refrigerator and stove, was about the size of our house on Sumner Welles. We didn't stop shivering until Papi set the apartment temperature to about eighty. Beads of water gathered on the windows like bees and we had to wipe the glass to see outside. Rafa and I were stylish in our new clothes and we wanted out, but Papi told us to take off our boots and our parkas. He sat us down in front of the television, his arms lean and surprisingly hairy right up to the short-cut sleeves. He had just shown us how to flush the toilets, run the sinks, and start the shower.

This isn't a slum, Papi began. I want you to treat everything around you with respect. I don't want you throwing any of your garbage on the floor or on the street. I don't want you going to the bathroom in the bushes.

Rafa nudged me. In Santo Domingo I'd pissed everywhere, and the first time Papi had seen me in action, whizzing on a street corner, on the night of his triumphant return, he had said, What are you doing?

Decent people live around here and that's how we're going to live. You're Americans now. He had his Chivas Regal bottle on his knee.

After waiting a few seconds to show that yes, I'd digested everything he'd said, I asked, Can we go out now?

Why don't you help me unpack? Mami suggested. Her hands were very still; usually they were fussing with a piece of paper, a sleeve, or each other.

We'll just be out for a little while, I said. I got up and pulled on my boots. Had I known my father even a little I might not have turned my back on him. But I didn't know him; he'd spent the last five years in the States working, and we'd spent the last five years in Santo Domingo waiting. He grabbed my ear and wrenched me back onto the couch. He did not look happy.

You'll go out when I tell you you're ready. I don't want either of you getting lost or getting hurt out there. You don't know this place.

I looked over at Rafa, who sat quietly in front of the TV. Back on the island, the two of us had taken guaguas clear across the Capital by ourselves. I looked up at Papi, his narrow face still unfamiliar. Don't you eye me, he said.

Mami stood up. You kids might as well give me a hand.

I didn't move. On the TV the newscasters were making small, flat noises at each other.

Since we weren't allowed out of the house—it's too cold, Papi said—we mostly sat in front of the TV or stared out at the snow those first days. Mami cleaned everything about ten times and made us some damn elaborate lunches.

Pretty early on Mami decided that watching TV was beneficial; you could learn English from it. She saw our young minds as bright, spiky sunflowers in need of light, and arranged us as close to the TV as possible to maximize our exposure. We watched the news, sitcoms, cartoons, *Tarzan, Flash Gordon, Jonny Quest, Herculoids, Sesame*

Street—eight, nine hours of TV a day, but it was *Sesame Street* that gave us our best lessons. Each word my brother and I learned we passed between ourselves, repeating over and over, and when Mami asked us to show her how to say it, we shook our heads and said, Don't worry about it.

Just tell me, she said, and when we pronounced the words slowly, forming huge, lazy soap-bubbles of sound, she never could duplicate them. Her lips seemed to tug apart even the simplest constructions. That sounds horrible, I said.

What do you know about English? she asked.

At dinner she'd try her English out on Papi, but he just poked at his pernil, which was not my mother's best dish.

I can't understand a word you're saying, he said one night. Mami had cooked rice with squid. It's best if I take care of the English.

How do you expect me to learn?

You don't have to learn, he said. Besides, the average woman can't learn English.

Oh?

It's a difficult language to master, he said, first in Spanish and then in English.

Mami didn't say another word. In the morning, as soon as Papi was out of the apartment, Mami turned on the TV and put us in front of it. The apartment was always cold in the morning and leaving our beds was a serious torment.

It's too early, we said.

It's like school, she suggested.

No, it's not, we said. We were used to going to school at noon.

You two complain too much. She would stand behind us and when I turned around she would be mouthing the words we were learning, trying to make sense of them.

Even Papi's early-morning noises were strange to me. I lay in bed, listening to him stumbling around in the bathroom, like he was drunk or something. I didn't know what he did for Reynolds Aluminum, but he had a lot of uniforms in his closet, all filthy with machine oil.

I had expected a different father, one about seven feet tall with enough money to buy our entire barrio, but this one was average height, with an average face. He'd come to our house in Santo Domingo in a busted-up taxi and the gifts he had brought us were small things—toy guns and tops—that we were too old for, that we broke right away. Even though he hugged us and took us out to dinner on the Malecón—our first meat in years—I didn't know what to make of him. A father is a hard thing to get to know.

Those first weeks in the States, Papi spent a great deal of his hometime downstairs with his books or in front of the TV. He said little to us that wasn't disciplinary, which didn't surprise us. We'd seen other dads in action, understood that part of the drill.

What he got on me about the most was my shoelaces. Papi had a thing with shoelaces. I didn't know how to tie them properly, and when I put together a rather formidable knot, Papi would bend down and pull it apart with one tug. At least you have a future as a magician, Rafa said, but this was serious. Rafa showed me how, and I said, Fine, and had no problems in front of him, but when Papi was breathing down my neck, his hand on a belt, I couldn't perform; I looked at my father like my laces were live wires he wanted me to touch together.

I met some dumb men in the Guardia, Papi said, but every single one of them could tie his motherfucking shoes. He looked over at Mami. Why can't he?

These were not the sort of questions that had answers. She looked down, studied the veins that threaded the backs of her hands. For a second Papi's watery turtle-eyes met mine. Don't you look at me, he said.

Even on days I managed a halfway decent retard knot, as Rafa called them, Papi still had my hair to go on about. While Rafa's hair was straight and dark and glided through a comb like a Caribbean grandparent's dream, my hair still had enough of the African to condemn me to endless combings and out-of-this-world haircuts. My mother cut our hair every month, but this time when she put me in the chair my father told her not to bother.

Only one thing will take care of that, he said. Yunior, go get dressed.

Rafa followed me into my bedroom and watched while I buttoned my shirt. His mouth was tight. I started to feel anxious. What's your problem? I said.

Nothing.

Then stop watching me. When I got to my shoes, he tied them for me. At the door my father looked down and said, You're getting better.

I knew where the van was parked but I went the other way just to catch a glimpse of the neighborhood. Papi didn't notice my defection until I had rounded the corner, and when he growled my name I hurried back, but I had already seen the fields and the children on the snow.

I sat in the front seat. He popped a tape of Jonny Ventura into the player and took us out smoothly to Route 9. The snow lay in dirty piles on the side of the road. There can't be anything worse than old snow, he said. It's nice while it falls but once it gets to the ground it just causes trouble.

Are there accidents?

Not with me driving.

The cattails on the banks of the Raritan were stiff and the color of sand, and when we crossed the river, Papi said, I work in the next town.

We were in Perth Amboy for the services of a real talent, a Puerto Rican barber named Rubio who knew just what to do with the pelo malo. He put two or three creams on my head and had me sit with the foam awhile; after his wife rinsed me off he studied my head in the mirror, tugged at my hair, rubbed an oil into it, and finally sighed.

It's better to shave it all off, Papi said.

I have some other things that might work.

Papi looked at his watch. Shave it.

All right, Rubio said. I watched the clippers plow through my hair, watched my scalp appear, tender and defenseless. One of the old men in the waiting area snorted and held his paper higher. When he was finished Rubio massaged talcum powder on my neck. Now you look guapo, he said. He handed me a stick of gum, which would go right to my brother.

Well? Papi asked. I nodded. As soon as we were outside the cold clamped down on my head like a slab of wet dirt.

We drove back in silence. An oil tanker was pulling into port on the Raritan and I wondered how easy it would be for me to slip aboard and disappear.

Do you like negras? my father asked.

I turned my head to look at the women we had just passed. I turned back and realized that he was waiting for an answer, that he wanted to know, and while I wanted to blurt that I didn't like girls in any denomination, I said instead, Oh yes, and he smiled.

They're beautiful, he said, and lit a cigarette. They'll take care of you better than anyone.

Rafa laughed when he saw me. You look like a big thumb.

Dios mío, Mami said, turning me around.

It looks good, Papi said.

And the cold's going to make him sick.

Papi put his cold palm on my head. He likes it fine, he said.

Papi worked a long fifty-hour week and on his days off he expected quiet, but my brother and I had too much energy to be quiet; we didn't think anything of using our sofas for trampolines at nine in the morning, while Papi was asleep. In our old barrio we were accustomed to folks shocking the streets with merengue twenty-four hours a day. Our upstairs neighbors, who themselves fought like trolls over everything, would stomp down on us. Will you two please shut up? and then Papi would come out of his room, his shorts unbuttoned and say, What did I tell you? How many times have I told you to keep it quiet? He was free with his smacks and we spent whole afternoons on Punishment Row—our bedroom—where we had to lie on our beds and not get off, because if he burst in and caught us at the window, staring out at the beautiful snow, he would pull our ears and smack us, and then we would have to kneel in the corner for a few hours. If we messed that up, joking around or cheating, he would force us to kneel down on the cutting side of a coconut grater, and only when we were bleeding and whimpering would he let us up.

Now you'll be quiet, he'd say, satisfied, and we'd lay in bed, our knees burning with iodine, and wait for him to go to work so we could put our hands against the cold glass.

We watched the neighborhood children building snowmen and igloos, having snowball fights. I told my brother about the field I'd seen, vast in my memory, but he just shrugged. A brother and sister lived across in apartment four, and when they were out we would wave to them. They waved to us and motioned for us to come out but we shook our heads, We can't.

The brother shrugged, and tugged his sister out to where the other children were, with their shovels and their long, snow-encrusted scarves. She seemed to like Rafa, and waved to him as she walked off. He didn't wave back.

North American girls are supposed to be beautiful, he said.

Have you seen any?

What do you call her? He reached down for a tissue and sneezed out a double-barrel of snot. All of us had headaches and colds and coughs; even with the heat cranked up, winter was kicking our asses. I had to wear a Christmas hat around the apartment to keep my shaven head warm; I looked like an unhappy tropical elf.

I wiped my nose. If this is the United States, mail me home.

Don't worry, Mami says. We're probably going home.

How does she know?

Her and Papi have been talking about it. She thinks it would be better if we went back. Rafa ran a finger glumly over our window; he didn't want to go; he liked the TV and the toilet and already saw himself with the girl in apartment four.

I don't know about that, I said. Papi doesn't look like he's going anywhere.

What do you know? You're just a little mojón.

I know more than you, I said. Papi had never once mentioned going back to the Island. I waited to get him in a good mood, after he had watched *Abbott and Costello,* and asked him if he thought we would be going back soon.

For what?

A visit.

Maybe, he grunted. Maybe not. Don't plan on it.

By the third week I was worried we weren't going to make it. Mami, who had been our authority on the Island, was dwindling. She cooked our food and then sat there, waiting to wash the dishes. She had no friends, no neighbors to visit. You should talk to me, she said, but we told her to wait for Papi to get home. He'll talk to you, I guaranteed. Rafa's temper, which was sometimes a problem, got worse. I would tug at his hair, an old game of ours, and he would explode. We fought and fought and fought and after my mother pried us apart, instead of making up like the old days, we sat scowling on opposite sides of our room and planned each other's demise. I'm going to burn you alive, he promised. You should number your limbs, cabrón, I told him, so they'll know how to put you back together for the funeral. We squirted acid at each other with our eyes, like reptiles. Our boredom made everything worse.

One day I saw the brother and sister from apartment four gearing up to go play, and instead of waving I pulled on my parka. Rafa was sitting on the couch, flipping between a Chinese cooking show and an all-star Little League game. I'm going out, I told him.

Sure you are, he said, but when I pushed open the front door, he said, Hey!

The air outside was very cold and I nearly fell down our steps. No one in the neighborhood was the shoveling type. Throwing my scarf over my mouth, I stumbled across the uneven crust of snow. I caught up to the brother and sister on the side of our building.

Wait up! I yelled. I want to play with you.

579

The brother watched me with a half grin, not understanding a word I'd said, his arms scrunched nervously at his side. His hair was a frightening no-color. His sister had the greenest eyes and her freckled face was cowled in a hood of pink fur. We had on the same brand of mittens, bought cheap from Two Guys. I stopped and we faced each other, our white breath nearly reaching across the distance between us. The world was ice and the ice burned with sunlight. This was my first real encounter with North Americans and I felt loose and capable on that plain of ice. I motioned with my mittens and smiled. The sister turned to her brother and laughed. He said something to her and then she ran to where the other children were, the peals of her laughter trailing over her shoulder like the spumes of her hot breath.

I've been meaning to come out, I said. But my father won't let us right now. He thinks we're too young, but look, I'm older than your sister, and my brother looks older than you.

The brother pointed at himself. Eric, he said.

My name's Joaquín, I said.

Juan, he said.

No, Joaquín, I repeated. Don't they teach you guys how to speak?

His grin never faded. Turning, he walked over to the approaching group of children. I knew that Rafa was watching me from the window and fought the urge to turn around and wave. The gringo children watched me from a distance and then walked away. Wait, I said, but then an Oldsmobile pulled into the next lot, its tires muddy and thick with snow. I couldn't follow them. The sister looked back once, a lick of her hair peeking out of her hood. After they had gone, I stood in the snow until my feet were cold. I was too afraid of getting my ass beat to go any farther.

Was it fun? Rafa was sprawled in front of the TV.

Hijo de la gran puta, I said, sitting down.

You look frozen.

I didn't answer him. We watched TV until a snowball struck the glass patio door and both of us jumped.

What was that? Mami wanted to know from her room.

Two more snowballs exploded on the glass. I peeked behind the curtain and saw the brother and sister hiding behind a snow-buried Dodge.

Nothing, Señora, Rafa said. It's just the snow.

What, is it learning how to dance out there?

It's just falling, Rafa said.

We both stood behind the curtain, and watched the brother throw fast and hard, like a pitcher.

Each day the trucks would roll into our neighborhood with the garbage. The landfill stood two miles out, but the mechanics of the winter air conducted its sound and smells to us undiluted. When we opened a window we could hear the bulldozers spreading the garbage out in thick, putrid layers across the top of the landfill. We could see the gulls attending the mound, thousands of them, wheeling.

Do you think kids play out there? I asked Rafa. We were standing on the porch, brave; at any moment Papi could pull into the parking lot and see us.

Of course they do. Wouldn't you?

I licked my lips. They must find a lot of crap out there.

Plenty, Rafa said.

That night I dreamed of home, that we'd never left. I woke up, my throat aching, hot with fever. I washed my face in the sink, then sat next to our window, my brother snoring, and watched the pebbles of ice falling and freezing into a shell over the cars and the snow and the pavement. Learning to sleep in new places was an ability you were supposed to lose as you grew older, but I never had it. The building was only now settling into itself; the tight magic of the just-hammered-in nail was finally relaxing. I heard someone walking around in the living room and when I went out I found my mother standing in front of the patio door.

You can't sleep? she asked, her face smooth and perfect in the glare of the halogens.

I shook my head.

We've always been alike that way, she said. That won't make your life any easier.

I put my arms around her waist. That morning alone we'd seen three moving trucks from our patio door. I'm going to pray for Dominicans, she had said, her face against the glass, but what we would end up getting were Puerto Ricans.

She must have put me to bed because the next day I woke up next to Rafa. He was snoring. Papi was in the next room snoring as well, and something inside of me told me that I wasn't a quiet sleeper.

At the end of the month the bulldozers capped the landfill with a head of soft, blond dirt, and the evicted gulls flocked over the development, shitting and fussing, until the first of the new garbage was brought in.

My brother was bucking to be Number One Son; in all other things he was generally unchanged, but when it came to my father he listened with a scrupulousness he had never afforded our mother. Papi said he wanted us inside, Rafa stayed inside. I was less attentive; I played in the snow for short stretches, though never out of sight of the apartment. You're going to get caught, Rafa forecasted. I could tell that my boldness made him miserable; from our windows he watched me packing snow and throwing myself into drifts. I stayed away from the gringos. When I saw the brother and sister from apartment four, I stopped farting around and watched for a sneak attack. Eric waved and his sister waved; I didn't wave back. Once he came over and showed me the baseball he must have just gotten. Roberto Clemente, he said, but I went on with building my fort. His sister grew flushed and said something loud and rude and then Eric sighed. Neither of them were handsome children.

One day the sister was out by herself and I followed her to the field. Huge concrete pipes sprawled here and there on the snow. She ducked into one of these and I followed her, crawling on my knees.

She sat in the pipe, crosslegged and grinning. She took her hands out of her mittens and rubbed them together. We were out of the wind and I followed her example. She poked a finger at me.

Joaquín, I said. All my friends call me Yunior.

Joaquín Yunior, she said. Elaine. Elaine Pitt.

Elaine.

Joaquín.

It's really cold, I said, my teeth chattering.

She said something and then felt the ends of my fingers. Cold she said.

I knew that word already. I nodded. Frío. She showed me how to put my fingers in my armpits.

Warm, she said.

Yes, I said. Very warm.

At night, Mami and Papi talked. He sat on his side of the table and she leaned close, asking him, Do you ever plan on taking these children out? You can't keep them sealed up like this; they aren't dead yet.

They'll be going to school soon, he said, sucking on his pipe. And as soon as winter lets up I want to show you the ocean. You can see it around here, you know, but it's better to see it up close.

How much longer does winter last?

Not long, he promised. You'll see. In a few months none of you will remember this and by then I won't have to work too much. We'll be able to travel in spring and see everything.

I hope so, Mami said.

My mother was not a woman easily cowed, but in the States she let my father roll over her. If he said he had to be at work for two days straight, she said okay and cooked enough moro to last him. She was depressed and sad and missed her father and her friends. Everyone had warned her that the U.S. was a difficult place where even the devil got his ass beat, but no one had told her that she would have to spend the rest of her natural life snowbound with her children. She wrote letter after letter home, begging her sisters to come as soon as possible. I need the company, she explained. This neighborhood is empty and friendless. And she begged Papi to bring his friends over. She wanted to talk about unimportant matters, and see a brown face who didn't call her mother or wife.

None of you are ready for guests, Papi said. Look at this house. Look at your children. Me dan vergüenza to see them slouching around like that.

You can't complain about this apartment. All I do is clean it.

What about your sons?

My mother looked over at me and then at Rafa. I put one shoe over the other. After that, she had Rafa keep after me about my shoelaces. When we heard the van arriving in the parking lot, Mami called us over for a quick inspection. Hair, teeth, hands, feet. If anything was wrong she'd hide us in the bathroom until it was fixed. Her dinners grew elaborate. She even changed the TV for Papi without calling him a zángano.

Okay, he said finally. Maybe it can work.

It doesn't have to be that big a production, Mami said.

Two Fridays in a row he brought a friend over for dinner and Mami put on her best polyester jumpsuit and got us spiffy in our red pants, thick white belts, and amaranth-blue Chams shirts. Seeing her asthmatic with excitement made us hopeful that our world was about to be transformed, but these were awkward dinners. The men were bachelors and divided their time between talking to Papi and eyeing Mami's ass. Papi seemed to enjoy their company but Mami spent her time on her feet, hustling food to the table, opening beers, and changing the channel. She started out each night natural and unreserved, with a face that scowled as easily as it grinned, but as the men loosened their belts and aired out their toes and talked their talk, she withdrew; her expressions narrowed until all that remained was a tight, guarded smile that seemed to drift across the room the way a splash of sunlight glides across a wall. We kids were ignored for the most part, except once, when the first man, Miguel, asked, Can you two box as well as your father?

They're fine fighters, Papi said.

Your father is very fast. Has good hand speed. Miguel shook his head, laughing. I saw him finish this one tipo. He put fulano on his ass.

That *was* funny, Papi agreed. Miguel had brought a bottle of Bermúdez rum; he and Papi were drunk.

It's time you go to your room, Mami said, touching my shoulder.

Why? I asked. All we do is sit there.

That's how I feel about my home, Miguel said.

Mami's glare cut me in half. Such a fresh mouth, she said, shoving us toward our room. We sat, as predicted, and listened. On both visits, the men ate their fill, congratulated Mami on her cooking, Papi on his sons, and then stayed about an hour for propriety's sake. Cigarettes, dominos, gossip, and then the inevitable, Well, I have to get going. We have work tomorrow. You know how that is.

Of course I do. What else do we Dominicans know?

Afterward, Mami cleaned the pans quietly in the kitchen, scraping at the roasted pig flesh, while Papi sat out on our front porch in his short sleeves; he seemed to have grown impervious to the cold these last five years. When he came inside, he showered and pulled on his overalls. I have to work tonight, he said.

Mami stopped scratching at the pans with a spoon. You should find yourself a more regular job.

Papi smiled. Maybe I will.

As soon as he left, Mami ripped the needle from the album and interrupted Felix de Rosario. We heard her in the closet, pulling on her coat and her boots.

Do you think she's leaving us? I asked.

Rafa wrinkled his brow. It's a possibility, he said. What would you do if you were her?

I'd already be in Santo Domingo.

When we heard the front door open, we let ourselves out of our room and found the apartment empty.

We better go after her, I said.

Rafa stopped at the door. Let's give her a minute, he said.

What's wrong with you? She's probably face down in the snow.

We'll wait two minutes, he said.

Shall I count?

Don't be a wiseguy.

One, I said loudly. He pressed his face against the glass patio door. We were about to hit the door when she returned, panting, an envelope of cold around her.

Where did you get to? I asked.

I went for a walk. She dropped her coat at the door; her face was red from the cold and she was breathing deeply, as if she'd sprinted the last thirty steps.

Where?

Just around the corner.

Why the hell did you do that?

She started to cry, and when Rafa put his hand on her waist, she slapped it away. We went back to our room.

I think she's losing it, I said.

She's just lonely, Rafa said.

The night before the snowstorm I heard the wind at our window. I woke up the next morning, freezing. Mami was fiddling with the thermostat; we could hear the gurgle of water in the pipes but the apartment didn't get much warmer.

Just go play, Mami said. That will keep your mind off it.

Is it broken?

I don't know. She looked at the knob dubiously. Maybe it's slow this morning.

None of the gringos were outside playing. We sat by the window and waited for them. In the afternoon my father called from work; I could hear the forklifts when I answered.

Rafa?

No, it's me.

Get your mother.

How are you doing?

Get your mother.

We got a big storm on the way, he explained to her—even from where I was standing I could hear his voice. There's no way I can get out to see you. It's gonna be bad. Maybe I'll get there tomorrow.

What should I do?

Just keep indoors. And fill the tub with water.

585

Where are you sleeping? Mami asked.

At a friend's.

She turned her face from us. Okay, she said. When she got off the phone she sat in front of the TV. She could see I was going to pester her about Papi; she told me, Just watch the TV.

Radio WADO recommended spare blankets, water, flashlights, and food. We had none of these things. What happens if we get buried? I asked. Will we die? Will they have to save us in boats?

I don't know, Rafa said. I don't know anything about snow. I was spooking him. He went over to the window and peeked out.

We'll be fine, Mami said. As long as we're warm. She went over and raised the heat again.

But what if we get buried?

You can't have that much snow.

How do you know?

Because twelve inches isn't going to bury anybody, even a pain-in-the-ass like you.

I went out on the porch and watched the first snow begin to fall like finely-sifted ash. If we die, Papi's going to feel bad, I said.

Don't talk about it like that, Rafa said.

Mami turned away and laughed.

Four inches fell in an hour and the snow kept falling.

Mami waited until we were in bed, but I heard the door and woke Rafa. She's at it again, I said.

Outside?

You know it.

He put on his boots grimly. He paused at the door and then looked back at the empty apartment. Let's go, he said.

She was standing on the edge of the parking lot, ready to cross Westminister. The apartment lamps glared on the frozen ground and our breath was white in the night air. The snow was gusting.

Go home, she said.

We didn't move.

Did you at least lock the front door? she asked.

Rafa shook his head.

It's too cold for thieves anyway, I said.

Mami smiled and nearly slipped on the sidewalk. I'm not good at walking on this vaina.

I'm real good, I said. Just hold onto me.

We crossed Westminister. The cars were moving very slowly and the wind was loud and full of snow.

This isn't too bad, I said. These people should see a hurricane.

Where should we go? Rafa asked. He was blinking a lot to keep the snow out of his eyes.

Go straight, Mami said. That way we don't get lost.

We should mark the ice.

She put her hands around us both. It's easier if we go straight.

We went down to the edge of the apartments and looked out over the landfill, a misshapen, shadowy mound that abutted the Raritan. Rubbish fires burned all over it like sores and the dump trucks and bulldozers slept quietly and reverently at its base. It smelled like something the river had tossed out from its floor, something moist and heaving. We found the basketball courts next and the pool, empty of water, and Parkridge, the next neighborhood over, which was full and had many, many children. We even saw the ocean, up there at the top of Westminister, like the blade of a long, curved knife. Mami was crying but we pretended not to notice. We threw snowballs at the sliding cars and once I removed my cap just to feel the snowflakes scatter across my cold, hard scalp.

1998

AS KINGFISHERS
CATCH FIRE

by COLUM McCANN

from STORY

As kingfishers catch fire dragonflies draw flame.
—*Gerard Manley Hopkins*

A FLOCK OF KINGFISHERS arrived the evening Rhianon Ryan died, in the middle of a winter so cold that other birds froze in the air. Thousands of them came on a brief and noisy migration with a gunning of wings, making it seem that the northern lights had arrived in the sky, iridescent blue and salmons and corals and emeralds and the fabulous yellows of a thousand converging beaks. They came with a marvellous bobbing action in the air, like a shoal of flying fish. It was the strangest thing—apart from Rhianon—to have ever happened to the small Roscommon town.

The kingfishers appeared from the south, low-flying and rapid, casting tenacious shadows over the farmlands. They swooped down on rivers and fed on fish found in icy water. Farmers on tractors shaded their eyes, women at storefronts held up umbrellas to keep off the bird shit, children stood in the town square and let the birds alight in their arms, teenage boys took out rifles that they would never use. Still the birds kept coming, letting out a high sound, like a musical keen. They lined the awning of the cinema. Gathered in the eaves of the dole office. Congregated near the video shop. Perched on goal posts in the football field. They even sat around the rims of beer kegs at the back of pubs. For the whole of that night and the following day, until Rhianon was buried, the town was stunned into silence, watching king-fishers as they burst their colours through the air. Her funeral was carried out, but talk of Rhianon was overshadowed—even at her wake the missing gaps in her life were not filled with the chatter of the locals, but with talk of how the strangest aurora had visited the town.

Rhianon left Ireland on a mail boat bound for New York in the spring of 1950. It was her nineteenth birthday and by the time she wrote her first letter, three months later, there were so many rumours about her the townspeople were a little disappointed, at first, to find out the truth.

She was, she wrote, on her way to Korea with American soldiers to help nurse democracy into the world. Rhianon had always cared for the sick and the dying. At the age of eight she had climbed the wall of the local lunatic asylum with a pair of scissors in her hand. The following morning the employees were amazed as old women with no teeth suddenly rose from their beds with beehives and bouffants. Bachelor farmers slicked back pomade. Young lunatics were proud of their short-back-and-sides, carrying tiny mirrors around in their overalls. Every Saturday after that Rhianon was seen in the asylum garden giving free hairdos, carefully applying lipstick, clipping nose hairs, twirling cotton sticks in ears to take out wax. Some of the local people came to get their hair done, although they were always relegated to the end of the queue. During the week she bicycled to the houses of the sick and listened to their life stories as she gave them makeovers, rinsing their hair, chopping stray ends, taking away straggly fringes. She even took a short apprenticeship with the undertaker, dressing the dead, but the dead didn't tell interesting stories, so she soon gave up on that.

Everyone hailed her as she cycled along the curvy grey streets, with her pellucid blue eyes under a giant umbrella of electric red hair.

A party was held for her outside the local cinema on the day she left, and people came from miles around to wish her farewell; a line of them gathered under a red-and-white canvas tent to get tips on the latest makeup. Young men scribbled their addresses on the inside flap of cigarette packages. Old women listened carefully to hints about how to stave off wrinkles. Rhianon chatted with everyone, but was too shy to make a speech—she simply stood at the cinema door and hung her head as the townspeople clapped. A car beeped impatiently to bring her to the mail boat.

When she left, all colour seemed to drain itself out of the town, down through the rain gutters, along into ditches, and out to the lowlands, leaving the streets pale and monochromatic.

When the first letter arrived, the people imagined Rhianon in nurse-whites, landing in Korea in a plane with a giant red cross on the side. World atlases were hunted out of libraries and youngsters located the port of Pusan where she said she was going. Great consternation rose up when the butcher claimed that Koreans were apt to eat dogs. A whiparound was made to send food to Rhianon, fruitcakes and long-lasting soda bread, with a stern warning: *Stay away from meat, girl!* Pictures of General Douglas MacArthur were clipped from papers and the talk was of whether the North Koreans would sweep further south or not. Her mother hung an American flag outside Rhianon's cottage, and it flapped through rainstorms.

Rhianon, for her part, began to send letters as long as skirts.

Helicopters flew in low, she said, carrying the injured. Korean women in the rice fields were shaped like sickles, backs bent into their work, stopping only to stare upwards at the flying machines. The canvas flaps of tents blew in the wind. The hospital was a symphony of moans. Soldiers screamed about the loss of their legs or arms. Bags of plasma were scarce. She had no time for hairdos and not an ounce of makeup was to be found anywhere. At night the scratchy voice of Nat King Cole came over the radios. American soldiers sat around and smacked chewing gum in their jaws. The Yanks called her "Popsicle" because they said she looked like a long white stick under an icicle of red hair. When evenings fell, mosquitoes raved delightedly around her and she had taken to drinking spoonfuls of vinegar to keep them at bay. Another Irish nurse had come down with malaria. Rhianon was nursing her. Don't worry about the meat, she wrote, there wasn't a dog in sight. The most abundant wildlife was kingfishers, tons of them, radiant and mysterious—they were often seen to dart around the camp, dropping the seeds of plants, then flying off again. At night bats flitted above the rice fields and somehow made her think of home, the movement of shadows on the land. She always signed off by saying that she would write again soon and drew a love heart underneath her name with a squiggle coming out at the end of the heart, like a tail of a tadpole.

The letters were carted by the postman around the town and people gathered in the tiny cinema, before Cagney appeared in a rerun of *Yankee Doodle Dandy*. Rhianon was discussed before the curtains were pulled back from the screen. Women wearing head scarves and brooches leaned into one another earnestly. Boys refused to believe that Rhianon didn't eat dogs. Men talked about the latest reports from the newspapers. And then one afternoon her letters burst into tropical bloom when Rhianon wrote that she was almost in love with a dying man, and people whispered of her affair even through the appearance of Hollywood stars in khaki uniforms re-enacting World War II.

The soldier, Rhianon said, had so much shrapnel in his body that he could have been a fallen meteorite, heavenly in the way he shoved his stubby arms to the sky as if he wanted to return to the patient black Korean night and utter some final rage. At evening the man gave off a glow in his army bed, the magnetism of the metal in his body attracting every packet of light in the tent around him. In the beginning the soldier had smelled of DDT—so much lice on his body that the tiny parasites had blocked out the light, but when a doctor doused him in insecticide he began to give off faint glimmers. Even the surgeons noticed the aura hovering around him, some of it coming from a sucking chest wound, more of it seeming to emanate from his eyes. They put it down to hallucination or perhaps chemicals—but Rhianon put it down to sainthood. He was the only one of her patients who didn't mind dying. He told her that there was a dignity to a good death, that to die well was the only thing a man could do honestly in life. Having almost fallen in love the soldier was happy to die. The *almost* was important to both him and Rhianon—to them love was like innocence, once you became aware of it, it was gone forever. Rhianon wrote, under a bare bulb where moths careened, that she sat by the soldier's bed—a metal frame with green canvas—and held his hand, feeling the light flow into her. The soldier smiled back under the cloth, a slow and spectral smile. In the distance firefights cleaved the oriental sky. Days piled themselves into weeks. Rhianon sometimes wasn't sure if he was already a ghost or not, so she broke the rules and kissed him gently on the lips to make sure he was still alive.

Under the soldier's bed, in a bucket filled with ice, lay three of his mangled fingers.

He had lost the fingers in a firefight near Inchon, when a grenade landed in the branches of a tree. Two hours later an army unit found

591

him lying on the ground, full of shrapnel, staring at his fingers spread out on his emergency blanket. He had been holding the detached fingers to his mouth every hour, trying unsuccessfully to spit the drying blood back into them. He was placed on a stretcher. The fingers were brought into camp with him, in the pocket of his fatigues, a trinity of remembrance. The doctors cast them into a bin, but Rhianon rescued them and tucked them into her nurse-whites. She placed blocks of ice in a bucket every evening, carefully packing it around the dismembered flesh. Each morning the vicious heat of that Korean summer turned the ice to water and the fingers lay there, floating, speaking of love and collapse, turning blue and black, the demise of another summer's day.

The fingers didn't give off any light but Rhianon was afraid to let them disintegrate. She picked them up one by one and fastidiously placed ice around them.

"I have only one wish," the soldier told Rhianon one morning during the rainy season. "Bury my fingers in a place where I was young, and someday you must return to see what grows there. Promise me that. You can do whatever you like with the rest of my body, but my fingers must be buried and you must return to see what grows." Rhianon wiped the soldier's brow, from which light continued to fulminate.

When the letters arrived there were long novenas hailed to the heavens of Roscommon; rosaries were incanted at fieldside grottos; yellow votive candles were lit at the back of the church; the cinema was packed as Rhianon's mother read aloud the letters; some of the townspeople stared at their own fingers in a sad empathy for the unknown soldier. The complexion of gossip was changed. Talk of Rhianon was a grand diversion from idle chat about the weather, baking formulas, and the disastrous milk yields. The postman swished on his bicycle through puddles, from house to house, carrying news. Some of the villagers even felt their own hearts creaking as they heard about the bold and inky handwriting. *My soldier will die soon, I am sure of it. The tent is full of light. I'm not sure what I will do without him. With all my love, Rhianon.*

It was soon decided that the soldier was an American corporal, tall, beautiful, with hair so slick and blond you could skate on it. The hillside he spoke of was probably somewhere in Nebraska or the Dakotas. He was a rancher's son, people imagined, hence the request for the finger burial—to see what would grow in the soil of his youth.

His eyes undoubtedly held the chimera of blueness. He had probably been a hero in battle, maybe raging through the firefight with another soldier carried on his back, or pitching a grenade at an advancing line of Chinese communists, or gallantly planting a flag on a hill. He would have a quintessential American name—Chad or Buster or Wayne—names that invoked movie stars who were capable of rising from the ashes of their celluloid dying. And he too would rise phoenix-like from his hospital bed, recover fully, return one day to the country town with Rhianon on his arm, down Main Street, past the butcher's shop without a second glance, waving his fingerless hand at passersby, using the good hand to fling his hat to boys on the bridge.

Mrs. Burke, the dressmaker, made a white taffeta gown for Rhianon's return. Hurley, the publican, promised a free keg for the celebration. The funeral director said he might even jazz up his hearse with white ribbons for the imminent wedding. Rhianon's mother rehearsed recipes in her mind—potatoes roasted in a bed of rosemary, flanked by a slicing of fresh carrots. And when Rhianon scribbled a single-line note that she was coming home, the excitement in the town was paralysing.

When Rhianon returned in the spring of 1953—a warm day when yellow bunting was hung from townhouse windows—there was no blue-eyed soldier at her side.

She walked down Main Street, her hair unwashed and strung like strawberry jam on the top of her head, a hand over her belly where a child had begun to show. People came out to greet her, uncoiled from their houses like a giant rope, but they were shocked at the sight of the bulge in the smock. They shook her hand and welcomed her, told her how beautiful she looked, but soon drifted off, disappointed. Shouts from the doorway of the pub melted down into whispers. A gramophone in the window of a house was turned off and a needle slowly scraped across a record. The yellow ribbons were slack in the breeze. "There's no soldier with her," the butcher incanted from his shop counter, "there's no soldier with her at all." Somebody mentioned the word "whore." At a curve in the road near the river, Rhianon's mother slapped her daughter's face and that night the dressmaker sent a small plume of smoke above the town, burning the taffeta gown in an old oil barrel.

Rhianon wandered around the town in a daze, telling the story to anybody who would listen, gently whispering that instead of the blue-eyed baby boy of an American corporal, she was carrying the bastard child of a black-haired Korean soldier who, when he died, had set off a backwards meteor shower over the landscape of his country, huge streams of light rivering upwards to the sky from some hillside where digit-shaped flowers burst out every spring in his memory. Nobody asked about the fingers and Rhianon didn't say a word, although a van arrived from Dublin at her cottage carrying a giant fridge that nobody had seen the likes of before, with a freezer section on top, to which Rhianon attached a strong lock.

Her son, Jae Chil, was stillborn, Rhianon bought a twenty-acre farm, dug him a plot in the easternmost field, arranged him for burial, said a few Confucian prayers over the mound, dressed herself in mourning-black from that day on. Two deep furrows inveigled themselves into the corners of her mouth, where she deceived her sadness by forever smiling.

She tended to a herd of twenty cows with a dog she called Syngman and was often seen driving them down a laneway, a stick raised high in the air, her Wellington boots covered in dung. She came to town carting pails of milk in a baby pram. She was still beautiful, walked tall and unburdened, offered her cosmetic services to the undertaker who tentatively avoided her, hid himself in a back office when she came calling. She could be sometimes seen on the grounds of the asylum arranging the hair of patients as they sat in white garden chairs by flower beds, but for the most part she lived out the tedium of her days without bothering anybody, just working away silently in her fields. She didn't talk about Korea, although there were times when she was heard gibbering in a strange language to herself. Sometimes children sneaked up to her house and tried to peer in the windows. When she came out, in black apron with baking flour on the front, they ran away. Rhianon would stand at the door and stretch her arms wide, questioning them, almost imploring. From a safe distance the children would point at her and make a slant of their eyes, but she simply shrugged and waited until they left, the children bored by her seeming indifference.

On a few occasions, when travellers came through, she'd invite them to stay. They said that Rhianon seemed to always have words dangling on the very edge of her lips, but they couldn't figure out if the words were to be swallowed or shared. In the end the old woman said nothing, just sat with her guests and watched the sunsets slide by.

Rhianon stopped selling milk, only came into town from her farm when there were electrical blackouts and she would run frantically through the streets seeking anyone who had blocks of ice they could give her. She tore at the roots of her hair—corrugated now into rows of grey—and ran back with plastic bags of ice to her cottage, a quirk soon forgotten when new, more reliable pylons were erected all around the country, leapfrogging through the lowlands. There were rumours, of course. She was hiding the soldier in a back bedroom. She was saving to make another trip to Pusan. She was going to get married to one of the lunatic farmers. But the rumours were tame, and like the ice, Rhianon herself might well have been forgotten but for her final trip to the undertaker on a freezing Monday morning when, at first, nothing stirred in the deep cyanic vault of the sky.

She arrived in a floral dress, the black of mourning jettisoned for some reason. She stood at the undertaker's desk, twisting a curl around her finger, and said she would arrange herself for her own death, thank you very much, which would be on the following Wednesday.

"Absolutely no frills," she said.

"None?"

"Not a sausage."

"Pardon me?"

"None at all."

She handed him a bundle of money in old currency and said that her clothes were not to be touched, nor her pockets rifled, nor her fingers uncurled, nor her eyelids closed, nor her face made up in any manner or means, and definitely nothing should be done with her hair. Word of the gesture slipped around town and dozens of locals followed the undertaker on his trip to check on Rhianon.

It was the coldest day of the year. Berries had shrivelled on hedges. Puddles had been seduced by ice. The people came on foot and, as they negotiated the long laneway to the cottage, the distant flocks of birds appeared to the south. Men and women stopped in their tracks, lifted up their anorak hoods and removed head scarves for a better view. Children whistled through their teeth. The skein of kingfishers seemed endless and the people were mesmerised by the sight, almost frozen to the spot.

Only the undertaker, rubbing his fingers like money, went into the cottage. Rhianon was found in bed, propped up by four pillows, a natural death, her feet frozen to the bedstead, her eyes open, her face painted, a curious look of contentment on her. A cup of green tea lay on her bedside table. There were no notes. She was lifted into a coffin hurriedly and arrangements were made, while outside the townsfolk still stared upwards.

The kingfishers continued their onslaught, a salvo of them through the Roscommon sky, with a liquid movement of their wings. A silence descended, like that of a half-forgotten prayer. Instead of going to the wake—Rhianon had prepared whiskey and sandwiches and left them on the kitchen table—the group of people stood outside and saluted the wash of colour. Even the gravedigger looked as he slammed his boot on the blade of the shovel to lift the first clod of soil for the coffin. He kept straining upwards to see as the hole got deeper and deeper.

The birds left when Rhianon was laid down into the ground, in a plot she had prepared beside her son.

The locals walked home, chattering amongst themselves about the fabulous sight. They weren't even angry that two whole days had to be spent cleaning the bird shit from all the windows of the town and sweeping feathers from the ground. A smell of ammonia hung for weeks. Everyone waited for another visit of the birds, but it never came.

They all stayed stupidly unaware of the three shrivelled fingers that lay in the hip pocket of Rhianon's burial dress when they dropped her down into the ground. It never even crossed their minds that the Korean soldier had found the place of his youth, and it was only the following spring, when exotic oriental azaleas burst up wildly around the old woman's grave, that the townspeople pondered the idea that the kingfishers hadn't arrived for them at all.

1999

THE BILL COLLECTOR'S VACATION

by PATRICIA HAMPL

from PLOUGHSHARES

ALL WEEK THE HEAT has been killing. Foolish to walk the distance to the credit union even so early in the morning, imagining you can beat the worst of it. Think of the walk back, the pavement baking, not a tree for blocks. *Foolish*—a Kenneth word. *Don't be foolish, Marilyn, take the Volvo.*

This, as so often now, was her cue. The tiny, greased gear of her willfulness downshifted away from him, revving at the barest stroke of his control. Or his contempt. She wasn't free to do the sensible thing—drive the air-conditioned car out of the cool garage to the credit union two miles away. She had to fight. Fight what?

Anyway, it was good to walk. A recent article she had clipped made the point: walking was as good, even for cardiovascular, as jogging. Better, really, less threat to the joints. Kenneth was a runner—he didn't like the word jogger. She had put the clipping on the kitchen corkboard: *Jogging Benefits Questioned.* Not that Kenneth bothered to read the clippings she put up, though he could be annoyed by the sight of grocery coupons pinned there. "What are you wasting time clipping coupons for?" he would say, walking out the back door to the garage. That shrug of disdain as he passed by.

Get to the credit union by eight when it opens, home by nine-thirty, before the real heat of the day: this was her plan. She wasn't due at the bookstore until afternoon. But already the day's new heat was adding itself to the surplus still standing from yesterday. The night had left it all to simmer.

At the credit union, she pulled on the big glass door. It didn't budge. Her eye went to a white rectangle on the glass, above the handle: Weekdays 9 a.m.-4:30 p.m. An added judgment, another cluck of contempt. *Foolish, not to check the hours.*

She turned, was struck by the sun. A man was sitting on the low retaining wall in the shade, apparently having made the same mistake. He held a check and a green deposit slip in a meaty hand. He smiled at her in a way she recognized was harmless. How could you tell that about strangers? Could you? Marilyn trusted her instinct on things like this. Strange, how she bristled at Kenneth, but she still trusted the world for no good reason.

"Plenty of room," the man said. He patted the low wall where he sat, and looked away, toward the state capitol and its immense greensward. She joined him on the retaining wall, ducking out of the sun.

She was annoyed by the hour wait—waste of time. Said so. Wasn't this something new, the nine o'clock opening hour? Were these temporary summer hours? Shouldn't the credit union have sent out notices of any change? "And in this heat," she added. She expected him to meet her on this. But he—beefy, younger than she, dressed in shorts and tee, stomach lazing over his waistband—veered away from the communion of resentment. "I'm on vacation," he said easily, gazing off. "Might as well wait."

Marilyn felt oddly annoyed, as if this fat stranger's contentment subtly betrayed her. *Foolish to be impatient.* She wished she hadn't settled in next to him, but it made no sense to walk back home (plus the question of facing Kenneth), and this was the only shaded place to sit.

A woman in cutoffs, her skimpy yellow hair raked high in a painful-looking ponytail, hurried to the door in flip-flops, her child trailing behind her. She took in the sign, sighed, squinted in the direction of the flower box. No room. Her feet smacked the steps as she rushed back to her car, the child's face impassive as a loan officer at her side.

Several others came by, mostly businessmen in suits too dark, too cruelly heavy, for the day. Sweating figures frowning theatrically at their watches. Each time the plot of discovery and disappointment looked stagier. Always, they walked off, got in their closed cars, drove away. People were becoming cartoons. Only she and the fat man sat there, waiting it out by the retaining wall, electric-blue lobelia rising from the flower boxes behind them.

The sharp edges of her annoyance melted, as she sat there regarding other people's irritation. What predictable animals we are. She was going to point this out to the heavy man sitting peacefully to her right. But her observation would seem to him, she sensed, mean-spirited. He wouldn't like it.

How did she know this—that he would be allergic to—to what? Irony? The basic unkindness of reading people, observing them? He would not like judging people. That was it, he wasn't a judger. He was—she hadn't the slightest idea. But how interesting, anyway, to know he wouldn't like a smart observation. You know these things about people. It's the way you size up anyone, quick brush strokes of assessment you hardly know you're making. It's how we make our way through the day, down the street, she supposed. Glancing and judging, feinting to the left, dodging to the right.

She asked what he did for a living.

"I work for the Consolidated Bureaus," he said.

What was that?

A smile, sad smile: "I'm a nasty bill collector."

Was it a hard job?

"Well, only eight to ten percent of the bills sent to me ever get collected. Ever. Believe it. And of all the people I talk to— it's a phone job—only five percent show *any* willingness to work with me on the problem. Can you believe that?" He shook his head in mild wonder.

"Do they admit they owe the money?" Marilyn asked. His earnestness seemed to require the question.

"Sure."

"And?"

"They could care less."

"I suppose it makes you pretty cynical," Marilyn said. God, what a hopeless job.

"You don't trust *anybody*," he said richly. But his voice gave him away, no edge to it. He was a great unflexed wad of trust. Wasn't cynical, wasn't bruised. He was intact. Rare sight.

She should not believe, however, the people on *Oprah* and *20/20* who told outlandish tales about bill collectors. The part about threats. "There are rules and laws, we can't do any of that stuff," he said, repelled. The very idea he would menace anyone. He shifted slightly, a shiver of disgust.

Imagine being married to such a man. That sweet disgust at his own supposed power, rippling from the center of his soft pudding self—it

599

was reliable, good. Something reassuring about disgust, less aggressive than contempt.

She had gone over this: it was contempt she had to contend with from Kenneth, not just the grit of his practiced will sparking against her worn-out compliance. At first (thirty-six years!—their daughter was a mother twice already) his abruptness had struck her as certainty. Impatient, yes. But the good kind of impatient—eager, ambitious, hungry. Men should be hungry. The growl of love and work, lean and hungry. She used to think that way—men are, women are. Everybody did.

She had been proud, secretly, to recognize that hunger in Kenneth, willing to admit that's what she wanted. A twilight boat ride around the harbor, sponsored by their two Catholic colleges, spring, 1959. Holding a glass of shrimp-colored punch, feeling bold, though she did nothing illicit. Thinking, calculating about him—that was illicit. She shrugged off, in an instant, the domesticated male virtues so prized in Father Sullivan's Attributes of Catholic Marriage class. "Does he give you a champagne feeling of well-being, girls?" the priest rang out to his roomful of putative virgins. A nun, still wearing the Renaissance habit of the Order, sat at the back of the room grading papers, a sardonic eyebrow raised occasionally like a mordant punctuation mark to the old priest's blather. The sins he had in mind were corny, middle-aged fantasies. He warned them about wife-swapping, for God's sake.

The truth was, Kenneth *had* given her a champagne feeling, though not of well-being. Something grainier, like the dry sandiness of real champagne hitting the roof of your mouth. Even the faint sneer on Kenneth's face had not scared her off. Had there been a sneer, even then? She had looked up at his smooth face as he said something—what?—something funny, something a bit unkind, a circle of people around him, crewcuts and candy-colored sweater sets. Whatever he said, it gave her the chance to tilt her face up to him, a kiss-me-angle, laughing, admiring. Oh, she wanted him. The big boat cut the water smoothly, then there was a shift as it turned. Her punch sloshed out of the glass, her hands got sticky. "Better watch that," he said, smiling. Had noticed her. They were married the weekend after graduation, to no one's surprise. They had become one of their campuses' solid "couples" since their sophomore year. Pre-law and el ed. "Great planning, Ken," an uncle whacked him on the back at the wedding, "she'll get you through law school."

Which Marilyn had, four years of second grade at Compton Elementary, using birth control without a qualm. *None of their business,* Kenneth said. He led them with amazing nonchalance, away from the crafted certainties of their parochial background. He had no crisis of faith. It wasn't spiritual, not even intellectual. He simply saw that life was elsewhere. He began growing his hair long, not crazy long, just curling over his collar. They marched together downtown to the Federal Building, to protest the draft. But they threw nothing, not rocks, not blood. They did not get arrested. He was *Law Review,* clerked for a state supreme court justice. Good firm, some teaching. Then the children, just two, a girl, then a boy.

By the time the children were in school, Marilyn didn't want to go back to teaching, cramming down a damp sandwich in the staff room choked with smoke, the pent-up aura of captives in the corridors, mayhem roaring from the lunchroom. Motherhood spoiled her. It was orderly—to her surprise. Days alone, doing little things, one after another. Reading books to the children, their small fingers pointing: Train, elephant! Giraffe, giraffe, giraffe!

She opened a bookstore with the mother of another boy in her son's Montessori class. Children's books and educational games. Now the place, Charlotte's Web, was hers. She'd bought out her partner, who had moved to Florida. Business was good, really good. Kenneth was impressed. She had been approached about opening a second store in a mall, books, interactive multimedia products, a whole area devoted to hands-on computers. The computer stations for the new store reminded her of the hi-fi booths of her high-school years, where you could go and listen to a record to see if you wanted to buy it. Sit in the little confession-box-size glass booth, headset clamped on like earmuffs, melting into Johnny Mathis.

She stared off at the green shimmer of the capitol grounds across the avenue from the credit union. Was it Johnny Mathis who had sung "Moon River"? Audrey Hepburn was dead. Marilyn had cried, actually sobbed, alone, looking at the pictures in *People* magazine. My era.

"I was sitting here before you arrived," the bill collector said, as if they had been carrying on a conversation—had they? had she missed something?—"and I was watching that man on the mower on the capitol grounds across the street there, trying to figure out how he runs that thing."

Marilyn looked across at the figure on the mower.

601

"I've been watching him really close—no hand levers, nothing with his feet. I can't figure it out. He just sits on it, and it goes on its own." Fascinated by the likelihood of magic at work, voice rippling with awe. "Do you see anything?"

"No, I don't," Marilyn said. "He just seems to go."

"That's what I'm thinking," the man said.

This thought seemed to connect him to many other thoughts. There is absolutely no point, for example, he said, in attempting to collect a bill during the full moon: people are *nuts* during the full moon. Ditto during the twelve-year period when he managed a skating rink: he always hired extra security on full moon nights. The kids were nuts then, too. Possessed. More murders on full moon nights, according to the police. More *everything*.

He expressed no irritation at the feckless and sometimes evil ways of the world. Apparently he lived in a state of astonishment.

From the full moon to astrology. He was a Taurus. Again the amazement of it all: most of his family were Gemini or Cancer—he had no *idea* why he was a Taurus. A unbidden mystery boring out of the core of his identity. There was meaning in all this. Believe it.

He also wondered why—as a Capitol Patrol car went by—there were city police and capitol police. Wasn't that a waste of money, an overlap? Marilyn mentioned the existence of the university police, another doubling of duty. Maybe there was a value in having this extra protection in sensitive areas? He thought that over, agreed. "There are lots of chemicals sitting around the university," he said. "Things can blow up."

"The university," he repeated, as if pondering a thesis. It was a place he had come to know well in the last year. Wasn't it incredible, the labyrinth of corridors at University Hospital, the confusion of the place for the non-university person thrust suddenly into that maze? Take himself. He'd gone there every day for months and months. Never figured the place out. Pause. "My brother was a patient there."

They were turning a dark corner, she sensed.

The brother was big in astrology, Tarot, all that. He had come home from California for a family visit, had read their father's cards. He told his brother that the father would be dead before Christmas. But it was himself who was gone before Christmas. Just six months ago. "He read his own cards," the bill collector said, something like reverence in his voice. "The one thing you cannot do is read your own cards. But you can read your own fate in another person's cards. You don't even know it."

Oh yes, the cards had sometimes told him more than he wanted to know, too. He stayed away from the cards now.

He turned abruptly from the occult, steered them toward his *amazing* four-year-old. This boy liked *his* cooking better than his wife's. Why? Because it was spicier. Imagine: a four-year-old who loves spicy food, really spicy, like an adult. Incredible, but true.

So many amazing facts. Flowers can grow out of sheer rock, you saw that a lot along Lake Superior where he, the wife, and the boy were going for the week, as soon as he deposited his check. Or the oddity of sundogs, and the fact that a significant percentage of the population does not believe we ever landed on the moon. Some pretty interesting arguments, you know? His brother had a book on it. Also, he and his brother had once seen a funnel cloud twirling along 61 North. The amazing thing? It looked just the way you always heard they looked: absolutely a funnel, skidding around like a bad fast dancer, touching down, and then, for no reason, up and off again. He leaned back against the flower boxes. Weather was *really* weird.

Not to mention the host of unpaid bills all about us, the carelessness of people. "They say, 'Fuck you,' just like that, and slam the phone down," he said, marveling, not insulted.

Then there's the big one, Big D. The sudden disappearance of blood relatives, their unbelievable dematerialization. You keep seeing people who look just like them. Or rather, you *start* seeing people who look just like them, the backs of heads. You never noticed that before, not till he passed away, was gone. Then he seemed to be everywhere. "My brother was younger than me," he said, "but he goes first. They say, 'Expect the unexpected.' It's easy to forget that." Blue lobelia appeared to sprout from his shoulders where he leaned against the retaining wall.

The day was heating up. The humidity felt intentional, vicious, needling away at the air. It would be another heavy day to live through.

The bill collector wasn't looking at Marilyn. He just gazed out, kept talking, seeing things. Galena, Illinois, used to be located on the banks of the Mississippi River, but no longer is. You see, a river is not a straight line between banks. It's a whole system, and you don't know where it starts or stops, what space it really takes up. They make a big deal about finding the source of the Mississippi. That's dumb. The Indians laughed at that. There *isn't* really a source. It's a big muddle up there. They just choose this stream or that, call it "the source." You don't *know*. What you see is *not* what you got. Nor are you necessarily safe from earthquakes just because you live in the Midwest. Remember that little town in Missouri? Gone. And raisins are not a fruit, not a berry. Raisins are really former grapes, shriveled up—but he bet she knew that one already.

The bill collector's voice wheeled through the heat, his marvels believable and meaningless at once, lovely harmlessnesses making the world work, gears in the great engine carrying us over the rough patches. The grass across the avenue on the capitol greensward had been watered earlier in the morning from jets buried in the ground. Now the green gave off a low weather system, a minute fog just above itself, tiny rainbows evaporating by the minute as the heat burned them into the day.

The man on the riding mower worked the grass like a tidy quarter section of alfalfa, without lever or foot pedal, hands visible on the steering wheel, but no sign of where the energy came from. Something at the knee? Marilyn's eyes shut a quick instant against the disloyal thought. It was too far to see now, anyway. Who knows?

A gray Volvo wagon—their own, she realized—turned the corner. Kenneth coming to get her. He pulled up near the sidewalk, the tires making the watery sound of tires slowing on dry pavement. He leaned across the seat toward the passenger window so she could see him beckoning. His face was filmy behind the gleam of the rolled-up window. *And now you see darkly, but then face to face.* But when, when do you see someone face to face? Not in this life. Was he smiling?— she thought he was smiling. A good smile. Concern there. She could make out a hand,gesturing. He wanted her to be out of the heat. Oh, and safe. He worries. Always has. Sees trouble. It's what he thinks imagination is for—worrying. Remember the first time? "I'll always protect you"—the little patch of movie dialogue, the champagne of well-being, the two of them meeting the length of their pure bodies for the first time, crazy to touch. Some dumb motel on University Avenue, the *l* blanked out on the neon sign. *Star Mote.* Looking for trouble, the sweet, safe kind, a month before the wedding. *I'll always protect you.*

Soon, the big glass door will open. But not yet. Kenneth must wait, just a sec, honey. She must stay here in the shade, the lobelia gushing over the cinder blocks. The fat stranger keeps talking, listing all the unlikely things that happen, that just are. She doesn't move. She will

604

go to the Volvo in a moment, explain it all. But for now, this extra instant, she stays put, here in the killing heat. She wants to look straight ahead at nothing for another minute, wants to keep listening to the bill collector, who, still in mourning, is describing the world as the wonder it must be.

1999

THE MANSION ON
THE HILL

by RICK MOODY

from THE PARIS REVIEW

T HE CHICKEN MASK was sorrowful, Sis. The Chicken Mask was supposed to hustle business; it was supposed to invite the customer to gorge him or herself within our establishment; it was supposed to be endearing and funny; it was supposed to be an accurate representation of the featured item on our menu. But, Sis, in a practical setting, in test markets—like right out in front of the restaurant—the Chicken Mask had a plaintive aspect, a blue quality (it was stifling, too, even in cold weather), so that I'd be walking down Main, by the waterfront, after you were gone, back and forth in front of Hot Bird (Bucket of Drumsticks, $2.99), wearing out my imitation basketball sneakers from Wal-Mart, pudgy in my black jogging suit, lurching along in the sandwich board, and the kids would hustle up to me, tugging on the wrists of their harried, underfinanced moms. The kids would get bored with me almost immediately. They knew the routine. Their eyes would narrow, and all at once there were no secrets here in our town of service-economy franchising: *I was the guy working nine to five in a Chicken Mask,* even though I'd had a pretty good education in business administration, even though I was more or less presentable and well-spoken, even though I came from a good family. I made light of it, Sis, I extemporized about Hot Bird, in remarks designed by virtue of my studies in business tactics to drive whole families in for the new *low-fat roasters,* a meal option that was steeper, in terms of price, but tasty nonetheless. (And I ought to have known, because I ate from the menu every day. Even the coleslaw.)

Here's what I'd say, in my Chicken Mask. Here was my pitch: *Feeling a little peckish? Try Hot Bird!* or *Don't be chicken, try Hot Bird!* The mothers would laugh their nervous adding-machine laughs (those laughs that are next door over from a sob), and they would lead the kids off. Twenty yards away, though, the boys and girls would still be staring disdainfully at me, gaping backward while I rubbed my hands raw in the cold, while I breathed the synthetic rubber interior of the Chicken Mask—that fragrance of rubber balls from gym classes lost, that bouquet of the gloves Mom used for the dishes, that perfume of simpler times—while I looked for my next shill. I lost almost ninety days to the demoralization of the Chicken Mask, to its grim, existential emptiness, until I couldn't take it anymore. Which happened to be the day when Alexandra McKinnon (remember her? from Sunday school?) turned the corner with her boy Zack—he has to be seven or eight now—oblivious while upon her daily rounds, oblivious and fresh from a Hallmark store. It was nearly Valentine's Day. They didn't know it was me in there, of course, inside the Chicken Mask. They didn't know I was *the chicken from the basement, the chicken of darkest nightmares,* or, more truthfully, they didn't know I was a guy with some pretty conflicted attitudes about things. That's how I managed to apprehend Zack, leaping out from the in-door of Cohen's Pharmacy, laying ahold of him a little too roughly, by the hem of his pillowy, orange ski jacket. Little Zack was laughing, at first, until, in a voice racked by loss, I worked my hard sell on him, declaiming stentoriously that *Death Comes to All.* That's exactly what I said, just as persuasively as I had once hawked *White meat breasts, eight pieces, just $4.59!* Loud enough that he'd be sure to know what I meant. His look was interrogative, quizzical. So I repeated myself. *Death Comes to Everybody, Zachary.* My voice was urgent now. My eyes bulged from the eyeholes of my standard-issue Chicken Mask. I was even crying a little bit. Saline rivulets tracked down my neck. Zack was terrified.

What I got next certainly wasn't the kind of flirtatious attention I had always hoped for from his mom. Alex began drumming on me with balled fists. I guess she'd been standing off to the side of the action previously, believing that I was a reliable paid employee of Hot Bird. But now she was all over me, bruising me with wild swings, cursing, until she'd pulled the Chicken Mask from my head—half expecting, I'm sure, to find me scarred or hydrocephalic or otherwise disabled.

Her denunciations let up a little once she was in possession of the facts. It was me, her old Sunday school pal, Andrew Wakefield. Not at the top of my game.

I don't really want to include here the kind of scene I made, once unmasked. Alex was exasperated with me, but gentle anyhow. I think she probably knew I was in the middle of a rough patch. People knew. The people leaning out of the storefronts probably knew. But, if things weren't already bad enough, I remembered right then—God, this is horrible—that Alex's mom had driven into Lake Sacandaga about five years before. Jumped the guardrail and plunged right off that bridge there. In December. In heavy snow. In a Ford Explorer. That was the end of her. *Listen, Alex,* I said, *I'm confused, I have problems and I don't know what's come over me and I hope you can understand, and I hope you'll let me make it up to you. I can't lose this job. Honest to God.* Fortunately, just then, Zack became interested in the Chicken Mask. He swiped the mask from his mom—she'd been holding it at arm's length, like a soiled rag—and he pulled it down over his head and started making simulated automatic-weapons noises in the directions of local passersby. This took the heat off. We had a laugh, Alex and I, and soon the three of us had repaired to Hot Bird itself (it closed four months later, like most of the businesses on that block) for coffee and biscuits and the chef's special spicy wings, which, because of my position, were on the house.

Alex was actually waving a spicy wing when she offered her life-altering opinion that I was too smart to be working for Hot Bird, especially if I was going to brutalize little kids with the creepy facts of the hereafter. What I should do, Alex said, was get into something positive instead. She happened to know a girl—it was her cousin, Glenda—who managed a business over in Albany, the Mansion on the Hill, a big area employer, and why didn't I call Glenda and use Alex's name, and maybe they would have something in accounting or valet parking or flower delivery, *yada yada yada,* you know, some job that had as little public contact as possible, something that paid better than minimum wage, because minimum wage, Alex said, wasn't enough for a guy of twenty-nine. After these remonstrances she actually hauled me over to the pay phone at Hot Bird (people are so generous sometimes), while my barely alert boss Antonio slumbered at the register with no idea what was going on, without a clue that he was about to lose his most conscientious chicken impersonator. All because I couldn't stop myself from talking about death.

Alex dialed up the Mansion on the Hill (while Zack, at the table, donned my mask all over again), penetrating deep into the switchboard by virtue of her relation to a Mansion on the Hill management-level employee, and was soon actually talking to her cousin: *Glenda, I got a friend here who's going through some rough stuff in his family, if you know what I mean, yeah, down on his luck in the job department too, but he's a nice bright guy anyhow. I pretty much wanted to smooch him throughout confirmation classes, and he went to . . . Hey, where did you go to school again? Went to SUNY and has a degree in business administration, knows a lot about product positioning or whatever, I don't know, new housing starts, yada yada yada, and I think you really ought to . . .*

Glenda's sigh was audible from several feet away, I swear, through the perfect medium of digital telecommunications, but you can't blame Glenda for that. People protect themselves from bad luck, right? Still, Alex wouldn't let her cousin refuse, wouldn't hear of it, *You absolutely gotta meet him, Glenda, he's a doll, he's a dream boat,* and Glenda gave in, and that's the end of this part of the story, about how I happened to end up working out on Wolf Road at the capital region's finest wedding- and party-planning business. Except that before the Hot Bird recedes into the mists of time, I should report to you that I swiped the Chicken Mask, Sis. They had three or four of them. You'd be surprised how easy it is to come by a Chicken Mask.

Politically, here's what was happening in the front office of my new employer: Denise Gulch, the Mansion on the Hill staff writer, had left her husband and her kids and her steady job, because of a wedding, because of the language of the vows—that soufflé of exaggerated language—vows which, for quality-control purposes, were being broadcast over a discreet speaker in the executive suite. Denise was so moved by a recitation of Paul Stookey's "Wedding Song" taking place during the course of the Neuhaus ceremony ("Whenever two or more of you / Are gathered in His name, / There is love, / There is love . . . ") that she slipped into the Rip Van Winkle Room disguised as a latecomer. Immediately, in the electrifying atmosphere of matrimony, she began trying to seduce one of the ushers (Nicky Weir, a part-time Mansion employee who was acquainted with the groom). I figure this flirtation had been taking place for some time, but that's not what everyone told me. What I heard was that seconds after meeting one another—the bride hadn't even recessed yet—Denise and Nicky were secreted in a nearby broom closet, while the office phones bounced to voice mail, and were peeling back the layers of our Mansion dress code, until, at day's end, scantily clad and intoxicated by rhetoric and desire, they stole a limousine and left town without collecting severance. Denise was even fully vested in the pension plan.

All this could only happen at a place called the Mansion on the Hill, a place of fluffy endings: the right candidate for the job walks through the door at the eleventh hour, the check clears that didn't exist minutes before, government agencies agree to waive mountains of red tape, the sky clears, the snow ends, and stony women like Denise Gulch succumb to torrents of generosity, throwing half-dollars to children as they embark on new lives.

The real reason I got the job is that they were shorthanded, and because Alex's cousin, my new boss, was a little difficult. But things were starting to look up anyway. If Glenda's personal demeanor at the interview wasn't exactly warm (she took a personal call in the middle that lasted twenty-eight minutes, and later she asked me, while reapplying lip liner, if I wore cologne) at least she was willing to hire me—as long as I agreed to renounce any personal grooming habits that inclined in the direction of Old Spice, Hai Karate or CK1. I would have spit-polished her pumps just to have my own desk (on which I put a yellowed picture of you when you were a kid, holding up the bass that you caught fly-fishing and also a picture of the four of us: Mom and Dad and you and me) and a Rolodex and unlimited access to stamps, mailing bags and paper clips.

Let me take a moment to describe our core business at the Mansion on the Hill. We were in the business of helping people celebrate the best days of their lives. We were in the business of spreading joy, by any means necessary. We were in the business of paring away the calluses of woe and grief to reveal the bright light of commitment. We were in the business of producing flawless memories. We had seven auditoriums, or *marriage suites,* as we liked to call them, each with a slightly different flavor and decorating vocabulary. For example, there was the *Chestnut Suite,* the least expensive of our rental suites, which had lightweight aluminum folding chairs (with polyurethane padding) and a very basic altar table, which had the unfortunate pink and lavender floral wallpaper and which seated about 125 comfortably; then there was the *Hudson Suite,* which had some teak in it and a lot of paneling and a classic iron altar table and some rather large standing tables at the rear, and the reception area in Hudson was clothed all in vinyl, instead of the paper coverings that they used in Chestnut (the basic decorating scheme there in the Hudson Suite was meant to suggest the sea vessels that once sailed through our municipal port); then there was the *Rip Van Winkle Room,* with its abundance of draperies, its silk curtains, its matching maroon settings of inexpensive linen, and the *Adirondack Suite,* the *Ticonderoga Room,* the *Valentine Room* (a sort of giant powder puff), and of course the *Niagara Hall,* which was grand and reserved, with its separate kitchen and its enormous fireplace and white-gloved staff, for the sons and daughters of those Victorians of Saratoga County who came upstate for the summer during the racing season, the children of contemporary robber barons, the children whose noses were always straight and whose luck was always good.

We had our own on-site boutique for wedding gowns and tuxedo rentals and fittings—hell, we'd even clean and store your garments for you while you were away on your honeymoon—and we had a travel agency who subcontracted for us, as we also had wedding consultants, jewelers, videographers, still photographers (both the arty ones who specialized in photos of your toenail polish on the day of the wedding and the conventional photographers who barked directions at the assembled family far into the night), nannies, priests, ministers, shamans, polarity therapists, a really maniacal florist called Bruce, a wide array of deejays—guys and gals equipped to spin Christian-only selections, Tex-Mex, music from Hindi films and the occasional death-metal wedding medley—and we could get actual musicians, if you preferred. We'd even had Dick Roseman's combo, The Sons of Liberty, do a medley of "My Funny Valentine," "In-a-Gadda-Da-Vida," "I Will Always Love You" and "Smells Like Teen Spirit," without a rest between selections. (It was gratifying for me to watch the old folks shake it up to contemporary numbers.) We had a three-story, fifteen-hundred slip parking facility on site, convenient access to I-87, I-90 and the Taconic, and a staff of 175 full- and part-time employees on twenty-four hour call. We had everything from publicists to dicers of crudités to public orators (need a brush-up for that toast?)—all for the purpose of making your wedding the high watermark of your American life. We had done up to fifteen weddings in a single day (it was a Saturday in February, 1991, during the Gulf War) and, since the Mansion on the Hill first threw open its door for a gala double wedding (the Gifford twins, from Balston Spa, who married Shaun and Maurice Wickett) in June of 1987, we had performed, up to the time of my first

611

day there, 1,963 weddings, many of them memorable, life-affirming, even spectacular ceremonies. We had never had an incidence of serious violence.

This was the raw data that Glenda gave me, anyway, Sis. The arrangement of the facts is my own, and in truth, the arrangement of facts constitutes the job I was engaged to perform at the Mansion on the Hill. Because Glenda Manzini (in 1990 she married Dave Manzini, a developer from Schenectady), couldn't really have hated her job any more than she did. Glenda Manzini, whose marriage (her second) was apparently not the most loving ever in upstate history (although she's not alone; I estimate an even thousand divorces resulting from the conjugal rites successfully consummated so far at my place of business), was a cynic, a skeptic, a woman of little faith when it came to the institution through which she made her living. She occasionally referred to the wedding party as *the cattle;* she occasionally referred to the brides as *the hookers* and to herself, manager of the Mansion on the Hill, as *the Madame,* as in, *The Madame, Andrew, would like it if you would get the hell out of her office so that she can tabulate these receipts,* or, *Please tell the Hatfields and the McCoys that the Madame cannot untangle their differences for them, although the Madame does know the names of some first-rate couples counselors.* In the absence of an enthusiasm for our product line or for business writing in general, Glenda Manzini hired me to tackle some of her responsibilities for her. I gave the facts the best possible spin. Glenda, as you probably have guessed, was good with numbers. With the profits and losses. Glenda was good at additional charges. Glenda was good at doubling the price on a floral arrangement, for example, because the Vietnamese poppies absolutely had to be on the tables, because they were so . . . *je ne sais quoi.* Glenda was good at double-booking a particular suite and then auctioning the space to the higher bidder. Glenda was good at quoting a figure for a band and then adding instruments so that the price increased astronomically. One time she padded a quartet with two vocalists, an eight-piece horn section, an African drumming ensemble, a dijeridoo and a harmonium.

The other thing I should probably be up-front about is that Glenda Manzini was a total knockout. A bombshell. A vision of celestial loveliness. I hate to go on about it, but there was that single strand of Glenda's amber hair always falling over her eyes—no matter how many times she tried to secure it; there was her near constant attention to her makeup; there was her total command of business issues and her complete unsentimentality. Or maybe it was her stockings, always in black, with a really provocative seam following the aerodynamically sleek lines of her calf. Or maybe it was her barely concealed sadness. I'd never met anyone quite as uncomfortable as Glenda, but this didn't bother me at first. My life had changed since the Chicken Mask.

Meanwhile, it goes without saying that the Mansion on the Hill wasn't a mansion at all. It was a homely cinder-block edifice formerly occupied by the Colonie Athletic Club. A trucking operation used the space before that. And the Mansion wasn't on any hill, either, because geologically speaking we're in a valley in here. We're part of some recent glacial scouring.

On my first day, Glenda made every effort to insure that my work environment would be as unpleasant as possible. I'd barely set down my extra-large coffee with two half-and-halfs and five sugars and my assortment of cream-filled donuts (I was hoping these would please my new teammates) when Glenda bodychecked me, tipped me over into my reclining desk chair, with several huge stacks of file material.

—Andy, listen up. In April we have an Orthodox Jewish ceremony taking place at 3 P.M. in Niagara while at the same time there are going to be some very faithful Islamic-Americans next door in Ticonderoga. I don't want these two groups to come in contact with one another at any time, understand? I don't want any kind of diplomatic incident. It's your job to figure out how to persuade one of these groups to be first out of the gate, at noon, and it's your job to make them think that they're really lucky to have the opportunity. And Andy? The el-Mohammed wedding, the Muslim wedding, needs prayer mats. See if you can get some from the discount stores. Don't waste a lot of money on this.

This is a good indication of Glenda's management style. Some other procedural tidbits: she frequently assigned a dozen rewrites on her correspondence. She had a violent dislike for semicolons. I was to double-space twice underneath the date on her letters, before typing the salutation, on pain of death. I was never, ever to use one of those cursive word-processing fonts. I was to bring her coffee first thing in the morning, without speaking to her until she had entirely finished a second cup and also a pair of ibuprofen tablets, preferably the elongated, easy-to-swallow variety. I was never to ask her about her weekend or her evening or anything else, including her holidays, unless she asked me first. If her door was closed, I was not to open it. And if I ever reversed the digits in a phone number when taking a message for her, I could count on my pink slip that very afternoon.

Right away, that first A.M., after this litany of scares, after Glenda retreated into her chronically underheated lair, there was a swell of sympathetic mumbles from my coworkers, who numbered, in the front office, about a dozen. They were offering condolences. They had seen the likes of me come and go. Glenda, however, who keenly appreciated the element of surprise as a way of insuring discipline, was not quite done. She reappeared suddenly by my desk—as if by secret entrance—with a half-dozen additional commands. I was to find a new sign for her private parking space. I was to find a new floral wholesale: for the next fiscal quarter, I was to *refill her prescription for birth-control pills*. This last request was spooky enough, but it wasn't the end of the discussion. From there Glenda starting getting personal:

—Oh, by the way, Andy? (she liked diminutives) What's all the family trouble, anyway? The stuff Alex was talking about when she called?

She picked up the photo of you, Sis, the one I had brought with me. The bass at the end of your fishing rod was so outsized that it seemed impossible that you could hold it up. You looked really happy. Glenda picked up the photo as though she hadn't already done her research, as if she had left something to chance. Which just didn't happen during her regime at the Mansion on the Hill.

—Dead sister, said I. And then, completing my betrayal of you, I filled out the narrative, so that anyone who wished could hear about it, and then we could move onto other subjects, like Worcester's really great semipro hockey team.

—Crashed her car. Actually, it was my car. Mercury Sable. Don't know why I said it was her car. It was mine. She was on her way to her rehearsal dinner. She had an accident.

Sis, have I mentioned that I have a lot of questions I've been meaning to ask? Have I asked, for example, why you were taking the windy country road along our side of the great river, when the four-lanes along the west side were faster, more direct and, in heavy rain, less dangerous? Have I asked why you were driving at all? Why I was not driving you to the rehearsal dinner instead? Have I asked why your car was in the shop for muffler repair on such an important day? Have I

614

asked why you were late? Have I asked why you were lubricating your nerves *before* the dinner? Have I asked if four G&Ts, as you called them, before your own rehearsal dinner, were not maybe in excess of what was needed? Have I asked if there was a reason for you to be so tense on the eve of your wedding? Did you feel you had to go through with it? That there was no alternative? If so, why? If he was the wrong guy, why were you marrying him? Were there planning issues that were not properly addressed? Were there things between you two, as between all the betrothed, that we didn't know? Were there specific questions you wanted to ask, of which you were afraid? Have I given the text of my toast, Sis, as I had imagined it, beginning with a plangent evocation of the years before your birth, when I ruled our house like a tyrant, and how with earsplitting cries I resisted your infancy, until I learned to love the way your baby hair, your flaxen mop, fell into curls? Have I mentioned that it was especially satisfying to wind your hair around my stubby fingers as you lay sleeping? Have I made clear that I wrote out this toast and that it took me several weeks to get it how I wanted it and that I was in fact going over these words again when the call from Dad came announcing your death? Have I mentioned—and I'm sorry to be hurtful on this point—that Dad's drinking has gotten worse since you left this world? Have I mentioned that his allusions to the costly unfinished business of his life have become more frequent? Have I mentioned that Mom, already overtaxed with her own body count, with her dead parents and dead siblings, has gotten more and more frail? Have I mentioned that I have some news about Brice, your intended? That his tune has changed slightly since your memorial service? Have I mentioned that I was out at the crime scene the next day? The day after you died? Have I mentioned that in my dreams I am often at the crime scene now? Have I wondered aloud to you about that swerve of blacktop right there, knowing that others may lose their lives as you did? Can't we straighten out that road somehow? Isn't there one road crew that the governor, in his quest for jobs, jobs, jobs, can send down there to make this sort of thing unlikely? Have I perhaps clued you in about how I go there often now, to look for signs of further tragedy? Have I mentioned to you that in some countries DWI is punishable by death, and that when Antonio at Hot Bird first explained this dark irony to me, I imagined taking his throat in my hands and squeezing the air out of him once and for all? Sis, have I told you of driving aimlessly in the mountains, listening to talk radio, searching for the one bit of cheap, commercially interrupted persuasion that will let me put these memories of you back in the canister where you now at least partially reside so that I can live out my dim, narrow life? Have I mentioned that I expect death around every turn, that every blue sky has a safe sailing out of it, that every bus runs me over, that every low, mean syllable uttered in my direction seems to intimate the violence of murder, that every family seems like an opportunity for ruin and every marriage a ceremony into which calamity will fall and hearts will be broken and lives destroyed and people branded by the mortifications of love? Is it all right if I ask you all of this?

Still, in spite of these personal issues, I was probably a model employee for Glenda Manzini. For example, I managed to sort out the politics concerning the Jewish wedding and the Islamic wedding (both slated for the first weekend of April), and I did so by appealing to certain aspects of light in our valley at the base of the Adirondacks. Certain kinds of light make for very appealing weddings here in our valley, I told one of these families. In late winter, in the early morning, you begin to feel an excitement at the appearance of the sun. Yes, I managed to solve that problem, and the next (the prayer mats)—because K-Mart, *where America shops,* had a special on bathmats that week, and I sent Dorcas Gilbey over to buy six dozen to use for the Muslim families. I solved these problems and then I solved others just as vexing. I had a special interest in the snags that arose on Fridays after 5 P.M.—the groom who on the day of the ceremony was trapped in a cabin east of Lake George and who had to snowshoe three miles out to the nearest telephone, or the father of the bride (it was the Lapsley wedding) who wanted to arrive at the ceremony by hydrofoil. Brinkmanship, in the world of nuptial planning, gave me a sense of well-being, and I tried to bury you in the rear of my life, in the back of that closet where I'd hidden my secondhand golf clubs and my ski boots and my Chicken Mask—never again to be seen by mortal man.

One of my front-office associates was a fine young woman by the name of Linda Pietrzsyk, who tried to comfort me during the early weeks of my job, after Glenda's periodic assaults. Don't ask how to pronounce Linda's surname. In order to pronounce it properly, you have to clear your throat aggressively. Linda Pietrzsyk didn't like her surname anymore than you or I, and she was apparently looking for a groom from whom she could borrow a better last name. That's what I found out after awhile. Many of the employees at the Mansion on the Hill had ulterior motives. This marital ferment, this loamy soil of romance, called to them somehow. When I'd been there a few months, I started to see other applicants go through the masticating action of an interview with Glenda Manzini. Glenda would be sure to ask, *Why do you want to work here?* and many of these qualified applicants had the same reply, *Because I think marriage is the most beautiful thing and I want to help make it possible for others.* Most of these applicants, if they were attractive and single and younger than Glenda, aggravated her thoroughly. They were shown the door. But occasionally a marital aspirant like Linda Pietrzsyk snuck through, in this case because Linda managed to conceal her throbbing, sentimental heart beneath a veneer of contemporary discontent.

We had Mondays and Tuesdays off, and one weekend a month. Most of our problem-solving fell on Saturdays, of course, but on that one Saturday off, Linda Pietrzsyk liked to bring friends to the Mansion on the Hill, to various celebrations. She liked to attend the weddings of strangers. This kind of entertainment wasn't discouraged by Glenda or by the owners of the Mansion, because everybody likes a party to be crowded. Any wedding that was too sparsely attended at the Mansion had a fine complement of *warm bodies,* as Glenda liked to call them, provided gratis. Sometimes we had to go to libraries or retirement centers to fill a quota, but we managed. These gate crashers were welcome to eat finger food at the reception and to drink champagne and other intoxicants (food and drink were billed to the client), but they had to make themselves scarce once the dining began in earnest. There was a window of opportunity here that was large enough for Linda and her friends.

She was tight with a spirited bunch of younger people. She was friends with kids who had outlandish wardrobes and styles of grooming, kids with pants that fit like bedsheets, kids with haircuts that were, at best, accidental. But Linda would dress them all up and make them presentable, and they would arrive in an ancient station wagon in order to crowd in at the back of a wedding. Where they stifled gasps of hilarity.

I don't know what Linda saw in me. I can't really imagine. I wore the same sweaters and flannel slacks week in and week out. I liked classical music, Sis. I liked historical simulation festivals. And as you probably haven't forgotten (having tried a couple of times to fix me up—with Jess Carney and Sally Moffitt), the more tense I am, the worse is the impression I make on the fairer sex. Nevertheless, Linda Pietrzsyk decided that I had to be a part of her elite crew of wedding

617

crashers, and so for a while I learned by immersion of the great rainbow of expressions of fealty.

Remember that footage, so often shown on contemporary reality-based programming during the dead first half-hour of prime time, of the guy who vomited at his own wedding? I was at that wedding. You know when he says, *Aw, Honey, I'm really sorry,* and leans over and flash floods this amber stuff on her train? You know, the shock of disgust as it crosses her face? The look of horror in the eyes of the minister? I saw it all. No one who was there thought it was funny, though, except Linda's friends. That's the truth. I thought it was really sad. But I was sitting next to a fellow *actually named Cheese* (when I asked which kind of cheese, he seemed perplexed), and Cheese looked as though he had a hernia or something, he thought this was so funny. Elsewhere in the Chestnut Suite there was a grievous silence.

Linda Pietrzsyk also liked to catalogue moments of spontaneous erotic delight on the premises, and these were legendary at the Mansion on the Hill. Even Glenda, who took a dim view of gossiping about business most of the time, liked to hear who was doing it with whom where. There was an implicit hierarchy in such stories. *Tales of the couple to be married caught in the act on Mansion premises were considered obvious and therefore uninspiring.* Tales of the best man and matron of honor going at it (as in the Clarke, Rosenberg, Irving, Ng, Fujitsu, Walters, Shapiro or Spangler ceremonies) were better, but not great. Stories in which parents of the couple to be married were caught—in, say, the laundry room, with the dad still wearing his dress shoes—were good (Smith, Elsworth, Waskiewicz), but not as good as tales of the parents of the couple to be married trading spouses, of which we had one unconfirmed report (Hinkley) and of which no one could stop talking for a week. Likewise, any story in which the bride or the groom were caught *in flagrante* with someone other than the person they were marrying was considered astounding (if unfortunate). But we were after some even more unlikely tall tales: any threesome or larger grouping involving the couple to be married and someone from one of the other weddings scheduled that day, in which the third party was unknown until arriving at the Mansion on the Hill, and at which *a house pet was present.* Glenda said that if you spotted one of these tableaux you could have a month's worth of free groceries from the catering department. Linda Pietrzsyk also spoke longingly of the day when someone would arrive breathlessly in the office with a narrative of a full-fledged orgiastic reception in the Mansion on the

Hill, the spontaneous, overwhelming erotic celebration of love and marriage by an entire suite full of Americans, tall and short, fat and thin, young and old.

In pursuit of these tales, with her friends Cheese, Chip, Mick, Stig, Mark and Blair, Linda Pietrzsyk would quietly appear at my side at a reception and give me the news—*Behind the bandstand, behind that scrim, groom reaching under his cousin's skirts.* We would sneak in for a look. But we never interrupted anyone. And we never made them feel ashamed.

You know how when you're getting to know a fellow employee, a fellow team member, you go through phases, through cycles of intimacy and insight and respect and doubt and disillusionment, where one impression gives way to another? (Do you know about this, Sis, and is this what happened between you and Brice, so that you felt like you personally had to have the four G&Ts on the way to the rehearsal dinner? Am I right in thinking you couldn't go on with the wedding and that this caused you to get all sloppy and to believe erroneously that you could operate heavy machinery?) Linda Pietrzsyk was a stylish, Skidmore-educated girl with ivory skin and an adorable bump in her nose; she was from an upper-middleclass family out on Long Island somewhere; her father's periodic drunkenness had not affected his ability to work; her mother stayed married to him according to some mesmerism of devotion; her brothers had good posture and excelled in contact sports; in short, there were no big problems in Linda's case. Still, she pretended to be a desperate, marriage-obsessed kid, without a clear idea about what she wanted to do with her life or what the hell was going to happen next week. She was smarter than me—she could do the crossword puzzle in three minutes flat and she knew all about current events—but she was always talking about *catching a rich financier with a wild streak and extorting a retainer from him,* until I wanted to shake her. There's usually another layer underneath these things. In Linda's case it started to become clear at Patti Wackerman's wedding.

The reception area in the Ticonderoga Room—where walls slid back from the altar to reveal the tables and the dance floor—was decorated in branches of forsythia and wisteria and other flowering vines and shrubs. It was spring. Linda was standing against a piece of white wicker latticework that I had borrowed from the florist in town (in return for promotional considerations), and sprigs of flowering trees garlanded it, garlanded the spot where Linda was standing. Pale colors haloed her.

—Right behind this screen, she said, when I swept up beside her and tapped her playfully on the shoulder, —check it out. There's a couple falling in love once and for all. You can see it in their eyes.

I was sipping a Canadian spring water in a piece of company stemware. I reacted to Linda's news nonchalantly. I didn't think much of it. Yet I happened to notice that Linda's expression was conspiratorial, impish, as well as a little beatific. Linda often covered her mouth with her hand when she'd said something riotous, as if to conceal unsightly dental work (on the contrary, her teeth were perfect), as if she'd been treated badly one too many times, as if the immensity of joy were embarrassing to her somehow. As she spoke of the couple in question her hand fluttered up to her mouth. Her slender fingertips probed delicately at her upper lip. My thoughts came in torrents: *Where are Stig and Cheese and Blair? Why am I suddenly alone with this fellow employee? Is the couple Linda is speaking about part of the wedding party today? How many points will she get for the first sighting of their extra-marital grappling?*

Since it was my policy to investigate any and all such phenomena, I glanced desultorily around the screen and, seeing nothing out of the ordinary, slipped further into the shadows where the margins of Ticonderoga led toward the central catering staging area. There was, of course, no such couple behind the screen, or rather Linda (who was soon beside me) and myself *were the couple* and we were mottled by insufficient light, dappled by it, by lavender-tinted spots hung that morning by the lighting designers, and by reflections of a mirrored *disco ball* that speckled the dance floor.

—I don't see anything, I said.

—Kiss me, Linda Pietrzsyk said. Her fingers closed lightly around the bulky part of my arm. There was an unfamiliar warmth in me. The band struck up some fast number. I think it was "It's Raining Men" or maybe it was that song entitled "We Are Family," which played so often at the Mansion on the Hill in the course of a weekend. Whichever, it was really loud. The horn players were getting into it. A trombonist yanked his slide back and forth.

—Excuse me? I said.

—Kiss me, Andrew, she said.—I want to kiss you.

Locating in myself a long-dormant impulsiveness, I reached down for Linda's bangs, and with my clumsy hands I tried to push back her blond and strawberry-blond curlicues, and then, with a hitch in my motion, in a stop-time sequence of jerks, I embraced her. Her eyes, like neon, were illumined.

—Why don't you tell me how you feel about me? Linda Pietrzsyk said. I was speechless, Sis. I didn't know what to say. And she went on. There was something about me, something warm and friendly about me, I wasn't fortified, she said; I wasn't cold, I was just a good guy who actually cared about other people *and you know how few of those there are.* (I think these were her words.) She wanted to spend more time with me, she wanted to get to know me better, she wanted to give the roulette wheel a decisive spin: she repeated all this twice in slightly different ways with different modifiers. It made me sweat. The only way I could think to get her to quit talking was to kiss her in earnest, my lips brushing by hers the way the sun passes around and through the interstices of falling leaves on an October afternoon. I hadn't kissed anyone in a long time. Her mouth tasted like cherry soda, like barbecue, like fresh hay, and because of these startling tastes, I retreated. To arm's length.

Sis, was I scared. What was this rank taste of wet campfire and bone fragments that I'd had in my mouth since we scattered you over the Hudson? Did I come through this set of coincidences, these quotidian interventions by God, to work in a place where everything seemed to be about *love,* only to find that I couldn't ever be a part of that grand word? How could I kiss anyone when I felt so awkward? What happened to me, what happened to all of us, to the texture of our lives, when you left us here?

I tried to ask Linda why she was doing what she was doing—behind the screen of wisteria and forsythia. I fumbled badly for these words. I believed she was trying to have a laugh on me. So she could go back and tell Cheese and Mick about it. So she could go gossip about me in the office, about what a jerk that Wakefield was. *Man, Andrew Wakefield thinks there's something worth hoping for in this world.* I thought she was joking, and I was through being the joke, being the Chicken Mask, being the harlequin.

—I'm not doing anything to you, Andrew, Linda said.—I'm expressing myself. It's supposed to be a good thing. Reaching, she laid a palm flush against my face.

—I know you aren't . . .

—So what's the problem?

I was ambitious to reassure. If I could have stayed the hand that flut-tered up to cover her mouth, so that she could laugh unreservedly, so that her laughter peeled out in the Ticonderoga Room . . . But I just wasn't up to it yet. I got out of there. I danced across the floor at the Wackerman wedding—I was a party of one—and the Wackermans and the Delgados and their kin probably thought I was singing along with "Desperado" by the Eagles (it was the anthem of the new Mr. and Mrs. Fritz Wackerman), but really I was talking to myself, *about work,* about how Mike Tombello's best man wanted to give his toast while doing flips on a trampoline, about how Jenny Parmenter wanted live goats bleating in the Mansion parking lot, as a fertility symbol, as she sped away, in her Rolls Cornische, to the Thousand Islands. Boy, I al-ways hated the Eagles.

Okay, to get back to Glenda Manzini. Linda Pietrzsyk didn't write me off after our failed embraces, but she sure gave me more room. She was out the door at 5:01 for several weeks, without asking after me, without a kind word for anyone, and I didn't blame her. But in the end who else was there to talk to? To Marie O'Neill, the accountant? To Paul Avakian, the human resources and insurance guy and petty-cash manager? To Rachel Levy, the head chef? Maybe it was more than this. Maybe the bond that forms between people doesn't get un-made so easily. Maybe it leaves its mark for a long time. Soon Linda and I ate our bagged lunches together again, trading varieties of pud-dings, often in total silence; at least this was the habit until we found a new area of common interest in our reservations about Glenda Manzini's management techniques. This happened to be when Glenda took a week off. What a miracle. I'd been employed at the Mansion six months. The staff was in a fine mood about Glenda's hiatus. There was a carnival atmosphere. Dorcas Gilbey had been stockpiling leftover ales for an office shindig featuring dancing and the recitation of really bad marital vows we'd heard. Linda and I went along with the festivi-ties, but we were also formulating a strategy.

What we wanted to know was how Glenda became so unreservedly cruel. We wanted the inside story on her personal life. We wanted the skinny. How do you produce an individual like Glenda? What is the mass-production technique? We waited until Tuesday, after the after-noon beer-tasting party. We were staying late, we claimed, in order to separate out the green M&Ms for the marriage of U.V.M. tight end

Brad Doelp who had requested bowls of M&Ms at his reception, *excluding any and all green candies*. When our fellow employees were gone, right at five, we broke into Glenda's office.

Sis, we really broke in. Glenda kept her office locked when she wasn't in it. It was a matter of principle. I had to use my Discover card on the lock. I punished that credit card. But we got the tumblers to tumble, and once we were inside, we started poking around. First of all, Glenda Manzini was a tidy person, which I can admire from an organizational point of view, but it was almost like her office was empty. The pens and pencils were lined up. The in and out boxes were swept clean of any stray dust particle, any scrap of trash. There wasn't a rogue paper clip behind the desk or in the bottom of her spotless waste basket. She kept her rubber bands banded together with rubber bands. The files in her filing cabinets were orderly, subdivided to avoid bowing, the old faxes were photocopied so that they wouldn't disintegrate. The photos on the walls (Mansion weddings past), were nondescript and pedestrian. There was nothing intimate about the decoration at all. I knew about most of this stuff from the moments when she ordered me into that cubicle to shout me down, but this was different. Now we were getting a sustained look at Glenda's personal effects.

Linda took particular delight in Glenda's cassette player (it was atop one of the black filing cabinets)—a cassette player that none of us had ever heard play, not even once. Linda admired the selection of recordings there. A complete set of cut-out budget series: *Greatest Hits of Baroque, Greatest Hits of Swing, Greatest Hits of Broadway, Greatest Hits of Disco* and so forth. Just as she was about to pronounce Glenda a rank philistine where music was concerned, Linda located there, in a shattered case, a copy of *Greatest Hits of the Blues*.

We devoured the green M&Ms while we were busy with our reconnaissance. And I kept reminding Linda not to get any of the green dye on anything. I repeatedly checked surfaces for fingerprints. I even overturned Linda's hands (it made me happy while doing it), to make sure they were free of emerald smudges. Because if Glenda found out we were in her office, we'd both be submitting applications at the Hot Bird of Troy. Nonetheless, Linda carelessly put down her handful of M&Ms, on top of a filing cabinet, to look over the track listings for *Greatest Hits of the Blues*. This budget anthology was released the year Linda was born, in 1974. Coincidentally, the year you too were born, Sis. I remember driving with you to the tunes of Lightnin' Hopkins or Howlin' Wolf. I remember your preference for the most bereaved of acoustic blues, the most ramshackle of musics. What better soundtrack for the Adirondacks? For our meandering drives in the mountains, into Corinth or around Lake Luzerne? What more lonesome sound for a state park the size of Rhode Island where wolves and bears still come to hunt? Linda cranked the greatest hits of heartbreak and we sat down on the carpeted floor to listen. I missed you.

I pulled open that bottom file drawer by chance. I wanted to rest my arm on something. There was a powerful allure in the moment. I wasn't going to kiss Linda, and probably her desperate effort to find somebody to liberate her from her foreshortened economic prospects and her unpronounceable surname wouldn't come to much, but she was a good friend. Maybe a better friend than I was admitting to myself. It was in this expansive mood that I opened the file drawer at the bottom of one stack (the *J* through *P* stack), otherwise empty, to find that it was full of a half-dozen, maybe even more, of those circular packages of *birth-control pills,* the color-coated pills, you know, those multihued pills and placebos that are a journey through the amorous calendars of women. All unused. Not a one of them even opened. Not a one of the white, yellow, brown or green pills liberated from its package.

—Must be chilly in Schenectady, Linda mumbled.

Was there another way to read the strange bottom drawer? Was there a way to look at it beyond or outside of my exhausting tendency to discover only facts that would prop up darker prognostications? The file drawer contained the pills, it contained a bottle of vodka, it contained a cache of family pictures and missives the likes of which were never displayed or mentioned or even alluded to by Glenda. Even I, for all my resentments, wasn't up to reading the letters. But what of these carefully arranged packages of photo snapshots of the Manzini family? (Glenda's son from her first marriage, in his early teens, in a torn and grass-stained football uniform, and mother and second husband and son in front of some bleachers, et cetera.) Was the drawer really what it seemed to be, a repository for mementos of love that Glenda had now hidden away, secreted, shunted off into mini-storage? What was the lesson of those secrets? Merely that concealed behind rage (and behind grief) is *the ambition to love?*

—Somebody's having an affair, Linda said.—The hubby is coming home late. He's fabricating late evenings at the office. He's taking some desktop meetings with his secretary. He's leaving Glenda alone with the kids. Why else be so cold?

—Or Glenda's carrying on, said I.

—Or she's polygamous, Linda said,—and this is a completely separate family she's keeping across town somewhere without telling anyone.

—Or this is the boy she gave up for adoption and this is the record of her meeting with his folks. And she never told Dave about it.

—Whichever it is, Linda said,—it's *bad*.

We turned our attention to the vodka. Sis, I know I've said that I don't touch the stuff anymore—because of your example—but Linda egged me on. We were listening to music of the delta, to its simple unadorned grief, and I felt that Muddy Waters's loss was my kind of loss, the kind you don't shake easily, the kind that comes back like a seasonal flu, and soon we were passing the bottle of vodka back and forth. Beautiful, sad Glenda Manzini understood the blues and I understood the blues and you understood them and Linda understood them and maybe everybody understood them—in spite of what ethno-musicologists sometimes tell us about the cultural singularity of that music. Linda started to dance a little, there in Glenda Manzini's office, swiveling absently, her arms like asps, snaking to and fro, her wrists adorned in black bangles. Linda had a spell on her, in Glenda's anaerobic and cryogenically frigid office. Linda plucked off her beige pumps and circled around Glenda's desk, as if casting out its manifold demons. I couldn't take my eyes off of her. She forgot who I was and drifted with the lamentations of Robert Johnson (hellhound on his trail), and I could have followed her there, where she cast off Long Island and Skidmore and became a naiad, a true resident of the Mansion on the Hill, that paradise, but when the song was over the eeriness of our communion was suddenly alarming. I was sneaking around my boss's office. I was drinking her vodka. All at once it was time to go home.

We began straightening everything we had moved—we were really responsible about it—and Linda gathered up the dozen or so green M&Ms she'd left on the filing cabinet—excepting the one she inadvertently fired out the back end of her fist, which skittered from a three-drawer file down a whole step to the surface of a two-drawer stack, before hopping and skipping over a cassette box, before freefalling behind the cabinets, where it came to rest, at last, six inches from the northeast corner of the office, beside a small coffee-stained patch of wall-to-wall. I returned the vodka to its drawer of shame, I tidied up the stacks of *Brides* magazines, I locked Glenda's office door and I went back to being the employee of the month. (My framed picture hung over the water fountain between the rest rooms. I wore a bow tie. I smiled broadly and my teeth looked straight and my hair was combed. I couldn't be stopped.)

My ambition has always been to own my own small business. I like the flexibility of small-capitalization companies; I like small businesses at the moment at which they prepare to franchise. That's why I took the job at Hot Bird—I saw Hot Birds in every town in America, I saw Hot Birds as numerous as post offices or ATMs. I like small businesses at the moment at which they really define a market with respect to a certain need, when they begin to sell their products to the world. And my success as a team player at the Mansion on the Hill was the result of these ambitions. This is why I came to feel, after a time, that I could do Glenda Manzini's job myself. Since I'm a little young, it's obvious that I couldn't *replace* Glenda—I think her instincts were really great with respect to the service we were providing to the Capital Region— but I saw the Mansion on the Hill stretching its influence into population centers throughout the northeast. I mean, why wasn't there a Mansion on the Hill in Westchester? Down in Mamaroneck? Why wasn't there a Mansion on the Hill in the golden corridor of Boston suburbs? Why no mainline Philly Mansion? Suffice to say, I saw myself, at some point in the future, having the same opportunity Glenda had. I saw myself cutting deals and whittling out discounts at other fine Mansion locations. I imagined making myself indispensable to a coalition of Mansion venture-capitalists and then I imagined using these associations to make a move into, say, the high-tech or bio-tech sectors of American industry.

The way I pursued this particular goal was that I started looking ahead at things like upcoming volume. I started using the graph features on my office software to make pie charts of ceremony densities, cost ratios and so forth, and I started wondering how we could pitch our service better, whether on the radio or in the press or through alternative marketing strategies (I came up with the strategy, for example, of getting various non-affiliated religions—small emergent spiritual movements—to consider us as a site for all their group wedding ceremonies). And as I started looking ahead, I started noticing who was coming through the doors in the next months. I became well versed in the social forces of our valley. I watched for when certain affluent families of the region might be needing our product. I would, if required, attempt cold-calling the attorney general of our state to persuade him of the splendor of the Niagara Hall when Diana, his daughter, finally gave the okey-dokey to her suitor, Ben.

I may well have succeeded in my plan for domination of the Mansion on the Hill brand, if it were not for the fact that as I was examining the volume projections for November (one Monday night), the ceremonies taking place in a mere three months, I noticed that Sarah Wilton of Corinth was marrying one Brice McCann in the Rip Van Winkle Room. Just before Thanksgiving. There were no particular notes or annotations to the name on the calendar, and thus Glenda wasn't focusing much on the ceremony. But something bothered me. That name.

Your Brice McCann, Sis. Your intended. Getting married almost a year to the day after your rehearsal-dinner-that-never-was. Getting married before even having completed his requisite year of grief, before we'd even made it through the anniversary with its floodwaters. Who knew how long he'd waited before beginning his seduction of Sarah Wilton? Was it even certain that he had waited until you were gone? Maybe he was faithless; maybe he was a two-timer. I had started reading Glenda's calendar to get ahead in business, Sis, but as soon as I learned of Brice, I became cavalier about work. My work suffered. My relations with other members of the staff suffered. I kept to myself. I went back to riding the bus to work instead of accepting rides. I stopped visiting fellow workers. I found myself whispering of plots and machinations; I found myself making connections between things that probably weren't connected and planning involved scenarios of revenge. I knew the day would come when he would be on the premises, when Brice would be settling various accounts, going over various numbers, signing off on the pâté selection and the set list of the R&B band, and I waited for him—to be certain of the truth.

Sis, you became engaged too quickly. There had been that other guy, Mark, and you had been engaged to him, too, and that arrangement fell apart kind of fast—I think you were engaged at Labor Day and broken up by M.L.K.'s birthday—and then, within weeks, there was this Brice. There's a point I want to make here. I'm trying to be gentle, but I have to get this across. Brice wore a beret. *The guy wore a beret.* He was supposedly a great cook, he would bandy about names of exotic mushrooms, but I never saw him boil an egg when I was visiting you. It was always you who did the cooking. It's true that certain males of the species, the kind who linger at the table after dinner wait-

627

ing for their helpmeet to do the washing up, the kind who preside over carving of viands and otherwise disdain food-related chores, the kind who claim to be effective only at the preparation of breakfast, these guys are Pleistocene brutes who don't belong in the Information Age with its emerging markets and global economies. But, Sis, I think the other extreme is just as bad. The sensitive, New Age, beret-wearing guys who buy premium mustards and free-range chickens and grow their own basil and then let you cook while they're in the other room perusing magazines devoted to the artistic posings of Asian teenagers. Our family comes from upstate New York and we don't eat enough vegetables and our marriages are full of hardships and sorrows, Sis, and when I saw Brice coming down the corridor of the Mansion on the Hill, with his prematurely gray hair slicked back with the aid of some all-natural mousse, wearing a gray, suede bomber jacket and cowboy boots into which were tucked the cuffs of his black designer jeans, carrying his personal digital assistant and his cell phone and the other accoutrements of his dwindling massage-therapy business, he was the enemy of my state. In his wake, I was happy to note, there was a sort of honeyed cologne. Patchouli, I'm guessing. It would definitely drive Glenda Manzini nuts.

We had a small conference room at the Mansion, just around the corner from Glenda's office. I had selected some of the furnishings there myself, from a discount furniture outlet at the mall. Brice and his fiancée, Sarah Wilton, would of course be repairing to this conference room with Glenda to do some pricing. I had the foresight, therefore, to jog into that space and turn on the speaker phone over the coffee machine, and to place a planter of silk flowers in front of it and dial my own extension so that I could teleconference this conversation. I had a remote headset I liked to wear around, Sis, during inventorying and bill tabulation—it helped with the neck strain and tension headaches that I'm always suffering with—so I affixed this headset and went back to filing, down the hall, while the remote edition of Brice and Sarah's conference with Glenda was broadcast into my skull.

I figure my expression was ashen. I suppose that Dorcas Gilbey, when she flagged me down with some receipts that she had forgotten to file, was unused to my mechanistic expression and to my curt, unfriendly replies to her questions. I waved her off, clamping the headset tighter against my ear. Unfortunately, the signal broke up. It was muffled. I hurriedly returned to my desk and tried to get the forwarded call to transmit properly to my handset. I even tried to amplify

628

it through the speaker-phone feature, to no avail. Brice had always affected a soft-spoken demeanor while he was busy extorting things from
people like you, Sis. He was too quiet—the better to conceal his tac-
tics. And thus, in order to hear him, I had to sneak around the corner
from the conference room and eavesdrop in the old-fashioned way.

—We wanted to dialogue with you (Brice was explaining to Glenda),
because we wanted to make sure that you were thinking creatively
along the same lines we are. We want to make sure you're comfortable
with our plans. As married people, as committed people, we want this
ceremony to make others feel good about themselves, as we're feeling
good about ourselves. We want to have an ecstatic celebration here, a
healing celebration that will bind up the hurt any marriages in the
room might be suffering. I know you know how the ecstasy of marriage
occasions a grieving process for many persons, Mrs. Manzini. Sarah
and I both feel this in our hearts, that celebrations often have grief as
a part of their wonder, and we want to enact all these things, all these
feelings, to bring them out where we can look at them, and then we
want to purge them triumphantly. We want people to come out of this
wedding feeling good about themselves, as we'll be feeling good about
ourselves. We want to give our families a big collective hug, because
we're all human and we all have feelings and we all have to grieve and
yearn and we need rituals for this.

There was a long silence from Glenda Manzini.

Then she said:

—Can we cut to the chase?

One thing I always loved about the Mansion on the Hill was its
emptiness, its vacancy. Sure, the Niagara Room, when filled with five-
thousand-dollar gowns and heirloom tuxedos, when serenaded by
Toots Wilcox's big band, was a great place, a sort of gold standard of
reception halls, but as much as I always loved both the celebrations
and the network of relationships and associations that went with our
business at the Mansion, I always felt best in the *empty* halls of the
Mansion on the Hill, cleansed of their accumulation of sentiment, utterly silent, patiently awaiting the possibility of matrimony. It was onto
this clean slate that I had routinely projected my foolish hopes. But after Brice strutted through my place of employment, after his marriage
began to overshadow every other, I found instead a different message
inscribed on these walls: *Every death implies a guilty party.*

Or to put it another way, there was a network of sub-basements in
the Mansion on the Hill through which each suite was connected to

another. These tunnels were well-traveled by certain alcoholic janitorial guys whom I knew well enough. I'd had my reasons to adventure there before, but now I used every opportunity to pace these corridors. I still performed the parts of my job that would assure that I got paid and that I invested regularly in my 401K plan, but I felt more comfortable in the emptiness of the Mansion's suites and basements, thinking about how I was going to extract my recompense, while Brice and Sarah dithered over the cost of their justice of the peace and their photographer and their *Champlain Pentecostal Singers.*

I had told Linda Pietrzsyk about Brice's reappearance. I had told her about you, Sis. I had remarked about your fractures and your loss of blood and your hypothermia and the results of your post-mortem blood-alcohol test; I suppose that I'd begun to tell her all kinds of things, in outbursts of candor that were followed by equal and opposite remoteness. Linda saw me, over the course of those weeks, lurking, going from Ticonderoga to Rip Van Winkle to Chestnut, slipping in and out of infernal sub-basements of conjecture that other people find grimy and uncomfortable, when I should have been overseeing the unloading of floral arrangements at the loading dock or arranging for Glenda's chiropractic appointments. Linda saw me lurking around, *asked what was wrong and told me that it would be better after the anniversary, after that day had come and gone,* and I felt the discourses of apology and subsequent gratitude forming epiglottally in me, but instead I told her to get lost, to leave the dead to bury the dead.

After a long excruciating interval, the day of Sarah Danforth Wilton's marriage to Brice Paul McCann arrived. It was a day of chill mists, Sis, and you had now been gone just over one year. I had passed through the anniversary trembling, in front of the television, watching the Home Shopping Network, impulsively pricing cubic zirconium rings, as though one of these would have been the ring you might have worn at your ceremony. You were a fine sister, but you changed your mind all the time, and I had no idea if these things I'd attributed to you in the last year were features of the *you* I once knew, or whether, in death, you had become the property of your mourners, so that we made of you a puppet.

On the anniversary, I watched a videotape of your bridal shower, and Mom was there, and she looked really proud, and Dad drifted into the center of the frame at one point, and mumbled a strange *harrumph* that had to do with interloping at an assembly of such beautiful women (I was allowed on the scene only to do the videotaping), and you were very pleased as you opened your gifts. At one point you leaned over to Mom, and stage-whispered—so that even I could hear—*that your car was a real lemon and that you had to take it to the shop and you didn't have time and it was a total hassle and did she think that I would lend you the Sable without giving you a hard time?* My Sable, my car. Sure. If I had it to do again, I would never have given you a hard time even once.

The vows at the Mansion on the Hill seemed to be the part of the ceremony where most of the tinkering took place. I think if Glenda had been able to find a way to charge a premium on vow alteration, we could have found a really excellent revenue stream at the Mansion on the Hill. If the sweet instant of commitment is so singular, why does it seem to have so many different articulations? People used all sorts of things in their vows. Conchita Bosworth used the songs of Dan Fogelberg when it came to the exchange of rings; a futon-store owner from Queensbury, Reggie West, managed to work in material from a number of sitcoms. After a while, you'd heard it all, the rhetoric of desire, the incantation of commitment rendered as awkwardly as possible; you heard the purple metaphors, the hackneyed lines, until it was all like legal language, as in any business transaction.

It was the language of Brice McCann's vows that brought this story to its conclusion. I arrived at the wedding late. I took a cab across the Hudson, from the hill in Troy where I lived in my convenience apartment. What trees there were in the system of pavement cloverleafs where Route Seven met the interstate were bare, disconsolate. The road was full of potholes. The lanes choked with old, shuddering sedans. The parking valets at the Mansion, a group of pot-smoking teens who seemed to enjoy creating a facsimile of politeness that involved both effrontery and subservience, opened the door of the cab for me and greeted me according to their standard line, *Where's the party?* The parking lot was full. We had seven weddings going on at once. Everyone was working. Glenda was working, Linda was working, Dorcas was working. All my teammates were working, sprinting from suite to suite, micromanaging. The whole of the Capital Region must have been at the Mansion that Saturday to witness the blossoming of families, Sis, or, in the case of Brice's wedding, to witness the way in which a vow of faithfulness less than a year old, a promise of the future, can be traded in so quickly; how marriage is just a shrink-wrapped sale item, mass-produced in bulk. You can pick one up anywhere these days, at a mall, on layaway. If it doesn't fit, exchange it.

I walked the main hallway slowly, peeking in and out of the various suites. In the *Chestnut Suite* it was the Polanskis, poor but generous— their daughter Denise intended to have and to hold an Italian fellow, A. L. DiPietro, also completely penniless, and the Polanskis were paying for the entire ceremony and rehearsal dinner and inviting the DiPietros to stay with them for the week. They had brought their own floral displays, personally assembled by the arthritic Mrs. Polanski. The room had a dignified simplicity. Next, in the *Hudson Suite,* in keeping with its naval flavor, cadet Bobby Moore and his high-school sweetheart Mandy Sutherland were tying the knot, at the pleasure of Bobby's dad, who had been a tugboat captain in New York Harbor; in the *Adirondack Suite,* two of the venerable old families of the Lake George region—the Millers (owners of the Lake George Cabins) and the Wentworths (they had the Quality Inn franchise) commingled their resort-dependent fates; in the *Valentine Room,* Sis, two women (named Sal and Martine, but that's all I should say about them, for reasons of privacy) were to be married by a renegade Episcopal minister called Jack Valance—they had sewn their own gowns to match the cadmium red decor of that interior; *Ticonderoga* had the wedding of Glen Dunbar and Louise Glazer, a marriage not memorable in any way at all, and in the *Niagara Hall* two of Saratoga's great eighteenth-century racing dynasties, the Vanderbilt and Pierrepont families, were about to settle long-standing differences. Love was everywhere in the air.

I walked through all these ceremonies, sis, before I could bring myself to go over to the *Rip Van Winkle Room.* My steps were reluctant. My observations: the proportions of sniffling at each ceremony were about equal and the audiences were about equal and levels of whimsy and seriousness were about the same wherever you went. The emotions careened, high and low, across the whole spectrum of possible feelings. The music might be different from case to case—stately baroque anthems of klezmer rave-ups—but the intent was the same. By 3:00 P.M., I no longer knew what marriage meant, really, except that the celebration of it seemed built into every life I knew but my own.

The doors of the Rip Van Winkle Room were open, as distinct from the other suites, and I tiptoed through them and closed these great carved doors behind myself. I slipped into the bride's side. The light was dim, Sis. The light was deep in the ultraviolet spectrum, as when we used to go, as kids, to the exhibitions at the Hall of Science and Industry. There seemed to be some kind of mummery, some kind of expressive dance, taking place at the altar. The Champlain Pentecostal Singers were wailing eerily. As I searched the room for familiar faces, I noticed them everywhere. Just a couple of rows away Alex McKinnon and her boy Zack were squished into a row and were fidgeting desperately. Had they known Brice? Had they known you? Maybe they counted themselves close friends of Sarah Wilton. Zack actually turned and waved and seemed to mouth something to me, but I couldn't make it out. On the groom's side, I saw Linda Pietrzsyk, though she ought to have been working in the office, fielding calls, and she was surrounded by Cheese, Chip, Mick, Mark, Stig, Blair and a half-dozen other delinquents from her peer group. Like some collective organism of mirth and irony, they convulsed over the proceedings, over the scarlet tights and boas and dance belts of the modern dancers capering at the altar. A row beyond these Skidmore halfwits—though she never sat in at any ceremony—was Glenda Manzini herself, and she seemed to be sobbing uncontrollably, a handkerchief like a veil across her face. Where was her husband? And her boy? Then, to my amazement, Sis, when I looked back at the S.R.O. audience beyond the last aisle over on the groom's side, *I saw Mom and Dad.* What were they doing there? And how had they known? I had done everything to keep the wedding from them. I had hoarded these bad feelings. Dad's face was gray with remorse, as though he could have done something to stop the proceedings, and Mom held tight to his side, wearing dark glasses of a perfect opacity. At once, I got up from the row where I'd parked myself and climbed over the exasperated families seated next to me, jostling their knees. As I went, I became aware of Brice McCann's soft, insinuating voice ricocheting, in Dolby surround-sound, from one wall of the Rip Van Winkle Room to the next. The room was appropriately named, it seemed to me then. We were all sleepers who dreamed a reverie of marriage, not one of us had waked to see the bondage, the violence, the excess of its cabalistic prayers and rituals. Marriage was oneiric. Not one of us was willing to pronounce the truth of its dream language of slavery and submission and transmission of property, and Brice's vow, *to have and to hold Sarah Wilton, till death did them part, forsaking all others,* seemed to me like the pitch of a used-car dealer or insurance salesman, and these words rang out in the room, likewise Sarah's uncertain and breathy reply, and I rushed at the center aisle, pushing away cretinous guests and cherubic newborns toward my parents, to embrace them as these words fell, these words with their intimations of mortality, *to tell my parents I should never have let you drive that night, Sis. How could I have let you drive? How could I have been so stupid? My tires were bald—I couldn't afford better. My car was a death trap; and I was its proper driver, bent on my long, complicated program of failure, my program of futures abandoned, of half-baked ideas, of big plans that came to nought, of cheap talk and lies, of drinking binges, petty theft; my car was made for my own death, Sis, the inevitable and welcome end to the kind of shame and regret I had brought upon everyone close to me, you especially, who must have wept inwardly, in your bosom, when you felt compelled to ask me to read a poem on your special day, before you totaled my car, on that curve, running up over the bream, shrieking, flipping the vehicle, skidding thirty feet on the roof, hitting the granite outcropping there, plunging out of the seat (why no seat belt?), snapping your neck, ejecting through the windshield, catching part of yourself there, tumbling over the hood, breaking both legs, puncturing your lung, losing an eye, shattering your wrist, bleeding, coming to rest at last in a pile of mouldering leaves, where rain fell upon you, until, unconsciously, you died.*

Yet, as I called out to Mom and Dad, the McCann-Wilton wedding party suddenly scattered, the vows were through, the music was overwhelming, the bride and groom were married; there were Celtic pipes, and voices all in harmony—it was a dirge, it was jig, it was a chant of religious ecstasy—and I couldn't tell what was wedding and what was funeral, whether there was an end to one and a beginning to the other, and there were shouts of joy and confetti in the air, and beating of breasts and the procession of pink-cheeked teenagers, two by two, all living the dream of American marriages with cars and children and small businesses and pension plans and social-security checks and grandchildren, and I couldn't get close to my parents in the throng; in fact, I couldn't be sure if it had been them standing there at all, in that fantastic crowd, that crowd of dreams, and I realized I was alone at Brice McCann's wedding, alone among people who would have been just as happy not to have me there, as I had often been alone, even in fondest company, even among those who cared for me. I should have stayed home and watched television.

This didn't stop me, though. I made my way to the reception. I shoveled down the chicken satay and shrimp with green curry, along with the proud families of Sarah Wilton and Brice McCann. Linda Pietrzsyk appeared by my side, as when we had kissed in the Ticonderoga Suite. She asked if I was feeling all right.

—Sure, I said.

—Don't you think I should drive you home?

—There's someone I want to talk to, I said.—Then I'd be happy to go. And Linda asked:

—What's in the bag?

She was referring to my Wal-Mart shopping bag, Sis. I think the Wal-Mart policy which asserts that *employees are not to let a customer pass without asking if this customer needs help* is incredibly enlightened. I think the way to a devoted customer is through his or her dignity. In the shopping bag, I was carrying the wedding gift I had brought for Brice McCann and Sarah Wilton. I didn't know if I should reveal this gift to Linda, because I didn't know if she would understand, but I told her anyhow. *Is this what it's like to discover, all at once, that you are sharing your life?*

—Oh, that's some of my sister.

—Andrew, Linda said, and then she apparently didn't know how to continue. Her voice, in a pair of false starts, oscillated with worry. Her smile was grim. —Maybe this would be a good time to leave.

But I didn't leave, Sis. I brought out the most dangerous weapon in my arsenal, the pinnacle of my nefarious plans for this event, also stored in my Wal-Mart bag. The Chicken Mask. That's right, Sis. I had been saving it ever since my days at Hot Bird, and as Brice had yet to understand that I had crashed his wedding for a specific reason, I slipped this mask over my neatly parted hair, and over the collar of the wash-and-wear suit that I had bought that week for this occasion. I must say, in the mirrored reception area in the Rip Van Winkle Room, I was one elegant chicken. I immediately began to search the premises for the groom, and it was difficult to find him at first, since there were any number of like-minded beret-wearing motivational speakers slouching against pillars and counters. At last, though, I espied him preening in the middle of a small group of maidens, over by the electric fountain we had installed for the ceremony. He was laughing good-naturedly. When he first saw me, in the Chicken Mask, working my way toward him, I'm sure he saw me as an omen for his new union. *Terrific! We've got a chicken at the ceremony! Poultry is always reassuring at wedding time!* Linda was trailing me across the room. Trying to distract me. I had to be short with her. I told her to go find herself a husband.

I worked my way into McCann's limber and witty reception chatter and mimed a certain Chicken-style affability. Then, when one of those disagreeable conversational silences overtook the group, I ventured a question of your intended:

—So, Brice, how do you think your last fiancée, Eileen, would be reacting to your first-class nuptial ceremony today? Would she have liked it?

There was a confused hush, as the three or four of the secretarial beauties of his circle considered the best way to respond to this thorny question.

—Well, since she's passed away, I think she would probably be smiling down on us from above. I've felt her presence through the decision to marry Sarah, and I think Eileen knows that I'll never forget her. That I'll always love her.

—Oh, is that right? I said,—because the funny thing is I happen to have her *with me here,* and . . .

Then I opened up the small box of you (you were in a Tiffany jewelry box that I had spirited out of Mom's jewelry cache because I liked its pale teal shade: the color of rigor mortis as I imagined it) held it up toward Brice and then tossed some of it. I'm sure you know, Sis, that chips of bone tend to be heavier and therefore to fall more quickly to the ground, while the rest of the ashes make a sort of cloud when you throw them, when you cast them aloft. Under the circumstances, this cloud seemed to have a character, a personality. *Thus, you darted and feinted around Brice's head,* Sis, so that he began coughing and wiping the corners of his eyes, dusty with your remains. His consorts were hacking as well, among them Sarah Wilton, his troth. How had I missed her before? She was radiant like a woman whose prayers have been answered, who sees the promise of things to come, who sees uncertainties and contingencies diminished, and yet she was rushing away from me, astonished, as were the others. I realized I had caused a commotion. Still, I gave chase, Sis, and I overcame your Brice McCann, where he blockaded himself on the far side of a table full of spring rolls. Though I have never been a fighting guy, I gave him an elbow in the nose, as if I were a Chicken and this elbow my wing. I'm sure I mashed some cartilage. He got a little nosebleed, I think I may have broken the Mansion's unbroken streak of peaceful weddings.

At this point, of course, a pair of beefy Mansion employees (the McCarthy brothers, Tom and Eric) arrived on the scene and pulled me off of Brice McCann. They also tore the Chicken Mask from me. And they never returned this piece of my property afterwards. At the moment of unmasking, Brice reacted with mock astonishment. But how could he have failed to guess? That I would wait for my chance, however many years it took?

—Andy?

I said nothing, Sis. Your ghost had been in the cloud that wreathed him; your ghost had swooped out of the little box that I'd held, and now, at last, you were released from your disconsolate march on the surface of the earth, your march of unfinished business, your march of fixed ideas and obsessions unslaked by death. I would be happy if you were at peace now, Sis, and I would be happy if I were at peace; I would be happy if the thunderclouds and lightning of Brice and Sarah's wedding would yield to some warm autumn day in which you had good weather for your flight up through the heavens.

Out in the foyer, where the guests from the Valentine Room were promenading in some of the finest threads I had ever seen, Tom McCarthy told me that Glenda Manzini wanted to see me in her office—before I was removed from the Mansion on the Hill permanently. We walked against the flow of the crowd beginning to empty from each of the suites. Our trudge was long. When I arrived at Glenda's refrigerated chamber, she did an unprecedented thing, Sis, she closed the door. I had never before inhabited that space alone with her. She didn't invite me to sit. Her voice was raised from the outset. Pinched between thumb and forefinger (the shade of her nail polish, a dark maroon, is known in beauty circles, I believe, as *vamp*), as though it were an ounce of gold or a pellet of plutonium, she held a single green M&M.

—Can you explain this? she asked.—Can you tell me what this is?

—I think that's a green M&M, I said.—I think that's the traditional green color, as opposed to one of the new brighter shades they added in a recent campaign for market share.

—Andy, don't try to amuse me. What was this green M&M doing behind my filing cabinet?

—Well, I—

—I'm certain that I didn't leave a green M&M back there. I would never leave an M&M behind a filing cabinet. In fact, I would never allow a green M&M into this office in the first place.

—That was months ago.

—I've been holding on to it for months, Glenda said.—Do you think I'm stupid?

—On the contrary, I said.

—Do you think you can come in here and violate the privacy of my office?

—I think you're brilliant, I said.—And I think you're very sad. And I think you should surrender your job to someone who cares for the institution you're celebrating here.

Now that I had let go of you, Sis, now that I had begun to compose this narrative in which I relinquished the hem of your spectral bed-sheet, I saw through the language of business, the rhetoric of hypocrisy. Why had she sent me out for those birth-control pills? Why did she make me schedule her chiropractic appointments? Because she could. *But what couldn't be controlled, what could never be controlled, was the outcome of devotion.* Glenda's expression, for the first time on record, was stunned. She launched into impassioned colloquy about how the Mansion on the Hill was supposed to be a *refuge,* and how, with my *antics,* as she called them, I had sullied the reputation of the Mansion and endangered its business plan, and how it was clear *that assaulting strangers while wearing a rubber mask is the kind of activity that proves you are an unstable person, and I just think, well, I don't see the point in discussing it with you anymore and I think you have some serious choices to make, Andy, if you want to be part of reg-ular human society,* and so forth, which is just plain bunk, as far as I'm concerned. It's not as if Brice McCann were a *stranger* to me.

I'm always the object of tirades by my supervisors, for overstepping my position, for lying, for wanting too much—this is one of the deep receivables on the balance sheet of my life—and yet at the last second Glenda Manzini didn't fire me. According to shrewd managerial strat-egy, she simply waved toward the door. With the Mansion crowded to capacity now, with volume creeping upward in the coming months, they would need someone with my skills. To validate the cars in the parking lot, for example. Mark my words, Sis, parking validation will soon be as big in the Northeast as it is in the West.

When the McCarthys flung me through the main doors, Linda Pietrzsyk was waiting. What unfathomable kindness. At the main en-trance, on the way out, I passed through a gauntlet of rice-flingers. Bouquets drifted through the skies to the mademoiselles of the Capi-tal. Garters fell into the hands of local bachelors. Then I was beyond all good news and seated in the passenger seat of Linda's battered Volkswagen. She was crying. We progressed slowly along back roads. I had been given chances and had squandered them. I had done my best to love, Sis. I had loved you, and you were gone. In Linda's car, at dusk, we sped along the very road where you took your final drive. Could Linda have known? Your true resting place is forested by white birches, they dot the length of that winding lane, the fingers of the dead reaching up through burdens of snow to impart much-needed instruction to the living. In intermittent afternoon light, in seizure-inducing light, unperturbed by the advances of merchandising, I composed a proposal.

2000

SEED

by MARY YUKARI WATERS

from SHENANDOAH

T HE NAKAZAWAS were in China barely a week when they first heard the drumming of a prisoner procession. They were sitting side by side on the hard seat of their new Western-style garden bench. Though it was twilight and turning cool, the ornamental wrought iron retained the sun's rays, reminding Masae of a frying pan slowly losing heat. Turning her head toward the sound, she stared at the concrete wall as if seeing through to the dirt road on the other side.

Clearly a small drum, it lacked the booming resonance of *taiko* festival drums back home. *Tan tan tantaka tan, tan tan tantaka tan,* it tapped in precise staccato, flat and almost toy-like, as if someone were hitting the drumhead with chopsticks. Moments later, like an afterthought, came the scuffling sound of many feet, and a man's cough less than ten meters away. The Nakazawas sat unmoving in the dusk. Out of habit, Masae's thoughts darted out to their baby girl: Indoors . . . noise didn't wake her . . . good. Above the wall, in sharp contrast to the black silhouette of a gnarled pine branch, the sky glowed an intense peacock blue. It seemed lit up from within, some of the white light escaping through a thin slit of moon.

"Ne, what'll they do to them?" Masae asked her husband Shoji once the drumbeats began to fade.

"Shoot them, most likely," Shoji said. He shifted forward on the hard iron seat and leaned down to tap his cigarette with a forefinger, once, twice, over his ashtray in the crabgrass. "Some might get sentenced to hard labor."

Masae turned her entire body to face her husband's profile. Its familiar contours, now shadowed by nightfall, took on for an eerie instant the cast of some other man: hollowed cheeks, eyes like strong brush strokes. "Araaaaa—" she sighed with a hint of reproach. Granted, these things happened in occupied countries and they had known about the prison camp before their move; still, they could do without such reminders while relaxing in their own garden. Masae wondered what people back home would think of this. In their old Hiroshima neighborhood, mothers went to great lengths to shield their children from unpleasantness, even pulling them indoors so they wouldn't watch two dogs circle each other in heat. Last winter, naturally, the neighborhood children had been spared any specific details of the Pearl Harbor incident. "I think," she now told her husband, "this is not a good location."

"H'aa, not so pleasant," Shoji said. He sounded humble; normally he would have been quick to point out that the company had chosen this house. They sat silent in their walled-in garden, on the bench which had, by now, lost all its heat. Masae could sense a faint shift in their relations. The drumbeats still rang faintly in her ears, like the aftermath of a gong. In the mock orange bushes behind them, a cricket began to chirp—slow, deliberate, unexpectedly near.

"Ochazuke might taste nice," Masae said, "before bed." Comfort food from home: hot green tea poured over leftover rice, flavored with salty flakes of dried salmon and roasted seaweed.

"Aaah! Masae, good thinking!" Shoji said, rising. His hearty exclamation was absorbed efficiently, like water by a sponge, into the silence of the Tai-huen plains.

The Nakazawas lived two kilometers from the main town, which was so small it had only six paved streets. If Masae looked out from the nursery window on the second floor (for she rarely ventured past the garden walls), she saw the dirt road leading straight into town. To her left were hills: wheat-colored, eroded over centuries to low swells on the horizon. Dark wrinkles wavered down their sides, as if the land had shriveled. Right behind those hills, the Japanese Army had built a labor camp for Chinese prisoners of war. On the other side of the dirt road, a flat expanse of toasted grass stretched out to a sky which faded in color as it approached the earth, from strong cobalt blue to a whitish haze. And somewhere past that skyline was the great Pun'An Desert.

Shoji was not in the Army. He managed a team of surveyors. His company back home, a construction conglomerate, had targeted this area because there was talk of building a railroad; Tai-huen might become a crucial leg in the Japanese trade route. Similar foresight in the Canton and Hankow provinces, which had come under Japanese rule three years ago in 1939, was paying off now in housing commissions. "The faster we take the measurements," Shoji kept repeating to Masae, as much for his own benefit, she felt, as hers, "the faster we go home. Next April, that's the goal. Maybe June, no longer than that." He worked late most nights in the Japanese tradition, flagging a bicycle-ricksha in town to bring him home over the long dirt road in the moonlight.

Each night Masae watched for her husband from the nursery window as she sang their daughter Hiroko to sleep. Hiroko, two years and nine months come the end of summer, was already developing her own idiosyncrasies. She fell asleep in one position only: curled up on her left side, right arm slung over the right half of her tiny bean-stuffed pillow, head burrowed under its left half. Masae didn't see how she could breathe, but she knew better than to tug away the pillow even if Hiroko was asleep.

Tonight, cranking open the window to feel the night breeze, Masae drew in a deep breath. With the climate so dry, the air had no real smell other than that of the dusty wooden sill over which she leaned. But Masae loved that instant when her face, dulled from the heat of day, first came into contact with the night air. She savored it so fully that if the cool breeze were a feather brushing her cheek, she could have counted its strands.

Two months ago, after the first enemy prisoners passed by, Masae had kept all the windows locked. Since then her vigilance had waned, but only slightly—enough to open a window, but not to leave it unattended. Even Koonyan, their heavy-set maid who came two afternoons a week, still unnerved her; the girl never spoke, merely taking in Masae's Japanese orders without any expression. Recently Masae dreamed that Koonyan turned toward her and revealed a face without features, as smooth and blank as an egg. She admitted this to Shoji, with a self-deprecating little laugh. "Nothing to be afraid of," he told her. "Hoh, behind that face she's busy thinking about her little pet birds!"

Shoji's wry comment referred to a company function two months ago, which they had attended shortly after the prisoner procession. It was a Western-style welcome dinner held in their honor, at someone's home in the main town. Masae was seated beside the company interpreter, an elderly Japanese man who had studied Chinese classics at Kyoto University. Shoji sat across the table from them, his chin partially obscured by a vase of thick-petaled indigenous flowers. Last year a prisoner had escaped, the interpreter told them with a lilting Kansai accent. This Chinese man had hidden in the dark on someone's pan-tiled roof, lying flat as a *gyoza* skin while the Army searched for him in the streets; he might have gone free if not for the Army's German shepherds. "See," Masae told her husband across the flowers, "it pays to play it safe!"

"But they're not overly antagonistic toward us," the interpreter had reassured them, "compared to occupied provinces I've seen. Tai-huen's been under one warlord or another for dynasties. Here their focus is on small things, pet birds for example. Every household has a pet bird in a bamboo cage."

"Aaa, well, they're peasants," Shoji said benevolently. He had studied global geological theory at Tokyo University, which held as much prestige as the interpreter's alma mater, and he was proud of his large-scale understanding of things.

"True, but it's not just that, I think. Sometimes the small focus is necessary. I myself find it crucial."

"Yes—no doubt." Shoji shot Masae a quick glance of confoundment over the flowers. It occurred to her that these fleshy petals might be indirectly related to a cactus species.

"Yes, it's crucial." A quality of sorrow in the interpreter's voice, deeper somehow than mere sympathy for the Chinese, threaded its way to Masae's sensibility through the muted clinks of silverware around her. "The immensity of this land. . . ."

At her window now, looking out over the darkening plain for the jig-gling light of Shoji's ricksha lantern, Masae's thoughts drifted out toward the great Pun'An Desert. She had never seen a desert; she imagined it much like these plains except hotter and bleaker, stripped of its occasional oak trees and the comforting motion of rippling grass. An endless stretch of sand where men weakened, and died alone. Masae, being from Hiroshima, had grown up by an ocean which had drowned thousands in storm seasons. Yet as a child she had sensed the water's expanse as full of promise—spreading out limitless before her, shifting, shimmering, like her future. She and her schoolmates had linked elbows and stood at the water's edge, digging their toes into the wet sand and singing out to sea at the tops of their voices: songs such as "Children of the Sea" or, if their mothers weren't around, the moun-taineering song that Korean laborers sang, "Ali-lan." She remembered the tug of her heart when, on the way to school, she had followed with her eyes a white gull winging a straight line out to sea. But those were the impressions of youth. Masae was now at mid-life, mid-point—Hiroko had been a late child—and for the first time she sensed the inevitability of moving from sea to desert.

THE NEXT NIGHT, for the third night in a row, Hiroko demanded that her mother read *Tomo-chan Plants her Garden*. Masae sat on a floor cushion before the dark nursery window, while Hiroko perched on her lap and turned the pages when told. Each page showed, with predictable monotony, yet another brightly colored fruit or vegetable ballooning up magically from its seed, hovering above it like the genie in their *Arabian Nights* book. They certainly looked nothing like the meager produce their maid brought home from the open-air market: desert vegetables, Masae thought. The big *daikon* radishes, for example. She was serving them raw as all Japanese women did in the summer, finely grated and mounded on a blue plate to suggest the coolness of snow and water. But these radishes had no juicy crunch. They were as rubbery as boiled jellyfish and required rigorous chewing. Shoji didn't seem to notice—he was often exhausted when he came home—and Masae fancied lately that he was absorbing the radishes' essence. Since they had come to Tai-huen, something about him had shrunk in an indefinable way, as if an energy which once simmered right below the surface of his skin had retreated deep within his body.

Yet Shoji denied having any troubles, and laughed shortly at what a worrier she was. As long as Masae could remember, Shoji's laughs had been too long—about two ha-ha's past the appropriate stopping point. They had always irritated her, those laughs, but lately Shoji stopped way before that point as if to conserve them. She missed his long laughter now, the thoughtless abundance of it.

"The End," Masae concluded, slowly closing the book. Hiroko squirmed on her lap, and Masae could sense the wheels in her mind starting to turn, thinking up new questions about the story in order to postpone her bedtime. To deflect the questions, Masae picked her up and carried her to the window, upon which their faces were reflected in faint but minute detail, as if on the surface of a deep pool. The child's head gave off the warm scent of shampoo.

"Way out past those lights," she told her daughter, cranking open the window with her free hand, "is the desert, *hora!*" Their reflections twisted and vanished; coolness flowed in around them. A coyote howled in the distance.

"What's a dizzert?"

"Lots of sand, nothing else. No people. No flowers."

"Ne, how come?" This, turning around to squint up to her mother.

"It's too dry for anything to grow."

Hiroko digested this in silence; then, "Are there rice balls?"

"No. There's nothing out there in the desert."

"What about milk?"

"No."

"What about—" she twisted in Masae's arms to peer back at the nursery—"toys?"

"*No.*"

"How come?"

Masae drew a deep breath. At such times she felt like she was floundering in a churning river. She longed for Shoji—or any adult, for that matter—with whom she could follow a narrow stream of rational thought to some logical end.

"Mama told you why, remember?" she said. "You already know the answer. Yes, you do."

"The dizzert lost all its seeds!" Hiroko cried, tonight's story fresh in her mind. "You got to get some seeds. And then you can grow things." Masae left the matter alone.

After Hiroko fell asleep, she returned to the window. The stars neither glimmered nor winked; they lay flat on the sky in shattered white nuggets. The town lights were yellower, a cozy cluster of them glowing in the distance with a stray gleam here and there. She imagined blowing the lights out, with one puff, like candles.

Seeds. As a girl Masae had read a book on deserts, how it rained once every few years. After the rain, desert flowers burst into bloom only to die within two days, never seen by human eyes. Such short lives, ignorant of their terrible fate. She had wondered at the time how a seed could be trusted to stay alive in the sand; wouldn't it just dry up from years of waiting? In the driest, bleakest regions of the desert, who was checking whether flowers still bloomed at all? Aaa, Masae thought, this is what comes of keeping company with a child.

But one fact was indisputable: the Pun'An Desert was expanding. Shoji had mentioned it, only last night—spreading several centimeters each year, according to the latest scientific report. Killing the grass in its path like a conquering army. Wasn't it reasonable, then, that seeds were actually dying in this part of the world, leaving fewer and fewer of them to go around? An inexplicable sense of loss overwhelmed Masae. When Shoji's ricksha lantern bobbed into view, its light refracted through her tears and gleamed brighter than any evening star.

A PRISONER PROCESSION was coming. Masae heard its faint *tan tan tantaka tan* from the living room, where she sat on the floor reading a letter from her mother. She had assumed, since that one procession in the beginning of summer, that prisoners would always come by after sunset. But it was still afternoon. Koonyan, the maid, was still here—her blank, egg-shaped face had just peered in at her mistress as she glided silently down the hall—so it wasn't even five o'clock yet.

Masae was aware of the strange picture she must make to Koonyan, sitting in the middle of the floor while surrounded by perfectly good imported furniture. The company representative who arranged their move must have been an Anglophile; he had stocked the house with a modish array of brocaded ottomans and chaise lounges, even the bench made of black iron out in the garden. The Nakazawas could not relax in such chairs. They installed *tatami* matting on the concrete floors, and Masae had Koonyan sew floor cushions for all the rooms. Shoji bought a saw and shortened the legs of the Western style dining table so they could sit at ease during meals.

Don't you worry so much, her mother's letter said. Masae noted the slowness of the mail; the letter was dated August 10, 1942, more than four weeks ago. *We're all just fine. There've been only those two air raid alarms—not a single hit. Rationing, though, has gotten much more inconvenient, and not having nice meals on the table can be demoralizing, especially for your father! But I am confident in my heart that all this will have blown over by the time you sail back. I can imagine how Hiro-chan will have grown. . . .*

There was the heavy click of the back entrance doorknob turning, then Hiroko's high-pitched voice: "Mama—Mama, the festival's coming—" To Hiroko, who had experienced the Koinobori Festival just before moving to China, drums always meant festivals.

Masae followed her child as she ran toward the garden gate, passing through the flickering shade of the pine tree. When Hiroko got excited, her right arm always swung harder than her left. The habit had started back in Hiroshima. She had been carried about so often on the arm of one relative or another, her left arm curled around the back of someone's neck, that when she was set down she forgot to move her "neck" arm. "Mama, I want to go!" Hiroko wailed without turning around. An image flashed through Masae's mind of a man pouncing, catlike, from the roof. But it faded. And she felt a sharp need to gaze at other living faces, even Chinese ones. She turned to Koonyan, who had followed her out, and nodded. Koonyan leaned a hefty shoulder into the solid weight of the wood, face impassive above her navy mandarin collar; Hiroko imitated her movements, grimacing. The rusty hinges yielded with a prolonged creak.

About forty men, dressed in khaki uniforms, shuffled toward them in three columns. Long shadows stretched out behind them, narrow and wavery like floating seaweed. Herding the prisoners were four Japanese guards with German shepherds at their heels, dogs as tall as Hiroko. "*Wan wan!*" shrieked Hiroko in delight, mimicking dog barks and leaning forward as far as Masae's grip on her hand would allow. "*Wan wan!*" The dogs' ears—huge black-tipped triangles of fur—flicked to attention, but otherwise the German shepherds ignored her, stalking past with the controlled intensity of wolves. One Japanese guard, noticing Masae's kimono, gave a curt nod; she acknowledged it with a slight bow. The Chinese stared ahead, their brown faces blurred with exhaustion and the dust of the plains.

Tan tan tantaka tan, tan tan tantaka tan, beat the little drum at the head of the line. Hiroko, eyes crinkled up with joy, let out a loud excited squeal. She began dancing; standing in place, bending and straightening her knees in jerks which didn't quite match the drum's rhythm. Her ponytail flopped limply on the top of her head.

One tall prisoner about Shoji's age looked over at Hiroko, bright-eyed in her red sundress. The corners of his mouth stretched out in a wistful smile. One by one the others began to grin, and Masae had a jumbled impression of teeth: stained teeth, buck teeth, missing teeth. The prisoners turned their heads and kept looking at the dancing child as they passed by, wrists bound behind them with strips of cloth; Hiroko beamed back, thrilled by the attention of all those adults.

And as the columns of men grew small in the distance, Masae felt this moment shrink into memory, shriveling and gathering into a small hot point in her chest. A stray seed, she thought. It could have so easily been lost. Hiroko would not remember this, nor would the dead prisoners. *The immensity of this land. . . .* Ancient land, stretching out to desert beneath the blank blue sky of late summer.

2000

THE FIRST MEN

by STACEY RICHTER

from MICHIGAN QUARTERLY REVIEW

I'M RIDING UP an escalator with Roxy explaining how she's the worst mother in the world. Some of my students, I say, have really bad mothers, but she takes the cake. Roxy, who's a real cunt, says something along the lines of "you ungrateful whore" and storms off to Ship and Shore, which is retailese for Fat and Ugly.

I go to the Ladies Lounge and vomit then proceed to Lingerie to buy a couple of push-up bras on credit. Look, it isn't my fault that Teddy drinks too much, okay? I just want to say that. EVERYBODY ACTS LIKE EVERYTHING IS MY FAULT AND IT ISN'T MY FAULT. I hate it, hate it, hate it. And I wanted that perfume, that's why I lifted it. What do you want me to say? That it's a disease? I have news for you baby. Greed is not a disease.

A little later, an ugly clerk at The Sunglass Hut is explaining why these three hundred dollar glasses are ultimately *me* when Roxy swoops past with her nose in the air, jingling her car keys so I'll notice she's leaving without me. I can tell she wants me to run after her, but I'm not going to give her the satisfaction—I·mean, is this any way to treat your own daughter? I'm stranded with no nutritional options but corn dogs and frozen yogurt and giant cinnamon buns that stink up all the stores west of The Gap. I've maxed out most of my cards. I am not drunk, I haven't scored in several days, nor have I been laid. I'm considering trying to go easy on drugs because of the children. Think of the children! That's what Roxy says, but give me one good reason why I should listen to her.

Besides, I do think of the children. Right now I'm thinking of Roger Wells, everyone calls him Pig Pen—cute. He's in my third period Health Ed class, and he sells me downers at a reduced rate in exchange for a guaranteed B+. This was a good deal for everyone until Pig Pen started skipping class entirely. How am I going to buy drugs when he won't fucking come to class? "It's no big deal, Miss Roberts. Whatever you say, Miss Roberts." That kid is a liar and a degenerate—B+ or not, I'm filling in the negative comment bubbles with a number two pencil on that one. I am TRYING to teach a unit on reproduction, very touchy vis à vis the school board, the PTA, the textbook company, and there are only so many things I'm authorized to say according to state law—the curriculum on this date is fully legislated. I keep repeating *abstinence, abstinence* when Pig Pen slinks in late and tosses a note on my desk that says I owe him big money. Through the window, I get a peek at his drones circling. This kid is a really bad kid.

You want to know how they get that bad? Some are born bad. Some of them have bad parents. Some of them watch too much MTV and it spoils them. You can spot the ones that have been corrupted by heavy metal music from the slogans on their t-shirts and their constant, vulture-like slouch. Some of them have been in accidents and received blows to the head. When they wake up, they're bad. Pig Pen may have been bad due to any of these influences, or he may have gone bad during a gym class trauma—getting picked last for a year, pantsing, taunts concerning penis size. It's been known to happen. One day they're little boys and girls, and the next they're criminals and drug addicts.

So after the bell rings I tell Pig Pen I need a few days to get the money together, and would he please get me some more of those good downers? For a while he had a pharmaceutical source and could obtain the best, best shit, and when I looked at him I swear I almost started to drool. Pig Pen said okay Miss Roberts.

God's honest truth, I was going to pay the kid. Good, bad, I didn't care, he had what I needed. Unfortunately I had to go and drop in on Roxy and have my entire head screwed up, a task that took her about twenty minutes. She's sitting in her kitchen, in a warm-up suit patterned after the British flag, trying to make me eat a pound cake. She's accusing me of having an eating disorder and keeps saying, "Let me look in your mouth, let me look in your mouth," as though I'm a farm animal she's thinking of buying. Then she puts a slice of cake with whipped cream and strawberries in syrup in front of me—a sort of witch test. If I don't eat it, I'm mentally sick. If I do, I'll turn into a fat slug like her.

I pick up the fork. Roxy informs me that I am a heathen, and that I have picked up the wrong fork. I pick up another fork. She sighs and wedges her lumpy hips more firmly in her chair, but after thirty-two years of this I'm certain that this fork is the one. I cut the cake into bite-sized pieces. I consume it daintily. I wait until she's running the insinkerator before I duck into the bathroom to vomit.

After that, she starts whining that we never go anywhere together so we make a date to go to the mall on Saturday. My friend Wanda won't talk to me anymore, but when she did, she used to say WHY DO YOU SPEND SO MUCH TIME WITH THAT WOMAN IF SHE DRIVES YOU CRAZY? But what she doesn't understand is that Roxy has accused me of taking her boyfriend Teddy out drinking when the truth is Teddy is an alcoholic and doesn't need anyone to "help" him drink. We went to the Golden Nugget once or twice, but HE called ME and asked for a ride. Shit. Do you want to know why I'm bad? My mother made me this way.

The upshot is that after the cake incident I was so stressed out I went to Rossingham's and bought four gold chains and a cubic zirconia tennis bracelet with instant credit and a small down payment and have Roxy to thank for this little spree. The next thing I know it's already Saturday and I'm broke, stranded at the mall, pausing in the food court to watch captive sparrows pecking crumbs off the floor. I think the smell lures them through the automatic doors and the poor things are too stupid to figure out how to get back out. Or, I don't know, maybe it's the greatest deal; maybe for a sparrow the mall is the lap of luxury, like living in the Hyatt for a human.

So I'm bird watching and calmly sipping my Diet Coke when I look up and who should be approaching? Not Pig Pen, thank God, but one of his worker drones, Seymour Jackson, to whom I'd given a D the year before in Biology. Seymour Jackson is a big white kid with a military crew-cut and arms that reach almost to his knees. He has the deadened, blank face of a jock but Seymour is not a jock because he's a bad boy and a drug dealer who smokes cigarettes incessantly. In class, he'd chew tobacco and spit into a Big Gulp cup that he liked to balance on the edge of my desk on his way out. Those of Seymour's peers not too frightened to refer to Seymour at all, refer to Seymour as "Action."

The way it goes for high school teachers these days is you generally don't want to chitchat with kids you've given a D, particularly strapping lads who work for an organization to whom you owe money for narcotics. Nevertheless, Action Jackson comes right up and looks at me—just looks. Very mean. Very tall.

"Miss Roberts?" He seems confused.

"What can I do for you, Seymour?"

"You're at the mall?"

Let me tell you a little bit about these kids. They're not bright. They sniff nail polish remover and drive around with handguns tucked under their registration slips. They wear sunglasses in the rain and get gum stuck in their braces. In my class they think it's really funny to act like a retarded mental idiot when I call on them. There are no class clowns anymore—the youth of today are too dim-witted for wise-cracking. When I see the instructions "shake and pour" on a carton of orange juice I think thank God, because these kids are in desperate need of instructions. So I say to Action, enunciating clearly: "Yes, Seymour. I am at the mall."

He's drumming his hands on his stomach, rolling his head around in a weak imitation of Stevie Wonder. Teenage boys, Jesus Christ. They can't hold still for a second and they can't look you in the eye. You can practically smell the hormones steaming from them—it's repellent, but at the same time it's a struggle not to take them home and fuck their brains out. I AM NOT referring to Brandon Murray here. Brandon Murray is a pathological liar who is "at risk" and any charges he's made against me should be regarded as impeachable fantasy.

Then Action wants to sit down. "Miss Roberts, Miss Roberts, can I sit here a minute?" What am I supposed to say? I am thinking this kid might have a gun in his jeans. I owe seven bills and some change to Pig Pen, which isn't all that much, considering these guys drive Camrys and carry cell phones in their backpacks, but they watch a lot of TV, a lot of movies, and they've picked up all manner of bullshit about loyalty, manhood, honor, prompt payment.

"Miss Roberts," he tosses a pack of cigarettes on the table, then his backpack, then a clump of keys with a little pot pipe on the ring. "That book you made me read, the one about the cave men. . . ."

"They're called *Homo erectus,* Seymour."

"Homo whatever. Look, I know I didn't pay attention in class, but I keep thinking about it. The whole thing about him hunting giant tree sloths and adapting and working in groups. . . ." Action's foot is going up and down as if it were electrified. It's possible he's on speed, but he's so hyper to begin with it's difficult to tell. He's puffing a cigarette too, pinching the filter really hard, like he wants to prevent something from escaping. "I keep thinking," he's saying, "about the acquisition of language."

"Hey Action. Do you have anything for me?"

"Like what?"

"Something powdered. Or in capsule form."

Action drums on the tabletop. He's moving so much of his body in such a fitful manner that looking at him is like watching something under a strobe light. "I can't do it Miss Roberts," he finally says. "Pig Pen says you gotta pay up first."

"What are you on right now? Can you get some for me?"

"Right now?"

"Yeah, right now."

"Okay," he says. "Wait here."

Action walks around to the other side of the carousel, by the booth where they sell personalized Barbie books imprinted with your child's name. It looks like he's talking on his cell phone, but I'm not sure. I'm thinking that if I manage to escape with my life, I might go to Dillard's and buy some Lancome eye shadow in smoky gold. Also, if I manage to escape with my life as well as score some drugs, I'll buy a pound of chocolates and eat them without vomiting.

After a few minutes Seymour comes back with a styrofoam cup in each hand. As he walks across the food court, I detect a bulge under his left arm, through his warm-up jacket. This is bad news. Seymour occasionally seems nice and vulnerable, like a kid, but the truth is he's also young in the sense that he doesn't understand how dangerous he is. It's too bad Roxy ditched me, because I'm thinking it might be a good idea to have already made an exit myself.

"Here you go, Miss Roberts." Seymour places one of the styrofoam cups in front of me and tucks his long arms under the table. The cup is half full of black liquid.

"What the hell is it?"

"Espresso. Rocket fuel of the gods."

"That's all you've got for me?"

"Hey. It's stronger than you think."

"Seymour, I have to go now." I gather my bags. Action scoots his chair over to my side of the table and touches my arm—very gentle. Very soothing.

"You can't go just yet, Miss Roberts. You gotta wait a while."

"Because. . . ."

"You gotta answer me about *Homo erectus,* okay? I read that First Man book and it was freaking me out." He's leaning toward me, suddenly calm, patient. There's something almost paternal about him and if you knew Action you would be terrified by this also. "I mean, it says that in monkeys, feelings go straight into the brain, right? Like an injection."

"There's something called the limbic system, Seymour. Fear, pleasure, pain."

"The reptile brain!"

"Sorta, right. Seymour, I have to go."

"Wait." His hand is on my knee, not in a sexy way, but in an anchoring way. "*Homo erectus*—he added another step. Like, a filter, right?"

"More or less. Speech centers. Symbolic thinking. Like, if I say the word 'cup' you can think of a generic cup, this cup on the table, whatever, and your brain sorts through the possibilities and figures out what I'm talking about. Ta da, you've got language. You and I communicating. Understand?"

"And this is like, an amazing leap, right? That book said it took a million years."

"Fuck, Seymour. I don't know how long it took. I wasn't there."

Seymour's big face goes slack. He's disappointed, but what do you want me to say? I'm not even trained in science but the district is so strapped that half of us cross-teach. My field is Spanish and I'm a licensed family counselor. For some reason the district has declared I'll teach Health, Biology, and Remedial Math. I am, however, familiar with the book Seymour is referring to, *The First Men,* a title in the Time-Life series I assign as extra credit when a student is failing because it has a lot of pictures. It also happens to have been written by Edmund White, father of the gay literary renaissance and author of a great biography of Jean Genet, a bad boy if ever there was one. If he could ever learn French, I'm sure Seymour would have gotten along great with Jean Genet.

His cell phone is ringing. "Will you please excuse me?" The more polite Action is, the more I figure I'm in trouble. He turns away but keeps his foot on top of my shoe—I have to pretend to ignore this. The more I act like everything is cool, the more likely it is that everything WILL be cool. I'm beginning to think, however, that I'm not going to score any drugs off Seymour on this particular day.

653

He's on the phone saying *uh huh, uh huh.* The way he looks at me with one eye, his body tense but motionless—it's giving me a chill. It's as though every trace of the little boy has been precipitated out of him and what remains is cool and gray. He reminds me of a pair of stiletto heels I tried on in Dillard's. When was that? Less than an hour ago.

"Okay," he says, hanging up the phone. "You're going to have to come with me, Miss Roberts."

"I have a lot of people waiting for me upstairs. My ex-husband. He's a cop."

"You're going to have to hook up with them later, Miss Roberts. I'm really, really sorry about this."

There's a car and then another car parked by a dumpster. Action nods at a pair of kids I haven't had in my class and urges me into the back of an Econoline van, license plate PMD 525. The two guys in front look like brothers—weak chins, slicked hair, sunken cheeks smothered in clumps of cystic acne. Both are so thin that their bones show through their clothes, but it's not like I could take them. They would have weapons.

"You boys," I ask, "do you go to Salpointe?"

They are not saying anything to me. They are not even turning around and acknowledging that I've spoken.

Action climbs in the back beside me and encourages me to buckle up. I feel he wants this not for safety, but to hold me immobile.

"Hey," I say, "I can get some stuff for your face that'll give you the complexion of a baby—my esthetician makes it. You can't buy it in stores."

The boy in the passenger seat twists around and fixes me with dull, sleepy eyes. His face looks like it got pinched by the forceps on the way out, and right where the tongs would have gone, there's a particularly nasty jumble of welts and pus.

"Miss Roberts," says Action, "would you mind keeping quiet?"

"This stuff is a miracle. If you boys hurt me, you'll throw away any chance of ever clearing up your skin."

"Hey, Miss Roberts. . . ." Action sounds pissed.

"And I know how devastating acne can be for kids your age. Okay. I'm through."

The boys start up the van and it feels like we're driving in circles. I can't see outside because the windows are covered with aluminum foil, though I could see through the windshield if Action would scoot over.

Action is on the cell phone again. He's calm, gliding in his movements, and I know this isn't good. He whispers something to the driver, then turns to me.

"We've gotta go see Pig Pen, okay Miss Roberts? You've gotta give him the money now, today."

"Give me the phone, Seymour."

"I'm not allowed."

"Give it to me or else you're expelled."

"I got expelled already."

"I can get you back in. Seymour. Are you listening to me?"

"It's not my choice, Miss Roberts. We got certain agreements between us. We use language to make agreements in order to do business. We're working together like *Homo erectus* did to hunt the wooly mammoths. I'm right about that, aren't I?"

"Yes, Seymour."

"You didn't know I was smart, did you?"

"You're a very bright boy."

"Then why'd you give me the D?"

"Because you didn't do the reading, you didn't take the tests, you didn't come to class. You left tobacco spit on my desk and bothered that girl Shelly, by always asking her if she was wearing a wig. Seymour, look at me." Seymour has started to vibrate again, subtly, in the fingers and feet. "I don't have the money."

The van is no longer traveling in circles. We could easily be out in the desert. People die in the desert all the time—hikers, thieves, Mexicans dodging immigration. They find them days, weeks or years later, beneath palo verde trees, huddled in pathetic disks of shade.

"Do you want to go to the prom? I could get you back into school. Take whoever you want. You could take Shelly."

Action scratches his ear and stares at the foil over the window. After a minute he lights up another cigarette. "Miss Roberts," he says, "I gotta ask you this thing about evolution. Millions of years of things building up—fire, language, hunting, society. I mean, all those stone tools, people trying to form words and their mouths aren't big enough or something. It all builds up to what? To me, like, riding in this van, talking to you?"

"Listen, Seymour. I don't have the money."

He looks away and pats at his hair cautiously, as though it were a toupee. "I know that, Miss Roberts."

"Call my mother—Roxy Ingram. She'll pay Pig Pen."

"Pig Pen already spoke to Roxy, Miss Roberts. She said she wasn't going to pay your debts no more. She said to tell you."

The van makes a right. After a while the ride turns bumpy and I'm almost certain we're on a dirt road. The sun pouring in the windshield is very bright. We all rock from side to side in our seats, the four of us looking very crisp, all the stains on our clothes visible, all of our wrinkles and pimples standing out in the light as though we were under a microscope, being examined for the defect that keeps our mothers from loving us.

"The thing that bothers me though," Action's eyes list sideways to some pensive arena, "is what it means. You know? Man evolving from guys with big jaws and shit—is that, what, science? x = y or whatever? Or is it some kind of miracle?"

Action is a handsome kid. His skin is dewy and he works out at the gym, I guess, because his arms are big and he doesn't have that inchoate, half-formed look a lot of juniors have. There's something oddly beautiful about the way he can't sit still and can't complete a thought and can't finish exhaling before he inhales, and even though it's likely he'll spend most of his life in jail, and fucking deserves it, at this point in his development it seems entirely obvious that he's a wonder of creation anyway—graceful and predatory, like a shark.

"Yeah, Seymour, I think it's a miracle. I think it's a miracle and a marvel that you've evolved to the point where we can sit here discussing evolution, even as you're driving me out to the middle of nowhere to stab me or shoot me or suffocate me with a couch cushion."

"Ha!" He sucks on his cigarette with deep satisfaction. "I thought so. I thought I was a miracle."

Action leans against the door so I can finally see outside. We're in the desert, clipping past saguaro and cholla, weird plants that look like freaks of evolution themselves. At least I can see the sky, rushing toward us, so blue I feel like if I took a swipe at it, pigment would come off on my hand.

"It's not just you, Seymour," I say. "It's me. I'm a miracle too."

He isn't listening. He's making funny noises with his mouth that are probably meant to mimic the sounds an electric guitar makes on the radio. I think the song is *Back in Black*. Also, he's playing a set of air drums and vibrating his knees, both of them, up and down with astonishing speed. I rip the foil off the window. We're moving through a valley carpeted with beautiful, thorny plants, about half of them dead. It's sleepy and still. There's a different time scale in the desert; things move slowly. Saguaro cacti don't sprout their first arms for a hundred years, and even then they're just adolescents.

The van rolls to a stop. The two boys in front twist around and look at me eagerly, like I'm suddenly going to put on a big show or something. Action opens the door and ushers me out to a place that's saved from being described as the middle of nowhere by very little—just the foundation to a house that was either never built or burned to the ground long ago. There's a border of concrete with four steps leading up a dirt lot—a rectangle filled with weeds and some bleached beer cans. It's an island of nothing in the middle of the desert, which is, as always, surprisingly green and filled with motion. I used to like to play in the desert when I was a kid but now I'd rather stay indoors; out here, without any people, everything seems strangely removed, like I'm taking in the view through a veil. The wind reminds me of other times I've felt the wind. The sun could be on film. And all the different plants growing in the dirt. They all have names.

"Is he going to?" The driver says this as though I'm not there.

"Could you do me a favor, Miss Roberts?" Action, again, is smooth and steady, taking my hand as the wind blows his shirt tight against his torso. In other times he would have been the model for a Greek statue, a Roman foot soldier, a quarterback, the one who invented the spear. Even now I can see that he's in his element, gliding. Nothing, for him, is veiled. "Could you go up there?" he says to me. "Would you mind please climbing up those steps now?"

I watch the wind blowing around scrub and trash on the little platform. Above, white clouds drift.

I start climbing. These boys aren't going to hurt me. These boys are good boys. These boys will let me go.

2000

657

THE ANOINTED

by KATHLEEN HILL

from DOUBLETAKE

My harp is turned to mourning.
And my flute to the voice of those who weep.
—Job 30:31

I

IN MISS HUGHES'S SEVENTH-GRADE MUSIC CLASS, we were expected to sit without moving finger or foot while she played for us what she called "the music of the anointed." At a moment known only to herself, Miss Hughes opened the album of records ready at her elbow and, tipping her head from side to side, cautiously turned the leaves as if they had been the pages of a precious book. When she had found the 78 she was looking for, she drew it from its jacket and placed it on the spinning turntable. But before lowering the needle she took a moment to see that we were sitting as she had instructed: backs straight, feet on the floor, hands resting on our darkly initialed wooden desktops.

While the record was playing, Miss Hughes's face fell into a mask, her mouth drooping at the corners. A small woman in high heels, she stood at attention, hands clasped at her waist, shiny red nails bright against her knuckles. She wasn't young, but we couldn't see that she was in any way old. The dress she wore was close-fitting. Often it was adorned by a scarf, but not the haphazard affair some of our teachers attempted. Miss Hughes's scarf was chosen with care, a splash of blue or vermilion to enliven a somber day, and was generous enough to allow for a large, elegant loop tied between her breasts.

Most of us had turned twelve that year and were newly assembled at the high school. The spring before we had graduated from one or another of our town's four elementary schools, where we had stooped to water fountains and drawn time charts on brown paper. Now we watched with furtive interest while the juniors and seniors parked their cars with a single deft twist of the steering wheel. This was the grown-up world we had been waiting for, fervently and secretly, but once here most of us knew we had still a long way to travel. Our limbs were ungainly, ridiculous. We twitched in our seats; our elbows and knees, scratched and scabbed, behaved like children's. We knew we couldn't lounge at our lockers with the proper air of unconcern, nor did we suppose we could sit upright and motionless for the duration of the "Hallelujah Chorus" from Handel's *Messiah* or a Beethoven sonata. Yet under Miss Hughes's surveillance, we learned to do so. If the grind of a chair's legs or a sigh reached her ears, Miss Hughes carefully lifted the needle from the spinning record and, staring vaguely into space, showing no sign that she recognized the source of the disturbance, waited until the room was silent before beginning again.

In other classes we doodled in our notebooks, drawing caricatures of our teachers, words streaming from their mouths in balloons. Small pink erasers flew through the air. On the Monday morning following a stormy bout with us on Friday, Mrs. Trevelyan, our math teacher, was tearful. "My weekend was ruined," she told us. "It troubles me very much when we don't get along together. Surely we can do better, can't we? If we make a little effort?" We looked at her with stony eyes. To our social-studies teacher, Miss Guthrie, we were deliberately cruel. Her voice was high, her mouth was tense, and often when she spoke a tiny thread of spittle hung between her lips. If someone answered a question in a strangled voice, mimicking her, she pretended not to notice.

Miss Hughes neither cajoled nor ignored us. Instead she made us her confidants. Music class met on Friday afternoons and through the windows the dusty autumn sunlight fell in long strips across our backs and onto the wooden floor. Behind us, flecked with high points of light, trees lined one end of the playing field. It was hard to tell, turning to look after a record had wound to its end, if the sun were striking to gold a cluster of leaves still green and summery or if a nighttime chill had done it.

The class always followed the same turn: first, Miss Hughes dictated to us what she called "background," pausing long enough for us to take down what she said in the notebooks we kept specially for her class, or for her to write on the blackboard a word we might not know how to spell. *To what class of stringed instruments does the pianoforte belong?* we wrote. *The pianoforte belongs to the dulcimer class of stringed instruments.* Or: *Name several forerunners of the pianoforte. Several forerunners of the pianoforte are the clavichord, the virginal, the harpsichord, the spinet.* If giggles rose involuntarily in our throats at the word "virginal," we managed to suppress them.

Following dictation, which she delivered without comment or explanation, she would ask us to assume our "postures." We had already written down the name of the piece we were about to hear, its composer, and usually some fact having to do with its performance— *on the harpsichord, the third movement of Mozart's Sonata in A Major, otherwise known as the "Turkish March," played by Wanda Landowska.* After she had set the needle on its course, we were for the moment alone with ourselves, a fact we were given to understand by the face wiped clean of all expression she held before us. We were then free to think of whatever we liked: a nightmare we had almost forgotten from the night before; a dog shaking water from its back, the drops flying everywhere like rain; a plan we had made with a friend for the weekend. Or we were free simply to watch the dust floating in the shafts of sunlight, to follow a path the sounds led us up and down.

We marveled that Miss Hughes always knew exactly when to turn and lift the needle, that she knew without looking when the record was almost over. After she had replaced the arm in its clasp, she turned her full attention to us. "You have just heard, boys and girls, in the 'Turkish March,' a great virtuoso performance. What do I mean by 'virtuoso'? A virtuoso performance is one executed by an instrumentalist highly skilled in the practice of his art, one who is able to bring to our ears music that we would otherwise go to our graves without hearing. The first great virtuosi pianists were Liszt and the incomparable Chopin, both of whom you will meet in due course.

"In fact, boys and girls," she said, lowering her voice a little so that we had to lean forward to hear, "we have our own virtuosi pianists, ones who regularly perform close by in New York City, only a half hour's ride away on the train. You have heard the name Artur Rubinstein, perhaps? You have heard the name Myra Hess? These are artists whose work you must do everything in your power to appreciate first-hand. We go to sleep at night, we wake in the morning, we blink twice and our lives are over. But what do we know if we do not attend?"

Miss Hughes suddenly held up her two hands in front of us, red fingernails flashing. "You will see, boys and girls, I have a fine breadth of palm. My fingers are not as long as they might be, but I am able to span more than an octave with ease. Perhaps you do not find that remarkable. But I assure you that for a woman a palm of this breadth is rare. I had once a great desire to become a concert pianist myself. A very great desire. And I had been admitted to study at Juilliard with a teacher of renown. A teacher, Carl Freidburg, who in his youth in Frankfurt had been the student of Clara Schumann. Who had heard Liszt interpret his own compositions. When I went for my audition, when I entered the room where the piano was waiting and Mr. Freidburg was sitting nearby, I was afraid. I do not hide that from you, boys and girls. I was very much afraid. But as soon as I began to play Chopin's Polonaise in A-flat, a piece that requires much busy fingerwork by the left hand and a strong command of chords, I was so carried away by the fire of the music that I forgot the teacher. I forgot the audition. I forgot everything except the fact that I was now the servant of something larger than myself. When I reached the end and looked up—and I was in a bit of a daze, I may tell you—the great teacher's eyes were closed. He bowed his head once, very simply. That was all. I left the room. Soon afterward I received a letter assuring me that he would be proud to have me for his student."

Miss Hughes's face had registered the sweep of feelings she was recounting to us. Her eyes had narrowed with her great desire to be a pianist; entering the audition room, her jaw had grown rigid with fear; and while the great teacher had sat listening to her play, her face had assumed the look we were familiar with, the mask. Now her dark eyes took on a dreamy expression we had not yet seen. She seemed to be looking for words in a place that absorbed all her attention, over our heads, out the window, beyond.

"It was that winter, boys and girls, that my destiny revealed itself to me. If it were not too dramatic to put it this way, I would say that my fate was sealed. Everything I had hoped for, worked for, practicing seven hours each day after I had finished giving lessons—everything was snatched away in a single instant. I will tell you how it happened. Because someday in your own lives you may wake to a new world in which you feel a stranger. And you will know, if by chance you remember our conversation here today, that someone—no, my dear boys and girls, many others, a host of others, have also risen to a dark morning.

"A friend, a friend whom I loved, had asked if I would accompany him on a skiing trip to Vermont. Of course I said yes. Why should I not? We were to spend a day on the slopes. I was a great skier—my father had taught me when I was a child—and I looked forward to this holiday with the greatest excitement. I had been working hard that winter, too hard. It may have been my fatigue that in the end brought about my ruin. Because taking a curve that at any other time I might have managed with ease, my legs shot out from beneath me, and in an attempt to catch myself I let go of my pole and put out my hand, as any good skier knows not to do. Instead of fracturing a leg or a hip, both of which I might easily have spared, I injured my left hand, breaking three fingers that never properly healed."

This time Miss Hughes raised her left hand alone. She must have been about to point out to us the fatally injured fingers when the bell rang and she immediately dropped her arm. "To each of you a pleasant weekend, boys and girls," she said, turning to replace her records in their sleeves.

By class the following Friday we had other things to think about, and perhaps she did as well. We had just listened to Bach's Fugue in G Minor, for the purpose of learning to recognize the sound of the oboe—and the room for once had an air not of enforced constraint but of calm—when Miss Hughes lifted her head and, looking out the window, told us that there was one of us, sitting now in our midst, who listened to music in a manner quite unlike the rest. "He listens as if for his life, boys and girls, and it is in this manner that the music of the anointed was written. For the composer, the sounds struggling in his imagination are a matter of life and death. They are as necessary to him as the air he breathes."

She kept us in no more suspense, but allowed her gaze to rest on a boy who always sat, no matter the classroom, at the end of a row. We had scarcely noticed him at all, those of us who had not gone to elementary school with him. But there he sat—at this moment, blushing. His hair was sandy, his face was freckled, and he wore glasses with clear, faintly pinkish rims. His name was Norman de Carteret, a name that in a room full of Daves and Mikes and Steves we found impossible to pronounce without lifting our eyebrows. During the first week of September, Miss Hughes had asked him how he would like us to say his last name, and he had answered quietly, so quietly we could scarcely hear him, that it was Carteret, pronouncing the last syllable as if it were the first letter of the alphabet. The "de" he swallowed entirely.

"Then," Miss Hughes had said, "your father or his father must have come from France, the country that gave us Rameau, that invaluable spirit who for the first time set down the rules of harmony. The country to which we are indebted as well for Debussy, who accomplished what might have been thought impossible: he permitted us to hear the sound of moonlight."

· · ·

I knew something about Norman the others didn't.

My mother had lived in our town as a child and occasionally met on the street someone she would later explain was once a friend of her mother's, dead long ago. Hilda Kelleher was one of these friends, even a cousin of sorts, and lived in a large, brown-shingled Victorian house, not far from the station. A wide porch, in summer strewn with wicker rocking chairs, ran along the front and disappeared around one side. The other end of the house was flanked by tall pines that in winter received the snow. Hilda was of an uncertain age—older than my mother, but maybe not a full generation older. Her hair was dyed bright yellow, and when she smiled her mouth twitched up at one corner uncovering teeth on which lipstick had left traces. Hilda had never married, but there was nothing strange in that. The town was full of old houses in which single women who had grown up in them lived on with their aging mothers, going "to business," teaching in the schools, supplementing their incomes in whatever ways they could. I supposed that they, too, had been girls, just as I was then, walking on summer nights beneath streetlights that threw leafy shadows on the sidewalks, that they, too, had listened to the murmur of voices drifting from screened porches, had heard the clatter of passing trains and dreamed of what would happen to them next. But life had passed them by, that was clear.

Hilda had dealt with the problem of dwindling resources by taking in boarders. An aunt of my mother's, a retired art teacher who, as my mother liked to say, "had no one in the world," was looking for a place to live. One afternoon in late summer, just before school opened, my mother visited Hilda to inquire about arrangements, and I went with her. While they sat talking in rocking chairs on the front porch I discovered around to the side a swing hanging from four chains. It was easy to imagine sitting there on summer nights behind a screen of vines, morning glories closed to the full moon, listening to the cicadas. Swinging back and forth I could hear their voices, my mother's telling Hilda how Aunt Ruth had lived in Mrs. Hollingsworth's house in Tarrytown, how this arrangement would seem familiar to her. I heard Hilda saying how glad she was that a room was available, that we would look at it in a moment. She went on to say that one boarder, who had been with her a year, had moved out of the room into a smaller one that better suited his means. Did my mother know a Mr. de Carteret? He had a son who was going to the high school, she thought, in the fall. The son lived with the mother but came to visit the father on Saturdays. The terrible thing was that when he came the father wouldn't open the door of his room to him.

Her voice sank so low that I got out of the swing and stood along the wall to listen. "The poor child," she said in a loud whisper. "He knocks, and when his father won't let him in he sits outside the door in the hall. Saturday after Saturday he comes to the house and waits outside his father's room and still his father won't see him. Sometimes—oh, the poor child, I wish I knew what to do—he is there all afternoon."

I was back in the swing by the time they called me to look at the vacated room. We followed Hilda up a staircase of wide oak steps and along a hall, passing mahogany doors on either side. At last she threw one open on a room that had a neat bed covered with a white spread, a desk, and a chest of drawers. The afternoon sun was sifting through the pines and falling on the bed. My mother said she couldn't imagine that her aunt wouldn't be happy here; the room seemed to breathe tranquility. We closed the door, then went down the hallway to the staircase and out of the house.

I had been wondering whether or not I should whisper to my closest friends what I had heard Hilda say about Norman, but after Miss Hughes had asked us to notice his perfect attention it seemed to me

I should not. Why not, I couldn't be sure, except it seemed that if he were listening "as if for his life," he had heard something in the music that I hadn't, and I didn't think the others had either. I felt out of my depth. And soon enough, by saying nothing, by keeping to myself what I took to be his secret, I came to feel that some understanding had sprung up between us, that we shared a knowledge hidden from the others.

Then, very soon, our paths crossed.

II

In our old school there had been a classroom filled with books which we called the library. Twice a week we sat in a circle around Miss Kendall, the librarian, while she read to us, turning the book around from time to time to show us the pictures. I knew the books I wanted to read in that library; they were not the history books urged on us by our teachers, or the books about boys running away to sea, or even the large and lavishly illustrated volumes of myths and fairy tales. It was stories about girls I wanted, mostly orphan girls, or at least girls, like Sarah Crewe, whose mothers were dead and who had been left to the care of cruel adults to whom they refused to be grateful— to whom, in moments of passion, they poured out their long-suppressed feelings of outrage.

I had tried to explain all this to the older girl in the high school library who was supposed to show us around, and she had said I might like to read *Jane Eyre*, pointing to shelves lodged in a corner. I should look under the B's, she said, but I ended up nearby, facing shelves where all the books were written by people whose names began with a C. I was stopped by a title: *Lucy Gayheart*, a book about a girl, and perhaps even the kind I had in mind. It was written by Willa Cather, a name I had never heard, and I quickly looked around for a place to read.

This library was much larger than our old one, and instead of a little table where books were set on their ends for display—picture books and books for older children with such titles as *The Story of Electricity* and *Abigail Adams: A Girl of Colonial Days*—here there were unadorned long tables stretching the width of the room, with chairs tucked in on either side. High windows filled one end, and beneath them the librarian sat at her desk, ink pad and rubber date stamps poised at her elbow. I had sat down and opened the dark blue cover of the book to the first page when I looked up and saw Norman de Carteret sitting across the table, poring over an immense open volume. One foot was drawn up to rest on the seat of his chair, and as he read he leaned his face against his knee. It was a book about ships, I could see that; there was a full-scale picture of a sloop, or a schooner, with all its sails unfurled. There was writing on the different parts of the ship and on the sails, too, probably to let you know what they were called. Norman was absorbed, and I began to read.

> In Haverford on the Platte the townspeople still talk of Lucy Gayheart. They do not talk of her a great deal, to be sure; life goes on and we live in the present. But when they do mention her name it is with a gentle glow in the face or the voice, a confidential glance which says: "Yes, you, too, remember?" They still see her as a slight figure always in motion; dancing or skating, or walking swiftly with intense direction, like a bird flying home.

Lucy was one of the vivid creatures I wanted to read about, that was clear, but there was something that seemed not quite right, some note I had not yet heard. The story was already over and she lived on the first page not as a living person but as a memory.

I read on and to my surprise saw that Lucy, like Miss Hughes, wanted to be a pianist. She had been giving lessons to beginners from the time she was in tenth grade and had left Haverford to study music with a teacher in Chicago. Now she had come home for the Christmas holidays and had gone skating with her friends on the Platte. A young man, Harry, had joined them, and at sunset Lucy and he had sat together

> on a bleached cottonwood log, where the black willow thicket behind them made a screen. The interlacing twigs threw off red light like incandescent wires, and the snow underneath was rose-colour. . . . The round red sun was falling like a heavy weight; it touched the horizon line and sent quivering fans of red and gold over the wide country. . . . In an instant the light was gone. . . . Wherever one looked there was nothing but flat country and low hills, all violet and grey.

These words, too, seemed remarkable, because I thought I recognized the place. In our town, if you followed the railroad tracks over the bridge that looked down on Main Street, on past the red-brick factory and Catholic church, you came to a reservoir that in spring was overhung with Japanese cherry trees, their branches weeping pink blossoms into the black water. During the winter months, when the reservoir had frozen over, we skated there. No prairie surrounded the water, only rocks and frozen grass and crouching woods; but the sky loomed wide overhead, and on winter afternoons the red sun was caught for a moment in the drooping silver branches of the cherry trees. I thought I knew how the Platte would look, the sun going down on it, thought I knew how afterward everything would turn ordinary and flat.

Norman was still contemplating the picture of the sailing ship. I could glimpse him sitting there as I lowered my head to continue reading. Now Lucy and Harry were settled in a sleigh that was, I read,

> a tiny moving spot on that still white country settling into shadow and silence. Suddenly Lucy started and struggled under the tight blankets. In the darkening sky she had seen the first star come out; it brought her heart into her throat. That point of silver light spoke to her like a signal, released another kind of life and feeling which did not belong here.

I closed the book, deciding for today to forget *Jane Eyre*. I knew I had never read a book like this one. I had been expecting someone else to come along, or for Lucy and Harry to say something surprising or romantic to each other—something to happen besides the round red sun falling on the prairie and the star speaking to Lucy like a signal. And yet I felt that in this book these were enough. The pages I had read threw open the strange possibility that looking at things, feeling them, were also things that happened to you, just as much as meeting someone or going on a trip. What you thought and felt when you were alone or silently in the presence of someone else also made a story.

I looked up to see that Norman seemed to have fallen asleep on his book. His glasses were standing on their lenses beside him on the table and his face was in his arms. When the bell shrilled through the room, his shoulders twitched and he raised his head from the picture of the boat with all its sails. Looking up, still half asleep, his short-sighted blue eyes came to rest on mine. Another time I might have looked away. But as I, too, was half asleep, entertaining visions of quivering fans of red and gold playing on the prairie, turning over my new thoughts, I realized only after a moment that Norman had smiled at me as if he were still dreaming, as if he had been alone and, suddenly seized by a happy idea, were smiling at himself in a mirror.

III

One Friday afternoon in October we filed into Miss Hughes's class-room to find her standing beside the day's album of records, dressed entirely in white. Her dress, made of soft white wool, fell just below her knees. There was no crimson or purple scarf tied round her neck; instead, a long necklace of pearls hung between her breasts.

"You will be wondering, boys and girls," she said to us as soon as we were seated, "why you find me today dressed as you see. I am in mourning, but a mourning turned to joy. White is the color of sorrow, as it is of radiance. And today I am going to play for you a piece of music that throughout your lives you will return to again and again. If ever you must make a decision, if ever you find yourselves tossing on a stormy sea—and life will not spare you, boys and girls; it spares no one—I beg you to do as I say. Find a spot where no living soul will disturb you, not even your dearest friend, and in the silent reaches of your soul listen to the music you are about to hear. Today we shall have no dictation, because it is my idea that Mozart's Requiem is best introduced without preliminaries. A requiem, you must know, is a prayer for the dead. Today we shall hear the opening section of this great work. One day—we shall see when—I shall play for you an-other."

Miss Hughes lowered the needle to the record that was already in place and spinning on the turntable. For a few moments a mournful sound filled the room, something that seemed to move forward, as if people were walking—a rhythmic, purposeful sound, with an echo for every step—when suddenly, without any warning, a blare of trum-pets and kettle drums broke it all up, a frightening, violent blast that made us jump in our seats. Then, into the clamor, a chorus of men's voices forced their way, low, solemn, moving forward as before, but confident, as if they were sure of what they were saying. We were just getting used to the chorus when high above all the rest floated a single woman's voice, a voice raised high above the world but sliding down to meet it, and so calm, so full of understanding, I could have cried.

Miss Hughes lifted the needle and allowed her face to keep the expression of the mask for a few moments longer than usual. Then she drew a deep breath. "To comment on this music, boys and girls, would be an impertinence. We must let it rest in us where it will. Rest: a word, as it is used in music, to mean the absence of sound, a silence, sometimes short and sometimes long, when we hear only the vibrations of what has come before and prepare for those that will follow. You will understand what I mean if you think of a wave, the kind you see in a Japanese painting, caught in that moment just before it breaks."

The record had remained spinning on the turntable, its black surface crossed by a silver streak of light. Now Miss Hughes bent down, turned the knob, and the record slowly wound to a halt. Then she again stood upright, facing us. "The word 'requiem'—a Latin word you of course already know—might best be translated by several words in English: may he find rest at last, the one who has died. But my own prayer, I shall tell you now, is that we, the living, may find rest within the span of our own lives. I mean that rest we know only when we are most awake to sorrow and to joy, when we find we can no longer tell the difference. Then we are living outside of time, as we are when we are listening to music such as that we have just heard. In such an instance, death is only something that happens to us, like being born or growing old, but is of less consequence than the many deaths we sustain in life. I mean the deaths, my friends, when our dearest hopes are blasted."

Miss Hughes had been speaking slowly, meditatively, choosing her words with care. Her eyes had gone from one of us to the other. Now she assumed the dreamy look we had seen once before. She looked beyond us, through the clear panes of the window, into the distance. "Because, boys and girls, death may come to us in many disguises. You see, I, too, have gone down into the waters.

"I think I have told you already that my great desire in life was to have become a pianist, to play for myself one of the late piano concerti of Chopin, let us say, or of Schubert's impromptus. To that end I was living in Paris, studying with a teacher who was drawing from me all those feelings that I had supposed—young as I was—must remain outside music, separate from it. I had embraced discipline, and practicing for hours and hours everyday was the only way I knew to approach a sonata or prelude. It was this teacher who showed me that music is composed by a spirit alive to suffering and to joy and must be played by another such spirit. That it was only by bringing every moment of my life to the music that I could hope to draw from it what the composer had put in."

For a moment Miss Hughes seemed to wake from a sleep and looked at us alertly. "As indeed, boys and girls, in this room we must bring every moment of our lives to the music as we listen."

I wondered, while she stared from face to face, if her damaged hand had healed by the time she arrived in Paris, or if all this had taken place sometime before the skiing accident. But I would no more have thought to question whether or not Lucy Gayheart had taken the train back to Chicago the night after she had sat on the log and seen the round red sun falling like a weight into the prairie. The facts, the before and after of events, had their own logic by which, trusting the source, I supposed they must take their place in some pattern hidden from me.

Miss Hughes was playing with her pearls, winding them around her fingers. Again her gaze had retired to a place beyond the window.

"The city of light, boys and girls; that's what you will hear Paris called. But it is also, I will tell you, the city of darkness. If you cross the Pont des Arts one day, you will see the Ile de la Cité, that great barge of an island, drifting up the river—the River Seine, I'm sure you know. And on that island, as you make your way across the bridge, you will see swing slowly into view a spectacle that has greeted the eyes of bewildered humanity for almost eight hundred years, the great square towers of Notre Dame. I say 'slowly,' you will notice, because like the opening of the requiem we have just heard, like Bach's Fugue that stirred our souls a few weeks ago, that's how many of the best things come to us. The catastrophes stop us in our tracks. I know, my friends, because I came to a halt on the bridge that day; I was unable to continue my walk. I had a letter with me that I had only just received and that had thrown me into a state of the most painful confusion."

In the silence that followed these words we could hear the excited cawing of crows on the playing field behind us.

"The letter was from a close friend at home relating the pitiable state into which my father had fallen. A debilitating illness from which he could not recover. The friend, who was old himself, did not ask me to return. But how could I think of anything else? Who would care for my father if I did not? I was all he had in the world, and it was to him that I owed my early life in music, he who had given me my first lessons on the piano. Of course I must return to look after him.

"And yet—and here, my dear boys and girls, I do not seek an answer—how would that be possible? To leave Paris, to leave the city in which I had been so happy! To leave all those feelings I had begun to put into my music! In short, to leave my teacher! It was not to be thought of. I leaned out over the edge of the bridge and looked down into the river flowing beneath. I could not see my way. I tasted the bitter waters of defeat. Oh, I was tempted! Finally, scarcely knowing how I got there, I found myself in my room, and after closing the door and pulling the shutters, I listened to Mozart's Requiem. By the time it had concluded I knew my way."

Miss Hughes, standing immobile in white, continued to gaze out the window. Surely the class would be over in a minute or two, but she didn't seem to recollect our presence. I stealthily turned my head to see sleek black crows lifting out of the trees and lighting back into them, their outspread wings glinting in the afternoon light, the branches with all their yellow leaves tossing up and down.

IV

In the days that followed, I decided that Miss Hughes had been in love with her teacher. She must have been, I thought, because I had now followed Lucy Gayheart to Chicago where she lived alone in a room at the top of a stairs. A room, perhaps, like the room in Paris to which Miss Hughes had stumbled and had drawn shutters on a bright day. Lucy Gayheart was not in love with her teacher, but her teacher had urged her to attend a concert given by a celebrated singer named Clement Sebastian who, although he lived in France, was spending the winter in Chicago. "Yes, a great artist should look like that," she had thought the moment he had walked onto the stage. And then he had sung a Schubert song.

> The song was sung as a religious observance in the classical spirit, a rite more than a prayer. . . . *In your light I stand without fear, O august stars! I salute your eternity.*

. . . Lucy had never heard anything sung with such elevation of style. In its calmness and serenity there was a kind
of large enlightenment, like daybreak.

I remembered that Lucy had struggled up in Harry's sleigh when
she had seen the first star flashing to her on the wide prairie, and I
thought perhaps this was what Miss Hughes had meant about listening for your life: what you heard in the music was something exalted
that you already knew, but weren't aware that you did—something
you had blindly felt or heard or seen.

But then, reading on, I learned that Lucy's mood had quickly
changed. There was to be no more serenity and calm. She listened to
Sebastian sing five more Schubert songs, all of them melancholy, and
felt that

> there was something profoundly tragic about this man. . . .
> She was struggling with something she had never felt be-
> fore. A new conception of art? It came closer than that. A
> new kind of personality? But it was much more. It was a
> discovery about life, a revelation of love as a tragic force,
> not a melting mood, of passion that drowns like black wa-
> ter.

Although I didn't understand exactly how the music had led to this
discovery, I knew that in this book, called by her name, I was not
reading about Lucy alone. The lines that came next made it clear she
was merely one member of a select company, a company set apart—
as Miss Hughes had set Norman apart—by a destiny determined
from within: "Some peoples' lives are affected by what happens to
their person or their property; but for others fate is what happens to
their feelings and their thoughts—that and nothing more."

V

One Saturday afternoon in late October my mother asked if I would
take Hilda and Aunt Ruth a lemon poppyseed cake she had made for
them. It was not only Aunt Ruth she felt had no one in the world, but
Hilda as well. "Poor souls," she said. "To be all alone like that." I put
the cake, wrapped in wax paper, in the straw basket that hung from
the handlebars of my bike. The leaves were now almost gone from

the trees, but the day was clear and warm, like a day in early September. In less than a week it would be Halloween, and although we now thought it childish to go out begging, it was nice to think about walking from house to house, the night with its bare branches stark against a sky filled with spirits riding the air. I was in no rush to arrive at Hilda's because Aunt Ruth made me uneasy. When she came to our house she would give paper and colored pencils to my sisters and me and tell us to let our imaginations run wild. Then she would look at our efforts and to mine she would say, "D minus." Just as she might say the same if one of us carried her a cup of coffee that was not hot enough. But how could you obey a direction to let your imagination run wild? It was like someone wishing you sweet dreams.

By the time Hilda's house came into view I was riding my bike in loops, swerving sharply toward one curb then the other, doubling back. In the middle of the street I made a circle, three times. I knew now it was not so much Aunt Ruth I was afraid of running into; it was Norman de Carteret. Suppose he was sitting in the dark hall outside his father's door? Or suppose I met him coming out of the house as I was going in?

And then, my bike making wider and wider loops both toward and away, going over in my mind what I would say to Norman if we happened to meet, I finally dared to look up and saw him there on the porch at the side of the house, sitting on the swing that hung from the four chains. The morning-glory vines were bare, and he was sitting with his feet against the porch railing, pushing himself back and forth. I could see, too, that when he saw me he flinched and lowered his head to hide his face. But then, as I was about to ride by, pretending I hadn't seen him, he looked up and—as he had done in the library—smiled. I parked my bike at the bottom of the steps, removed the cake from the basket, and went around the corner of the porch to where he was sitting.

"Hi," he said. His brown high-top sneakers were resting on the porch railing. Behind his glasses his blue eyes floated a little.

"Hi," I said. There was a long pause before I thought of something to say. "My aunt lives here."

"I know." His voice was high and childish. "So does my father."

I sat down on the railing not far from his feet, swung my legs up and leaned back against one of the round white pillars. It seemed surprising that Norman spoke of his father. Had he knocked on his door this morning and, like all the other times, been greeted with si-

673

lence? Had he been waiting in the hall for hours, not knowing what to do, and finally come down to sit on the swing?

"Did you come here to see him?" I asked, both fearful and eager that he say more.

"Yes," he answered, looking straight ahead, out between the vines that in August had made a screen from the sun. Now a few shriveled leaves hung in the warm afternoon. Just as at school, Norman was wearing corduroy trousers a little too big for him, and a plaid flannel shirt buttoned at the neck. The sleeves came down almost to his knuckles. "I'm waiting till he wakes up. He told me not to go away. He wants me to wait for him here."

"Oh," I said and came to a stop. His voice had something in it I thought I recognized. It was in Miss Hughes's voice when she stared out the window while the crows were squawking and flapping in the trees. But Miss Hughes, as she stood there with her hands clasped at her waist, seemed to be communing with something only she could see. Norman's face, on the other hand, had lost its dreamy quality: his freckles stood out while he spoke; his eyes looked sharp and aware. He was looking at me as if he had made a point that he expected me to respond to.

Suddenly overcome with anxiety, not knowing what to answer, wanting only to erase the look in his eyes that made me afraid, I started unwrapping the cake. "Want some?" I asked.

"Sure," he said, and when I broke off a large chunk and held it out to him he leaned forward in the swing and took it in a hand I could see was trembling. I broke off another chunk for myself. At first we ate demurely, silently, spilling a few crumbs around us and brushing them away. I would find a way later on, I thought, to explain to my mother about the cake. Then I swallowed a piece that was too big for me and choked and sputtered, and then, on purpose this time, crammed a fistful in my mouth, pretending to frown at him disapprovingly, as if he were the one stuffing his mouth, until suddenly I was aping convulsions, bent double, holding my side, almost falling off the railing. Norman at first looked on, snorting with laughter. Then he, too, snatched a handful of cake and shoved it in his mouth, and soon we were both grabbing for more, exploding in high giggles, looking at each other cross-eyed, holding our sides, pretending to be on the point of collapse, pretending to be falling and dying, until the cake had disappeared, lying around us in half-eaten pieces.

Gradually we subsided, our shoulders stopped shaking, and we could breathe without gasping for air. The afternoon grew quiet around us. We could hear children playing up the block and the sound of someone raking leaves. Inside the house someone began to play the piano, some song from a time before we were born, something the grown-ups had sung when they were young. On the other side of the hedge, the late sun struck a large window into a flaming pool of orange. We avoided each other's eyes as if we had shared a secret we were ashamed of. After a while whoever was playing the piano broke off abruptly in the middle of a song and closed the cover with a bang. The sun slipped from the window, the branches of the trees reached ragged above our heads. When I finally got to my feet, taking leave of Norman without saying a word, it was almost dark.

For a few days afterward I tried falling in love with Norman de Carteret. I passed him in the halls sometimes, and once caught sight of him at his locker, turning his combination lock. But since our afternoon on Hilda's porch we were shy with each other, lowering our eyes when we met. Once, in music class, when Miss Hughes was playing a Brahms quintet for clarinet and strings, I tried to imagine how he might be listening, perhaps in the way Lucy had listened to Sebastian sing the Schubert songs. He was seated behind me, at the end of the row, and when I turned my head very slightly I could see him sitting there, his eyes sharp and aware, as they had been when he talked about his father. But at the end of the class when he walked through the door, his corduroy pants hanging from his hips, I could see he was only a child like myself.

VI

During the following weeks I pursued the story of Lucy Gayheart in fits and starts. I read with a sense of exaltation and impending doom, dipping back from time to time, for reassurance, into the world of Sara Crewe and Anne of Green Gables. There was some new strain in the voice telling the story, something I had not encountered in any other book. It ran along beneath the words like a stream beneath a smooth surface of ice, some undertone murmuring, "This is the way life is, this is the way life is." It was a voice—dispassionate, stern—I listened for with joy, as if it brought news from a country for which I had long been homesick. And yet my nightly dreams told me, too, it was a country where terror and brutality might strike out of a benign blue sky. It seemed not so much that my child life was fading into the past. It was more that my entire future life was rising before me, as if it were already known to me, as if it had already happened long ago and was waiting to be remembered.

Despite my fitful reading, Lucy's story was quickly running its course. She had already become Clement Sebastian's piano accompanist, already fallen in love with him. He was Europe, the wide world, the life of feelings, unabashed and unashamed, not cramped or peevish as in Haverford. He was a singer, an artist. And although he was married, he had fallen in love with Lucy, with her youth, her enthusiasm, perhaps with her rapturous admiration of himself, he who was disillusioned and tired of the world. And so when Harry came to see her in Chicago, to take her to a week of operas and to propose marriage, she told him desperately that she couldn't marry him, that she was in love with someone else.

None of this seemed surprising. The undertone I listened for, I knew, had something to do with desire, with wanting someone who wasn't there. Or maybe someone who was there but whom you couldn't reach out and touch. It had to do with feelings that couldn't be spoken and yet had to be spoken, the space between.

But now Lucy's story was taking an unexpected turn, was moving in directions my daytime self would not have thought possible. In response to what Lucy told him, Harry, in a fit of pique, married a woman lacking in that quick responsiveness he had loved in Lucy, and regretted the marriage immediately. Sebastian left Chicago for a summer concert tour in Europe and met a sudden death. In despair, Lucy returned to Haverford, to a "long blue-and-gold autumn in the Platte valley."

Then January came and "the town and all the country round were the colour of cement." Lucy left the house one afternoon to skate on the river, just as we would soon be skating on our reservoir with its weeping cherry trees. What she didn't know was that the bed had shifted, that what once had been only a narrow arm of the river had become the swift-flowing river itself. She skated straight out onto the ice, large cracks spreading all around her. For a moment she was waist deep in icy water, her arms resting on a block of ice. Then "the ice cake slipped from under her arms and let her down."

I was incredulous. Despite the opening sentences of the book, I thought I hadn't understood and read the passage over and over, looking for some hint, some odd word or phrase, that would change its meaning. And yet, even while searching, even while trying to re-

676

assure myself that I must have missed something, I was aware—by some inner quaking that echoed the sound of splintering ice—I had understood very well. Harry is left to take up a life wracked with remorse that only time will soften, and Lucy slips into the regions of the remembered. It was as the undertone running beneath the story had assured all along: Lucy's response to Sebastian's songs, her bleak sense of foreboding, would be fulfilled. An early death—anticipated by the intense life of feelings—had been her destiny, and at the appointed time her death had risen to meet her. This, I supposed, was what people called tragedy.

VII

Because of Haverford whose sidewalks Lucy had walked in the long autumn of her return, the houses and streets of our town looked different, the late gardens of chrysanthemums and Michaelmas daisies, the silver moon rising above them. In the November afternoons we ran up and down the hockey field in back of the school, and even at four o'clock the red bayberries flickered in the twilight. Walking home, thinking of Lucy, I noticed the cracks in the sidewalks, the way the roots of trees had splintered them. Beneath the sidewalks ran a river of fast-flowing roots that could throw slabs of cement into the air, make a graveyard of the smooth planes where we used to roller-skate and sit playing jacks. From the end of one street I could see the train station, its roof black against the orange sky, and could imagine the tracks running over the bridge and past the reservoir into the city. Even now Myra Hess might be practicing the Chopin she would play tonight to a crowd at Carnegie Hall. Perhaps Miss Hughes was sitting on the train that would take her to the concert; perhaps she would return late at night to a room in a big house like Hilda's, a room that looked on pines.

For Thanksgiving my mother invited Hilda and Aunt Ruth, who must not be left alone. Hilda's lipstick, a wan hope, had left traces on her teeth, I took note as she leaned across the table to ask if I had met Norman de Carteret in any of my classes. Before answering I vowed I would not, cost what it might, be trapped as she had been, would not become an old woman in a town where life was one long wait. Hilda went on to recount to the table at large that Mr. de Carteret, who had scarcely stirred from his room for months, had been busy during the last days buying a turkey to cook for his son.

677

He had bought cranberry sauce and sweet potatoes, she told us, and a bag of walnuts. It was all assembled on the table in the kitchen, and she herself had contributed two bottles of ginger ale. She had helped him put the turkey in the oven several hours before and at this moment it must almost be done. She hoped he wouldn't leave it in so long that it dried out. She hoped, too, that he remembered to turn off the oven once he took it out, because something might catch fire. She wondered if she should telephone him now to warn him but was persuaded by my father that a fire was unlikely.

On Monday we were back in school. I didn't see Norman that day, or the next, or the next, not until Friday, when, passing in the hall, I caught sight of him standing at his locker. He was standing idly there, staring into it in his usual absentminded way, not looking for anything in particular, it seemed. That was in the morning. By lunch a rumor had run through the school like fire through grass. One friend whispered it, and then another. Had I heard? Norman de Carteret's father had killed himself. Yes, it was true. He had drowned himself in the reservoir on Saturday. He'd done it by putting stones in his pockets. Someone's father had been there, had been part of the group that had pulled him from the water on Saturday night. That's why Norman hadn't been in school. All the teachers had been sent a notice, but Norman was in school today. Had I seen him? I had? What did he look like? Was he crying?

I absorbed the news as if it were of someone I knew nothing about, someone I had to strain to place or remember, someone whose name I barely recognized. Norman had again become a stranger, someone wrapped in an appalling story. My exchanges with him had separated me from the group; for a while I had shared his isolation and in drawing near him had drawn closer to my dreaming self, my reading self. Now I wanted nothing more to do with him. I was terrified that recalling our shared silences might draw me into some vortex of catastrophe. My fear was akin to what I had felt when, reaching the end of Lucy's story, I had looked frantically for something to tell me that I had not understood, that the words printed so boldly in black on the white page spelled out a meaning I had not grasped.

All day there had been the promise of snow in the air, and when we filed into Miss Hughes's room a few stray flakes had begun to fall. They were there in the window, the first of the season. Norman was already sitting in his place at the end of a row and the snow was falling behind him. He was sitting bolt upright in his seat, staring straight ahead, the corners of his mouth twisted up into something like a grin. But we only glanced at him, we didn't stare, sitting down as quickly as we could in our own places to get him out of our sight. We were overwhelmed with curiosity but also repelled. It would have been better if he hadn't been there at all, if we could have gone over the story, embellishing it with each retelling, without having to look at him, without having to sit with him in the same room.

Miss Hughes was, as usual, standing in her place beside the phonograph, the album on the table beside her. She was wearing a dark gray dress with a scarf that shimmered blue one moment, green the next. We had not met for two weeks because of the Thanksgiving vacation, but she had told us the last time we had seen her that she would welcome us back by introducing us to that consummate artist, Chopin. Now, rather brusquely, without the preliminary remarks with which she usually asked us "to silently invite our souls in order to prepare for the journey ahead," she asked us to open our notebooks and she began to dictate. "For Chopin," she pronounced, "the keyboard was a lyric instrument. He told his students, 'Everything must be made to sing.'"

For a few moments there were the sounds of papers rustling and of pencil cases coming unzipped. Then we settled to writing down her words.

"Chopin was a romantic in his impulse to render passing moods, but he was a classicist in his search for purity of form. His work is not given to digression. The Preludes are visionary sketches, none of them longer than a page or two. 'In each piece,' Schumann said, 'we find in his own hand, "Frederic Chopin wrote it!" He is the boldest, the proudest poet of his time.'"

We wrote laboriously, stopping as Miss Hughes carefully wrote on the board the words "classicist," "digression," "visionary." She made sure we had written quotation marks around Schumann's words, the exclamation point where it belonged. Out of the corner of my eye I saw that Norman was hunched over his notebook, writing.

Miss Hughes had turned to the album. "Now, boys and girls, we shall listen to one of Chopin's Preludes, the fourth, in E minor. It is very brief."

She drew a record out of its sleeve and placed it on the spinning turntable. After three months' training, we knew to assume our postures, so she had only to glance quickly around the room before lowering the needle. We heard the chords, the chords going deeper and deeper, and I pictured pine trees pointing to the sky at sunset; a darkness was about to overwhelm them, but for the moment they were lit by the setting sun. Everything was disappearing, the chords were telling us; a deep shadow was falling over the side of the mountain, yet the melody was singing of the last golden light thrown up from behind the rim.

"Do you hear it, boys and girls?" Miss Hughes asked us as she lifted the needle from the record. "Do you hear there the voice of desire? Not for one thing or another, not for a person or a place, but desire detached from any object. What we have heard in this fourth Prelude is the voice of longing when it breaks through into the regions of poetry, into the regions of whatever lives closest to us and furthest away."

Miss Hughes's scarf flashed blue then green against her gray dress, against the dark square of the blackboard behind her. Her eyes assumed the dreamy look we had seen before. "It was for this I had hopes of becoming a pianist," she told us, looking out the window. "To coax that voice from the instrument, to allow others to hear it in the way that I did." She was gazing into the snowflakes, it seemed, into the bare, black branches through which they were falling in the waning afternoon. She was watching them spill from the gray sky; in a trance she was following their white tumble. But all at once, as if she, too, were falling from some high place, as if she, too, were whirling through deep silent spaces, she seemed to catch herself. I had turned in my seat to look at the snow but also to catch a glimpse of Norman. He was sitting now with his face buried in his arms, as he had sat that day in the library.

Miss Hughes looked around her sleepily, and for the first time we saw her face, without the prompting of music, assume the mask. For a long moment she stood before us, impassive, mouth pulled down at the corners, eyes closed. When she opened them they rested darkly on Norman's lowered head. She allowed them to remain there a few seconds, taking her time, as if she were inviting us to consider with her which words she might choose.

"Is there anything we can do for you, Norman?" she asked at last.

There was silence in the room. I thought of the snow hitting the ground and wondered whether it had already begun to cover the brown grass beneath the trees, thought of Norman's father lying somewhere in the earth, his body in its coffin perhaps already beginning to rot, his grave still raw and exposed. The snow would hide all that, the dirt piled on top, and if Norman went to look where his father was, he would see an even cover of white.

"Because," Miss Hughes continued, "we would like you to know that you are sitting in the company of friends."

She brooded, frowning, while we sat rigidly in our seats. Then she turned her eyes from Norman to us. "You are perhaps not aware, boys and girls, that Mozart was Chopin's favorite composer. I shall now tell you a story. When Chopin died at the age of thirty-nine, in Paris, his funeral was held at the Madeleine, a church of that city. Afterward he was buried in a cemetery called Père-Lachaise, where you may someday wish to visit his grave. But at his funeral, it was Mozart's Requiem that the gathered mourners were given to hear. I once told you that before long we would listen together to another section of it. Today we shall hear the Lacrimosa. The word means 'full of tears.' "

We waited while she returned the record we had heard to its sleeve and drew out another.

She brooded over us now as a moment ago she had brooded over Norman. "We cannot see into the mysteries of another person's life, dear boys and girls. We have no way of knowing what deaths a soul has sustained before the final one. It is for this reason that we must never presume to judge or to speak in careless ways about lives of which we understand nothing. I tell you this so that you may not forget it. We may honor many things in life. But for someone else's sorrow we must reserve our deepest bow."

Miss Hughes had placed the record on the turntable and now paused before lowering the needle. "You will hear in the music that I am about to play for you a prayer for the dead, a prayer that they may at last find the peace that so often escapes us in life. Because, boys and girls, in praying for the dead we are praying for ourselves in that hour when we, too, far away as that hour might seem to us now, shall join their ranks. But even more—and you will understand me in time—we are honoring the suffering in our own lives, those of us who barely know how we shall survive the day. If you listen closely I know you cannot fail to hear something else: the tale of how our grief, the desire for what we do not have, the desire for what is forever denied us, may at length—when embraced as our destiny—become indistinguishable from our joy. Indistinguishable, you will understand, my dear friends, in that moment when time, as in the most sublime music, has ceased to be.

"When the record comes to an end I ask that you gather your things and silently take your leave. I shall look forward, in a week's time, to the return of your company."

We heard strings draw out one note and then two more, a little higher, the same pattern repeated three times, very sweet, very light, as if we might all float on these blithe strains forever. Into this—not denying but blending—broke a chorus of plaintive voices repeating something twice, voices asking, imploring, like a wind that moans in the night; then quickly gaining strength and conviction, they began an ascent, a climb, in which they mounted higher and higher, at each step becoming bolder, a procession like the first section we had heard weeks before. But now the voices surged as if straining toward something nobody had ever reached, up and up, the procession climbing higher and higher, the kettle drums pounding, the trumpets blaring, the echo falling in the wake of each step, until they could mount no higher and then—with utter simplicity, with utter calm—the voices returned to the point from which they had begun and pronounced their words in an ordinary manner, foot to earth.

When the record had spun to its end, when there was nothing more to listen for, we slowly picked up our books and filed out of the room. At the door I turned to look back and saw Miss Hughes still standing at attention before the phonograph, her hands together in front of her. Norman had not moved; his face was hidden in his arms. It was early December and already the room was filling with shadows, but the snow swirling at the window cast a restless light, the flickering light of water, over Miss Hughes's frozen mask, over Norman bowed at his desk. For the moment Miss Hughes was standing watch. But soon Norman would raise from his arms the face we had not yet seen and that would be his until, in life or in death, he opened his eyes on eternity.

2001

PRAIRIE

by SALVATORE SCIBONA

from NEWS FROM THE REPUBLIC OF LETTERS

Rosalie and i are twins. We were born here in Manitoba where our parents had settled after fleeing the war in Kentucky and President Lincoln's Conscription Act of 1863. Our father was a Quaker and so a pacifist and so unwilling "to kill any man for any cause, however righteous," as he told us. When the draft officials in Bowling Green, Kentucky informed him that—as he was sane, thirty-two years old, had all his fingers and sight in both eyes—he must either enlist or pay $200 to a substitute, he persuaded Mother that they should move north. Our mother was not a Quaker, she was Methodist, but all three of her brothers had gone to Tennessee and joined the Confederate army to whip the "miscegenist baboon" (as they called Lincoln), and she had no desire to see her husband and brothers on opposite sides of a war. They intended to return once the war ended, but Father soon found that the prairie so cleared his mind that he could not recall what it was in Kentucky he'd planned on missing, and Mother was so smitten with him, she claimed, that if our father asked her "to move to the south pole and live on penguin eggs" she thought it would be a fine life, if he was there. So he stayed and she stayed with him, and they never left Manitoba. I have never left it either.

We were born on June 3, 1864, the day of the Confederate victory at Cold Harbor in Virginia. Mother told us that she had thought her baby was still another month away and on that day she'd been picking strawberries two miles from the house. When the birth pangs struck, she tried to walk back home but the contractions crippled her, and she lay down in a thicket of poplars and gave birth to Rosalie. I, she had assumed, was the afterbirth. Father found us early that night. Mother had bit off our umbilical cords, cleaned us with her skirts, laid us down in the dry leaves beside her, and passed out.

I have only a few memories from early youth: the shushing sound of Rosalie's boots through unbroken snow, the snap of her leg bone after she fell out of a tree, her cold feet against my knee after I woke from a nightmare. However, when we were eight, Father began to take us with him on his semiannual trips to Winnipeg to trade for the supplies we could not produce on our own, paper for example, and sugar. I remember that first trip clearly.

Rosalie and I had never seen a town, had never traveled further than five miles from home. We hardly slept the night before we left. In the morning, Father hitched Isaiah and Chester, our oxen, to the barley wagon and Mother packed us rye bread, a sack of onions, pemmican and a jar of gooseberry preserves. We headed southeast, Mother stayed home.

The prairie around our farm rolls slightly; wide patches of junipers and poplars interrupt the grasses and line the creek shores. When my sister and I were young, bison herds passed over the prairie around us so regularly that we didn't need to keep cattle or pigs, since bison meat and the pemmican we made from it were so easy to come by. But as we rode toward Winnipeg that October, Rosalie and I sitting on either side of Father at the front of the wagon, the prairie turned dead flat for as far as you could see in all directions, empty of almost anything but short, dry sedges covering the ground. We went a whole day's driving, forty miles, without seeing a tree, and there was no game at all except groundhogs and a pack of wolves we heard. The aurora those nights, with nothing on the ground and no moon even to distract your eyes from it, seemed brighter than it was at home. I had never paid much attention to it before.

Rosalie asked Father why the lights seemed to move sometimes and sometimes to be still, and why they were green and blue one night but almost red the next. He said, "I have no earthly idea, Rosie."

It took us six days to get there. As we entered Winnipeg, a noise rose up around us. It was the ugliest sound I'd ever heard. I thought it might be river rapids, but I couldn't see the river, and it sounded harsher than water rushing; there were shrill noises in it. I covered my ears as we drove past the people walking and talking hurriedly in the street. After about a minute, I realized that I was hearing the sound of many people speaking at once. This was a crowd. Rosalie was leaping in the barley, and laughing.

I also recall a blue storefront in the middle of town. Mother had taught both of us how to read the Bible, and had told us many stories—of children who had disobeyed and been switched, of men who had sinned and been cast out of their towns, and of unrepentant old people who had died and been damned forever. Until our first trip to Winnipeg however, Rosalie and I believed that the Bible was the only story anyone had written down. Imagine our astonishment then, amid all the uncountable wonders and noises of Winnipeg, when we entered that blue building and saw hundreds of books on the walls. Rosalie and I began to trap badgers and raccoons so that we could sell their pelts twice a year in Winnipeg and buy books with the money.

We had learned to read as most children do, I suppose: by saying, in order, the sounds of the letters. After we recognized the words by sight, we continued to read them out loud, as our parents did. As far as I could tell, even reading by ourselves, all of my family spoke the words as we read them. I hadn't imagined that one could read silently until I was seventeen. And I wish I had known that before. Because for all the time I read aloud, regardless of how taken I was with the characters or the scenes of the stories, I still had to endure my own awkward, gruesome voice speaking. Mother and Rosalie had high, liquid reading voices. They often sounded as if they were singing as they read. The words came out so casually, with none of the stutters which ruined my voice, that you'd think they were talking about the weather. So usually Rosalie read our books to me. I would often take over her chores, work twice as long in the field, the barn or our kitchen and she would follow me reading Roman history or English novels or American adventure stories aloud.

While Father and I waded far out in the Assiniboine River, gathering stones with which to build the house where I still live, the house which replaced the windowless sod one that became the granary, Rosalie sat on the shore yelling out *A Tale of Two Cities* over the sound of the current. Father kept stopping her to say, "Go back a piece. I lost you." And, "Is he the scruffy one or the rich one?" By the time she finished it, we were laying the foundation. Father looked up out of the hole in the ground and said, "Go on, Rosie, start over." We heard that book three times while building the house, then Father let her move on to *David Copperfield*.

When we were sixteen, in the summer of 1880, Father began to cough, hard. His lips turned purple. One bright afternoon in late October, while Rosalie was reading *Great Expectations* to him, he died; we buried him under a patch of tamaracks on the hill. Five days later, before dusk, telling us, "Dears, nothing so confirms my faith in the Lord's grace as His sunset, I think I shall go to watching it now," Mother stepped out our front door.

An hour later, I looked on the front porch and Mother was gone. She had been taking long walks by herself along the river the last few days and not eating much so Rosalie and I decided to have supper without her. We ate dried sturgeon, onions and buckwheat cakes. By the time we'd finished washing our dishes outside, it had gotten much colder, begun snowing, and the wind had picked up some; Mother still wasn't home.

Rosalie said, "If we don't start looking now, her tracks might get too snowed over to see." So we filled up our lanterns with bison oil and followed mother's tracks through the mud toward the river. It had rained hard all morning, so the mud was soft and her tracks were clear but our boots were sinking past our ankles and it was slow going. Just as we reached the river, the snow covered over her trail completely and we didn't know which direction to go.

I looked over the river but it was too dark to see anything further than three feet away from our lamps, except for the snow disappearing on the surface of the water. "Why don't you go upstream and I'll go down?" I said to Rosalie, then turned to her, and saw in the lamplight that she had covered her mouth with her hand and was weeping. "Or we can go together and then check back the other way."

She took her hand away from her face and said, "Yes, let's do that."

We doused the lamps so we could see further ahead of us, and walked about four miles upstream but saw only trees, mud, snow and the river, then we turned back downstream. Just before the sky began to grow light again, Rosalie said she saw something move on the other side of the river, but as we got closer to it, we saw that it was a young black bear, and then it ran off. We found Mother's body just after sunrise, washed up on the east shore of the Assiniboine, five miles downstream from the place where we had first reached the river the night before. The snow was still falling when we found her, and it continued to fall the rest of the day.

It took us about three hours to walk back home through the snow. I hitched Isaiah and Chester to the sleigh and put our canoe in the back, then we drove to the river, dropped the canoe into it, and paddled to the other shore where Mother was. Her legs and arms were twisted so I tried to straighten them out but they wouldn't bend. The canoe was too slight to hold the three of us so I paddled Mother back over the river and left Rosalie on the far shore. Then I returned for Rosalie. By the time we had gathered Mother into the sleigh and rode back home, it was dark.

As Isaiah and Chester climbed up the slope toward the stable, Rosalie said, "I have to sleep a little, Julius. I'm tired."

Then I realized that neither of us had eaten or slept since the day before. I was tired but not hungry, and knew I wouldn't be able to sleep. So I said, "You go in and sleep then and I'll get you once I'm done digging," and I went into the barn to get a spade.

"Julius, we can't leave her out here!" she said. Mother lay in the back of the sleigh, partly covered with snow.

"She's already frozen."

"Bring her into the house," she said.

"Sister—"

"Listen to me, Julius," she said, "please bring her inside." So I did.

After I'd cleared the snow away from an open place next to Father, I found that only the top of the ground had frozen and it was still wet underneath, so the earth was soft. But the tamarack roots were hard to get through. Once I'd finished the grave, I went back home to wake Rosalie. She had wrapped Mother in a bison skin, washed Mother's face, braided her hair, and wound it in a bun at her nape.

As we carried Mother up the hill, the wind was fierce. My face was too numb to sting, but the wind had stiffened it, and I could not have moved my lips to sing "Shall We Gather at the River" with Rosalie even if I had wanted to. Once she finished singing, I closed the ground up over Mother. And we went back home and slept for a long time.

So we were alone. As the winter wore on, I grew quieter and quieter. When I poured out my whiskey at night, I began to take care to keep the bottleneck from clinking against the edge of my glass. And outside, where the wind nearly deafened one to all other sounds anyway,

I tried to drive nails into stockade posts with one swing, not out of a desire to conserve my labor, but because all the sounds I made, even breathing, became hideous to me. I hardly spoke at all.

The wind that winter was harsher than any I had experienced. Blizzards followed blizzards. I went outside only rarely, to fish through the ice on the lake two miles north of our house and to keep my eyes open for bison but they had grown scarce by that time. The winter of 1880 to 1881 seems to have killed all the bison left in western Manitoba. After that time, I never saw one again. In the mornings and late afternoons I piled and repiled the snow up along the west and north walls of our house and the stable, to stifle the wind. Even so, during one especially windy and frigid week, I couldn't keep the walls buried for very long before the wind, blowing from the northwest at an angle to the walls, swept the snow away and three of our seven hens froze in the stable.

The summer before, at the bookstore in Winnipeg, Rosalie had discovered a Greek New Testament and a Greek primer, which fascinated her for some reason. She seemed to spend much of that winter studying those books at the desk in front of the window, which looked south and so was shielded from the wind. At breakfast, we had much the same conversation every day.

"That's unbecoming, Julius," Rosalie said. I was picking at my ear with the blunt end of a pencil.

"Beg pardon," I said.

She watched me eat. "Do you want more pemmican?"

"No, this's all right."

"If you want more, Brother, it won't trouble me." She had pulled up the hatch in the floor and started climbing into the cellar.

"It's enough. I'm full."

From the cellar she said, "If I were a girl you were courting and I saw that thing in your ear at my table you wouldn't get any more food from me."

"I don't want more," I said.

"It reflects poorly on one's sister, such behavior from a boy, you know that don't you? They'll think you're a boor, which may be true, but they'll think I had no sense at all, couldn't train you to eat at table."

Later, as I was cutting the second helping of eggs she had made me, my fork squeaked on the plate and I winced. It turned my stomach, that noise. How she failed to notice the sound or just failed to be bothered by it bewildered me. She kept talking and asking my opinion of what she said but every day I had less to reply.

Maybe I got lazy. Talking had always felt like labor to me, like an obligation to respond to other people for whom speaking came easily—people, like Mother and Rosalie, who seemed to enjoy the sounds of their own voices. It satisfied me so much only to listen, not because I had nothing to tell them, but because, before I spoke, I had to steel myself against the revulsion I felt for my voice and that steeling took effort, and maybe I was sick of the effort.

Rosalie begged me to speak to her, and the more she asked the less able I felt to do it. By February I could manage little more than "I reckon not," "yes" and "thank you," and those with tremendous effort and shame. By March I was not speaking at all. Honestly, I do not understand it, even now. I can only say that I hated the sounds of my feet and the sounds of my tools striking their objects and more than all by far, I hated the sound of my voice.

Hated my voice I say, in the past tense, because I no longer remember it. One night during that winter, when Rosalie finished reading the Gospel of Mark to me, I said, "Thank you" because I was so grateful to hear her voice telling the story, grateful to her for abiding my quietness. But the next morning I could not thank her for breakfast nor say good-bye as I left the house. I have not spoken since I thanked her for reading to me that night. Probably my voice has changed much since I last used it when I was sixteen. Even if I wanted to speak now I cannot remember which muscles are used to form spoken words. I may have become a mute out of choice or complacency but by now, I believe, I am as incapable of speech as a dead man.

The thaw came early that spring and three or four acres of the field near the hill were dry enough in April that I could start plowing for seed potatoes and rye. The prairie was green everywhere and the wild strawberries seemed about to bloom already, which worried me because another frost seemed almost inevitable and if they bloomed too early they might get frozen and not bear that year. Still, the day I started plowing was warm, and there was a breeze, and no mosquitoes yet. Rosalie swept the stable and patched its roof with new shakes. When I came in for supper, she had roasted the last of our bison meat and made some rye bread. We finished supper and washed the dishes. I sat down next to the stove with Father's pipe and some willow bark to smoke while Rosalie read a history of the recent war in the United States to me. It was from the second volume of this history that we learned about the battle that had taken place on the day we were born. When she finished, she pinched out the tallow flame between her thumb and first finger and we went to bed.

After a while she said, "Are you awake, Julius?"

I rolled over.

"So tomorrow, I'll wake up and you'll wake up and it will be just like today was, won't it?" I shrugged my shoulders. There was a long silence. I was almost sleeping when she said, "Do you think it will snow again?" I thought about it. "Maybe we should get a dog in Winnipeg, hm?" she said. Her voice was getting louder.

Then she said, "Goddamn it! Will you please say something?"

I did not speak. "Damn you!" She got out of bed and paced in front of the windows. "It's as if you were a stone! As if you were sitting there on the ground and someone picked you up and threw you into the river and now you were under water, but you don't care because you're just going to sit there where you fell just as before. What difference does it make to you? Nothing. Well you're not a stone, Brother. You're not. And I'm not either. You think you can just work all day like before and pretend somebody else is talking to me. But nobody is. I am all alone."

She was screaming, "And you're thinking, To hell with my sister. Then to hell with you!"

I sat up in bed. She walked outside barefoot. I could hear her pacing on the porch and got up and sat at the desk and watched her pacing through the window. I tried to think of something to say and to find the will to say it. Then I couldn't see or hear her anymore. I took a piece of paper out of the drawer and wrote on it, "I am sorry." When I went outside to the front porch, she was sitting on its floor, leaning against the house. I gave her the paper. She looked at it, crumpled it, and threw it onto the grass.

In June, Rosalie moved us into Winnipeg. "I'm asking your opinion about this but I know you won't answer me. If you don't want to go, speak," she said, and laid her hand on the side of my neck. "I don't want to leave either, Brother, but I must have someone to talk to." Eggs snapped in the skillet and the prairie wind spilled in through the open doorway; there were no other sounds in the house. Winnipeg, I thought, would be a crowd of awful sounds. I did not wish to go there. But I did not wish my sister misery either. So I said nothing and we left home.

690

All we owned of value was Father's deed to our 160 acres of the prairie, our chickens, and Isaiah and Chester. We didn't want to sell the farm, though in 1881, the land boom in Manitoba was near its height and we could have gotten a fair sum for it; so we sold the chickens and our oxen who were old by then and we got only £21 altogether. We lived on that money until Rosalie was hired as the apprentice to the cook of a wealthy Quebecois named Papillon. His house was four stories tall, built from American limestone. It had eight chimneys, fifteen-foot ceilings in all its rooms, seventy-eight windows, a chapel, a kitchen ten times the size of our home on the prairie, five French crystal chandeliers and quarters for fifteen servants in the basement. The Premier of Manitoba was said to have exclaimed one night, after a formal dinner in Papillon's house, that once Papillon died, the King of France might use his house for a second Versailles. Rosalie and I moved into a room, with one ground level window, in the basement.

I had no skills for urban life, and because I did not speak, people assumed, absurdly I have always thought, that I could not hear. In her free hours, Rosalie walked with me around the city to mills, smiths, butchers, and just about anybody, asking them if they had work for her brother who was standing beside her.

"What's he need his sister to ask for?"

"He does not speak, you see, but—"

"Then no I don't," they answered, and we moved on.

Depending on my sister's wages for my food humiliated me, but even so my inactivity was worse. Some days, I walked through town from sun-up until dark, just to keep the sloth from stealing my mind. Twice I tried to ask for work at the railway office, even wrote down my request before I walked in. But as the secretary stood staring at me, my hand froze around the paper in my pocket until finally I ran back outside. I did not understand looking for work, as if it were hidden. On the farm, work was always there, like a great feast whose abundance outstripped the most ravenous appetite, there was always, always more to do. But in Winnipeg I starved for it. And because I was not working, I had no appetite, and I ate almost nothing of what Rosalie brought from Papillon's kitchen. Sometimes a potato in a day. I grew thin.

I woke in darkness one December night. The darkness was pure, more absolute than the blue light of nighttime, because there was no light at all. The perfect blackness was familiar vaguely. I felt Rosalie's back at my side and was suddenly very happy but I didn't know why. Then I realized that we were in our old house, the sod house with no windows, and all that had come after it—the riverstone house Father and I had built and laid the three windows in, Father and Mother's deaths, our move to Winnipeg and so much sadness were all a dream, and here was Rosalie beside me, and the coals in the stove were dying out so I must go outside to get more wood, and there was the door, right over there, and the prairie lay outside it. I leapt from the bed, pulled on my trousers and boots, and as I reached my hand over to the wall where my hat hung from a hook, I didn't feel the hat, but something cold, flat and smooth.

The window. It had snowed that night and the snow had piled up and blocked out the usual dim light from outside. We were in Papillon's house after all.

"Julius?" Rosalie said. I only stood there, with my hand pressed against the cold glass. She didn't say anything for a long time. It was cold and deadly quiet and all I wanted at that moment was to listen to her talking, which she knew. I didn't care what she talked about. She sat up in bed and told me about the recipe for honeyed pheasant; about the recent shooting of the President of the United States by a man who had sought office in his administration; she told me the names of clouds which she had overheard while serving lunch to Papillon's son and his tutor; and about the university student who was teaching her, on Saturday and Tuesday evenings, to read Greek. She talked for a long time, an hour maybe, and finally, just after I had taken my boots and trousers back off and got in bed and just before I fell asleep, she said, "It's so dark now. It reminds me of the old house."

That spring, Papillon and his chief of staff, a short half-Blackfoot named DuPage, were inspecting leaks in the basement walls and came into our room in the afternoon. Rosalie was working in the kitchen, and I sat under the window reading. I stood as they came in.

DuPage was running his fingers down the brown cracks in the wall and saying something in French to Papillon who nodded and rubbed his eyes. Papillon did not seem to notice I was in the room until he turned around and put his glasses on.

"Who is this?" He asked DuPage in English.

"He belongs to your undercook, Monsieur."

"You pay my servants enough to have servants do you, Mr. Du-Page?"

"No. He is her brother I think."

"How do you enjoy living here then, Sir?" Papillon asked me. I looked at my feet.

"Why doesn't he answer me? Do you like my house?"

"He's an idiot, Monsieur, he can't answer." I looked up quickly and glared at DuPage.

"He understands you, apparently," Papillon said to him and looked back at me. "What is your trade, young man?" He waited for me to answer. "I see that you understand me, so either you can't speak," he held out his right hand, "or you have no trade," and held out his left, "which is it?"

By now his voice had changed tone. At first he seemed annoyed to have found me there, but now he was looking at me with a wide-eyed expression I have seen people use when addressing their dogs.

"Which is it?" he said again holding out his hands, and after an uncomfortable silence he folded his hands together and said, "Perhaps it's both."

I nodded.

"His sister is the one who came in from the wild last fall, yes?" he asked DuPage.

"Yes, Monsieur."

"Probably you can hold a plow then, grow things?" he asked me.

I nodded again.

"Delightful." He told me about the twelve acres on the back of his property which he had hired a young man to cultivate with wheat, broccoli and "vegetables, you know." How this young man had recently run off, allegedly to Chicago, in the middle of his planting. I could have his job if I wanted it. By the time he finished, DuPage had left the room. I nodded to him that I would take the job, and then pulled from the desk at my right a piece of brown paper and wrote on it, "I am very grateful to you." And gave it to him. He looked down at the paper then back up at me and whispered conspiratorially, "You can write! You're not an idiot at all then!" But I did not respond to this.

Many years passed.

I often longed for our return home. But in lieu of that, living in Papillon's house and working in his fields suited me as well as any

693

other arrangement I could imagine. I worked alone and outside, as I wanted to. The other servants had never heard me speak and never expected me to, so my silence was never a point of contention with them. Rosalie seemed to reconcile herself to it.

Rosalie continued to study Greek with her tutor, who had graduated university and taken a teaching position at a boys' school in town. His name was Benjamin. Usually he would come to Papillon's house and they would walk back to the school together and use an empty classroom there. If Rosalie was not finished working in the kitchen when he came, he would sit at the desk in our room and he and I would converse, so to speak. Except for Rosalie, Benjamin was the only person I knew in Winnipeg who was willing to have conversations of longer than a minute with me. Those who knew that I could hear and wanted to know something from me would ask, read my response, thank me, and walk away. But Benjamin acted as if talking on paper were no different from talking in speech. We had long discussions, about the mountains in the United States where he was born, about the ocean and about books that we had both read. Sometimes we both wrote. He said it made him think more slowly. Then Rosalie would come in and they would go.

I was allowed to leave Papillon's house on one of his horses for three weeks every summer, so that I could go back home and keep up our house and the outbuildings on the farm. All the buildings were small and so their repairs were small. I made no additions or improvements; I kept things as they were.

Throughout the year, I imagined that I could live on the farm by myself and be happy and only lacked the nerve to do it. But by the second week, I would stay up long hours to finish painting the stable and clearing the spider webs from the eaves of our house so I could get back to Winnipeg sooner. The quiet which in my youth I had been terrified to leave was, in adulthood, almost as frightening to endure.

Rosalie never came with me. She talked about the farm endlessly, to me, to Benjamin, and to the other servants, but between our leaving, in 1881, and our return here, in the spring of 1895, she never saw this place. Maybe the painting of it in her mind became too perfect to risk violating by seeing it again.

I grew to abide the sound of many people speaking together. At dinner, the housekeepers, horsekeepers, groundskeepers and ladykeepers talked up a swarm of words and often I stayed in the dining

694

room after dinner and picked out a person's voice from the crowd and listened to it for a while.

At the end of all the day's work, after we had put down our books and our journals, we would lay down to bed and Rosalie would tell me about the news or a passage from Aeschylus she'd been working on. We lived this way a long time.

Of course, Greek is a difficult language. What my sister tried to explain of its grammar seemed perfectly ridiculous. It was painful to listen to. When she read it out loud, I wrote on my pad of paper "it sounds like hoofs on slag to me." The characters, even, looked designed to be inscrutable. Even so, after twelve years of instruction, the last nine of which were free of the small tuition she had paid Benjamin, I suppose I should have suspected that my sister had that language more or less under her belt. The one time it occurred to me to wonder about this, I thought that maybe they had started in on Latin together, and put the thought away and forgot to ask her about it. I didn't suspect anything, I suppose, because it was unthinkable that my sister would ever deceive me. And she didn't deceive me, maybe she withheld some of her life from her brother—Lord, what I withheld from her—but she never lied. I'm certain that if I had asked, she would have told me the truth.

My blindness seems shocking, even reprehensible, to me now. That the darkest period of melancholy in her life—in which deep black rings grew up under her eyes; and her hitherto ceaseless talking thinned out to two or three mumbled "no thank you's" or "how do you do's" in a day; and I, in straightening our bed one morning, turned over her pillow and found it wet on the bottom—happened to coincide with Benjamin's engagement to the daughter of the boys' school's headmaster, that I who have never loved a person that way, should have been incapable of seeing that my sister did was perhaps the greatest failure of my brotherhood. For which I have been deservingly punished.

I began to fear that she would stop talking altogether. Each day her silences grew longer and my panic deepened. I found myself privately furious with her for keeping her voice from me though she knew how much I relied on it. How, I thought, could she be so treacherous, so cruel? Then for the first time I realized the extent of my own cruelty. For the first time I felt what Rosalie must have felt when she told me, "I am all alone." I had done, had continued doing for fourteen years, precisely the same thing to her. Rosalie's silence was only just.

I decided that something must be done, something drastic. I decided to speak to her. We were walking together along the edge of the field behind Papillon's house as the sun was setting red behind the trees and the wind bent the tops of rye. Then we stopped, and I turned to her, and tried to shape my mouth so that if I breathed properly, I would make the letter 'r'. Rosalie's mouth fell open. I tried to breathe out, but my throat seized. I tried to remember how to say the letter 'r'. Or to say any letter. The wind blew dust in our faces.

After five minutes, I saw that I could not do it and covered my mouth with my hand. Then she leaned over and kissed my cheek as the sun disappeared into the woods.

Two months after the engagement, Rosalie's lessons, which had stopped, began again, and although her depression seemed slowly to lift, and she began to speak and read to me at night again, she didn't talk as much or as loudly as she had before.

In the fall of 1891, while his son was at university in France, Papillon paid me a visit in the field. He was seventy-three then, but continued to ride his horse through the rye on his way out to speak to his "man" as he called me to his friends. "This is my man, Mr. Julius," he would introduce me. I would tip my hat. "Don't be offended, he's a mute, that's why he doesn't greet you. Ha ha!" he would say. On that day in 1891, he was trotting up to me where I was picking a burr from the mule's foot at the edge of the field and his mouth was open—maybe he had already started talking—and then his one eye started to twitch and his tongue came out of his mouth and he fell off the horse. I heard his head strike a rock. Of all the noises I have heard and hated in my life, that one was the ugliest, a skull on a rock. It was loud enough that I could hear it over the horse's legs rustling the rye, and I knew he must be dead. He wore very short riding boots, and when he fell from the horse, one of the boots remained on his foot but the other got caught in the stirrup. So as the horse bolted away, one boot went with it and bounced against the horse's ribs, looking as if there were a ghost, with its foot in the boot, kicking the horse clumsily along. When I reached his body, I took off one of my shoes for his naked foot and brought him to the house, slung over the mule's back.

Papillon's son returned from Europe and took control of his father's household, sold off all the asbestos mines, and invested his fortune in the securities market in New York. His wealth grew enormously. On one dinner, with three hundred guests, for which Rosalie had to hire twelve extra cooks, he spent £10,000. But he held many such dinners, and by 1893 nearly all the money was gone.

After his bankruptcy in 1894, the younger Papillon managed to hold on to his house for only another year. He sold everything of value in it, the chandeliers, the wine in the cellar. Eventually he even sold the land I had tilled since his own early youth. He let all the servants go, though he let us continue to live in his house. Then finally he sold the house too, or his creditors sold it. We all had to move out.

"Why shouldn't we go back?" Rosalie said. "Why've you been tending it all this time if we weren't going back eventually?"

"We have enough money to take a flat in town," I wrote.

"If you want to go, we should go," she said.

"It's not necessary."

"Julius, you never wanted to be here. I understand that. Let me pay you back."

"It will bore you."

"It will not. If you want to go, I will be happy to go. Besides, I am tired of this place. There are things I could stand to be rid of."

"Such as what?" I wrote.

"Oh, things. Things I'd rather be far from than near to."

"I don't understand."

"Don't fret yourself about it. I miss the prairie, I do."

"Promise me you'll say if you've changed your mind," I wrote.

"I won't change my mind," she said.

"Nevertheless."

"Anyway, I promise."

We left the next week. All the property we'd amassed in the fourteen years we lived in Winnipeg fit inside two trunks that lay under our feet on the train. At Brandon, we bought two horses and a wagon and rode north. After the first day's riding, we had reached Virden and spent the night in a stopping house there. We got home just before sunset the next day. That was two springs ago.

The prairie is a jealous place. My family and countless others laid claim to broad portions of it, or thought we did. In fact it was the prairie that claimed us. It permits you the delusion that you own it, while all the time it behaves with such perfect indifference to your wishes and so frigidly refuses to return to you any of the attention you give it that you begin to suspect, if it has a will or feeling, they do not concern themselves with you. After three months without rain, you ask that the grasses do not catch fire; maybe it rains peacefully and the prairie goes damp again, maybe lightning strikes and your fields turn to ash all around. You hope that the blizzard will hold off until the unaccounted-for heifer finds her way home; and she may or she may not. The prairie does not seem to hear you. However, if you leave the open prairie, if you move into town, as Rosalie and I did, you may find that, though it could never hear, it does speak, you may find that the prairie calls out to your thoughts, as if in longing, that though you may have no desire to return to it, you find yourself pulled back as by responsibility to leave whatever happiness you may have found elsewhere and return to the prairie, not for yourself, but out of loyalty to it. And if you return the jealous prairie will rob your mind of nearly all the tastes and sounds and smells of your other home. Like a wife burning the love letters her husband's mistress sent him. You may find, as I now do, watching the snowy bluff in the distance through this window, that you cannot recall the taste of an orange, the sound that a collection of tired people make as they settle in for supper, or the smell of a room you lived in for fifteen years even. Perhaps the prairie longed for you, perhaps it wanted only to dominate your imagination.

The trees were thicker now, Rosalie said, and there were more wild strawberries, and the trout in the Assiniboine seemed smaller than she remembered, but everything else looked the same. I grew barley, corn and wheat and kept the pigs and the cattle and fished a little more than I had in my youth. Rosalie did the canning and tended the vegetables and the chickens. She spent long hours watching the prairie. In the winter, from behind the window glass, and in the summer, from a chair on the porch. Even in the terrible mosquito season of June and July, she would watch calmly and smoke in Father's pipe some awful smelling plant she'd found in the woods which seemed to keep the insects away from her. She'd stare out at the bluff south of here, rapt, and looked fairly sad at these times.

Nine months ago, Rosalie and I rode into the town that had grown up about twenty miles southwest of here over the time we were away, and found that there was a letter for her at the post office. She didn't read it right then. She put it in her pocket, and tried to look calm but I saw that her hands were shaking. That night, she brought a lamp and walked to the bluff over the creek to read it. There was no moon and I could see the lamp on the bluff, even a mile away, from the window here. It was the only light anywhere. When she came back four hours later, she was still crying. I offered her a shot of the Scotch we'd bought in town, but she refused and handed me the letter.

I wrote, "This is to you. I shouldn't read it."

She pushed the letter into my chest.

The postmark said "PM January 24 1897 Baltimore MD"

I told her that I wanted her to go to him. What I meant was, since you are going, I will not keep you. Since a brother's love is not the same, since Benjamin postponed his other marriage repeatedly until he realized why, since he has asked you, and since you, I can see, said yes years ago, then I wish I wanted you to go to him, and though I want you to stay, I will say the opposite.

She has written four times since she left last May, imploring me, in each letter, to come live with them in Baltimore. Benjamin is now a professor at a college there and says that I am welcome and that he could find me work, but I do not feel capable of leaving the prairie again.

When Father came here, he forgot Kentucky. He said that he felt incapable of telling lies on the prairie, that this place asserted itself as the only possible reality—the sun set here and no place else; this particular rush of wind along the face of the grasses in spring was the only sound of wind in spring—and so you could not make fictions of other faces or other voices because the prairie did not permit you even to imagine them. Nor to imagine the true faces of your past. In time, he said, it stole Kentucky from his brain. It robs you piecemeal—one day you cannot remember the name of a face, the next you cannot picture the face either, the next you forget what it was you were trying to remember the day before, the next you forget that you were trying to remember something. Two months ago, I remembered the names of all of Papillon's horses; today I cannot remember how many of them there were. Today I remember why Rosalie did not take her Greek books with her when she left.

But since she is no longer here, I don't know that I will remember that in a week. Soon I will not remember her voice, as I do not remember mine. This place will have taken it. Eventually, it seems, the prairie will disburden my mind of all those strange memories and I will forget that I ever had a sister and will think only of what I am seeing and hearing on the plain.

2001

PU-239

by KEN KALFUS

from PU-239 AND OTHER FANTASIES (Milkweed Editions)

Someone committed a simple error that, according to the plant's blueprints, should have been impossible, and a valve was left open, a pipe ruptured, a technician was trapped in a crawlspace, and a small fire destroyed several workstations. At first the alarm was discounted: false alarms commonly rang and flashed through the plant like birds in a tropical rain forest. Once the seriousness of the accident was appreciated, the rescue crew discovered that a soft drink dispenser waiting to be sent out for repair blocked the room in which the radiation suits were kept. After moving it and entering the storage room, they learned that several of the oxygen tanks had been left uncharged. By the time they reached the lab the fire was nearly out, but smoke laced with elements from the actinide series filled the unit. Lying on his back above the ceiling, staring at the wormlike pattern of surface corrosion on the tin duct a few centimeters from his face, Timofey had inhaled the fumes for an hour and forty minutes. In that time he had tried to imagine that he was inhaling dollar bills and that once they lodged in his lungs and bone marrow they would bombard his body tissue with high-energy dimes, nickels, and quarters.

Timofey had worked in 16 nearly his entire adult life, entrusted with the bounteous, transfiguring secrets of the atom. For most of that life, he had been exhilarated by the reactor's song of nuclear fission, the hiss of particle capture and loss. Highly valued for his ingenuity, Timofey carried in his head not only a detailed knowledge of the plant's design, but also a precise recollection of its every repair and improvised alteration. He knew where the patches were and

701

how well they had been executed. He knew which stated tolerances could be exceeded and by how much, which gauges ran hot, which ran slow, and which could be completely ignored. The plant managers and scientists were often forced to defer to his judgment. On these occasions a glitter of derision showed in his voice, as he tapped a finger significantly against a sheet of engineering designs and explained why there was only a single correct answer to the question.

After Timofey's death, his colleagues recalled a dressing down he had received a few years earlier at the hands of a visiting scientist. No one remembered the details, except that she had proposed slightly altering the reaction process in order to produce a somewhat greater quantity of a certain isotope that she employed in her own research. Hovering in his stained and wrinkled white coat behind the half dozen plant officials whom she had been addressing, Timofey objected to the proposal. He said that greater quantities of the isotope would not be produced in the way she suggested and, in fact, could not be produced at all, according to well established principles of nuclear physics. Blood rushed to the woman's square, fleshy, bulldog face. "Idiot!" she spat. "I'm Nuclear Section Secretary of the Academy of Sciences. I fucking *own* the established principles of nuclear physics. You're a *technician!*" Those who were there recalled that Timofey tried to stand his ground, but as he began to explain the flaw in her reasoning his voice lost its resonance and he began to mumble, straying away from the main point. She cut him off, asking her audience, "Are there any other questions, any educated questions?" As it turned out, neither Timofey nor the scientist was ever proved right. The Defense Ministry rejected the proposal for reasons of economy.

Timofey's relations with his coworkers were more comfortable, if distant, and he usually joined the others in his unit at lunch in the plant's low-ceilinged, windowless buffet. The room rustled with murmured complaint. Timofey could hardly be counted among the most embittered of the technical workers—a point sagely observed later. All joked with stale irony about the lapses in safety and the precipitous decline in their salaries caused by inflation; these comments had become almost entirely humorless three months earlier, when management followed a flurry of assuring memos, beseeching directives, and unambiguous promises with a failure to pay them at all. No one had been paid since.

Every afternoon at four Timofey fled the compromises and incompetence of his workplace in an old Zhiguli that he had purchased precisely so that he could arrive home a half hour earlier than if he had taken the tram. Against the odds set by personality and circumstance, he had married, late in his fourth decade, an electrical engineer assigned to another unit. Now, with the attentiveness he had once offered the reactor, Timofey often sat across the kitchen table from his wife with his head cocked, listening to their spindly, asthmatic eight-year-old son, Tolya, in the next room give ruinous commands to his toy soldiers. A serious respiratory ailment similar to the boy's kept Marina from working; disability leave had brought a pretty bloom to her soft cheeks.

The family lived on the eighth floor of a weather-stained concrete apartment tower with crumbling front steps and unlit hallways. In this rotted box lay a jewel of a two-bedroom apartment that smelled of fresh bread and meat dumplings and overlooked a birch forest. Laced with ski tracks in the winter and fragranced by grilled shashlik in the summer, home to deer, rabbits, and even gray wolves, the forest stretched well beyond their sight, all the way to the city's double-fenced perimeter.

His colleagues thought of Marina and the boy as Timofey was pulled from the crawlspace. He was conscious, but dazed, his eyes unfocused and his face slack. Surrounded by phantoms in radiation suits, Timofey saw the unit as if for the first time: the cracked walls, the electrical cords snaking underfoot, the scratched and fogged glass over the gauges, the mold-spattered valves and pipes, the disabled equipment piled in an unused workstation, and the frayed tubing that bypassed sections of missing pipe and was kept in place by electrical tape. He staggered from the lab, took a shower, vomited twice, disposed of his clothes, and was briefly examined by a medic, who took his pulse and temperature. No one looked him in the eye. Timofey was sent home. His colleagues were surprised when he returned the next day, shrugging off the accident and saying that he had a few things to take care of before going on the "rest leave" he had been granted as a matter of course. But his smile was as wan as the moon on a midsummer night, and his hands trembled. In any case, his colleagues were too busy to chat. The clean-up was chaotically underway and the normal activities of the plant had been suspended.

Early one evening a week after the "event," as it was known in the plant and within the appropriate ministries (it was not known anywhere else), Timofey was sitting at a café table in the bar off the lobby of a towering Brezhnev-era hotel on one of the boulevards that radiated from Moscow's nucleus. A domestically made double-breasted sports jacket the color of milk chocolate hung from his frame like wash left to dry. He was only fifty years old but, lank and stooped, his face lined by a spiderwork of dilated veins, he looked at least fifteen years older, almost a veteran of the war. His skin was as gray as wet concrete, except for the radiation erythema inflaming the skin around his eyes and nose. Coarse white hair bristled from his skull. Set close beneath white caterpillar eyebrows, his blue eyes blazed.

He was not by nature impressed by attempts to suggest luxury and comfort, and the gypsies and touts milling outside the entrance had in any case already mitigated the hotel's grandeur. He recognized that the lounge area was meant to approximate the soaring glass and marble atria of the West, but the girders of the greenhouse roof impended two stories above his head, supported by walls of chipped concrete blocks. A line of shuttered windows ran the perimeter above the lounge, looking down upon it as if it were a factory floor. The single appealing amenity was the set of flourishing potted plants and ferns in the center of the room. As Timofey watched over a glass of unsipped vodka that had cost him a third of his remaining rubles, a fat security guard in a maroon suit flicked a cigarette butt into the plant beds and stalked away.

Timofey strained to detect the aspirates and dental fricatives of a foreign language, but the other patrons were all either Russian or "black"—that is, Caucasian. Overweight, unshaven men in lurid track suits and cheap leather jackets huddled over the stained plastic tables, blowing smoke into each other's faces. Occasionally they looked up from their drinks and eyed the people around them. Then they fell back into negotiation. At another table, a rectangular woman in a low-cut, short black dress and black leggings scowled at a newspaper.

Directly behind Timofey, sitting alone, a young man with dark, bony features decided that this hick would be incapable of getting a girl on his own. Not that there would be too many girls around this early. He wondered if Timofey had any money and whether he could make him part with it. Certainly the mark would have enough for one of the kids in ski parkas waving down cars on the boulevard. The young man, called Shiv by his Moscow acquaintances (he had no friends), got up from his table, leaving his drink.

704

"First time in Moscow, my friend?"

Timofey was not taken off guard. He slowly raised his head and studied the young man standing before him. Either the man's nose had once been broken, or his nose had never been touched and the rest of his face had been broken many times, leaving his cheeks and the arches beneath his eyes jutted askew. The youth wore a foreign blazer and a black shirt, and what looked like foreign shoes as well, a pair of black loafers. His dark, curly hair was cut long, lapping neatly against the top of his collar. Jewelry glinted from his fingers and wrists. It was impossible to imagine the existence of such a creature in 16.

Shiv didn't care for the fearlessness in Timofey's eyes; it suggested a profound ignorance of the world. But he pulled a chair underneath him, sat down heavily, and said in a low voice, "It's lonely here. Would you like to meet someone?"

The mark didn't reply, nor make any sign that he had even heard him. His jaw was clenched shut, his face blank. Shiv wondered whether he spoke Russian. He himself spoke no foreign languages and detested the capriciousness with which foreigners chose to speak their own. He added, "You've come to the right place. I'd be pleased to make an introduction."

Timofey continued to stare at Shiv in a way that he should have known, if he had any sense at all, was extremely dangerous. A crazy, Shiv thought, a waste of time. But then the mark abruptly rasped, in educated, unaccented Russian, "I have something to sell."

Shiv grinned, showing large white canines. He congratulated him, "You're a businessman. Well, you've come to the right place for that too. I'm also a businessman. What is it you want to sell?"

"I can't discuss it here."

"All right."

Shiv stood and Timofey tentatively followed him to a little alcove stuffed with video poker machines. They whined and yelped, devouring gambling tokens. Incandescent images of kings, queens, and knaves flickered across the young man's face.

"No, this isn't private enough."

"Sure it is," Shiv said. "More business is done here than on the Moscow Stock Exchange."

"No."

Shiv shrugged and headed back to his table, which the girl, in a rare display of zeal, had already cleared. His drink was gone. Shiv frowned, but knew he could make her apologize and give him another drink on the house, which would taste much better for it. He had that kind of respect, he thought.

"You're making the biggest mistake of your life," Timofey whispered behind him. "I'll make you rich."

What changed Shiv's mind was not the promise, which these days was laden in nearly every commercial advertisement, political manifesto, and murmur of love. Rather, he discerned two vigorously competing elements within the mark's voice. One of them was desperation, in itself an augury of profit. Yet as desperate as he was, Timofey had spoken just barely within range of Shiv's hearing. Shiv was impressed by the guy's self-control. Perhaps he was serious after all.

He turned back toward Timofey, who continued to stare at him in appraisal. With a barely perceptible flick of his head, Shiv motioned him toward a row of elevators bedecked with posters for travel agencies and masseuses. Timofey remained in the alcove for a long moment, trying to decide whether to follow. Shiv looked away and punched the call button. After a minute or so the elevator arrived. Timofey stepped in just as the doors were closing.

Shiv said, "If you're jerking me around . . ."

The usually reliable fourth-floor *dezhurnaya*, the suppurating wart who watched the floor's rooms, decided to be difficult. Shiv slipped her a five dollar bill, and she said, "More." She returned the second fiver because it had a crease down the middle, dispelling its notional value. Shiv had been trying to pass it off for weeks and now conceded that he would be stuck with it until the day he died. The crone accepted the next bill, scowling, and even then gazed a long time into her drawer of keys, as if undecided about giving him one.

As they entered the room, Shiv pulled out a pack of Marlboros and a gold-plated lighter and leaned against a beige chipboard dresser. The room's ponderous velvet curtains smelled of insecticide; unperturbed, a bloated fly did lazy eights around the naked bulb on the ceiling. Shiv didn't offer the mark a cigarette. "All right," he said, flame billowing from the lighter before he brought it to his face. "This better be worth my while."

Timofey reached into his jacket, almost too abruptly: he didn't notice Shiv tense and go for the dirk in his back pocket. The mark pulled out a green cardboard folder and proffered it. "Look at this."

Shiv returned the blade. He carried four knives of varying sizes, grades, and means of employment.

"Why?"

"Just look at it."

Shiv opened the folder. Inside was Timofey's internal passport, plus some other documents. Shiv was not accustomed to strangers shoving their papers in his face; indeed, he knew the family names of very few people in Moscow. This guy, then, had to be a nut case, and Shiv rued the ten bucks he had given the *dezhurnaya*. The mark stared up through the stamped black-and-white photograph as if from under water. "Timofey Fyodorovich, pleased to meet you. So what?"

"Look at where I live: Skotoprigonyevsk-16."

Shiv made no sign of being impressed, but for Timofey the words had the force of an incantation. The existence of the city, a scientific complex established by the military, had once been so secret that it was left undocumented on the Red Army's own field maps. Even its name, which was meant to indicate that it lay sixteen kilometers from the original Skotoprigonyevsk, was a deception: the two cities were nearly two hundred kilometers apart. Without permission from the KGB, it had been impossible to enter or leave 16. Until two years earlier, Timofey had never been outside, not once in twenty-three years. He now realized, as he would have realized if he hadn't been so distracted by the events of the past week, that it wasn't enough to find a criminal. He needed someone with brains, someone who had read a newspaper in the last five years.

"Now look at the other papers. See, this is my pass to the Strategic Production Facility."

"Comrade," Shiv said sarcastically, "if you think I'm buying some fancy documents—"

"Listen to me. My unit's principal task is the supply of the strategic weapons force. Our reactor produces Pu-239 as a fission by-product for manufacture into warheads. These operations have been curtailed, but the reactors must be kept functioning. Decommissioning them would be even more costly than maintaining them—and we can't even do that properly." Timofey's voice fell to an angry whisper. "There have been many lapses in the administration of safety procedure."

Timofey looked intently at Shiv, to see if he understood. But Shiv wasn't listening; he didn't like to be lectured and especially didn't like to be told to read things, even identity papers. The world was full of men who knew more than Shiv did, and he hated each one of them. A murderous black cloud rose from the stained orange carpeting at his feet and occulted his vision. The more Timofey talked, the more Shiv wanted to hurt him. But at the same time, starting from the moment he heard the name Skotoprigonyevsk-16, Shiv gradually became aware that he was onto something big, bigger than anything he had ever done before. He was nudged by an incipient awareness that perhaps it was even too big for him.

In flat, clipped sentences, Timofey spoke: "There was an accident. I was contaminated. I have a wife and child, and nothing to leave them. This is why I'm here."

"Don't tell me about your wife and child. You can fuck them both to hell. I'm a businessman."

For a moment, Timofey was shocked by the violence in the young man's voice. But then he reminded himself that, in coming to Moscow for the first time in twenty-five years, he had entered a country where violence was the most stable and valuable currency. Maybe this was the right guy for the deal after all. There was no room for sentimentality.

He braced himself. "All right then. Here's what you need to know. I have diverted a small quantity of fissile material. I'm here to sell it."

Shiv removed his handkerchief again and savagely wiped his nose. He had a cold, Timofey observed. Acute radiation exposure severely compromised the immune system, commonly leading to fatal bacterial infection. He wondered if the hoodlum's germs were the ones fated to kill him.

Timofey said, "Well, are you interested?"

To counteract any impression of weakness given by the handkerchief, Shiv tugged a mouthful of smoke from his cigarette.

"In what?"

"Are you listening to anything I'm saying? I have a little more than three hundred grams of weapons-grade plutonium. It can be used to make an atomic bomb. I want thirty thousand dollars for it."

As a matter of principle, Shiv laughed. He always laughed when a mark named a price. But a chill seeped through him as far down as his testicles.

"It will fetch many times that on the market. Iraq, Iran, Libya, North Korea all have nuclear weapons programs, but they don't have the technology to produce enriched fissile material. They're desperate for it; there's no price Saddam Hussein wouldn't pay for an atomic bomb."

"I don't know anything about selling this stuff . . ."

"Don't be a fool," Timofey rasped. "Neither do I. That's why I've come here. But you say you're a businessman. You must have contacts, people with money, people who can get it out of the country."

Shiv grunted. He was just playing for time now, to assemble his thoughts and devise a strategy. The word fool remained lodged in his gut like a spoiled piece of meat.

"Maybe I do, maybe I don't."

"Make up your mind."

"Where's the stuff?"

"With me."

A predatory light flicked on in the hoodlum's eyes. But Timofey had expected that. He slowly unbuttoned his jacket. It fell away to reveal an invention of several hours' work that, he realized only when he assembled it in the kitchen the day after the accident, he had been planning for years. At that moment of realization, his entire body had been flooded with a searing wonder at the dark soul that inhabited it. Now, under his arm, a steel canister no bigger than a coffee tin was attached to his left side by an impenetrably complex arrangement of belts, straps, hooks, and buckles.

"Do you see how I rigged the container?" he said. "There's a right way of taking it off my body and many wrong ways. Take it off one of the wrong ways and the container opens and the material spills out. Are you aware of the radiological properties of plutonium and their effect on living organisms?"

Shiv almost laughed. He once knew a girl who wore something like this.

"Let me see it."

"It's *plutonium*. It has to be examined under controlled laboratory conditions. If even a microscopic amount of it lodges within your body, ionizing radiation will irreversibly damage body tissue and your cells' nucleic material. A thousandth of a gram is fatal . . . I'll put it to you more simply. Anything it touches dies. It's like in a fairy tale."

Shiv did indeed have business contacts, but he'd been burned about six months earlier, helping to move some Uzbek heroin that must have been worth more than a half million dollars. He had actually held the bags in his hands and pinched the powder through the plastic, marveling at the physics that transmuted such a trivial quantity of something into so much money. But once he made the arrangements and the businessmen had the stuff in *their* hands, they gave him only two thousand dollars for his trouble, little more than a tip. Across a table covered by a freshly stained tablecloth, the Don—his name was Voronenko, and he was from Tambov, but he insisted on being called the Don anyway, and being served spaghetti and meatballs for lunch—had grinned at the shattering disappointment on Shiv's face. Shiv had wanted to protest, but he was frightened. Afterwards he was so angry that he gambled and whored the two grand away in a single night.

He said, "So, there was an accident. How do I know the stuff's still good?"

"Do you know what a half-life is? The half-life of plutonium 239 is twenty-four thousand years."

"That's what you're telling me . . ."

"You can look it up."

"What am I, a fucking librarian? Listen, I know this game. It's mixed with something."

Timofey's whole body was burning; he could feel each of his vital organs being singed by alpha radiation. For a moment he wished he could lie on one of the narrow beds in the room and nap. When he woke, perhaps he would be home. But he dared not imagine that he would wake to find that the accident had never happened. He said, "Yes, of course. The sample contains significant amounts of uranium and other plutonium isotopes, plus trace quantities of americium and gallium. But the Pu-239 content is 94.7 percent."

"So you admit it's not the first-quality stuff."

"Anything greater than 93 percent is considered weapons-grade. Look, do you have somebody you can bring this to? Otherwise, we're wasting my time."

Shiv took out another cigarette from his jacket and tapped it against the back of his hand. Igniting the lighter, he kept his finger lingering on the gas feed. He passed the flame in front of his face so that it appeared to completely immolate the mark.

"Yeah, I do, but he's in Perkhuskovo. It's a forty-minute drive. I'll take you to him."

"I have a car. I'll follow you."

Shiv shook his head. "That won't work. His dacha's protected. You can't go through the gate alone."

"Forget it then. I'll take the material someplace else."

Shiv's shrug of indifference was nearly sincere. The guy was too weird, the stuff was too weird. His conscience told him he was better off pimping for schoolgirls. But he said, "If you like. But for a deal like this, you'll need to go to one godfather or another. On your own you're not going to find someone walking around with thirty thousand dollars in his pocket. This businessman knows me, his staff knows me. I'll go with you in your car. You can drive."

Timofey said, "No, we each drive separately."

The mark was unmovable. Shiv offered him a conciliatory smile.

"All right," he said. "Maybe. I'll call him from the lobby and try to set it up. I'm not even sure he can see us tonight."

"It has to be tonight or there's no deal."

"Don't be in such a hurry. You said the stuff lasts twenty-four thousand years, right?"

"Tell him I'm from Skotoprigonyevsk-16. Tell him it's weapons-grade. That's all he needs to know. Do you understand the very least bit of what I'm saying?"

The pale solar disc had dissolved in the horizonal haze long ago, but the autumn evening was still in its adolescent hours, alive to possibility. As the two cars lurched into the swirl of traffic on the Garden Ring road, Timofey could taste the unburned gasoline in the hoodlum's exhaust. He had never before driven in so much traffic or seen so many foreign cars, or guessed that they would ever be driven so recklessly. Their rear lights flitted and spun like fireflies. At his every hesitation or deceleration the cars behind him flashed their headlights. Their drivers navigated their vehicles as if from the edges of their seats, peering over their dashboards, white-knuckled and grim, and as if they all carried three hundred grams of weapons-grade plutonium strapped to their chests. Driving among Audis and Mercedes would have thrilled Tolya, who cut pictures of them from magazines and cherished his small collection of mismatched models. The thought of his son, a sweet and cheerful boy with orthodontic braces, and utterly, utterly innocent, stabbed at him.

The road passed beneath what Timofey recognized as Mayakovsky Square from television broadcasts of holiday marches. He knew that the vengeful, lustrating revision of Moscow's street names in the last few years had renamed the square Triumfalnaya, though there was nothing triumphant about it, except for its big Philips billboard advertisement. Were all the advertisements on the Garden Ring posted in the Latin alphabet? Was Cyrillic no longer anything more than a folk custom? It was as if he had traveled to the capital of a country in which he had never lived.

Of course hardly any commercial advertising could be seen in 16. Since Gorbachev's fall a halfhearted attempt had been made to obscure most of the Soviet agitprop, but it was still a Soviet city untouched by foreign retailing and foreign advertising. The few foreign goods that found their way into the city's state-owned shops arrived dented and tattered, as if produced in Asian, European, and North American factories by demoralized Russian workers. Well, these days 16 was much less of a city. It was not uncommon to see chickens and other small livestock grazing in the gravel between the high-rises, where pensioners and unpaid workers had taken up subsistence farming. Resentment of Moscow burned in Timofey's chest, alongside the Pu-239.

Plutonium. There was no exit for the stuff. It was as permanent and universal as original sin. Since its first synthesis in 1941 (what did Seaborg do with that magical, primeval stone of his own creation? put it in his vault? was it still there?) more than a thousand metric tons of the element had been produced. It was still being manufactured, not only in Russia, but in France and Britain as well, and it remained stockpiled in America. Nearly all of it was locked in steel containers, buried in mines, or sealed in glass—safe, safe, safe. But the very minimal fraction that wasn't secured, the few flakes that had escaped in nuclear tests, reactor accidents, transport mishaps, thefts, and leakages, veiled the entire planet. Sometime within the next three months Timofey would die with plutonium in his body, joined in the same year by thousands of other victims in Russia and around the world. His body would be brought directly to the city crematorium, abstractly designed in jaggedly cut, pale yellow concrete so as to be vaguely "life-affirming," where the chemistry of his skin and lungs, heart and head, would be transformed by fire and wind. In the rendering oven, the Pu-239 would oxidize and engage in wanton couplings with other substances, but it would always stay faithful to its radioactive, elemental properties. Some of it would remain in the ash plowed back to the earth; the rest would be borne aloft into the vast white skies arching above the frozen plain. Dust to dust.

Yet it would remain intangible, completely invisible, hovering elusively before us like a floater in our eyes' vitreous humor. People get cancer all the time and almost never know why. A nucleic acid on a DNA site is knocked out of place, a chromosome sequence is deleted, an oncogene is activated. It would show up only in statistics, where it remained divorced from the lives and deaths of individuals. It was just as well, Timofey thought, that we couldn't take in the enormity of the threat; if we did, we would be paralyzed with fear— not for ourselves, but for our children. We couldn't wrap our minds around it; we could think of it only for a few moments and then have to turn away from it. But the accident had liberated Timofey. He could now contemplate plutonium without any difficulty at all.

And it was not only plutonium. Timofey was now exquisitely aware of the ethereal solution that washed over him every day like a warm bath: the insidiously subatomic, the swarmingly microscopic, and the multi-syllabically chemical. His body was soaked in pesticides, the liquefied remains of electrical batteries, leaded gasoline exhaust, dioxin, nitrates, toxic waste metals, dyes, and deadly viral organisms generated in untreated sewage—the entire carcinogenic and otherwise malevolent slough of the great Soviet industrial empire. Like Homo Sovieticus himself, Timofey was ending his life as a melange of damaged chromosomes, metal-laden tissue, crumbling bone, fragmented membranes, and oxygen-deprived blood. Perhaps his nation's casual regard for the biological consequences of environmental degradation was the result of some quasi-Hegelian conviction that man lived in history, not nature. It was no wonder everyone smoked.

For a moment, as the hoodlum swung into the turning lane at the Novy Arbat, Timofey considered passing the turnoff and driving on through the night and the following day back to 16's familiar embrace. But there was only one hundred and twenty dollars hidden in the bookcase in his apartment. It was the sum total of his family's savings.

Now Shiv saw Timofey's shudder of indecision in his rearview mirror; he had suspected that the mark might turn tail. If he had, Shiv would have broken from the turning lane with a shriek of tire (he savored the image) and chased him down.

In tandem the two cars crossed the bridge over the Moscow River, the brilliantly lit White House on their right nearly effervescing in the haze off the water. It was as white and polished as a tooth, having been capped recently by a squadron of Turkish workers after Yeltsin's troops had shelled and nearly gutted it. Shiv and Timofey passed the Pizza Hut and the arch commemorating the battle against Napoleon at Borodino. They were leaving the city. Now Timofey knew he was committed. The hoodlum wouldn't let him go. He knew this as surely as if he were sitting in the car beside him. If the world of the atom were controlled by random quantum events, then the macroscopic universe through which the two Zhigulis were piloted was purely deterministic. The canister was heavy and the straps that supported it were beginning to cut into Timofey's back.

He could have even more easily evaded Shiv at the exit off Kutuzovsky Prospekt; then on the next road there was another turnoff, then another and another. Timofey lost count of the turns. It was like driving down a rabbit hole: he'd never find his way back. Soon they were kicking up stones on a dark country road, the only traffic. Every once in a while the Moscow River or one of its tributaries showed itself through the naked, snowless birches. A pocked and torn slice of moon bobbed and weaved across his windshield. Shiv paused, looking for the way, and then abruptly pivoted his car into a lane hardly wider than the Zhiguli itself.

Timofey followed, taking care to stay on the path. He could hear himself breathing: the sound from his lungs was muffled and wet. Gravel crunched beneath his tires and bushes scraped their nails against the car's doors. The hood slowed even further, crossing a small bridge made of a few planks. They clattered like bones.

Timofey's rearview mirror incandesced. Annoyed, he pushed it from his line of sight. Shiv slowed to a stop, blinked a pair of white lights in reverse, and backed up just short of Timofey's front bumper. At the same time, Timofey felt a hard tap at his rear.

Shiv stepped from his car. Pinned against the night by the glare of headlights, the boy appeared vulnerable and very young, almost untouched by life. Timofey detected a measure of gentleness in his face, despite the lunar shadows cast across it. Shiv grimaced at the driver of the third automobile, signaling him to close his lights. He walked in front of his own car and squeezed alongside the brush to Timofey's passenger door.

"We have to talk," he said. "Open it."

Timofey hesitated for a moment, but the lengthy drive had softened his resolve and confused his plan. And there was a car pressed against his rear bumper. He reached over and unlocked the door.

Shiv slid into the seat and stretched his legs. Even for short people, the Zhigulis were too goddamned small.

"We're here?"

"Where else could we be?"

Timofey turned his head and peered into the dark, looking for the businessman's dacha. There was nothing to see at all.

"All right, now hand over the stuff."

"Look, let's do this right—" Timofey began, but then comprehension darkened his face. He didn't need to consider an escape: he understood the whole setup. Perhaps he had chosen the coward's way out. "I see. You're as foolish as a peasant in a fairy tale."

Shiv opened his coat and removed from a holster in his sport jacket an oiled straight blade nearly twenty centimeters long. He turned it so that the moonlight ran its length. He looked into the mark's face for fear. Instead he found ridicule.

Timofey said, "You're threatening me with a knife? I have enough plutonium in my lungs to power a small city for a year, and you're threatening me with a *knife*?"

Shiv placed the shaft against Timofey's side, hard enough to leave a mark even if it were removed. Timofey acted as if he didn't feel it. Again something dark passed before Shiv's eyes.

"Look, this is a high-carbon steel Premium Gessl manufactured by Imperial Gessl in Frankfurt, Germany. I paid eighty bucks for it. It passes through flesh like water. Just give me the goddamned stuff."

"No. I won't do that," Timofey said primly. "I want thirty thousand dollars. It's a fair price, I think, and I won't settle for anything less. I drove here in good faith."

Timofey was the first man Shiv had ever killed, though he had cut a dozen others, plus two women. He wondered if it got easier each time; that's what he had heard. In any case, this was easy enough. There wasn't even much blood, though he was glad the mark had driven his own car after all.

Now Shiv sat alone, aware of the hiss of his lungs, and also that his armpits were wet. Well, it wasn't every day you killed a man. But Timofey hadn't resisted, it hadn't been like killing a man. The knife had passed through him not as if he were water, but as if he were a ghost. Shiv sensed that he had been cheated again.

He opened and pushed away Timofey's brown sports jacket, which even in the soundless dark nearly screamed Era of Stagnation. The canister was there, still strapped to his chest. The configuration of straps, hooks, and buckles that kept it in place taunted Shiv with its intricacy. He couldn't follow where each strap went, or what was being buckled or snapped. To Shiv it was a labyrinth, a rat's nest, a knot. To Timofey it had been a topographical equation, clockworks, a flow-chart. "Fuck it," Shiv said aloud. He took the Gessl and cut the thin strap above the cylinder with two quick strokes.

Already the mark's body was cool; perhaps time was passing more quickly than Shiv realized. Or maybe it was passing much more slowly: in a single dilated instant he discerned the two cut pieces of the strap hovering at each other's torn edge, longing to be one again. But then they flew away with a robust *snap!* and the entire assembly lost the tension that had kept it wrapped around Timofey's body. The effect was so dramatic he fancied that Timofey had come alive and that he would have the opportunity to kill him again. The canister popped open—he now apprehended which two hooks and which three straps had kept it closed—and fell against the gearshift.

Powder spilled out, but not much. Shiv grabbed the canister and shoveled back some of what was on the seat, at least a few thousand dollars' worth. He couldn't really see the stuff, but it was warm and gritty between his fingers. He scooped in as much as he could, screwed the cylinder shut, and then dusted off his hands against his trousers. He cut away the rest of the straps, leaving them draped on Timofey's body. He climbed from the car.

"Good work, lads."

The two brothers, Andrei and Yegor, each stood nearly two meters tall on either side of their car, which was still parked flush against Timofey's bumper. They were not twins, though it was often difficult to recall which was which, they were so empty of personality. Shiv, who had called them from the hotel lobby, thought of them as pure muscle. By most standards of measurement, they were of equally de-ficient intelligence. They spoke slowly, reasoned even more slowly, and became steadily more unreliable the further they traveled from their last glass of vodka. Nevertheless, they were useful, and they could do what they were told, or a satisfactory approximation of it.

"What do you got there?" said Yegor.

"You wouldn't understand, believe me."

It was then that he saw that Andrei was holding a gun at his hip, leveling it directly at him. It was some kind of pistol, and it looked ridiculously small in Andrei's hands. Still, it was a gun. In the old days, no one had a gun, everyone fought it out with knives and brass knuckles and solid, honest fists, and pieces of lead pipe. You couldn't get firearms. They never reached the market, and the mere possession of one made the cops dangerously angry. But this was democracy: now every moron had a gun.

"Put it away. What did you think, I was going to cut you out?"

Yegor stepped toward him, his arm outstretched. "Hand it over."

Shiv nodded his head, as if in agreement, but he kept the canister clutched to his stomach. "All right, you've got the drop on me. I admit it. I'll put it in writing if you like. They'll be talking about this for years. But you're not going to be able to move it on your own."

"Why not?" said Andrei. He raised the gun with both hands. The hands trembled. For a moment, Shiv thought he could see straight down the barrel. "You think we're stupid."

"If you want to show me how smart you are, you'll put down the fucking gun."

"I don't have to show you anything."

"Listen, this is plutonium. Do you know what it is?"

"Yeah, I know."

"Do you know what's it's used for?"

"I don't got to know. All I got to know is that people will buy it. That's the free market."

"Idiot! Who are you going to sell it to?"

"Private enterprise. They'll buy it from us just like they'd buy it from you. And did you call me an idiot?"

"Listen, I'm just trying to explain to you"—Shiv thought for a moment—"the material's radiological properties."

Shiv was too close to be surprised, it happened too quickly. In one moment he was trying to reason with Andrei, intimidate him, and was only beginning to appreciate the seriousness of the problem, and had just observed, in a casual way, that the entire time of his life up to the moment he had stepped out of Timofey's car seemed equal in length to the time since then, and in the next moment he was unconscious, bleeding from a large wound in his head.

"Well, fuck you," said Andrei, or, more literally, "go to a fucked mother." He had never shot a man before, and he was surprised and frightened by the blood, which had splattered all over Shiv's clothes, and even on himself. He had expected that the impact of the shot would have propelled Shiv off the bridge, but it hadn't. Shiv lay there at his feet, bleeding against the rear tire. The sound of the little gun was tremendous; it continued roaring through the woods long after Andrei had brought the weapon to his side.

Neither brother said anything for a while. In fact, they weren't brothers, as everyone believed, but were stepbrothers, as well as in-laws, in some kind of complicated way that neither had ever figured out. From Yegor's silence, Andrei guessed that he was angry with him for shooting Shiv. They hadn't agreed to shoot him beforehand. But Yegor had allowed him to carry the gun, which meant Andrei had the right to make the decision. Yegor couldn't second-guess him, Andrei resolved, his nostrils flaring.

But Yegor broke the long silence with a gasped guffaw. In the bark of his surprise lay a tremor of anxiety. "Look at this mess," he said. "You fucking near tore off his head."

Andrei could tell his brother was proud of him, at least a bit. He felt a surge of love.

"Well, fuck," said Yegor, shaking his head in wonder. "It's really a mess. How are we going to clean it up? It's all over the car. Shit, it's on my pants."

"Let's just take the stuff and leave."

Yegor said, "Go through his pockets. He always carries a roll. I'll check the other guy."

"No, it's too much blood. I'll go through the other guy's pockets."

"Look, it's like I've been telling you, that's what's wrong with this country. People don't accept the consequences of their actions. Now, *you* put a hole in the guy's head, *you* go through his pockets."

Andrei scowled but quickly ran his hands through Shiv's trousers, jacket, and coat anyway. The body stirred and something like a groan bubbled from Shiv's blood-filled mouth. Some of the blood trickled onto Andrei's hand. It was disgustingly warm and viscid. He snatched his hand away and wiped it on Shiv's jacket. Taking more care now, he reached into the inside jacket pocket and pulled out a gold-colored money clip with some rubles, about ten twenty dollar bills, a few tens, and a creased five. He slipped the clip and four or five of the twenties into his pocket and, stacking the rest on the car's trunk, announced, "Not much, just some cash."

Yegor emerged from the car. "There's nothing at all on this guy, only rubles."

Andrei doubted that. He should have pocketed all of Shiv's money.

"I wonder what the stuff's like," said Yegor, taking the closed canister from Shiv's lap.

He placed it next to the money and pulled off the top, revealing inside a coarse, silvery gray powder. Yegor grimaced. It was nothing

718

like he had ever seen. He wet his finger, poked it into the container, and removed a fingerprint's worth. The stuff tasted chalky.

"What did he call it?" he asked.

"Plutonium. From Bolivia, he said."

Andrei reached in, took a pinch of the powder, and placed it on the back of his left hand. He then closed his right nostril with a finger and brought the stuff up to his face. He loved doing this. From the moment he had pulled the gun on Shiv he had felt as if he were in Chicago or Miami. He sniffed up the powder.

It burned, but not in the right way. It was as if someone—Yegor— had grabbed his nostril with a pair of hot pliers. The pain shot through his head like a nail, and he saw stars. Then he saw atoms, their nuclei surrounded by hairy penumbrae of indeterminately placed electrons. The nuclei themselves pulsed with indeterminacy, their masses slightly less than the sum of their parts. Bombarded by neutrons, the nuclei were drastically deformed. Some burst. The repulsion of two highly charged nuclear fragments released Promethean, adamantine energy, as well as excess neutrons that bounced among the other nuclei, a cascade of excitation and transformation.

"It's crap. It's complete crap. Crap, crap, *crap!*"

Enraged, Andrei hoisted the open container, brought it behind his head, and, with a grunt and a cry, hurled it far into the night sky. The canister sailed. For a moment, as it reached the top of its ascent beyond the bridge, it caught a piece of moonlight along its sides. It looked like a little crescent moon itself, in an eternal orbit above the earth, the stuff forever pluming behind it. And then it very swiftly vanished. Everything was quiet for a moment, and then there was a distant, voluptuous sound as the container plunged into the river. As the two brothers turned toward each other, one of them with a gun, everything was quiet again.

2001

719

Westminster Public Library
3705 W. 112th Avenue
Westminster, CO 80031
www.westminsterlibrary.org